# The Barnabas Chronicles

## Volume 1

Baird:  Encouraged to Trust
Book 1

Benen:  Encouraged to Protect
Book 2

Blair:  Encouraged to Believe
Book 3

Bradon:  Encouraged to Overcome
Book 4

Brady:  Encouraged to Heal
Book 5

Branigan:  Encouraged to Hope
Book 6

By

Ronna M. Bacon

## *Baird: Encouraged to Trust Book 1*

When Berneen Dakin agrees to marry Baird Cassidy to save his life, she becomes involved a fight to save not only his life but her own and that of her beloved younger brother, Darby. Clues to their adventure lay in their past. Who is after them and why? Berneen and Baird must learn to trust one another, trust his fellow team mates from The Barnabas Foundation, but more importantly, learn to trust God in ways they never have had to. Finding the ones after them is difficult, but bringing the men and women to justice for crimes in the past is even more difficult, and tests their growing love for one another. Will they survive?

## *Benen: Encouraged to Protect Book 2*

When asked to fly to a Latin American country, Benen Carroll doesn't hesitate. When asked to marry his longtime friend, Cadee Daniell, to help her escape the country, Benen doesn't hesitate. What the young couple doesn't know is that there are forces gathering around them to defeat them, destroy them and damage their reputations. Poisoned on the way out of the country Cadee almost meets death but survives. Surprises and struggles clash with their determination to resolve the mystery while clinging tight to God's promises to protect them.

A trip to a foreign country. A request by an old friend. Married to keep someone safe and return them to their home country. Danger shadows them. Will they survive? Do they trust God enough for Him to protect them?

## *Blair: Encouraged to Believe Book 3*

Reuniting with his lost love, Blair Campion is devastated to learn that Devaney Daubney had spent years moving across the country, on his trail, trying to find the man or woman responsible for separating them. When Devaney is shot and almost killed, Blair's love for his lady grows even deeper, knowing he will do whatever he can to keep her safe and find the culprits. Devaney is sure there is more than one. A deceptive detective adds confusion to their mystery. Devaney has lost her belief in God, only to find it come back stronger than before, Blair's support the catalyst to this. Will they survive? Will the culprits win?

## *Bradon: Encouraged to Overcome Book 4*

When Bradon Cahill comes to her rescue in an abduction attempt, Ennis Dacre is convinced he is the one sent to free her from her stalker. Little do they know the attempts that will be made on their lives, with both critically injured at one point. They face danger together and apart, their lives melding to one as they fall in love, Ennis' fear of dogs overcome by the persistence of Bradon's dog, Kade. Abductions and assaults draw Bradon's friends from The Barnabas Foundation into the fray as they race to uncover the culprit and the ones behind him, and at the same time, help Ennis overcome the fear she has lived with for years. Their faith in God is tested and strengthened as they fight through to the finish.

## *Brady: Encouraged to Heal Book 5*

Stumbling on a body was not how Brady Coghlan had planned his vacation. Meeting the beautiful, Dr. Fynn Daley, forensics entomologist, who was called in on the investigation drew him into her world and the danger that was stalking her. Running from her hometown and giving up the work she loves, Fynn moves back to Brady's town. Abducted and assaulted, left to die in the forest, Fynn struggles to determine who is actually after her. Brady is adamant he will protect the lady he has come to love and draws in his friends from the Barnabas Foundation, with an unexpected visit from friends of Fynn. Into the mix is Fynn's recollection of her brother, Farr, who disappeared when she was two and he was six. Reuniting with Farr and trying to find who is after her leaves Fynn desperate to heal from old and new wounds, as she learns to trust in God in a whole new way.

## *Branigan: Encouraged to Hope Book 6*

When Branigan Clery is contracted to set up a security system for a local trucking company, he does not expect to save the owner's daughter, Guenivere Danby, from an abduction and then an attempt on her life. Drawn in to the mystery surrounding the beauty, both Guenivere and Branigan face assaults, kidnappings and threats. To find hope in herself and in her Lord, Guenivere must reach into her past as a preteen, face the assault from then and the threats that have shaped her life. Branigan's friends from the Barnabas Foundation and the ladies who are part of the family there are once more drawn in to investigate and help to keep them safe and solve the unknown stalker.

ISBN 978-1-989699-68-3

# Table of Contents

2 Corinthians 1:3-4 (NKJV)


Blessed be the God and Father of our Lord Jesus Christ, the Father of mercies and God of all comfort, who comforts us in all our tribulation, that we may be able to comfort those who are in any trouble, with the comfort with which we ourselves are comforted by God.

# Baird: Encouraged to Trust

*The Barnabas Chronicles*

*Book 1*

*By*

*Ronna M. Bacon*

Joshua 1:9

Have I not commanded you? Be strong and of good courage; do not be afraid, nor be dismayed, for the Lord your God is with you wherever you go. (NJKV)

Table of Contents

The fallen crisp leaves crunched under his feet as Baird Cassidy shuffled around the perimeter of the enclosed yard, the high board fence preventing him from seeing what lay beyond his prison. And prison it was, even though he had been allowed out that day, day three, he thought.

He had awakened in a rough cell two days earlier, his head pounding as he felt the lump under the tousled waves of dark brown hair, his light hazel eyes squinting against the meagre light coming in through the dirty windows. He had rolled to his side, fighting the nausea that roiled in his stomach. He had finally pushed himself upright, his legs swinging over the edge of the bunk he had apparently just been dumped on, no blanket to cover him against the chill.

He stood, his hand reaching to steady himself against the rough stone, his head spinning for a moment, before he made his way around the small room, finding the windows and then the door. He had shaken the door, eventually banging on it, without rousing anyone. He had slumped back on the bunk, his head drooping before he flopped over on his side, losing the fight to keep himself awake. He didn't hear the quiet whispers of sound as the critters that shared his room crept out and observed him before scurrying away, knowing they would find no food there. Not yet.

He was roused by the hands that shook him roughly and then hauled him to his feet, hands gripping his arms shoving him forward, his feet stumbling over each other until he gained enough balance to walk on his own. He was thrust down into a chair, a bowl of soup set in front of him, and ordered to eat. That was all he would get that day, he was told. He finally nodded, his eyes slipping open and closed as he picked up the spoon and began to eat.

The scene was repeated the next two days, but on the third day of his captivity, he got a glimpse of a woman, no, lady, he thought as she moved silently around the room, not looking at anything but what she was working on. He watched through lowered eyelashes as he ate as slowly as he could, taking in her tousled, unkempt black hair, the thinness of her face and arms, what he could see of them.

He saw the bruises on her arms and grew angry and then sighed. Lord, what have I gotten involved in?  We were sent out, what three days ago, four, told to find a certain house and that we needed to find the thumb drives and packages left for our boss, Barnabas?  That went well until we were on the way back to our vehicles and we were ambushed.  I don't remember what happened.  Lord, let the other five on my team have made it out.  Please, Lord?  I don't care about me, but don't let them have been hurt.

Berneen Dakin tried hard to watch the man that had been brought to the prison, or whatever it was that she was kept in, without it being obvious.  She had no idea who he was, but she prayed he made it out alive.  He was not the first one brought there.  But any of the others had lasted only a few days and then disappeared.  When she had first asked about them, the blows from the leader's hands had sent her to the floor, a huddled heap.  She had pulled herself up after a while and dragged herself to the room next to the jail cell, the dampness and chill of it a welcome respite from the coarse voices and even coarser words she had to endure when she was on the main floor of the building.  She spent as little time there as she could, seeking refuge and protection in her room, the door locking on the inside.

She watched from the corner of her eye that day as the man ate and then was roughly handled and shoved through the door to the backyard.  He would be only allowed out there for thirty minutes, less if he tried to escape.  That she knew.  She looked around, her tasks done for the day, and then she too slipped through the door, shrinking back into a corner, knowing she could not be seen.  Some of the guards would punish her for being out there, that she knew, but the one who was there that day, wouldn't.  He seemed kinder than the others, but she didn't trust him.  She had lost her trust in people, having been imprisoned in this place for two months, she thought.  Three, perhaps?  God had abandoned her, that she had decided.  She had prayed for release but none had come.

Her face raised to the sun, she closed her eyes, relishing the few moments of freedom she would have.  She would be dragged back in soon, meals to prepare, laundry to do, the building to clean.  She despaired of ever getting free.  Her gaze shot around as she heard a whisper of a sound, not sure what it was.  Her gaze landed on the other prisoner, watching as he turned, his head tilted, trying to determine, she thought, what the sound was and where it came from.

The guard moved towards Baird, his hand out to shove him towards the building when Baird's fist flew towards his jaw, knocking him down and out. Baird watched as his team mates, or some of them, appeared at the top of the fence, dropping down near him, their voices muted as they approached.

"Baird, come. We need to leave now." His team leader, Branigan Clery, was at his side, pushing him towards the wall, not understanding why Baird hesitated, his eyes on the building.

Then, Baird saw her, huddled in the corner, her hands covering her mouth. "Branigan, we need to take her with us."

"Take who?" Branigan swung, his eyes meeting those of Berneen, before one of the other men was at her side, tugging her towards Baird, even as she fought him, struggling to free her arm, dragging herself backwards, her feet digging into the ground, her long hair flying loose around her, fear on her face.

Blair Campion finally just swept her into his arms and ran for the wall, handing her up and over and then scaling the wall, dropping lightly beside her, watching closely as Baird reached for her hand and pulled her with him. His eyes dropped to her feet and then he was beside Baird.

"She has no shoes on, Baird!"

"What!" Baird slid to a halt, his eyes on Blair before he stared at Berneen, finally dropping his gaze to her bare feet. He mumbled something and simply swept her into his arms, a small cry coming from her before her arms were around his neck.

They heard the yells of outrage from behind the walls and quickened their pace, finding the vehicle they had hidden, leaving Brady Coghlan behind the wheel. Once they were all inside, he sped away, not caring that he was driving over the speed limit.

Baird dropped to a seat, his breath in gasps, his head pounding afresh, his eyes sliding closed for a moment before they popped open, his gaze finding furious gray eyes that had flecks of blue, green, and amber in them glaring at him.

His hand went up, even as Blair spoke.

—

"Miss? Cut the anger. We couldn't leave you there."

She spun in her seat, her glare directed at Blair. "You have no idea what you just did. I can't leave there." She struggled to reach for the door, her hands clasped gently but tightly in Baird's. "Please, I need to go back."

"We can't let you. Why is it so important that you do?"

"They'll kill someone close to me. They threatened that already." She slumped back, her hands, freed from Baird's grasp at her words, covering her face even as sobs shook her body.

"Miss, we'll make sure they're safe. Let me know the names."

She shook her head. "I can't. They're in hiding and I can't send anyone to them."

She sank back further, Baird's eyes on her before sudden pain in his head caused a groan to be torn from his body and he collapsed, a hand reaching for her, even as she turned, fear on her face.

"They hurt him, didn't they?"

Blair nodded, his eyes exchanging glances with the men even as he reached for Baird, easing him back on the seat, seeing Berneen reaching to cradle him, a shuttered look covering her face.

"Do you know who did this?" Blair's voice was stern, matching the look on his face.

She nodded. "I think I do. He's vicious. I prayed to get away but couldn't. He'll be beyond furious that this man escaped. They never do. I think, if you look, you'll find graves around the walls. Men would be there and then just disappear." She sounded defeated, drawing the attention of the five men to her before their eyes dropped to Baird, wondering just how close it had been for him.

Baird was carried carefully to the infirmary on the first floor of the main building in their headquarters compound and gently laid on a hospital bed, and Brady had then disappeared, on the hunt for Doc Whitson. The men that had carried him in stood back, their eyes watchful, hurting for their comrade, even as Blair had carried Berneen in and set her on a bed in a neighbouring room, despite her protests. He had to physically restrain her from fleeing the room, finally standing in the doorway, arms crossed, a frown on his face as he watched her pace. He could not understand her attitude. His head turned as he heard footsteps and saw the physician heading his way, stopping at Baird's room.

He turned back, to find Berneen in front of him, her arms wrapped around herself.

"How is he?" She had an unreadable look on her face, but her eyes showed her concern. Those she could not shutter, no matter how much she wanted to.

"Baird?" At her nod, he just shook his head. "Doc's with him now. We'll see what he has to say. But we need to do something about you."

She snorted, spun and walked away, leaving him staring after her in disbelief. He stepped back from the doorway in the hall as he heard his name called and Breck Curran walked his way. Breck was over the two teams of men, reporting directly to their employer, Barnabas Carey.

"Blair? Talk to me. What's going on?"

Blair simply shook his head. "We found Baird, tried to get him out, and he insisted the lady imprisoned there as well just had to come with us."

"Lady? We had no reports on a female there." Breck watched over Blair's shoulder for a moment. "She needs someone to take care of her."

"She does. I asked Anna to come over."

---

Breck nodded. "Good. Have Doc take a look at her." He paused, a thoughtful look on his face. "Do we have a name?"

"Not yet. She has not been exactly cooperative with us. In fact, she has been hostile, not happy that we removed her as well. She stated that she had someone close to her that had been threatened with death but refused to tell us who or where they are."

The two men looked around as they heard brisk steps on the wooden hallway floor and saw Anna Whitson headed their way, stopping first to check on Baird before she appeared in front of them. Anna mothered all, Blair thought, and then sighed. She was Barnabas' housekeeper, had been housekeeper to his parents until they retired, when they told Anna they were buying a small condo and that she could retire. She had snorted, simply held out her hand for a key and showed up at their condo once a week to clean. She took interest in all the men employed by Barnabas, including Barnabas, shaking her head at the fact that he had hired only men who were single, orphans, and had the same initials as his. She had stared at him at first, but then informed him that that would never last. These educated men, as she termed them, would never stay with him.

She had been proven wrong, a loyalty to Barnabas burning within each one. She prayed daily for her boys, as she called them, and for life mates for them.

She looked up at Breck and then Blair, before she stood where she could watch Berneen.

"What's her story, Blair?"

"We have no idea. Baird refused to leave the place without her. She's not happy about that, says someone close to her has been threatened with death. And no, we have not been able to find out her name."

Anna nodded, before she turned. "I'll be right back. Sarah left some clothes that I think will fit her. I know my slippers will. She can't be walking around at this time of year in her bare feet."

She was back in no time, dropping the clothing on the bed, and then turning to find Berneen. Berneen had dropped into a corner, her arms around her knees, her face buried. Anna's heart broke for the young woman but knew she had to get her up and on her feet, showered, hair shampooed, and dressed in clothes that were clean.

She stood in front of Berneen for a moment, her eyes assessing the younger woman, seeing the neglect and abuse that she had undergone, subtle signs that the men would have missed.

"Young lady, let's get you on your feet." Anna's voice was soft but firm. She watched as Berneen ignored her. She reached down at that point, a hand grasping Berneen's arm gently.

Berneen flinched, her arms going up to cover her head. Anna heard an exclamation from the two men, who moved towards her, stopping as she raised a hand and shook her head.

"Come on, dear. On your feet. I think you would like to get cleaned up and into some clean clothes. Doc wants to check you over but I asked him to wait until you had a chance to have a shower or a bath, whichever you prefer."

Berneen lowered her arms, her gaze finding the kindly one of the older woman and frowned. "I can't. I'm not allowed."

Anna heard the low growls from the two men and waved them back. "Well, I have no idea who told you that. But that person is not here and not in charge of you anymore. You're here visiting me and I know after travelling I always like to get washed and into clean clothes." She gently drew Berneen to her feet and, an arm around her, led her over to the bed. "My granddaughter's about your size. These will do until we can get you your own clothes. Now, pick out what you want and I'll take you somewhere you can clean up."

Berneen reached out a tentative finger at last, touching the clothing, tears near the surface. Anna gave a sound and then swept the younger woman into her arms, holding her as she wept. Berneen finally moved back, wiping at her eyes.

"Thank you."

"And we do need to know your name. We can't continue to call you by the names we have been, although they all suit you."

"Berneen." That was all Berneen was able to get out, overcome with emotions. At Anna's questioning look, she spelt it out for her.

———

"Berneen! A lovely name for a lovely young lady. But you must have two names, as my grandson would say."

Berneen looked up at the ceiling, blinking past the tears, knowing that once she gave her name, she was losing her anonymity and that anyone searching her name would find the one she was trying so hard to protect.

"It's Dakin. I'm Berneen Dakin."

"Beautiful names for a beautiful lady. Now, pick what you want and I'll show you the guest room where you can clean up. Doc will want you back here to look you over, make sure you're not harmed, but he's in no rush."

"But he has to be." Berneen rushed to pick up the first outfit she touched.

Blair spoke from beside her, causing her to jump, fear on her face as she turned to him.

"Anna's right. Take your time." He nodded at the clothing. "Pick what you want to wear, not what you think you should, or the first thing you touch. Doc's in no rush. He's still with Baird, and then he muttered something about a piece of apple pie with his name on it." He grinned at Anna. "I just want to know if there's one with your name on it."

Anna laughed, even as she turned him around and shooed him from the room. "Those boys! Always hungry and always teasing! But they have hearts of gold, every single one of them."

Thirty minutes later, Anna tucked Berneen into the bed in the infirmary room. Berneen had hardly been able to stay awake, feeling clean for the first time in months, she realized, her hair washed and braided. She snuggled down under the blankets, relishing the warmth and feeling with her sock-covered feet the hot water bottle Anna had tucked in the bottom of the bed. She had finally chosen a long-sleeved T-shirt and leggings, feeling the leggings over, knowing that the teal coloured would suit her. She had stared around the guest room in Anna's apartment, amazed at the cleanliness she hadn't seen in months, the bright cheerful colours of jade and cream. She had inspected the soaker tub and then chosen the large shower, relishing the heat of the water and the selection of shampoos and soaps.  The fluffy jade towels had her in tears.  She had never known such luxury, she thought.

Doc stood for a moment, his arm around Anna, thankful for his helpmeet, and watched as Berneen slept.

"Any concerns?"

Anna shook her head.  "No, I don't think so.  Physically, I saw a few bruises and her feet are rubbed almost raw in some spots.  There are some minor cuts on her hands and feet but they can be dealt with tomorrow.  It's her emotional state that I am worried about."

Doc nodded.  "I'll look her over tomorrow.  Tonight, let her sleep.  She may be up and down, but I think we're okay for now."  He looked behind him.  "Some of the boys will be up, watching over Baird, and will come get us if they need us."

"Good.  Head off, Aaron.  I'll be along shortly.  I just worry about her."

Doc dropped a kiss on his wife's cheek, thinking she was more beautiful than when they had wed in their late teens.

Brady looked up from where he sat near Baird's bed as Doc stopped beside it, his hand reaching for Baird's wrist, and then reaching for his stethoscope.

"Doc?"

Doc looked up at Brady, knowing how close the men on each team were with each other.

"He's hurting, Brady.  I won't kid you that way.  But he's sleeping naturally.  The IV will help rehydrate him."  He watched Baird closely before he nodded.  "We'll need to keep him quiet for a couple of days.  He's had a rough go."

"And the lady?"

"Berneen? Anna finally found out her name.  She's hurting emotionally.  I'll assess her tomorrow.  We're concerned about her emotional health.  You know nothing about her?"

Brady shook his head.  "They hadn't seen her.  They just couldn't figure out why Baird wouldn't move to the fence.  He's the one who wanted her to come, refused to move until they had her with us.”

"He’ll need to debrief, won’t he?” Doc simply shook his head after he spoke and walked away.

Rolling to his side early the next morning, Baird felt the blankets over him before his hand ran along the sheet, a frown on his face. His eyes opening, he waited for the dizziness to hit him. When it didn't, he rolled to his other side, his eyes on the room, wondering for a moment where he was. He took in the hospital atmosphere and then sat up, abruptly, not knowing if he was still a captive or not. He fumbled for the side rail, finding the lock to release it and lower it before he swung his feet over the edge, looking down to find slippers waiting for him. He stood, slipping into them and then reaching for the robe someone had dropped on the end of the bed, studying it for a moment, thinking it looked familiar before shoving his arms into the sleeves and tightening the belt around his waist.

He shuffled slightly as he walked to the door, not quite steady on his feet, but better than he had been. Cracking open the door, he peeked out and then realized he was home. This was their building. He shot a look behind him and knew he had been taken care of. He just didn't remember much after seeing his team mates drop down in front of him, what day that was, he wasn't sure. He moved towards the stairs, staring at them for a moment before he headed for the elevator, taking it to the third floor, finding his apartment door and entering, sighing as he did so. He spun abruptly, his hand coming out against the wall to steady himself as the door opened behind him and Branigan entered.

"Baird? Should you be up?"

Baird stared at him for a moment before he carefully shook his head. "I need to be. I need to get cleaned up." He rubbed at his face, feeling the days-old stubble on it .

Branigan nodded, knowing how he would feel if it had been him. "I can see that, but what has Doc said about you being on your feet?"

Baird went to shake his head again and stopped. "I have no idea. He wasn't there. If you're going to harass me about this, Branigan, leave."

Branigan's hands rose in the air. "No, not that, Baird. Just concern." He nodded down the hallway towards Baird's bedroom. "Go on. Find some clean clothes. Get yourself put back together." He watched carefully as Baird walked away from him, his hand out, tracing along the light cream paint on the hall wall as he walked towards his bedroom, his head hanging down.

Branigan shook his own head. Lord, he shouldn't be on his feet. He's been through something none of the rest of us can understand. He didn't get the care he needed at the first of his trouble. Now, dear Lord, we're playing catch up with that. Help us to help him. He's going to need You like never before, Lord. And I fear this is just beginning for him. Bless my friend, Lord.

He headed for the kitchen, opening first the fridge and then the freezer, finding the cinnamon raisin bagels he knew Baird preferred, finding the toaster tucked away in a cupboard. He listened for the water to stop and then dropped the bagels in the toaster, reaching for the butter and jams to set on the table, making coffee for them both. This kitchen was almost as familiar as his own, the men sharing meals with one another on a frequent basis.

Baird shut the door to his bedroom, leaning on it for a moment, his head back, his eyes closed, knowing just how close to the edge of collapse he was. He didn't remember what he had been through, and wished he did. He needed to process it but couldn't if he didn't know what had happened. He finally moved to his dresser, rifling through the drawers to find clean clothes, staring at a T-shirt for a moment, before he sighed, his eyes closing. He seldom let himself remember his mother but at times when he was down or not well, that was when he wished she was still there, not in heaven. I need her today, Lord. I just need my Mom. He blinked back tears as he headed for the closet, finding clean jeans, and then heading for the attached bathroom, standing for a moment staring at the navy blue towels before he reached to turn on the water in the shower.

Staring at himself in the mirror over the sink a while later, he frowned. He looked haggard, he thought, and then shook his head carefully, waiting for the dizziness to hit once more. He rubbed at

—

his face, knowing he needed to shave but not having the energy to do that.  No, he thought, as he tilted his head, he needed to do that, and reached for his razor.

Finally heading for the kitchen, following the aroma of the toasted bagels, he paused in the doorway to his spare room, frowning.  Something seemed off in there, but he wasn't sure what.  He shrugged, heading for the kitchen, a quiet word of thanks for the food.

Branigan eventually pulled him to his feet, a hand on his shoulder directing him back down in the elevator towards the infirmary.

"I don't need to be there, Branigan.  I can rest just as well in my own place."  Baird's protest echoed through the elevator.

"Doc hasn't released you yet, Baird.  You know how it works."  He followed Baird from the elevator, watchful as always.

Baird stared down the hallway in one section of the building, where the infirmary was located, noting the door closed to the other infirmary room.

"Branigan?  Who got hurt?"

"What do you mean?  Who got hurt?"  Branigan had a frown on his face, not quite sure what Baird was meaning.

Baird pointed to the door.  "There.  There's someone in there, isn't there?  Which one of our guys got it?"

Branigan's eyes slid shut.  Baird had forgotten.  Lord, why me?  Why do I get to tell him about Berneen?  He felt the poke on his shoulder from Baird's finger.

"Branigan?"  When his friend didn't respond, Baird turned to the door, tapping quietly.  When there was no response, he slowly opened the door, staring inside for a moment before he entered, fully expecting to see one of his team mates there.  He could hear water running slowly in the sink in the attached washroom, the door to it open, but his focus was on the bed.  His feet carried him forward, slowly, until he stopped, mesmerized by the young woman lying there, asleep.  He turned back to stare at the door, Branigan standing in the doorway, his eyes watchful, hands shoved into his sweatshirt pockets.

---

Baird turned back to the bed, his hands in his cardigan pockets, staring down at the sleeping lady, he guessed to be somewhat his own age. He glanced up briefly to see Anna standing across from him, her eyes on first him and then the lady before she moved away, her feet taking her to Branigan. He could hear their soft conversation, but watched the lady instead.

Who is she, Lord? I know I've seen her but not just sure where. He reached out tentative hands and tucked the blankets up tighter around her neck, seeing her tiny movement away from him and then she lay still, a soft sigh coming from her. He touched a wayward curl that had escaped her braid, marveling at the softness of her raven black hair, before his hand rested lightly on the side of her face. She shifted slightly, first turning away from his touch, and then leaning into it. He watched carefully, seeing her relax slightly at his touch. And then he saw it. A tear, glistening on her cheek, quivering with the movement of her breathing, reflecting back the light as it moved, momentarily showing a rainbow in its movement. His thumb came out, wiping it gently away, his heart raised in prayer for the lady he didn't know. He turned at last, reluctant to leave her side, but knowing he needed to.

Branigan's hand rested briefly on Baird's shoulder as Baird paused in the doorway to look back at Berneen.

"Branigan?"

"Come on, Baird. You need to get back to bed. You're getting shaky on your feet." Branigan's hand turned his friend towards the other infirmary room. "And I will explain the lady to you."

Baird settled back into the bed, the head of it raised for him to almost sit up. Branigan pulled up a chair, taking a quick look at his watch, knowing he needed to be off to his work shortly, but Baird came first. When he looked up again, Baird had dozed off. Branigan just shook his head and then left, the door closing quietly behind him.

—

Mid-morning, Bradon Cahill watched Berneen as she stood in the lobby, a look of awe on her face as she slowly turned in a circle, her head raising and lowering as she took in the rich wooden paneling on the walls, the heavy dark green drapes at the windows, carefully selected paintings and framed photographs on the walls, the dark wooden floors, the security counter set off to one side near the corridor that led to the offices. He also knew she would see the seating areas at each end of the lobby, gas fireplaces facing each other from the side walls. He waited for her to turn towards him, leaning a shoulder against the wall near the elevators.

Berneen stopped her circle for a moment, her eyes on a painting and she walked over to take another look. Her eyes slid closed. It was one of her mother's. Tears pushed at her eyelids and she blinked hard to push them back in. She refused to cry. She jumped as she heard a voice beside her and then felt a dog's tongue licking at her hand.

She looked down, staring at the Australian Shepherd standing beside her, looking up at her, mouth open and tongue reaching to lick her hand once more. She carefully touched its head and the dog leaned against her. She looked up startled as she heard the voice again.

"Sorry, I didn't mean to startle you. You seem entranced with that painting." Bradon watched for a moment before he spoke again. "I'm Bradon Cahill. This dog that seems to have fallen in love with you is my dog, Kade."

"He's beautiful." She looked back at the painting, sorrow coursing through her, causing a frown on Bradon's face. "The painting? I thought it was lost. My mom painted it when I was young. She never told me she had sold it. It just disappeared when I was 18 after they were killed in a riot while overseas."

Bradon stared at her, his eyes finally looking behind her at Barnabas, who stood, shock briefly showing on his face. "Your

---

mother painted this?  Barnabas?  Berneen, Barnabas Carey is behind you.  He's run the foundation here."

Berneen spun, her hands on her face, as she faced Barnabas. "I'm sorry.  I'm sorry.  I didn't mean to say you stole it. I'm sorry."

The two men stared her, watching carefully as she tried to compose herself.

Barnabas spoke finally, his hand out to take her arm gently. "How be we find seats in my office?"

She stepped back, her head shaking.  "No.  I can't take your time.  Just let me know where I can find a ride to the nearest town and I'll leave."

Barnabas shook his head, as he once more gently took her arm, guiding her down the hallway to his office and seating her in a comfortable chair away from his desk.  Bradon sat near her, Kade on the alert, his eyes not leaving Berneen.  Barnabas walked away, returning in a short time with a tray of coffee, tea, and cold drinks. He pointed to the tray he set on the table.

"Take your pick."  He finally seated himself across the table from her, looking up as he heard a soft tap and then the door opened, Baird appearing, a frown on his face that smoothed out as he saw Berneen.  He seated himself near her, realizing as he did so she had not heard him enter, her gaze on Barnabas.

Barnabas watched, a slight smile on his face as Berneen continued to stare at him.  "Please, Miss Dakin.  Take your pick of what you want.  We can't until you do."

She reached for a bottle of water, stopping to stare at the hand that came to rest on her arm.

"Don't take what is closest or easiest.  Take what you really want.  If it's not there, tell us."  Baird's voice startled her and she looked up at him, a frown in place that disappeared, leaving her face blank, as she recognized him.

"You're here?"

"I am."  He gave a quick grin before he nodded at the tray. "Now, what do you really want?  If it's not there, we'll see if we can find it."

—

She sighed, not liking that he was forcing her to make a choice. "Is there peppermint tea?"

Baird took a look and then handed her a mug of water and a teabag. "Here. Barnabas always keeps a selection of different teas for whoever wants them. Not all of us like regular tea or coffee."

Berneen took the mug, a quick word of thanks to him, before she looked up at Barnabas, to finding him watching her closely.

"Miss Dakin? May I call you Berneen instead?" At her nod, Barnabas grinned. "You'll find we're not much on formalities here." He paused for a moment, his eyes thoughtful. "We need to have a talk, but I think first we need to spend time in prayer."

The men's heads bowed even as Berneen stared at first one and then the other, her eyes finally resting on Baird, sitting close to her, his hand once more on her forearm. She heard a whisper of sound and looked to her other side, to find Kade sitting tight to her, his chin on her leg. She sighed to herself. What now, Lord? What kind of group did I walk into? I'm afraid, Lord, but the fear is not from these men. The fear is from outside. I just know if I leave I'll disappear again and never return.

—

Berneen heard the quiet conversation among the three men as she sat, head bowed, her eyes on her mug sitting on the table in front of her, but her thoughts miles away. She jumped slightly as she felt Baird's hand on her arm again and realized then someone had been speaking with her.

"Berneen, Barnabas had asked you a question." Concerned that she didn't respond, he reached to tuck her hair behind her ear, just so he could see her face. "Are you okay?"

Hesitating, she finally shook her head, blinking hard. She refused to cry. Her captivity had taught her that. Any sign of a tear was a reason for belittling, if not a beating, and she just couldn't go through that ever again.

"Berneen, what can we do for you?" Baird shot a look at Barnabas, who had leaned forward in his chair, elbows on his knees, chin on his linked hands. When she didn't respond and wouldn't look at him, he was on his knees beside her, his arm around her, the other hand gently gripping the hands she had clasped on her knee. "What is it you are afraid of? Or who? Or for whom?" He could feel her body shaking, but frowned as he saw her fight with her tears.

"Berneen?" Barnabas' quiet voice had her finally looking up, the men drawing in quick breaths at the look of fear and devastation on her face. "Talk to us. We want to help you. We won't let you fight this on your own. Not anymore. Tell us who you are so scared for."

She shook her head, not wanting to speak, turning her head to watch Baird as Barnabas spoke. He shouldn't be here, she thought, taking in the whiteness of his face, the dark circles under his eyes, the fatigue in his movements.

"Baird, you shouldn't be here."

"No, I need to be. We need to determine who and why. You were just not taken. I get that. It had to be planned. And I was taken for a reason, and I would very much like to know why."

She stared at him. "Sit in your chair, please? You're going to fall over if you don't."

He watched her for a moment before he rose, pulled his chair over as close to her as he could, and then seated himself, reaching for a mug of coffee. He shared a look with Barnabas and Bradon before studying her once more.

"Berneen?" The slight tremor of her hand as she reached for her own mug showed him she had heard him. "What are you afraid of?"

She once more shook her head. "I can't tell you."

"No. It's more than that. You can but you won't." Barnabas smothered a sigh. He was not used to working with women, other than Anna, and his own secretary, Amy. "Who are you afraid for?"

Berneen, in a sudden movement, dropped her mug to the table and was on her feet and out the door, running through the hallways, slamming open the outside door, her feet slipping a bit on the wet step before she was running from the building, not caring or knowing exactly where she was heading.

The three men stood in shock for a moment, and then Baird was right behind her, stopping as he reached the outside, not knowing which way she had run.

"Baird?"

Baird spun as he hear his name called. Blair Campion, a good friend as well as one of the six men on his team, ran towards him, stuffing a rag into his pocket.

"Berneen?" Baird was afraid, afraid that she would disappear before he found her again.

"Towards the lake. I don't know if she even knows where she's heading."

Baird shook his head. "She doesn't. She's terrified for someone and won't tell us." He reached for the jacket Bradon held out, a word of thanks coming from deep within him.

"We'll spread out and find her, Baird. We won't let your lady disappear." Bradon was gone, Kade at his side, leaving Baird staring after him, finally remembering to snap his mouth closed.

---

"Come on, Baird. I'm with you. The other fellows who are around will be out shortly." Buckley Cullen, the minister in their group who served the community in an old-fashioned stone and clapboard church, stood beside him. "Where to?"

"The lake. I just pray she's safe."

"We all do." Buckley shrugged into his own jacket before pointing to Baird's. "Jacket on, Baird, and then let's move."

"Wait. I need a jacket for Berneen." Baird turned to head back to get one, stopping short as he saw one in Buckley's hands. "Buckley?"

"Anna saw her run and knew she needed this. She handed it to me, told me to stick with you, and to find that child, as she termed it, quickly and bring her home."

Baird nodded, his feet moving him quickly towards the lake. "It will be cold coming in off Lake Erie. I have no idea if she's used to this kind of weather or not."

"She's never said?"

Baird shook his head at the question in Buckley's voice. "We, none of us, have really had a chance to talk to her, it's only been a couple of days. That's what we were doing when she ran. She's afraid for someone and when Barnabas pushed her to tell us, she took off. She's hiding something really deep."

"We all are, Baird, when you come down to it." Buckley slowed his walk, his hand coming out to stop Baird. "Has she family?"

"That we don't know, at least I don't. I imagine by now that Barnabas may have someone looking into that."

—

Berneen slid to a stop in the sand, her balance off for a moment, as she stared out at the lake. She spun, stumbling slightly in the sand, before she dropped to her knees, not caring that the sand was cold and damp. She rose suddenly, hearing a voice behind her before arms were wrapped tight around her, trapping her own to her body before she was dragged towards a pile of rocks. She struggled to get free but the arms were too strong. A hand was clapped across her mouth to stifle her screams for help. She continued to struggle even as she heard voices.

No, Baird, she thought. Go away. It's too dangerous for you here. She watched, helplessly, as men moved away from the rocks, circling behind Baird and the man with him. She didn't know him, but realized he was a friend of Baird's, trapped now because of her.

"She was here, Buckley. Those are her tracks." Baird searched the area, moving slowly forward, until he saw the disturbance in the sand. "She's been taken again. Where?" His eyes raised as he searched the area, seeing the tracks leading towards the pile of rocks. "Come on. This way."

When Buckley didn't respond, Baird turned to face him, his hands raising into the air as he saw the weapon pointing at Buckley's head and the one pointing at his own.

"Whoa! What's going on here?" Baird frowned when the men didn't respond, merely motioned for him to move. "I'm not moving until you tell me what you want."

He watched as Buckley looked behind him and turned, his hands dropping slightly as he saw Berneen held captive, horror on her face that he had been taken again.

"Again, I have to ask. What is going on?"

Baird received no answer, other than a shove from behind that sent him stumbling through the sand towards Berneen. He could hear mumbling from Buckley behind him. The three were then

---

forced to walk along the beach, almost into the icy waters at times, until they reached a ramshackle cottage and were shoved into it.

Baird was kept separated from the other two, forced to stand near the door, watching closely as Berneen and Buckley stood in the kitchen area, her eyes on him, Buckley watching the men closely. He heard the faint murmurs of talk before he was once more shoved forward, this time back out the door, and then into a waiting vehicle. His heart sank as he twisted to stare back at the cabin, not knowing what was happening and not knowing if he would see those two again.

Left on their own in the cabin, Buckley and Berneen stared at each other for a moment before Buckley made a systematic search of the cabin, turning to face Berneen.

"We haven't been introduced. I'm Buckley and you are Berneen." He grinned at her for a moment. "What happened?"

"What happened? I was grabbed out there, forced to watch you two taken captive, and now I'm left locked up in a cabin. What do you want to know, besides that?" Her words had a bite to them, she was that angry. She sighed. "I apologize. It's not your fault."

"No, it's not. And I don't know that it's either yours or Baird's." Buckley spun to face the door, not sure where Baird had disappeared to. "I suggest we make ourselves as comfortable as we can."

Berneen shrugged, then searched the cabin herself. "There's not much here. No chairs. No couch. Just this table."

"But there is some straw." Buckley scraped it into two piles, and then motioned to her. "Have a seat, my lady. It's rough but it's not the bare floor."

She sank down, grateful for somewhere to sit, her back resting against the rough boards behind her, her arms wrapping around her bent knees. "Why did you follow me?"

Buckley shrugged, a grin appearing on his face for a moment. "Baird was intent on finding you. We couldn't let him go on his own."

She looked at him horrified. "You mean there are more of you out there?"

—

He nodded. "About six or seven of us. The rest were off site." He tilted his head, a puzzled look on his face. "Why?"

She just shook her head. "You can't be doing that. You just can't."

"And why not? It's who we are, Berneen. We don't walk away from anyone."

"Well, you should. I've brought danger to Baird, I think."

He watched her closely, a frown on his face. "Why would you say that? Maybe it's the other way around. Baird brought danger to you."

She stared at him, remembering to snap her mouth closed. "In case you forgot, I was there when they brought Baird in. So it has to be me."

Buckley shook his head, his heart raising in prayer for Berneen. "Maybe. Maybe not." He looked towards the door as he heard voices and the door swung open, Baird shoved through it, stumbling a bit as he struggled to keep his balance. Buckley was on his feet, fists clenched, ready to fight for his friend, pausing as he saw the weapon pointing at Berneen.

Baird shook his head at Buckley, reaching to wipe at the blood dripping from a cut on his cheek, a bleak look on his face. It had not gone easy with him, not when he realized what they were asking of him. His refusal had gone hard with him. With the escalating threats against Berneen, he had just finally nodded, not willing to put her in any more danger than she was.

Berneen stood as well, tight to the wall, her hands covering her mouth, eyes huge and full of fear and worry, as she stared first at Baird ,then at the man behind him.

"You'll do what we ask, Miss Dakin, or he dies." The voice was low, harsh, and full of menace. The eyes showing through the mask were hard, cold, reminding her of the ice that would soon envelope the lake.

"I don't know what you mean." She gave a small scream as a heavy fist drove itself into Baird's abdomen, bending him forward at the waist. "What did you do that for?" Anger laced her words.

Berneen kept shaking her head at the escalating demands made towards her, struggling to release herself from the strong arm around her, her eyes flickering towards Buckley, who stood, weapon to his chest, unable to help either one, his mind racing to find a solution and finding none, and then to Baird, who took a blow somewhere on his body each time she refused a request.

The final blow Baird took sent him to his knees, bent over at the waist, sitting back on his legs even as his arms wrapped around his abdomen, his head touching the dirty, worn wood floor. Blood dripped from the cuts on his face and from his lip, bruising beginning to show.

Berneen grasped the thumb of the man holding her, pulling it backwards as far and as hard as she could. A cry of pain sounded from the man and his arm loosened enough so that she could shove away from him and scurry to Baird. She dropped to her knees, her arms around Baird, her head buried against his neck as sobs shook her body. Buckley moved to try and get to them but stopped as he felt the weapon dig harder into his chest. His heart broke for Berneen as he listened to her sob-filled pleas for Baird not to be hurt anymore, for them not to kill him.

"It's your choice, Miss Dakin. You do what we want, he lives. You refuse once more and he dies." The man who spoke studied his nails, not really caring which way she decided. He had been given his orders and he was following them.

Berneen finally nodded, agreeing to their demands. She was pulled to her feet, her hands reaching for Baird as he too was hauled upright, her arms around him to help steady him as he swayed.

Buckley made a sound, drawing her attention to him, shaking his head at her. "Berneen. No."

"I have to, Buckley. There's no other way." She caught her breath, trying to still the sobs. "He'll die if I don't."

"That is correct, Miss Dakin. Your decision has saved his life, for now."

She stared at the man, unable to see his face for the mask he wore, shudders running through him. "I don't understand."

"You will." He turned to one of his men, who held out a paper for him. "We have the license. We have the minister. Let's have a wedding."

Berneen turned to Baird, sobs shaking her body once more. "Baird?"

"It's okay, Neen. We're okay." His voice was low, halting, and he had difficulty forming his words.

Buckley was shoved towards them, barely keeping his balance. He studied his friend and then Berneen, sighing to himself, knowing there was no way out of this. Not unless someone friendly walked through the door right now and he couldn't count on that. His heart raised in prayer, asking for guidance, for permission to perform the ceremony, but knowing he had little choice.

"Buckley?" Berneen's broken question caught his attention. "Who's the minister?"

"That would be him." The leader of the men shoved at Buckley, causing him to sway slightly. "He's a minister. Much better than a JP."

Berneen stared at Buckley, horror on her face for a moment. "You're a minister? Is that why they took you?"

He shook his head. "No, I just happened to be there." He sighed, rubbing his hands up and down his arms. "Are you sure, Berneen? Baird?"

Baird mumbled something, his consciousness fading a bit more with each moment. Buckley sighed once more. It was now or never, he thought. *Lord, I have no idea what Your plans are for my friend and this young lady. Please, Lord? Is there any way to avoid this?*

Buckley stood for a moment, his eyes closed, before he felt the weapon poke him once more in the back. He sighed, his eyes opening, taking in his friend and the young woman standing beside him, knowing he had no choice but to perform the ceremony.

The words spoken, the "I do's" said, signatures on the paper, Buckley finally drew a deep breath. He had no idea what to expect at this point. A sudden sound from Berneen had him reaching for Baird, catching at him as he fell forward, taking Berneen with him. The couple hit the floor with a thud and lay still, Buckley prevented from reaching them. He was shoved backwards into the wall, his own vision darkening and swirling in front of him as his head hit a stud and then he too was still, his eyes open but his body not responding to his commands. He didn't feel the paper tucked into his jacket nor hear the men leave.

Buckley finally roused, shivering in the chilliness of the cabin. He scrubbed at his face, as his eyes searched for the men and not seeing them. He was on his feet, stumbling towards Baird and Berneen, dropping to his knees to feel for pulses. His head dropped to his chest as he realized they were still alive.

Berneen roused slightly, her head raising before it dropped once more to her out-flung arm. Buckley sat back on his heels, his eyes assessing the two, before he rose and headed for the door, not knowing if the captors were out there or not. A sound at the door stopped his progress in mid-step and he raised his hands, fisted, in an effort to be ready to protect himself. His hands dropped as he recognized the men coming through the doorway.

"Brady! Bradon! Brody! Burney! What? How did you find us?"

Brady shook his head as he took a swift look at Buckley. "You okay?"

"I am, I guess. It's Baird. He took an awful beating."

Brady was on his knees beside Baird, assessing him, before he turned to Berneen. "How long, Buckley?"

"I'm not sure. A couple of hours at least. What day is it?"

"It's Tuesday." Bradon Cahill watched Buckley closely.

"Late Tuesday?"

Bradon shook his head. "No, early morning.  The sun's just up."

"Then twelve hours, maybe?"  He started for the door, Brody Corcoran after him.  "Where are they?"

"Who, Buckley?"

"The five men.  They were here.  Where are they?"

"Gone.  What happened?"  Burney Cummins was torn, not sure whether to follow his team mates or wait with Brady.

Buckley shook his head.  "First, those two need seen to. Brady?  Can we just take them to Doc?"  He was desperate to get out of there but didn't know if Baird could or should even be moved.

"We can, for now, Buckley."  Brady stood, his eyes on the couple.  "Let's get them out of here. Brody, Burney.  You two take Baird.  I'll take Berneen."

Buckley followed them, not sure of anything anymore, other than they needed to be out of there.

Berneen roused as she was buckled into a seat, fighting against the hands holding her.  "I need to stay with Baird.  Please?  Where's Baird?  I can't leave him."

Brady sat back on his heels, before he turned to look at Buckley.  "Buckley?  What is she talking about?"

Buckley just shook his head.  "I need to talk to Barnabas."  His head dropped back against the headrest and his eyes closed.

Barnabas stood, his eyes on Buckley, not quite sure he understood what the other man had said, fingering the folded paper he had been handed. Buckley leaned against the wall outside the infirmary room, his head back, his eyes closed, fatigue in every line of his posture.

Looking through the open door, Barnabas watched as Doc and Brady worked over Baird. He could tell their concern by their movements, even though he couldn't hear their words. His eyes lifted to where Berneen stood at the head of the bed, not moving, her eyes on Baird, her hands clenched around the railing of the bed. She swayed too with fatigue and something else Barnabas couldn't put his finger on. She had been adamant when they tried to separate the couple. She just refused. When they had physically removed her, she fought them, finding her freedom from them and running back into the room, to stand where he now saw her. Doc had looked at him and just shook his head, stating that they should just let her be for now.

"What are you saying, Buckley?" Barnabas' attention went back to his friend.

"They're married, Barnabas. They forced me to marry them. They almost killed Baird before she agreed." Buckley looked up, devastation in his eyes as well as worry and something else Barnabas just couldn't place, shame, perhaps? "I had no choice." He nodded to the paper. "They took Baird away first and then came back with that."

"Married?" Barnabas unfolded the paper, reading it, before he folded it again and dropped it into a pocket on his shirt. "It's legal?"

Buckley nodded. "They made sure of that. I suspect when they took Baird away, that's what they went and did. I don't remember Berneen signing anything though."

"This sounds as if it was well planned. She could have signed the application when she was held captive the first time, without knowing what it was she was signing. This sounds like a sophisticated group."

Buckley shook his head, even as he shoved himself away from the wall. "I'm not seeing that. I see revenge in it." He walked away, shoulders stooped with fatigue and another emotion he refused to admit to.

Barnabas watched him go, seeing Breck walking up beside Buckley, before he turned and walked towards the bed where Baird lay.

"Doc?"

Doc looked up for a moment, then swinging his stethoscope around his neck, he walked to where Barnabas stood at the end of the bed.

"He's hurt, Barnabas. He'll heal but it will take a while. No broken bones. I don't see any evidence of internal bleeding. Whoever did this was a pro."

"That's what I was thinking. Has he spoken at all?"

Doc nodded. "Just to ask where Berneen was. When he found out she was safe and standing near him, he just nodded and passed out again." He paused, not quite sure how to express himself. "Barnabas, what do you know of what happened? They're both wearing rings, wedding bands, that they weren't yesterday morning."

Barnabas drew a deep breath, knowing his next words would be a shock, and would change the dynamics of their group. "Buckley married them. He was forced to. From what he said, if Berneen had not agreed, we would be having a funeral for Baird."

Doc stared at him for a moment, no longer shocked by what he heard anymore, working as he did in a low-cost clinic in the downtown area of their nearby town. "You're sure?"

"We are. Buckley said if he hadn't agreed, they would have found some other way to make it happen. He gave me the license. I'll check it out but I would suspect the marriage is already registered. They're not amateurs, whoever they are."

Brady had moved closer to them, a frown on his face. "But why? Why Baird? Why Berneen?"

"That's what we'll need to investigate, Brady. Some of the guys are already at work on that, without knowing the full extent of what the three went through. We'll meeting in ten minutes in the boardroom."

"I'll be there." Brady walked away, his head shaking at the news.

"What about Berneen, Doc?" Barnabas studied her, moving quickly to catch her as she swayed and then collapsed. He looked around for somewhere to set her, moving to the recliner Doc pushed towards the bed.

"She won't move from the room, Barnabas. And I would like to know why."

"Buckley said she was threatened after he finished the ceremony. She was told she had to stay with Baird at all times. If she didn't, he would be dead. Just like that."

"What?" Doc stared at him even as he reached to assess Berneen. "Who does this? This young lady has been through enough already."

"I know. But she's still hiding something. She's afraid for someone and won't tell us who."

"She's an orphan, right?" When Barnabas nodded, Doc continued. "I don't see a boyfriend, so it must be a sibling. Have you looked into that?"

"We are now. I spoke with the police. They're not saying much, but they don't have much to go on. No one reported her missing and we think she was held for at least three months, just for what little she has said."

"A brother." Baird's soft voice interrupted them.

"What was that, Baird?" Barnabas walked to the head of the bed, bending over to catch Baird's words.

"A brother. Darby. She whispered his name when we were in the cabin. I don't know where he is though."

"We'll find him." Barnabas straightened up, his eyes on Berneen. "We'll find him and bring him to her, to safety." He spun on his heel and walked rapidly from the room, knowing that he needed to speak with the other twelve men and send them searching for Darby.

42

Pausing in the doorway to the conference room, Barnabas drew a deep breath. He watched the eleven men who were working away, laptops, phones, tablets in front of them. He could see someone had been using the whiteboards as well. He gave a small smile as he watched Burney Cummins working away with pen and paper. As an author, Burney thought differently from the other men and worked with what he called old-school tools. Breck stood beside him, concern on his face. Barnabas knew that when he spoke, what he would have to change would change the dynamics of the group. This was not how he ever thought it would, but God knew, he understood. God had allowed this, why, he had no idea.

Breck finally spoke. "Barnabas?"

"Yeah, Breck?"

"What happened out there? Buckley won't say, Baird isn't talking, and Berneen won't leave his side. She fought us too hard to get back to him for it to be something minor."

"It's something major, Breck." He sighed, raising a quick prayer for words and guidance before he walked over to drop into the chair at the head of the table, his eyes searching each man's face as they looked up at him.

"Guys. We need to talk. But first we need to pray and pray hard. What I have to tell you is not easy."

An hour later, Barnabas rose, heading for the table that held the coffee pot and the kettle. He hesitated for a moment, his head dropping down as he thought through what had happened in a week or so. He sighed to himself before he picked up his mug and turned watching as the men milled around, each uncertain as to what was coming. He finally dropped back into his seat, watching closely as the men selected their tea or coffee of choice and then sat back down, their eyes on him. Breck had left for a moment and was even now heading back into the room, a sheaf of papers in his hand that he set down in front of Barnabas.

Barnabas drew a deep breath, one of the deepest he thought he had ever had to draw.

"Guys. This is not easy. Our group dynamics have changed, without our input. Yesterday, while Baird, Buckley and Berneen were held captive, Baird was beaten severely. You all know that. What you don't know is why. And this is so hard. It affects Baird in a way I never thought it would. Berneen was asked a question and every time she refused, Baird was beaten. She finally agreed to their demands. What were their demands? That she marry Baird." He waited as he heard the indrawn breaths, the quiet comments, and the questions that spilled from the men. He finally held up a hand. "Buckley told me she had no choice. If she hadn't finally agreed, Baird would not be here. They were adamant that she do what they demanded, or Baird would be killed. Buckley was forced to perform the ceremony, even though he resisted. We have no idea as to why or who yet. That's what we need to dig in and find out."

He nodded as Benen Carroll raised a hand. "What do we know about Berneen? Other than what we have been told by her, and that's not a lot."

Barnabas shook his head. "We're finding out more. She was afraid for someone, we can all agree on that. It is her brother, Darby. Baird was awake enough to tell me that. Where he is, that we need to find."

"Do we know how old he is? What he looks like?" Branigan was reaching for his laptop, already to search.

"We don't know that. That's what we need to find out. We do know that she is an orphan, she's admitted to that."

"How long?" This from Blair, who was reaching for his phone, searching for newspaper articles.

"I'm not sure, but I would suspect a while." Breck finally spoke. "If he's younger than her, she would have likely had custody of him."

Brody spoke up, looking up from his phone. "She was 18 when her parents died. Apparently it was in a riot overseas." He drew in a deep breath, looking up at Barnabas, sorrow and worry combined on his face. "Her brother was only five."

"Five?" Barnabas too drew in a deep breath before he shoved back from the table. "Find out everything you can and get it to me as soon as you can. I'm heading to see if Berneen is awake."

Barnabas hesitated in the doorway of the infirmary room, not sure how to proceed. He walked forward, stopping by Baird's side, watching as he moved restlessly in his sleep. He walked around the bed and crouched down in front of Berneen, finding her awake.

"Berneen?" He watched as her eyes moved to him and a look of devastation and shame came across her face. "We don't blame you. Not one of us. We thank you for keeping Baird alive. Buckley told us what happened." He watched as her eyes slid closed, her throat working as she swallowed hard, tears trickling down her face. He reached out for a damp cloth that sat on a table beside her and handed it to her, watching as she twisted it in her hands.

"I'm so sorry, Barnabas. I can't imagine what the other men think." She looked up at him, tears clouding her eyes. "I tried to stop them. I didn't want to do this. They would have killed him. I couldn't let them do that."

"We know that, Berneen. None of us blame you. We want to help you." He watched her closely.

She looked over at the bed. "How is Baird?"

"He's alive. He's hurting but he will for a while. Now, Berneen, we need to talk. Baird mentioned your brother's name. You said it when you were trying to protect him."

"I was. Someone threatened us. I had to hide him."

"Do you know who?"

She hesitated, then shrugged. "I'm not sure. I think the lawyer was involved." She turned as she heard a sound and then was on her feet, bending over Baird as he roused. "Baird?"

"Neen? Are you okay?" His words were barely audible and he slipped into a natural sleep before she could answer.

"Baird? Baird?" Berneen made a sound of disappointment before she felt Barnabas' arm around her shoulders.

"Berneen, can you come with us? I know. I know. You were told not to leave his side, but I have security at his door. No one will get to him.  We need to talk to you and I want the other men to hear what you have to say.”

She stared at him in horror.  “Oh, no!  I can’t face them.  Look what I did!”

Breck spoke from beside her.  “You did nothing wrong.  Not that we are aware of.  The other guys know that.  They all want to see you, to speak with you.”

Barnabas’ arm around her shoulders drew her away, much to her distress, and then he guided her to the conference room where the men were working away.  He noted with no surprise that Buckley was there, providing the encouragement they all needed.  He made a mental note to talk to Buckley himself or have his father do that.

Barnabas seated Berneen at the table, setting a cup of the peppermint tea she seemed to prefer in front of her before he stepped away to speak with Breck.  She refused to raise her eyes, not wanting to see the looks of condemnation she was sure she would see.

"Berneen?"  Buckley's low voice caught her attention.  "Are you okay?"

"I think so.  I'm not sure."

Barnabas slid into the chair beside her, his eyes on her, knowing the men were watching her.

"Berneen, can you look up for a moment?"  When she didn't respond, he repeated himself.  "Baird would want you to."

She hesitated, then finally raised her head, dreading the looks she just knew she would be facing.  She sought the faces of each man, reading in each one their compassion for her and their concern.  She shook her head.  "I shouldn't be here."

"No, you need to be."  Barnabas sipped at his mug of coffee before he set it back down.  "First, before we do anything else, Buckley?"

Buckley nodded, his head bowing as he petitioned God for peace for the young woman seated at the table and for each one of them, for wisdom as they sought answers, for protection for them all.

Barnabas hesitated for a moment before he began to speak.

"I need to explain our situation here.  It's a unique group of men I have working for me."

Berneen's eyes were trained on him, a puzzled look on her face.

"The Barnabas Foundation was started by my father when I was born, named for me, but based on the Barnabas in the Bible.  It was set up to encourage people to get ahead. He provided no-cost loans and grants to organizations, churches, individuals, etc, who needed them. When he retired and I took over the Foundation, we changed how it works. I employ these men. They work in various occupations in the community but their wages come from the Foundation. They are also volunteers in various groups in the community, being mentors, those who come along side of those who need their help and encouragement. We take no credit for what we do. That credit belongs to God. We meet weekly for a time of prayer to refresh ourselves and then to search through the applications and requests that we receive for help."

"Just men?" Berneen's quiet question had Barnabas pausing, his eyes on her.

"That's correct. It is hoped that as the men meet their life mates and marry, we can expand our services to women and children. That is what our prayer is." Barnabas watched as her eyes slid closed and she reached to swipe at the tears on her face. "Berneen?"

"I wish you had been doing that for women and children. I could have used your help." Her head went down on her folded arms when she finished speaking.

"Berneen? Can you tell us your story? We all want to help you. You're part of our family now."

She looked up at Breck as he spoke, her head shaking. "No, I'm not. I'm an interloper."

Breck shook his head, a slight smile on his face. "No, you're family. Talk to us, please? The men have been searching, finding bits and pieces, but there are things that you know that we won't find, no matter how we search."

She watched Breck as he spoke, knowing he was speaking from his heart and that she really did need to talk to them. She sighed, not seeing the looks the men were exchanging, puzzled looks to be true, but with compassion on their faces. She finally nodded, and when she spoke, her voice was low and broken.

"I have to go back a few years. Mom and Dad were wonderful. Dad provided well for us, and always had everything in order. That's why what happened after they died puzzled me so much.

"Dad had to go overseas on business. For some reason, he really didn't want to go, but went. Mom went with him. While there a riot broke out. They were killed. But they were the only ones hurt or killed." She looked up at Barnabas. "That was just so strange. Their bodies were brought home. The day after the funeral, the lawyer approached me, told me the house and everything in it was gone and we had to leave right away. He gave me thirty minutes to pack what I could and what I needed for Darby before he shoved us into his car and then dropped us off downtown, with nowhere to go and nowhere to stay." She blinked back tears as she stared up at the ceiling. "How do you explain to someone that their parents are gone and now their home is?"

"Berneen, how old were you?"

'Eighteen." She looked at Barnabas as she answered his question, not hearing the quickly indrawn breaths from the men.

"And Darby?"

She shook her head, tears making it impossible for her to speak for a moment. "Five. Dad had changed things so I became his guardian if anything happened to them."

"Eighteen and suddenly responsible for a child. Did you have a boyfriend?" Breck's quiet question startled the other men for a moment.

She nodded. "I did. Until he found out I wouldn't put Darby into foster care. He pushed for that. When I refused, told him he was my only living relative left, that I wouldn't let him go, he laughed at me and walked away. Told me that no man wanted to be saddled with a child."

She once more didn't see the thunderous looks of anger on the men's faces as they shared glances, or hear the angry mutterings. Barnabas did, but watched Berneen closely.

"How did you survive?" Breck asked the question the other men wanted to but didn't ask.

"For the first couple of nights we slept in abandoned buildings. Then I was able to get into a shelter. I had to prove over and over

—

that I had custody of Darby.  Finally, someone helped me to find a furnished room and work at a convenience store.  It was a struggle, still is.  I wanted to go to college, but won't, not while I have to provide for Darby."

"And where is Darby now?"  Barnabas waited for an answer, seeing her struggling with whether to trust him or not.  "Berneen?  Where is Darby?"

"So far, I think he's safe, but it's been three months since I saw him, so I don't know for sure."  She raised her eyes to Barnabas.  "I need to see him, to see he's okay."

"We'll find him and bring him to you.  Trust us, he'll come to no harm.  Just tell us where he is."

Berneen studied his face before she raised her eyes and did the same to each man seated there, finally realizing that for now she was safe and that Darby would be to.

She sighed, reaching for a paper, writing down an address.  "There is one thing.  He won't come willingly unless you give him the code words."

"Code words?  Not just one?"  This comment came from Brandon Conaghan.

She nodded.  "It's what he wanted.  He wanted to be safe and he felt if we had a system of words then no one could persuade him to go with them."  She reached for a pad of paper and dashed off a quick note.  "Give him this, after you give the code words."

Barnabas nodded to the men he wanted to go.  Brandon stopped by Berneen.

"What are the words, Berneen?"  His words were quiet as he reached for the folded paper.

"They are carnation and daisy."  She sighed, a slight smile on her face.  "He wanted flowers and would only take the names of the ones I like best.  There is a phrase as well."  She paused, sorrow flicking across her face.  "It's like this:  Go with Berneen.  Mom and Dad.  He chose it as well."  She rose suddenly and ran from the room, seeking solace with Baird.

---

Her head resting against the pillow, Berneen pulled the blanket up over her more, her eyes on Baird as he tossed and turned, his sleep restless. She wasn't thinking of anything, keeping her mind blank on purpose, not sure if Barnabas would be successful in finding and convincing Darby to go with his men. She looked around at the quiet steps, a frown coming on her face as she saw Breck with one of the other men.

"Berneen? We have a question for you. Buckley said you were told not to leave Baird at all. How do they know if you do?" Breck's question caught at her thoughts and she shrugged.

"I have no idea."

"Do you have any other jewelry other than your rings?"

She finally nodded, her hand reaching for a necklace that she wore. "Just this."

"Can we see it for a moment?" He waited until she nodded and then took it off, handing it to him.

Branigan reached for it, inspecting it before he nodded. "What we thought, Breck. There's something here that would track her. I can remove it." He walked away with her necklace, leaving her staring after him.

"Hey, wait! You can't take that." She shoved at her blanket, her hands stilling as she saw Breck shaking his head. "What? Did he really just do that?"

"He did, Berneen. He'll be right back with your necklace. I promise. There's a tag of some kind on it that tracks you."

Her face paled, and she drew in a deep breath. "How long?"

Breck shrugged. "We don't know that. Not until we catch the men responsible." He shot a quick glance back at the door. "Can you give us any names?"

She sighed. "You're not giving up on that, are you?" When he grinned at her and shook his head, she stared at him. "Okay. The lawyer is Owen Small. I don't know of any others."

She didn't see the closed look come over Branigan's face at the name or the look the two men exchanged. That was a name they knew, had been looking into for a long time, just waiting to find something to hold him responsible for what they suspected.

"Have they found Darby?" She looked up at Breck with a plea on her face.

"Not yet. They're searching for him. They haven't gone to the house door yet, not wanting to spook him or let someone know where he is." Breck turned slightly as he heard a sound. "Excuse me."

Berneen rose, moving to stand beside Baird, watching as he awakened slightly, her hand reaching for his. Baird's eyes flicked open, and she could tell he was more aware of where he was.

"Baird?" Her soft voice drew his attention to her.

"Berneen? Where are we?"

"You are in the infirmary at your home. I just happen to be here as well." She watched closely as he nodded before glancing around and then reaching to raise the head of the bed. "How are you feeling?"

"Sore, but I want out of here. Where's Doc?"

"He won't be back until this afternoon." Breck stood at the end of the bed, assessing Baird. "You're not going anywhere until he says you can."

Baird's head went back as he groaned. "I need out of here, Breck. I need to keep Berneen safe. I can't do that from here."

"We hear you, Baird, but no, not until Doc comes back." Breck excused himself as he heard his name called.

"Berneen? Help me up, please?"

"No, you need to be here." Her hand on his stilled his motions. "Let me see if I can find something for you to eat."

He shook his head. "No, don't leave me."

---

Breck had returned, his face thoughtful, as he approached the bed.  "Why is it so important that she not leave you?"

"They told me that if she did, she would die."  Baird looked up at the silence that greeted his words.  "What?"

"When did they tell you that?"

"When we were separated.  Why?"

"Because I was told the very same thing after they made us marry.  Who are these monsters?"  Berneen ran from the room, not sure where she was heading, but finding her way to the chapel on the main floor of the building.  She slid into a seat, her arms wrapped around herself, not sure if she should be there, but not knowing where else to go.

—

Brandon watched the young man approaching them, his eyes dropping to a photo he held before he tucked it away in his jacket pocket. He nodded to Benen, Blair and Brady, knowing that Darby Dakin was nearing them. He deliberately stepped into Darby's path, causing the youth to stop suddenly and look up at him, fear flickering briefly in his eyes.

"Excuse me? I need to pass, please." Darby stood, waiting for the men to move, frowning when they didn't. "I'm sorry. I really do need to go by you." He moved to the side, finding his way still blocked. "Is there a problem?"

Brandon finally spoke, a smile playing across his face. "If you're Darby Dakin, and I have no doubt you are, we need to talk." He watched closely Darby's face, seeing a slight quiver on the lips. "Your sister sent us."

Darby remained still, his eyes trained on Brandon, but noting the three other men.

Brandon grinned. "Berneen was right. She said you wouldn't respond. Here are the words she gave us. Carnation. Daisy. And a phrase. Go with Berneen. Mom and Dad." He watched as Darby's shoulders slumped and put out a hand to steady the youth.

"She's safe?" Darby's desperate question was barely above a whisper. "I haven't heard from her in weeks."

"She's safe. Now, do you need to go into the house or can you come with us right away?" Benen spoke from beside Darby.

"No. I carry everything with me. She told me to."

"Prepared. Good. We like that." Been gentle hand shoved him into the car. "In you go. We'll take you to your sister."

"She's okay? She's not hurt?" Darby was anxious, desperate to know how his sister was. She was the only relative he knew. He could barely remember his parents.

"She has had what you might call an adventure." Brandon turned to him, his eyes meeting first Blair who was behind the wheel, taking them away from the house and towards Berneen. "She was kidnapped and held captive. Some of us men managed to get her free."

"Kidnapped? When? Three months ago? That's when she stopped communicating with me."

"That sounds about right." Brady finally spoke, his eyes having assessed Darby's condition as best he could. "Do you know anything about who would want to do that?"

Darby's face darkened. "That lawyer. Or her boyfriend from when we had to leave the house. He was nasty to me. Berneen never saw what he did and I was too scared to say anything."

"He's not in the picture as far as Berneen in concerned." The four men exchanged a glance before Brady sighed. "We have to tell you something though. Your sister was married yesterday. Not by choice. She chose to do that to save the life of a friend of ours."

"Married?" Darby's voice rose sharply. "How? No way!"

"I'm sorry, Darby." Brandon's soft voice caught his attention. "She is. Baird was beaten almost to death."

"It can't be legal, can it?" Darby's eyes searched each of the men's faces before he slumped back against the seat. "It's not. It can't be."

"I'm sorry, Darby." Brady's voice cut through his dark thoughts. "A friend of ours was forced to perform the ceremony. Whoever the men were who had abducted the three of them made sure it was done legally. We searched. The marriage is recorded as happening."

Darby's face was buried in his hands by the time Brady finished. "This can't be happening. Why Berneen?"

"That's what we're working through to find out. If you know anything, we'll want to talk to you."

Darby was silent, his thoughts in disarray. "I need to see Neen." His voice was barely above a whisper, as he stared through the windshield, watching as the darkness deepened and the stars came out. "I just need Neen."

The men nodded soberly, knowing she needed her brother as well.

Brady led Darby quietly through the hallways of the building, stopping for a moment at the infirmary door. "They should be here. Doc wasn't sure if he would let Baird go to his apartment or not." He cracked open the door and paused. "It looks as if he let them go."

He turned Darby around, walking with him towards the elevator, hesitating as he saw Barnabas heading their way.

"Darby, this is Barnabas. He's the one we work for."

Darby studied the older man before his hand went out for Barnabas to shake. "Thank you. Thank you for finding Berneen. Where is she?"

"Doc released Baird and let him go home. They're upstairs in his apartment. That's where Brady's taking you." Barnabas watched as the youth struggled to control his emotions, not willing to cry in front of the older men. "Come on, Darby. We'll get you to your sister in a couple of minutes."

Barnabas tapped lightly at the apartment door and then opened it, moving through with Darby and Brady following. He paused as he heard heated words from the couple in the living room. He watched their standoff for a moment before he spoke.

"Baird. Berneen. Stop, you two. I have someone here who wants to see Berneen."

The words halted as Baird looked towards the three standing in the entranceway, Berneen not moving.

"Berneen? Sweetheart?" Baird's voice finally broke through her stillness. "I think you need to turn around. Sweetheart? Please?"

She glared at him. "I'm not your sweetheart." She finally turned, not sure what or who was there, her hands flying to her face as she saw Darby and then she was across the floor, sobs shaking her

—

body as the siblings clung to each other, Darby's face wet as well from his tears.

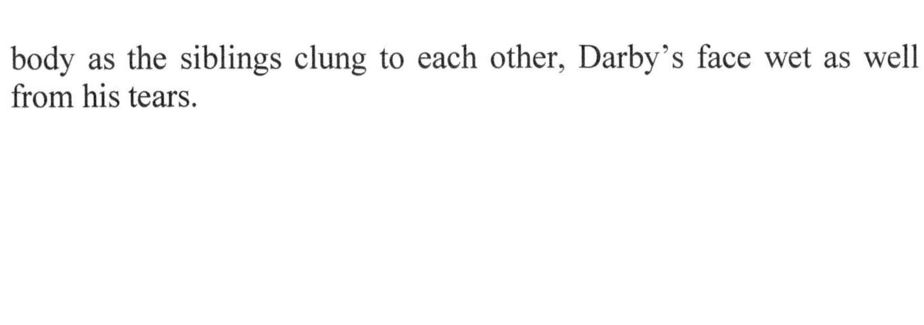

57

Berneen tried to control her sobs, bring her emotions back under control, knowing she needed to do that, not just for herself but for her beloved brother. Her thanks raised to God, knowing He was the one who had kept her brother safe and brought him back to her. She looked up at Brady, mouthing her thanks to him. He nodded, spoke quietly to Barnabas and Baird and then walked away, closing the door quietly behind him.

Berneen finally stood back, her arms wrapped around herself as she studied her brother.

"Darby? You're okay?"

He nodded, not wanting to trouble her with the feeling he had been followed more than once.

"No, you're not. How many times?"

"A few. I couldn't see them but I know someone was there." He lifted his eyes to Barnabas. "I was followed. I don't know why."

"That's okay, we'll figure it out. Right now, though, I think you're needing something to eat. Come on. Baird won't mind if we raid his fridge. I hope he has something besides bagels and cream cheese." Barnabas winked at Darby as he turned the younger man towards the kitchen, laughing at Baird's protest that the fridge was stocked, Anna had seen to that.

Baird watched Berneen closely for a moment before he approached and just enveloped her into a hug. She clung to him, her tears wetting his shirt once more.

"You okay?" His voice was low enough so that only she could hear him.

"I'm not sure, Baird. Not anymore. I'm glad Darby's here, but it just complicates things."

His chin on the top of her head, he sighed, tightening his hold on her. "It does, but we'll work it through. Do you want him here with you or do you want him to stay with Doc and Anna?"

"Here. I can't leave him anymore." She gave a groan of frustration. "This is so unfair, Baird."

"I know, Sweetheart. I know. You've been shoved into something you don't want, may never want, and don't know why or who."

She finally stepped back, almost running for the bathroom. He could heard the tap running, knowing she was seeking to control her emotions. He sighed, his gaze looking up as he sought wisdom from God as to what he did or didn't do. He finally moved towards the kitchen, peace in his heart, but hurting physically. He was ready to lay down again, to take some pain medications, but he was reluctant to, not until he had talked to Barnabas.

Barnabas shoved away from the counter he had been leaning against, holding out a mug for Baird. Baird nodded, his eyes on Darby.

"Where am I to go?" Darby's question caught the two men off guard for a moment. "I mean, you just got married, right?"

Baird pulled back the chair beside Darby, and slid down, grateful to be off his feet, his eyes closing for a moment against the pain. Barnabas watched, a frown on his face, as he searched Baird's face, seeing the deepening colours of the bruises, the cuts and scrapes from his beating.

"Berneen wants you to stay here. We'll work it out, Darby. You two need each other." Baird laid a hand on the youth's arm. "You two have healing you need to do. We'll keep you as safe as we can here."

"But I have school. How do I go back and forth?" Darby ignored Baird's words for the moment.

"We'll work out something that you can do here. Baird here mentors young men in high school."

"You do?" Darby was surprised. "As a volunteer?"

—

"That's correct. We all have normal occupations but we all volunteer in an organization that helps encourage others to get ahead." Baird's eyes slid closed and he swayed slightly in his chair.

Barnabas moved towards Baird, pulling him to his feet, and then directing him down the hall, meeting Berneen as she walked towards them.

"Baird?"

"He needs to be laying down, Berneen. I'll get him settled." Barnabas shot a glance behind him. "You need to talk to Darby. He's not sure where he should be."

She nodded, her eyes on Baird, her thoughts muddled as to which of the men who she now had in her life that she should go to. She walked towards the kitchen, watching Darby as he moved around, making himself another sandwich, and saw his look of gloom and defeat and worry.

"Darby?"

Darby spun, his eyes on his sister. "Neen?"

"We'll talk, Darb. Tonight, I've made up the guest room for you. Not that I had to do much. Baird is so prepared for anything and everything it seems."

"We do need to talk, Neen. I tried to find you, but couldn't." He blinked rapidly, not willing for the tears to fall again. "I just need to understand what happened to you."

"I'm not sure I even know. Once you're done that sandwich, head off for bed. I left the light on for you."

"Neen?" She turned back at his questioning voice. "Are you okay? I mean, with marrying like you did. The men who found me told me what happened. It shouldn't have been that way."

"I know, Darb. But God allowed it. He could have stepped in at any time. We'll work it through." She turned as Barnabas stopped beside her. "Baird's settled?"

"He is. He almost refused his pain medications but thought better of that idea." Barnabas studied the young woman in front of him, sorrow in his heart for what his friend and his lady had been put

—

through. "We'll talk more tomorrow, Berneen." He walked away, leaving the siblings staring after him.

Snuggling down further under the blanket, Berneen laid her head against the pillow she had dropped on the living room couch earlier, a yawn drawn from her.  She glanced at the clock, only two in the morning, she thought.  It's been a long night and it's not over.  She had been up and down, making sure her men were asleep.

She had just gotten Baird settled again.  He had been up and had refused her requests to take his pain medications until the pain had almost doubled him over.  It had taken a while to work but she knew he was sleeping now.  He had wanted to talk and she had refused, knowing his body needed the sleep, that he wasn't ready to hear what she had to say.  And just what did she have to say, she wondered?

She had stopped to check on Darby on her way back to the living room, dropping to her knees beside his bed, a hand on his hair, desperate pleas raised to God.  She knew what she was facing was far from over.  That was a given, she thought.  She just wanted her men safe.  She didn't care about herself.

She reached for her Bible, her hand rubbing along the well-worn leather.  She had left it with Darby when she sent him into hiding.  She blinked rapidly for a moment, willing the tears away.  I've cried enough, she decided.  I need to be strong and not cry at anything anymore.  Lord, where do I search for help?  What verses do I go to? I know You've promised safety, that I am never alone, but some days it feels like that.  I need to have something I can cling to, a verse or verses, something, please, dear Lord.

She lifted her head hours later, then shoving back her blanket, stumbled to her feet, running for Baird as she heard muttering coming from him.  Darby met her in the hallway.

"Berneen?"

"It's Baird."  She shoved the door to the bedroom all the way open and was on her knees beside him, her hand on his face, her other hand tight in his, watching as his head tossed and turned and his muttering finally subsided.

"Baird?" Berneen's voice finally reached to him and he roused.

"Berneen? What?" He shifted his position, his hand reaching for hers, not realizing he already held her other hand.

"You were dreaming. At least, I think you were." She studied him, seeing the darkening bruises. "Who is Art?"

"Art? He was someone my Dad knew. Why?"

"Because you've mentioned him in your dreams."

Baird sighed, squinting at the clock, seeing Darby standing in the doorway, not sure where he needed to be. "Let me get up, and we'll talk."

She frowned at him. "You're not that strong yet, Baird."

"I'll manage. You go put on your tea and my coffee. Darby here can help me if I need help." He sighed as she refused to move. "Neen? I promise. I'll be careful."

Berneen stood for a moment, leaning back against the closed door, listening to the groans from Baird and the quiet comments from Darby, before she headed for the kitchen. Baird was right. They needed to talk. But they also needed to talk to Barnabas and whoever it was that was the leader of Baird's team. She knew the men were divided into two teams, but that they walked back and forth between the teams as necessary. That, Buckley had explained while they were captive.

She turned as she heard footsteps in the hall, leaning back on the fridge, watching carefully as Baird sank into a chair, Darby right behind him, hands held up in case Baird stumbled. He shared a look with his sister, shaking his head slightly. She sighed, knowing she was going to have to send for Doc, and not wanting to awaken him.

Their meal finished, Baird reached for the hands of the siblings, bowing his head for prayer. It took him a while to find his voice, emotions roiling within him. Darby studied his sister and her husband before he bowed his head, not sure what it all meant for them or where he fit in.

Barnabas' fingers tapped against the papers Berneen had slid across the table to him.  He watched her closely, not quite sure how to read her.  He didn't know her well enough to do just that.  His gaze shifted to Darby, finding him a hard read as well.  Darby's eyes were on his sister and they were communicating in a silent manner.  He then looked at Baird, a frown on his face as he watched his friend study his wife, a look in his eyes Barnabas had never seen before.  He sighed even as he prayed, asking for safety for his friend.

"What is this, Berneen?"  He flipped through the papers, not reading anything, as he waited for her answer.

She rubbed her hands along her legs, not sure how to even answer him.  "It's names, dates, addresses.  Anything Darby or I could think of."  She turned her face to Baird, disconcerted to find him studying her so intently.  "Baird has added some names and data as well."

"Baird?"  Barnabas' voice finally cut through whatever or wherever Baird had drifted to and he looked up at his friend.

"Barnabas?  What did you say?"

Barnabas ducked his head even as he shook it, to hide the grin he couldn't quite contain.  Lord, I do believe my friend is falling in love right in front of me.  Bless these two, dear Lord.  They have a lot to overcome.

"Baird?  What exactly have you given me?"  He looked down at the papers once more, a frown on his face. "What have you three gone and done?"

"Just listed names, addresses, dates, thoughts, whatever came up.  We tried to organize it according to which one of us remembered what or who."  Baird watched Barnabas closely, not quite sure if what they had done would help.

---

"This will help. Let me look through it and then we'll talk." Barnabas was soon engrossed in reading, his pen out marking spots on the pages, writing comments.

Baird shook his head, regretting it as it pounded. Berneen was on her feet, heading for the door as a knock came, and Doc walked in, a quiet word or two spoken to Berneen, before he was beside Baird, drawing him to his feet and back to the bedroom.

"How are you feeling, Baird? Don't try and hide it from me. You know you can't." Doc had his stethoscope out, ready to listen to the younger man's heart and lungs.

"I hurt, Doc, like I have never hurt in my life. I don't want Berneen to know how bad." Sweat beaded along his forehead as he spoke.

"She knows, Baird. She knows. You can't hide it from her. She's too perceptive." Doc turned as he heard a tap at the door and then Berneen slipped into the room.

"Doc? How is he?" Worry laced her voice.

"He's starting to heal, Berneen, but that will take time. Physically, that is. There are other emotions that he needs to deal with, that you need to deal with, and that as a couple you need to deal with." He stepped back, his eyes assessing the bruising. "The bruising is changing, Baird. You're healing. I would suggest you not go back to work before next week."

"I have to, Doc. I have plans I promised to have ready by Friday. I can't let that couple down."

Doc shook his head. "Just how far along are the plans?"

"Almost done. But then I have another couple coming in Friday afternoon to see me." Baird sighed, knowing what Doc would say. "I have to, Doc. I can't put them off."

"I'll allow it on one condition. Berneen there is with you." He held up a hand. "She's with you, calls me if she needs to, and you will rest when you can. Do you understand?"

Baird finally nodded. "I do, Doc, better than you think." He looked past Doc to where Berneen stood, hesitating as to what had

—

been asked of her, emotions flowing across her face. He frowned for a moment. "Berneen?"

"Baird? Just what is it you do? I know you tutor and mentor youths from the local high school, but what your occupation is? That I have no idea. I won't agree to anything until you fully explain what you do." There was a bite to her words as she grew angry, not at Baird, but at the circumstances that had joined their lives together and anger at the men who had caused it.

Doc shook his head. "You two need to talk. Baird's an architect, Berneen. He provides house drawings and plans, I think is how he words it, for low-income families and single people. He is paid by The Barnabas Foundation, as are all the men, but he does charge a nominal fee, which I understand goes back to the families once the house is built." His gaze steady on Berneen, he saw the moment she understood the character of the man sitting in front of her.

"Baird? Is this true?"

Baird sighed. "It is. Not many people know it, outside of the Foundation. That's how Barnabas has chosen to work it. I mean, they don't know that I am paid through the Foundation. That's confidential." He glared at Doc for a moment, who just laughed at him.

"She has to know, Baird. She has to know. And from what I understand, she now draws a salary from the Foundation as well, doesn't she?"

Berneen stared between the two men, finally remembering to snap her mouth closed. "No, that can't be right. I have to work. I have to support Darby and myself."

Baird rose, a hand resting on Doc's shoulder for a moment, before he walked to stand in front of Berneen. "That's what we have to talk about. I hadn't known how you felt. Barnabas can explain it. But yes, once we men marry, our wives draw a salary from the same source as we do. That's how Barnabas and his father wanted it. That way, we can both serve God where He wants us to be, whether in a work place or as a volunteer somewhere. We'll need to watch where you go for now. As for Darby, I imagine Barnabas has already taken steps to provide a source of income for him as well."

—

Berneen studied Baird, then looked past him at Doc, who was nodding, before her eyes slid closed and the tears she could not stop flowed down her face.  She swiped at them angrily before she felt Baird just envelop her into his arms and hold her tight.  She didn't hear Doc's quiet prayer before he walked from the room.

"Baird?"

"Neen?  It's true.  Barnabas will look after you two.  And before you ask, it's okay.  His father was a billionaire, investing over the years and just growing his finances.  This is how he has chosen to use it, to help others out.  It's part of how they see being a Barnabas, an encouragement."

She leaned back, to study him.  "Just what do you mean, be a Barnabas?  You all keep saying that, but not explaining it."

Baird wrapped an arm around her shoulders and led her from the room, heading for the kitchen, where he could heard Barnabas and Darby laughing over something Doc had said on his way out of the apartment.

"Barnabas?  Have a moment?  Can you explain what your Dad was thinking when he set up the Foundation?  Berneen has asked."  He slid back a chair for her, seated her and then chose the chair beside her, his hand coming out to grasp hers.

Barnabas shot Baird a quick look before his gaze dropped to Berneen, seeing her confusion.

"Sure. You're a believer, I know, Berneen. You are familiar with Paul and his companion of his trips, Barnabas? Paul indicated that Barnabas was an encouragement to himself and other believers. Dad believed we needed people in today's world like Barnabas. He set up the Foundation, when I was born and named it for me, in order to do just that. The low-cost loans and grants helped out many. When he decided to retire and turned it over to me, we had a long, sometimes heated, discussion of where we wanted to go. He wanted to change the focus of it. I didn't. I wanted it to stay the way he had set it up. We finally came to see eye to eye on it. So, now our focus is mentoring, walking alongside those who are down and out, those who need a hand up. Do you understand?"

Berneen nodded, her eyes not having left Barnabas' face. "I do. I think it's wonderful. And why has no one else done this?" She shared a look with Darby, who had a slight frown on his face. "But I don't understand. Baird said that you had planned to provide an income for the wives as the guys married. Why?"

"Why? Because we want to. Because you ladies are worth more than the most precious jewel in the world. You will come in as helpmeets to my guys. It is only right that you have an income. You can work out in the work place, if you desire, or in volunteer situations. That is your choice. It makes no difference to your income." He turned to watch Darby, seeing the longing on the youth's face. "Darby, as of today, you have an income as well." He held up a hand as Darby went to protest. "No, it's only right. We need to help you out, to encourage you. You've had a rough life, both you and your sister. You are the people we look for to help."

"I wish you had been there years ago." Darby's broken words showed how deep his emotions ran before he was on his feet, heading for his room. They heard the door shut quietly behind him.

---

Berneen reached to hug Barnabas. "Thank you. You don't know what that means to Darby and to me. We've struggled for so long, making do with what I could manage to earn, going without so many things, even necessities."

Barnabas shared a look with Baird, before he spoke. "It's who we are, Berneen. All of us. We just want to help those who need it." He looked down at the papers in front of him as he heard her settle back against Baird, whose arm had come around her.

"Those names you wanted to take about, Barnabas?" Baird spoke, his eyes on Berneen.

"Those names. Yes. We need to talk about them." He sorted through the pages. "Berneen, Owen Small?"

"Him? That's a name I never wanted to hear again." She shivered, her arms wrapping tighter around herself

"Talk to me. Tell me about him." Barnabas pulled over a pad of paper and drew out his pen, catching Berneen's frown. "I work best with pen and paper. That's how I do it." He grinned at her before he sobered. "Who was he to you?"

"He was a lawyer Dad had used at work. Dad was a building inspector for the town over from here. He inspected commercial buildings. Small worked for the town, or so he said. Dad never was quite sure of him. He didn't have him do any personal work for him." She stared at Barnabas before she twisted to look up at Baird. "That's why I couldn't figure it out."

"Figure out what, Sweetheart?" Baird prompted her when she didn't speak for a few minutes.

"He said he was the lawyer Dad had used to draw up his will and his powers of attorney." She blinked back tears, her emotions still raw after all that time. "He told us the night after we buried Mom and Dad that we had to get out. That the house had been taken back over by the mortgage company and that Dad knew that was happening when he went overseas. He said he was Darby's guardian but he wanted nothing to do with the brat as he called him." She struggled with her anger. "He gave us thirty minutes to pack and leave. He dropped us off down town. I never knew who to turn to. I didn't think I could go to the police. He told me that if I did, I would never see Darby again."

—

Barnabas' mouth had tightened as she spoke, knowing that she was repeating herself but also knowing she had to. "Do you know who your father used for personal legal matters?"

"I think it was Walter Trevor, but I can't be sure. I know he was a good friend of Dad's." She dropped her head to her hands. "I should have gone to him but I didn't."

"You were in shock. You were trying to look after yourself and your brother. I can have Brody approach him. He's the paralegal in the group. Is that okay?"

She nodded, her eyes thankful. "I guess. I should have but I was afraid."

"Afraid you'd lose Darby?" At her nod, Barnabas shook his head. "You were an adult at that point, right? There would have been no reason for them to take him away from you, unless it was played that you were homeless and incompetent to care for him." He looked at Baird as he drew in a deep breath.

"How wealthy were your parents, Berneen?" Baird's question had her turning her head once more to look at him.

"I'm not sure. We had a nice house, enough food, not extravagant, that I know. Dad was saving for our college funds, that's what he said."

Barnabas nodded. "Now, how did they die? And where?"

"They were in Europe. I'm not sure which country now. There was a riot and they were involved as bystanders. But I don't get it. They were the only ones hurt or killed. That doesn't sound right. It never did."

"We'll look into that as well." Barnabas paused as he flipped through the paperwork in front of him, pausing once in a while to read a sentence or paragraph. "Baird, your turn. Some of what you need to say, I know. But you have hidden depths that you have not told anyone, or if you have, it's been years."

Baird nodded, then sipped at his coffee, a grimace in place as he realized it had cooled. "We've talked many times, you and I, Barnabas, but you're right. There are things I have not said." He dropped his gaze to Berneen, who sat, leaning on his without realizing what she was doing, and waited for a moment, trying to gather his thoughts.

"Baird?" Barnabas' voice drew his attention and Baird sighed.

"Okay.  So, where do I start?"

"Your mother, Baird?"  Berneen had twisted once more so she could watch him.  She saw Darby quietly taking a seat, knowing he needed to hear this as well.

Baird drew a deep breath, knowing he needed to talk, had needed to for years.  Lord, let me release this, please?  You know I need to.  Is this where I change to who You want me to be, to let go of baggage I've carried, baggage like that those I've mentored I've told to let go of?

He watched Darby closely, not sure how the youth would take what he had to say.

"Barnabas, you know my mother was killed in a bus accident when I was seven."  He heard Berneen's softly indrawn breath and saw the tightened look that came across Darby's face.  "Dad and I were a team, just the two of us.  He was a commercial architect.  I think he knew your father, Berneen, Darby, if he was a building inspector.  I seem to remember a man named Dakin that he mentioned once or twice."

Berneen nodded.  "He was.  He inspected commercial buildings."

Baird continued.  "Dad said there were some inspectors who were what he called 'shady', that took graft money.  He knew your father didn't, Berneen.  Somewhere he left a paper that named them all but I could never find it.  Our house was searched after he died.  I think that was what they were looking for."

Barnabas paused, his pen poised above the paper.  "You never mentioned that your home was searched.  Is there a police report?"

Baird nodded.  "I have a copy.  It happened when I was 19." He paused, working to control the anger he had felt at that invasion. "Dad was called to a commercial building.  It wasn't one of his own, but the builder felt something was off and wanted a second opinion on it.  He was there with Dad and a couple of other men.  The building collapsed before they could get out.  Shoddy workmanship was how the city termed it.  I heard that a private investigator had been hired, but I never heard the outcome of that."  He looked up at Barnabas.  "I have notes that I can copy for you.  We need to resolve

———

this. Somehow I think this is all involved, Berneen's father, my Dad, and the lawyers."

"That's what the fellows are picking up. They know your father was clear, Berneen, Darby. They have determined he was not involved in any inspections of that building. And they know that your father was not the architect on record, Baird." Barnabas studied his notes. "Baird, what happened to all your belongings?"

Baird stiffened, sorrow on his face. "There was a fire about a month after Dad died. Everything was destroyed. It was always felt that it was arson, but no one ever confirmed that with me."

Barnabas nodded. "We'll look into that and pull reports as we can. Brody I think had come across that and was working on obtaining the reports he could." He paused as his phone chimed and he excused himself to take a call. He spun quickly as he listened, his eyes on Darby who had returned to sit beside his sister, their words quiet as they spoke to one another. He sighed as he pocketed his phone. Things just got more complicated, Lord. How do we solve this and keep these three safe at the same time? He was worried, he knew, not just for these three but for whoever else ended up in the path of the men who were after them.

Berneen watched him closely as he sat back down, her eyes thoughtful before they shifted to her brother, knowing somehow that whatever it was Barnabas had learned involved him.

"Barnabas?" Her quiet voice raised his head and he sighed once more.

"How close were you to the couple you were living with, Darby?" His question startled the siblings.

"They were people we knew through someone else. Why? What has happened to them?"

"They're safe. We moved them from their home after the guys found you." Barnabas watched Baird closely, knowing he had a good idea of where he was heading with his words. "But their house burned down last night. No one was inside, thank God."

"Burned down? How?" Darby shot to his feet, not sure if he should be heading for that couple or stay where he was.

—

73

"We're talking with the arson investigator now and the investigating officer. We'll know more." Barnabas pointed to the chair. "Sit, Darby. They're safe. We moved them and all their possessions out of there last night."

"You did? How?"

Barnabas gave a quick grin. "We had friends, more than we really needed, who went in, packed them up, and moved them. I won't tell you where they are but they are safe. They were worried about you and Berneen."

Darby sat back. "But how did they know where I was?"

"That we're working on as well. Branigan would like to see your backpack, if he can. They may have slipped something in there to track you."

Darby was on his feet and back with the pack. "Do you need anything that was in it?"

"Not at the moment, but Branigan may want to look it over, only if it's okay with you and Berneen."

"Do what you need to, Barnabas. I want this over." Berneen's voice once more had a bite to it, drawing Darby's eyes to his sister. He was not used to the tone of voice she was using.

'We'll do our best to keep you both safe, you and Darby, Berneen."

"But will it be enough?" She was on her feet and they heard the sliding door to the balcony open and close.

"Baird? You're off to work?" Barnabas' change of subject brought Darby's eyes to him.

"I am. Branigan's with me. That's the condition Doc put on me going back."

"Then, I guess, Darby, you're with me. Come on. I'll show you around and introduce you to some of the men who may be around. I know Doc's Anna will be looking for you. She's told me that." Barnabas gathered his papers, rose and then followed Darby from the room, his heart raising in prayer for Baird, knowing they were not done, not by a long shot, he thought, with the men after them.  They really hadn't figured it out yet, either, and that worried him more than he let on.

A cup of her tea in her hand, Berneen wandered Baird's office, her fingers coming out once in a while to trace a picture, a portrait, a model.  She could see the intensity he put into his work, the desire to provide the best he could for those who were less well off.  She finally turned, perching against a credenza and watched as he work, his concentration on the drawing he was finishing off, seeing the ruffled curls he had been running his fingers through.  She also saw the pain on his face and sighed.  It was time for him to take a break and just how did she get him to do that?

She walked quietly back into the reception area, studying the desk there, knowing he worked on his own without a secretary.  She sat for a moment, her eyes searching the desk, before she rose and walked over to a canvas of Lake Erie at its wildest, she thought.  She looked for the artist name and could not find it.  She stepped back a bit, her mind searching through the Scriptures about storms, and feeling a calmness and peace come over her.  God, You're here, right in the midst of my storm.  You are here.  I am not alone.  I don't need to fear the storm.  You can calm the waves, the wind, the rain.  But You can and do bring peace to me.  Thank you.

She felt an arm come around her and then leaned back against Baird.  She was slowly learning to trust him, even though it had only been a few days she had known him.  She realized she had read his character correctly when they had both been captive first.

"Are you ready to go, Baird?"

"Almost.  You seem entranced with that photo."

"I am.  I was just remembering verses about God and storms. We're in the middle of a huge one, I think."

"That we are, but we are not alone, never alone."  He waited for her to ask about the artist.  "I took that just after Dad died.  It suited my mood at the moment."

"It's beautiful, Baird.  I can see why you would say what you just did about it."  She looked down at his hands lightly grasping

---

hers and frowned again, studying the engraved red gold ring on his finger and then the matching band on hers. "Baird?"

"Yes, Sweetheart?"

"The rings. Who picked them out?"

"I did. They had picked out plain thin gold rings. I didn't like them."

"And how hard a time did you have?" She felt him shrug. "Do you think they had placed something in them to track us?"

"That's what I guess I was thinking. I was also thinking that a plain gold band didn't suit you. You needed something more, something special."

She sighed once more as she leaned back on him, feeling him sway slightly. "Thank you. Now, are you done enough that you can leave?"

"I am. I need to check my messages, though." He released her and moved to the reception desk, sliding heavily into it.

"Teach me how to check them. I can do that. I can't just sit here and do nothing." Berneen was at his side, perching on the corner of the desk. "Please, Baird? I need to feel useful. I haven't felt needed or wanted in months."

"Darby needs you." He sat back, his eyes on her downcast face. "I need you, Berneen. I don't think you realize how much."

She shook her head, not looking at him, sliding from the desk. "No, you don't. You just think you do. Come on, Baird. You need your medications, don't you?" She walked through the door, not looking back, leaving Baird staring after her, sorrow on his face, but also determination to show her exactly how much she was needed.

Lord, I'm falling in love with her, even in such a short time, and I have no idea where to go with that. I don't know how she feels and I won't ask. She'll need to tell me, if and when she is ready to. Even if it takes fifty years, I won't leave her.

He rose, feeling the pain but not as bad as he had. He healed quickly, he knew, and prayed that this time, he would heal even quicker. He turned out the lights, closed and locked the door behind him, and then reached for Berneen's hand, not catching her look at him or their linked hands.

Breck watched the couple walk away, then down at the papers in his hands.  He needed to talk to Berneen, but shrugged, walking back to his own office, not willing to disturb them at that time.  He would catch up with them later.  He looked up to see Darby standing in front of him, a forlorn, lost look on his face.

"Darby?  Looking for me?"

Darby shrugged.  "I don't know.  I just need to be doing something and don't know what.  I've managed to get through that pile of homework someone left for me."  He grinned at Breck.  "Thank you for talking to my teachers.  I can keep up with the class now."

Breck shrugged off Darby's thanks and then dropped the papers on his desk before he turned Darby around.  "Come on.  Have we shown you our gym?  It even has a walking track and when the weather is cold, we have an outdoor rink.  Play hockey?"

"Shinny.  I do.  Say, this is great!"  Darby's face glowed at the thought of playing shinny, a favourite sport of his.  "Do you guys play hockey or shinny?"

"We do, as much as we can.  Barnabas is in the planning stages for a rink near the edge of the property that can be used by community groups.  We get to use it anytime it's free, when it's finished."

Keeping his eyes on Berneen seated on the couch, Baird reached for the papers Breck was endeavouring to get her to take.

"They won't bite, Berneen." Breck grinned at the dark look she shot him. "Just some paperwork to complete. Routine stuff."

"Routine stuff. That's what they all say before they ask for a complete life history on you. Why?"

"Why? Because we need this for you. You're part of our family now and we need to put data on file for you. If not for our records, then for the government's."

"Right. The good old government. The government that never helps." Berneen knew she was grumbling but couldn't stop herself.

Breck shook his head. "Just complete them and get them back to me, please? It's likely nothing more than what you would complete for employment and likely a lot less. Name. Address. Both of which we do know. And banking information so we can begin to deposit your cheques."

"Can I refuse that?"

Breck stared at her, shocked before he looked at Baird, who was shaking his head. "Refuse the cheques? Berneen, did Barnabas not explain what is laid out in our charter? That when the men marry, their wives collect earnings from us?"

"He did. I'm just not sure on that." She was being obstinate, she knew, just why, she wasn't sure.

"It doesn't matter if you're sure or not. It goes into your account. You are now an employee of the Foundation." He rose, disappointment on his face. "You're the first one of the guys' wives. Don't let what you've been through colour how you look on what we do or what we provide." He walked away, the door closely quietly behind him.

Baird stared at her for a moment, then walked away, leaving her on her own, her thoughts jumbled and dark. She wasn't up to this, she thought. She didn't deserve any of this. Then, she heard a small voice speaking to her, telling her that God had seen what she had been through, that He had been there with her, and that He had planned this for her. All she had to do was accept it. But could she? That was the question she couldn't answer. She reached for the papers Breck had dropped on the chair and then searched for a pen, filling out what she needed to.

She hadn't heard Baird for a bit and went looking for him, finally finding him in his home office, stretched out on the couch, sound asleep. Covering him with the afghan that lay on the back of the chair, she slipped to a sitting position beside him, her hand on his face, wincing at the various colours that showed, knowing she owed him her life. She was aware that she not likely would have survived much longer her captivity.

She rose, heading for the outside door, Breck's papers in her hands, stopping for a moment to stare back down the hallway, not sure if this was where she was meant to be. All she knew was that she felt safe and secure, even though danger still swirled around her.

Breck watched Berneen closely as she paced his office, her papers dropped in front of him.

"Berneen? What's up? It's not about this, is it?" He tapped the papers.

"No, it's not. I'm just so confused. Does that make sense? I mean, I feel safe. I feel secure. I know you all will look out for me. I have Darby back with me. But I feel as if I'm in a holding pattern, not able to move forward, certainly not backwards. That there is danger ahead, not just for me, but for Baird, Darby and all of you."

Breck nodded. "It's all that, Berneen. You have had to make a major decision in your life, to save someone else and yourself. You have been living on the edge for too many years, not able to grieve for your parents, raising Darby since he was what five? You have not been able to do things a young lady should have been able to do. Now, you find yourself in a situation where danger is all around you, and you don't know who or why. That, we are working on."

"Have you found out anything at all? Why would they want me to stay with Baird all the time? That doesn't make sense."

—

Breck motioned to a chair and waited until she had seated herself. "It does, if what we're looking at is true. We're thinking revenge of some kind."

"Revenge?" Her voice rose and she clapped her hands over her mouth. "Revenge? But why? Who?"

"We're looking at the original architect on the building that collapsed on Baird's Dad. At the men who were with him. Their relatives. Friends. Business associates." He looked down for a moment before looking back at her. "At your parents. Who they knew. Who your Dad worked with." He held up a hand as she went to speak. "Just bear with me for a moment, please?" He thought quickly through what he knew. "We know for sure that your parents were murdered. We have that documentation from overseas. Why it was never followed up on here, we are working through that. It appears that the reports ended up on an investigator's desk, and he just buried them."

"He buried them? You mean, this could all have been solved years ago and maybe I wouldn't have had to do this? Wouldn't have had to live pay cheque to pay cheque and that not well at all?"

"That's possible, Berneen. We're working with the new investigator. He's heading overseas tomorrow to see what he can learn."

She just shook her head. "But you really don't know who or why, do you?" She was on her feet, running from his office, leaving him to come after her.

Breck watched as Baird stopped her, his arms around her as she struggled to escape his embrace. Baird just tightened his hold, his eyes on Breck as he approached.

"Breck? What happened? I woke up, found Berneen not there, and came looking for her."

"She brought me her paperwork, but she didn't like the fact the original investigator had the documents from overseas and didn't investigate anything." He looked down at Berneen, who by this time had calmed enough to stand still in Baird's embrace. "We have definite word that they were murdered. It was a setup, Baird, and we don't know why or who, or how it affects Berneen and Darby. Not yet, anyway."

—

Berneen shoved herself away from Baird, a dark look on her face. "How do I tell Darby?"

Breck looked behind the couple, a sigh rising but not released. "I think he knows, Berneen. He's right behind you."

Berneen spun, her eyes on her brother, seeing the devastation on his face before she moved to him, hugging him tight, feeling the tears he shed, knowing he didn't want her to see them.

A blanket tucked around her, a pillow beside her, Berneen curled up in a corner of the couch, a tablet of paper in front of her, pen tapping quietly.  She had left only the lamp beside her on, knowing that if there were more lights, either one of the men in her life might come and send her to bed, and she just wasn't ready to sleep.  She had made the rounds of the two bedrooms, finding both Baird and Darby asleep.  She brushed at the hair that had escaped her braid, not realizing what she was doing, it was just a habit.

She stared at the paper, knowing she needed to start working through her memories, and not sure if she was ready for that, if she ever would be.  Her pen finally began to move, as she wrote paragraph after paragraph, stopping every once in a while to ease the cramp in her hand.  She stared at the conclusion she had come to.  No, she thought.  No him or her!  Why?

She didn't hear the soft footsteps on the hardwood floor heading her way until the papers were gently removed from her hands and dropped to the table in front of the couch.  Hands shifted her so that Baird could stretch out beside her, her pillow tucked behind him, the blanket covering them, her body cradled in his arms, her head on his shoulder.  She started for a moment and then relaxed.

"You need to sleep, Sweetheart."  Baird's quiet voice was barely audible.

"I can't.  I need to solve this."

"No, you need to sleep.  Darby said you only sleep for an hour or two at a time and are then up wandering around."

"I thought I hid that from him."  She twisted her head to look up at Baird.  "You need to shave."

He gave a light laugh.  "And here I thought the beard would cover the bruising.  Guess not, eh?"  He tucked the blanket tighter around her.  "Darby knows you're not sleeping.  He told me he's known for years.  He's that worried about you he couldn't not share with me."

She dropped her face back against him. "I didn't know. I thought he was sleeping when I was up." She yawned, fatigue suddenly hitting her hard. "I figured out who it is. I wouldn't have suspected them."

"Did you? Care to share?" Baird waited and then realized she was asleep. He reached for her papers, careful not to disturb her and flipped through them, his breath catching as he saw who she had named. Lord, why now? Why did she come to this conclusion? It is going to be hard to prove, but You know where the proof is. Just protect my lady and my sweetheart, please, dear Lord? I don't want her hurt, not again. He too slept, what he cared for most in the world tight in his arms.

Darby walked quietly through the house a few hours later, surprised at finding Baird's door open. He squinted at the clock on the microwave, noting it was only five in the morning. He saw the low light in the living room and stopped in the arched doorway, his eyes on his sister, before he looked at Baird. He had heard Baird moving around the apartment about midnight. He sighed, praying that his sister had slept for longer than her normal. She needs it, Lord. Baird is good for her. He challenges her without putting her down. She's had that enough, been driven to her knees in more ways than one, and that not always to pray. He turned, heading for his bedroom, quietly shutting the door and reaching for his Bible. He felt the danger around them and desperately needed to feel safe. When or how that would happen, he had no idea, but he needed to find solace in the Scriptures. That was what Berneen had taught him.

Baird finally roused, his eyes on his watch, before he looked down at Berneen, who still slept, her hand clutching his T-shirt tightly. He touched her hair lightly before he moved, sliding away from her and upright, reaching to tuck the blankets around her. He walked away, finding Darby in the kitchen, blinking at the daylight coming in the window.

"Darby? You're up?"

"Well, yeah! It is after eight after all. I thought you had to be in the office by ten."

Baird nodded. "I do." He looked back at the living room. "Berneen's still asleep."

"She is? That's unusual. She never sleeps like that." Darby rose to pour Baird's coffee, setting the mug in front of the older man. "How long?"

"About seven hours or more I would say."

"You're good for her, Baird. She needs you in her life." Darby looked down, blinking back tears. "So do I."

"I don't plan on leaving anytime soon, not if I can help it. That I promise you." Baird finished his coffee and rose. "I was told I needed to shave. Let your sister sleep. If she's not awake when I have to leave, can you stay with her?"

"I can. I have some studying to do." Darby searched Baird's face. "What did she do?"

"She came up with some names. I need to pass them on to the guys. I can do that later." Baird walked away, not seeing the look on Darby's face.

Branigan stared at Baird as he slumped in his desk chair, worn out from his conference with the new clients, before his eyes dropped to the papers Baird had just handed him.

"She did what?"

"She named a couple of people she thinks are responsible. I have no idea how she came up with them. I just scanned through her notes. That's a copy. I couldn't take the originals. I needed to leave them with her." He nodded at the papers. "I saw who she's named. I would never have suspected them. Now, how do we prove what she's come up with?"

"Your lady has a very scary mind, Baird." Branigan slid down into a chair as he read through her notes. "She's good. Very concise. Gives facts. Provides suppositions and questions. Gives a very clear reason for why she suspects who she does." He looked up and then around as he heard footsteps and Berneen appeared in the doorway, worry on her face.

"Baird? When did you come down here? I couldn't find you."

Baird was on his feet, drawing her to him and then down to his chair with him as he seated himself again. "Didn't Darby tell you?"

"Darby? He knew? He left a note that he was away with Benen and Bradon." She looked up then, and flushed, seeing Branigan watching them, a smile on his face. "Branigan? I'm sorry. I didn't know you were here."

"That's okay, Berneen. I was just leaving. Baird has taken the opportunity to pass on your thoughts. We'll be working on them."

She stared, open mouthed, as he walked away. "Baird? What did you do?"

"Gave him a copy of your notes. You know we needed to do that. Now. About us."

"What about us?" She twisted in his arms. "Have you solved the mystery yet?"

"Not quite. I just was wondering if I could take you out for a meal."

She gaped at him. "Baird! How can we? It's not safe!"

"We also can't hide." He didn't put into words his thoughts, that if they were out and about, just maybe they could draw out the ringleaders, have them arrested, and solve this so they could go on with their lives.

Berneen rose, shaking her head. "Absolutely not. We are not going out in the open."

Baird rose as well, staring down at her. "We can't hide forever. You can if you want. I don't intend to." He walked away, heading for the room he kept his samples of materials in.

Berneen watched and then fled, tears on her cheeks. Anna saw her coming, stopped her and then swept her into an empty room.

"Berneen? What is going on?" Anna's hug was welcoming before she seated Berneen and drew up a chair, her hands reaching for the younger woman's.

"Baird wants to take me out somewhere. I don't think it's safe. He can't be hurt again because of me." Berneen refused to look up until Anna's hand under her chin raised her face.

"Berneen, what are you really afraid of? Being left on your own again? Losing Darby too?" Anna's voice held compassion as she prayed for the younger woman.

Berneen finally nodded. "I am. I don't want anyone else hurt." She stared at Anna, grief on her face. "I don't think I had a chance to grieve for Mom and Dad, things happened too quickly and too harshly."

"And now it's all coming out, all these emotions, a new living situation. A husband you never expected to ever have, one who wants to cherish you and treat you as you should be treated." Anna sat back, her hands folded in her lap. "Baird has never dated, has shown no desire to get to know any of the young women who throw themselves at him. We see how he watches you, even in such a short

—

time that we've known you.  He treats you as a lady should be treated.  He treats you as an important part of his life.  I know Baird well enough to know that even if you decide to move on, seek an annulment, and leave him, he will never marry again.  It's not who he is.  However you two managed to come together as a couple, forced as it was, he is determined to protect you and prove to you that you are a person of value, someone who he would like to get to know, to be that important part of your life.  He knows what he was asking when he wanted to take you out for a meal.  He knows the danger you would face.  He's willing to take that risk. Are you?"

Anna's eyes raised as she heard the footsteps stop at the doorway and saw Baird standing there, heart on his face, his eyes on Berneen.  Berneen didn't raise her eyes from Anna's face, her mind working with what Anna had said.  She drew a quivering breath, not sure how she wanted to proceed, if she even did.  She had not been asked if she wanted to marry Baird.  She had been given little choice, that she knew.  She had known she could not have his death on her hands and that's what would have happened.

She shook her head.  "I'm so confused, Anna.  So confused."  She bent over, her face covered by her hands.  "I need to talk to someone but I don't know who."

Anna's hand rested on Berneen's head.  "You do, love.  I would have suggested Buckley in other circumstances, but he's too close to the situation.  The best person to talk to is Baird.  And I'm not sure that you're ready to do just that.  Are you?"  She felt the slight shrug Berneen gave.  "How can we help you, Berneen?"  She moved back as Baird approached, dropping to his knees beside Berneen, his arms going around her.

"Neen?  Don't cry.  Please.  Let's talk.  I'm okay with not going out to dinner, if you're that worried about it."

Berneen turned to watch Baird, finding his face close to hers.  She was torn, not sure what to do, wanting to trust, but not sure if she could.

"Can you trust me, Neen?"  He watched her face, seeing subtle signs of the struggle she was going through that she refused to let him know about.  "Don't hide from me, please?  Let me walk through this with you.  You need someone there."

—

She finally leaned into him, her voice broken as she spoke. "I want to, Baird. I really want to, but it's been so long. Too long, I think. I haven't been able to trust anyone but myself to keep Darby and I safe. It's hard to let go of that."

"We know, Sweetheart. We know." He stood, pulling her to her feet, walking towards Anna. "Anna, I think a shopping trip is in order. Are you game?"

"About time, is what I think. I'm game. In fact, Blair and Brady are waiting out front for us."

Berneen's eyes grew huge. "They are? Why?"

"Just because. They want a trip to town and want you and I and Baird to go with them."

Baird snorted. "Yeah, right. As if they need us."

"But, you see, Baird, they do. They want to make sure you and Berneen can get out and this is their way of saying welcome to the family, Berneen."

Berneen stopped, bringing the two with her to a halt. "It is? Why?"

"Because you are a part of the family. This is where part of your desire to trust comes in. Baird knows these men, he works with them. They know Baird. They are getting to know your brother. He's not letting them away with not getting to know him. They want to know the woman who has captured Baird's heart." Anna walked away from them at that point, heading for the outside door.

Baird watched the changes that flickered across Berneen's face, the emotions, and saw the instant that she gave in and then reached for his hand.

"I guess, then, Baird, we're off to town."

Two days later, Berneen watched as Baird walked back towards her from the rear of the church parking lot. He had driven them to church, the church Buckley pastored, and she was not sure she should be there. He reached for her hand, his eyes thoughtful as he studied the building.

"You don't want to go in, do you, Baird?" Darby asked the obvious question.

"It's not that, Darby. It's your sister I'm concerned about. This is so sudden. No announcements or anything of what was coming. I'm not sure the people will understand."

Darby stopped walking, his hand out to stop Baird. "Will they judge her, condemn her?"

Baird shrugged. "I have no idea. I am sure some will. We'll try and keep it as low key as we can. That's why we're coming in almost at time for the service to start. The other guys will be around us. We leave before the last song. We're trying to keep your sister safe, and I'm not sure that we can."

"We don't have to go, Baird, if it's that much work." Berneen tried to back away, but Baird just swept an arm around her and nudged her forward.

"It's no work. We always sit together at the back, all of us, except for Barnabas. He's usually up front. So there's no problem. Six of them and Darby will be in the row in front of us. We'll do our best to keep you safe." He looked around, feeling eyes watching them, not seeing anyone that stood out, but knowing at that moment just how much of a risk they were taking. He urged the siblings into the church and then to the pew they would sit in, timing it so that they entered as the congregation was standing for the first song.

Berneen sat, fascinated as she listened to the sermon Buckley brought, a sermon about learning to trust. She shivered every once in a while and glanced behind her, knowing someone was watching her.

———

"Someone's there?" Baird low question caught her attention.

"There is, but I don't know who." She looked up at him and then across the aisle to the other side of the church, finding curious eyes on her with no condemnation shown.

"Buckley's almost finished and then we'll go." Baird rose, caught her hand and led her from the church, his team members surrounding them until Baird had closed the door to his car, after seating her in the passenger seat.

"Did you see anyone?" Baird's eyes searched each of the five men.

"No one that we would suspect. But then, she's named people we would never have suspected." Benen spoke, his voice low as he searched the area. "Let's get you two home again. I don't like the feeling I'm getting."

"Me neither." Brady headed for his vehicle, Benen beside him. The other three men would follow in Branigan's vehicle.

Berneen watched as they pulled away from the church. "Is this really necessary? Isn't it overkill?"

Baird shook his head. "No, it's not. Branigan got a text message during the service from one of our security guards. They received a direct threat aimed at you. They plan something today. We need to get you home and safe."

Berneen stared at him before she shifted in her seat to stare out the side window. "This is too much, Baird. When does it end? Darby?"

"He's safe. They won't try for him unless they can't get to you. The other team knows what's up and will take precautions." He glanced at her as he parked in his designated spot and laid a hand on her arm. "Wait until the other guys are here. We'll go in together."

She shuddered, a sudden chill running through her. "We can't do this all the time, Baird. There are times when we'll be on our own or out together without them." She turned once more, a thought crossing her mind. "Do they know if we're not together all the time? And just what did they mean by that?"

"That's what we're working through. I think Barnabas was correct when he said revenge. This is what it feels like. The not knowing. The worry. The fear. The uncertainty. We don't know when or why they'll hit."

"That's what I don't get. I was held against my will. There were at least four men they brought in before you. Those men disappeared. They were only there for a couple of days. But now that I think of it, I'm not sure they were even prisoners. They could have been part of the gang, brought in to terrorize me."

Baird stared at her before he was out of the car, yanking open her door, and running with her towards the building.

"Baird? What on earth?"

He led her to his office, unlocking the door, shoving her down into a chair, before he turned to the five men who had followed them. "I think Berneen just solved part of the puzzle."

"How so?" Benen reached for the coffee pot and headed for the kitchenette, knowing that it would be needed. "Berneen? Do you want some of your tea?"

She was on her feet, brushing by Baird to help Benen. "I do. I can't sit still and be waited on."

"Baird? Care to explain your comment?" Blair opened up a package of food Anna had handed him earlier that day, knowing that they would likely want something.

"Berneen commented that the men that were brought in may have been part of the gang."

Branigan nodded as he sorted through the mugs, setting out utensils that might be needed. "That's what we're beginning to think. That this was all a ploy, Baird, and that you were the one they wanted there all along. Why? As we've decided, revenge. It's the only answer. But who? That's the question. We think it's the family of one of the men who died when your Dad did. But we haven't got enough evidence or information to go to the police. Berneen? We'll need you to work through your captivity. I don't think anyone has had you go over it in a detailed manner."

"No, we haven't." She stood, leaning against a door frame, her mug in her hand, her eyes on Branigan. "That's what we need to do." She moved to set her mug down, but Brady's hand stopped her. "Brady?"

"First we eat, Berneen. We'll get to your observations in a bit." He pulled out a chair and shoved her down, grinning at her comment of bossy men and why did she need them anyway?

Baird had stepped back, his eyes on Berneen and his friends, watching how they interacted. He could see that she was relaxing around them, her attention on something other than trying to be herself around them. He raised his eyes, meeting Branigan's eyes, who nodded.

Berneen listened closely as Baird interacted with his friends and team mates.  She could see and feel the trust the men had for one another.  She turned as Bradon sat down beside her, Kade nudging at her arm for attention.

"Bradon?  You have a puzzled look on your face."

He nodded.  "I do.  I've read over what you wrote.  I just don't get how the lawyer managed to get away with this."

"I was eighteen, Bradon, in shock, grieving.  I had a five-year-old brother I was trying to comfort and keep everything as close to normal for him as I could.  I didn't know any better."  She bit back the anger she was beginning to feel.  "I never had a chance to look through any paperwork.  I know Dad had a safe and he gave me the combination to it, but we were out of the house before I could even do that."  She blinked back the tears of frustration and anger that prickled at her eyes.

"We get that, Berneen.  Believe me, we get that.  But do you know if the house was sold or not?"

She stared at him.  "I have no idea.  Dad always said it couldn't be sold.  That it was to be a  family home for as long as there were descendants.  Can we look into that?"

He grinned and pulled his laptop over to him.  "We can and we will.  Now, the address."  He typed rapidly as she spit it out, Baird having come to stand behind her, his hands on her shoulders.  "There.  Now, let's see."  Bradon perused various articles, clicking rapidly through screens.

Berneen watched, envy growing inside her as she watched how he maneuvered his laptop with ease.

"We'll get you a laptop, Sweetheart, and we'll teach you to use it."  Baird spoke quietly in her ear.

---

"You will? I can? I never had a chance. We didn't have the money for extras. Darby is learning at school, but other than the cash register at work, I don't know computers." She groaned. "Work! I never thought, Baird. I need to talk to them. I left them in the lurch." She was becoming upset, and the men in the room hesitated in their work to study her and then Baird.

Baird dropped to a crouch beside her, an arm around her, as he shared a look with Bradon. "We can do that. I have to work tomorrow morning, but in the afternoon, we can head to town and you can pick out your very own lap top. And we can call your work or you can go in, whichever is the easiest for you."

Her hand touched his face lightly and then her attention was drawn to a photo on Bradon's computer. "That's my home. It looks the same. What year?"

"That was taken a month ago, from what I am reading. The comments are that there has been no one living in it for years, but the taxes and utilities are paid. The town can't do anything about that." He sat back, a frown on his face as he rubbed the back of his neck. "That's strange. You were told the house had been forfeited, but no one is living there." He looked around. "We need Brody. He has sites he can search that we don't have access to."

Brady was out the door, running through the hallways, finding Brody as he was heading up the stairs.

"Brody? Do you have a few minutes?" Brady slid to a halt, a hand on the wall to balance himself.

"I do. Why?"

"Because we've found Berneen's old home on the internet. She was told it was forfeited. Bradon has found evidence that it's not. We need you to research for us, if you've time."

Brody walked rapidly back the way Brady had come. "Where are you working? Baird's office?"

"We are. Anna sent in food, if you haven't eaten."

"I have." He stopped in the doorway, assessing what was happening before he moved to a chair beside Bradon. "Bradon? Talk to me."

"Brody, you know that Berneen was told her home was forfeited.  But it doesn't seem that it was.  I found evidence in a newspaper article from a month ago that it is still being cared for, taxes and utilities paid.  This is strange."

Brody nodded, then with a question on his face, reached for Bradon's laptop.  "May I?"

Bradon motioned with his hands.  "Go ahead.  This is part of the puzzle we need to solve."  He rose and stepped away, turning back to watch Berneen and then looking up as Darby found his sister.

Darby's quiet words to his sister had her sitting back and staring at him.

"You're sure, Darby?"  At his nod, she sighed.  "This just makes it worse, doesn't it?  When did you find out?"

"Just now."  He thrust a phone at her that he had been holding.  "Baird gave me this.  I haven't given the number to anyone but the couple I was staying with.  Someone is trying to find them.  They're looking for me, Berneen.  How do they stay safe?"

Baird looked around Berneen at him.  "They're safe, Darby.  We have them tucked away where they can't be found."

"Are you sure, Baird?"  Darby was worried but trying hard not to how it.

"Trust me, Darby.  Barnabas has made sure of that."  He looked around at a sound from Brody.  "Brody?"

Brody's eyes rose from where he had been studying a website.  "This is worse than we thought, Baird.  Far worse."

All eyes were on Brody as he spoke, before Baird stood and walked to stand behind him, his eyes on the laptop screen.

"What did you find out?" Baird could see Berneen reach for Darby and grasp his hand.

"Someone has tried to change the ownership on the house, tried to change the name the utilities are in. Apparently a copy of a will was presented, but it didn't match the documentation on file." Brody looked around at Baird. "I have a name, but I'm not sure if it's correct."

"Who is it?" Berneen's voice was tight, her hand gripping Darby's just as tightly.

"Owen Small. He's not the attorney that your father put on record, though."

Berneen gave a harsh laugh. "He's the one who chased us from that home." She rose, coming to stand beside Baird, not conscious of how his arm encircled her. "Can we get into the house?"

"I don't see why not. According to the record here, you're listed as the owner, with Darby listed as a minor, to become part owner at age 18." Brody looked over at Darby as he made a sound. "You never knew, Darby?"

Darby shook his head, as he walked to stand beside his sister, his eyes on the family home. "No. I don't know that we ever discussed that. Did we, Berneen?"

"We didn't, not that I remember. I thought if the house was gone, there was no point." She stared at her brother. "I'm sorry, Darby. I should have fought harder to keep you there."

"I don't think you had much choice, Berneen. Not from what you've said." Brody pointed at an article he had pulled up. "It says here that Small had taken over your father's office and was removed forcibly by the authorities. They are still trying to find evidence that he has hidden about his activities."

"It will be hidden in the house somewhere. Would he have changed the locks?" Berneen began to pace, not sure where she was going with her questions, only certain that she wanted back into her home.

Branigan shared a look with Baird before he spoke. "I do security systems, Berneen. As such, I am a trained locksmith. I'll get you into your house. Do we have what we need in documentation, Brody?"

"We should do. I'll talk to the police tomorrow morning. We need to get in there as soon as we can."

Late that evening, Baird clicked off the kitchen light and, coffee mug in hand, he headed for the living room, settling down into his favourite recliner, feet up, and watched Berneen silently as she huddled on the couch, wrapped in a blanket, her eyes on the floor in front of her. He didn't think she was looking at anything in particular, but he was hesitant to speak. He finally sighed, set aside his mug of coffee, and moving to the couch, he swept her into his arms, settling back where she had been sitting and wrapping the blanket around them. His feet went up on the table, and his head tilted so he could watch her face.

"Neen? Talk to me. You haven't said much said Brody found the picture of your house."

She shook her head. "What can I say, Baird? What is there to say?"

He heard the defeat in her voice. "It's not your fault, Neen. You didn't know. You were too young."

"I still should have known. I should have checked it out. I should have gone to the police." Her head dropped to his shoulder as her anger abated. "It's not fair, Baird. Just not fair. So much has been taken from Darby."

"And from you. Ssh. Sleep, Neen. Brody will let us know tomorrow when we can get it." He dropped a kiss on her hair, not even realizing he had done so, and rested his cheek against her head.

———

Berneen stilled, feeling the kiss, a wonder starting to move in her heart, softening the hardness she had worked to install in it, not willing to love again.

"Who hurt you so bad, Neen?" Baird's quiet question was unexpected. He didn't think she would answer, she just wasn't ready to trust him that far, not with her heart at any rate.

She shrugged, then yawned, her eyes closing as she slept. Baird waited and then slept himself, shifting to a more comfortable position.

Darby squinted at the clock hours later as he made his way to the kitchen, not surprised to find Berneen in the living room, but when he saw Baird, he stopped, the slight noise of his socked feet on the floor rousing Baird.

"Darby? You up?"

Darby snorted before he grinned. "Considering it's morning, then yeah, I'm up."

"What time is it?" Baird shifted, his eyes on Berneen as she still slept.

"After six. Didn't you say you had to be in your office by eight?"

"I do." Baird yawned but made no effort to move.

Darby shook his head as he reached for Baird's cup of cold coffee. "I'll make fresh." He studied his sister, then spoke once more. "Thanks, Baird."

Baird twisted his neck, working at the stiffness, as he watched Darby. "For what?"

"For being you. For taking me in when you didn't have to. For that." Darby nodded at his sister.

"For what?" Baird repeated himself.

"For that. She doesn't trust easily, if at all. To see her sleeping like that? I don't think she's slept more than an hour or two at a time for the last ten years. Thank you." Darby walked away, his shoulders hunched as he tried to control his emotions.

"You're welcome, Darby. You're family. This is what family does." Baird shifted Berneen away from him, rose, and then watched as she settled back down on the couch, a slight smile on her face, before he tucked the blanket around her once more. He stood, watching her, feeling the ice in his heart melting more. He shook his head and then headed for his shower, rubbing at his face, noting the pain was less and the swelling was going down. He wouldn't scare the clients too much, he thought.

Watching Berneen intently, Brody moved through the group of men towards where she stood with Baird and Darby, uncertainty on her face. Brody glanced around, seeing Branigan talking with the officers on hand before he glanced at the tidy grounds surrounding the two-story house they all stood in front of. It was Tuesday afternoon, and all fourteen men had taken the time to be there, to support Baird, but more importantly, to support Berneen and Darb.

"Brody?" Baird's quiet voice barely broke through the stillness surrounding them. He glanced around, seeing neighbours on their porches, curious as to what was happening.

"We're almost ready to go in. We'll let the officers go in first with Branigan. Then, we'll walk you through." He peered closely at Berneen as he spoke, seeing the tension, fear, anxiety and whatever emotions she was feeling flickering on her face. Darby just stood, his eyes on the house, not sure how he felt. It had been too long, and he had been too young.

Berneen gave an abrupt nod, her eyes intent on the officers as they moved towards the front door, watching in amazement as Branigan used the key she had handed him to unlock the door. For some reason, she had never been able to throw the key away, bringing in out in the darkness of the night, to feel it in sorrow and grief, to clench it in anger. She lost track of the number of times she had pitched into a garbage can only to go back and dig it out, tucking it away in a pocket. She moved slightly, her hand tucked tight in Baird's, her other hand tight in Darby's. She turned her head to watch Darby, finding interest on his face but not the emotions she was feeling.

"Darby?"

Darby turned his head to study his sister, seeing the emotions she was endeavoring to cover. "It's okay, Neen. I'm okay. But you? Are you?"

She shrugged, her eyes going back to the open front door. "No, I don't think I am. I have no idea what we'll find, what he has done inside. It's almost too hard, Darb." She spun suddenly, seeking solace in Baird's arms, realizing as she did so that she had learned to trust him in a way she hadn't trusted anyone before.

Baird's arms held his bride tight, his chin on the top of her head, before he reached out an arm and swept Darby into a hug as well. Darby leaned against Baird, realizing he now had a complete family. He studied his sister for a moment before he looked around at the footsteps approaching them.

"Berneen?" Baird's voice was low and she looked up at him. "Barnabas is here. I think we can go in now."

She turned her head, and the two men drew in a deep breath, seeing the devastation on her face, realizing just how hard it would be for her.

Barnabas looked around, spying Buckley and motioning him over.

"Buckley? Pray, please." Barnabas' words were almost curt, to cover his emotions.

Buckley's prayer sought wisdom, peace, guidance and protection for them. Berneen swiped at the tears on her face, pausing as a large white handkerchief appeared in her line of sight. She hadn't known that Baird carried one. Then she sighed. There was so much she didn't know about him and wasn't sure if she ever would.

Baird's hand gripped hers tight as she walked up the steps to the wide covered porch and then squeezed harder as she hesitated at the door, her own hand reaching for Darby.

"Darby, do you remember anything?"

He nodded. "I remember us playing on the porch. I don't know that anything has changed here." He walked through the door, curiosity on his face as he studied the hallway and then walked through the rooms.

Berneen stood in the hallway, staring around, then looking up the oak stairway to the second floor, before she too moved through the lower floor, stopping every once in a while as memories stirred in her mind, reaching for objects, books, pictures. She finally stood in the room that had been her father's office, one arm around her waist, the other hand on her face, as her head moved. She fought back the tears. She knew Barnabas and the men were around, she could hear quiet footsteps and low conversation. She also knew that there were still police officers around. The chief had come to her, stating that her father had been a good friend of his, and he was sorry for how it had all been handled. She had been gone before he knew what was happening. They were searching, he said, for proof of what she had just reported.

She moved away from the office, heading for the stairs, finding Darby standing staring into the room that had been their parents. She stood with him, arms around one another.

"Has anything changed, Neen?"

She shook her head. "It's exactly as we left it that night. I mean, cleaners have been through but I don't see anything missing." She moved forward, towards the dresser. "Mom had a secret compartment she kept her jewelry in. Let me see if it's still there." She reached behind the mirror, feeling for a moment, before a section of wall moved and a shallow closet appeared.

Darby stared at it and then at Berneen, watching as she moved towards the closet, her hands reaching for the drawers and pulling them open.

Baird stood in the doorway, not sure what she had just done, watching as she came back out, laying what she had in her hands on the dresser.

"Berneen?" Darby's voice questioned her.

"Just a sec, Darb." She looked through the jewelry cases and boxes and then re-entered the closet. She breathed a sigh of relief as she came back out. "It's all here. Nothing is missing,"

"Berneen? Will you take that with you?" Baird walked towards her. "I know the guys brought boxes with them in case there were things you wanted to take with you."

She looked up at him, relief on her face. "There are some things, if you have room for them in your apartment."

"Ours." She frowned at him. "It's our apartment, Berneen. Not mine anymore. And yes, we have room for whatever you want to take."

———

103

She nodded. "Okay, then. What's here on the dresser." She looked around. "I think that's all for this room." She walked away, stopping in the doorway of her own bedroom, tears suddenly blinding her.

Darby reached for his sister, the siblings clinging together, before she moved forward, looking around. "Just the photos in here, I think, Baird." She reached for one, his hand stopping her.

"The guys will pack what you want. Just tell them." He looked back at Barnabas, who nodded.

"Oh. Okay, then." She moved away, not seeing the look on his face as she did so. "Darby? I'm not sure what to take from your room."

Darby stared around, not really remembering anything. It was a child's room, he thought, and then sighed. That's what he had been when he had been forced to leave. He picked up a stuffed bear, memories coming with it.

"This, Neen. I want this."

She nodded, her hand touching it lightly. "They gave that to you just as they were leaving. Mom said it was full of hugs and kisses, enough to do until they came back."

He nodded soberly. "I remember. I felt so lost when I knew we didn't have it with us."

"We didn't have time to plan. Small made us leave so quickly."

Baird watched Berneen closely as she moved through the main floor of the house, indicating what she wanted to take with her, worried at her silence and withdrawal. Buckley stood beside him, concern colouring his face.

"Are you okay, Baird?"

Baird shrugged. "It's hard, Buckley. I see them doing this, coming back to their home after so many years, having to fight their grief once more. I never really got to do that. The house was destroyed so soon after Dad went home."

"She's trusting you and she's trusting us, whether she realizes it or not."

Baird nodded. "I see that. It will take time for her to do that fully though, if she ever does." He paused, not quite sure how to proceed. "How do we go on, Buckley? How do we get through the next few weeks? Coming back here will open up a wealth of emotions she has just buried, both for herself and for Darby. She's grieving for both of them."

"I know, Baird. I've put a call into a friend, asking if she would talk with her." Buckley stared at Berneen as she stood at her father's desk before she sank into his chair, her hand rubbing along the polished wood. "Baird, do you have room for the desk?"

Baird stared at him, uncertain as to the change of topic. "I can do. In the den. Why?"

"Because she needs it. She needs that contact with her father. Darby muttered something about his mother giving the desk to their father."

"Okay." Baird looked around, stopping as Buckley's hand came to rest on his shoulder.

"We'll look after it. Find out if there is anything else in furniture she wants. We can put it in one of the storage units for now."

"Thanks, Buckley." Baird moved towards Berneen, crouching down beside her, an arm around her. "You okay?"

She nodded, slowly. "I think so. There have been so many memories, I'm overwhelmed. I need to pack his desk and the filing cabinets. Do we have room for boxes, Baird?"

"We do. I have a storage unit that we can put things in when you've sorted through them." He looked around. "Didn't you say your father had a safe?"

"He did." She shoved back the chair, rising, and walking towards the entry, pausing at a certain point, her hands feeling along the chair rail molding, before Baird heard a click and a section of the wall popped open.

"What is it with these?" He was trying to lighten the mood for her.

She gave a half smile. "Dad liked mysteries and puzzles. He did these two. I think there is another one but I don't remember for sure." She punched in the digital code and then turned the handle on the safe, pulling it open. She stared at what was inside, her breath in her throat. "I think we'll just clear it all out, Baird, and take it with us."

"That sounds like a plan."

Berneen took one last walk through the house, her arms wrapped around herself. She knew Darby had done that and then gone out to explore the yard and outbuildings, some of Baird's friends with him. Baird waited patiently for her, one shoulder against the arched doorway to the living room. His thoughts were bleak, wondering how she would leave this to live in his apartment. He sighed to himself, knowing that he had never planned to move from there. It was his home, his sanctuary, but now he knew he had to face giving it up, moving from there, away from the men he considered his family. He just wasn't sure he could do that.

"Berneen?" She had stopped in front of him, not looking at him, her eyes on the floor, her arms wrapped around herself. "We have time. We don't have to leave yet."

"No, it's okay. I'm ready to go." She looked up, her emotions hidden. "I needed this, Baird. It's not home anymore. Not with

Mom and Dad gone.  It's Darby's if he wants it.  If he doesn't, then I don't know what I'll do."

"You mean that, don't you?"  At her nod, he just swept her into a hug, a kiss dropped on her head.  "Don't make any rushed choices.  We'll keep it and over time, we can discuss it and decide from there."  He turned her to face the front door.  "Just know that no matter what you decide, I back you every step of the way."

She looked up at him, wonder in her eyes.  "You mean that, Baird?"

"I do.  You're my wife.  I can't do anything else but that."  He looked down at her, tumult in his heart as the ice melted more and more and he admitted to himself finally that he was beginning to care deeply for the lady he held right at that time.

Sudden yells from outside the house had Baird shoving Berneen down and covering her with his body despite her struggles to get up.  He could hear distinct popping sounds as well as shouts to put down the weapon.  An officer was beside them suddenly, a hand on Baird's back keeping them down.

"Darby!  Baird!  Where's Darby?"  Berneen struggled to free herself, unable to as Baird's weight kept her on the floor.  "Baird? Get off me.  I need to find Darby."

There was sudden silence outside, then more calls, this time for paramedics.  Baird knew Brady would in the thick of it.  He sat up, his arms still around Berneen, the officer's hand still on his shoulder.

"Baird, let me go.  I need to find Darby."  Berneen's anger flared as she shoved at him.

"No, we wait, Berneen.  We have to wait.  They'll let us know when we can leave here."  His arms tightened on her even as his heart raised in prayer.  Please, Lord, not Darby.  Don't take him from her.

A few minutes, Baird looked up as quiet footsteps approached, and Barnabas and Buckley stood for a moment, worry, concern, and another emotion he couldn't place.

"Barnabas? Buckley?"

His voice raised Berneen's head and she stared at the men before she shoved away from him, on her feet, running for the outside door, slipping on the polished hardwood, and then she was outside, her voice calling for Darby.

"I'm sorry, Baird.  He was hit.  How bad, we're not sure. Small took us by surprise, coming in from the back of the lot. Brady's with him."  Barnabas' voice held sorrow and concern, knowing how this would affect Baird's Berneen.

Baird scrambled to his feet, his only thought finding Berneen.

Berneen struggled to reach her brother, held back by some of Barnabas' men, her eyes wide in shock and horror as she watched them work over him, Brady right there in the thick of the paramedics.  She couldn't tell how bad it was, but she knew he was unconscious.  She watched as they finally lifted him to a stretcher, and then ran with the stretcher towards the waiting paramedic rig, his coat and shirt cut away, blood covering his arm, a large bandage wrapped around it, oxygen mask in place, IV line running to his hand.  Berneen tried to follow but found herself held in Baird's arms.

"We'll follow, Berneen.  Come on.  Brody has a car for us.  They'll give us an escort there."  He shoved her into the waiting vehicle, his eyes on her, following her to a seat and slamming the door behind him..

He pulled her from the vehicle as Brody stopped at the Emergency entrance and ran with her inside, stopping at the clerk's desk.

"Darby Dakin was just brought in.  This is his sister.  She's his next of kin for medical purposes."

The clerk looked up and then nodded to some chairs.  "Wait there.  I'll let them know you're here."

Berneen huddled against Baird, her eyes not moving from the door, not sure if Darby was even alive.  She had noise around her but didn't stir.  She felt a hand on her arm and finally looked around, seeing Barnabas there.

"Barnabas?  What happened?"

"Small snuck up on us all.  He had been under surveillance and somehow managed to slip away."  He looked down for a moment, swallowing hard.  "I'm sorry, Berneen.  We thought we had you two safe."

"You did, I think.  You did what you had to."

"I know, but it wasn't enough. Darby shouldn't have been hurt. We had men with him and he was still got to." Barnabas bit back the anger he was feeling. This had never happened to him before, and he didn't like it, not one bit.

She looked up as she heard footsteps heading her way and was on her feet, moving the meet the physician before Baird could stop her. He was right after her, his arm around her.

"Doctor? How is Darby?"

"A lucky young man. It looked a lot worse than it was. The bullet winged his arm, but didn't break anything. A few stitches and he'll be good to go. He informed me that he was not staying in here."

"No, he won't. Doc will look after him, as will Brady. And I'm sure Anna will smother him with care." Baird spoke up at that point.

The physician peered at Baird. "Baird? You here?"

"I am, Bill. This is my wife, Berneen, and that's her brother, Darby."

"Married? I hadn't heard, Baird." Bill studied his friend and then Berneen. "Congratulations. I didn't know you had been dating."

"Long story, Bill, for another day. Can we see Darby?"

"In a few minutes. The nurse is just getting him cleaned up. He's not a happy camper."

Berneen laughed, tears not far off. "He never is when he's sick. I should know. I've nursed him on my own for the last ten years." She moved away from the two men, intent on finding Darby.

"What did she just say?" Bill spun to watch her.

"She's raised him since he was five and she was eighteen. Their parents were killed overseas, and there was no one else. Again, another long story."

"You and your long stories. We need to do coffee soon." Bill walked away, his hand already reaching for the chart the charge nurse was holding out to him.

———

110

"Baird? How's Darby?" Barnabas stood beside him.

As Baird turned, he saw the rest of the men standing behind them, stern looks on their faces.

"Just a graze, I think he said. Nothing serious. He'll be ready to go home soon." He looked around to where Berneen stood, her eyes on her brother. "This is not going to help, guys. Not at all."

"No, it won't. And it won't help when she hears Small is dead. He didn't give the officers any choice." Brody stood next to Baird. "Who gets to tell her that?"

"I guess I do."

Barnabas shook his head at Baird's words. "No, the chief will come and talk to her later tonight. He wants to tell her himself."

Her head cushioned on her folded arms, Berneen rested at the kitchen table later that evening. Baird had set a cup of her peppermint tea in front of her, rested his hand on her back, and then walked away, his mug of coffee in his hand. He was making room for her things, he said. She just shook her head, not even able to think about that. She thought back over the afternoon, a frown on her face. There had been something off in her father's office and she didn't know what. She jumped to her feet and then caught herself as her head spun.

She ran for Baird, finding him standing staring at her father's desk, looking around as she ran into the room.

"Baird? Can someone take pictures or a video of my Dad's office?"

He shrugged. "We can. Why?"

"Something was different. I don't know what. Maybe if I have pictures, I can tell."

Baird nodded, made a quick phone call and then reached to pull her into a hug. "Benen will look after that. He still has the keys. He said he'd head over there now."

"Now? Baird, it's too late."

Baird shook his head. "He wants to. He'll bring copies by tomorrow." He turned her in his arms, making her face the room. "Your Dad's desk fits just right."

"It does. Thank you, Baird. I thought it would be too crowded." Her heart was hurting for her brother, but she knew it was opening up to Baird. He was wiggling his way in without even trying. She sighed to herself, knowing she was beginning to care deeply for him, if not love him, and that scared her.

"The police chief wanted to come by tonight, but I put him off." Baird's quiet voice broke into her thoughts.

"Small's dead. What more can he say?"

———

"How'd you know?"

She shrugged. "I just did."

His chin on her head, he waited, knowing that she would speak when she was ready. If not tonight, then maybe tomorrow.

"I don't know how well Dad knew him. That's the thing. How did he get involved in our lives? What was he after?" Berneen moved away from Baird, leaving him to sit back against his desk, arms folded across his chest. "How do we find out?"

"We'll find out. The police are investigating now, the chief has said that. Barnabas won't rest until he finds out why and how."

"It's too dangerous. Today proved that." Berneen walked away, leaving Baird to drop his head in frustration before he was out of the room and after her.

"Neen? Take the bed tonight? No arguments?"

She glared at him before she gave an abrupt nod, heading for the bedroom, stopping first in Darby's doorway to watch him, a prayer rising for healing for her baby brother.

Baird watched her disappear and then walked to the front door as he heard a quiet tap at it, opening it to find Breck standing there. He stepped back, Breck walking through the doorway, hesitation in his manner.

"Breck?" Baird was puzzled at his friend stopping by that late.

"Baird, go. Get some sleep. I'll watch for Darby." Breck watched as Baird's eyes slid closed before he nodded and walked away.

God, I have no idea where we're going with this. Protect these three. It was too close today for Darby. Breck headed for the kitchen, knowing it was going to be a long night, and he would need coffee to keep him awake.

Baird hesitated for a moment before he pulled a blanket from the closet and then laid down on top of the bedspread, covering himself with the blanket, his arms reaching for Berneen, pulling her close to him, his head against hers as he drifted off to sleep, trying to pray, but unable to form any words, confident in his heart that God knew what he wanted and needed to say.

———

Berneen scowled at the photos spread out in front of her the next morning, not sure what she was seeing or if she could even trust her memory any more.  She closed her eyes to envision, if she could, what the office had looked like.  A sudden thought had her eyes open and her hands scrambling through the photos, stilling as she found the one she wanted.  She stared at it, and then was on her feet, running through the apartment.  Breck looked askance at her.

"Baird?  Where is he?"

"I think in his office."  Breck was on his feet.  "Why?"

"Because I found out what is wrong in Dad's office."  She spun, heading for the door.  "Does he have clients, do you know?'

Breck shrugged.  "I'm not sure.  He might have."  He was torn, wanting to go with her, but needing to stay with Darby, who had been up and then gone back to sleep.  "Berneen!  Wait.  Let me get someone to go down with you."

She spun.  "I'm only going to the first floor.  Is that an issue?"

Breck's hand drew her back from the door.  "It might be.  We have security, but someone could conceivably get in.  We need to take steps to make sure you're safe even here."

She paled, not realizing that she could be in danger in the Foundation building.  "Here?  Breck?"  She turned as she heard a knock at the door.

Breck opened it slowly to find Anna standing there, crock pot in hand, a smile on her face.

"Good morning, Breck.  Just bringing in a meal for all of you."  She walked past him, deposited the pot on the counter, plugging it in, and then turned to sweep Berneen into a tight hug.  "Now, your brother?  Is he up?"

"Darby was up earlier, before Berneen was.  He's sleeping again."  Breck reached for Berneen's arm.  "Now that Anna's here, we can go find Baird."

———

Berneen hesitated at the door to Baird's office, as she watched him deep in his work, not willing to disturb him. She clutched the photo in her hand, knowing that when she spoke, it would change things for her. It would change a memory that she had of her father.

Breck had no trouble disturbing Baird, showing he had done that very thing many times before.

"Baird. Can you mark your place and take a moment?"

Baird's finger went up as he ignored Breck. Fifteen minutes later, he sat back, his eyes on his drawings before he nodded and then looked around, coming to his feet and approaching Berneen as she stood, hesitating, ready to turn and flee.

"Berneen. I didn't know you were here. You need to speak up, Sweetheart. I would have stopped where I was if I had known."

She stared at him before she snapped her mouth closed. She wasn't used to that, she thought. "It's okay. You needed to finish that. You just thought Breck was here."

"No, it's not okay. You have a voice. You need to use it to let me know where you are and what you want and how you feel." He wrapped her in a hug, a frown on his face as he looked at Breck.

Breck just shook his head. Lord, you need to work with these two. They're in love with one another, afraid to speak about it, afraid to trust one another. Bring that trust to them. Help them to trust You more and more each day.

"Berneen has a photo, I think, in her hand that she needs to talk to you about." Breck turned, hand on the doorknob, when Berneen's hand gripped his arm and pulled him back.

"No, please, Breck. You need to stay. Maybe you'll see something I have missed." She slipped from Baird's arm and slapped the photo on his desk. "This. This is what has me puzzled."

Baird studied it, then shook his head, his gaze on Breck, who stood beside him, studying first the photo and then Berneen.

"Berneen? What is it you see that you don't like?" Breck spoke finally, when Berneen had just stood there, staring at Baird, a puzzled look on her face.

"I'm sorry. What did you ask, Breck?" Berneen finally looked at him, and then at the photo.

"Talk to us. Tell us what that area should look like and what you see that makes it different."

Baird reached for a white china marker. "Here. Use this. We can get other copies of the photo. Do you need it enlarged?"

Berneen stared at him, her thoughts muddled, before Breck sighed, reached for the photo and headed for Baird's copier, enlarging the photo and bringing it back, placing it in front of her. He reached for her hand that held the marker and set it against the photo.

"Berneen? If you can? Can you mark what's different?"

"I guess." She shrugged as she moved to stare down at the photo. Her thoughts traced back to playing in that office with her father working away, looking up every once in a while to interact with her. She thought of being in there the night before her parents flew out, somehow knowing that trip would change their lives, but never imaging how much it would.

Her fingers traced through the photo, her mind working, before she began to mark what she knew and what she thought was different.

"There. I think that's it. Those pictures. The knick-knacks. Dad hated things like that in his office. He said it was distracting to have odds and sods sitting around, as he put it. Those books. They're not his. He disliked that author."

She looked up. "Can we go back there, Baird? I didn't pack those things. I need to see them in real life."

He glanced at his watch, made a quick calculation, and then nodded. "Just let me make a quick phone call. I'm not quite where I should be with the plans. Not your fault!" His hand went up as she opened her mouth to protest and then clamped it shut. "They knew it might take a bit of time. I'm sourcing materials right now for them, not what I usually do, but they asked. I have to wait for some replies."

Berneen watched as Baird unlocked the door to her childhood home, not sure she wanted to be there again, but knowing she had to. She would likely have to come back again and again, just to dispel the sadness she felt, but she wasn't even sure that would work. She prayed for peace, for the burden to be lifted, and felt a lightening of her burden.

Breck and Benen stood behind her, their backs to them, watchful. They knew Small had not been working alone. What they were not sure of was how much the other person or people were involved with this house.

Baird opened the door, stepping through, his hand reaching for hers, waiting as she hesitated in the hallway, a frown on her face, before she walked through to the office. She reached for the box he carried but he shook his head, setting it on a small table, and then reaching to hug her. She could hear his softly-uttered prayer and then stepped away from him, her eyes on the photos as she gathered them and held them out to him, working quickly to gather everything she had noted different.

Benen finally spoke. "Is there anything else that seems off here, Berneen?"

She looked at him in surprise, not having thought of that, just wanting to get in and out. "I don't think so. Let me walk around here and I'll see." She walked the office, hesitating every once in a while to indicate something off and that object was gathered up into boxes as well.

The three men watched as she walked the whole house, finding objects she said were not theirs, had not been there before, and they gathered each one for her.

Finally, she stood on the back porch, looking around the yard. "I just don't know, Baird. Everything has grown so much in the last ten years. I can't tell if things are different."

"That's okay, Sweetheart. We'll work with what you've taken." He turned as Breck approached from around the house. "Do you want anything more from here today?"

She shook her head, walking down the steps and along the flagstone path to the front yard.

Baird stared after her before he spoke. "I don't think she'll want to come back here."

"No, I don't think she will. Darby will, but he doesn't have the memories that she does." Breck walked beside Baird as they followed Berneen. "What happens to the house?"

"It stays as it is until Darby is 18. I mean, they can live in it, or rent it, but Berneen said they can't sell it. I'm not sure, but I think she said it can't ever be sold."

"Wow! That's something. It's a nice house, has good bones as you would say."

"It is. But I don't think she'll want to live in it. And I'm not sure if she could even come visit Darby here. There's been too much taken away from it and her."

"I can see that." Breck stood and watched as Baird approached Berneen, moving her to the vehicle and into it, before he too stood, his eyes on the house before they dropped to Breck and he shook his head.

Breck sighed, knowing that whatever these two were going through, it was not over, not by a long shot, he thought. He approached the car, his eyes catching the forlorn look on Berneen's face before her gaze met his and then flickered away quickly, but not so quickly that he didn't see the sheen of tears in her eyes.

Baird stood later that afternoon, back from his office in the lower floors, and watched Darby. He was standing in the office doorway, his eyes on his sister, wanting to go to her but making no move to do so, not sure how to approach her as she worked through the material she had brought back with her.

Baird stopped beside Darby, an arm around his shoulder for a moment, before he nodded towards the kitchen.

"Has she eaten at all?" He kept his voice low.

118

Darby shook his head, and Baird could see the worry in his eyes. "No. I can't get her to leave that stuff. She won't talk to me, won't leave it, has stayed in there since she came back."

"Leave it to me. How's the arm?" Baird grinned at the grimace Darby made. "Like that, huh? How be you do what you can to find us a meal? I'll deal with Neen."

"Baird, why do you call her Neen? That's what we've always done. I guess that's my fault. I couldn't say her full name, just Neen, and it stuck."

Baird shrugged, not sure himself why he did. "I have no idea. It just suits her."

Baird stood for a moment, his eyes on Berneen, before he moved behind her, his arms coming around her and stilling her movements. "Have you taken a break since we got back?"

She shook her head. "I wanted to keep working at this. There's something here. I'm just not seeing it."

"You need to step back and take a break. I found Darby in the doorway, wanting to talk to you, but not wanting to interrupt you."

"That's crazy. He could have." She could feel anger starting to build in her, not directed at Baird or Darby.

"He didn't know, Berneen. He thinks he can't." Baird just stood, his arms dropping to his side. "You two need to talk, Berneen. He's hurting, not just physically. He's been back to a house he really doesn't remember. He sees you're hurting and upset but won't talk to him."

She spun. "Don't tell me how my brother is. I think I know."

"Berneen, you know him, but this is something neither one of you have faced before. You need to communicate with him."

She shoved at him, not able to move him. "Baird, I know him. He would talk to me. He always has."

"Berneen, listen to me. You're married now. In his eyes, that changes things. He knows your relationship has changed all of a sudden. He's been thrown into a new home, been hurt, sees his sister shutting him out."

They continued to argue back and forth, neither giving way, until Baird sighed, swept her into his arms and kissed her, silencing the hurt angry words she was about to speak. He raised his head, his eyes on her, watching as she stared up at him and then opened her mouth to argue once more. His face dropped to hers as he kissed her again.

Darby slid back into his chair in the kitchen. He had opened the door to Blair, who entered and headed for the coffee pot, his head tilting as he heard the voices in the office.

"They're arguing? Baird never argues."

Darby grinned. "She's trying. He's not." He looked around as the voices went silent and his grin grew bigger.

Blair stared at him. "You think this is funny?"

Darby shook his head. "I do. Berneen is trying her best to argue but Baird isn't."

Blair stared at him for a moment before he too grinned. "I see. It's like that is it?"

"What's the saying? Kiss and make up?" Darby began to laugh as Blair just shook his head. "I would say Berneen is doing the fighting, Baird's doing the making up part."

Berneen leaned against Baird, her head to his chest, hearing the strong steady beat of his heart, knowing that he cherished her. But did he love her? That was what she was not yet sure of. If she could be, then maybe life would be different. But would she walk away from him, taking Darby with her? Would Darby even go?

Baird regretted his hastiness at kissing Berneen, without asking her if he could. But she looked so cute, he thought, standing up to him, her hair loose around her shoulders for once. He figured that whatever was left of his heart for her to steal would be considered stolen. He wanted to spend the rest of his life with her, God willing, but he didn't know if that was how she felt.

The next morning, Baird stood where Berneen had stood, seeing what she had seen, and he felt the fear running through him once more that he had felt when Darby was hurt. The people after Berneen were vicious, he could see that. He wasn't sure if she had picked up on what he was seeing. His phone in his hand, he hesitated, staring at it, not sure who to call. He turned as he heard footsteps on the floor behind him. Barnabas walked towards him with a man he didn't know.

"Baird? This is John Paul. He's a friend, an investigator, that I spoke with. I didn't say anything to you or Berneen as I wasn't sure he would be free. He informs me he freed up his schedule just to work on this."

Baird reached to shake the older man's hand, noting the graying hair and the lines of life on the man's face. "Thank you. Now, what do you need to know?"

"I need to talk to you, to your wife, and her brother. Are they available?"

"I think so. Berneen was still sleeping a few minutes ago. Darby had been up and was heading to see Doc." Baird moved to reach for his phone sitting on his desk.

Barnabas' hand stopped his moving away. "Let me call Doc. He'll bring him back. You wake Berneen."

"I'm behind you, Barnabas. Did you grab yourself a coffee on the way by?" Berneen moved past the two men, handing Baird his mug of coffee, positioning herself so she was tight to his side, his arm coming around her, as she sipped at her tea.

"No, we didn't but we can. John?"

"Sounds good, Barnabas." John studied the younger couple in front of him. "Berneen? May I call you that?" At her nod, he set the folders he had been carrying down on Baird's desk. "Thank you. I worked with your father a few times. I am sorry for your loss."

She tilted her head, a frown on her face.  "You did?  And thank you."  She wasn't quite sure of the man standing in front of them, not quite liking what she was reading from him.  "I don't remember Dad speaking of you at all."

John shook his head.  "He wouldn't have as it was work related."  He looked around.  "Barnabas has done a nice job on these apartments."

Neither one of the couple responded, leaving John to move restlessly, before Barnabas was back, handing him a mug of coffee.

"So, Berneen?  What have you found?"  Barnabas watched her closely, seeing the shuttered look that came over her face.  What is wrong, Lord?  Who doesn't she trust?  His eyes shifted to Baird, watching as the other man studied John, a frown on his face.

Barnabas sighed to himself, not sure if he had done the right thing after all.  He motioned to Baird, who moved towards him, and then followed Barnabas into the hallway.

"Barnabas?"

"I'm sorry, Baird.  I should have asked you first."  Barnabas took a sip of his coffee, watching Berneen, who had shuffled the photos into a pile and then into a folder before she moved away from John, setting the folder on Baird's desk.  She then moved around the desk to sit in his chair, her eyes on John.

"No problem, Barnabas.  I just don't get Berneen's reaction.  She's reading something about him that I'm not."

"She is."  Barnabas paused, his eyes on John.  "You know, he just doesn't sound like the John I knew."  He walked away, his phone out, heading for privacy to make a call.

Baird moved back towards Berneen, perching on the side of the desk, his hand on hers where they rested on the desktop.

"So, John, tell me.  What all have you worked on for Barnabas?"

John looked at him, shaking his head.  "Can't tell you that.  All my investigations are kept confidential."  He leaned back against a table, setting his mug down, and folding his arms.  "I feel like you two don't trust me."

"Why should we?" Berneen's words had a bite to them. "We don't know you. Have never seen you. I doubt very much if what you have in those folders will help at all."

"And why would you say that? You have no idea what I have."

Berneen shook her head, her eyes narrowing. "I just have a feeling, Mr. Paul. And I have learned to go with my gut instincts. That says you are not who you are saying you are."

John Paul laughed. "Your gut instincts? Really?" He looked with amusement at her before he spoke again. "Is that how your wife goes through life, Baird?"

Baird's face tightened as he too became suspicious of the man in front of them. "I trust her instincts. I doubt she is saying what she is without knowing something." He looked down at Berneen, a question of his face for a moment, before he nodded. He stood, tall and strong, Berneen thought, ready to face anything that was thrown at him. She trusted him with her life and now her heart. He would do his best to protect her.

John Paul shook his head. "You two have no idea what you're talking about."

Baird's attention was caught for a second by a whisper of sound from the kitchen area, not sure what was going on. He heard a muted sound from Berneen and looked back at John Paul, seeing him standing now in front of him, a wicked looking knife in his hand.

"Whoa!" Baird backed away, standing in front of Berneen. "Wait a minute! What's going on here?"

"Your wife is what's going on here. She needs to come with me." The older man moved towards them, Baird shoving Berneen away from him.

"Run, Berneen. Get out of here." Baird felt the angry slash of the knife in his abdomen, a shocked, disbelieving look covering his face even as his hands reached for the area, one hand coming back as he stared down at it in horror, before his legs crumpled and his body slumped to the floor, not moving. The older man stood over him, reaching down to wipe the blood from the knife on Baird's shirt before he walked over, picked up his folders and his mug and then left.

Berneen hesitated before she ran for the doorway, sliding to a stop as she saw the man standing there, his hands reaching to grasp her arms, a hand coming around her mouth as he grappled with her. She fought him, desperate to escape, to find help for Baird and Barnabas. Where was Barnabas, she thought? A sharp prick in her arm sent her mind whirling as darkness swirled around her and she slumped, gathered quickly into the man's arm and carried from the apartment, down the back stairs and then dumped into a waiting vehicle. She didn't see John Paul slide into the front seat, his head turned for a moment as he watched her closely before he nodded and the vehicle sped away, out of the back driveway and away from the building where she had felt safe.

Doc tapped at the door of the apartment, frowning when he had no answer. His hand stopped Darby from walking in.

"Wait, Darby. I don't like this." He spun the young man around and headed for the next apartment. "Stay in here."

Doc walked back to Baird's apartment door, hesitating for a moment. He heard footsteps approaching and turned to see Branigan and Bradon approaching.

"Doc? What's going on?" Branigan stopped, his eyes worried. "We got a call from Barnabas that he needed us here."

"That's what I was afraid of. I've stuck Darby away in Benen's apartment for now." He reached for the doorknob, before Branigan's hand stopped him.

"Let us go first, Doc." He cautiously opened the door, not speaking, Benen right behind him.

They stopped, frozen in time for a moment, as they spied Barnabas' body, sprawled face down on the kitchen floor, not moving, a large wound on the side of his head, the blood not congealed as yet. Benen stooped, feeling for a pulse, and nodding, before he pointed to the rest of the apartment.

The two men searched quickly and then when they reached the office, gave a cry of alarm and sprang forward to where Baird lay, hands assessing him.

"Go get Doc, Benen. See if Brady's around too."

"He's on duty. I'll put in the call." Benen's phone was in his hand even as he moved quickly to find Doc and point towards the office. "In there, Doc. Baird's hurt bad. I'll stay with Barnabas."

Doc shot him a quick look before he too bent over Barnabas. "That's a nasty blow. I'll be back as soon as I can." He almost ran for the study, seeing the look of distress on Benen's face.

He paused for a moment, finding Branigan with his hands pushing a towel against Baird's abdomen. Branigan had shifted Baird carefully to his back and then ran for towels to try and stop the bleeding.

"How long?" Doc was on his knees, his hands moving the towel, looking around for scissors. "Scissors?"

Branigan searched, finding a pair in a desk drawer, and handing them to Doc.

"I don't think that long, Doc. Barnabas called me not five minutes ago." He looked around. "Where's Berneen?"

"She's not here? Look for her, boy." Doc's attention was directed at assessing the wound, frustrated that he didn't have the supplies he needed. "Where are the paramedics?"

"Benen called." Branigan searched the apartment, standing aside as the paramedics rushed in, followed by the police officers. He frowned. She was nowhere to be seen. He looked up as he heard a sound at the door and saw Darby standing in the entrance, fear, no terror, Branigan thought, on his face and moved towards him, not realizing how much blood he had on his hands or shirt.

"Darby?"

"Branigan! You're bloody! Where's Berneen? Where's Baird?" Darby's voice was rising in his panic even as Branigan moved him backwards.

"I need to clean up. Back to Benen's." He waited, Darby not moving. "Darby!" Branigan's voice was sharp and lashing, not his normal voice, causing Darby to jump. "Move! Back to Benen!"

Branigan scrubbed at his hands and then looked down at his shirt, pulling it from him and ditching it into a trash can. He quickly reached in Benen's closet, pulling out a sweatshirt, knowing Benen would tell him to do just that.

He turned and watched Darby, who stood, eyes frozen on the door, not moving, before he walked over to him, an arm around the youth's shoulder.

"I don't know where your sister is. She's not there. Barnabas is down with a head wound. It looks as if he was struck from the side."

"Baird?" Darby's voice was barely audible. "Where's Baird?"

"He's hurt, Darby, hurt bad. He was stabbed. Doc's working on him as are the paramedics." He paused as he heard a tap at the door, and shoving Darby behind him, reached to open it.

He walked out to speak with the police officer, standing so he could watch Darby. He nodded before he motioned for Darby to come with him.

"We'll head to the hospital, Darby. They've taken them in."

"Is Baird alive?" Darby could barely get the words out.

"He is. I'm not sure how serious it is. I wasn't told." An arm around Darby's shoulder provided support to the youth, who stumbled as he walked.

"Berneen?"

"I'm sorry, Darby. She's not there. They don't know where she is."

Darby's heart sank, as worry for his sister filled his mind and heart. "Then, where is she?"

"We don't know. She was there when you left, right?"

Darby nodded. "She was still sleeping, I think, or just waking up. I wasn't gone that long, was I?"

"No, I don't think you were. These people move fast, that's the problem. They see an opportunity and take advantage of it." He pulled to a stop in a parking spot outside the hospital, and reached to grab Darby's arm as the youth opened the door. "We need to pray, Darby. This is testing your faith and your trust in God. Don't let it move you away from Him."

Darby stared at him, wondering how he knew just what he was feeling, before he nodded and bowed his head.

Darby paced the waiting room, his eyes on the door the examination room.  He needed to see Baird, needed that desperately and so far hadn't been allowed back.  Brady had come through, wheeling a stretcher in, and when he was done, had stopped by him.

"Darby?"

"Brady?  How's Baird?"

"Baird?"  Brady spun, his eyes on the door as well.  "What do you mean?  How's Baird?"

"You didn't know?  He was stabbed, Branigan said.  They have him back there.  Barnabas was hurt as well."  His voice faltered for a moment.  "Berneen's gone.  We don't know where she is."

"Berneen?"  Brady's eyes met Breck, who stood beside him, a grim look on his face.  "Breck?"

"We don't know much yet.  We need to talk to both Barnabas and Baird, and that's not possible, not right at the moment.  The police will want their statements first before we can talk to them."  He nodded at Darby.  "We need him to see Baird."

Brady nodded.  "Let me see what I can do."  He walked away, his hand rubbing at his face, before he stopped, turned to watch Darby and then disappeared through the doors.

Ten minutes later, he was back, his hand reaching for Darby's arm.  "I have permission for you to see Baird, but only for a couple of minutes.  They're getting him ready to go to surgery."

"Surgery?  He's hurt that bad?"  Darby's voice died away.  "Brady?"

"He was stabbed, Darby.  Didn't you know that?"  When Darby shook his head, Brady spoke once again.  "He was stabbed in the abdomen.  They need to take him to surgery to assess and repair the damage."

Brady watched as Darby slowly approached the stretcher Baird lay on.  Darby gripped the railing, his eyes on his brother-in-law, not sure if he should speak or not.  He didn't see Baird's hand raise slowly and jumped when it touched his.

"I'll be okay, Darb.  Stay with Barnabas."  Baird dropped off again and Darby was forced to move way as the attendants moved the stretcher out of the room and towards the elevator.

Brady pulled Darby with him.  "Come on.  Up to the surgical waiting room.  I hear the guys are up there as is Anna."  He punched the button to the elevator in an angry manner and then dropped his head.  Lord, we need You right now.  How we need You!

Darby sat once more, his eyes on the doors to the waiting room, watching for the surgeon to come, for a police officer to enter to say they had found Berneen.  He didn't hear the muted, angry conversation around him.

"Where's Barnabas?"  His question stilled the words around him.

"Barnabas was hurt too, Darby.  Didn't we tell you that?" Benen spoke from where he was seated beside him.

Darby shrugged.  "How bad?"

"A concussion for sure.  He had a nasty cut on his head.  He's still unconscious, Darby, so we can't talk to him.  His secretary said he had a friend come to see him this morning and that friend and he headed to talk to your sister and Baird."

"Is he responsible?"

"We don't know.  He wasn't there.  There were no signs of anyone but your sister, Baird, and Berneen, other than for the condition we found the two men in."  Benen's hand rested on Darby's shoulder.  "We'll find her, Darby.  That's a promise from all of us."

"Don't let it take so long!"  Darby was angry, not at the men he considered his friends, but at the situation he found himself in.

"We'll do our best, Darby."  Benen moved his head, hearing footsteps approaching the door, and the surgeon walked in, pulling off his mask and then his surgical cap before he sank into the empty chair by Darby.

---

"Darby?  Is that correct?"  The surgeon watched the youth closely as he nodded.

"That's right.  How's Baird?"

"He's in recovery right now.  He's a lucky man that he was found so quickly."

Darby's face whitened as he took in the words.  "Doctor? What do you mean?"

"I mean with as quick of a response as he had and with Doc there right away, he'll pull through.  Without that, we wouldn't be having this conversation."  Compassion showed in the physician's eyes as he watched Darby's eyes close and then as he raised his gaze to take in the men sitting and standing around the youth.  "I'll get you in to see him once we've moved him to the ICU."

Darby nodded, his eyes on the door, not hearing the quiet conversation around him as the physician walked away.  He felt an arm around him and leaned for a moment against Anna before he rose, walking away, searching for what he had no idea.  Benen followed, careful to stay back to let him have the space he needed, but eyes watchful still the same.

Two days later, Baird rested back against the raised head of his bed. He had been moved to a private room, the surgeon declaring he no longer needed to be in the ICU bed. Darby paced the room, not looking at Baird, who finally sighed, his eyes raised to the ceiling as his heart raised in prayer for his young bride and for her brother, and for his friends. Barnabas had been in, seated in a wheelchair, having been told he could not walk on his own just yet. He would need to stay in the hospital for another day or so.

Baird knew Barnabas was angry and had asked for the folder of photos to be brought in to him. The men had refused, but Darby had snuck them in. That folder even now lay on his legs, unopened. Barnabas had simply handed it to him, stating he had made notes. He needed Darby to look at the photos and see if he could remember anything. He had shaken his head at the unspoken question of Baird's face. Berneen was still missing and they were no closer to finding her than they had been.

Darby finally stopped by Baird's bedside, his eyes on the folder.

"What's with the folder?"

Baird handed it to him. "Take a look. It's what your sister was working on when she disappeared. It's your Dad's office. She found some things that were off. We went back and boxed them up. I think they're likely in the storage unit."

Darby reached for the folder. "Is she alive, Baird?"

"I would think so. I doubt they have done anything to her yet." He watched as Darby's eyes slid closed and a tear trickled down his face. "Come here, Darby. I need to pray for you." His arms wrapped around the youth and he felt the hard grip Darby had on him even as Darby's body shook with sobs. "It's okay, Darby. It's okay to weep. God bottles our tears, you know. He sees your sorrow and grieves with you."

"He does?"

"He does.  That's part of Who He is."

Darby finally stepped back, placing the folder on the table, and opening it, a frown on his face.  "I'm not sure if I can see what she saw.  I don't have the memories that she does."

"We get that, Darby.  Just take a look.  That's all we ask." Baird looked around him as the door squeaked open and Branigan entered, followed by Buckley.

"Okay."  Lost in his thoughts, Darby studied the photos.  "Do you know why she circled what she did?"

"She said that those objects and books weren't her father's. That he wouldn't have had them there."

"Oh, okay."  Darby frowned.  "This statue?  I know it.  It was in the house where I had been staying.  It has the same scrapes on it."  He looked up at Baird.  "How did it get to our place?"

"That's what we're looking at.  We think Small did that, but we can't prove it."

Darby stared at him, horror suddenly on his face.  "He was there.  He was a friend of theirs.  I met him many times."  He slid his eyes closed.  "He knew exactly where I was all the time."

"That changes things."  Branigan's voice caused Darby to jump.

"It does, doesn't it?"  Baird agreed.  He shoved at the blankets. "I need out of here and now."

"No, you don't.  You're not released yet.  That won't happen for a couple of days."  Benen shoved him gently back.  "Even with Doc and Brady on site, they won't let you go."

Baird's head went back on the pillow as his hand went to his abdomen, pain slicing through him.  "You're right, Benen.  But I need to be doing something."

"Work on healing.  Pray.  That's what you can do."  Branigan reached for the folder.  "Anything else, Darby?"

Darby shrugged, before he looked at Branigan.  "Baird says the stuff is in the storage unit.  Can I look at it?"

"That you can. You come with me now. We'll leave Benen here to make sure Baird behaves himself." He smirked at the scowl Baird sent his way.

An hour later, Darby sat back, his hands resting behind him on the floor. "I don't see anything other than that statue. Do you have the photos?"

"I do." Branigan spread them out. "How be we find what she has circled and I can take them up to my office. We'll work through them there."

Darby nodded, knowing that he didn't want to go back into Baird's apartment. Not until his sister and Baird were home. "What happens with Baird's apartment?"

"We've sent in cleaners. They've looked after getting everything back to normal." He watched Darby closely as they walked up the stairs to Branigan's office. "You're not wanting to go back there. That's a given. I'm not sure if Baird will or not. We haven't discussed that yet."

"He may not. I'm not sure Berneen will feel safe there."

"I know. We've been discussing it. Barnabas will talk to them and see what they want to do. Right now, Baird has asked for it to be painted. He needs to know the colours your sister likes."

Darby's steps slowed and then stopped, shock and surprise on his face. "He wants to know them? Why?'

"So we can repaint the apartment in the colours she feels comfortable with. He's okay with that. In fact, he asked for that before we had a chance to talk to him."

Darby's steps resumed, even as he tried to sort through his muddled thoughts. "He would do that?"

"He would, Darby. And let us know what colour you want your bedroom. He stressed that." Branigan unlocked and then shoved open his office door, depositing the box on a table in a conference room. "Here. We need to eat. Let me call in an order and then we'll get to work."

———

Two days later, Baird moved slowly around the same table, his hand on his abdomen, Darby following him, watching closely. The man finally stopped, his hands reaching for the statue Darby had identified.

"This is the one, Darby? What is wrong with it that you two picked up on?"

Darby shrugged. "I have no idea. I know Berneen knew it didn't belong to Dad." He reached for it and in the transfer between hands, it slipped from their grasp and hit the floor, breaking into pieces. "I'm sorry, Baird. I'm so sorry. That was my fault." He was done on his knees picking up the pieces and handing them to Baird.

"It's not your fault, Darby." Baird set the pieces on the table, a frown on his face. "It looks as if it had already been in pieces and just broke along the repair lines." He picked up a piece to study it more closely. "Here, what's on this?"

Darby reached for another piece. "There's something on this as well."

Baird looked around. "Find Branigan. See if he has his camera here."

Branigan followed Darby back in, camera in hand. "Darby said you wanted this."

Baird nodded, even as he swayed on his feet. Darby shoved a chair at him and made him sit. "We dropped the statue and it broke. But I think it's been broken before. There is something on each of the pieces. I can't make them out, but if we take photos, we can enlarge them and see what we find."

"That's true." Branigan began to take pictures and then headed for the computer he had set up in the room. "Give me a moment to upload these and then we'll look at them." Even as he worked away, his eyes kept straying to Baird and then to Darby, his heart raised in prayer for the two.

He finally reached for the pages on the printer, shuffling through them as he walked back towards Baird, pausing for a moment.

"Branigan, what did you find?"

"Something interesting.  I think it involves your Dad as well."

Baird's hands reached for the photos.  "Why would you say that?"

"Because his name is there.  On the second photo."  Branigan pointed to the pile of photos Baird had dropped on the table.  "It gives his name, occupation and the last building he designed.  Another photo also gives your Dad's name and the last inspection he did, Darby.  Somehow, your Dads are connected in a way we have determined yet."

"How is that?"  Baird paused, his eyes focused on the way in front of him.  "But how would that play into what's happened to Berneen?"

"That's what we have to determine and as quickly as we can.  Darby?  Has your sister ever said anything about your Dad's work?"

Darby shrugged.  "She told me what he did, but nothing more than that."  He paused.  "Didn't she clear out his desk and safe?  Can we look through that material?"

"We can and will."  Baird was on his feet, gathering up the photos. "Branigan?"

"Right with you.  Benen is here as well."

"Good.  We may need to bring in all the guys.  I doubt we'll keep them away."  Baird moved slowly, Darby's arm linked with his to provide support.

Baird sank down in his desk chair, the photos in front of him, his eyes sliding closed for a moment before he looked up at Darby as he sorted through boxes, pulling out the ones he wanted.

"Here, Baird.  I think this is it.  Berneen marked them all as they were packed."  He sat back for a moment.  "Where do we start?"

"We start by organizing by year, I would think, or by topic." Bradon reached for some of the papers, the other men's hands there as well, Brady just coming in, still in his paramedic uniform.

"Baird?" Brady stopped beside him. "Are you sure you should be up?"

"No, I'm not. But I have to." Baird looked up at Brady. "I need to do this. I told Berneen I would back her in what she was doing. I have to do the same with Darby." He blinked rapidly for a moment to clear his eyes. "Have you heard anything yet?"

Brady shook his head. "Nothing. And I would hear rumours of some kind on the street. It's silent."

"So where is she then?" Baird reached for the papers he was being handed. "How do we do this, Brady?"

"We start with names, dates, addresses." He looked around. "Can we put up paper somewhere, Baird?"

Baird nodded. "We can. There are some small rolls of newsprint there. Tape in the cupboard."

He watched as his friends worked through what they had found, Anna bringing in a meal, Doc finally hauling him to his feet and hand on his back, directing him to his bed.

"You need to rest, Baird." Doc examined his wound and then watched closely as Baird laid back before pulling a blanket over him. "You need to sleep and recover. Not doing that won't help Berneen."

"I know, Doc. I just want to be part of what they're doing."

"And you will be. Give yourself some time." Doc watched as Baird slept, before he turned, shaking his head as he did so. The men were all like sons to him, and he hurt when they hurt. This time, though, there was nothing in his medical bag to help heal a broken heart.

———

136

Branigan looked up at a sudden sound from Buckley, and then walked towards where he was sitting.

"Buckley?"

"I think I'm figuring it out, Branigan. Look. There are the fathers' names. Their occupations. Addresses where they were involved in either construction or inspection. They overlap in ways we didn't see, did we? There are a number they don't connect on, but these five? They were involved in them." Buckley rose, searching for a clear sheet of paper and marking down the addresses. "Now, we have to determine if anything happened to these properties. Who the owners are now. Insurance. Debts. Mortgages."

They stared at Buckley for a moment before Brody shook his head.

"Are you sure you're not an investigator, Buckley?"

Buckley just grinned. "It goes with how I approach my messages. I search Scripture for connections and confirmation. I don't get up and make Scripture match what I say. I make what I say match Scripture." He pointed to the paper. "This is the same idea. We are just making the facts speak for themselves. They point to someone and something, with proof there."

"And we need the proof in order to go to the authorities." Braden looked around. "Breck, are they okay with us doing this?"

Breck shrugged. "They don't know about this. They would just look it over, likely, and then give it back to us. There is nothing that we have seen that would lead conclusively to anyone or any company."

"Okay, so where does this lead us?" Branigan walked over to study the paper, his face suddenly paling. "Benen, did you see this?"

Benen stood beside him in an instant, his face paling as well. "Isn't that the client Baird was working with that suddenly withdrew their plans? He had a bad feeling he said all along about him."

"He did." Branigan pulled out his phone. "I need to talk to the detective. Then we need to talk to Barnabas."

"We do." Benen was out of the door, heading for Barnabas, stopping as he met him in the hallway. "Barnabas?"

"Benen. I take it you are all in there?" He pointed towards the door.

"We are. I was just coming to find you. Buckley has sorted through everything so quickly, I can't get over how he did it. He's come up with some names and details we need to talk about."

"That's good." Barnabas paused for a moment. "Baird? Darby?"

"Doc sent Baird to bed. Darby is right there in the office, in the midst of what we're doing. He's bringing a new outlook to what we searching for, asking questions to understand what we want to find, who his father was, who Baird's father was, their occupations. Things that we take for granted that he is striving to understand. He's hurting in a way I had hoped not to see him hurt."

Barnabas nodded, his mind working through who he knew that could help him. "I might have a friend who could help him. His kids went through something."

"That would help. Barnabas, are you okay?"

"Not really. I hate this. I hate that Berneen is again missing. As for me, I have a headache that won't stop but it won't stop me. I won't let it." He walked away from Benen, coming to a stop in Baird's office doorway, his eyes searching his men, seeing their hurt for their friend but also their determination to solve whatever it was they had to solve and bring Berneen back home. He trusted them with that, that whatever they needed to do, they would do.

Branigan paused on the way past him. "I'm heading over to the house. Blair's going with me."

"Take Bradon and Kade as well. Let Kade run a search before you go in. I won't be surprised that you found some hidden objects." The men shared a glance before Branigan nodded and then called for Bradon to come with him.

Barnabas moved around the room, speaking with each one, until he stopped by Darby, dropping into a chair beside him, his eyes closing for a moment. He opened them to find Darby staring at him.

"You shouldn't be here, Barnabas." Darby's words were quiet.

"I need to be, Darby. I need to be. Benen tells me you instigated this."

Darby shrugged. "Someone had to. This is how they do it in detective movies and books, inside it? They set up white boards and cover them with data."

"That they do. Are you planning on going into that line of work?"

Darby shrugged. "I have no idea. They want me to settle on something in high school, so I know whether I want to go to college, university or trade school. Right now, I'm not sure where I want to be."

Barnabas agreed with him. "Take your time. You have your whole life ahead of you. I have friends in all trades and professions. You can talk to them, perhaps work with them for a day or so just to get a feel of what they do."

"You'd do that for me?" Darby was surprised and it showed on his face.

"Darby, it's what we do with our volunteer work. Any one of these guys would welcome you to work with them and go on their volunteer assignments if we can get approval for that."

"That's great." Darby blinked rapidly, thinking how it would have felt if his father had still be alive and able to arrange that for him. "About this?"

"Yes, this. I understand Buckley has narrowed it down."

"He has. Here are the names." Darby slid over a neatly written list. "I think I know one of them. The last name. I can vaguely remember Mom and Dad talking about him. But I can't be positive. I was so young, and it was so long ago."

Barnabas studied the youth, knowing Darby was seeking approval. "I trust you on this, Darby. If you say it's the name, we'll investigate it until we prove it otherwise. That's who we are. That's what we do."

Darby nodded, his eyes on the paper. "I think too I heard the couple I was staying with mention him. And it wasn't in a very pleasant manner. They didn't like him."

"We'll look into him." Barnabas paused. "The couple you were staying with? Did we ever get their names?"

Darby looked at him. "I have no idea if Berneen mentioned them or not." He added their names to the list. "I never did feel comfortable there but I stayed because that was where Berneen knew to reach me."

The next day, Barnabas rose from behind his desk and walked through his building, stopping every once in a while from the pain of his headache. He wanted it done with but it would take time, that he knew. He rubbed at the smaller bandage Doc had put on that morning before telling him to leave the investigation to others. He had enough to do with his own work. His secretary had kept everything up to date for him, organizing the material and requests, adding her comments to them.

He stopped at Baird's office and tried the door, finding the knob turning under his hand. He entered, not surprised to find Baird there.

"Baird?"

Baird looked around, and Barnabas drew in his breath. He knew Baird had not fully recovered from his first adventure as they termed it. To see the haggard, pale face of his friend was heart-wrenching.

"Barnabas? I thought Doc had told you to stay still."

Barnabas sank into a chair. "I thought he had told you the same."

Baird sat back, his coloured pencil tapping for a moment. "He did, but I need to finish these plans. I almost had them done the other day but had to wait for some material specifications before I could. I'm sending them off shortly to the homebuyer, to see if they're what he wants."

"That's good." Barnabas just sat for a few moments. "How are you really doing, Baird?"

Baird shrugged. "Hurting. Having trouble trusting. Want Berneen back. Trying to stay strong for Darby."

"I get that. What can we do for you?"

———

"Find Berneen. Bring her home." Baird's voice lowered to a whisper. "I need her home, Barnabas, but I don't know if she'll be alive when she comes back."

Barnabas could hear the sorrow in his friend's voice. "We're praying that she is, Baird. I know it's likely hard to trust at this time."

"It is." Baird looked past Barnabas as the door opened and Bradon walked in.

"Bradon?"

"We have some news, Baird. Barnabas, I'm glad you're here." He pulled over a chair, his eyes on his clasped hands for a moment before he looked up. "Barnabas, your friend? John Paul? We just received word they found his body yesterday. The coroner puts his time of death as last Sunday."

"Sunday? Then, who was that who was here?" Barnabas was shaken, not sure what to think.

"He had a twin brother, who walked on the wrong side of the law. I've seen their pictures. It's hard to tell them apart."

"That's what I was picking up then. I knew something seemed off but I couldn't understand what. He had to have been the one I talked to on Monday then." Barnabas blew out a breath even as he sat back in his chair. "What did I do?"

"Someone pulled a fast one on us. Likely they didn't think you'd know until after they pulled what they did. It was a setup, Barnabas, directed at getting to Berneen." Bradon looked between the two men. "You two were incidental casualties. That's how the police have worded it. I don't think so."

Baird shook his head, even as his hands were moving to package the house drawings for courier pick up. "No, we weren't. They wanted us out of the way. They were looking to make a statement and they did. Now, what do we do with this information?"

"We look harder at him and his contacts." Barnabas drew in a deep breath. "Does the brother know the family Darby stayed with?"

"That we're looking into but it seems as if he does.  The contact was Small."

"This just gets worse and worse, doesn't it?"

"It does.  But does it bring us closer to finding Berneen?" Baird sat back down, his eyes on his friends.  "I worry about Darby. She's all he has.  I don't want to face what we've all faced, being orphans and alone."  He shook his head.  "Sorry, Barnabas, that didn't come out right.  You're not an orphan."

"No, I'm not.  But my friends are and I need to be able to understand them and how they feel.  We've talked this over many times in the past."  He looked around as he heard the door open and more footsteps approach.  "Darby?  What is it?"  Barnabas was on his feet, his hand out to draw Darby closer.

Darby looked at the men, as best he could through his tears.  "I got this."  He held out a photo.  "It's Neen.  She looks as if she's dead."

Baird was on his feet, Darby wrapped in his arms as he sobbed, heartbroken at the thought his sister was dead, even as Bradon took the photo and peered at it.

"No, I don't think she is, Darby.  They want her alive, why, we haven't yet figured out.  They're letting us know they have her. They want to work on your emotions, Darby, Baird.  We need to watch you two closely.  Who's to say they won't come after one of you?"

"But why, Barnabas?  What is they want?"  Darby spun, fighting free to stand in front of the older man, anger radiating from him.  "What do we have that they want?  Or that they think we have? If Dad had been into computers and he was alive today, I would think there was a thumb drive or something that he had hidden with information on it."

Bradon's hand froze as he raised it to rub at his head, a sudden light coming to his face.  "That's it. Darby, I do believe you have solved what we've been struggling with.  What was in your father's office that would hide something like this?"

Darby shrugged.  "I have no idea.  I guess we need to go through what Berneen brought back."

———

"We did that.  She is adamant that your father didn't place those items there."  Bradon watched as Baird rose to his feet. "Baird?  What are you thinking?"

"I'm thinking we need to go back to that house and if we have to pack up everything and bring it back here, we will."

"I think that is a good idea."  Benen waved his phone.  "I spoke with Charles.  His trucks and guys are on their way there.  We just need to meet them with a key."  Charles was a good friend of theirs from church and owned a moving company.

"Great work."  Baird was out of the office, Darby at his heels, before the other men could make a move.

Baird stood in the empty house as the movers carried the last of the boxes from it, his eyes on Darby. He walked towards the youth, his hand coming to Darby's shoulder.

"Do you know of any more hiding places?"

Darby shook his head. "We talked about that. Berneen was sure there were only the two safes. The one in the bedroom. And the one in the office." He swiped a hand across his eyes before he walked up the stairs and stood in his bedroom, sorrow working through him. Please Lord? I need my Neen. Bring her home soon, Lord. I just need my sister.

Baird had followed, stopping in the doorway, his eyes on the youth and then roaming the room. He frowned and walked towards the wall opposite the door. "What's this, Darby?"

Darby looked at Baird and then the wall, finally moving to stand beside him. "What's what?"

"This? Don't you see it? The paper doesn't quite match. It was hidden behind the photo." Baird worked at the paper, removing it and then stopped, surprised at the small door he found there. Opening it, he reached in, finding a cloth sack. He felt around, finding nothing else. He felt the sack and his eyes lighted. "Come on, Darby. We hit pay dirt, I think." He moved as rapidly as he could from the room and down the stairs, Darby on his heels, even as he tucked the bag into an inside pocket of his jacket. He slid into Benen's vehicle, Darby beside him on the back seat.

"All set?" At their nod, Benen pulled from the curb, watchful but not seeing anyone that concerned him.

"They'll unload into one of the storage units, Benen?"

"They will, Baird. Blair is looking after that." He watched Baird in the mirror for a moment. "What did you find?"

"I think we found a missing piece of the puzzle. There was another hidden door in Darby's room. We would not have found it if we hadn't cleared out the house." He looked over at Darby. "We're not giving up your house, Darby. But Berneen has said she can't live in it. It's yours, she has told me. But you can't live in for three or more years."

"I don't know that I want to, Baird. Neen won't come to visit me there. I know that." Darby stared out the window, sorrow on his face, not seeing the looks the men with him were exchanging.

"We'll work it out, Darby. Don't worry about it. If we have to, it can be rented out." Baird paused. "Or it could be used for short-term stuff, like missionaries coming home on furlough and needing an address to work from."

Darby spun on the seat, the first interest in something else on his face they had seen since Berneen disappeared. "Can we do that? Or use if for people who are between homes? Like women and children?"

"That's another thought. We'll talk it over with Berneen and Barnabas."

Darby nodded. "That bag, Baird? What's in it?"

Baird pulled it out, staring at it. "I think a thumb drive." He opened the bag and shook out the contents into his hand. "I was right. A thumb drive. Thank you, Darby. You may have just solved the riddle we've been working on."

"I hope I have. We need Berneen home, safe and sound. If that does it. I hope it does." Darby turned away once more, falling silent, his eyes staring out the window again.

Baird's hand rested on Darby's shoulder before he dropped the thumb drive back into the bag and pocketed the bag.

Once in Benen's office, Baird pulled the bag out and handed it to Benen. "Can we open it, do you think?"

"I'll take a look. We may be able to." He sat down at his desk, bowed his head for a moment, and then inserted the thumb drive to his computer, running a scan on it first to ensure there were no bugs or viruses. "It's clean. Now, let's see what we can do with it."

———

He found he was able to open it, scanning what was coming up before he sat back, his face pale, his eyes raising to Barnabas who had followed them into his office and then to Baird and Darby. "This is bad, guys. Names, dates, addresses, information on shoddy inspections and poor designs. This is what they were after."

Barnabas pointed to the computer. "Make a copy of that. I'm taking it to the detective now." He turned as he heard Doc's voice.

"Barnabas. I just came through the lobby. Security says there's a detective to see you."

Barnabas shook his head. "No, there won't be. Benen?"

Benen tossed him the thumb drive. "Take Blair or Breck. They're driving."

Barnabas nodded and was gone before they could say another word.

Late that afternoon, Baird opened the door to his apartment to find Barnabas standing there and then stepped back so he could enter.

"Baird, you need to be in bed. You look horrible."

Baird nodded. "I will. I can relax now, I think." He walked away, a hand to his abdomen, his steps slow and hesitant.

"Doc?" Benen's voice broke the silence.

"I don't like his colour. Someone needs to check on him later tonight."

Baird walked back towards his kitchen, Benen following him, late that evening.  He poured their coffee, handing Benen his mug, and then stood, back to the counter, watching his friend.

Benen sat, his eyes on Baird, a frown on his face.  "Have you slept, Baird?"  He was concerned about the look of pain on Baird's face, the paleness, the dark circles under his eyes.

"I did for a while, then I had to get up."  He sighed, his eyes dropping to his mug.  "I'm trying to stay as normal as I can for Darby, but it's not working for either one of us."  He turned, setting his mug on the counter, his hand going to his abdomen.  "Have you talked to Barnabas?"

"Just briefly.  The detective was quite interested in that material.  He's going to have his techs go over it and then hand it off to one of the detectives helping on the case.  They want this solved, Baird."

Baird swayed for a moment, then his eyes closed, his body sagged and he crumpled to the floor as his knees gave way, an arm wrapped around his abdomen, just missing the handle on the oven door, taking the towel hanging there down with him.

Benen was on his knees, his hands rolling Baird to his back, even as he shouted for Darby.

"Darby!"  When he heard no response, he yelled again.  "Darby!  Now!  I need your help!"

Darby appeared in the doorway, hair sticking up, eyes half closed against the light, rubbing at his face.  "Benen?  What's up?  Why are you yelling for me?"

"Call for help.  Baird just collapsed."

Those words had Darby awake and alert, reaching for the phone on the counter, dialing for emergency services.  He stood back, beside Benen, and watched as the paramedics worked on Baird before he was bundled onto a stretcher and then wheeled away.

"Go on. Get dressed, Darby. I'll take you after him."

Darby ran for his room and then ran for the door, Benen after him, watching as Darby slammed the door, lock in place. Benen smiled to himself, noting that Darby seemed to have grabbed the first pieces of clothing he had laid his hands on, not caring about style at all.

Darby sat once more in the surgical waiting room, his foot bobbing up and down with his stress, his eyes on the entrance door, willing the surgeon to come, but afraid to have him come. Buckley sat beside him, his arm around Darby's shoulders. Anna sat on his other side, his hand tight in hers. As many of the other men who could be there, were. Doc had sent word he'd come as soon as his shift finished at the clinic in the shelter downtown.

Darby was on his feet as he saw the same surgeon approaching.

"Doctor? Baird?"

"He's alive, but he wouldn't be if he had been on his own. He was bleeding internally, likely had been all day. What was he doing?"

"Moving around too much, likely." Buckley spoke up. "I'm sure you're aware his wife has been kidnapped, and he is doing everything he can to help find her."

"He needs to rest. He'll not survive another one of these episodes. As it is, right now, it's touch and go. We're sending him to an ICU bed when we can. You, young man, you can see him but only for a bit." The surgeon searched the faces of the men around him. "All of you can in shifts. But I want it understood. He can't continue as he has been. He left too soon the last time. This time, we won't let him go." The surgeon spun on his heel and walked away, anger emanating from his very stride.

"He won't stop. He can't. It will kill him if he has to." Darby's words were quiet but heard by everyone around him. Anna's arm around him kept him close to her.

"We're praying, Darby. We're praying. I'm getting a sense from God that this will end shortly." Anna's words were whispered to the youth.

———

"I hope so, Anna.  Please, God. I pray so."  He turned, his head down, unable to control his tears, pushing his way through the men, to drop onto a chair, his head buried against his upraised knees.

Moving restlessly, Berneen raised her head slightly and rubbed her face against her sleeve, before she rolled to her side from her stomach, her hair flowing around her. She slept again, not moving, the sleep deep and drugged.

The man stood over her, anger on his face. He needed to talk to her, to give her orders as to what she was going to do, but he couldn't. He couldn't get her to wake up. He had no idea how much of the sedative she had been given or how often, but it was wreaking havoc with his plans.

He spun on his heel, slamming through the door and locking it behind him, leaving Berneen enclosed in a windowless room, on her own. He would find the men responsible for this and make them pay. This was not acceptable, he thought, as his heavy footsteps stormed through the house, causing the men there to raise their heads and share a glance. They knew that Berneen had not been given too much sedative but how to explain that to their leader. That was a question none of them wanted to face but they would have no choice, not given the mood he was in.

Berneen stirred again, how much later, she wasn't sure. She dragged her body to a sitting position, pushing her unkempt hair behind her, and then scrubbing at her face, her eyes barely open. She saw the bottle of water beside her and reached for it. Uncapping it, she drank thirstily before she set it back down, her body slumping once more in sleep. She just couldn't stay awake, she thought.

How long she had been like this, she didn't know, awakening again, more alert but still sleepy and not quite aware of what was going on. She sat up, looking around, seeing no windows and only a door. She dragged herself to her feet, stumbling over them as she fell against a wall. Her hands feeling her way along, she searched for a way out, not finding any. She moved more rapidly and more in a panic, finally stopping at the door, her hand clutching at the door knob and shaking it. Her hand still on the knob, she began to strike at the door with her open hand.

"Hey! Open the door! Let me out!" She continued to strike at the door. "Please! Someone? Anyone? Open the door, please? Let me out?"

Her hand fisted, and she began to hammer at the door, finally stepping away as she realized no one heard her, or if they did, that they were not going to open the door as she demanded and let her out. She backed away from the door until she hit the wall opposite it, standing for a moment before she slid to a sitting position on the floor. She shoved her unkempt hair away from her face, scrubbing at her cheeks, feeling the stickiness from the tears she didn't remember shedding. She climbed to her feet once more, heading for the rudimentary sink that stood in a corner, a curtain hiding the toilet from view. She turned the tap cautiously, not sure if there would be water, her eyes sliding closed as water poured from the tap. She scrubbed at her face and hands, not sure if she was getting the dirt and stickiness away from them. She reached for the thin worn towel that hung there, and then changed her mind. She couldn't use it, not knowing if it had been used by someone before her. She pulled up the sweatshirt she was wearing, using the inside to wipe at the wetness on her face and hands.

That someone else had been held there for a time, she had no doubt. She could see the damage done to the drywall where someone had tried to pry it away from around the door but had been unsuccessful. She had no idea who had taken her. All she could remember was seeing Baird drop to the floor, his hand on his abdomen, and then trying to run, before she was stopped. She rubbed at her arm where she had felt the prick of a needle before her consciousness had fled.

She slumped back to the floor, this time in a corner of the wall that contained the door, her legs out in front of her, ankles crossed, as she wrapped her arms around herself, her thoughts going to the man who had appeared with Barnabas. She knew the name he had given wasn't right but she couldn't place where she had seen him.

Then, as she sorted through her memories, a tiny thought tickled at her memories and then grew. Her eyes shut as she concentrated, then flew open at the memory that surfaced. She groaned. She knew the man, and it wasn't from a pleasant experience. She remembered her father telling her to avoid any contact with him if she could and if she couldn't, then to find him. He would protect her.

She shuddered at her memory. He had approached her one day as she had stood in the local bookstore, his hand clenching her arm in a tight grip as he demanded she call her father. He wanted to speak with him, and her father had been avoiding his calls. She had stared at him, panic setting in, as she jerked at her arm, finally freeing herself as a saleswoman approached them and his grip loosened. She had fled from the store, wanting to find her father, and then realizing he had just left on his trip with her mother. She had hidden herself in the house, making Darby stay inside, much to his dismay. He had protested loud and long, she remembered.

Her head back on the wall, her mind drifted. Why, Lord? She questioned Him. Why me? Why this? Who is doing this? I thought that being a Christian meant safety, peace, happiness, joy, protection. This certainly doesn't feel like this. I don't know that I can trust, not like Your Word says I need to. I feel isolated, alone, forgotten. I doubt I'll make it out of here alive. So, where is Your protection? Where are You? How can I trust? My husband is likely dead. I don't know what has happened to my brother. So, tell me, how do I trust You?

———

Berneen didn't stir or look up as the door finally opened, and the man walked in, looking for her, stopping just short of her feet. She studied the shoes, the shiny black patent leather, the pointed toes, the dark socks showing just a bit below the creased black dress pants. She didn't respond as he stood there, a foot starting to tap as her refusal to look up.

"Look at me!" The words came out in a staccato manner, harshness behind them, a coarseness she recognized from years gone by. "I said, look at me!"

She refused to look up, even when his hand reached out and clutched her hair at the scalp, pulling backwards, making her face turn up. She kept her eyes down, not wanting to see the cruelty in the face she feared.

"I said, look at me!" Her chin was then grasped and her head tilted further up, her eyes closing.

The man finally stepped back, knowing that for now, she would not obey him. "You will look at me at some point, young lady. If you don't, you'll never go back to your family." He cackled out a cruel laugh. "Those that are still living, that is."

She shuddered at the thought of someone else she loved dying, but she just could not look up. Lord? Is this where I'm supposed to trust You? That You will bring me to safety? Just how do I do that?

She heard his heavy footsteps walk across the floor and out the door, the door slamming behind him, the lock clicking into place.

Now what, she thought? Where do I go from here? He wants something from me, or he wants me to do something for him. That's definitely not an option.

She rose, pacing the room, trying to think of a way to escape, to get away. She turned the door knob, shaking it slightly, finding it locked. She searched for hinges, not seeing them on the inside of the door. Well, she thought, there goes that idea. I can't remove the hinge pins, even if I had something to work with.

She paced more, finally dropping down into the same corner, this time her knees drawn up, her arms folded on them, her chin on her arms. Lord? Where are You? This isn't supposed to happen to Christians, you know. We're supposed to be safe. Or is that what You want me to learn? That no matter where I go, I'm not safe. That's a frightening thought, that I can't be safe anywhere. Mom and Dad sure weren't.

She paused as she thought about that, wondering who had been responsible for their deaths. Her eyes slanted towards the door, knowing that the man who had left her here was likely responsible in some way. She shuddered at the thought.

Her head rested against the wall and she slept, not hearing the door unlock again and lighter footsteps approach her, setting down a tray on the floor beside her, before the man stepped back, his eyes on her, a look on his face that said he would do his best to get her out of there. He was low man on the totem pole, he thought. He didn't realize he had signed on for this. He didn't like it, not one bit.

He walked away, locking the door, but not wanting to do that. He had no choice. The boss expected the key to be returned to him, and the younger man knew he would check the door himself.

Berneen eventually roused, not sure what had awakened her. She stood, feeling the floor shaking under her. She spun, her eyes huge with fear, then ran for the door, shaking at the knob, pounding on the door, unable to elicit any response. She felt the building shaking and she spun once more, unable to escape, not knowing what was happening, fear coursing through her body in a deeper and deeper wave. She headed for a corner, not sure if she would even be safe there. Then, the floor gave way beneath her, and she fell the few feet to the crawlspace under the floor, her head hitting against the flooring and her eyes closed as her body sagged and went limp, her head dropping back against the floor. She didn't hear the yells of the men as they ran for safety, leaving her the only occupant of the now shaky, almost demolished building. They didn't know that this had been planned, that they were to have died along with Berneen, when the building collapsed, and that for some reason, the building didn't collapse all the way, allowing their escape, and allowing a small space that kept Berneen safe.

Red and blue emergency vehicle lights played across the scene, highlighting the fragility and instability of the building as men and women milled around, shouts and answers ringing through the air.

Barnabas stood for a moment, staring at the building, then down at a paper in his hand, his heart falling as he realized that he stood in front of the building that they had tracked Berneen to. Was he too late? Had she escaped? He looked around, finding the fire captain walking towards him.

"Ron?"

"Barnabas? What are you doing here?" Ron Walker turned to face the building. "We're looking but we don't think anyone was inside."

"I think there was." Barnabas' voice was barely audible.

"What?" Ron spun back to face him. "Whatever do you mean?"

"I mean this." He held up the piece of paper. "We tracked Baird's wife to here. We think she was held captive here. Oh, God! Please! Don't let her be dead!" Barnabas cry went to the heart of the man standing beside him.

"How sure are you?" Ron took the paper Barnabas held out to him and read it. "You're sure?"

"As sure as we can be." He looked around, seeing Brady walking towards him. "And now I have to tell a friend she's in there."

"Barnabas?" Brady's voice held a question. "Why are you here?" His voice died away as he began to shake his head and turned to the building. "No! She's not, is she?"

"Benen and Burney tracked her to here. I don't know how, but they did."

Brady stared at him and then turned to the fire captain. "Captain? Can we search?"

"No, it's not stable enough." He walked away, his arm waving at some of his men, who ran towards him and then ran towards the engine, pulling equipment from it.

"They'll search, Brady, from outside. That looks like a heat sensing camera." Barnabas had followed Ron to where he was sending his men to searching.

"It is, Barnabas. Pray that if she's in there, we can find her and that she's in a spot we can access." Ron looked up at the building. "Pete. Call for a crane. Have it ready to move in when I say."

Hours passed. Brady sat on the step of his paramedic rig, the light from the huge spotlights reflecting from the stripes on his uniform. Barnabas had been back and forth, returning this time with Buckley, Bradon and Breck. Bradon had Kade with him, just in case he said. He didn't elaborate but they knew what he was referring to and their hearts sank. Their prayer was to find Berneen alive and that they could get to her.

A sudden shout had all heads turning towards the back corner of the house and Brady was on his feet, running that way.

"Captain?" His question was almost breathless, he was so afraid of what he would hear.

"We have a heat source here, Brady." Ron moved his men away. "The crane will stabilize  the building enough so that I can send someone in."

"Me." He stared at the captain. "Please sir. Let me go."

Ron finally nodded. "Okay. Get yourself geared up as you need to. I want someone to go with you."

"It's a crawl space, Captain. There won't be room for more than me, I suspect." Brady ran for the rig and then was back, ready to enter through a shattered window when he was given word. A heavy tarp dropped to the ground at his feet, ready to cover the window frame.

Barnabas stood as close as he was allowed, the three other men nearby as they watched Brady speaking with the captain before, with a clap of the older man's hand to his shoulder, he picked up the tarp and headed for the window. The four friends exchanged glances, knowing they were praying that it was Berneen who had been spotted and that she was alive now. It had seemed like hours since the heat source was found.

Brady draped the tarp over the window frame, pausing to pray for a moment, before he slid feet first into the crawl space, the light from the torch he held shining eerily around. He could hear the drip from pipes that still held a bit of water. He knew the utilities had been shut off, so that wasn't a concern. He just didn't know how clear a path he would have to where the person was. He prayed it was Berneen, not someone else. They needed to find her for Baird. Baird was still being kept unconscious, the surgeon concerned about the bleeding.

He moved forward, his gloved hands feeling his way, until he felt a small object in his way and stopped, digging through the sand and dirt, uncovering match-box sized tin boxes, five of them. He frowned for a moment as he studied them, then scooped them up, sticking them into a pocket on his uniform cargo pants and zipping the pocket closed before he shone the light around. A foot showed briefly as he flashed the light by it and then he trained the light on the foot, playing it around, seeing the body lying there, almost lifeless, he thought.

He crept forward, hearing the groaning and squeaking of the building, knowing that at any moment it could give way. The crane had support chains and ropes running to the building, but that didn't help inside. He reached for the foot, feeling how small it was, and knew it was a woman. He crept closely, not minding the stones and debris he was crawling over, not seeing the dust and bits of debris dropping into his line of sight, ducking below the jagged edges of the wood. He felt for the arm, found the wrist and with a quick motion, had his glove off feeling for a pulse. His head dropped briefly. She was alive.

He moved carefully to edge her nearer him, mindful that she could have injuries he would worsen by that very activity, but he had no choice. He had to do this. There wasn't room for a backboard or neck collar. He paused for a moment and then with a sigh, reached for the scissors in his other pants pocket, reaching to carefully cut away the hair that was trapped under a beam, hurting for her with each strand his scissors sliced through.

He worked his way carefully backwards towards the window, his movements gentle, his eyes on the woman's face until he could see it. Thank you, God, he thought. It's Berneen. She's alive. Please, hold up the building until we're out. That's all I'm asking right now.

He moved back until he was at the window and saw the men, the captain among them, watching for him. Eager hands reached to take Berneen from him as he gently lifted her up and through the window, to be placed carefully on a backboard and then rushed to the waiting stretcher. Brady reached for the hands and arms that pulled him through the window and once on his feet, ran for Berneen, wanting to be the one who took her in for treatment. The captain nodded, his eyes raising to where Barnabas and the others waited.

The captain walked towards them. "We have her, Barnabas. She's alive." He watched with compassion as the men's faces relaxed and almost tears clouded their eyes.

"How is she?" Barnabas could barely get the words out. He had not known Berneen long he thought, but she had become an important part of their lives, just because of Baird.

"I don't know. She's unconscious. Brady didn't say much when he handed off to us, other than to be careful." Ron turned, his eyes on the paramedics as they were loading the stretcher. "Head off with them, Barnabas. Stay right behind the rig. I'm sending an escort with you. The police chief has authorized it.

A sudden yell had them all turning, watching both in fascination and horror as the building shuddered and then collapsed on itself, tearing away the restraints from the crane. The four friends stood in shock, realizing how close it had been for Berneen and Brady not making it out.

His feet sounded quietly on the tiled floor, Barnabas headed for the ICU rooms, Buckley keeping step with him. They needed to find Darby and knew he would be around that area somewhere.

"Did Brady give any hint as to her condition when you talked to him, Buckley?"

Buckley shook his head. "Not really, other than she was likely dehydrated and unconscious. He asked that we pray it's not serious."

"That we can." Barnabas paused at the entrance to the chapel, peeking through the doors, seeing Anna there. "Anna's in there. She needs to go home."

"She won't. Not while her boys, as she calls them, need her. And now that Berneen is here? She definitely won't. She always wanted a daughter, but only had sons. She has quite taken to Berneen."

"That she has. I'm glad for Berneen's sake. She needs her." Barnabas sighed as they walked towards the waiting room, finding Darby huddled in the corner, his eyes on the door to the rooms. "He just won't leave."

"No, he won't. Not until Baird can tell him to. And that's not happening any day soon." Buckley paused, his thoughts muddled for a moment. "The church has had the prayer chain working every day, all day, and the board members and trustees have kept the church open."

"That helps."

Even though it was late at night, Darby was making no effort to leave. He couldn't, he told them. He needed to be with Baird. He didn't look up as the two men sat on either side of him.

Barnabas' arm came out around Darby's shoulders, knowing that when he spoke, Darby would be on his feet, running for the Emergency Department, and they needed to prepare him, for what he would see when he found his sister.

"Darby?"  When the youth didn't respond, Barnabas shared a looked with Buckley.  "Darby, I need you to listen to me."

Darby looked around, a bleak look on his face, fatigue showing, his face white.  "What is it, Barnabas?  More bad news about Baird."

"There has been news?"

Darby nodded.  "They took him back to surgery a bit ago.  There was an area the surgeon was concerned about.  They're talking about needing to transfuse him, I think they said."

"No, I hadn't heard.  Was someone with you when they talked to you?"

Darby nodded.  "Doc and Anna.  Branigan was here as well."  He sighed, his eye closing as he fought his tears and lost the battle.

"Okay.  So we pray harder.  But that's not what I wanted to talk to you about."  Barnabas' voice was gentle, but Darby's head shot around and he stared at him.

"No!  Please, God.  No!  She can't be gone!"

"Whoa, there, Darby.  She's not.  We found her but she is hurt.  She's downstairs right now being looked after."  His arm tightened on Darby as Darby made a move to rise.  "Wait, please.  We need to tell you what happened."  He went on to explain how they had tracked Berneen to the house, only to find the house was collapsing, that they had searched and found her, Brady going in to bring her out.  He looked up at that point to see Brady approaching, staring down at something in his hands.

Darby looked up and then was on his feet away from the two men, almost running towards Brady.  "Brady?  Thank you."  He hugged Brady, his arms tight before he stepped back.  "Can I go to her?  Can I see her?"

"You can.  I'll take you down in just a moment.  First, I need to give these to Barnabas."

"What are those?"  Darby peered closer.  "They look like old match tins."

"That's what they are. They have something in that that I can't get out. We'll figure it out." He handed them to Barnabas. "I found them before I found Berneen."

Barnabas studied them, feeling the weight of an object inside each one, before he dropped them into a pocket. "We'll look at them. Right now, Darby needs his sister."

Brady nodded, as hand on Darby's shoulder, he turned him and walked him back to the elevator, not knowing or caring how dirty his uniform had become during his crawl under the house.

Darby stood at his sister's bedside, watching as her head turned slightly in a restless manner. He saw the bruise on her forehead and winced. He hadn't spoken to the doctor yet although he could hear him talking to a nurse outside the curtain. He was just thankful his sister was back with him.

Sore, battered, tired, her mind still foggy, fighting a headache, but showered and in clean clothes, Berneen stood at Baird's bedside, her hand resting against his cheek, seeing the hollows that had appeared in them. She felt the stubble that she knew he would not like. How she knew that, she wasn't sure. It was just something she knew.

She watched as he slept, the intubation tube still in place, IVs running to his arms, the heart monitor leads. She knew he had had a blood transfusion and knew just who had given his blood. She would need to find Doc at some point and thank him.

She had heard about his three surgeries, her heart breaking for him, knowing that even now, he was still in danger. She had been told that bluntly by the surgeon. In fact, she was told Baird should not be alive. The surgeon had no idea why he was. Berneen had given a small smile at that, knowing exactly Who had kept him alive.

She had talked at length with the detective, letting him know who had abducted her and how she knew him. She told him how terrified of the man she was, given his actions in the past. She now had a police officer assigned to her all the time. It was a given, she was told, that the man would make another try for her.

She had had no words to thank Brady, just gave him a long hug, for his part in rescuing her. He had just nodded, dropped a kiss on her cheek, and said you're welcome. He had not wanted her thanks, that she knew. She understood just how much of a risk he had taken, but he had said it was all part of his job. She knew better. She had been told he had been the one to volunteer to go in, not wanting anyone else to risk their lives for her.

Darby wouldn't move from her side, desperate to make sure she kept safe. He had told her that he had been so afraid she wouldn't come back, that he couldn't handle losing anyone else in his family. His eyes had strayed to Baird at that point, and Berneen understood without words how worried he was and just how much Baird had come to mean to him.

She heard the nurse's footsteps coming towards her and looked up at the clock. Her time was up for now. She reached to kiss Baird's cheek, a whispered I love you to his ear, and then stood back, wiping at the tears on her face before she turned and headed for the waiting room.

She had sent Darby home to sleep, Branigan staying with him. She had objected, but Branigan had just shrugged, saying this was what they did. Their employers gave them that flexibility. Because Barnabas was the one who paid them and if he didn't object, how could they?

She slumped into a chair, reaching for a blanket to wrap around herself. A bottle of water appeared in her line of sight and she took it with a word of thanks. Buckley seated himself beside her, his eyes watchful.

"How is Baird?"

"The same, I think, Buckley. They still don't know if he'll rouse or not." Her head went back against the wall behind her, and she pulled at her hair. "Brady felt so bad."

"About what?"

"That he had to cut my hair to free me. I don't care. Hair will grow. He can't feel guilty."

Buckley gave a small laugh. "Then you don't know?"

"Know what?" Her head twisted to watch him.

"That Baird loves your long hair. He made some comment to Brady just after you two were married, something along the lines that he hoped you never cut it."

"I didn't know that."

"There are a lot of things you two need to talk about. That is one of them." Buckley sighed. "It shouldn't have happened how it did."

"But you said God allowed it, didn't you? So how can we doubt? I had a lot of time to think this last time. I got mad at God, told Him off, yelled at Him." She looked shamefaced as she said this.

"I think at times we all feel something like that. It's all part of growing as His child. It's part of learning to trust." He gave her a long look. "And that is something you've been dealing with."

"It is, Buckley. It's been so hard to trust, for the last ten years. I have wanted my parents, needed them, and had no one I could turn to."

"We get that, Berneen. We get that Darby feels the same. You two need to talk at some point." He turned his head as he heard rubber-soled footsteps heading their way and was on his feet as a nurse hurriedly approached.

"Mrs. Cassidy, can you come with me? The surgeon needs to speak with you."

Berneen's face whitened and she reached for Buckley's hand, not letting go until she stood in Baird's room, her eyes on the surgeon before flickering to Baird, a frown coming on her face as she saw the intubation tube gone.

"Doctor?"

"Mrs. Cassidy, if I had been a betting man, I would have said your husband would be gone by now. Instead, he is breathing room air with the help of oxygen by nasal prongs. We've begun the process of weaning him off the medications. All the imaging done today is clear, not like yesterday that still showed a huge area of concern." He stared at her before looking at Buckley. "So you tell me, why?"

"God. Plain and simple, Doctor. God." Buckley spoke for them.

"You almost make me believe."

"Believe, Doctor. You have been part of a miracle." Berneen moved away to stand at Baird's side, her hand on his cheek, her other hand holding his, feeling his fingers close around her, even as his eyes flickered open and a small smile creased his face, before he dropped off into a normal, natural sleep.

Berneen stood, hands on her hips, watching in frustration as Baird moved slowly around his office in the apartment a week later. She wanted him to rest, to lie down, or at least sit down, and he was refusing. He needed to work, he said. She argued with him, finally throwing up her hands in defeat and turning to walk away from him. She didn't hear the soft sound of his socked feet approaching her until his arms came around her.

"I heard you, Berneen. That's what brought me back. I was almost Home, I think. I could see the light of heaven. But your voice and your words brought me back to you." His head rested against her. "I love you, too. I didn't want to live if you weren't here. I couldn't go on."

She stood still, listening to him, before her hands were raised to grip his. "I know, Baird. I know. I didn't think I could live either. I was sure you were dead. You went down so fast and there was so much blood."

"Can you live here still? Given what happened? Barnabas has had it all repainted, new flooring, new window treatments. He said he will change anything you don't like. Or if you can't live here, he'll move us to another apartment."

She turned then, her arms around him, being mindful of the hurt and incision area. "I can. As long as you are here, I can. Can you?"

He shrugged. "I can live wherever you are. We need to talk over things, we need to talk to Darby too, but that can wait."

She nodded before she moved away, heading for the kitchen. She had put on coffee for him and was determined to get him to sit somehow. He needed to. She had been warned to have him rest as much as she could.

She frowned as she heard a tap at the door, glancing down the hallway at Baird as he approached, his hand on his abdomen, a frown on his face.

"Were we expecting anyone?" His voice was quiet.

"No, not that I am aware of. Darby's off with some of the guys, hiking some of the Bruce Trail. Barnabas said he had put out the word that you needed to rest and no one was to come near you. Unless it's Doc or Anna."

She gave a scream as a hard kick at the door broke the lock and sent the door flying to crash against an inside wall. She stared at the sledge hammer held by the man who entered and realized it had been that he had used to break in. She backed away, backed into Baird, whose arms encircled her, even as he spoke.

"Who are you?"

"You're coming with us."

"I don't think so." Baird simply shook his head, his arms tight around Berneen. "We're not going anywhere."

"Oh, I think you are." The man raised the sledge hammer, bringing it down on the hallway wall, leaving a huge hole in the drywall. "This says you do."

"And this says they don't." Branigan stood there, a weapon to the man's neck. "Drop it! I said, drop it!"

The man finally dropped the sledge hammer, his eyes burning with hatred at Baird and Berneen.

Branigan shoved the man at the officer who was just entering. "He's wanted, I think, on multiple charges, including abduction, attempted abduction, assault, breaking and entering, just for starters."

Berneen stared at him for a moment. "How did you know?"

Branigan shrugged. "I was coming to see how you were and heard the commotion." He shared a look with Baird, shaking his head slightly.

Baird nodded, knowing they would talk later.

"Well, now that he's gone, coffee anyone?" Berneen moved to the kitchen, reaching for mugs, pouring the men their coffee, reaching for her tea and realizing she didn't want that anymore. Her mug in her hand when Baird was hurt had turned her off her tea.

———

"Berneen?  Your tea?"  Baird's arm came around her.

"I can't, Baird.  I need to find something else."  She swiped his mug of coffee, sipping at it.  "This isn't so bad after all."

She slid into a seat at the table, leaving him staring openmouthed at her, as Branigan rubbed at his upper lip, trying to hide a grin.

"So, Branigan, what else was it you wanted?"  She smirked as he laughed, Baird's comment that she should know better than to ask that ringing in her ears.

Walking through the church parking lot after church the following Sunday, Berneen felt content, her hand in Baird's, knowing just how much they had been prayed for. She was thankful. She had found that God was faithful. She was learning to trust. To trust God in a way she had never thought she could. Learning to trust Baird. Learning to trust his friends, who counted her as a sister now. Learning to trust Darby. Learning also that she had to leave everything in God's hands.

Baird had watched Berneen's face during the service, seeing the peace and contentment that was beginning to show. He knew the men were still out there, that they had been spotted in the area, but that they had so far eluded arrest. That worried him, and that worry he was learning to leave with God.

Darby had run ahead of them, eager to be home. Baird had promised to show him some plans for tutoring that he was working on, and that was something Darby was interested in. He had energy to burn he thought, and hoped one of the men would be willing to run the beach near their home today. They quite often did that.

He slid to a halt, his hands rising as he saw the man appear from behind the car, a weapon pointed at Darby's head. He motioned Darby closer and when Darby didn't move, the man stalked towards him, roughly grabbing him by the arm before he spun him around and snaked his arm around Darby's neck, the weapon muzzle digging into Darby's temple. Darby froze, not sure what he should be doing or what the man wanted. He hadn't said and Darby was too afraid to ask.

Baird stopped suddenly, his eyes on Darby, causing Berneen to frown up at him, her words dying on her lips as she followed his line of sight. She paled, moved to run towards him, and was only stopped by Baird's arm around her. That caused him pain, but he didn't care. He needed Berneen to stay safe and somehow they needed to free Darby.

"What do you want?" Baird voice echoed through the stillness that ensued when onlookers realized what was happening.

"You know what I want. That thumb drive."

"We don't have it. We can't get it." Baird was playing for time, watching Bradon move around behind the car, Kade by his side, alert, ready to attack when he was given the order. That couldn't happen, not yet.

Berneen dropped to the ground, her hands covering her mouth, not sure what was going on.

"That's him, Baird. That's the man who held me captive. Each time. I recognize his voice." She paused. "But I know it from when I was a teen. He's the man who tried to snatch me when Mom and Dad were still alive. But there's someone else."

"That's right, little lady. There is someone else. And he's behind you." The man moved his weapon enough to gesture with it. That was all Kade needed. Without warning and with only a slight movement of Bradon's hand, he was moving, flying over the car, the man's arm in his grip as he took him down, Darby rolling away, hands reaching for him to pull him to safety.

Baird dove for Berneen, driving her down, a groan coming from him even as he covered her body with his. She shivered from fear, hearing the calls and shouts, then felt the hands on her, raising her to her feet. She stopped, her eyes on Baird even as she flung herself into his arms, hers tight around him.

"You're okay? You didn't get hurt again?"

"I'm okay. It hurts but that's okay. You're okay?" Baird leaned back, studying the face of the woman he knew he loved beyond anything he thought possible. "You're okay, Sweetheart. I love you." He kissed her, then heard a throat clearing beside him. "Go away, Barnabas. Let me kiss my best girl."

"That's fine. You can do that. But I have a young man here who needs his sister."

Berneen struggled to release herself from Baird's grip, her eyes on her brother before she had him in a tight hug. She felt his tears on her face, knowing they mixed with hers. She looked around at Baird finally, not having noticed his arms surround them both.

"Is it over, Baird?"

"It is, Sweetheart.  Barnabas tells me that the man behind it all was standing back of us.  He was ready to shoot us."

She shuddered once more.  "I'm glad.  Can we just go home now, please?"

He laughed, even as his arms tightened around the two he held. "We can.  We'll find out what it's all about later."

Holding his mug of coffee, Barnabas leaned against a table in the building conference room, a smile on his face as he listened the conversation, the laughter, the teasing and feeling the relief that it was all over for Baird. The men and women, yes, women, he thought, were all in custody. The authorities were still sorting through everything but he had been told enough so that he could share with his men, Doc and Anna, and Baird, Berneen and Darby. It was only fair, he thought. All of them had been through a lot in such a short period of time.

"They're doing okay, Baird and Berneen."

"They are, all things considered. Darby's had to grow up faster than he should have, given what has happened in his life." Barnabas sipped at his mug of coffee before he set it behind him on the table. "Now, if I can get their attention, I can let them know what was going on and why."

"You start at this side of the room. I'll do the other." Breck moved away, a quiet word spoken to each man, watching at Barnabas did the same, before his friend halted beside Berneen, a comment from him making her laugh.

Barnabas studied each man in front of him, praying that none of the rest would go through what Baird had done, but knowing in his heart what likely faced all of them.

"I spoke with the detective earlier today. This meal that Anna and Doc has provided for us is the right time and right opportunity to tell you what was going on.

"Baird, your father had been called in on that job site. He found major issues in the design. The building was brought down around them. The authorities have been trying for years to find the men responsible, and couldn't until now. It is up to the courts what they face. I'm sorry. I wish I could have said it was an accident but it wasn't.

"Berneen, Darby. Your parents were sent overseas on that trip. Your mother was not to have gone but the woman who arranged it insisted that she go. Your father provided a wealth of information on that thumb drive. He also provided the information in those little boxes Brady found the day he rescued you. We don't know why they were there. Only God does. But suffice it to say there was enough information there for the authorities to bring down a group who had been plaguing the city with numerous bad builds. These people no one could or would name. He did that. We have been told that is why he was sent overseas. Their thinking was that if he was involved in a riot overseas and killed, no one would question it. You did. A word from you was all it took to set the men after you.

"The man at the head of it, Tom Paul, had a grudge against both your fathers. He set them up for murder. He also had his brother killed. He's the one who was here that day. We didn't realize it in time, he didn't give us an opportunity to do that.

"The building you were held in? It belonged to a numbered company traced back to him. We have experts examining it but it had been damaged in a way that would bring it down. He thought you would die in it and that would be the end of it.

"Darby. Berneen. Baird. The authorities have asked that I extend their thanks to you three. You have helped bringdown a group of men and women they have been after for years. Your courage and faith have spoken loudly to them. There will be court to face but we'll have the lawyers that you need."

Barnabas stopped speaking for a moment, unable to continue. He looked around at the other men.

"My thanks to each one of you, guys. This is what friendship is. This is what we do. You have all been an encouragement to each other, in many ways and forms."

Baird finally spoke. "That place Berneen was kept in at first. Why?"

"One of the men said that it was to break her spirit and bring her down. They had plans for her but when they saw you that day and had heard you would be in the area, the plans changed. They saw an opportunity to seek revenge. The plan all along for you two was what they forced on you. Marriage. Then the death of one or the other of you.  It didn't matter to them which one.  The men Berneen saw before you, Baird?  It was what was suspected.  They were men from the gang, made up to look as if they had been beaten. That was all part of wearing her down.  It didn't seem to work."

He looked over at Doc and Anna.  "Doc.  Anna.  I know your prayers were there, helping get us through.  Thank you."  He walked away, his hands stuffed into his pockets, not speaking, leaving quiet murmurs behind him.

Baird was on a search. He couldn't find Berneen anywhere. It had been three weeks since Barnabas had talked to them. He needs to see her, to talk to her. He searched through the apartment and then headed for his office, walking better than he had, the pain in his abdomen lessening each day.

Darby just smirked when he was asked where Berneen was. "Lose your wife already, Baird?"

Baird stared at him, laughed and then hugged the youth he thought of as a brother. "No. She's just good at hiding."

He finally walked from the building a frown on his face, before Bradon took pity on him.

"Try the beach. She likes to walk there."

"She does? I didn't know that."

"She heads there every day at some point. You need to learn what your wife does, Baird." Bradon ducked the playful swat Baird aimed his way before he headed for the path to the beach.

Baird stopped, leaning against a rock pile, his eyes on Berneen as she stood, arms wrapped around herself, her hair flying loose around her face. He didn't know if he liked her hair better loose or in the braid she wore most days.

He finally walked through the sand, his arms reaching to encircle her and pull her back against him, content just to stand and watch the waves beating against the shore, even though the wind was cold.

He finally spoke. "Ready to go home, Sweetheart?"

"I am, Baird, my love. I am. We can finally get on with our lives, can't we?"

"We can. And you are staying with me, aren't you?" A little bit of fear and uncertainty came through.

---

She turned, her face raised to study him. "I am. I wasn't sure if that's what you wanted. I know it's what I want."

He bent to kiss her, then studied her face. "It's what I want. I used to wonder why my wife would look like, I mean, hair colour, eyes, height. You are more than what I ever imagined."

"I never thought I would ever marry. Not raising Darby. Men would ask me out but when I said I had a little brother to look after, they backed away. You didn't, even if you could have. You just made him part of your family. He needed that. Thank you."

"God has blessed us, Sweetheart. And you are the sweetest part of my heart, did you know that?"

"I am. Thank you, Baird." She stood on tiptoes to kiss him, her arms around his neck in a hard hug. "God is good, Baird. I have learned to trust Him in ways I didn't think I could."

"He does that to you, you know? Makes you trust Him."

He turned her to walk back towards the buildings, her hand tight in his, content, knowing that God had protected them through everything. He knew there had been times neither thought they would survive, but they had been encouraged by their friends to keep on trusting. That's what, he thought. That's what got us through. Trusting.

Dear Readers


Thank you for choosing to read the story of Baird and his Berneen. What an adventure they had! Learning to trust along the way! God does that, you know. Brings us to a point where we have to trust and lean only on Him.

Trust has been on my mind a lot in the last few weeks. It was not what I had envisioned for being so strong in this story, but that's how the characters work the plot line. They decide the story, I'm just along for the ride and as a scribe.

During this time, I have taken in a six-year-old Shetland Sheepdog named Summer at the request of her breeder, a good friend of mine. We have been working through trust issues, Summer and I. She has been learning to trust me in so many ways and seeing how she has opened up to me, seeing her tail wag as she greets me, feeling her poke me with her nose. I know the trust has come.

The concept for this series is based on Barnabas, companion to Paul on some of his journeys. Barnabas has always been a favourite of mine. The idea of being an encourager, a Barnabas, has been something I have sought to do throughout my life. Only God knows how successful that has been.

As you journey through life, remember. Trust God. Encourage someone. In encouraging someone, you are encouraged yourself.

God bless.


Ronna

# Benen: Encouraged to Protect

## The Barnabas Chronicles

### Book 2

By

Ronna M. Bacon

Psalm 59:1 Deliver me from my enemies, O my God; protect me from those who rise up against me… (KJV)

## *Table of Contents*

His hands shoved into his navy hooded sweatshirt pockets, Benen Carroll stood outside the hospital room, his eyes trained on the door, just waiting.  Waiting for what, he wondered?  The last few days, no, a week or ten days, he thought, had been a whirlwind of activity, and that not always of the good kind.  He leaned his head back, his eyes sliding closed, fatigue weighing him down.  His thoughts drifted as the sounds of the activity normally found on a hospital floor faded around him.

He thought back to two weeks ago, when a letter had arrived, a letter from people in his past, people he no longer saw, but had been a frequent guest in their home in the past.  The couple, now serving as missionaries in a Latin America country, had asked for his help.  He could not refuse.  They had become family, almost, to him when his mother had passed away from cancer when he was twenty.  He didn't remember his father, losing his father when he was so young, to cancer as well.

He had read the letter and then set it aside, knowing he needed to pray over it.  What they asked would change his life, that much he knew.  He had finally gone to his friend and boss, Barnabas Carey, who ran The Barnabas Foundation, an foundation that provided help to those in need.  Benen worked as an IT specialist but his wages were paid for by the Foundation.  He had asked for two weeks off, to travel to see the family.  Barnabas had shot him a long look, scrutinized his face for a few minutes, and then nodded, asking that he call if he needed any help.  Benen had nodded, knowing he would not do that.

He had taken a private flight down, the airplane part of the Foundation arsenal of transportation, and landed, heading for the mission where he knew he would find his friends.  He had not expected to land in a country torn apart by riots and war.  He had feared for their lives, knowing that they would be targets.

After clearing customs, he had shouldered his backpack and headed away from the airport, knowing Andy would fly home and then return in about five days.  He wended his way through the crowds, mobs almost, he thought, noting the high presence of police and military personnel. He shook his head as he was jostled roughly. What had he walked into and just what did it mean for his friends? His eyes constantly searched the crowds, feeling himself being watched but he could not find who it was.

The couple, Mary and Ted Daniell, had greeted him, welcomed him into their home. They had been there for years, and were scheduled to leave for their furlough back at home. Only this time, they wouldn't be coming back. That much they knew. Their mission board had deemed it too dangerous and were pulling their people out.

The day before he was to fly home, Ted approached Benen with a request. Benen had stared at him and then at Mary, his eyes then moving to their daughter, Cadee, who was his age and had been a good friend of his in college. He watched the emotions flickering across her face before he agreed. Even as he did so, he was not sure he was doing right, but God had not spoken to stop him. And Benen had enough faith to know that God would step in.

The parents had fled very early the next morning, heading for another country and safety and then a flight home to Ontario, Canada, where they had a home on the shores of Lake Erie. Cadee, they knew, would be safe with Benen.

Benen had stared at the door as it closed behind them, then turned to Cadee.

"Cadee?" He ran his hand through his thick blond hair, his intense dark blue eyes troubled.

She had turned, her dark brown eyes hiding her emotions, her own dark blond hair, cut to shoulder length, swinging around her face as she did so. "Benen? Now what?"

"Now what is that we grab what we can stuff into our backpacks and then head for the airport. Andy said he'd be there by this morning." He stood for a moment, not sure if she would even come with him, feeling his jacket pocket for the envelope of paperwork he had been handed by Ted.

She nodded, her steps rapid as she moved to pack what she could, handing him his own pack. She looked around, sorrow briefly showing on her face. "Let's go. We'll need to walk. It's a hike, you know."

"I know." He reached for her hand, stopping her movements. "First, we need to pray. We're not going to make it unless God goes ahead of us."

Their movements hampered by the crowds milling in the streets, they walked away from the mission and headed for the airport, Cadee's hand tight in his. Jostled, almost torn away from one another, they forged ahead, Benen's eyes watchful. He heard a whimper from Cadee at one point and turned, finding her rubbing at her shoulder.

"Cadee? What happened?"

"I felt a sting. Likely a bug of some kind." She pulled him with her. "There's the airport. We made it."

He glanced down at the watch on his left wrist and nodded. "We did. Just in time." After clearing customs, which didn't take long to his surprise, he rushed her towards the airplane and up the stairs into it, nodding at the pilot, before he pointed to a seat.

"Sit there, Cadee. Buckle up. Andy's ready to take off as soon as we're situated." He tucked their packs away, then chose a seat near her, nodding to Andy's question of were they ready as he did so. He felt the plane lift off, the start of a long flight, he knew.

Towards the end of the flight, he had turned to Cadee, concerned. He watched as she slept, her head against a pillow he had tucked behind it, wrapped in the soft yellow blanket he had found. He was concerned, that was a given. He moved to touch her, dismayed at the clamminess of her skin, the dark shadows that were appearing under her eyes, her paleness, the occasional spike of a fever he had felt over the last couple of hours.

He moved forward to stand in the cockpit doorway.

"How long, Andy?" He squinted through the darkening skies, knowing it was getting to the early evening on that winter day.

"Just coming up to start the descent. Making it through customs a bit ago was a breeze, for some reason. I've never seen it go so fast." He studied his instruments before him, then glanced at the runway lights as he prepared for their approach. "Buckle up, Benen." He shot a quick glance at Benen. "How's your lady?"

"She's not well. I don't know why. She was fine earlier this morning." He returned to his seat, his eyes on Cadee.

He carried her to his car, his thanks ringing in Andy's ears as the pilot placed their luggage in the car trunk, and then stood back, watching before he slammed the door and ran for his seat, speeding away, instinct telling him that he needed to get to the hospital and fast. Something was wrong with her and she needed medical attention.

He roused as the nurse touched his arm, pointing to the door, before he nodded, his footsteps heavy as he moved that way, coming to stand at the end of the bed, watching Cadee, wishing he knew what the problem was.

He finally pulled a chair close to the bed, and sat, his elbows on his knees, hands clasped, chin resting on his thumbs, his eyes not moving from Cadee as she lay, motionless. He studied the heart monitor, the IV pole and its bags of IV fluid and antibiotics, heard the slight hiss of the oxygen from the nasal prongs as she struggled to breathe. He didn't look around as he heard the door swish open and footsteps approach.

"Benen?" Barnabas spoke, his eyes on his friend, a frown in place. "What's going on? Andy said you were back but that you headed right here with the lady you brought back with you."

Benen didn't move, simply shifted his eyes to stare at Barnabas before they shifted to the man with him, Branigan Clery, his own team leader. He sighed, knowing that when he spoke, things would be changed. Lord, he thought, I had no idea this was in the works when I agreed to help the Daniells. I really didn't, but You did.

"Benen?" This time, it was Branigan who spoke, his eyes full of concern, before he turned as the door opened and a physician entered.

Benen was on his feet, swaying slightly from fatigue, watching closely as the physician assessed Cadee and then motioned for the nurse to hang another bag to the IV pole.

"Doc?" Benen's voice was quiet, hopeful, yet with a tone to it that said he accepted the inevitable. By this time, it was early morning and he had been anxiously awaiting the results of the testing.

"Benen, we ran the blood work we spoke of. You were correct. What she thought was a bug bite wasn't." The physician gently moved the hospital gown closer to her neck, exposing the area on her shoulder that showed a red, almost angry looking mark. "She was poisoned. It looks as if she moved the dart or whatever it was before she took in too much, but there was enough to cause this. Who does she have for enemies?"

Benen shrugged, his mind sorting through what little Ted had been able to tell him.

"Considering where we just came back from, who knows, Doc." He spoke with the physician for a few more moments, and watched as he walked away.

"Benen? Care to explain? I know where Andy took you and brought you back from." Barnabas watched Benen, a frown on his face. "Who is she?"

"Cadee?" Benen's hand traced down her hair, stopping to rest on her cheek. "She's an old friend, Barnabas." He paused, swallowing hard, his eyes still on Cadee, wishing she would awaken and help him say what he needed to say. He finally spoke once more. "And my wife."

When he uttered those words, Benen had no idea of the effect they would have on his friends, or the relief that he felt when he acknowledged it. He knew, he thought, that he would have to tell them, but just not like this. Not with Cadee laying there, not knowing if she would live or die. His heart raised in prayer for her, for her parents, for the ones they had had to leave behind in the war-torn country.

"Benen? What on earth are you talking about? You're not married! You're not even dating anyone."

Barnabas' voice broke through his thoughts. He heard the questions, the concern, in it. He finally looked around, seeing Barnabas and Branigan exchanging looks.

"Barnabas? It's too long a story for now." He sank back into his chair, fatigue washing through him, a bleak look around his eyes. "Can we talk tomorrow? Or rather later today?" He amended this question as he glanced at his watch, seeing it was early morning by then.

"Benen?" Branigan's voice came from beside him, Branigan's hand on his shoulder. "We have no idea what you're facing or what's going on. Let us pray for you."

Benen nodded, his eyes not leaving Cadee's face. "Listen, guys. Can you tell the others before I bring her home? If I even get to do that." He blinked at the moisture blocking his vision. "You heard the physician. She was poisoned as we were almost to the plane. We still don't know why or who."

"Benen? What did you go and get involved in?" Barnabas' voice held concern, but also a touch of frustration and worry.

"You know the country we came from. Her parents were missionaries there. Cadee had been visiting them for a few months, working in the office for them. I didn't know when they asked me for help just what all was at stake. They couldn't put it into writing. It was too dangerous for them, for Cadee, and for myself, if I chose to go there." Benen turned slightly to watch his friends. "The Daniells themselves slipped away to another country to escape and make their way back here. That's how afraid they are for all of them. I had to bring Cadee back. The only way to do that safely was for her to have a name change. That's what they asked of me, yesterday. They asked if I would give her the protection of my name and then bring her back with me. The minister from their church married us."

Barnabas approached him, standing with his hand on Benen's shoulder as he prayed.

"Now, is there a chance they have followed you?"

Benen shrugged. "I guess. Andy wasn't on the ground too long." He looked down at Cadee for a moment, watching her restless movements. "The thing of it is, Barnabas? There is a contract out on her. She saw something, someone, knows something, has something that she shouldn't have. We just don't know what."

"And you're afraid they'll follow you to here?" Branigan spoke up.

"I am. We don't know who, so we can't be prepared." Benen watched Cadee as she moved more restlessly, her mouth working as she tried to swallow, her tongue flicking out between her lips as she tried to moisten them. He reached to cradle her head in one hand as with the other he carefully fed her ice chips, the only thing the physician would allow her.

Barnabas and Branigan moved away, their eyes on the young couple, as they spoke quietly, before Barnabas walked away, leaving Branigan leaning against the wall outside the room, his eyes on Benen. He finally shook his head. First Baird, marrying Berneen like he did, saving his life. Branigan gave a small smile. That couple was working out just fine, he thought, deeply in love despite what they had been through. He tilted his head to study Benen, a frown on his face. Something else was going on there, he thought. Then he sighed. They're more than old friend, aren't they, Lord, at least on his part.

Benen finally sat back down, his eyes on Cadee, willing her to awake, but knowing that she couldn't, not just yet. He had been warned that it may take days. He twisted in his chair, trying to find a comfortable position, pulling the blanket tight around him, his eyes finally sliding closed as he slept, exhausted from the trip, the worry, and his fear for Cadee.

Branigan watched before he turned as he heard his name called gently. Doc Whitson stood there, a frown on his face.

"Branigan?"

"Benen's here, Doc." He looked towards the partly open door. "He's in there."

Doc stepped to the door. "That's why I'm here. Tom called me in. He wants me up to speed on her for when she goes home."

"She will be going home, Doc? Benen doesn't seem to believe that."

"She will be. Thanks to Benen's question, she will be. Tom said I need to be aware of what's going on with her." Doc looked around before he handed Branigan the cup of coffee he was carrying for him. "What's this I hear though? Benen's wife?"

"Apparently so. It's quite the story, though." He looked around as he heard footsteps approaching and a nurse entered Cadee's room. He frowned and then shrugged. What did he know about schedules in the hospital?

*Chapter 3*

Her eyes flickering open and closed, Cadee finally roused, her hand searching for her aching head, the very touch on it sending the pain wafting through it stronger.  She squeezed her eyes shut, wondering just what she had gone and done that she didn't remember going and doing.  She tried to moisten her dry mouth and lips and couldn't.

She felt a gentle hand raising her head, the touch soft and careful.  A glass touched her lips and she swallowed, greedy to drink, protesting with a whimper when the glass was moved back before she had had enough of the water.

"It's okay, Cadee.  You can have more."  A voice, familiar, from her past she thought, spoke but before she could respond, she drifted back to sleep.

Doc stood and watched for a moment before he looked at Benen.  "That's a natural sleep, Benen.  Given what she's been through, I would not have expected it yet."

"She has always healed quickly from whatever she's had."  Benen stood, an arm leaning on the side rail of the bed, the other hand gently moving her hair back from her face.

Doc nodded, then spoke.  "We'll get her home likely by tomorrow, if all goes well."

"Plan for this afternoon, Doc.  I know her.  She'll walk out of here today if she can."

Doc shook his head, before he laughed.  "I'll have Anna go through your place, tidying it up for you.  Any special instruction?"

Benen hesitated, then nodded.  "The yellow room?  The spare room?  Can you put some yellow roses in there for her?"  He didn't see the look Doc gave him, his attention back on Cadee as she moved.

———

He didn't hear Doc walk away, didn't hear the footsteps that approached quietly and then turned and walked away. His sole focus was Cadee.

Cadee roused once more, feeling a hand touching her face gently and a voice talking to her, asking her to awaken. She turned into the hand, thinking it was familiar, but not sure.

"Cadee? Come on, darling. Time to rise and shine. Wake up, sleeping beauty."

Cadee cracked an eye open, then closed it, the light bright for a moment. She blinked, trying to clear her vision before her eyes opened once more and stayed open. She glanced around, searching for what she didn't know, before her eyes landed on the man standing by her bedside, his head tilted to see her face, a smile on his.

"Benen Carroll?" She swallowed from the glass he held to her mouth. "What are you doing here?"

He shook his head. "You don't remember?"

She shook her own. "No, I don't." She looked around the room once more. "Where am I?"

"In the hospital back in Ontario. You've been sick." He hesitated to tell her exactly what had happened.

"Sick? By the way I feel, it's much more than just that." She stared at him before he nodded.

"It is, Cadee. You were poisoned over twenty-four hours ago. We didn't know until you wouldn't wake up when we landed and I got you to treatment here."

"What is going on, Benen?" She shifted in the bed, trying to sit up, nodding when he raised the head of the bed. "There's more to that than what you have said."

He sighed, knowing he would have to tell her, holding out the glass, this time her hands reaching for it, his cupping hers gently.

She stared at his hand, catching the light reflecting off his wedding band. "Benen! You're married! When? Where's your wife? You shouldn't be here with me!" She was growing agitated before her hand raised and she stared at her own finger, seeing a wedding band on it. "This can't be happening. I'm not married. I'm not even dating!" She searched the room again. "Mom? Dad? Where are they? Are they safe?"

"I'm not sure where they are at this moment, Cadee. They crossed the border to make their way back here. They were recalled by the mission."

"We were? I don't remember?"

"What is the last date you remember?"

She thought, giving him a date, the day before he arrived in the country.

"I landed there the next day. Your parents wrote to me, asking me to come." He paused, sorrow in his heart as he realized she had forgotten him being there. "You don't remember?"

She shook her head, her eyes wide as she watched him. "No. Should I?"

He reached for her left hand, laying the palm of his left hand along the top of hers, his fingers curling between hers, their rings side by side, his face thoughtful, not quite sure how to say what he needed to say.

"Benen? What are you doing?" She tugged at her hand but he refused to release it.

"You have no memory of your dad writing to me, asking me to come?"

She shook her head again. "No, they didn't tell me that they had. It's been so many years."

"It has been." He bit at his upper lip, pulling it down, his eyes on their hands. "They wrote me for a specific reason, not telling me until the day before we left to come back here. They told me you were in a danger, that they had had word a contract was put out on you for what reason, we don't know. They feared for your very life." His eyes lifted to her, a look in them she could not read. "They felt they knew me well enough to ask something of me, something that would keep you alive and get you back here."

"Benen?" Her head began to shake and he felt her hand trembling under his. The dark shadows had deepened under her eyes, the shadow of pain and something else in them. "What did they ask of you?"

"They asked me to bring you home while they made their own way back. There was a catch. They were told the only way to get you out safely was by a private plane but there was something else. Someone would be watching for you flying out under your name." He paused again, once more biting at his lip, as his eyes traced her familiar face, seeing the changes the last few years had brought and seeing also the fear she was living under.

"What did you do?"

"Your father asked if I would marry you, giving you the protection of my name and myself. He knows the organization I work for. He has spoken any times with Barnabas, without your knowledge of that."

"We did what?" Her voice rose to a squeak even as her head shook. "Tell me we didn't."

"I'm sorry, Cadee. I can't tell you that. We discussed it and both agreed it was the only way. You did say you would marry me. The minister from your church performed the ceremony. We fled the next day. We spent the time between our wedding and early the next morning packing up, making arrangements for your things to be shipped back to here, your father making sure the people there would be all right."

She was shaking her head. "We didn't. We couldn't have." She watched as his head nodded. "Benen? Tell me we didn't."

"I'm sorry, Cadee. We are married. You are my wife." He released her hand and walked away, out of the room, knowing her well enough to know she needed some time on her own, to absorb what he had just said, given that she didn't remember it.

Cadee watched him walk away, her hand to her mouth, even as her mind tried to take in what he had said. Exhaustion overcame her will to think it through, and she slept.

―――

Cadee pulled the blanket up tighter around her neck, not used to the colder weather now, she thought. She had protested when Benen had wrapped it around her, saying she didn't need it. It was the next day after the earthshaking news that they were now married, husband and wife, and that she just couldn't comprehend. They had been good friends at college and then drifted apart once they graduated.

She turned her head to stare at Benen, finding him with his face turned towards the window of the vehicle, not watching her. She sighed to herself. How did they do this, she wondered?

Benen knew Cadee was uncomfortable with him and that he regretted. He prayed for her memory to return, but the physicians hadn't been too sure on that. He had heard her protests when he had wrapped her in the blanket, positioned her in the wheelchair and headed down to the lobby doors where Branigan waited. She had protested when he had gathered her into his arms and placed her in the backseat of his car, Branigan at the wheel, before he walked slowly around, his eyes on her the whole time, to take a seat beside her, making sure she was buckle into her seatbelt.

They needed to talk, he thought, not just about them. They needed to find out who was after her and why. Right now, he didn't think she knew, but if she did, she might well have hidden it deep into her mind. She did that with unpleasant things, he remembered only too well.

He didn't see his friends in the truck ahead of them or the SUV behind them as they pulled away. Branigan and Barnabas had called a meeting early that morning, explaining to the men about Benen and Cadee, bringing surprise and shock to most of their faces, acceptance on Baird Cassidy's face. Baird and his wife, Berneen, had been married not long before this, Berneen agreeing to it to save Baird's life. They only had one question: What could they do to help Benen?

Benen stood for a moment, his eyes on the building that housed not only their own offices, but their homes as well, staring at it, realizing he had no idea how changed his life would be when he returned, that he would not be coming home just by himself. He sighed, not seeing Barnabas standing in the lobby, his own eyes on Benen.

Benen once more gathered Cadee into his arms, walking towards through the lobby, his eyes on her face for a moment, ignoring her protests.

"Benen! I can walk!" She waited for a moment. "Put me down!"

Benen leaned back in the elevator, a nod to Barnabas as he stepped in, pushing the button for the third floor. He waited until the doors closed and then spoke.

"Cadee, you are not strong enough to walk. If we didn't have a physician on site, you would not have been allowed out yet. The physicians recommended against it."

"I wasn't that sick. I would know if I had been." She coughed, trying to hide it.

Benen's mouth tightened in frustration and almost anger. "Cadee, this is not the time or place for this conversation. Suffice it to say, a day and a half ago, they had no idea what was wrong with you. You were getting sicker and sicker. They had prepare me, you know, that you would not recover. That this was it for you." He stared down at her for a moment, seeing the shock on her face. "That's right. You were that close. God worked in your life, healing you enough that you could come home. The physician told me that if you had received just a tiny bit more of the poison, you would not have made it to the plane."

She grew quiet, her eyes huge, her mind trying to absorb what he had said. She didn't see the look of compassion on Barnabas' face as he listened to the two.

Barnabas unlocked and then opened the door for Benen, stepping in after him, setting the keys on the countertop in the kitchen before he reached for the coffee pot. He knew Benen would want something. Just what Cadee liked, he had no idea.

Benen set Cadee down on the double bed in his spare room and then knelt to remove her shoes, rising to set them tidily in the cupboard. He reached into the dresser, pulling out her night clothes, silently thanking whoever of the men had brought their luggage. He knew it was likely Anna who had unpacked for Cadee.

"Do you want a shower, Cadee? Something to drink? Or just to change and climb into bed?"

She stared at him, not sure what to think, or even what she wanted to do. "A shower would be nice, but I'm really not sure if I can manage."

He nodded, then turned to walk away. "I'll be right back."

He paused as he saw Barnabas. "Thank, Barnabas, for all you've done."

Barnabas shrugged. "It's what we do for each other. Is she settled?"

"No. Do you know if Berneen is home?"

"She should be. She told me last night she'd be around today, at least for a while." He watched as Benen headed for the door and the apartment next door.

Benen tapped at the door of Baird's apartment, not sure if he should be even doing that. He stepped back, turning to walk away, when the door flew open and Berneen stood there.

"Benen! You're home. Welcome home." She reached to hug her friend before stepping back.

"Berneen! Good to see you." Benen began to smile. "Does Baird know you're wearing his favourite T-shirt?" Berneen had on Baird's T-shirt with the logo of his favourite sports team.

Berneen smirked. "No, he doesn't. It will be back in his drawer before he's home."

Benen began to laugh as he saw Baird appear behind Berneen. "Sure about that?"

"I am!" She gave a squeal as arms came around her and Baird dropped a kiss on her cheek.

"Now I know what you're up to when I'm not home." He reached to shake Benen's hand. "Benen? How are you? Really."

Benen shrugged. "Struggling. Doubting. Knowing I need to protect her but not sure how or from whom."

Baird nodded, knowing somewhat how he felt. "Katie?"

"I'm sorry?"

"Katie? Isn't that her name?" Baird was puzzled, not sure why Benen had questioned him.

"No, it's Cadee. C-a-d-e-e. Unusual, I know. I have a favour to ask, Berneen. Say no if you have to."

Berneen took one look at him and then nodded. "She needs help, doesn't she?"

Benen sighed, grateful that he didn't have to put it into words and beg. "She does. Thank you, Berneen."

She was away and into his apartment before he was finished, leaving Benen staring after her.

"Benen, now that we're alone, how are you really? I know what you said, but there's more."

Benen leaned against the door, a hand drawn down his face, praying that he could put into words how he felt. "She doesn't remember, Baird. She doesn't remember me arriving there."

Baird's face tightened and his heart felt for his friend. "She doesn't remember marrying you, is that what you're saying?"

Benen nodded. "It is. The physician I talked to said that can sometimes happen. Trauma drives recent events away from the mind. She may or may not remember. He couldn't tell me that." Benen turned. "Thanks for praying, Baird."

"It's a given, Benen. You know that." Baird walked beside Benen back to his apartment and then stood in the kitchen, his head shaking at Barnabas. He could hear quiet words down the hall before Benen's footsteps were heard returning to the kitchen.

Late that afternoon, Benen looked up from his computer where he had been trying to sort out a complex problem for a client and then saved what he was working on before he arose and walked out into the hallway, intent on finding Cadee. He found her right outside the office door, a frightened look on her face that didn't disappear when she saw him.

"Cadee?" He stooped to peer into her face, his hands on her upper arms.

"Where are they, Benen?"

"Where are who?" He really wasn't sure what she was meaning, but fear began to grow within him. He knew then, without a shadow of a doubt, that she was aware of what had been threatened.

"Them. Whoever they are that are after me. They won't let me go. They'll follow you here." She blinked back sudden tears, something he knew she regretted and didn't want him to see.

"The ones after you? I don't know, darling. You know who they are, don't you?" He swept her into a tight hug as she nodded. "Can you tell me about it?"

She shook her head. "I can't, Benen. I don't know enough about them or why they're after me to know what to say."

He turned her towards the living room, one arm around her, and made her sit on the couch, walking to the kitchen and back with a bottle of water for her.

"Here, drink this first. Then you can tell me what you want to drink. Anna left soup for you. She was by last night with it."

"Who's Anna?" She was puzzled, knowing there were people in his life she didn't know and for some reason that scare her.

"Anna is Doc's wife. She mothers us all." Benen sat beside her, his back against the couch arm, watching her. "Tell me what you can, Cadee. We'll research it. I know my friends. They won't stop until they solve it."

She looked horrified and terrified at the same time. "They can't. They'll be hurt." She watched him shake his head. "They will be."

"They know that. Some day, ask Berneen to tell you their story. It's not one I would believe if I hadn't been involved." He paused, watching her, knowing he would have to explain. "It's like this. Berneen had been abducted and held. Baird was abducted. We went in and got them out. They were abducted again the next day or so along with Buckley, who is a minister. He was forced to marry them to save Baird's life. It all came down to revenge against them for something that had happened in the past with their fathers."

She looked shocked. "What? You would never know it. Berneen is so much in love with him."

"And he with her. God worked it out. If Berneen had asked for her freedom, Baird would have given it to her, but he would never ever have married again."

"That's sad, you know." She leaned her head back on the couch, shifting so she faced him. "Is that what will happen with us? We'll go our separate ways?"

"I don't know, Cadee. God brought us together. He could have stopped the wedding, but He didn't. We prayed about it and agreed that we should go ahead. If one of us had had any doubts, we would not have. You know how your parents are."

She nodded, a yawn catching her by surprise. "We do need to talk, Benen. I just don't think today's the day."

"It's not." He grinned at her, impishness in his eyes. "Do you want something to eat?"

"That sounds good. Did you say soup?"

"I did. If I know Anna, it's likely her homemade chicken soup. It's so delicious." He rose, his hand extended for her to grasp.

She studied his hand for a moment, studied the wedding band she could see, and then took his hand, reaching out in faith, knowing from past experience with him she had nothing to fear from him but that he would do his best to protect her.

*Chapter 6*

Two days later, Cadee slumped into a chair in Benen's office, not saying a word, watching him hard at work, recognizing in his posture the friend from years previous when he was determined to solve a problem.  She wished he would solve hers, and then they could get on with their lives.  Would it be with him, she wondered?  She had tried hard to hide the crush she had had on him during college, not sure if he returned her feelings or not, and if he had, he had not shown it.

Benen had glanced up with a smile and asked how she was before his attention was back on the problem.  She could hear his side of the conversation and realized he had changed what his planned occupation had to have been.  He had been determined to teach, but now it looked as if he worked with computers.  She shook her head.  She wasn't the only one who had changed then, she decided.

Benen finally sat back, rubbing at his neck, rotating his shoulders and neck to relieve the stress.  This problem had been a long one to solve, with the computers of a small company, but he was confident he had managed to do just that.  He had no desire to fly across the country to work on them.

He looked up to find Cadee's eyes on him, a frown in place, as she curled up in a chair, unknowing taking the one he favoured, the afghan he kept there wrapped around her.

"I'm sorry, Cadee.  How long?"

"How long?  What do you mean?"  Her voice was low, and he could hear the fatigue in it.

"How long were you here?  I tend to get lost when I'm working."  He rose to move beside her, crouching down and resting an arm on the chair.

"You always did.  No one could get your attention if you were problem solving."  She watched him closely, seeing the changes life had made in him.  "Were you finished?"

———

"I am." He watched her closely. "You're about to ask me something."

"Stop doing that." She shoved at him with her socked foot, causing him to grab for the chair arm as he laughed. "I was. I need to find work. If I can't go back to the mission down there, I need to find something to do. There's no point in going back to the office in the headquarters here. There's no place for me."

Benen nodded, then rose, reaching for her hand. "Up for a bit of a walk? We need to go talk to Barnabas."

She slid her feet into her slippers and then looked down. "I'm not dressed to meet someone that rich."

Benen began to laugh, drawing a cross look from her. "Darling, it doesn't matter. Barnabas doesn't flaunt his wealth. If you were to meet him on the street, you would never know."

"I highly doubt that." She walked with him, her hand in his, waiting for the elevator, before she spoke again. "You did say he pays your wages?"

"He does, darling. He pays them, so that frees up a company to hire someone else if they need to, without having to worry about finding the money to do so. We all also volunteer in various capacities in different organizations. You met Baird. He volunteers as a tutor. Berneen is still trying to decide if she wants to work or just volunteer."

"What is your volunteer work, Benen? I should know."

"That you should. I go to the nearby prison and teach computer basics, helping to train the prisoners to find work when they're released."

She stared at him. "You never used to want to go anywhere near a jail. What happened?"

"God. And then Barnabas. He encouraged me to do that, telling me that I had nothing to fear. That God was my Protector and He walked in there with me." He held the door open so she could exit, watching in amusement as her mouth dropped and then snapped close.

———

She turned slowly in a circle, her hand pulling Benen with her. "This can't be real. It's like something out of a movie."

"It's real. Barnabas and his father spent a lot of time designing this, choosing the materials very carefully." He tapped his foot on the floor. "Real hardwood floors. The tiling, the walls, the seating arrangements at either end, the fireplaces?" When she nodded, he continued. "They are not that expensive, not really. He put this in to welcome clients that we have come through, but more importantly, he wanted this building to be home to each of us. He lives here himself. His parents used to until his dad retired. He wanted something warm and welcoming for us."

"I would say he succeeded." She frowned as she spied the security desk. "But you have security."

"We need to. Barnabas is very wealthy in his ow right but The Barnabas Foundation could be a target. It's not common knowledge what he does with that. Security is there as a protection for us all. We don't always have the best of clients come through."

She shook her head. "And here I thought I left danger behind."

"No, unfortunately, you didn't. We still need to talk about that, though." He opened the door to The Foundation Office, grinning at Barnabas' secretary. "Amy, this is Cadee."

Cadee stared at her. "I thought you were Anna."

"She's my younger sister. They say we do look alike." Amy reached to hug Cadee, surprising her before she hugged Benen. "Welcome to the Foundation family, Cadee. Benen, Barnabas is free. He's been expecting you this afternoon." She threw up her hands as Cadee stared at her. "I have no idea how he knows these things. He can't explain it himself, other than to say God."

Barnabas appeared in his office doorway, leaning against the doorframe as he watched Benen and Cadee speaking with Amy. He shook his head. *What is it with these guys of mine? These two, anyway. Both of them married, and I would say that these two in front of me love each other but are afraid to say anything. Lord, protect them. Bring them through the fire I just know they are going to face.*

Benen looked up at that point, a grin on his face at the teasing Amy had been sending his way.

"Barnabas? You're free?"

"That I am. Come on in and bring your lovely bride with you."

Cadee started at Barnabas, not quite sure if he was serious or not, before her eyes lifted to Benen, who was smiling down at her.

"He means it, Cadee. I can see the question in your eyes." Benen seated her on the soft leather sofa before he headed for the kitchenette off the office, returning with the spiced apple tea she seemed to like and a coffee for himself and Barnabas, who had sat in a deep leather chair facing the couch, having dropped a folder on the table between them.

Barnabas gave a quiet thanks, watching as Benen slid to a seat beside Cadee and reached for her hand. "Welcome, Cadee. I don't think you remember me speaking with you in the hospital."

She shook her head. "Not really. Did you?"

Barnabas grinned at her. "I did. You weren't very clear on your answers though."

She groaned. "Please tell me I didn't answer stupidly."

"No, you didn't. You just couldn't answer some things, told me to ask you later." He sipped at his coffee before setting it on the table beside his chair. "We need to talk about what you're going through. The guys are all wanting to help, to free you from the fear and yes terror you're under. Don't deny it. We know that's what's been going on." He nodded at Benen. "Benen has been able to tell us what your father has told him. We need to talk to you."

She sighed. "I know you do, but Dad knew everything I did. I have no idea who or why. I don't remember seeing something or someone I shouldn't have."

"Let it rest. You'll remember, likely at the worst time possible. We will want you to go through your things when they arrive, see if there's something that doesn't belong to you." He looked at Benen for a moment. "Benen tells me that your father asked that your belongings be shipped here. That is not a problem."

"He did?" She turned to study Benen, finding him nodding at her. "I wonder why."

"Because this is your home, Cadee, darling. At least for now." Benen looked over at Barnabas. "We need to explain something to you, Cadee, and I fear you will have the same reaction as Berneen."

Barnabas began to laugh at that, drawing Cadee's shocked look to him. "She did protest, very vehemently, if I recall." He reached for the folder, handing it to her, hesitation on her part to take it. "Benen has explained about the Foundation and how the men are paid?"

She nodded. "He did. I don't understand how it affects me."

Barnabas nodded. "Berneen was the same. It is written into our charter that when the men marry, their wives will receive a salary from the Foundation as well. That frees them to either stay at home, work out in the community, or volunteer."

She stared at him, her mouth open until she felt Benen's finger tapping her chin. She shut it was a click, a dumbfounded look on her face. "Are you for real?" At his nod, she slumped back on the couch, her eyes shifting between the two men. "For real?" Benen nodded this time. "I don't believe this." Her eyes filled with tears. "Do you know what this means to me? I can do so much now that I couldn't before."

Benen's arm around her, he hugged her to him. "That's what it was set up for, darling. For you to use as you want. If you have plans you want to put in place, talk to Barnabas. There is funding available."

She stared at him, a hand reaching to swipe at the tears on her face. "Benen, do you know how many women and children I can help? Help them to assimilate into life here? Learn about God?"

Barnabas blinked back tears himself. He had not expected that reaction, not after Berneen being adamant that she didn't want him to pay her. They had finally agreed that he would, but she was still reluctant to take the money.

"Cadee, when you're ready, come talk to me. This is what the Foundation does - what you want to do. We'll work it out." He paused, his eyes on the floor for a moment, before he looked up. "Now, I have word your belongings will be here next week. For now, do what Doc has suggested. Rest. Eat well. Sleep when you need to. You were through a trauma in more ways than one." He looked at Benen, finding him watching his bride. "You and Benen need to talk at some point. But for now, we'll focus on what happened to you and why and who is responsible. Anything you can tell us, anything that you don't think is important, let us know."

She nodded, a shadow crossing her face, leaving paleness in its wake. "I will. It's just so hard to concentrate and think right now."

Barnabas nodded once more. "We get that, Cadee. We really do. All the fellows have approached me, Benen, offering to help in any way they can."

"I've talked to my team and I know the other team is the same." He rose, drawing Cadee to her feet and then scooping her into his arms, his eyes on her face as her eyes slid closed. "We'll talk, Barnabas. Soon."

"Let's. The men want to meet in the morning. Does that work?"

Benen thought through his work outlined for the morning. "It should. If it doesn't, I'll let you know."

"And Anna said she'll be up to stay with Cadee."

## Chapter 8

Dropping his portfolio on the table in the conference room, Benen headed for the coffee and poured a mug, turning to return to his seat, finding Buckley Cullen, the minister in the group, standing in front of him, his hand extended.

"Congratulations, Benen. I hope to meet your bride soon."

"You do need to do that." Benen ran his hand through his hair, deep in thought. "You all do. I just don't know though."

"She's recovering?"

"She is, but stress can tire her." Benen turned as Branigan spoke from beside him.

"We'll do a meal on the weekend, Benen. One of our potlucks. We're due for that. You two come, introduce her to us, and then we eat. You can leave at any time." He reached for his own mug of coffee. "No pressure. We want to do what we can to alleviate that for you, and to solve the mystery. None of us want to see you two go through the horror that Baird and Berneen did."

"No, we don't want that. Not for any of us." Benen slid his chair closer to the table, arranging his mug on the table to his liking and then looked towards the middle of the table where Barnabas had seated himself. "Barnabas? We're ready to start?"

"We are. First, though, prayer. What requests to we have? Benen?"

The men shared their requests and then broke into groups of two to pray, finishing as Barnabas pulled his Bible towards him.

"I have felt led to study protection in the last few days. God is our Protector. The Psalms are filled with cries for protection and praise for it. Benen, you and Cadee have been on my mind today. I fear for you two. May God hide you in the hollow of the rock and cover you both with His hand." He looked around the table. "Now, where do we stand?"

Brody Corcoran, the paralegal in the group, stood, passing around a folder to each man. "This is what I have found out about the mission the Daniells were with. It's not on the up and up. It seems to have been sabotaged somehow in the last month. Were you aware of that, Barnabas?"

"I was. I have sent in a team to work with the mission. We are trying to contact the Daniells but have had no luck as yet. Benen?"

"I haven't heard from them, and I know Cadee hasn't. They were to be here tomorrow. If they're not, they agreed to send me a text and let me know where they are. I told them we'd go in and get them."

"That's correct. Any way to contact them before then?"

Benen shook his head. "Ted wanted it that way. He wanted to make sure I had time to get Cadee out before they made contact. We weren't sure if we could even get out of the country."

"That's what I thought." Barnabas looked around at the men sitting there. "Breck?"

Breck Curran, second in command to Barnabas, looked up. "We can leave this for now. Benen, you and I will talk. I need to talk to Cadee as well. Let's pray we don't overwhelm her in any way when we do. Now, Burney, your team. We need to send you six out to British Columbia. There are some people out there we need to talk to. Your team's up. You'll leave in the morning."

Benen finally stood, stretching. For some reason, it had been a long meeting, many items to discuss. He headed for the door, not seeing the looks following him, intent on finding Cadee.

"Buckley? How is he?" Breck stood beside Buckley.

"To tell you the truth, I really don't know. I need to talk to him and meet Cadee. Maybe this afternoon." He groaned. "No, I can't. I have a couple coming in for counselling."

"Try this evening then. You don't have any meetings?"

Buckley shook his head. "No. This is hard, you know."

"I know. It's tough for us. Think of how it is for them."

"True." Buckley walked away, leaving Breck staring after him, a frown on his face.

Cadee turned from the kitchen sink. She was more stable on her feet, feeling a bit stronger, and had insisted that she would and could get her own breakfast. Benen had laughed at her, dropped a kiss on her cheek and walked away, leaving her staring after him, a hand on her cheek at the spot of the kiss. Now that he was back, she had no idea how to face him.

"Cadee, are you up to a group potluck this weekend?"

"Why?"

"Because we are invited to the potluck here. We usually get together for a meal at least every four or five weeks. We're a little late doing that this time. There's been so much going on."

She shrugged, leaning back against the counter, her arms folded. "I guess. What do we take?"

It was Benen's turn to shrug. "Whatever you want. I usually take a salad and rolls. If you want to do something different, that's good. Just let Anna know. She coordinates us."

"Sounds as if she was dressing you all in different clothing that had to match." She smirked as he laughed. "Now, Benen? What's on for today? You have commitments."

"For this morning. Then we need to head to the bank and get you set up with an account here." He walked towards her and drew her into a hug, feeling her hug him back, finding a crack opening in his heart.

"We can do that. But I do need to shop for some clothes. I don't have winter clothing. I haven't needed them."

Cadee looked behind her later that afternoon, feeling eyes watching her, but not seeing anyone. But then everyone here was a stranger to her. She turned back to the jacket Benen was holding out, insisting the jade colour was just what she needed. She shrugged. Clothing was clothing, she thought. I don't need special stuff. Just everyday stuff. She paused, as she saw the sweater that he had picked out for her, a soft green, knowing he wanted to her buy it, but not sure she should.

"You need these, Cadee. Don't worry about the cost. We can afford these." He studied her and then sighed, telling her what his wage was.

He watched her mouth drop open and then snap closed. Her eyes narrowed as she thought of her own salary.

"And just what will mine be?" Benen told her, reaching out to catch her arm as she swayed. "It can't be that much."

"It is. Trust me. Barnabas and his father considered everything when they set out our wages."

She was jostled by the crowd, not feeling the hand that was quickly stuck into her jacket pocket and then remove, the man disappearing in the crowd without being seen.

Feeling her jacket pocket later, making sure the pockets were empty before she laundered it, Cadee frowned as she pulled out the folded piece of paper. It wasn't hers, that much she knew. She hadn't put it there.

She unfolded it and read it, her face turning white as she did so. She spun, steadying herself against the wall as her vision clouded for a moment. She needed to find Benen. Only, he wasn't there.

She paused in the lobby of the building, not sure where she should go. She knew he had an office on the main floor, just not where. The paper was clenched in her hand, as she stood in front of the elevators, debating whether to go back up to the apartment or not.

She jumped as a voice spoke beside her and turned, a frown on her face. She didn't know the man standing there.

"Cadee? Are you okay?" Blair Campion, one of the men on Benen's team, watched her closely.

"I'm sorry?"

He grinned. "I'm Blair. I asked if you were okay."

She shook her head. "No, I'm not. I was looking for Benen."

"He's not here. I saw him drive away about an hour ago. Did he not tell you?" Blair's hand under her arm kept her upright.

"He did. I forgot." She stared at the paper in her hand. "I just so needed to talk with him."

Blair reached and gently removed the paper from her hand, a dark frown on his face as he did so. "Where did you get this?"

"In my jacket. We had been shopping. Someone must have slipped it into my jacket. I never saw them. Never felt it."

Blair nodded, his head up, searching. "Come with me. It's okay, Cadee. I just want to head to Branigan's office. He's in and can help you with that."

"But Benen?"

"We'll let him know where you are. It's okay. We don't bite." He grinned as she stared at him for a moment before her mouth snapped closed.

"I need to stop doing that. I'll be catching flies if I don't."

Blair heard her muttering and stared at her in his turn. "What did you just say?"

She looked up, flushing for a moment. "Mom used to tell me to close my mouth or I'd catch flies. Sorry. Old habits of talking to myself die hard."

Blair began to laugh, knowing that Benen had found himself quite a lady. "That's okay. I talk to the cars all the time." He grinned at her again. "I'm a mechanic."

Branigan looked up from his desk as they entered and rose, walking towards them.

"Blair? Cadee?"

Blair handed him the slip of paper even as he seated Cadee in a chair in front of the desk. "Cadee found that in her jacket, she thinks from this afternoon when they were shopping."

Branigan watched Cadee closely, not being familiar with her enough to read her face. "Cadee?"

His voice brought her face up to him and she shook her head. "I'm sorry. I just found it. I don't know who put it there."

Branigan stared at her before he looked down at the paper he held and his face grew stern.

"Cadee?"

She shrugged. "I didn't see who did it. But I wouldn't have known them anyway. I'm a stranger here, remember?" She sank back, her face pale, her strength almost depleted. She didn't hear the tap at the door and then quick footsteps across the floor towards.

She didn't see Benen drop to his knees beside her until she felt his arms around her and his voice talking with Branigan.

Her face turned towards him, almost nose to nose with him, as he studied her face, seeing the fatigue in her face and how she was sitting.

"Cadee, darling, what did you go and find?" His words were soft.

She shrugged again. "I don't know, Benen. Just a slip of paper that threatened me." She blinked, her eyes misting with tears that he knew were not like her. She never cried, he thought.

"We'll look into it. Blair brought you to the right person. Branigan is a security expert. He's likely already been doing that." He looked up to see Branigan nodding. "When he finds something, he'll talk to us."

Cadee gave a slow nod, her strength fading, her mind becoming somewhat foggy. "I haven't heard from Mom and Dad."

"No, we haven't, Cadee. They would contact the mission. I spoke with them about thirty minutes ago. They have heard nothing and should have. I talked to Barnabas. He said he's sending a couple of the guys down that way, to try and trace their tracks."

"Thank him for me." She yawned, her eyes closing as she settled back into the chair. "Wake me up when he calls, please?"

Benen began to chuckle, even as the other men stared at her. "Come on, Cadee, darling. We need to get you back to the apartment. Branigan needs his office, you know."

"No, he doesn't. I can use it." Cadee drifted off even as Benen, laughter sparkling on his face, gathered her close in his arms and rose.

"Did she really just say that?" Branigan asked, a smile lurking on his face.

"She did. She doesn't always make sense when she's tired like this." Benen grinned. "You wouldn't believe some of the conversations we've had over the years."

Blair began to laugh. "I can believe that."

Benen stood back from the door early that evening to let Branigan and Buckley enter. He frowned at them before pointing to the living room.

"I'll be right back. Do you need to talk to Cadee?"

The men exchanged a look. "We should, if she's available."

"Let me go see. There's fresh coffee, by the way."

The two men watched him walk down the hall before exchanging glances and then heading for the kitchen, filling mugs with coffee. They stood for a moment, not quite sure about entering the living room before Buckley shrugged and headed that way. He figured Benen knew where he wanted them. He sat, his eyes sliding closed as he prayed, knowing this would be a difficult meeting.

Benen paused for a moment outside the closed door to Cadee's room, his hand on the door itself, his heart praying for his bride. He had seen the looks on his friends' faces and didn't like them. He was afraid for her, afraid for her parents.

He tapped and then opened the door before moving to crouch beside the bed, his hand resting on Cadee's face.

"Cadee? Can you wake?" He waited, a slight smile on his face. "Cadee, darling, I need you to wake up."

Cadee's one eye opened and she glared at him from the pile of blankets she was buried under. "I'm sleeping, Benen. Go away.'

"Sorry, Cadee. I do need you to wake up. Branigan's here and wants to talk to you." He brushed back the hair from her face. "Come on, darling. Rise and shine." He stood, staring down at her for a moment. "Five minutes, or I'll come back and carry you out looking like that."

She continued to glare at him even as she shoved back the blankets. "Go on. I'll be out. I'm up now. You've made such a racket."

Benen laughed as he shut the room door behind him, shaking his head.  She hadn't changed, he thought, didn't like to be awakened and told to get up.  He leaned against the wall as he waited, his heart in prayer for his lady, not sure what they would be expecting to hear from Branigan.  And Buckley here as well.

He turned as the door opened, and Cadee peeked out, a smile on his face as he wrapped her into his arms.  "Let's pray first, darling.  We'll need it, I suspect."

She nodded against his chest, feeling safe for the first time in months, she thought.  Now, where did that thought come from, she wondered?

She watched Branigan closely as she waited for him to speak.  Benen had sent her in to sit on the couch and he was just heading back with her tea and his coffee.  He set the mugs down before seating himself and then wrapping an arm around her, drawing her close to him.  She frowned at him for a moment, thinking he was being bold, and then realized that, no, he really wasn't.  They were married, after all, of sorts, and he was always caring and concerned about her.  She never had realized that before.

"Buckley, will you pray first?  I think we'll need it."  Branigan's face was sober, and his words clipped.  Benen stared at him, and then down at Cadee, knowing it was not likely to be good news.

"I can."  Buckley's voice filled the room as he petitioned for safety, healing, protection and wisdom for the couple in front of him.

Branigan hesitated to speak when Buckley had finished, not quite sure how to proceed.

"Spit it out!  That's usually the best way."  Cadee's words startled him for a moment before he began to laugh.

"I can do that."  He still hesitated, his eyes on Benen, wondering just how to proceed.

"Did you find anything on the note?"  Benen's question didn't surprise Branigan.

"Not really.  I kept a copy and turned the original over to the detective I spoke with.  He'll have his lab take a look at it, but it's down the line as to when it can be done.  There's no urgency he said.

Yes, there is a threat there against Cadee, but we have no idea or evidence to indicate who or why. He did say that if it was from the country you fled from, Cadee, he may need to talk to the police there."

She snorted. "That won't help. There is a lot of corruption, unfortunately, in the force. I couldn't tell him who to talk to that would help." She leaned against Benen, her face sober. "But why me? I don't remember seeing or hearing anything that I shouldn't have."

"It may be something that was so innocent to you hearing it that you have forgotten it. It may be someone who was out of place where you were that you noticed and forget. It may also be an object that you have in your belongings. They're here now and in a storage unit. At some point, we'll have you go through them." He held up a hand as she opened her mouth to speak. "Right now, Doc has said you can't. Not for a couple of days. He said to remind you that you almost died and are still recovering."

She snapped her mouth closed, anger building inside her at the thought. "Yeah, well, there is that, isn't there? I need to do this, Benen. I need to." Her faced turned up to his even as she was pleading, no, begging him to let her go through her belongings. "Please?"

"We'll see how you are in the morning, darling. But I think there's more, isn't there, Branigan?" Benen's eyes never left Cadee's face as he spoke, seeing the fatigue and pain mingling there.

"There is." Branigan didn't speak for a moment, Buckley's eyes shifting between his friends. "We have been looking into where your parents are, Cadee."

She looked at him, hope in her eyes. "They're back? They're here?"

"No, I'm sorry, Cadee. They're not. We do know they crossed into the neighbouring country and managed to make their way onto a bus. But since then, they seem to have disappeared. We're working on that. I have sent a couple of men down there with Andy to try and trace their whereabouts."

Cadee sat back, devastated that her parents were missing. *God, why? You promised to protect us. I'm safe. But are Mom and Dad?*

Moving restlessly through the apartment, Cadee finally stood in the office doorway, watching Benen at work, not wanting to disturb him, but not wanting to be too far away from him. She knew she needed to sort through the feelings she had for him, but not today, she thought. Not today. I need to start going through my stuff, as Dad calls it.

She turned, heading for the living room, and reaching for her Bible. She needed reassurance and confidence from God that He was in control, that He would protect her and her family. Her eyes sought the hallway, hearing Benen's voice, and included him in her prayers.

Benen had looked up as he heard Cadee move away. He had wanted to go to her, to pray with her, but his client was demanding his attention. He finally stood after what seemed too long a time and moved away from his desk. He stretched, his muscles sore from sitting for so long, hands reaching for the ceiling, before he lowered them and tucked his flannel shirt back in. He walked down the hallway, stopping for a moment to watch Cadee as she sat on the couch, legs spread out in front of her under a blanket, her Bible on her lap, her head bent as she read. He headed for the kitchen, squinting at the clock. Lunchtime, he thought, reaching for bread and sandwich fixings, making her tea and his coffee, before he loaded everything on a tray and carried it into the living room, setting her meal before her.

She looked up as he moved her feet, sitting where they had rested, and then resting them back on his legs, tucking the blanket around them, and leaving a hand on them for a moment.

"Benen?"

"It's lunchtime, Cadee. Not much for now, but I think you should eat." Benen watched as she sighed, and then nodded, reaching to set her Bible on the table.

Cadee sighed, knowing she needed to eat, but also wanting to fast and pray until her parents were found.  She watched Benen from under her eyelashes, knowing he would understand but that he would still push her to eat, given that she had been sick.

"Benen?"  When he looked up at her, she continued.  "What is it you actually do?"

"I work in IT, problem solving for small companies and individuals.  A lot of what I do can be done remotely.  I sometimes travel, but not often."

"But someone said you volunteer.  Where and why?"  She bit into her sandwich, pulling it back to look at it.  "You remembered."

"What?  That you dislike mustard on your ham and cheese?  Of course, I would.  We've made too many of them for me to forget."  He bit into his own sandwich, his thoughts straying to years earlier, not seeing the surprised but pleased look on her face.

He finally set his plate aside and reached for his mug of coffee, watching her face as he did so.

"Cadee?  Talk to me."

She shook her head.  "What do I say, Benen?  You're taking care of me, trying to protect me.  I just don't want you keeping anything from me.  That's all."

"And I'm not, darling.  I'm not.  Branigan and the guys are working on stuff."  He stared across the room, his eyes on the clock sitting on the fireplace mantle.  "We can work on your things, if you like.  I just don't want you getting overtired."

"I know."  She looked around the room, liking the soft peach he had chosen for the walls, the wooden and leather furniture, the tasteful pictures.  "So, tell me.  What do you volunteer at?"

He shook his head.  "Not giving up on that, are you?"  He laughed as she glared at him for a moment.  "Cool it, darling.  I'm not hiding anything from you.  I volunteer at a local camera club, helping the members learn how to properly edit their photos."

She stared at him and then at the photos.  "Those are yours?"

"They are."

"Nice." She moved restlessly. "Have you heard anything on Mom and Dad?"

"Not yet. Barnabas said it might take a couple of days for the guys to find out anything." He lifted her feet to the floor, standing with a hand out to help her stand before he gathered their dishes and carried them back to the kitchen and the dishwasher.

"I can't get used to all these conveniences." Cadee stood and watched him as he worked. "We didn't have all this before Mom and Dad left for the mission."

"No, you didn't." Benen paused, before he turned to her. "How did they come to go out?"

She shrugged, her hands in her sweater pockets. "I don't really know. I know they wanted to when I was young. I came home one day to find out they had applied and been accepted. I was at a loss. This was right after college. I applied to work in the office down there as well."

"Didn't you have to fundraise or find support?"

She shrugged again. "We did to a certain extent. But we were told that someone had offered to sponsor us, so we didn't have to raise a lot." She frowned, before a distressed look crossed her face. "Benen? Who would do that?"

"They didn't tell you who?"

She shook her head. "No. Whoever it was wanted to remain anonymous, but we were told it was specific to us." She looked up, sudden fear on her face. "Benen? What if it was a set up to get us down there for some reason?"

"We'll talk to Barnabas. He knows the mission board you went out under. He'll see what he can find out. It has now become a matter of life and death for all of you."

She shuddered, his arms going around her. "I'm scared, Benen. Scared for Mom and Dad." Her voice was barely above a whisper.

His heart breaking for his bride, Benen wrapped her into his arms and prayed for her and her parents.

———

Benen stood at the entry to his storage unit, staring at the few boxes inside. He had no idea where Cadee's parents belongings had ended up. Here, he thought, but he wasn't sure. He wrapped an arm around Cadee and pulled her tight to him, his eyes dropping to her face, a sigh suppressed at the look on her face.

"We'll take our time, darling. If it's too much, we'll stop and come back. Doc told me to watch you. It's not been that long since we almost lost you."

She nodded, her hand wrapping around his, tightening with her emotions. "I know. And that I don't get. Why me?"

"We'll figure it out. Barnabas sent a text message a bit ago. He's onto something and wants to talk with us later."

"Has he heard anything?" She looked up, hope in her eyes.

"He didn't say." Benen studied the boxes. "Where do you want to start?"

"I'm not sure." She moved away, stopping to stare down at the first box. "This is Mom and Dad's." She looked around. "It's not much to show for a lifetime, is it? They sold off just about everything before they went out. I think they put some boxes in a friend's attic, but I'm not even sure they're still in there. Mom said something a couple of years ago of moving them, sorting through them again, and getting rid of anything that didn't matter."

She knelt, reaching for the box, finding Benen's hand there with his pocketknife to slit the tape, and then reaching to fold back the flaps for her. She hesitated, reaching for a moment to rub at her eyes, before she picked up the first thing, a picture of the three of them. She handed it to Benen, who took it, his eyes on her.

She continued to look through the box, even as he too examined each item she handed him, pulling the pictures apart to search inside the frame.

"Benen?" Her soft question had his head coming up. "Why look inside?"

"Just in case something has been put in there." He stopped for a moment, sitting back on the floor, his eyes on her. "Would you recognize something that's not your parents?"

"I don't know. I would hope I would. Unless it was something that they had hidden away and not shown me." She paused, deep in thought. "About a year ago, Dad was acting strange. I thought it was because they had just come back from a neighbouring country where they had been to a conference. Maybe it was more."

"Give Branigan the details. He'll find someone to look into it." He reached for the next box as she tidily packed away the first one.

Two hours later, she reached for the last box, one of her, her hands hesitating, fear suddenly running through her. She moved back, on her feet, her arms wrapping around herself. Benen had stepped out of the room to take a call and stood where he could watch her, wanting to go to her but unable to end his call with a client. He nodded as Brady moved past him into the room.

"Cadee?" Brady's voice startled her.

"I'm sorry." She spun, her eyes huge as she studied him.

"Sorry, Cadee. I'm Brady. I don't think we've had an opportunity to meet." He reached out to shake her hand.

"No, I don't think we have." She sighed. "There are just too many of you. I'll never keep your names all straight."

"Sure you will. It's easy. We all have the same initials as Barnabas." He began to laugh as her eyes seemed to grow in size. "That's it. All our first names start with B and our last names start with C. Barnabas had a reason for that. He'll explain it if you ask."

"I just might." She studied the box in front of her.

"Something wrong with that box?"

She nodded as she looked up at Brady. "There is. I felt evil in it. And I shouldn't."

His face growing stern, Brady crouched down beside it. "It's the same box you packed?"

"I think so. Why?"

"Because it looks as if the original tape was removed and then the box re-taped." He looked up at her, seeing Benen walking towards them as he pocketed his phone. "Benen? I think this is the box you might be looking for."

"Is it? Then how be we take it to the conference room. Blair said they had set up in there." Benen reached for the box, finding Brady's hands there first, Brady's head nodding at Cadee.

"Come on, Cadee darling. We're moving to a conference room. We can spread out what's in this box." Benen reached for her hand, waiting as she stood still. "Cadee? Anything else?"

She finally shook her head before pulling her hand free and walking away, deep in thought.

"Something more is going on with her, Benen." Brady's assessment of her told him that.

"I know. I can't get her to talk. That's not her. At least the her I knew." Benen sighed deeply as he moved forward, locking the storage room door, and then reaching to wrap an arm around Cadee, finding her shaking. "Cadee?"

She looked up at him, fear on her face. "There's something in there, Benen. I don't know what, but I can feel the evil from it. I don't want to know, but I have to, no, need to know."

Benen carefully opened the box, Cadee standing away from it, her eyes on his hands. Brady stood near him, ready to take the articles from Benen as he emptied the box. Brady laid them down carefully, then reached to take the box from Benen, searching it carefully, frowning as he found an envelope under one of the bottom flaps. He stared at it, seeing no name or any writing on the envelope before he touched Benen's arm, holding out the paper for him to take.

Benen looked at it, then at Cadee as he heard an exclamation from her, dropping the envelope to scoop her into his arms as her eyes closed and her body dropped suddenly towards the floor.

Brady pointed to a chair, moving quickly in. As a paramedic, he understood how shock could work on a body, and knowing what she had been through, he was concerned. He looked around as he heard footsteps, and Bradon Cahill and his dog, Kade, appeared.

"Bradon? Is Doc around?"

"No, he said he's on duty at the clinic. Do you need something?"

"Yeah. The kit from the infirmary. I don't want to move her yet, if I can help it. And some blankets. I need to lay her flat."

Bradon was off on a run before Brady had quite finished, returning in short order, shoving the kit Brady wanted at him, then spreading blankets on the floor, stepping back as Benen gathered Cadee into his arms, finding her rousing and fighting him. He sat back into the chair, keeping her close to him, his voice a mere whisper.

Brady crouched in front of her, concern on his face. "Benen, you're old friends. Has this ever happened before?"

Benen thought for a moment. "Not that I'm aware of. But she's been through too much already. When does it end?"

Brady nodded, stethoscope in his hand, as he paused. "I need to assess her vitals, Benen."

"Go ahead. I'll make sure you can." He looked down at Cadee, seeing her eyes opening. "Cadee, darling, Brady needs to check you out, make sure you're fine."

"Brady? Who's he? Where am I?" She stared at Benen. "Benen? Don't we have to pack up everything? Dad said we needed to leave in the morning." She stared around, jumping at the close proximity of Brady and then jumping again as she felt a tongue on her hand, staring at Kade. "Who are these?"

"We're home, Cadee. You had an adventure that took a few years off my life. It's been about a week or so." Benen watched as she thought through that and then nodded.

"What happened?" When he paused, he felt the anger in her, anger that he knew was not normal for her.

"When we were heading for the airplane, you received what you thought was a bug bite but the doctors think was a tiny dart full of poison. I almost lost you, darling."

She stared at him for a moment, before looking down at her hand. "We really did that, ddin't we?"

"We did, Cadee. We did. Your dad thought it was the only way."

She nodded before she laid her head down on his shoulder. "Thank you. I'm sure Dad was right. He was disturbed the last month or so, but wouldn't tell Mom and I why. He was afraid for us, wouldn't let us go out anywhere on our own. He had men and youths from the church guarding our home. Did he say why?"

Benen shook his head in turn. "He didn't. He said we'd talk when we reached a safer place."

"Where are they, Benen? They're in danger, aren't they? I can feel that. I wish they had waited and come with us."

"I wanted them to. They slipped away on us when we were cleaning up the kitchen. Your Dad seemed to think you needed to come back first." He sighed as he exchanged a look with Brady and Bradon, who stood watching, grim looks on their faces. "The last thing he said to me was to watch you closely. Someone had put out a contract on you, and he didn't know why."

"A contract?" She gave an unbelieving laugh. "Benen? Why? I worked in the office at the mission. I didn't see anything I shouldn't have. I was very careful with the people I met, where I went, who I was with. Again, why?"

"That we don't know. Your Dad might but he hasn't got here yet. I think they've gone into hiding, darling. Some of our guys are down there right now, trying to find them."

"They won't unless he wants them to.  He had made plans, told us about them, but we didn't believe him.  I guess he was right after all."  She shoved at his arms, rising, and walking to the table, her hands touching the objects laying there.  "There are all trinkets they picked up down there.  It's strange that they were all in one box."

"I think your Dad packed this one."  Benen stood behind her, his arms around her.  "I think he put these together for a reason.  We have to figure it out."

She nodded, her head rubbing against his chin, before she stared at the envelope.  "That's what I felt, Benen.  That's what I felt."  Her memory rushed back, engulfing her in a violent storm of shaking.  "What is in it?"

Brady took a look at her and left the room on the run, knowing they needed Buckley there.  Buckley looked up from his desk and the notes he was working on for his Sunday sermon, rose and ran after Brady without asking any questions.

Buckley stood beside Cadee, his eyes on her, before he looked up at Benen.

"Benen?"

"There's something about that envelope that is scaring Cadee badly.  We need to bath her in prayer, for protection, for safety."

Buckley simply bowed his head and prayed, asking for that from the God who he knew was in control of all.

Pulling out the flap on the envelope, Benen hesitated for a moment before he handed it to Buckley.

"Buckley? Would you, please?"

Buckley stared down at the letter and then up at Benen before his eyes shifted to Cadee, who was staring at the envelope. "You're sure?"

She looked up, an unreadable expression on her face. "Please. I can't."

Buckley pulled out the folded paper inside, feeling what she had felt, unfolding it and then frowning. "It's in another language. Can you read it, Cadee?"

She leaned over as far as she could from the safety of Benen's arms and then nodded. "I can. It's not nice." She spun, her arms around Benen, fear, no, terror shaking her body.

Benen stared down at her. "Is Brenden here?" Brenden Conroy was a interpreter.

"No, but Brennen is." Buckley looked around as he heard the door softly closed. "Brady's gone for him. Benen, get her sitting down and something hot into her."

Bradon set a tray of hot drinks of the table at that point. "I figured we'd need something." He turned to look behind him. "Anna's on her way and she has Berneen with her. Is that okay?"

Benen hesitated and then nodded. "That should be okay, I guess." He drew Cadee down into a chair, crouching down beside her, his arm around her, his hand on hers. "Cadee?"

She finally turned to look at him, and he drew in a sharp breath at the look in her eyes, one he had never seen before

"They're not in hiding, are they? They're missing? He has them!"

"Who has them?" All eyes were on her before they looked around at one another, Anna and Berneen walking in at that point and halting, not quite sure what they had walked in on.

"He does. I don't know his name. He used to come to church and then to the house to talk to Dad. Dad never liked him. He made sure Mom and I were visible when the man came around." She looked up at Benen again before poking at the paper Buckley still held. "He threatened me in that. He said I had something of his I needed to give him. I don't. I would remember if I did. And I don't." She looked up at Benen again before throwing herself at him, only Buckley's hand on his back stopping him from falling backwards. "It's all my fault. It's my fault they're missing."

"Tell me exactly what the letter says." Benen looked up at Brennen entered the room, concern on his face for his friend and his wife

"Benen? Brady said you had a letter you needed translated?"

Buckley handed it to him. "Cadee has basically told us it threatens her and asks for something she says she doesn't have."

Brennen studied it and nodded. "That's quite a condensed versions of what it says. There's a whole lot more to it, isn't there, Cadee?" His voice sounded harsh, but that was the concern he felt coming through.

She threw her head back to stare at him, their looks dueling with one another, before she nodded. "There is. Benen, they threaten to kill Mom and Dad, say they know where they are and that they can get to them at any time. They threaten you, telling me they'll kill you if I don't turn over the object to them. They know where I am and have threatened Barnabas and everyone else here. They said they can reach out to any one of us and harm us. I have to turn over whatever it is in the next two days." She didn't look away from Brennen as she spoke. "I have no idea what it is, so how can I?"

"So, we go through what we've pulled out of the box." Benen rose, his hand resting on her head in a caress. "Buckley, we'll need to pull that box apart as well. When did they put in that letter?"

———

230

"Who knows?  It wasn't after it got here, that's for sure." Brennen pointed with the mug he held.  "She's pretty much put it into a nutshell, but it's a lot worse sounding that what she says."

"Can you write out the translation?  Let Barnabas know and then whoever is working on this."

"We all are, Benen."  Brennen paused in setting his mug down. "You know right well that we are all involved.  We can't do anything less than that."

Benen turned as he felt Cadee rising, moving to stand near Berneen.  He couldn't hear their soft conversation, but he could see Cadee relaxing some.

"Anna, when is the dinner?"  Buckley spoke up.

"Sunday after church.  That two days from now.  Got your sermon ready yet?"  Anna, Doc's wife, grinned at Buckley as he shook his head.  "I know you do.  It's always ready by now.  You just refine it."

"And does everyone know what they're to bring?"  Buckley's smile widened as Anna shook a finger at him.

"What we always do.  You know that, Buckley."  She paused, her china cup of tea in her hand, as she studied the items on the table.  "Some of this is really bizarre, isn't it?"  She looked around, then called for Cadee.  "Cadee, can you come here?  I know you don't want to, but these things won't hurt you.  You need to talk to us, tell us what you know about them."

Cadee moved towards her, her hands once more touching the objects.  "This one.  I have never seen it before.  I've seen the others. Dad collected them from artisans down there.  But this one?  I have no idea what it is."

Benen reached to take it from her.  "I do.  It's an pestle, used in their cooking.  But why would your father have it?"

Brady reached for it, his face paling as he did.  "I've done some reading on poisoned darts.  This could well have been something that was used in the preparation of the poison."

Cadee paled and moved away.  "What did Dad go and do?"

———

Benen quietly shut the bedroom door he had opened and walked away.  Cadee was sleeping at last, he thought, knowing he would be back there to check on her.  It was late evening, and he had not been able to settle down to his work, and he needed to do that.  He sighed, reaching to pour yet another cup of coffee, and then walking through to his office, sinking into his chair, exhausted beyond belief.  He reached for his phone and then reached past it for his Bible.  He needed some God time, time to refresh his heart and soul with verses about trusting God, about God's protection.

He finally rose, heading for the kitchen to rinse out his mug and set the coffee for the morning, and then turning out lights as he moved through the apartment, standing at the living room window, the room dark behind him, staring out at the night, searching the heavens and the bright stars, feeling God's peace in his heart, but knowing their troubles were far from over.

He finally turned, reaching to close the drapes, not seeing the two men standing in the shadows of the trees that lined the parking lot, their eyes on his windows before they too walked away.

He showered, finding clean towels and clean pyjamas waiting for him.  He felt them, knowing that Cadee had done that, taking care of him.  He smiled and then, dressing, turning to walk to her bedroom door, tapping lightly before he entered and crouched down beside her, his heart breaking at the tears on her face before he kissed a cheek and rose, heading for his own bed and sleep.

He awoke in the night, his head raising, listening, before he was on his feet and running for Cadee, his bare feet hitting the floor hard at each step.  Hand to the door knob, he twisted it, throwing it open, the light from the hall shining into the room.  He paused for a moment not seeing her before he saw the doors to the walk-in closet open. He hastened across the room, pausing for a moment to search for her, finding her huddled into a corner, her arms wrapped around herself as she wept.

He dropped down beside her, reaching to catch her to him, his arms strong around her, his heart breaking at her sobs.  When she finally settled down, he spoke.

"Cadee?  What happened?"

"A bad dream!   A nightmare!  I dreamt Mom and Dad were dead.  They had been killed."  She shuddered even as she spoke, her voice hoarse.

Benen's heart broke for his bride and he began to pray, pray as he never had before.  She finally stirred after a while, shoving at him and then to her feet, to pace the bedroom even as he watched, a shoulder leaning against the closet door, an eye on the clock.  Only two in the morning.  They both needed to sleep.  He finally approached her, standing in her way, causing her to stop and raise her face to stare at him.  He simply swept her into his arms and walked from the room, settling her down into his place on his bed and pulling up the covers.

"Benen?  What are you doing?"  Cadee tried to rise but his hand on her shoulder kept her still.

"You need to sleep.  You won't sleep in there.  I know that. Not tonight.  So you sleep here."  He rose, heading for his closet, finding a blanket, and then covering himself as he stretched out beside her, his arms reaching to pull her close.  "Go to sleep, darling. I'll keep watch for a while and God will watch over us both."

They slept, not knowing that in less than a week, their world would be turned upside down in a way neither one of them expected.

*Chapter 16*

Sunday morning found Benen and Cadee standing outside the church, her hand tight in his, even as she hesitated about moving forward.

"They'll judge me, Benen. I just know they will. We married too quickly. They don't know me." Her voice rose in panic even as his hand squeezed hers.

"Benen? Who do you have here you're not letting go of?" The older gentleman stopped, his hand on Benen's shoulder, a look of interest on his face.

"Jace, this is my wife, Cadee. Cadee, darling, this is the trustee board chair, Jace Enger." Benen watched as Jace stared at him and then Cadee.

"Took a page from Baird's book, did you, son, and didn't let the love of your life escape?" He laughed, before he reached to hug Cadee, surprising her. "Welcome to our church family, Cadee. We don't bite, at least not much. Benen, you and your bride must join Martha and I for dinner one night this week. Martha will be in touch." He walked away, leaving Cadee staring after him, her mouth open until Benen gently tapped her chin.

"They're mostly like that. They welcome you in as a family member." He walked her into the church, finding a seat beside Berneen and Baird, letting Cadee sit next to Berneen. He looked around, a frown on his face for a moment, feeling someone watching him but now seeing anyone.

"Feel that too, do you?" Baird spoke quietly over the heads of the two women.

"I do. I know what you mean now." He listened to the sermon Buckley brought and his eyes frequently sought Cadee's face, seeing the thoughtfulness his words brought to her.

They walked away from the church, heading for home, having decided to walk that morning, not seeing some of the men following them.

---

"He's good, Benen."

"He is, Cadee. I have learned more from him that I have any minister I have sat under. He encourages us to search the Bible, to prove what he says. He wants to know if we are in disagreement with his messages and he'll spend time talking them through. We have some interesting discussions at times."

"Dad will like him." A troubled look flitted across her face. "You said the men are back from down there?"

"They are. Barnabas wants to have a meeting tomorrow with us all. You as well. You know the area, so perhaps you'll bring a different perspective to what they say."

"Oh, I'm sure I will. I just don't know the area Mom and Dad fled to." She sighed, her head resting against his arm for a moment. "It's hard, Benen. Very hard. I feel like I abandoned them down there, even though they left us."

"I know, darling. I know you do."

Seated at last in another conference room, this one set up with a kitchen, and with the potluck set up as a buffet, Cadee listened as Doc asked a blessing on their meal. She poked at her food at first before she began to eat, listening to the conversation and teasing around her, Berneen sitting beside her by choice, asking her questions, some of which Cadee's missed.

Brady finally looked across the table at her. "Cadee? Did you do this kind of stuff when you were young? Like at church?"

She shrugged. "Not really. The church we went to was huge, so we didn't have many meals, other than a formal Christmas dinner." She turned her head to Benen. "I don't know that many of the people really associated with one another."

He shook his head. "I don't think they did. Yours was a very formal church. Your family never seemed to fit in."

She sighed. "We didn't. I hated it. The youth group was brutal."

"It was, that I can remember, even though the leaders tried."

"They tried, but failed, miserably. I finally quit going. There was too much competition there."

"Competition?  What do you mean?"  Berneen leaned forward, eager to hear Cadee's response.

"I guess I mean with personalities.  A lot of the girls were only interested in catching one of the guy's eyes, especially the popular ones."  She smirked at Benen.  "You never noticed or knew, did you?"

"Knew what?"  He was puzzled, not sure what she meant.

"Benen!  How could you not?  You didn't see them throwing themselves at you?"

The table had silenced, waiting to hear his response.

"No, I didn't.  I wasn't interested in ladies at the time.  I was too busy with my studies."  He stared at her, his eyes narrowing as she began to laugh.  "You find this funny?"

"I do."  She shared a look with Berneen who began to laugh as well, thinking she knew where Cadee was heading with her words.

"Why?"  He took a bite of his apple pie, his eyes on her.

"Because they all wanted to be your girl, to date you."  She smirked once more.  "And I did it."

"Did what?"

"I'm your girl."

The members of the group began to laugh at the expression on her face.

"She's got you there, Benen."  Doc reached to wipe tears of laughter from his face.  "She really does have you, doesn't she?"

Benen reached to hug her, dropping a kiss on her cheek.  "You always did, darling.  You always did."  His voice was low enough that only she could hear him, causing her to stare at him in wonder.

———

Barnabas was on a search. He needed to talk to both Benen and Cadee and could find neither one. He stood in the lobby of the building, rubbing at his cheek, looking around before finally heading outside, shrugging into his jacket. It's winter, he thought, but not cold. It feels more like early spring than mid-December. He paused, knowing Christmas was coming, but with Benen in whatever it was he was involved with, he wasn't sure how to plan the usual Christmas dinner. He would leave it to Amy and Anna, making sure that Berneen and Cadee were involved in the planning if that was what they wanted to do.

He searched the buildings outside, not finding them before he headed to the large building that housed the gym. He knew Benen liked to work out, but wasn't sure about Cadee. He stopped, realizing he knew very little about her after all.

He cracked the door open, hearing the sound of equipment in use and laughter, both men and women. He stepped through the door, finding Berneen and Cadee walking the track, the men on the equipment, Berneen's teasing voice raised to be heard over the sounds. He stood for a moment, watching before Berneen saw him and waved.

Benen sat up on the weight bench he had been laying on, Brady spotting him, before he rose, reaching for a towel and then heading for Cadee, his hand coming out automatically to take hers before he walked towards Barnabas.

"Barnabas? You looking for us?" Benen's voice was quiet, holding questions he didn't voice.

"I am, Benen. Are you tied up for the next couple of hours?"

Benen glanced at his watch. "Not until about 11. Then I have to call a client." He pushed open the door. "Let me change and I'll meet you there. Cadee?"

"I'm fine. Hurry. I think Barnabas is in a rush."

The two men stared at her until they saw the sparkle of mirth in her eyes and began to laugh, walking quickly to the main building.

Cadee wandered the conference room, stopping in front of the objects still sitting on the table. She hesitated once more as she searched them, reaching for a small clay box, a frown on her face.

Barnabas looked up from where he was sitting, then rose, walking to stand beside her.

"You seem fascinated by this box." He pointed at it.

"I am. I don't remember that I've seen it before. It's not something Mom or Dad would have had." She reached to remove the lid, Barnabas' hand stopping her.

"I think we'll have someone look at that before you open it." He looked around, finding a large manila envelope and gently removing the box from her hand and inserting into the envelope. "I have a friend who can look at that for you." He wrote on the envelope, before he clicked his pen closed and set it down. "Cadee? How are you doing? Really?"

She shrugged, turning to watch the door, wanting Benen there. She wasn't comfortable talking to Barnabas, and she just didn't know why.

"I'm not sure. I just want my parents here." She saw Benen heading her way, and sighed. This was not how she pictured being married, not as a newlywed, anyway.

Benen paused for a moment, his arm around Cadee, a question on his face.

"Cadee found a small box she didn't recognize. I'm sending it to a friend to have them take a look at it." Barnabas pointed to where he had been sitting. "Let's sit. Brenden and Brandon will be here in just a few moments."

"They have news?" Benen sat into a chair beside Cadee, hope on his face.

"I'm not sure. They got in late Saturday and wanted time to go over what they found before they spoke with you two." He looked down at his notes. "Cadee, have you thought of anything or anyone at all that you could name, tell us about?"

———

She shook her head, then paused, a frown on her face. "About six or seven weeks ago, there was a letter that came to Dad, from somewhere in that country. He was with me when the mail came and took it from me before I could open it. He was really quiet and withdrawn for a few days after that."

"Did he say what it was about?" Barnabas shared a look with Benen.

"No, he didn't." She rubbed a finger along the edge of the table. "That's when he started talking of taking a furlough. I didn't think he meant it."

Benen's face was thoughtful, Barnabas watching him closely.

"Benen?"

Benen shook his head, bringing himself back to the present. "That's when he wrote to me, Barnabas, asking if I could come down there." A pained look crossed his face even as Cadee turned to look up at him. "He knew, Cadee. He knew then what he would ask of us. He knew I wouldn't and couldn't say no to coming and seeing all of you."

Cadee sat back, her hand going to her mouth, distress on her face. "Dad planned this? He planned for us to marry?" Her head shaking in denial, she turned, ready to rise and run, when Benen spoke.

"He did, Cadee. I am sure he did. You're his little girl, his daughter. No matter that you are a grown woman, he was still that worried about you. He could have chosen anyone. He could have taken a chance and sent you home on your own or with your mother. He was that scared. I saw it. I didn't know why and he wouldn't say."

"But it's not fair to you, Benen. You should have been able to choose your own wife."

Barnabas watched the two closely, not sure if he should leave and let them work it out on their own, or stay and support them. He made to shove his chair back, pausing as Benen spoke.

"I did, Cadee, my darling. I did. I could have said no, but I didn't." His heart was in his eyes as she turned, her eyes on him, wonder growing on her face. "We'll talk, my darling. We'll talk.

———

Your Dad knew, I think.  Right now, you need to digest what you've learned, and I think Barnabas has things he needs to talk to us about."

Barnabas stared down at the papers in front of him, conflicted for a moment, his head raising as the door opened and Brenden and Brandon entered, dropping their files on the table before heading to grab mugs of coffee for themselves, and the others as well, setting a cup of tea in front of Cadee, before sliding into chairs opposite the young couple.

"Barnabas? I think we need to pray and pray earnestly right now." Brenden's voice was tired and they could see the lines of fatigue in his face.

"Not a problem. I would have, anyway."

Once they had raised their heads again, Brenden's gaze was on Cadee, who hadn't look up, her thoughts far away, or as far away as the man sitting beside her, his hand on hers, clasping hers tightly. She hadn't known how he felt and to hear him voice what he had, it had shaken her,

"Cadee? Brenden needs to talk to you." Benen's words caught her attention and she looked up and across the table.

"Brenden?"

"Cadee, we did find your parents. They had hidden themselves away." He watched with compassion as she turned to Benen, her arms around him, hiding her face against him as she wept. He blinked back tears from his own eyes as he suspected the rest of them were also doing. He rose, heading for the bathroom off the room and returning with a warm damp cloth he handed to Benen.

She finally raised her head. "They're safe? They're okay?" Hope rose in her face.

"They are." He looked down for a moment before he looked up at her, hoping to reassure her. "They were followed from their home and had to make some quick decisions. They took the bus, but got off before they reached their destination, hoping to avoid being seen. They found a friend who has them safe, setting them to watch for someone looking for them. They found us. We have spoken with that person, but not them.  We didn't think it safe for them to do so."  He paused to let her compose herself.  "That person had a letter from them for you."

Cadee watched as the envelope was pushed across the table to her, her hand resting on it, before she looked up.

"They're okay?"  She repeated herself, needing that reassurance.

"For now, they are.  We've sent word we'll get them out.  We're working on a time frame for that."  Brandon looked at Barnabas.  "Barnabas, we'll need Andy."

"That's a given.  We'll talk."  Barnabas looked down at his notes.  "Were you able to find out any information on who or why?"

"The person we talked to didn't give us any information but from what they didn't say, your father knows, Cadee.  And this person not named is very dangerous and has a far reach.  He is concerned about your safety even here, and that of Benen, and then the rest of us."  Brandon sat back, his eyes on Benen, watching the emotions roil over his face.

"I figured that out.  What else?"  Cadee didn't take her eyes from the men across from her.

"He may have said something in that letter. That was the impression we were given.  As to getting them out, we'll receive a text message when it's the right time."  Brenden paused and pulled out his phone, a soft groan rising from him, as he read the message.  "Barnabas, we need to head back today.  Is Andy available?"

"He is.  He's hanging around all day, suspecting this."  Barnabas nodded at the two.  "Just you two or do you want others?"

"I think just us."  Brenden looked over at Cadee.  "I'm sorry, Cadee.  We need to leave now.  I wish I could stay and help relieve your worries."

She nodded before her eyes dropped to the envelope.  "Barnabas?  You said you needed to talk to us."

"I do, Cadee.  It won't take long."  He sighed to himself, not sure how to proceed given what had just happened.  "It was about your parents.  It seems that the mission they were out with has been taken over without any of the donors being aware of it. All the missionaries, except your parents, have been recalled in the last two months and told the mission is folding. Your parents were the only ones not told. They were led to believe there was nothing wrong, that it was business as usual."

Benen's hand tightened on Cadee. "Then, who are they after? Cadee or her parents?"

"Cadee. We need to find out why. And we need to come up with a plan for protecting her." Barnabas raised his hand as she went to protest. "You're family now, Cadee. We take care of our family. Your parents are as well. The guys will bring them here. Anna and Amy will set up an apartment for them to use. Is this what you want, to have them here?"

Overcome with her emotions and unable to speak, Cadee simply nodded. She rose abruptly, her letter in her hand, and almost ran from the room, Benen standing and staring after her.

"She'll be okay, Benen. Go to her." Barnabas stood as well.

Benen shook his head. "She needs a few minutes. She always does if her emotions get the better of her." He looked down at the fingers he was rubbing together, his thoughts muddled.

"Did you mean that?" Barnabas' quiet question raised Benen's head to watch his friend.

"Mean what?"

"What you told her. That you had made your own choice."

Benen nodded, a softened look coming over his face. "I did and I do. She's always been the one. I never saw the other girls, just her. I think that's why I kept in touch with her parents, not her. I was planning on going down there on my next vacation in the summer. I just didn't plan on this."

Barnabas laughed. "No, I don't think you did, but God did. He knew she needed someone to protect her. And that someone had to be a person she knows well. You are he, Benen."

Cadee pushed the envelope around on the kitchen table, not willing to open it but also not willing to set it aside. She was torn and conflicted by her emotions. Knowing that the guys were heading back down to find her parents and bring them home added to the mix. She knew Benen had returned, he had stopped, a hand on her shoulder, a kiss on the top of her head before he walked away and to his office.

She grabbed the envelope up quickly and ran to find him, halting in his office doorway as he sat, watching that very spot, hoping and praying that she would come to him. He rose, his arms open to wrap her into a hug as she threw herself at him.

He drew her down with him on the couch he had in the office, an arm around her.

"Cadee?"

"I can't open this, Benen. Why not?" She shoved the letter at him. "You do it."

"You're sure?"

She nodded. "Please. I need you to read it first."

He nodded, his finger finding the flap to unseal the letter, pulling out the folded paper, and frowned. "Your Dad didn't write much, Cadee. There's only one sheet and that is only used on one side."

She gave a small smile. "Dad has become very concise lately, only saying what he really needs to." She pointed at it. "Aren't you going to read it?"

"I will." He unfolded the paper and scanned it, his face paling as he did so.

"Benen? You went white. What did Dad say?" She reached for the letter as he moved it away from her.

"Cadee, your Dad has basically said what Brenden said.  He doesn't know the name of the man who has put out the contract on you.  He is working on that. He has an idea but needs to be back here to find out more information.  He thinks the man is connected with the mission and from this province."

"That's not good.  He didn't say who?"

"No.  It seems as if he knows but doesn't want to tell you.  Not yet.  He said he would talk to you when he saw you."

She reached again for the letter, reading it before she frowned and then read it aloud.

"Cadee, girl

"Your life is still at risk.  You need to take extra precautions.  Stay close to Benin.  He will keep you safe.

"Your mother and I are on our way back, but the man looking for you is in Ontario.  I won't give his name until we see you and even then I am not sure of it.  He may be connected with the mission.

"Father."

She frowned once more.  "That's not Dad's handwriting.  It's close but it's not.  And he never calls me girl, or refers to Mom as mother or himself as father."  She looked up at Benen.  "And your name is spelt wrong.  This is bizarre."

Benen took the letter from her.  "That's that then, isn't it?"  He reached for his phone he had set on the table in front of him.  "I need to alert Barnabas."

Barnabas sat back in his chair, his eyes on the couple, before he reached for his own phone.  He had been on his way to their apartment when Benen had called.

"Brenden?  Where are you ?  About halfway, you say?  Cadee and Benen read the letter.  It's not from her father.  What's that? You know?  How?  Okay.  What was that?"  Barnabas' eyes were on Cadee as he listened.  "You're landing when?  No, that's fine.  We'll see you when you get back."

Barnabas pocketed his phone, deep in thought, his eyes on the floor, before he looked over at Cadee.

———

"Brenden and Brandon are on their way back. They went to where they had found out your parents were at. They had already left. Apparently someone found them and they ran. Brenden's not able to say where they are."

Cadee leaned against Benen, feeling his arm tighten around her. "So, where are they?"

"That we don't know. Brenden and Brandon are working on that. Andy's been stopping at out of the way airports for them to search. If they find them, they'll bring them with them." He watched Benen closely. "They won't be in until late tonight or early tomorrow morning."

"Have they any idea where Mom and Dad are?" Cadee was desperate for news on her parents.

"No, but he says they seem to be moving fast. He suspects they have help." He looked at Benen. "In fact, he seemed to think they may have found a flight."

Benen nodded. "I would suspect that. But does it land in Canada or the United States?"

"I would say the States, as near to the border as they could get."

Hearing her name called, Cadee spun the next morning as she walked through the lobby with Benen, intent on heading out to town. She stopped, her hands on her mouth, and then she was running across the lobby, to throw herself into the arms of the woman who stood there, the man with her wrapping both women into a hug. Benen stood in shock and was then across the lobby, his hand out to shake the man's. Brandon and Brenden entered behind them, standing just inside the door, fatigue evident in their stance and on their faces, dropping their duffle bags to the floor.

"Mom! Dad! How?" Cadee looked around her mother towards the two men and then ran to hug them as well. "Brandon? Brenden? You found them?"

"Not really. It's more like they found us. They were at the airport when we landed, not sure where to head from there. I think they have quite a story to tell, but they need to rest first." Brandon turned her back towards her parents. "We'll talk, Cadee. Benen. Right now, these two people need to find somewhere to rest and also find some food."

Cadee's arm around her mother, she led her to the elevator, hearing her father's footsteps beside her, and then Benen's rapid steps as he hastened to catch up with them. She searched her parents' faces, seeing the deep-rooted fatigue in them and also the worry in their eyes. Why, Lord? What did they go through that You protected them from?

Hearing Ted talking with Benen in the kitchen, she led her mother to the spare room, taking a deep breath.

"You two can have this room." She rushed to gather her belongings, almost running to dump them into the master bedroom. "It's fine, Mom." Her words were low as her mother went to protest. "It's just for now. Barnabas said they'd arrange an apartment here for you."

Mary stopped her daughter with a hand to her back. "Cadee?"

Cadee shook her head. "It's okay, Mom. We're talking." She turned her face to her mother, a slight smile on it. "It's okay. He told me I was his choice all along."

Mary breathed a sigh of relief, glad that at least one thing in her daughter's life was going as it should. "He always did, Cadee. I could see it in how he looked at you and treasured you. So could your father. Ted told me that's the only reason he asked that of him, suspecting how he felt. And I know from watching you that he's the only one for you."

Cadee gave a slow nod before she hugged her mother. "We'll need to talk. Let's get some food into you two and then you sleep. You'll need it. Tomorrow is sufficient to find out what happened."

"Actually, Cadee, it's not, but it will have to be." Her father's voice had her spinning to face the doorway, seeing the distress on his face and the fear in Benen's eyes.

"Dad?" Cadee moved towards him, finding herself wrapped into his hug, before he turned her towards Benen.

"Let your Mom and I sleep for a bit. We need it. We're not thinking clearly right now." He nodded towards Benen. "Go on with what you had planned for the day. Benen said he'd talk to Barnabas and see if we can meet in the morning. It will take a while to tell our tale."

Benen led Cadee towards the outside door, her hand tight in his. "He's right, darling. Let them sleep. We'll have a chance to talk."

He paused their walk through the lobby, his eyes on Barnabas and Breck as they walked towards them.

"Benen?" Breck's voice was hopeful.

"They're getting ready to settle down and sleep. They've asked if we can meet tomorrow."

Barnabas and Breck exchanged glances, having already spoken with Brenden and Brandon.

"That shouldn't be a problem. I'll call a full meeting of all the guys. They need to hear firsthand what's going on." Breck spoke up. "Cadee, is there anything your parents need today?"

She shrugged.  "I have no idea.  I didn't see any luggage with them."

"There wasn't."  Breck shared a look with Benen.  "Brandon said they had nothing with them."

"Then, I'll need to shop for them, to get them some things."  Cadee chewed at her bottom lip, deep in thought, not seeing the looks exchanged between the three men.  She looked up, a frown on her face.  "Benen?"

"We'll get the basics for them.  Then, you and your Mom can go shopping."

Benen paced the conference room the next morning, his hands dug into his jeans pockets, his thoughts miles away. Some of the other men were already there, and he vaguely heard conversation and laughter around him. He finally paused behind the chair he had chosen, not wanting to sit until Cadee showed up, not really wanting to get the meeting underway, but he knew they needed to. They needed to heard what her parents had to say. That, he knew, would likely change everything. That scared him. He feared for Cadee's life.

He turned as he heard his name called and Ted walked towards him.

"Benen? We can't thank you enough for getting Cadee out when you did." Ted was agitated and Benen tilted his head, a frown on his face.

"Ted?"

Ted shook his head. "Cadee doesn't know yet, but the home we had down there was burned down the night after you two left."

Benen froze, his eyes on Ted, hearing the noise of conversation die away around him. "It was?" He rubbed at his head. "Then, if we hadn't left, we may not be here. Is that what you're saying?"

Ted shrugged. "It's impossible to know. A friend is quietly looking into it." He paused, his head turning to where he heard the women's voices approaching the room. "There's more. Dear Lord, I can't share it with Cadee, but I must. He's the only One who can truly protect her."

Cadee slipped into the chair Benen pulled out for her, suddenly shy. They had had words the night before and she knew she had to apologize to him. He had told her to take the bed, he would sleep in his office on the couch. She had protested, her hands folding the sweater he had picked out for her, placing it in one spot before she picked it up and repeated the process.

Benen had stood, his heart breaking for his bride, a prayer in it as well for patience, before he shoved away from the door he was leaning on and reaching to take her hands, stilling the movement, telling her it was okay, he had slept there before. It would be for one night, and he was fine with that. He had hugged her, dropped a kiss on the top of her head, murmured a prayer, and then walking to the door, opened it, hesitated a moment, before he walked out of the room, closing the door softly behind him. She didn't know that he had stood for moments outside the room, a prayer lifting to heaven before he could no longer utter any words, knowing that God understood his heart.

Benen scooted his chair into the table, his hand reaching for Cadee's, feeling the chilliness on it, and turned his head to watch her face. She's scared, Lord, and I don't want that for her. I want her at peace and happy. Please, dear Lord? Can we solve this and soon?

Barnabas looked around at the thirteen of his men sitting there, stern, sober looks on their faces before he looked at Ted and Mary, seeing the fatigue and worry and strain on their faces. His eyes then moved to Cadee and stopped, a frown appearing on his face. She was lost in thought and he needed her attention. He sighed. She was not an easy person to read, after all, and he would need to rely on Benen for that.

He cleared his throat, bringing all eyes to him, before he looked at Ted.

"Ted? Will you open our time of prayer? When we gather like this, we spend time in prayer, praying for one another and then the situation we find. Now that two of our men are married, their wives have become part of that prayer time." He smiled briefly at Cadee as she looked at him, wonder on her face, her mouth rounded as she took in what he said.

"That I will, Barnabas. I count it a privilege to do so." He looked around at the men, whose attention was focused on him. "You have all been prayed for over the many years that I have known of you. " He bowed his head, his throat working as he controlled his emotions, before his mouth opened and he prayed.

Barnabas finally raised his head, his eyes once more on Cadee, before moving to Benen and then her parents, knowing that when

Ted spoke, everything changed. He shared a look with Breck, who had been researching the Daniells, finding something in their past that needed to be addressed and he wasn't quite sure how to do that. He needed to talk to Benen alone first. Breck nodded, knowing that Barnabas had made his decision about that.

"Ted?" Barnabas turned to him, finding Ted studying him closely. "We need to hear your story."

"That you do. And to do that, I think we'll need to go back a few years. Something happened a number of years ago that I am just now realizing does have an impact on what we faced." He turned to Cadee. "I'm so sorry, Cadee. If I had known back then what I know now, your life today would be different."

Cadee stared at her father, her mouth opening and closing. "Dad? What are you talking about?"

He sighed, reaching for Mary's hand, feeling hers tighten on his, aware that she knew just what he was talking about.

"It's like this, Cadee. God help us, we never meant to keep it a secret." His head bowed, Mary's arm around him.

"Mom? Dad? You're scaring me! What are you talking about?" Cadee's voice rose in fear, Benen's arm around her the only thing keeping her in her place. "Benen? Do you know?"

He shook his head. "No, Cadee darling. I don't." He watched with concern as Ted struggled to control his emotions.

"It's like this, Cadee." Ted looked at his daughter, sorrow on his face. "You're not our own. We adopted you when you were a week old. We should have told you years ago but we kept putting it off. Now, we have to bear the consequences of that."

There was dead silence in the room at his confession, the men exchanging glances, Breck's eyes on Benen, sorrow in them for his friend and his bride.

Cadee's head began to shake and they could see the dismay, distress, confusion on her face before she was on her feet running from the room, Benen on her heels, trying to catch up to her. Ted rose, staring after them, Mary's hand on his arm keeping him in place.

Buckley was on his feet as was Brady, following the two, knowing they were not safe. They searched for the two, finding Benen standing in the parking lot, staring around.

"Benen? Where's Cadee?" Brady slid to a stop, Buckley heading away from them.

"I have no idea. She was ahead of me and then just disappeared." Benen spun in a circle, not sure where she had got to. "She can't be far, but I need to find her."

The two men spun as they heard the roaring of a motor, Benen shoving Brady to one side as the van clipped him, sending him flying towards a snowbank that he landed awkwardly in, before laying still. The van doors flew open, and men approached both Benen and Brady, weapons pointing at them. Brady's hands raised and then he was roughly shoved into the van, watching helplessly as Benen was dragged to the van and dumped into it, the men following, doors slamming shut as the van sped away, leaving the men who had ran for the outside staring in dismay after it.

Barnabas ran for his vehicle, Brandon beside him, calling orders to the other men, who scattered, some to stay with Ted and Mary, the others to search for Cadee and Buckley. He shoved the truck into gear and sped away, searching desperately for the van, finally slowing as he reached town.

"I don't see it, Brandon. It couldn't have gotten that much of a start on us." His head swiveled as he searched.

"It didn't. They took a side road, likely the first one near our place. They would have been out of sight before we even hit the main road." Brandon turned in his seat, looking behind them before he pulled out his phone and made the call he didn't want to make. He pocketed his phone when he was finished. "There are officers responding."

"Good. Let's go back to that road and see if we can figure out which way they took. Were either of the men hurt, do you know?"

"I think Benen. I saw him shove Brady to one side before he was clipped by the van. The van blocked my view after that." His closed fist hit the door. "How did they know? How did they know they would come out at that particular time?"

"They've been watching. The security people said there have been different vehicles driving around the place on the roads. Not one that they can pinpoint as to being a problem." Barnabas' fingers on his left hand tapped at the wheel even as his eyes kept moving, desperate to find the van. "I have no idea where Cadee disappeared to. Do you?"

Brandon shook his head. "I don't. I would suspect Buckley went after her when Brady went after Benen."

Shutting his door carefully, Barnabas studied the activity going on, waiting at Breck approached.

"Breck? Any word?"

Breck shook his head. "Buckley found Cadee and she's in your office. We've kept her separate from her parents. Anna has a place ready for them, and they've agreed to move there. I'm sending Berneen and Baird in to shop for them as soon as we've been cleared to some extent." He looked around, the activity disturbing to him. "Any sign of our guys?"

"Not a one. We think they took the first road but with all the traffic that has come in since then, we can't get a sense of which way they turned." Barnabas walked towards the police chief who had responded.

"Will?" Barnabas' hand was out to shake the older man's, a friend of his father.

Will Peters shook his head. "Barnabas, what happened? You and I spoke last night. I would not have thought this could happen."

"There was a development this morning that shook Cadee's world and she ran, Benen after her. She was told she had been adopted at one week of age and she never knew this."

Will stared at him, his eyes narrowing. "And this just opens up a new game, doesn't it?" He shook his head. "We'll need to talk to her parents, as well as to her."

"We've Cadee in my office. Would you talk to her?"

"I can do that. Her parents?"

"Anna's put them into the guest suite on the main floor for now. I'm not sure how long they'll stay, given this. They have caused a whole lot of hurt to a young lady I cherish as a friend."

"They have." Will turned to walk with Barnabas towards the building. "Were either of your men hurt?"

"We think Benen. Brandon said he saw him clipped by the van but we can't be sure of that."

Will nodded, his hand on the door to open it. "Is there someone who can be with Cadee?"

"Berneen and Baird are. Anna is looking after her parents. Amy's away today - she had planned a trip with her husband." Barnabas hesitated at the office door, his hand on the handle. "Will, we need to activate the prayer change."

———

"Already done.  I called Jace first thing."

"Thanks."  He still hesitated before he opened the door, walking into his office, hearing soft voices from his office, stopping as he saw Cadee almost running his way, his arms coming out to hug her.

"Barnabas?"  Her voice was full of emotion as was the face she tilted back to him.

An arm around her, he turned her back to the office.  "No word.  It's too soon.  We're looking, Cadee.  We'll find him for you."

She nodded even as she sat back down into her chair, her hands rubbing along her jeans.  "I know you'll do your best."

"We'll do more than our best."  He perched on the corner of his desk, glancing quickly at Berneen and Baird.  "Will Peters is the police chief of our town, Cadee.  He needs to talk to you."

She nodded, not taking her eyes from Barnabas.  "Mom and Dad?"  She dropped her face to her hands.  "How do I call them that, given what they have hidden?"

"They're still your parents, who love you deeply, Cadee.  They didn't make the decision lightly not to tell you.  There has to be a reason they didn't."

"I know, but that doesn't find Benen, does it?"  She rose and was gone once more before they could stop her.

Berneen was on her feet, running after her friend, finding her standing in the lobby.  Her arm around her, she drew her to the elevator.

"Come, Cadee.  Come to our place.  Baird will find us."  She looked over her shoulder to see Baird and Barnabas standing there, Will behind them.  "You need to get out of here.  It's too open."

Cadee stopped, bringing Berneen to a halt as well.  "No, I need to talk to them.  I can't keep running.  This doesn't solve anything."  She turned, finding the men behind her.  "Oh!"

"Berneen's right, Cadee."  Baird spoke.  "We'll go up to our place.  That way, Berneen will feed us.  We all need to eat."

Cadee shook her head.  "I can't."

"You need to, Cadee."  Will spoke up, years of experience behind his words.  "I think Benen would want you to.  Even just some soup."

She finally nodded, her hands reaching out to help Berneen, her mind not on what she was doing.  Her thoughts drifted to what her parents had said, and her movements stopped, knowing she needed to confront them, but unwilling to do so without Benen.  He was her support, her life, she thought.  She needed him here with her, now.

Cadee's thoughts drifted, the hum of conversation and activity around her fading as she returned to a few hours previously.

She had awakened that morning, was it only that morning, she thought, her arms wrapped around Benen's pillow. She shoved back her hair, and sat up, staring around the room, not sure where she was for a moment before she quickly slipped in for a shower and dressed rapidly, knowing Benen would need the room. She had quietly made her way to the kitchen, Benen soon there to help her.

They had eaten, she remembered, with not much conversation between then, her father shooting her glances she couldn't understand. They had walked down together to the conference room, she and her parents, finding seats before Barnabas started the meeting.

She couldn't remember now what she had said as her parents had told her that she was adopted. She had sprung from her chair, running from the room, shock on her face, sorrow deep in her heart. She heard Benen calling for her and had dodged out the door and around the side of the building, taking the walk that led to the garden area. She had hidden, her face covered with her arms as she waited, knowing he would find her, not willing to look up and around. She had heard the squealing of tires and then shouts from the men before she heard another vehicle leave. She crouched down even further before she jumped, feeling a hand on her arm, raising her to her feet.

She looked up, afraid, the fear dissipating as she saw Buckley, his face grim as he studied her before his head turned towards the commotion that they could both hear. He hustled her into a back door and then to Barnabas' office, shoving open the door and then seating her into a chair in the office itself, leaving and returning with a bottle of water he commanded her to drink.

She had glared at him, seeing the amusement lurking in his eyes before she had drunk, not hearing the quiet footsteps that had approached the door, just seeing Buckley step away for a moment before she was on her feet, facing the door, seeing Baird and

Berneen there, speaking quietly with Buckley before Berneen approached her.

"Cadee? You're okay?" Berneen reached to hug her, before she stood back, searching her face.

"No, I don't think I am. Where's Benen?" Her eyes flickered between the three of them before her head began to shake. "No! Where is he?"

"We don't know, Cadee. That noise you heard? He and Brady disappeared into a van and then the van disappeared. We're looking for them."

She shook her head, sinking back into her chair, her hand out to feel for the arm, eyes huge with fear.

"No, it can't be. He's here. He'll be here. I know he's here somewhere."

Buckley crouched down beside her, his hand on hers to still the motion. "I'm sorry, Cadee. He's not."

"He's not?" Her voice was broken, low, as she responded, seeing his head shaking. "Where is he?"

"We don't know. The guys are searching. The police are here."

"It's their fault."

"Whose?" Baird took the seat beside her, his eyes on her face, a frown in place.

"My parents. Or the couple that says they are." She slumped back in her seat, her hands rubbing at her face, tears she refused to shed shining in her eyes. "They did this."

"I don't know if they did, Cadee, but we'll talk with them. Bradon was making that his task. Do you want them to come here?"

She shook her head. "No, not right now. I need to sort through my thoughts, and I can't. Not with Benen missing." She was on her feet, pacing before she spun, her eyes on Buckley. "Buckley, what does God say?"

"That He loves you dearly. That He is here, no matter what you are facing. That He will protect Benen and Brady. That He knows what you are going through and is there, each step of the way. He has promised never to leave you, never to forsake you, to hide you in the hollow of His hand and cover you there."

She had listened soberly, her body relaxing as she heard his words. "He is. He is here." Her voice was very low, low enough the ones with her had to strain to hear them. "And he's with Benen. With Brady." She returned to her chair, reaching for the bottle of water, stopping to frown at it. "Berneen, there's something about a water bottle that I need to remember and I can't. What is it?"

Baird's hand was there, taking the bottle from her. "It will come. Let it rest. God will recall it to your memory when you need it. How about a cup of tea instead?"

"Do you have any juice, do you think? Orange juice sounds good." She sank back, her eyes closing, her face white, dark shadows under her eyes. She had not yet fully recovered from her poisoning and today she felt old, ancient, beyond a count of years. Her body ached as did her heart. Her head was pounding and she jumped as she felt a hand touch her. Her eyes opened, to find Berneen in Baird's chair, painkillers in her open hand. She stared at them before she took them, knowing she couldn't fight the headache or the pain wafting through her on her own.

Barnabas crouched down beside her, speaking to her. She looked around, finally just overcome with it all and just ran, stopping in the lobby, afraid to go outside, afraid to go back, just afraid. Too afraid to even pray.

Cadee finally came back to the room she was in, her mind telling her it was time to pay attention to the conversation around her. She looked down at the table where she was sitting and the empty bowl in front of her. She had not even been aware that she had eaten. She sighed, the sigh welling from deep within her, not allowed to vocalize.

Barnabas had been watching her, knowing that she was sorrowing in more than one way, but not knowing how to help her. That frustrated him.

Berneen rested her arm around Cadee. "Cadee? You did eat some soup, but do you want anything more?"

Cadee shook her head, finally raising it to look for Barnabas, finding him sitting beside her.

He grinned at her momentary look of discomfort. "Didn't know I was that close?" He laughed and the sobered. "We do need to talk, Cadee. Will wants to go over what they're doing to find Benen and Brady."

She looked across the table at Will, finding his kindly eyes on her. "I'm sorry. I wasn't nice to you before."

Will shrugged. "I've had way worse. Don't worry about it. But Barnabas is right. We do need to talk." He shoved aside his plate, reaching for his cup and drinking from it before he put it back down, his hands cradling it. "Cadee, we are doing our best to find them. I have patrol officers scouring the surrounding neighbours, going door to door, working their way out in an ever-increasing circle. We will find them, make no doubt about that."

"Will they be alive?" Her words were barely above a whisper.

Will shrugged. "We pray they are. It would be my guess they will be. Benen was taken for a reason and that reason seems to be you. Brady is incidental to that." He shared a look with Barnabas. "It is my guess that whoever was with him would have been taken.

The good thing is that Brady is a paramedic, that if Benen is hurt, he can treat him as best he can.”

“Are they together?  You are sure of that?”  Cadee voiced the question they all had been hesitant to.

“We have no reason to think they’re not.  In fact, I would suspect they will keep them together and use one against the other.”  Will smiled grimly as her face paled at his words.  “I will not mince words with you, Cadee.  I understand you like to be told what’s going on.  I would feel the same in your case.”

She nodded, a frown on her face.  “Why did they taken Benen?  I was out there and hidden until Buckley found me.”

“We know that.  We think he was taken to use against you.”  Will watched as she swayed, Berneen’s arm around her.  “That’s how they seem to be working.”  He looked up as he heard a tap at the door and then excused himself as Baird reappeared, beckoning for him.

Cadee looked around, knowing she was surrounded by friends, something she had missed for so many years, not having them down where her parents had served.

“Barnabas, what about the mission?”

“What about it?”  His voice was quiet, controlled, not showing the anger he was feeling, anger he would need to deal with.  Right now, his focus was on the young woman sitting beside him, and finding both Benen and Brady.

“The mission.  Was it ever legitimate?”  She heard the others gasp at her words but not Barnabas.  “It wasn’t, was it?”

“Our Foundation researched it before we became supporters.  It was up until about two months ago, about the time your father received that letter.  From what we can understand, it was taken over, a hostile takeover if you want to term it that way.  The other missionaries out with it were told to come home, the mission was closing.  Supporters were notified.  We only received notification this past week.  They delayed it, knowing we would launch a full investigation, which we have done.  Breck is working on that, and he’s not happy, to say the least, with what he’s finding.”

She nodded.  "And you need to talk with Dad and Mom."  She paused, biting at her lip, fighting back tears.  "This has been a horrible day.  How do I talk to them?"

Barnabas shook his head.  "None of us can tell you that.  We will pray with you.  We will pray with them.  Buckley is willing to sit in as your pastor, if you want.  Anna and Doc have both come to me, saying they want to be there.  Doc in particular is concerned as you have never fully healed yet from what you went through.  If it helps, any one of us will be there.  All of us if that's what you want.  Berneen has specifically asked to sit with you."

Cadee's eyes searched the faces in the room, seeing only love and concern, not the condemnation she expected to see.  She finally nodded.

"Tomorrow?  I can't today."  She shoved back from the table and walked away.  They heard the outside door open and close.

Berneen was on her feet, following, watching as Cadee stood outside their apartment door, her hand on the knob before she twisted it and walked in, shutting out her friend and shutting out the world.

Cadee slowly slid down the door to sit in a crumpled heap against it, tears she didn't know she was shedding on her face, before she was on her feet, running for the bedroom, throwing herself down on the bed, her arms wrapping around Benen's robe that he had thrown carelessly on it that morning, sobs finally shaking her body.  Her sobs spent, she slept.  Unable even to pray, her sobs wafted to God as those very prayers.

———

Rousing slowly the next morning, Cadee raised her head, not aware of where she was for a moment. Her arms tightened for a moment on Benen's robe before she set it aside and rose, heading for a shower, finding clean clothes and then making her way to the kitchen. She stood, fridge door open, not wanting to eat, but knowing that she had to. Squinting as she looked at the clock, she sighed. It was late, later than she thought.

She turned as she heard a tap at the door and cautiously made her way to it, peeking through the pinhole, before she stepped back, pulling the door open, letting Berneen and Anna enter.

Anna took one look at her young friend and simply swept her into a hug, holding her as she shuddered with her intense emotions. Berneen stood, her hand rubbing Cadee's back before she moved away, heading for the kitchen.

"Have you eaten yet, Cadee?"

Cadee turned at Berneen's words. "No. I just got up. I never sleep this late." She yawned as she slumped down into a chair, watching as Anna reached for the tea kettle and the tea and Berneen reached for bread.

"French toast coming up. We haven't eaten either."

Conversation was quiet among the three women as they ate. Cadee finally rose as she heard a knock at the door, stepping back to let Barnabas and Bradon enter, pointing to the kitchen.

"There's coffee. I made it without thinking." She slid into her chair, staring down at her unfinished breakfast before she pushed it away. "Barnabas? Why are you here?"

He grinned at her from is seat on the other side of the table. "Direct and to the point. I like that about you, Cadee." His smile faded as he sipped at his coffee. "Have you seen your parents since yesterday?"

She shook her head. "No. I need to. Why?"

"Because they're not here."  Shocked silence followed his words.

"They're gone?"  Cadee sat back, thinking through the few hours she had spent with them.  "That wasn't them.  They would have had baggage with them.  There was something off about them all along."  She raised her eyes to Barnabas and Bradon.  "Imposters?  What did they leave here in the apartment?"

"That's what we need to find out.  We're moving you out of here for now until Brandon can do a sweep.  Bradon will bring Kade through as well."  He looked down at their dishes.  "Just leave everything for now.  Grab what you need - your purse, Bible, clothes."

She stared at him for a moment, before she was on her feet, running for the bedroom.  They could hear drawers opening and closing, the sound of hangers hitting the floor, and then her hurried footsteps to the office, before she appeared in the kitchen doorway, a bag in her hand, her jacket on, sneakers on her feet.

"Where am I to go?"

Barnabas held up a hand and simply pointed to the door.  They followed him out and then down to his office, Brandon staying in the apartment.

He spoke on the phone for a while before he turned to Cadee.  "Cadee?"  He slipped into the chair beside her, not moving behind his desk.  "Security shows the couple leaving about two this morning.  They walked out to the road where a car was waiting for them.  We don't have enough information on that car to track it."

She nodded.  "It just didn't seem like them.  They looked like them, sort of sounded like them, but there was something off."

"What do you mean?"

"Just the way they spoke.  It was as if they were playing a part, with a dialogue they had been given."  She looked up at them.  "Dad would have wanted to pray first, and that man didn't.  He just ignored that."  She studied Barnabas.  "You don't know him, so you wouldn't have known."  Her eyes slid shut.  "That's why."

"Why what, Cadee?"  When she didn't respond, Barnabas shared a look with the other two women and then with Breck who had entered silently, closing the door behind him and leaning on it.

"Benen.  That's why he was taken.  He would have known.  I think he did.  I could see him watching them closely, a puzzled look on his face."

Barnabas nodded.  "That's the conclusion we've come to.  Our guys are out there searching, they've taken leave from their employment for now."

"They can't do that!"  Cadee was horrified.

"They can and will.  I think we've talked about this, but The Foundation pays them.  That means I can call on them when I need their help.  Their employers are all hand picked by The Foundation and in agreement with this."

She finally nodded herself.  "I remember."  Her voice was low.  "What about your volunteer activities?"

"They know as well.  Right now, we are searching.  They can't have been taken too far away.  That's a given.  They need to watch you.  You have been shaken by what you were told.  We need to work through that, and we will.  Right now, we need to get you settled into a new place."

"Here?"  Cadee had no hope that it would be and that Benen would never find her

Barnabas nodded again.  "It is.  There is a small suite beside Doc and Anna's and next to mine.  We'll put you there.  It's one that has full security in it.  We've needed it before and likely will again.  For now, it's yours and Benen's, until we find whoever it is that is after you."

She reached to hug him before she rose, Anna's arm around her, before Barnabas stopped her.

"Your things?  Did you notice anything odd about them?"

She shook her head.  "No.  Should I have?"

Barnabas thought for a moment.  "Have Anna look at them.  She knows what to look for.  Who would suspect her of finding something?  Anna, the other office here before you go up."

Two days later, Cadee rose, walking through the small suite. It was smaller than Benen's she knew, with just one bedroom and other rooms. She sighed. She wanted Benen home but then she would have to face her growing feelings for him and right now, that was something she was so unsure of.

She thought of her parents, praying they were still alive, and safe. Lord, protect them, please? I need them. Benen needs them. I feel so bad for Brenden and Brandon. They feel guilty but they would not have known. There is just no way. I think they planned on that, whoever they is.

She paused in the kitchen, her hands automatically reaching to make a cup of tea, her eyes on the window over the sink. She finally turned as she heard a tap at her door, moving that way slowly, feeling beaten up and beaten down.

Baird watched her closely as she moved around the kitchen, not really thinking of what she was doing, before she set a mug of coffee in front of him and pushed over the open cookie jar.

"Anna left some cookies. I am sure they are delicious. I just haven't had an appetite to try them."

"That's understandable." He sipped at his coffee before he replaced his mug on the table and folded his hands. "Cadee, I'm not here by chance. Barnabas asked me to be here with you. Berneen would be but she had a commitment she couldn't get out of. She'll be by later."

She studied him, her eyes narrowing. "This sounds like an all-day babysitting job."

He laughed at her nonsense. "I guess you could say that. Barnabas has to be away with some of the men. The others are here on site."

"And why would he be away?" Hope flared in her eyes. "They've found them?"

"We have a lead on where they may be. Barnabas is going in, taking Bradon and Kade for one, to see if they can really spot them or if it's another false lead. We have been swamped with those as have the police."

"But will that be okay with the police?"

Baird nodded. "Will has gone with them. He said he could do nothing other than that." He paused, gathering his thoughts. "They don't know when they'll be back. Barnabas was hoping by early afternoon, but it depends on what they find."

"I get that." She rubbed at the table, wiping away an imaginary spot. "About that couple?"

"Yes, that couple. Breck has found that they are connected to the takeover of the mission. How he did that, I have no idea, but he found that out. He stated to me that he still had a lot of research to do, but that somehow that couple is connected to your parents. He's shown their photo to some of the other missionaries, ones who know your family. They are adamant that couple are imposters. They have given us some leads to follow to find your parents. One of them has heard from your Dad. They are in the States, making their way slowly this way."

"They're alive?" Cadee's face lit up with joy, hope, and relief. "Oh, thank God. I was so afraid they were dead and buried somewhere I would never find them." She sobered. "Did they leave anything in Benen's?"

"They did. I can't tell you what as the police have now become involved, but yeah, they did. Some of it was down right dangerous. Food stuff that could have killed either one of you. I think that was the plan. Somehow, they are using you and also Benen to try and get at your Dad. That we need to talk to your Dad about."

Baird and Berneen finally left late that evening, leaving Cadee to lock up after them, and then wander the suite, her arms wrapped around herself, not wanting to retire but not wanting to stay up. She was on edge, Baird's words to her earlier puzzling her. What did they want from Dad? And who are they, anyway? Do I know them?

She finally sighed, headed for the bedroom, and then ready for bed, sat for the longest time on the side of her bed, not thinking, not praying, not sure what she should be doing or thinking.  She finally looked up, breathing a prayer that was inaudible but knowing God read her heart and understood her unspoken words, hopes and dreams.

She slept, not hearing the lock click open and closed and then the quiet footsteps heading her way.  She didn't see the tall familiar form that stood staring down at her before he too headed for a shower.  Benen stood once more staring down at her before he crawled in beside her, wrapping his bride in his arms, tears wetting her hair, his words too inaudible to any one but God.

Rousing early the next morning, Cadee felt disoriented for a few moments. She laid still, her senses warning her she was not alone. She slowly opened her eyes, staring at the wall in front on her before she shifted her body, feeling weight on her abdomen. Afraid, she twisted even more, her face coming close to Benen's as he sleep, his body totally relaxed in his fatigue and weariness, his arm anchoring her to him. Her eyes grew round, and she struggled to free an arm, her hand coming up to touch his face before tears clouded her eyes and she wept, her heart raising in praise that he was back. She wiped at her eyes, taking in his face, the changes she could see that hurt her.

She laid back, her hand locked around his arm before she slowly shifted away from him and stood, her eyes on him, then rushing to find her clothes, the bathroom door clicking softly behind her. Once dressed, she stood again, her eyes taking in his face before she stooped, a gentle kiss on his cheek, and then she headed for the kitchen, her eyes squinting at the time. Just after seven. She reached for her phone, hesitating for a moment before she dialled.

A rough voice answered. "Hello?"

"Barnabas?" She was hesitant, it didn't sound like him. "I'm sorry. I woke you up."

"It's okay, Cadee. Are you all right?" She could hear him shifting around.

"What time did you get back?"

"Around midnight. That's after we had them checked out at Emerge. They're okay, Doc said. Tired. Beaten up a bit. Need some food." Barnabas' voice didn't tell everything, and that she knew. She would have to wait.

"Thank you." She set down her phone, staring at it, then spinning in a circle. Anna had made sure to stock their kitchen with essentials as she called them. Cadee stood back in the kitchen doorway, her eyes on the bedroom before her feet took her back that way, finding Benen had arisen as well, the sound of the shower coming to her ears.

She turned once more to the kitchen, knowing she needed to feed him, just not what.  She finally pulled out food, set his coffee, made her tea, and then waited, her arms folded around herself, her eyes staring out the kitchen window.  Lost in thought, she didn't hear Benen approaching the kitchen door, stopping as he saw her there, waiting for him, before he was across the room, enfolding her in his arms, his tears wetting her hair.

She spun, her arms round him as sobs shook her body.  They finally stood back from one another, his hands on her arms, studying her face.

"Benen?  How?"

"God.  That's the only way they found us.  We were hidden quite well.  Somehow, Kade picked up the slight scent and followed it, finding us yesterday afternoon.  It took them a while to reach to us where we were.  And no, they didn't find the men responsible."  He shook his head at her.  "Will, the police chief, will be by later today, he said.  They took our statements yesterday but he wants to talk to us both."

She nodded, before pointing to a chair.  "You need to eat.  We can talk later."  When he didn't release her, she looked up, a puzzled look on her face.  "Benen?"

He simply cupped her cheek, bent and kissed her, a lingering kiss that neither wanted to end.

She stood, her eyes on him when he stepped back, not sure what had happened, only knowing her heart had warmed.

"Benen?"

He turned, a smile just for her on his face, and spoke.  "Cadee, my darling.  I missed you.  We'll talk, my darling.  But first, you've told me I need to eat."

She stared at him, her mouth dropping open until he winked, and then she laughed.

"Benen!  Only you!"

Barnabas studied the two of them later than morning, even as he set his mug down on his desk, and pointed to the chairs near the couch in his office.  He reached for a folder, knowing he needed to break some bad news to Cadee, but not willing to just yet.  He looked up as Will entered followed by Brandon.  He nodded at Will, knowing Will likely had details to hash out with Benen.

Cadee looked up at that point, her face paling at the grim looks on the men's faces, her hands reaching for Benen's.

Benen looked between the three men and sighed. He was still feeling not himself and that he knew would be a while. He reached to wrap an arm around Cadee, pulling her close to him. Barnabas had told him the night before how they had had to move Cadee from his apartment, that Brandon and the police had gone through it, finding dangerous objects planted there. He had stared at Barnabas before he questioned him, learning that the couple was not Cadee's parents after all.

Cadee broke the silence. "Will?"

"Cadee? We have some news. Some good news. Some bad news."

"Good news first, please and thank you. I can use all the good news I can get."

Will laughed at her, the sound breaking the solemnity of the moment. "Well, you will like this. We have found your parents. The real ones, this time. A friend on a force in the States found them at a homeless shelter. I understand Andy is on his way down with Breck to bring them home for you."

She stared at him. "Mom? Dad? You found them? Oh, thank God!"

Will smiled. "That we have. Andy told me they'll likely wait until tomorrow to come back. My friend wants to talk to them, to find out what they can tell them. He said what you're going through sounds too familiar to him."

"You mean, another mission?"

Will nodded. "That's correct. He didn't give a lot of information, so I don't have much to share with you." He looked over at Benen. "Now, for the bad news."

"There's always that, isn't there?" They laughed at Cadee's quiet muttering.

"The couple who were here?  They were found. Unfortunately, we'll not be able to speak with them.  Their bodies washed up on the lakeshore a few miles from here."

Cadee paled.  "Murdered!  How cruel!"

"It is cruel, Cadee, but they would have known that would likely be their fate, if they had really sought about it."  Brandon spoke this time.  "The research we've been doing shows us that it is a very vicious, vindictive, cruel, evil man behind all this.  We don't have the evidence we need at this point to arrest him."

Cadee had been watching him closely, her hand gripping Benen's tightly before she sighed.  "House arrest!  I just know it! We're not going to have any freedom, are we?"

They laughed at her grumbling and at her smirk, knowing she had done that on purpose.

"Seriously, Cadee.  It will seem like that, but we'll let you have as much freedom as we can let you have.  Benen can work from his office here as much as he can.  Now you, what are we to do with you?"  Barnabas shook a finger at you.  "Doc tells me you're not well enough yet to work.  So, tell us.  What do you want to do in the meantime?"

She shrugged.  "All I know is the work from the mission office.  I mean, I did study at college, getting my diploma in music, but I have no idea what to do with that.  I never did.  I'm not sure why I took that."

Benen watched her closely, knowing she was reluctant to say what she had played.  "She plays the violin and viola, Barnabas."

Barnabas sat back, wonder on his face, before he turned to Will.  "Will?"

Will was nodding.  "Just who we need.  Cadee, we'll like to ask something of you, but feel free to say no.  Our youth are putting on a concert this Sunday night.  We had a violinist booked but he fell ill and is unable to make it.  We can manage without one but if you would be willing, we'd appreciate it."

She stared at him, then turned to Benen, finding him watching her closely, knowing without being told he would back whatever decision she made.  "I don't know, Will.  I have no instrument.

Mine disappeared about six weeks ago. We found it shattered in our garden. We have no idea who did that."

Will shared a long look with the other men before he spoke. "Jace."

Barnabas was nodded. "Jace. He'll help."

"Jace? I'm sorry, I don't understand."

"Jace has a music store, Cadee. If he doesn't have an instrument to suit, he will track one down within hours." Benen hugged her tighter. "It's your choice, my darling. We will do what you want."

She sighed, knowing she missed her music. "I would need to see the instrument. But first, what about Benen? Where did you find him?"

Benen's hug tightened even more as he watched her face. "We were about three miles from here, Cadee. Kade found us. It's not going to be easy for you to hear, that much I know."

She nodded, her eyes searching the faces of the men. "I didn't think it would be pretty or easy to hear, but I need to. It's my fault, somehow, that you and Brady were taken."

"That's the interesting part, Cadee. We're not so sure on that any more." Barnabas' words had her eyes on him, puzzlement on her face.

Cadee rose, heading for the coffee pot and refilling their mugs, the kettle whistling softly until she unplugged it and made her tea. She glanced at the clock. Lunchtime, but who felt like eating?

She slid down beside Benen again, feeling his arm around her, her eyes on Barnabas, then Will, and then Brandon.

"Who talks first?"

Barnabas just shook his head. He was beginning to understand Cadee, to some degree, to know how she covered her feelings. This was one way, going on the offensive.

"I will, I guess." Barnabas sipped at his coffee, before sitting back, his mug cradled in his hands. "I have to take you back to the day it happened. You know how we tried to find them. We had suspicions all along that they had simply taken the first road and then disappeared on it. That is exactly what happened. Will's patrol officers finally found the car two days ago, hidden in an abandoned barn."

"Is that the one that's near the lake?" Cadee spoke up. "I saw it one day and wondered about it."

"That's the one." Will took over the conversation. "We had to search a large area around that barn. Kade picked up the scent of one of them and took off, Bradon after him. We lost them for a while but eventually connected. The men were in the basement of an abandoned, collapsed house. Sheltered from the weather for the most part. For some reason, the place was warmer than outside and it shouldn't have been."

"God." Cadee breathed only one word. "God provided and protected."

"That He did, Cadee." Brandon took over now. "We had to crawl to the back of the basement and there was only room for two of us to go in. We found Benen and Brady with their wrists fastened to the wall, unable to move very far. We were able to release them and then send them out one at a time, Burney going first, then

Benen, Brady and lastly myself. We made it out and before we could more than move away, the building finished collapsing. It had only been held up by a few rafters as far as we could see and it appears our going in and out jostled them in some way."

Cadee had paled, her hand gripping Benen's. "Tell me you found some evidence."

They all shook their heads. "We didn't. The men who put them in there were very careful. Both Benen and Baird were unconscious at the time and can tell us nothing of how they were placed in there. We suspect the building wasn't as demolished as we found it. Will has a team going over it now to see what they can find."

Cadee paled even more before her face turned up to Benen. "You never said. How bad?"

"How bad?"

She nodded. "How bad were you hurt?"

He shrugged. "Knocked out. Bumps and bruises. Nothing that will not heal, Cadee." He looked up at Barnabas. "But you have news other than this."

Barnabas nodded, a sigh welling within him that he kept down. "I do and I'm not sure how to even tell you." He held out the folder, Benen hesitant to take it. "It seems as if your past has come back as well."

Benen frowned. "My past? I have no past."

Cadee was staring at him. "Benen? Didn't you say something about a grandfather or an uncle at some point? They were into smuggling."

Benen groaned, his eyes sliding shut. "Great uncle Benjamin. I had forgotten. There were rumours that he was into smuggling, particularly during the Thirties and the Depression, but nothing was ever proven. Dad said he always denied it, but he was never comfortable with that denial. Dad always felt there was a sliver of truth to it." His hand rubbed at his jeans leg, his eyes on the floor. "I don't know if I could ever deny it or prove it, Barnabas."

"Not at this point. But Breck did find some evidence of a link to the mission, a large sum of money given by your Grandmother. It appears it came from your Great uncle. She told the staff there that she had no idea where he got it. They mentioned something about proceeds from smuggling, having heard the rumours but she shook her head at them, according to what was recorded. She states he had received money from his wife's family and that was what they had been living on. When he died, he asked that she give it to someone who needed it. They had no children."

"No, they never did. Uncle Ben was a quiet man, never saying much. He could have been into smuggling or it could have come from his wife's family. How do we prove that as this point?"

"Breck is still looking into that, but he doesn't seem to think he can prove it either, it's been too long." Barnabas sat back, his eyes shifting between Cadee and Benen. "That's not all. The mission you were under, Cadee? I know we've talked about what happened. The board that was there have been let go. The mission is essentially closed. We are still looking into the men who did the takeover. Will seems to think it was done illegally and has asked a detective to investigate."

Will nodded. "It's too big an issue to let go, Cadee. I'm sure you, your parents, and everyone else, including the supporters and sponsors, want answers."

They finally rose, not much further ahead in what they knew or suspected. Cadee felt they were keeping things from her and resented that before she shook her head, knowing they had to. It was a police investigation after all.

Cadee stood again in the kitchen of their suite, listening to Benen and Brandon talk, knowing they would soon head her way. She glanced at the clock, mid afternoon, she thought. None of them had had lunch, too busy talking to remember. She reached for the fridge, pulling open the door, and then closing it. She didn't feel like eating, her stomach in too many knots from what they had been told, and knowing how close it had been for Benen. She turned, a frown on her face. He had glossed over his time away from her too quickly. That was something she meant to ask him. She headed for the door as she heard a knock, pulling it open to find Brady standing there, his hand raised to knock again.

She stood for a moment before reaching to hug him and then pulling him into the suite, to the kitchen where she silently pointed to a chair before placing a mug of coffee in front of him, sliding into a chair opposite him, her eyes on him.

Brady frowned, and then smiled. "You want to know what happened?"

"I do. I was told about how they found you and what happened to that building." She shuddered at the thought. "But not what happened before then, after you were taken." She pointed at his chin. "You didn't have that bruise before that day."

He rubbed at it, a grimace on his face. "No, I didn't. Benen hasn't said anything?"

She shook her head. "We really haven't had a chance to talk, but there'll be things he doesn't now or doesn't remember. I need you to tell me it all, Brady. All."

He searched her face, a prayer for wisdom drawn from him, before he nodded. "Okay, then. It's not pretty."

"It never is. I have been around the block a few times, Brady. You have not seen what I have seen. But you're a paramedic. You'll understand, that I know."

"I gathered it wasn't the nicest of places you lived. And with the war on, that makes it even worse."

"It does." She shivered in remembrance, jumping as she felt a hand on her shoulder, looking up to find Benen sliding into the chair beside her. "Benen?"

"It's okay, my darling. I've been told. And I told them you would want to know, would demand to know in fact." He laughed as he ducked the elbow she aimed at him.

Brady grinned even as he shook his head at them. "Enough, you two. Let's behave."

"I always do. It's Benen that has trouble with that." Cadee smirked at Benen, hearing his protest that he had no trouble acting like an adult.

Brady shook his head once more before he sobered. "Benen, for a while there, I thought you were dead. You do know that?"

Benen nodded. "I remember you telling me that, but it's all so hazy, even getting out of there."

"Doc said you took more than one blow. The first one was when they hit you with the van and you were knocked out. The second one must have been when I was unconscious too."

"You were unconscious? Brady, what did they do to you two?" Cadee's horrified voice broke through the silence after Brady's words.

"That we don't know, Cadee. We'll have to ask them when we find them. And we will find them, trust me on that. Our guys are mad and you don't make them mad. They're a force to be reckoned with at any time, but when they're angry, look out world." Brady's thoughts drifted for a few moments before he looked back at Cadee.

"Cadee, to go back to the beginning. You had disappeared. I followed Benen, thinking to help him look for you. The van was there before either one of us saw it, coming in-between us and the building. Benen, you shoved me aside, I think, but didn't make it away in time. The doors flew open, they dragged you in and just dumped you on the metal floor. I was on my feet, ready to fight for you when they pointed a weapon at me and then forced me into the van. They wouldn't let me near you, and I fought them on that. That's when they knocked me down with the blow to the chin. I must have hit my head because I don't remember anything until we were being pulled from the van later that day. I don't know what they did to avoid being found. We were shoved through a woods to that building. I had to help you, you could barely put one foot in front of the other."

Brady's mind slipped back to that day and the kitchen faded from his vision. He remembered the fear he felt as he had been forced into the van, seeing Benen sprawled face down, lifeless, he thought. He had demanded to tend to him, but had been prevented from getting to him. He had insisted, fighting the men in the back of the van until a blow to his chin sent him tumbling backwards, his head striking metal before he laid still himself.

He had aroused hours later, how many he wasn't sure, feeling himself being pulled from the van, reaching for Benen as he tumbled from the van, helping him to stand upright, his eyes on the masked men in front of him, protesting that Benen needed medical attention.

They were forced through the woods, stumbling over the hidden fallen branches and debris, brought to a halt in front of a ramshackle house, that had begun the process of falling in on itself. He shifted Benen's arm around his shoulders and his grip around Benen's back, waiting for what he had no idea.

They were forced to walk to the edge of the building, to an open area, when sudden movements on the part of the men sent first Benen, and then himself, tumbling over the edge and through a hole in the floor, to land awkwardly on the basement floor. He groaned, turning himself over and then reaching for Benen, finding men in his way, dragging him backwards to a wall. He fought them, trying to get free and to Benen. He knew his friend needed medical attention. Shoved roughly down, his head slamming back again the foundation, his vision darkened for a moment, before he aroused, feeling his wrists encased in something. He tugged at them, desperate to escape, hearing the hoarse laughter of the men before they were gone.

He tugged again, not able to get loose, searching for a way out. He finally looked at his wrists, first one and then the other, despair darkening his vision. Shackles held his arms to the wall, giving him little room to move them. His head went back again, as prayers poured from his heart.

Benen, he thought, his attention turning to his friend, finding him chained in a similar manner, his head down. I need to get to him. He's hurting, and I need to take care of him. He tugged harder at the shackles, not finding them giving way.

Night came and went as did the next day. Brady tried repeatedly to escape to no avail. The next night came and went. The men had appeared that evening, bring food and water, letting them rise for a few minutes before they were once more shackled to the wall. Brady despaired of ever getting away. He was concerned about Benen.

Then, he frowned. Nothing had been asked of them. They had not had to answer any questions. No photos had been taken with them holding that day's paper. So, why had they been taken? He knew he was incidental to Benen's captivity, in the wrong place at the wrong time, but it didn't make a lot of sense. He prayed that Cadee was safe, that his friends or the police would find them.

The next morning, he shivered slightly in the cooler air, being struck by the thought that they had not suffered from the cold. God, is that You? Protecting us? Thank you.

His eyes went to Benen, his head tilting as he studied him as best he could in the darkness, not able to see him very clearly.

"Benen?" There was no response, so he kicked lightly at Benen's foot, rousing him somewhat. "Benen? Come on. Wake up."

He heard Benen moving slightly before his raspy hoarse voice responded.

"Brady? What? Where are we?"

"Not at home, that's for certain. How are you feeling?" He waited, his mouth opening to repeat his words when Benen responded.

"I hurt. All over. Where are we? What happened?" Benen tugged at his wrists. "What are these things?"

"We're shackled to a wall, in a basement of that abandoned house near the lake. You know the one about five miles from home?"

"Oh, that one.  Why?  What time is it?"

"Better question would be what day.  We've been here a good day and a half.  You were knocked flying by a van, knocked out, thrown in the van.  I tried to get you out, but was taken captive myself."

"That was real smart of you.  It doesn't explain why."  Benen's voice was fading.

"Stay with me, Benen.  I need you to stay awake."

"Sorry, my head is aching and it's hard to keep my eyes open.  Did you get a look at the guys that did this?"  A hopeful note crept into Benen's voice.

"No, I didn't.  They were wearing masks.  Benen, do you have any idea why?  Benen?"  Brady sighed to himself.  Benen had faded away on him again.  He didn't like that.  Benen needed medical attention and soon.

Hours passed, with Benen awake on and off.  Brady tried to occupy his mind, running through all the verses he had memorized, spending time in prayer, thinking through the next few weeks and what he needed to accomplish.  His head turned and he frowned during the late morning, hearing a sound.

He tensed, hearing the sound coming closer to him.  Then a head appeared through the debris.  His friends were there.  Quietly they studied the shackles, finding a way to release them and then shoving the men forward through the area that they had just used.

Hands outside pulled Benen and Brady to their feet and hurried them away, intent on getting them to safety.  Cracking and groaning behind them had them all spinning, watching in horror as the building settled even more.

"Thanks, guys.  That was just in time."  Brady shared a look with Barnabas before nodding at Benen.  "He needs medical attention."

"And so do you."

Late that evening, into the early morning of the next day, Benen and Brady walked towards their building, surrounded by their friends and police officers Will had sent with them, their hearts grateful for their friends' determination not to stop until they were found.  Words would never express their thanks, that much they new.

Brady watched as Benen stumbled slightly as he climbed the stairs, refusing the elevator.  He knew why.  It would fcel too confining.  He himself wasn't sure he could ever enter an elevator again.

He returned to the present, to find Cadee's face filled with horror and shock, her body shaking with her emotions, her hand tight on Benen's before she rose and came and hugged him.

"Thank you, Brady.  I can only imagine how hard it was for you."  Her emotions getting the better of her, she turned and ran from the room, leaving Benen and Brady staring at one another, knowing that their lives would never be the same again, not after what they had been through.

—

Two days later, Cadee stood in Jace's music shop, her eyes huge as she looked around, wandering the shop, studying the instruments there before she turned to Benen.

"Benen?  I didn't know this store was here."

"I didn't have a chance to tell you.  I knew I'd lose you if I did."  He simply grinned at her pleasure, glad he could help with her time recovering.  "Jace said he had a violin or a viola, whichever one you wanted to try."  He nodded to the counter.  "Over here."

Jace watched with pleasure as Cadee studied the two instruments, her hands gentle as she picked one up and then the other, finally taking the violin and tuning it, the bow tightened as well.  Her eyes closing as she raised the violin to her shoulder, the bow was drawn across it, music poured from it, hymns of thankfulness filling the store.  She played for a while, before setting it aside and reaching for the viola, repeating the steps she had just taken.

She looked up, her face happy, a smile on it.  "Jace. These are wonderful instruments.  Don't tell me you had these for sale."

"Actually, I do.  They are part of an estate sale that I was asked to be part of.  I have spoken with the family.  They wish you to take both, at no charge."

"I can't do that."

"It's their wish, Cadee.  All they want is for them to be used. It's their way of saying thank you for your service in the missions. That's what they've told me."

She turned to Benen, finding him shrugging.  "Benen?"

He shrugged.  "If it's what they want, Cadee, I don't see that you can say no."

She struggled with her answer, finally turning to Jace.  "I guess I have to say thank you.  I never expected this quality of instruments though."

"The previous owner played with an orchestra and travelled the world as a solo artist. They just wanted them loved and used." Jace laid a hand on hers. "You have a wonderful talent, Cadee. It would be a shame not to use it."

She nodded. "I was told they needed me for Sunday night. I haven't seen the music." She looked up at him as he laughed, then started to laugh herself. "You were that sure?" She reached for the music.

"No, I was that hopeful. We have prayed about this. God told us not to worry, that He would provide and He did. If you're not comfortable with this, we understand. Barnabas and Brandon have talked to us. We can set you up so you're not in sight. That had been the original wish of the violinist we booked, but the committee overruled him. We won't let them do that to you."

"Thank you. I would like to be out of sight. I think it would be much safer, given what we've been through."

"That it will, Cadee. Now, Jace, is there a practice coming up tonight or tomorrow night?"

"Tomorrow night. If Cadee can make it, we'd appreciate it. But again, no pressure. If you're not able to, that's fine."

Jace watched them walk away, not sure if Cadee would be there. She's got talent, Lord, talent she should be using. But it's Your timing, isn't it? Not ours. Protect this young couple.

Benen placed the instruments in the trunk, watching Cadee as she leaved through the music.

"Can you do it?" His quiet words broke into her thoughts.

She nodded. "I can. I just need to know it's safe for everyone if I do this. I don't want anyone hurt because of me."

"We get that, Cadee. We do. Barnabas and Will have assured me they will take care of that." He hugged her, then opened the car door. "Do you want to do some shopping while we're in town?"

She shrugged. "I guess I should. Christmas is almost here." She sighed. "How many do I buy for?"

"Only the ones you really want to."

She glared at him. "Then, that's everyone. Do you know that?"

He began to laugh. "I do, my darling. That I do. Who do you want to start with?"

"I need to find a good music store that sells CDs. Is there one in town?"

He laughed even harder, pointing to the shop they had just left. "Jace has the best selection in town."

She groaned, her hands covering her face. "How did I know you would say that?"

Drawing a deep breath Sunday night, Cadee drew the bow across the violin for the first note. She had opted to bring both instruments, not sure which one she wanted to use. Benen sat near her, his eyes on her, just as he had many times in the past. She watched him for a moment, before she was caught up into the music, as always, and then forgot about where she was and who was around her. Barnabas stood where he could see her, but hidden from her view, surprise on his face. She's good, he thought, good enough to tour. Will she choose that, I wonder? Then his attention was drawn to those few around them, most of them his men or police officers in plain clothes, volunteers Will had told him. It didn't surprise him that there were so many.

Cadee finally put the instrument away, carefully packing it into its case, coming back to the present as Benen hugged her.

"You're better than you ever were."

"I just got lost in the music. I shouldn't have. That was dangerous." She looked around, not seeing the men and women who had been there.

"It's okay. Barnabas and Will looked out for you."

Barnabas stood for a moment watching her, before he spoke. "Cadee. Benen. Let's get you two home. We can go out the back door. Breck has the van there for us."

Cadee followed, not seeing the couple standing watching her, Brandon and Brenden beside them.

Ted spoke. "She has always had a talent for that instrument. She was devastated when hers was destroyed. We could never figure out why."

"That's part of what we're looking into. Come on, you two. Let's get you to your suite. Tomorrow is time enough to let Cadee know you're here."

Mary nodded.  "I just don't know how she'll take it, given what she went through."  She sighed, her hand reaching for Ted's as they watched the traffic from the back seat of the car.  "How did they manage that?"

"That's something we don't know."  Brenden turned to look at them.  "They really did look and sound like you two.  I think Cadee was hesitant, picking up on something, but not sure what.  She did say you didn't protest at staying in Benen's apartment, not like she thought you would."

"And we would have, given they're newlyweds, no matter how or why they married.  We wouldn't have intruded, but this other couple seemed to insist on that?"

Brandon's head flipped around before his eyes sought the road again, his hands tight on the wheel.  "That's what puzzled me.  They insisted they had to be with her."

Ted shared a look with Brenden.  "How much did they do?"


Brenden sighed, knowing he would have to tell them.  "They left a lot of dangerous items and materials planted throughout the apartment.    With Cadee running like she did and Benen disappearing, we moved Cadee to the secure suite we have.  The couple left, Cadee not wanting to talk to them after them telling her she had been adopted at one week of age."

"They told her what?"  Ted's voice hardened as he worked to control his emotions, Mary's hand tightening on his.  "How cruel!"

"That's why she ran.  With her running, Benen took off after her.  That action of her saved both their lives.  If she hadn't run, the police think some of the objects would have been triggered and Cadee and Benen killed."

Mary's face whitened.  "These people are just so cruel. They haunted every step we took after we left Cadee and Benen.  I understand they even set you two up."

"They did.  Fortunately for them, we were aware of what was going on.  The lady who first approached us has disappeared.  The police in that country are on the look out for her but don't expect to find her."

Brandon pulled into his parking space. "I know we didn't have time to bring you here before the concert. You wanted to hear that. Let's get you in and get you settled. Tomorrow, Barnabas wants to meet with you two early in the morning. He knows you're the right ones this time, but he wants to talk with you. Our police chief wants to sit in."

"We have no problem with that. In fact, if he hadn't asked, I would have asked. Is it still Will?"

"It is. Do you know him?"

"I would say I do. We're old friends. He just doesn't tell people that." Ted reached for his bags, drawing back his hand as the two younger men shook their heads and then pointe dtowards the door.

Benen finally arose from his computer, stretching to release the muscles that had tensed. He had been afraid that he would be far behind in his work, but surprisingly he hadn't been. He would need to find out which one of his friends had stepped in. He knew one of them had. He had heard Cadee on the violin at different times over the morning and felt soothed by the hymns she had played. She was quiet now, and that concerned him, sending him looking for her. He found her in the living room, curled up on the couch, her Bible open on her knee, but her eyes raised to his.

"Benen? When you were captive, did you pray or could you pray?"

He sat down at the end of the couch, tucking the blanket around her feet. "What do you mean?"

"I mean, you're a praying man. Did you pray?"

"I guess I did. It's so automatic with me that I have no doubt I did. Why ask that?"

She shrugged. "I have no idea. I've been reading about how God protects us and just wondered if you had prayed. I know we were all praying for you. The church had a prayer chain going all day and night. But it's different when you're in the midst of the difficulty. We're told to pray, but sometimes our words are not audible or we can't."

"That's when the Holy Spirit steps in and prays for us. Brady said he prayed but he felt a presence with us. We should have frozen or been hypothermic but weren't. Now, you tell me, how did that happen?"

"God!" She turned her head as the door bell rang. "Of course, someone would interrupt us at this point."

Benen laughed. "We'll talk again. You have raised an interesting question." His hand on the open door, he froze, unable to speak, staring at the couple standing there, their eyes on his face, not quite sure of their reception.

"Ted. Mary. I didn't know you were back." He reached to hug them, and then pointed towards the living room. "Cadee's in there."

"Thank you, Benen." Ted was overcome with emotions for a moment. "We can't thank you enough for getting our girl out."

Benen shrugged, embarrassed for a moment, before he heard Cadee's feet on the floor as she headed his way.

"Benen? Which one of the guys is here and won't come in all the way?" She appeared in the hallway, stopping, her hands to her mouth in surprise. "Mom? Dad? Is that really you this time?"

Benen began to laugh. "It's really them. We can ask for ID but I don't think we'll need it."

Cadee shook a finger at him. "Not funny, buster." She turned back to her mother, hesitant about going near her.

"Cadee Rose, come here, dear. It really is your mother this time. I understand I had a stand-in that wasn't such a hot item."

Cadee began to laugh as she reached for her mother, hugging tightly before she turned to her father. "Yep, it's you. When did you get in?"

"In time enough to hear a girl play a violin."

"You were there, Dad? I didn't see you." Cadee backed up to Benen, finding his arms around her.

"That was the plan, dear. Barnabas didn't want us together last night. He wanted to talk to us first." Mary looked around the suite. "This is nice, Benen. I know it's not your regular one, but this is really nice."

"And just where are you?" Cadee's eyes narrowed as she headed into the kitchen.

"Right above this one, I think." Mary moved to help her daughter. "We'll talk, Cadee. We will talk when we get a chance. Both of us have been through too much."

"I know, Mom. That I know." She shared a look with Benen, not seeing the look her parents shared, or the relief that they felt

———

shown on their faces.  "What time does Barnabas expect to meet with us all?"

Mary's mouth dropped open before she snapped it closed. "Cadee, that's not nice."

She shrugged, a smile on her face.  "Barnabas knows me.  He knew I would ask that."  She dug an elbow into Benen who had moved to stand right behind her.  "Benen, stop your laughing.  We have serious things to talk about."

"We do at that, my darling.  We do, but as Breck says, you bring a sense of levity to the situation that is so needed."

She paused, then nodded.  "You are all so sober.  Berneen and I have to do that."

Barnabas looked up from his desk as Amy entered the office, shutting the door behind her.

"Amy?"  He peered around her at the closed door.

She was laughing almost too hard to talk.  "Cadee's here and in fine form.  She just asked me if you were ready to meet with them and just what did you have to say this time?"

Barnabas had begun to grin as Amy started talking, the grin turning to laughter.  "She's a character.  Benen and she make a great pair."

"They do.  Let's pray this adventure or misadventure or whatever you want to call it ends soon.  They need to get on with their lives.  And Ted and Mary?  Just where do you see them in the Foundation work?"

"Got me there, didn't you?  I've been praying about that.  The director of the homeless shelter told me a couple of days ago he needs to move back to Alberta to be with family that are unwell.  I feel Ted and Mary would do well there, but I need to pray more about that and then talk to him."

"Perfect.  Just the ones we need."  She turned to open the door. "But are you ready to face Cadee?"  She smirked at him as he laughed and said to send them in.

———

294

Barnabas watched with amusement as Cadee entered his office, seeking the chair she normally sat in. Her parents were more hesitant, Ted nodding at him before Cadee pointed to chairs for them. Benen was behind him, laughter on his face, his hands raised in a helpless manner as he caught Barnabas' grin.

"Good morning, Cadee." Barnabas moved to a chair beside her. "Thank you for last night. You added just the right touch to the concert for the families. We have been inundated with calls asking who was playing."

She shrugged. "I guess you can tell them. But that's not why I did it."

"We all know that, Cadee." Benen reached for her hand. "But I think we need to turn our attention now to what's going on with us."

Cadee shuddered. "I know we do. I wish it was all over with. Barnabas?"

"We're working on that. Will should be here shortly. He wants to update us. And no, he could send his detective but he wants to do the updating. This spans more than one country and continent and he has to be involved."

Cadee stared at him. "It does, doesn't it?"

"What does?"

"More than one country. More than one continent. What did I go and get involved in. Or rather, what did we?"

Ted spoke. "It does, Cadee. And we may need to go back to that country." He turned to Barnabas. "What do you have on the mission?"

"What you suspect, I think. It was taken over, all the others were sent home, except for you three. We're starting to get a sense of why, but not definite enough that we can go to anyone for an investigation."

"We were told about the couple. That's sad, but how do they relate to us? If they do." Ted watched his daughter as he spoke.

"Plastic surgery to make them look more like you. Cadee, I think you were picking up on something with them."

"I did. I felt evil around them and couldn't figure it out. Not from my parents." She looked up at Benen. "Benen?"

He nodded. "There was something." He looked around as Will entered. "Good morning, Will."

"Good morning, all." Will slid into a seat, his eyes on Ted and Mary. "The right ones, this time?"

Cadee began to laugh. "They are. God brought them back, protected them. They tell me they felt His hand many times over."

They fell silent at that point, before Ted began to pray. Cadee looked around as he finished, knowing that their adventure, as she termed it, would soon be over, she prayed and hoped. They couldn't go on much longer, she thought.

Will wasn't able to give much more details than they already knew. "That house, Benen? It is connected to that couple. His father owned it before it was abandoned. So they are local to the area. Their names are not for release at this time."

"That's fair." Benen finally rose, and reached for Cadee's hand. "If that's all, I need to be at work. Cadee has volunteered to help." He grinned down at her as she stared at him. "You promised to play those hymns again for me. And we have that discussion on prayer to continue."

She rose, her hand in his. "If you insist. Mom and Dad? I'm not sure about lunch but can we get together for supper?"

"We can do that, Cadee." Ted watched until the younger couple had walked away and the door had closed before he spoke. "Okay, Will. What are you not saying?"

Will stared at the closed door before he finally spoke. "I know you, Ted. Barnabas, we've talked. There are contracts out on Cadee and now Benen. Who put the one on Benen is still unknown, but with him being abducted like he was, they are serious. We need to

put a better guard around them.  At least until we can identify who is
it."

Barnabas nodded.  "The guys are pushing here, trying to find
out any information they can for you.  Branigan is just back from his
conference and I know he'll be putting long hours of his own time."

Ted nodded, his eyes on Will.  "Will?"

"We need to talk, Ted.  Do you have any idea of who it was in
the mission that set you up down there?"

Ted shook his head, his eyes on Mary.  "We don't.  We've
done our best to find out, but down there, it's totally different.  You
would never find out by asking.  That's a given."

Will sighed.  "That is about what I thought you would say."

Branigan walked towards Benen's office the next morning, a puzzled look on his face. He had been away at a conference and had just returned late the night before. He had spoken with Breck, who had brought him up to date on what was happening with Benen and Cadee. He had stared at Breck, shock on his face.

"Benen too? What is going on?"

"That is what we're not sure of, Branigan. We'll want you to go through Benen's place. The police did, but we'll feel better knowing one of our guys has done that." Breck had paused at that point. "You know that Ted and Mary are back. Cadee is still hesitant about them. I can understand why."

"To tell the truth, so would I be. How is Benen handling all this?"

Breck shrugged. "He's quiet, not saying much. But then again, that's him."

"It is. Do you know where I can find him?"

"Likely in his office. He's been working there some and in the suite a lot as well, just to be near Cadee. Now that Cadee! She has a wicked sense of humour."

Branigan just shook his head as he walked away, finding Blair waiting for him.

"You're heading to find Benen?" Blair's question raised Branigan's eyebrows.

"I am. Why?"

"Because I need to talk to him. I had his vehicle in the shop." Blair held out a hand. "I found this on his brakes."

"What?" Branigan looked at that. "What is it?"

"I'm not sure, but I don't think it was placed there for his health."

Branigan's face hardened as they walked towards Benen's office.  "This is getting worse and worse, Blair.  Breck talked to me this morning."

"Good.  Then you're up to speed on what's going on."

Branigan paused at Benen's office door, a prayer rising from within him.  He could feel danger approaching his friend.

Benen looked around and waved at his two friends, motioning towards his computer.  They nodded, knowing he would be with them as soon as he was able.  Branigan wandered the office, feeling something odd about it but not sure what.

The two men had finally found seats, hearing Benen's voice as he worked with a client. Their heads turned as the door opened and Cadee came in, a tray in her hands that she placed on Benen's desk, a quick kiss to his cheek, and then she was gone.

Branigan stared after her before turning to Blair, finding his face alight with laughter.

"Cadee?"

"She's like that, Branigan.  She's quiet when she needs to be.  I understand this has become a habit, that if Benen is here working, she'll bring a tray mid-morning for him."  Blair rose as he heard Benen moving about in his office.  "How did she know?"

"How did she know what?"  Branigan stared in turn at the tray. "She brought enough for all of us?"

"She did."  Benen reached to shake Branigan's hand.  "Don't ask how she knows.  She does.  She can put a finger on the pulse in this building and find the one who needs her help."

"She's been here, what about two weeks?"  Blair took the mug offered him and then studied the plate of goodies Cadee had left.

"About that.  She knew you two were here.  Ask her sometime how she knows.  She can't explain it."

Blair nodded before he dropped the object he had been holding on Benen's desk. "Know what this is, Benen?"

Benen stared at Blair for a moment and then down, finally reaching to pick up the object. He sighed. "I do. Ted showed me one when I was down there. Where'd you find it?"

"On your brakes. It was meant to take them out." Blair was growing angry, not at Benen, but at the culprits responsible for this.

"My brakes?" Benen sat back, his eyes thoughtful. "Which one was he after?"

"What do you mean?" Branigan leaned forward, his mug down on the desk.

"Cadee drives it sometimes. In fact, she asked this morning if you were done with it, Blair."

Blair paled. "I was until something nudged me to check the brakes. It wasn't due for that, just the oil change." He looked around as the door opened and Cadee reappeared.

"Benen, is your vehicle ready? Mom and I want to head into town." She stopped as she saw the two men sitting there and then her eyes were drawn to the object Benen still held. "Benen? Where did you get that? I thought I left all those explosive devices behind me."

"Obviously not. It was on the brakes of my car."

She paled and then nodded. "Of course it would be. They are obviously not done with us, are they?" She tamped down the anger she felt. "Guys, talk to Dad. He might have an idea of who, but don't count on it."

Benen watched her closely, seeing the fear she was trying hard to hide. "Cadee, we can get you two into town. In fact, I'll borrow a vehicle and take you."

She just shook her head and walked away, leaving the three men staring after her.

"Did she just do that?" Blair's head turned back to Benen.

He sighed. "She did. Now, she won't go, and I know Ted and Mary need things." He rose, his eye son his computer. "I can leave for a while, but I have a conference call in two hours. That won't give much time."

Branigan and Blair shared a look before Branigan spoke. "I booked today off, Benen, knowing I'd get in late. Let me take them."

Benen finally nodded. "Let me go get her and you can talk to her." He turned, finding Cadee right behind him, fear on her face. "Cadee?"

She held out her hand, a small box in it. "I found this in our kitchen, Benen. Who put it there?"

The three men crowded around her, Benen's arm holding her close to him, as they peered into the box.

"What is that?" Blair's voice was low and unsure.

"It's a warning. That's what it is. It's similar to what you pulled off Benen's car, only it goes on a door to a house. This was sitting on the counter. Someone has been in our place, Benen. How?"

His face grim, Barnabas stood in the conference room, watching his men as they milled around before finding places at the table. The news that someone had been in Benen's apartment has disturbing, but finding someone had made their way into the secure suite was even more disturbing. His security captain was running videos trying to find the exact time the explosive object was left, but he had not heard back from him. He suspected that they wouldn't, that a blip would be found in the security feed for the length of time it took the person to get in and out. There was also the security log from the door. Branigan had taken a look at it and then shook his head. Again, someone seemed to have hacked into their system, and they had one of the best available.

He finally sat, staring down at the folder in front of him, before he looked up, seeing Buckley. Buckley nodded, his head bowing as he led them in prayer. They all knew that only God would provide the answers they sought and the protection that was needed.

"Branigan, where do we stand?" Barnabas' question came quickly after their heads were raised.

Branigan shook his head. "About where you expected. Someone hacked into our systems. I have a friend who is working on tracing it. I'm not sure if he'll be able to."

"Okay. Benen?" Barnabas watched as Benen's attention returned to the room. "Did you talk to Ted?"

"I did, but he can't help. He hasn't seen those before. He was puzzled that Cadee had. I asked her. She said the boys in her Bible class showed one to her, warned her to watch for them. They didn't tell her why, but she took it as a warning. She's shaken, Barnabas. And it takes a lot to shake her."

Bradon looked across the table at Benen. "She's asked about getting a dog. Did you know that?"

Benen nodded. "I do. We had talked about that but decided not to at this point. I'm not all that convinced that she wants one."

He looked around at his friends, knowing they would do their best to solve this and protect his lady.

Finally rising, no further ahead with information or planning, Benen walked away, heading for Cadee, not finding her. That didn't surprise him. She was likely with Mary or Ted he thought.

He stood for a moment in the kitchen, a frown on his face, wondering just how safe Cadee was, wherever she happened to be at the moment. He turned as he heard the door open and close, and then Cadee's voice muttering to herself.

Cadee stopped, a smile lighting her face as she saw Benen.

"Benen? Are you working? You can't be done for the day?"

"No, I'm not. I just needed to make sure you were okay." He paused and then shook his head. "I have to head into town now for the camera club meeting. Want to come with me?"

She shrugged. "No, not really. I think I'll just relax."

He studied her for a moment, seeing the fatigue and whiteness on her face. "You've been doing too much." He walked towards her, reaching to hug her. "That's okay. I don't need to go."

"No, you need to. The club needs you to."

Late that afternoon, Benen quietly closed the door, toeing off his shoes to leave on the boot tray and hanging up his jacket in the closet. Low lights shone in the apartment and he moved slowly through it, looking for Cadee. He frowned when he didn't find her. Searching again, he saw nothing that showed him where she was.

A soft sound had him spinning, heading for the walk-in closet in the bedroom. Shoving open the door, he reached for the light switch, flooding the area. He frowned, not seeing anything, before he searched again.

Phone in his hand, he headed for the door, knowing it had been locked, before he spun, heading for the French doors in the living room that led to the outside. Unlocked! He frowned once more as he stepped through.

"Ted?" He spoke into the phone as Ted answered. "Is Cadee with you?"

"She was but headed home about ten minutes ago.  Why?"

"She's not here."

"What?  I walked her down and went in with her to check."  Ted's voice faded for a moment.  "I'm on my way down."

Benen clicked off his phone, watching the early night sky for answers before he looked down, a sound coming from him as he ran across the patio, intent on finding Cadee.  Following footprints, he slid to a halt, his heart in his mouth at the dark object in front of him.  Dropping to his knees, he carefully rolled the person over, fearful that it was Cadee.  It was Mike, the night security guard.

Benen was on his feet, his phone out to call Barnabas as he heard his name called.  Swinging around, he found Bradon there, Kade beside him, his hackles raised as he stared off into the night.

"Benen?"

"It's Mike.  I can't find Cadee.  Ted walked her down to the apartment about fifteen minutes ago.  She's not there."  Benen spun suddenly, a cry sounding in his ears and was running for the lakeshore, Kade in front of him, ears back, a low growl coming from him.

Bradon stood for a moment in shock, watching his dog run from him without being sent, and then he was racing after them, not seeing some of the other men who had heard the commotion and came from their apartments.

Brandon, Blair and Burney were after Benen and Bradon as quickly as their feet could take them.  Brady was on his knees beside Mike, helping him to sit up, turning as Breck crouched down beside him.

"He's okay?"

Mike nodded.  "I am.  I was blindsided.  I saw Cadee being hauled away and came to help her.  I didn't see the other man."  He shifted, frantic to find her.  "Where is she?"

"She's not here.  Benen and Bradon are after her."  Brady helped him to his feet.  "Let's get you in and get you assessed."

Mike shifted away from him.  "Go after them.  They can't have gotten far.  They were heading for the lake."

Brady stared at him before Mike shoved him. "Go. If she's hurt, she'll need you. I'll find Doc if I have to."

Brady shook his head and then was running as well, hearing shouts from in front of him, sliding to a stop as he saw Benen and Bradon standing still, hands in the air and then his focus went past them to where Cadee stood, a man's arm around her keeping her still, a knife held to her neck.

Barnabas watched from behind the pile of rocks, knowing others of his men were around, and that a call had gone in to the police department for assistance.  It was a question whether they would make it in time.  He watched as Kade circled, his eyes on Cadee, whom Barnabas knew he adored, just waiting for an opportunity to take down the man holding her.  Barnabas turned as he felt a hand on his shoulder.  Buckley stood there.

"Can we move in?"

Barnabas shook his head.  "Not yet.  He's keeping that knife on her."  He tried to see through the darkening sky.  "If we don't though, he'll be gone in the darkness."

Buckley nodded.  "I know.  Blair, Brandon and Brody are heading around them with the huge spotlights we have.  That should help."

They ducked as the lights suddenly lit up the night, causing the man who was holding Cadee to jump. Benen watched carefully, seeing her flinch, and made a move towards her, stopping as something in the tree line caught his eyes, before he shook his head. He wasn't sure he had even seen anything there.  He heard Bradon give a soft sound and his attention was back on Cadee.

No words were uttered by the man holding her as his gaze was locked with Benen's once more.  Benen frowned, thinking he knew the man but then shook his head.  He didn't, did he?  He watched closely, see the fear Cadee was trying her best to hide.  Then, the man began backing towards the water, wading into the icy cold lake, dragging Cadee with her.  She began to struggle, the shock of the water moving her to try to escape.  She shoved at the man's hand, pushing it away before she kicked at his shin, loosening his grip. She shoved away from him and dove into the water, her breath gone at the cold, and tried her best to swim.  She didn't hear Benen's shout or Bradon's yell at Kade.

As soon as Cadee had started her move, Kade had crept closer, his eyes intent on the man.  And then he sprang, his powerful jaws clamping on the arm still holding the knife, taking the man down on the sand.

Benen gave a shout, his feet pounding across the sand, trying to see where Cadee was.  He plunged into the water, diving down, frantic to find her.  Surfacing, he heard the calls from his friends and then he saw Brody heading for shore, Cadee's limp motionless form in his arms.  He plunged through the water, not caring that he was soaked, stumbling as he hit the sand, catching his balance and then running towards his bride.  He didn't feel the blanket draped around him as he dropped to his knees, his hands reaching for her, fighting the hands that held him back.

Pulled to his feet and back from where she lay, he struggled to get back to her, but his arms were held in a firm grip.  Buckley stood on one side of him, Brennen on the other, their eyes full of concern, their faces grim.  Their grips tightened on him.

Brady was on his knees beside Cadee, working frantically to revive her, doing CPR, Doc on his knees with him.  They could hear the sounds of the sirens and then the calls of the responding officers and emergency personnel.

Brady looked up as the paramedics dropped beside him.

"She was in the lake.  Not for long, maybe five minutes at the most."  He continued his work before stepping aside and letting the paramedics take over, his body turning so he could search for Brody and then Benen. Brody shook him off, nodding towards Benen.

"Look after him, Brady."

"You're okay?"

Brody shrugged, pulling the blanket around him tighter.  "I'm okay.  I'll get someone to take me in but I'm fine.  Benen needs you."

Benen stood, desperate to be with Cadee, watching as the men and women worked around them, hearing Barnabas talking to someone, asking that they find Ted and Mary and get them to the hospital.  He watched as Cadee was lifted to a stretcher, a blanket wrapped tight around her before he broke free and moved with the stretcher, his hand on her arm.  He refused to back away when she was loaded into the rig, hopping up and sitting in a corner, his eyes on her, not taking in the continued activity.  He was vaguely aware that Brady was with them.

Benen stood once more, blanket still around him, his arms folded, leaning against the wall in the Emergency Department, his eyes on the room where they had taken Cadee, his mind echoing with the words he had heard.  They didn't know if she'd awaken, or how she would be.  The lake water had been frigid and that concerned them all.

Doc watched for a moment before he nodded to Barnabas and both men walked towards Benen.  Benen's eyes never moved from the room door.

"Benen?"  Doc's voice finally brought his eyes around.  "Here. You need to get into dry clothes."

Shaking his head, Benen refused to move.  "I can't.  I need to see her."

"They won't let you in.  Not yet.  They're working on her." Doc's hand was firm on his shoulder, turning him and then gently shoving him into a room.  "Change and then I'll be back to assess you.  The ER physician told me to."

Benen stared at the closing door before he stared down at the bag holding his dry clothes.  Lord, save her, please.  I can't go on if she doesn't make it.  He knew full well what Doc and Brady hadn't said.  He remembered losing a friend to hypothermia when he was a teenager.  That was his fear.  That he would lose his lady love.

———

His hand holding open the door, Barnabas watched as Benen paced the exam room.  He knew Doc had been back in, warning Benen not to leave, that someone would be around to examine him, shaking off his protests.

"It will be done, Benen, and soon.  You were in the lake.  As was Brody.  He's been assessed and cleared.  I can tell you this much.  If you refuse, they will not let you in to see Cadee.  They need to ensure you are not harmed."  Doc had stared him down, compassion on his face.

Benen swung as he heard the door open, his eyes hopeful, then his face whitening as he saw the grim and sober looks on Barnabas and Buckley's faces.  His head began to shake as he backed away, until the bed behind him stopped his movements.

Barnabas halted his steps, knowing that they had frightened Benen without intending to.

"No, they're working on her still, Benen.  I'm sorry.  I didn't mean to frighten you."  Barnabas shared a look with Buckley.

"Can I see her?"  Benen felt like he was begging, but he just wanted to be with her.

"In about ten minutes or so."  Buckley's hand rested on his friend.  "First, we need to pray for you both."

Benen stared at him, his thoughts muddled, a puzzled look on his face, before he nodded, his head bowing.

His head raised as the door opened and a physician entered, Doc walking beside him.

"Benen?"  Doc spoke first.  "This is  George Forrest.  He's been treating Cadee."

"Doctor?"  He studied the man in front of him, a man near Doc's age he thought.  "Cadee?"

"She's starting to warm up, Benen.  It will be a while.  We'll take you in to her but be prepared for all sorts of lines and machines.  It's standard."  He shared a look with Doc.  "But there is one thing you need to be aware of."

Benen waited, not sure what was going on.  "Doctor?  What aren't you telling me?"  He shifted his focus to the door, seeing the light green of the walls, the various equipment in his peripheral vision.

"Her throat was sliced, likely when she made her move to escape."  Barnabas's hand steadied Benen as the physician continued.  "It wasn't deep but deep enough to be of concern."

Benen moved away from Barnabas, shaking off his hand, intent on finding Cadee, not hearing the voices calling him to wait.  He almost ran from the room, pulling the door open in an almost violent manner, heading for the room where Cadee was, pausing for a moment before he opened the door, his eyes focused on her, his feet moving forward without a conscious thought on his part.

He didn't focus on the equipment surrounding her, the hum and deep of the equipment itself, the moving of the nursing staff as they worked.  His focus was strictly on her, his hand reaching to touch her face, mindful of the oxygen line that lay across her cheeks.  He blinked rapidly, willing the tears not to fall.  He ignored the sound of the rubber soled shoes moving around him, the swish of the door as it opened and closed, and the footsteps that moved to stand beside him.  He didn't raise his eyes to study the light cream walls.  His vision remained locked on Cadee.

"Benen?"  Doc's quiet voice had him turning his head to the older man.

"Doc?"

"You heard George.  She's a survivor.  But what she went through a couple of weeks ago has affected her recovery today.  She was still not over the poisoning."

Benen just stared at him, before his attention went back to Cadee.  "Did they catch the guy?"

"The one who had her?  They did.  Kade kept him down until the police could move in.  The man's not talking though."

"He knew Cadee.  I could see it in his face."  He looked up, frowning at the heart monitor.  "I just don't understand why she was outside.  Did Mike say anything?"

"No.  He didn't see anything, but his impression was that there was more than one man.  He vaguely recalls seeing Cadee being dragged towards the lake."  Barnabas' voice sounded from behind him.  "That's what we can't understand.  Why the lake?"

"A boat?"

"That's what Will said they were looking into.  But there's no proof a boat was out there."  Barnabas was frustrated.  "The man's not from here."

"I didn't think he would be.  He seemed familiar to me.  I think I might have seen him hanging around the mission."  Benen sighed even as his hand rested on Cadee's cheek, feeling the chill in her skin.  "That means he won't speak much English."

"Will thought of that.  He's bringing in an interpreter but the only one available on short notice is Brenden."

"And that's a conflict of interest right here, isn't it?"  Benen turned to face his friends, his eyes rising to the door where Ted and Mary stood, hesitant about entering.  He walked towards them and into Mary's hug, Ted's arm around the two before they headed back to the bedside.

Cadee stared at Benen two days later as he stood in front of her, a mug of tea extended. She had insisted on moving home, telling the physicians that was what she wanted. She hated the hospital, it reminded her too much of the episode just a couple of weeks ago. Her eyes moved away from Benen, studying the living room of yet another suite they had been moved to, this time on the second floor of the building. She decided the pale amber of the walls was suitable but not her and not Benen. Nor was the leather furniture. She disliked the TV on the wall. She was nitpicking, she knew but just couldn't help herself.

Benen watched her closely before he sighed and walked away, knowing she wanted to fight and just not wanting to do that. He stood where he could watch her, seeing her shove herself back onto the couch before he approached, dropping a blanket over her despite her protests.

"You need this, Cadee. Now, the doctor said light food. Anna brought in some as did your mother. What would you like?"

She glared at him, her arms crossed, not happy with her situation.

"Give it a rest, Cadee. These are orders. What would you life? If you don't tell me, I'll find something and then stand over you until you finish it." Benen was losing patience with the situation, and didn't need Cadee's stubbornness.

She refused to answer him, her eyes daring him to follow through on his threat. He shook his head, knowing they needed to talk, but right now, she wouldn't. Lord, please? Protect her. Show me, show us, how we do just that. I'm at a loss to know just how. He meditated on that as he prepared a tray with soup, jello and the tea she favoured, setting it on a table beside her before he sat once more at the end of the couch, his mug of coffee on the table, tucking her feet under the blanket, one hand resting on her ankle, the other elbow on the back of the couch as his hand rested on his cheek, his eyes on her.

She finally reached for the mug of soup, knowing she did have to eat, but with little appetite.

"Who all was hurt last night?" Her question when it came was not unexpected.

"Mike has knocked out but is fine. Brody went into the lake as did I. He's the one who found you. And then there's Kade."

"Kade? What do you meant?" She sipped at her soup, a perplexed look on her face.

"He left Bradon behind, running after you. He broke his trust with Bradon to do that. He crept around and then attacked the man without being commanded to because you were in trouble. He has never done that before, and now Bradon is not sure how much he can trust him."

Cadee looked shocked. "He did what? Why?"


"Because it was you. Because to him, you're family and he has to look after his family." Benen's hand tightened on her foot. "And in doing that, he broke his training. He should have waited to be sent out and didn't."

Cadee was shocked. "I didn't know he'd do that. I mean, I never went overboard with anything to do with him. I only would pet him or play with him if Bradon said it was okay."

"We know, my darling. We know. Now, that man?"

She shuddered. "That man." She refused to look at him.

"Cadee, my darling. I know you know him. He's refusing to speak. Who is he?"

She sighed, finally setting her mug aside and wrapping her arms around herself. "I know his first name. It's Juan. But I don't know anything else about him. I don't even know if Dad or Mom saw him hanging around the mission. He watched me all the time. I think that's part of what Dad was warned about. But I don't know why he was there." She lifted eyes that were frightened and distressed.

Benen nodded.  "That is what Will thought.  That he was someone from down there.  But why did he do what he did."  He watched as she shuddered again.  "What did he say?"

She shook, her hands clenching at the blanket.  "I can't."

Benen's head came around as he heard the doorbell and he rose with a muttered sound.  "This is not over, Cadee.  Not by a long shot."

He stood at the open door, eyeing Will and Barnabas and then Ted.  "Come on in.  I'll need your help."

"For what?"  Will dropped his coat on the table in the entryway.

"Cadee's given me a name.  She just won't tell me what he said.  And she needs to."

"Cadee?"  Will's voice brought her head around and she blanched, knowing she would need to confess what was said.  "What's this I hear?"

"What did you hear?"  She was playing for time and refused to meet her father's eyes.

"Cadee Rose.  Enough.  If you can tell us what was said, it will help.  It may mean the difference between life and death for you, for Benen, for any of us.  They showed that last night when they attacked Mike.  They could have very easily killed him."

She finally nodded, her eyes on Benen, who had at back down at her feet.  "He told me I had to go with him.  That I belonged to someone else.  That if I didn't, he would kill Benen."

Her words caused the men to draw in their breath sharply, their eyes first on her and then on one another.

"Ted?  Did you know that?"  Will's voice was harsh.

"No, I didn't.  I wish I had.  I would have taken steps long before I did.  I had heard rumours that the drug lord had his eye on someone but never heard a name."

Cadee refused to look at the men, before Benen was on his feet, pulling her up and then sitting back with her wrapped in his arms. He felt her shudders.

"Cadee? He wasn't alone."

She shook her heard. "No, he wasn't. He grabbed me when I stepped out on the patio for a breath of air. I shouldn't have. I knew that, but I had seen Mike just walking by and thought I was safe." Her shudders deepened. "He had me before I could move. I knew there was another man. I could hear them talking but I couldn't understand what they were saying. I didn't know the language."

"Why didn't you tell me that before?" Will's voice though firm was still gentle.

She shrugged. "I couldn't. I didn't know who would hear me."

The men finally left, Ted lingering a moment to watch Cadee, who refused to look at him, her focus on her hands. Benen walked him to the door.

"What do we do now, Ted?" Benen was worried, knowing that one of the men was still out there.

"Pray and pray hard. You need to work. You can't be with her all the time. We'll pick up where we can. Barnabas is talking to his security team to see what they can do." He sighed. "But she will fight us all on that."

"Not if I can help it. Just pray this is over. Christmas is in ten days. I would like to enjoy our first Christmas without this over our heads." He turned to look back towards Cadee. "Barnabas has said we can move home tomorrow. That may help."

Cadee was nowhere to be found when Benen retired and he went looking for her, hearing the shower running and knowing she needed that time. He headed for the kitchen, tidying it for the night, before he reached for his laptop. He had to work. There were some calls that needed to be returned, only he had no heart for that tonight. Instead, he reached for his Bible, searching for words of comfort, of peace, of strength, knowing he would need them if he wanted to protect his lady. His head bowed in prayer, he didn't hear Cadee until her hand caught his as she sat beside him, her own head bowing.

The next afternoon, Cadee wandered Benen's apartment, not sure what she should be doing. Benen, she knew, was hard at work in his office and she was trying to be quiet for him. She turned as she heard a tap at the door and cautiously approached it, peeking out to see Berneen and Mary standing there. She pulled opened the door, her mouth dropping open as she saw the tree Berneen was holding.

"We've come to bring cheer." Mary reached to hug her daughter. "Now, tell us where you want it. You two girls can decorate." She held up the bag she was holding. "I'm baking, something I've wanted to do for five years."

Benen's head lifted for a moment later that morning as he heard the ladies' laughter and smiled. This would do Cadee good. He would need to talk to her later. Barnabas had called as had Will. Their news had not been good.

Cadee leaned back on Benen late that afternoon as his arms came around her.

"You're done for the day?" She had a wistful note to her voice.

"I am. The house looks nice." He looked around at the decorations. "You had fun."

"I did. Berneen is such a character. And her brother was by, as well."

"Darby? I thought he had school all day."

"He was off. Something about teachers striking."

"That's right. They are." He turned her towards the couch, gently shoving her down before his arm was around her as he sat beside her. "Will and Barnabas both called."

"They did?" She studied his face. "It's not good news."

"No, it's not.  Somehow the man who captured you killed himself last night.  They're investigating but they can't figure it out.  No one was in to see him.  The guards were by every ten to fifteen minutes."

"Well, that's that then.  I would gather that he didn't speak."

"No, he didn't.  But something has puzzled me.  Why back into the lake and take you with him?  Was that part of his original plan?"  His head tilted at he watched her.

She shook for a moment before she rubbed at her face.  "I think he was supposed to go down the beach, or up the beach.  Towards my right.  Then he saw you two.  I heard him muttering in whatever language that was and he started to pull me backwards."  She twisted to look at him.  "Did Dad know anything?"

Benen hesitated to speak, his mouth opening before he closed it, trying to gather his thoughts.

"Benen?  What did he say?"

Benen finally looked down at her, trying to figure out how to protect her.  "He said he had heard rumours of a drug lord or someone like that and a young lady, he could never determine exactly who or why.  And that bothers him."

"I had heard the same rumours.  Those kind of rumours are rampant down there, as you can well imagine."  She looked down before she raised her eyes again.  "You looked away from me that night and to your left.  Why?"

He shook his head.  "There was something or someone there.  I couldn't get enough of a look to know for sure.  Just an impression."

"And those impressions are usually right."  She sighed, her head coming down on his shoulder.  "When will this end, Benen?  When will it end?"

———

Standing in the church entryway on the following Sunday, Cadee watched for Benen to enter, her thoughts really not on being there. She had felt someone following her whenever she had left the building for the last few days, and it didn't help that Benen made sure someone was with her, one of his friends or one of the security people. She shook her head. He seemed to be taking things too far, she thought. She felt eyes on her and looked around, not seeing anyone who didn't seem to belong.

Benen stood at the entrance, deep in conversation with Jace, his eyes on Cadee. Something was up with her, he thought, before he finally excused himself, and walked over to her. An arm around her, he led her away from the crowds.

"Cadee? What's going on?" His voice was full of concern as was his face.

She shrugged, feeling herself growing more and more tense. "Someone is here, Benen, and I don't know who or why." She looked up at him and he drew in a sharp breath at the fear in her eyes. "It's coming to a head, as Dad says. I don't want anyone else hurt, but I don't seem to be able to prevent that."

"None of us seem to be able to do that." He bit at his lip as he looked around. "Do you want to stay or leave?"

"We can't leave! What would Buckley think?" She was horrified at his question.

"He would understand completely. He's like that." Benen watched her face closely before he sighed to himself, wrapped an arm around her and led her to the pew at the back he usually sat in. Brady stood and let them sit before he sat back down, leaning forward to watch Cadee before he looked at Benen, who simply shook his head.

Cadee tried hard to listen to Buckley, but her mind kept wandering. She tucked her hand into Benen's and felt his grip tighten on her.  Buckley's word finally reached to her, and she sat up and listened.  Not a normal Christmas message, she thought.

Buckley's voice resonated through the sanctuary, causing the congregation to exchange puzzled glances.  What was he saying? They had never thought of it before.  They had never thought how God had protected Mary, protected Joseph.  To have traveled in those times, he said, would have been a risk.  It was not like today, where they could travel in a vehicle.  Cadee thought about that, realizing that God did provide protection.  She was sure He had with her.

She stood close to Benen as she waited for him to make the move to leave, not sure why he wasn't.

"Benen?  It's over.  Are we leaving?"

Benen shook his head.  "Not yet.  Branigan found something on our vehicle and wants us to wait."  He turned slightly to watch her, seeing the sunlight reflecting through the stained glass windows on her face.

She stared at him, finally snapping her mouth closed.  "When did he tell you that?"

"Just as the last song was finishing.  You didn't see him?"  He frowned as he watched her, not sure what was going on with her.

She shook her head.  "No, I didn't.  I guess I was concentrating too hard on something else."  She flopped back down on the pew. "How long will it take?"

Bene shook his head.  "They're trying to keep us both safe, Cadee". He looked around from where he stood as he heard his name called.

Branigan approached him, slowly, a grim look on his face, Blair and Bradon keeping step with him.

"Branigan?"  Benen's voice died away as he looked down at the hand Branigan extended.  "What?"

"This box, Benen?  Cadee?  It was sitting on the hood of your car, Benen.  A warning.  We opened it.  In it are pictures of the two of you, alone, together, with whoever they could find to take pictures of.  The last one is a nasty one."

Benen didn't take his eyes from Branigan, but he felt Cadee leaning against him.

"Why is it nasty?" Her voice was calm, but Benen could feel the tremor in her body.

Branigan exchanged a look with Blair and Bradon, before he tilted the box so Benen and Cadee could see it.

"That's a grave!" Cadee's voice was shocked.

"It is.  It has Benen's name on it.  They're after him now, Cadee, and we need to find out why."

Cadee's gasp echoed the sound from Benen.  "Who?"

"That's what we want to know.  Now, we're taking you two home.  Your car has been impounded for now.  I spoke with Will. He will have officers here shortly to escort us."  Branigan walked away, leaving the four to stare after him.

Cadee found herself tucked between the men, her hand tight in Benen's, as they walked out to Bradon's truck. She frowned as she saw the three police cruisers waiting.

"Isn't this overkill?"

"Bad choice of words, Cadee." Bradon shook his head at her. "That's what will happen if we don't take precautions, and even then, there's no guarantee that will even keep you safe. They've proven they can get to you."

She slid into the car, Benen on one side of her, Bradon on the other, Branigan and Blair in the front seat. Barnabas ducked his head to look in before he nodded at Branigan and backed away.

Barnabas watched the cars drive away, wondering if they would make it home safe, and if they did, how did they proceed. Will stood at his side.

"What now, Will? How do we do this? This is nothing like Baird and Berneen."

"it's never the same, no matter how many times we do this. For now, I'll have officers in the building, outside their door, in his office. They will go nowhere they are not escorted."

Barnabas nodded, knowing just how bad it could get. He turned to walk away, turning back as Will spoke.

"She's going to go after them, you know."

Barnabas stared at him. "What did you just say?"

"Cadee. She's not going to sit back and let them come after her or Benen. She'll go on the offensive and I would say by tomorrow. Whether or not she tells Benen and he agrees with her, that's another question." Will paused, his thoughts muddled for a moment, his eyes narrowing as he pondered just what to do. "She'll slip away from anyone I have with her."

"We'll watch, but I think you're right. I've called a meeting with all of the guys for this afternoon. Hopefully we can come up with a plan."

"Make sure Benen is included."

"That's a given. Any suggestions?" Barnabas pulled on his gloves as they walked towards their vehicles, his shoulders hunching slightly against the cold wind blowing in off the lake.

"You're aware of what needs to be done. I know that. We've talked. Just keep an eye on her, and that is going to be difficult with your guys working and volunteering."

"Their volunteer work is done until the new year, and some have time off this week. Their places of employment are closed." Barnabas hit the key fob to unlock his doors. "I am just afraid, Will. Afraid that they will use one of them against the other or go after her parents."

"And that they will do." Will paused. "I can send someone out today to sit in on your meeting, if you like."

Barnabas nodded as he opened his door. "That would be appreciated. We're meeting in my office at about two." He smiled. "And I can almost guarantee Cadee will want to be there."

"You know, that's not a bad thought. Engage her. Get her involved. Don't hide from her what your plans are." Will waved as he walked away.

Barnabas stared down at the sandwich Cadee had handed him, a shuttered look on her face. He prayed for words, knowing he needed to reach her but not sure how.

"Barnabas? You're meeting with everyone?" Cadee's words roused his attention from his prayer.

"I am, Cadee. If you would like to be there, you can." He watched her closely, her eyes on him before she nodded.

"I would like that. I've been thinking about this. I may have an idea who it is, and if it's him, God help us, is all I can say." She blinked rapidly before Benen gave a sound and wrapped an arm around her. She just shook her head at the question on his face. "I need to use your computer for a moment after we finish."

"I'll help you. Barnabas?" Benen looked over at him.

"We all will, Cadee. You are not alone in this. Neither is Benen. God has you in the hollow of His hand. The other guys are mad and want whoever this is. Will is sending someone this afternoon for our meeting. At the moment, he has officers stationed with you two at all times." Barnabas regretted his words as he saw Cadee's face pale even more than it was. "I'm sorry, Cadee. We have to do this. We have to figure out how to end this."

"He's right, my darling." Benen's arm tightened around her, even as his chin rested on her head before he bent and dropped a kiss there. "We can't go on like this."

"I know. I'm just so afraid. Where are we meeting?"

"I thought my office." Barnabas watched as Cadee shook her head. "Not there? Why? What are your thoughts?"

"Have you searched your office, Barnabas? Have any of you? Who's to say they haven't hidden things in there, just waiting for a time like this. Those guys from there are brutal. They have no respect for law and order." Cadee shoved back from the table and walked away, her feet taking her to the master bedroom where she sank to the side of the bed and bowed her head, struggling to control her emotions.

Benen had risen to his feet as she left, before he sat back down, his hands scrubbing down his face, fear in his eyes, before he looked over at Barnabas, seeing in his face a reflection of his own emotions.

"Barnabas, what are you thinking?"

"I'm thinking that she's likely correct in her assessment. And how do we plan for that, then?" Barnabas pulled his phone out and scanned the text message he received, his face growing grimmer. "Will's had officers go over my office. Cadee was right. How did she know?"

"I have no idea. There will be people who say she's planned this herself." Benen turned his head to look towards the hallway. "I know she hasn't. No one knows the sleep she has lost, up pacing at night, tossing and turning, not sleeping except in fits and starts."

Barnabas snorted at his words. "I am sure they will. We know differently." He stopped, overcome with his emotions for a moment at the life his friends were forced to live.  "I didn't realize it was that bad."

"She hasn't wanted to tell anyone, not even her parents.  It has been draining."  Benen rose, reaching for the coffee pot.  "Where do we meet then?"

"Where they would least expect us.  No one will be in today. We'll meet in the open.  In the lobby.  We'll be comfortable there. In the meantime, I will have Will send people to start searching our suites and offices.  Our security guys can do that as well."  He dropped his head into his hands for a moment.  "I pray this ends with you two and the rest of us don't face something."

Pulling her sweater tighter around her, Cadee slumped back into a corner of one of the couches in the lobby, her eyes on the fireplace.  She watched the dancing flames, knowing it was a gas one, but still enjoying that vision.  She didn't hear the men milling around her, or their quiet grim conversation.  She jumped as she felt something touch her hand and looked down to find Kade standing there, his tongue out, his tail wagging.  She stared at him before looking up, looking for Bradon.  She was afraid to touch Kade, not wanting to interfere in his duty.

Bradon sat on the table in front of her, a grin on his face.  "It's okay, Cadee.  You can pet him.  I've dealt with him taking off like that."

She shook her head and tucked her legs up, her eyes back on Kade.  "No, I can't do that.  Please?"

He shrugged and then called Kade back, who lay, his chin on his paws, his eyes on her.  Bradon looked up as Benen sat beside Cadee.

"Benen?"  He frowned at the look in Benen's eyes.

Benen shook his head.  "They've been in all our suites, our offices.  How?"  He looked around, a frown on his face.  "They have to have gotten to someone but who?"

"That's what we think.  We're looking into that."  Branigan spoke from where he had seated himself near them.  "I don't think we'll be safe, any of us, until these people are caught."

"It's not just men, Branigan.  Try women.  Children.  They will use whoever they can to get to us."  Cadee shifted closer to Benen, her eyes rising as she heard footsteps heading their way.  "Will's here.  I thought you said he wouldn't be."

"He changed his mind when he was told what was found."  Benen reached to hug her with one arm.  "He's that worried, Cadee."

"Is he? What has he found out that he hasn't told us?" Cadee watched closely, seeing the worry on his face. "Will?"

Will just shook his head. He had news that he didn't want to share with her, but knew he needed to. "Cadee? Once we get started, let me speak. Then I have some questions for you."

She nodded, her eyes raising to Buckley as he stood, ready to pray for them all.

Will hesitated before he spoke, his thoughts on Cadee, his eyes on the folder he held before he handed it to her.

"Cadee, in this folder are photos I want you to look at." Will shook his head. "First, I have something to say and I need you to listen. Your response is important." He raised his eyes to Benen, finding him watching his bride closely.

"Will? You're scaring me." Cadee's voice was barely a whisper.

"That is the intent of what I am about to tell you and then show you. We have identified men and, yes, women who are involved in this plot against you. It is not what you have thought it was. There were rumours put out there that were meant to scare you and make you run. They had planned to take you and disappear when you did just that. But you didn't. You did the smart thing. You stayed with Benen or one of his friends, not letting them have a chance to get to you, other than that one time. They have been watching you closely. We have found evidence of that, not shared with anyone other than Barnabas. He has had security watching you both closely." Will paused, gathering his thoughts. "Your parents have been safe. They have not been targets. Now as to the reason, this is what we think. This is based on the investigations we have been pursuing. Our detective even made a trip down to the mission. He found some interesting data. That we can't share totally with you, but we'll share what we can."

He paused once more to sip at the mug of tea he had been handed, sorting through thoughts before he continued.

"Cadee, there was no drug lord down there looking for you. There wasn't anyone in that country looking for you. We have traced those rumours, with great difficulty, back here to Ontario. To the mission you worked under."

Cadee's mouth opened as she went to speak, and then snapped closed, anger on her face. "That mission again. When did the rumours start?"

"Just before the mission was taken over. We're working through that. Trust me. We want these people even more than you do. You're not the only one that has been targeted. I can't go into any details on that as it is an active investigation." He shook his head. "But, you. What they wanted? That's what we working through. You need to take all the precautions you can. Benen does as well. They will use him to get to you. Do you remember anything at all?"

Cadee shook her head, searching her thoughts. "There was one man who came down, said he was with the mission. That was in the summer. Dad and I questioned him closely. He couldn't or wouldn't say why he was there. We didn't know him, so we were really cautious in our dealings with him. He sent out strange vibes, if you want to call it that. I felt evil in him. Dad did too. He mentioned it in passing one day." She said a name, her eyes on Will as she did, seeing his nod. "You've been looking at him, haven't you? Is he in the area?"

"He is, Cadee. We have been asked by other forces to watch for him. He's not a very nice person. In fact, he is a very dangerous person. What we don't know is how he managed to take over the mission." Will looked around. "All I can say is this: all of you need to be very careful. They have been as close as the parking lot here. We know that. You know that. Mike took the brunt of it that night."

Branigan spoke up, his eyes searching the faces of his friends. "They'll be getting desperate, won't they? Trying to get to her. But why?"

"Cadee has something they want. We have some thoughts on that but we need to confirm that. Cadee, I want to go over any paperwork or files you brought back. Confidentiality is important, but we need to keep you alive. The rumour is that they want you dead, that you have something they need back."

Cadee blanched, her hands tightening on Benen's. "Why Benen?"

———

"To get to you.  Plain and simple.  Who can stay as close to you as he does?  And he is the one who took you away from down there.  Part of it is revenge or vengeance.  Part of it is a terror or fear campaign to make you flee from where you are safe."

Benen walked quickly across the parking lot towards the building in the late morning the next day, his thoughts not on his surroundings but on Cadee. He felt sudden fear for her and quickened his steps to an almost run. He slid to a stop as a man appeared in front of him, a revolver pointed at him. His briefcase dropped from his hand as he raised both of them at a motion from the weapon. He sighed. What Will had feared had come to pass. Lord, please? Have Cadee somewhere she's safe. I can't lose her. I love her too much.

He was shoved into the building and then down to an empty office, stumbling at the violent shove he received that sent him through the door, barely able to keep to his feet. He spun, his eyes on the man, whose face was covered with a ski mask, before he backed away, hands once more in the air. His back hit the wall and he stood, almost afraid to breathe at the evil and violent that came from the man. Hearing a sound he glanced sideways, his heart falling as he saw his five team members there.

Benen's only thought was Cadee, praying she was safe, that someone had been able to get her to safety. Their captor backed away, the door closing behind him. The six men waited, not sure if they could move.

"Benen?" Branigan's voice was low. "Did you see Cadee?"

Benen's head dropped. "No. I was on my way there when he stopped me in the parking lot. The rest?"

"We don't know. We were each taken one at a time and brought here. That has happened over the last hour. Bradon sent Kade to Cadee, but I'm not sure she'll let him in with her." Branigan moved away from the wall, searching the room. "They'll have cameras or microphones in here. Guaranteed."

Brady pointed at the wall that contained the door. The other five men nodded and continued their search, finding the items Branigan had named. They spun as they heard the door open and stared as Cadee was shoved into the room, spinning in anger as she did so, her voice harsh as she told the men off in another language.

Benen froze, waiting for what he didn't know. He reached for Cadee, pulling her back, his arms holding her close to him, his eyes on the men who had followed her through the door. He couldn't see their masked faces, but the glittering cold angry eyes told the story. They were not likely to walk out of here, any of them, unless God intervened. He could hear the sharp breaths of the men around him.

The apparent leader approached, his eyes on Cadee, before he pulled her from Benen's arm and shoved her into a chair one of the men had placed in the centre of the room. He then turned to the six men, ordering them to the floor, to place their hands behind their necks, and to not move. The men exchanged glances before they heard a whimper from Cadee and saw the first man standing beside her, his weapon against her temple.

Benen dropped to the floor, keeping his eyes on his bride, praying harder than he had ever prayed before, begging, pleading that Cadee would survive. He didn't care about himself. He just wanted his bride and his friends to live.

He listened to the words, not understanding what the man saying, his gaze on Cadee, watching as she shook her head. Her eyes sought his, a plea for understanding in them, signalling her love to him.

She spoke to him, her voice calm, belying the fear he knew she felt. "It's okay, Benen. He doesn't want you men at all. I don't know what he wants. He's asking for a photo or a file. I don't have that. We went through everything. I have nothing that he describes."

Benen gathered himself to rise as the man struck Cadee across the face, before he was slammed back to the floor, pain ricocheting through him as he hit hard and then a booted foot has stamped on his neck, holding him still. He heard sounds from his friends and then a voice commanding silence. They all froze. Benen was not able to watch Cadee any more, not from the angle his head was at.

Cadee yelled at the man to let Benen go, to let him alone. She suffered another slap to the face, her hand rising to cup her cheek, her tongue finding the cut on her lip and the coppery taste of the blood. She blinked back tears as she glared at the man.

"Let him alone! He's done nothing!"

"On the contrary, my dear, he has. He brought you back here. He has kept you from me. You have something I want and you will give it to me." The man stood, arms folded, legs shoulder width apart, his eyes narrowed through the slits in the mask as he stared at her, anger in him.

"I don't have what you want. In fact, I have no idea what you want. You need to give me more details." Cadee prayed that the wire Will had worked up for her was working.

Will had approached her earlier that day, startling her with his request.

"A wire? Why?" She had stared at him and then Barnabas and Breck as they stood beside her.

"Because we have word they'll make an attempt today to get to you. If they do, a wire will help us to track you and we can listen in on what is being said." Will held up the tiny transmitter he had for her. "Only you can trigger it on. It will fit behind your watch, or in your shoe. Wherever you want to wear it."

She stared at it for the longest time, biting at her lips, her arms folded across her body, before she looked up at Barnabas and then Breck. Both men nodded at her.

"We need to, Cadee. We don't want to invade your privacy, but we need to ensure we can track you." Breck felt like he was pleading with her.

"But it's not just about me, is it, Barnabas?" Her question startled the men, Will turning to Barnabas, a frown on his face.

"What's she talking about, Barnabas?"

Barnabas shrugged, his eyes still on Cadee. "I have no idea. Cadee? Care to explain?"

"I'm sorry, Barnabas. I don't know why I said that. It's just I get hunches like this sometimes that are usually correct. It's like God uses me to warn someone. I dislike that so much and have told Him so. I've asked that He not do it any more, but He still does."

———

The three men had shared a look.  They had heard of God working this way, but had never met someone He used.

"Cadee, do you know for sure what you are saying?  Do you have any information or leads at all?"  Will's voice was soft as he spoke, hushed by the presence of God.

She shook her head.  "No, I'm sorry."  Her eyes pled with them to understand.  "I don't, not at the beginning.  I just get impressions.  But I can see evil approaching Barnabas.  What shape or form, I'm not told.  I may be told.  I may not.  Usually all I can do is say something to the person.  It's up to them from there."

"And this has happened a number of times?"  Breck spoke, his eyes on her before he looked at Barnabas, a frown on his face as he watched his friend and employer.

"It has.  More frequently over the last two or three years.  At times, I hate it."  She turned away, rubbing at her eyes, before she turned back, her hand held out to Will.  "Let me have that.  I trust you."  She slipped out of her runner, attaching the transmitter and then slipping her foot back into the shoe.  "Will this really work?"

"It should, Cadee.  As long as you don't lose your shoe.  And it is waterproof."

She shrugged.  "Then you'll be able to hear me the next time I'm dragged into the lake."

"Cadee!"  Barnabas' voice had a note of shock as well as reproof.

"And you can't tell me something like that won't happen again, can you?"  She stared down the men, who acknowledged she was right.

Benen had no idea that Will had approached Cadee. He had been away since early in the morning, a client needing in-house help on an IT problem. He had been headed home when he was taken captive. He had no idea how the others had been taken. His heart raised in desperate pleas. He knew his friends were praying.

He felt the foot lift from his neck. He waited for it to return before he moved his head enough to watch Cadee. She was staring at him, a slight frown on her face before she looked down at her foot and then back at him. He frowned himself, wondering what she was trying to say.

Branigan's voice was low when he spoke. "Will's given her something."

"What?" Benen's voice was barely audible.

"Will was working on transmitters for you two. He has likely given her one."

"Silence!" The leader's voice rang through the room. Benen and Branigan both felt his wrath in the blows they took, pain searing through their bodies. Benen heard Cadee's voice but couldn't make out the words, only heard the rage in it as she yelled at the men. Cadee, he thought, this isn't helping. Please, Lord, get us out of here.

Cadee watched in horror at the abuse Benen and Branigan took, before she glared at the leader, who watched her closely, his eyes still narrowed, the evil and anger she felt from him showing in them.

"You need to cooperate with us. Otherwise, these men will be hurt. And when we're done with them, we have eight others we will use." His words were harsh and brutal.

Benen tilted his head as he listened. He knew that voice, just could not place where he knew him from. His eyes found Brody who nodded. Brody knew him as well. Benen watched as Brody shot a look at the leader and then back to him, mouthing a name.

Bene's heart sank. Brody was right. Now, how did they survive and bring this monster to justice?

The man left after a while, leaving two men in the room as guards. Cadee watched them closely, waiting for a chance to move. She knew she had the transmitter working. She had activated as she was grabbed, pretending she was losing her shoe, before she was roughly dragged through the building, first to Benen's office, which they had broken into, and then here. She had been captive for at least two hours, she thought, not taking a chance to glance at her watch to be sure. Her gaze shifted to the men where they lay on the floor, a frown on her face as she watched them. Cadee just knew that they were plotting something. She knew them well enough to know they weren't just laying there. Their minds were working on how to get them all free.

Barnabas stood behind the police barricade, at Will's side, his eyes on his building. He knew seven of the men were fine. They were lined up behind him, shoulder to shoulder, their eyes on the building as well.

"Will?"

Will shook his head. "Her transmitter is working. Smart lady to get that done. She's with the men now." He looked around, towards the command centre. "We'll get word if we have to move in."

"How many?" Breck's voice spoke up as he moved to stand beside Will.

"As far as we can tell, there are four plus the leader. Cadee's been feeding us information as she can, usually contained in her sentences to the leader." He paused, shaking his head. "She's good. We need her on our force."

"That will never happen." Buckley spoke up. "We've talked. She's not sure what she wants to do but it isn't that. She's afraid of police work. She saw too much down there. Cadee knows it's not the same but she told me the bad taste lingers."

Will excused himself as he heard his name called and walked towards the tech, spending a few moments in deep conversation as he studied the pages he had been handed. He shook his head as he turned to watch the building.

Barnabas had turned to watch him before he walked towards him.

"Will?"

"It's who we thought, Barnabas. Lance Logan. We have a rap sheet on him. He's brutal." He looked up at Barnabas. "We need to get in there and get them out. Any way in from the outside other than the door."

"There are windows, but it's a small office. If there are men in there, we wouldn't get in and out without them being aware of it."

Will nodded, his mind racing. "There's no one else in the building?"

Breck shook his head. "No. They were all away for the day. Amy was in Barnabas' office and we got to her and got her out."

"Good. I have my people moving in." Will stepped away as an officer ran towards him, before Will headed back that way with him.

Barnabas turned to his men. "We have to wait, guys. We have to let them do their job."

"I know we do, but what room are they in?" Burney spoke up.

"The one at the end, on the right, near the back entrance." Barnabas' voice slowed. "Come on, guys. We need to find Will. I had forgotten for a moment."

Will stared at Barnabas, not quite sure he had heard correctly. "What are you saying?"

"There's a tunnel. We put it in years ago, because we needed to have a way out if there was trouble. I had forgotten it. Until Burney asked." Barnabas ran his hands through his hair. "How could I forget?"

"We've never used it, but I know it's inspected regularly." Breck stood with his back to the building and pointed carefully. "It comes out near that pile of rocks. They were put there to hide the entrance."

"Okay. We'll look into it. Which one of you comes with me?"

Breck stepped forward. "I'll go. I'm usually the one who is in on the inspections." He turned to Barnabas. "They'll be watching us, Barnabas. How do we hide the fact that Will and I are gone?"

Brennen spoke up. "Head back to the Command Centre and then for your car, Will. Breck goes with you. They'll think your leaving. Breck can show you where to park so that you and some officers can head in through the woods. I doubt they'd be looking too hard that way."

Will and Breck headed away from the other men. Barnabas stood for a moment, undecided as to what to do, before he turned to the six remaining men.

"We can't just sit by. What can we do?"

"Come with me. Head off to the gym. We'll meet in there." Barnabas glanced around. "No one's watching us." His phone came out as he felt it vibrate. "Now, how did he manage that?"

"Who?" Buckley spoke for them all.

"Brady. He's gotten a text message off to me. There are two men in the room with them. Two other men beside the leader.

They've left. Benen and Branigan have been beaten. He says Cadee's been hit, blood on her mouth."

"That's not good. We don't have much time, then, do we?" Brandon moved quickly towards the rear of the building, heading for the office there. "What do we need to do?"

"First, Buckley? Prayer." Barnabas stood beside him as the men circled, arms linking, as they prayed.

"Buckley, where are the packs?" Barnabas looked up as they finished.

"Here." Buckley reached for them. "I'm not sure we'll be able to get in, though. Will has his people all around."

"That's true, but there is one way." Barnabas spun in a circle before he headed for the gym again, for the wall facing the lake. "Here. Breck told them of one tunnel, but not this one. This one leads to Benen's office, right?"

"It does." Brandon shouldered his pack, the contents of which no one but the men knew. "I'll lead."

They quickly moved through the tunnel, Brennen in the rear, closing the door behind them. They stopped Brandon reached for the lock on the door, carefully opening it, before stepping through, the other six men behind them.

"Now what? Barnabas?" His voice low, Brody spoke for them all.

"We see where they are." Barnabas stood by the door, the door opened slightly. "I don't hear anyone in the hallway." He reached for the stick with the small camera on it that Brenden had pulled from his pack. "Let's see what they're up to."

They watched intently in the small screen of the tablet that showed the camera view.

"They're not out there. Where are they?"

"Lobby?"

Barnabas pulled the stick back quickly and shut the door, motioning for the men to flatten themselves along the wall, a finger to his lips as he set the stick and camera down behind him. They heard the footsteps and then the door knob turned, the door opening and a man entering.  Brody had him on the floor, a hand over his mouth, before he could react.  Hands quickly bound him and gagged him, and then carried him into Benen's office, the door closing to shut him in.

———

Cadee watched through her lashes as the leader entered again. She had finally placed him, knew his name, but just didn't know why he wanted something from her. She had nothing but her own belongings. She was sure that was true for her parents as well.

She simply kept shaking her head as his questions, not seeing the looks of concern on the men's faces. They all knew she couldn't keep refusing to answer, that they would all pay for that if she did.

Cadee sought to find Benen, tears of pain blinding her eyes for a moment before she blinked them away. This man was getting more and more brutal. How could she stop him? She knew of no way. He was watching her, his face grim and sober, sorrow and concern for her in his eyes. He gave a subtle shake of his head, his eyes roaming the room before coming back to rest on her. She looked at the other men, frowning slightly as she saw their inattention to the men and their attention of the wall across from her.

She watched the leader as he left the room, taking one of the men with him, before she saw Branigan rise as the remaining man walked in front of the men. He had him down and unconscious from a blow to his chin before she could react. She drew in a deep breath, went to rise and then slumped back as the door reopened and the man entered, the other man with him.

The two men stopped, weapons drawn, as they stared around, not seeing their partner.

"Where is he?" The leader's voice was loud as he almost shouted the words. "Where is my man?"

Cadee's mouth was open to reply when a sound from behind him drew her attention. She screamed, drawing his eyes to her. His weapon raised even as Benen threw himself towards him. A scream broke from Cadee at the same time that a shot rang out. Benen's hand went to his head even as his body hit the floor, blood streaming from the crease mark left by the bullet, that traced along the side of his head.  He didn't move after he went down, leaving Cadee staring at him in horror before she looked at the man.

"Why?"

"Because he was interfering with my plans for you."  The man reached for her, pulling her to her feet.

She fought him, her hands and feet flying before she escaped and backed away, the five friends of Benen's on their feet, ready to attack when an opportunity arose.

He stared at her, before turning back to stare behind him, hearing a sound and then seeing the wall opening towards him, Will and four officers emerging, their own weapons drawn and pointed at the man.

"Put it down, Logan.  Put your weapon down."  Will's voice was hoarse with his emotions.

The man, known as Lance Logan, refused, his weapon still pointing at Cadee.

"Not a chance.  She's my ticket out of here."

"You're not going anywhere.  Your men outside?  They're under arrest.  It's just you and this one man now.  You shoot, we shoot."

Their words volleyed back and forth, the eyes of everyone watching them.  Cadee's eyes were on Benen, not sure if he was alive or well.  Her eyes flew to Logan as she heard him yelling, seeing the weapon pointing directly after her, before he fired.  The shot hit her in the chest, sending her flying backwards to land on the floor with a thud.

Baird was running towards her, on his knees, his hands reaching to try and stem the flow of blood even as commotion erupted around them.  He ignored the shouts and struggle, not daring to look around.  Bradon's hands were there to help him, Blair and Bradon working on Benen, Branigan standing with Will, watching as the men worked.

Will watched as Logan and his men were led away, Logan loudly demanding medical attention and crying police brutality.  He shook his head before he turned back to the room, moving aside as paramedics were rushed in.  Barnabas appeared at his shoulder, the other men standing in the hallway staring in, concern on their faces.

"Will?"

Will turned slightly, a frown on his face.  "I have no idea how you got in, Barnabas, but we will talk about that.  I hear you captured one of the men."

"No, two.  They're in Benen's office."  He looked past him at Breck.  "We used the tunnel to Benen's office.  You came in the one you needed to."

"You shouldn't have."

Barnabas shrugged.  "We took a chance, Will.  Now, what about Benen and Cadee?"

"Benen took a bullet along the side of the head.  They're moving out with him now."  Will moved them back so the stretcher bearing Benen could move past them.  Benen was still unconscious, his face covered in blood, a large white bandage wound around his head.

"Cadee took a bullet to the chest.  Baird was there right away, but I've called in an air ambulance."  Will strode from the room, Barnabas at his side.  "We need to clear this place, Barnabas.  Get your men out."

Barnabas motioned to Burney's group, pointing to the door. "Come on, fellows.  We need to clear out of here.  We'll give our statements at some point.  Right now, Branigan's team is stuck here. I want you with Doc and Anna, Ted and Mary, Berneen and Darby. I know they were kept away and kept safe.  But now we need to meet at the hospital.  Breck?  I need to be here.  Can you talk to them?"

Breck nodded.  "I was going to suggest that.  Come on, guys. Let's hit the road."

Barnabas watched the men as they walked away before he turned back to stare through the door at the men and women milling around, knowing that Brady was still in there, his hands helping to save Cadee.  Or at least, that was his prayer.  He knew she was hit hard and bad just by the look on Will's face and on the faces of the four of his men stalking in anger and worry from the room.

A hour later, Barnabas stood at Benen's bedside in the Emergency Department, his eyes on his friend, listening as the physician spoke.

"He'll have a headache when he awakens. No fractures. I don't see that any damage has been done to the eyes."

"That's a relief and an answer to prayer. Thanks, Doc." Barnabas reached to shake the physician's hand. "You said you were moving him to a floor?"

"We are. I understand a private room?"

"That's correct. A private room." Barnabas sighed. "When he awakens, we'll have to tell him about his wife."

"His wife? What about her?" The physician turned from where he had been headed for the door.

"His wife. Cadee. The gunshot to the chest." Barnabas had turned to the physician. "She was shot just after he was."

"That's his wife? I'm sorry. I didn't know that. I hadn't heard her name, only her condition." He sighed, returning to stare down at Benen. "Then, he's her next of kin."

"If you need authorization for treatment, her parents are in the waiting room, or in a conference room on this floor. I think that's where Will has them."

The physician nodded. "Someone else is treating her. I'll let them know." He looked down at Benen. "It will likely be a while before he awakens. If you need to have someone with him until he does, that can be arranged."

"Thank you. I know my friends would like that."

Barnabas finally headed for the conference room, his hand on the door before he opened it, a prayer raising for the people inside, for the two he had left behind him. He had no idea how bad Cadee had been hurt.

All eyes turned to him as he entered and then Ted and Mary were in front of him.

"Any word on Cadee?" Ted's voice held hope.

"Not that I know of, Ted. I did let them know you two were here. They'll be speaking with you shortly, I suspect."

"Benen?" Berneen spoke from his side, Baird's arm tight around her. It had been too close once more for them.

"He's still out. But other than a headache, the doctor doesn't expect any lasting damage."

"But Cadee? How is she?" Baird spoke, knowing what he had seen.

"I haven't been told yet." Barnabas turned as the door opened and Brady entered, wearing a pair of hospital scrubs.

"Brady?" All eyes were on him as Mary spoke.

"Mary, Ted. They asked me to find you. They need to talk to you about Cadee." His voice was calm, but the ones who knew him best read in his eyes his emotions and prayers began to flow.

"She's alive?"

Brady nodded. "She is, but barely. They're wanting to take her to surgery, but they need signatures for that. Benen can't, but you're listed as next of kin after him."

He watched as they walked away from him before he motioned for Barnabas to follow him.

The two men stood back from where Ted and Mary had been met by the physician, Ted's arm going around Mary as she collapsed against him.

"Brady? What couldn't you say?" Barnabas turned to him, his eyes watchful, his heart praying.

"She may not make it through surgery, Barnabas. It's close to the heart. They aren't sure if they can even remove it."

"So, Logan may win after all."

Brady shook his head. "No. Will was through. Logan tried to run, grabbed an officer's gun."

———

"And they shot him." Barnabas' hands clenched. "He's dead?"

Brady nodded. "He is. Will regrets that. They will be questioning the men with him but they don't think the men know much. He thinks there's someone else out there. Someone who hired Logan."

"He's the hit man?"

Brady nodded, even as he turned at footsteps behind him and saw the men encircling them. "Logan was the hit men. The others were ones he hired. I would say they not likely knew exactly what he was up to."

Buckley spoke up. "We have the prayer chain at church going. Jace has seen to that." He stopped speaking, his face whitening. "It has to be someone from the church. But who?"

Barnabas' hand stopped on his face as he heard the words. "Of course. It has to be. We need to talk to Will."

"And here he comes." Breck moved aside for Will to enter their group.

"Barnabas? Word on Benen and Cadee?" He was worried, he had seen the looks on the faces of the paramedics as they had rushed Cadee to the air ambulance and knew just how close it was for her.

"Benen's moving to a room soon. I gather you have men waiting for that?" Barnabas watched Will nod. "Cadee's headed for surgery." He turned as he heard wheels on the floor and the men stepped aside, their faces tightened in anger as they watched Cadee move past them, Ted and Mary following. Doc and Anna appeared in the doorway of the conference room, Berneen and Darby with them, before they walked to Cadee's parents and arms around them, walked with them to the elevator. No words were necessary.

Two days later, Benen sank into a chair beside Cadee's bed, his eyes first on all the equipment that surrounded her, before he reached for her hand, feeling the limpness of it. This was not how he expected to spending two days before Christmas, sitting in a hospital ICU room, not knowing if his bride would live or die. He reached to touch her face, what he could see of it, speaking words to her that he could not remember speaking. When a nurse touched his shoulder and told him he needed to leave, he shook his head and then nodded, rising to kiss his wife and then walk slowly from the room, grief weighing him down.

His five team members were waiting for him as he approached, ready to sit with him, to pray with him and for him. He nodded at their words, sinking down into a chair, his head pounding. He had been warned but didn't care. The only one that mattered was in the room down the hall. Cadee's surgeon had spoken at great length with him and her parents, indicating just how serious it was for her, how close it had been. He had finally sent Ted and Mary home for a break, telling them they would be needed when she awoke, and awake she would, he was adamant on that.

Two days later, Christmas morning dawned bright and sunny. Benen stood once more in the ICU room, his eyes on Cadee's face, his hand on hers, the other hand around her shoulders as his tears wet her hair. The ventilator had been removed the night before, but she still had not awakened. That concerned her surgeon. He had stated that she should have.

His thoughts turned to prayer. Benen knew they were both bathed in prayers of many, but he still felt so alone, as if there wasn't anyone but him. He knew God had protected them, even when he hadn't been able to protect her.

He felt Cadee moving, something she had not done yet, and he straightened up, his eyes on her face as she blinked, opening her eyes and then closing them again.

"I hurt." Her voice was rough and hoarse.

Benen grinned slightly. That was his Cadee, he thought. Honest to a point.

"Cadee, my darling, you're awake."

Her eyes opened and she stared at him for a moment. "Benen? What are you doing here? What time is it?" Then, she groaned. "Logan. Where is he?"

"He won't bother you again, my darling. He's gone to face a higher judge than one on earth. And it's Christmas morning."

"Christmas morning? We have the dinner in a few hours. I need to help." She tried to push back the blankets and found she had no strength to do that.

"Cadee, you can't. You had surgery five days ago. You're still in ICU." Benen's hands reached for hers. "You have to lie still."

She stared up at him, a frown on her face. "You were shot."

"Just a crease that knocked me out. Not like you."

"Why? What happened to me? And why am I in ICU?" She looked around, her head twisting to stare at the various pieces of equipment before she touched the IV line running to her hand.

"I almost lost you. You were shot. The bullet was close to the heart but they were able to get it out. The surgeon stated he shouldn't have but he felt other hands on his. I told him that was God. He stared at me and then nodded."

"That is what God does. I have seen it before. Now I have experienced it." She yawned, her eyes sliding closed as she slipped away into a natural sleep just as the nurse entered the room.

A week later, she was home, pampered to the point she was frowning at Benen every time he approached her. She was tired of being in bed and told him that. He had stood before he reached to wrap her in a blanket and carry her through to his office, making a place for her on the couch before he tucked blankets around her.

"Thank you, love." She snuggled down, her eyes on him as he sat behind his desk. "I didn't really mean to grumble."

———

"I know you didn't. You're not used to being still. Just rest." Benen's attention went to his work, not on her, missing her watching him.

Two hours later, he rose and stretched, standing watching her sleep, before he padded on socked feet through to the kitchen, pausing as he heard a tap at the door. Opening it, he stepped aside for Barnabas and Breck to enter.

"Coffee?" At their nod, Benen poured three mugs of coffee and pointed to the living room. "Cadee's asleep in the office. What can I do for you?"

"We need to talk to you both. It's important enough that I think you should wake her." Barnabas looked up at a sound and then rose. "Cadee?"

Benen was on his feet, reaching for her. "Cadee?"

She looked distressed. "I know who it was, Benen. I know who hired Logan." She hid her face against her husband. "It was Jace's brother. John."

"That's correct, Cadee. Will arrested him this morning. He has confessed. He had a grudge against your father for some slight in the years past. What it was? He was in love with your mother but she chose your father instead. He had never forgiven him that. He didn't tell Logan that was why he was after you, for revenge, but told him that you had something of his that he wanted back."

"All this over that? He almost killed me. Hurt Benen. How many others did he destroy?" Cadee's voice was sad.

"We'll never know. With the mission closed, all those that could have been reached haven't been." Barnabas grew silent, sorrow for that in his heart.

"Your Dad's reopening it, isn't he, Barnabas?" Benen's voice was quiet, but assured.

"He is. How did you know?" Barnabas stared at him.

"He talked to us, got our thoughts on that. Ted and Mary's as well. He wants to use them in the office, with their experience. Cadee has been offered a position there as well."

Breck spoke. "But she won't." He simply grinned as she frowned at him.

"And why not?"

"Because you can't keep track of us all if you're not around here. You do that well, Cadee." Breck looked at Benen, his head tilted as he studied the other man. "Do you know what your wife did for Christmas?"

"No, I don't. I didn't think she could do anything for Christmas, being in ICU at the time." His arm tightened around her as he gazed down at her.

"Each one of the men received a gift bag from her. In it was a CD of their favourite artist, autographed at that. One of your photos with their favourite verse on it, framed. A devotional book that she knew we all wanted. That's what your wife has done. She looks at a person, delves deep and finds what each one needs to be encouraged. Not many people have that gift. She needs to be used by God for that."

Cadee had stilled as Breck had begun to speak, knowing what he was going to tell. "I had to, Breck. I couldn't not do that. You all welcomed me into the family here, not knowing me. Welcomed me first for God's sake, then for Benen. Then we became friends and I felt your welcome for me. You took in my parents. You have shown Christ's love in that. You put your lives on the line for me. How could I not do what God prompted?"

Barnabas had to clear his throat before he spoke. "That's the embodiment of Barnabas in the Bible, Cadee. You have put hands and feet to what Dad and I envisioned with The Foundation. I think we need to bring you on staff."

She shook her head, her eyes huge. "I couldn't do that. I couldn't work for a company that has that much money behind it."

The men laughed even as Barnabas assured her she was just the person they had been looking for and hadn't know it. They would talk in the new year, he said.

Cadee watched as Benen walked back towards her, before he sat on the couch and just wrapped her in his arms, his voice praying for them both, before he grew silent and just held her.

A month later, Benen leaned against Cadee's desk in her office down the hall from his, watching with amusement as Barnabas and Cadee argued amicably about her duties. She was adamant she was the wrong person, but Benen knew she was where God wanted her. They had talked many times about it.

Cadee finally turned to Benen when they were alone, walking into his arms, her own around him. She still struggled with weakness and fatigue, but had been told that was to be expected, given what she had been through. She sighed, thankful that God had protected them, kept them safe, kept them alive. The court cases were upcoming, but she had no fear of facing her enemies. God had spoken to her, helped her to forgive them and move on. She knew Benen struggled at times, not sure how to forgive but he assured her he was working on that, him and God.

Benen tilted his head to look down at her. "Still not sure?"

"I'm not but everyone else seems to be. I just need time, Benen. I've been through so much, and this is something I have thought about for years, but never thought I would have an opportunity to serve God in this way. Mom and Dad are happy where they are. Did you know they are planning to move into a bungalow near the mission office?"

"I knew that. Your Dad and I talked. They feel that's where they need to be." He looked down at her, all his love for her in his eyes and on his face. "I never dreamed all those years ago, when we were such good friends in college, that you would be mine for life. I love you, Cadee Rose."

"And I love you, Benen. It's not fair." Her voice grew grumpy.

"What's not fair?" He was puzzled.

"I have two names. You only have one. What were your parents thinking?"

He shouted with laughter. "It's tradition that the males only have one name in my family. Just the way it works." He grinned at the face she pulled. "Are you telling me that any sons we have will have two names?"

"You'd better believe that." She looked up at him. "Thank you, Benen, for being my protector. I know at times it was hard and there were those incidents where you couldn't, but you tried."

"I know, my darling. I know. God was gracious. Now, we need to go out to lunch to celebrate?" He turned her towards the door, reaching for their coats, turning out the lights to the freshly painted and decorated office in the colours and theme that Cadee loved.

"Celebrate?" She slipped into the coat he held for her before he reached for her hand.

"Celebrate. Yes, we need to celebrate. Your new job. Our marriage, which we haven't had a chance to celebrate yet. That I have the love of my life with me. Too many things to enumerate."

She laughed, a carefree one that echoed through the lobby of the building as they headed for the outside doors. "Only you, Benen, could put it that way. And I have the love of my life with me as well."

Dear Readers

Thank you for choosing to pick up the story of Benen and his lady love, Cadee.  What a wild ride they took me on as an author!  Not what I had planned, but God gave the words to me, moved my fingers to work.

Evil is all around us.  As Christians, we can sometimes sense it stronger at times than at others.  I have had this happen to me.  At those times, that is when I feel the protection God provides surrounding me, bringing me through.  We will never know on earth just what or who God had protected us from.

God bless each one of you.


Ronna

# Blair: Encouraged to Believe

## The Barnabas Chronicles
## Book 3

By

Ronna M. Bacon

Jeremiah 29:13
And you will seek Me and find Me, when you search for Me with all your heart.
NKJV

# *Table of Contents*

Shrugging deeper into his red and black plaid winter jacket and tugging his woollen hat further down over his ears and his light brown curls, Blair Campion studied the vehicle perched precariously on the side of the road, nose down into the ditch. He shook his head as he slipped from behind the wheel of his truck, his feet sliding slightly on the icy mess underfoot. He caught himself, drawing in his breath, knowing if he fell, he would have trouble getting back up. The sleet and snow had accumulated during the day, and he didn't envy the tow truck driver the task of pulling out the car ahead of him. He himself had been late getting away from the garage where he worked as a mechanic.

Blair ducked his head to glance into the window on the driver's side, opening the door and closing it again, before he studied the ground once more. Whoever had been driving seemed to have made it out, he thought. Now to find them. They wouldn't survive for long, he thought, not in this weather if they were out in the open. His warm brown eyes searched the area, finding indentations he thought were footsteps. His eyes moved constantly as he walked slowly forward, stepping to the side as he saw the lights of an approaching vehicle. Recognizing it, he raised a hand and then moved to stand at the driver's door of the truck as it stopped beside him.

"Bradon? Branigan? What are you two doing out here?" He watched closely as his friends and teammates exchanged glances.

The three were part of a group of men whose salaries were paid for by The Barnabas Foundation, a foundation operated by Barnabas Carey. By paying their salaries, Barnabas made it possible for their employers to hire others to work in their businesses without having to worry about finding the money for their wages. The men also volunteered in various capacities.

"Looking for you?" Bradon grinned, an arm resting on the driver's door, his other hand on the steering wheel. "Anna, Doc's wife, was worried about you. She said you had promised to be home in time to eat with them and you're late."

"That's right, I was." Blair groaned. "I had to finish off a vehicle before I left, and then I found that." His thumb pointed behind him.

"Found what?" Branigan stared past him, his eyes narrowing. "That car? There shouldn't be any vehicles on this road."

"I know. The driver's not there. And it looks like they were run off the road. We'll need to call it in." Blair turned back to face the car. "I had just started searching when you came along." He stared down at the work boots he was wearing. "Except I'm not exactly dressed for the weather."

Bradon stared at the car and then moved to open his door. "I didn't bring Kade. I should have." He was referring to his dog, who was trained in search and rescue. "We'll search, and if I have to, I'll go get him."

"Thanks, guys."

The three spread out, finally meeting by the car once more.

"We'll have to call it in." Blair swiped at the sleet on his face. "Whoever it is can't survive much longer."

"I called it in already, Blair." Bradon stopped for a moment, stooping to peer at the car. "This isn't good." He spun. "Which way would they have gone?"

"We're assuming that they are still here, aren't we? What happens if they were pulled into the other vehicle and disappeared?" Branigan was running scenarios through his mind.

"That's what I'm afraid has happened." Blair spun in a circle, seeing the red and blue flashing lights of the emergency vehicles as they approached. "There's John with the tow truck as well. He'll take it back to work for us."

"Once it's released. That doesn't solve this." Bradon moved away, his eyes down. "I almost need to go and bring Kade back."

They all turned to the responding officers, answering as best they could, before looking up to see another friend, Brady Coghlan, standing near the paramedic rig.

"Brady's here." Branigan Clery's voice was low.

———

"So he is. He'll have had a busy day, no doubt." Bradon Cahill responded. "Now, let's spread out more. We've checked the ditches. Let's check on the other side."

The three men conferred with the officers, who nodded, knowing the men Barnabas employed. Blair searched once more around the car and then stood, his eyes on the trees, a thoughtful look on his face.

"Blair?"

He turned as Brady spoke from beside him. "Brady? Glad you're here."

"No sign of the driver?" Brady winced as he looked at the car. "That's not good."

"No, no sign." Blair sighed to himself, offering a prayer for their own safety and the safety of whoever it had been in the car. "We're not even sure the driver is still around."

Brady nodded. "I see. How about we look up in the trees? Maybe they made it that far and have hidden themselves."

Blair nodded, heading that way, slipping and sliding down the slope to the ditch and then back up the other side. Brady watched him closely, eyeing his footwear and then shaking his head. He knew Blair had just reacted to the situation, not thinking about his own safety. But then again, Lord, he muttered, we all do. We've already proven that with Baird and Berneen and Benen and Cadee, haven't we? You protected them. Now, please, protect us?

Blair ducked under the low-lying branches, thick with sleet and wet snow, and stared around, standing still for a moment before Brady's hand touched his arm.

"This way, Blair. I can see tracks that haven't been covered."

Blair frowned. "It has to be a woman. Those tracks are too small to be a man's."

"That they are." Brady was suddenly running forward, dropping to his knees beside a still form. "Blair, go get Tom. I've found our driver. Then, I need you to stay back." Brady looked around, catching the nod of acknowledgement before Blair turned and moved as quickly as he could away from the area.

———

Blair stood, anxious for some reason, his heart raised in prayer, his eyes on the area that he had just returned from, Branigan and Bradon on either side of him. They watched as the police officers milled around, finally releasing the vehicle for the tow truck to remove.

Blair moved forward as he saw the stretcher gently lowered to the road and then raised to full height as Brady and his partner moved forward to the paramedic rig, his eyes on the form laying so still. He frowned. Something was familiar about the person.

Brady watched closely as Blair approached, his mouth open to speak before he snapped it closely, his puzzled eyes turning to Branigan and Bradon, who both shrugged.

Blair stood for a moment, his eyes on the lady laying there, his heart sinking. He knew her. His hand reached out to touch the dark auburn hair, willing her curiously-coloured jade eyes to open.

"I need to go with her, Brady." He finally spoke.

"You can't, Blair." Brady was puzzled as to Blair's reaction.

"I have to, Brady. She's a friend." Blair didn't feel the hands on his arms as Branigan and Bradon both reached to restrain his movements and move him backwards.

"It still doesn't matter, Blair. You can't go with her."

"She's a really good friend, Brady. I have to."

Brady and his partner shared a look, Tom shaking his head and motioning towards the rig.

"Blair, come on. You can't go with her. We need you to step back." Brady waited but Blair made no effort to move. "Blair? Come on. Please? Let us load the lady and go."

"I have to go with her, Brady." Blair looked up, his friends drawing in their breath at the look of devastation, worry, concern and something unreadable in his eyes.

"You can't, Blair. Now, move." Brady nodded to the other two men, who once more gently restrained Blair from moving forward.

"I have to, Brady. I just have to." Blair's eyes were on the lady's hand, studying the rose quartz ring on her finger, before Brady tucked her hand back under the blanket. "I have to go with her."

"No, you don't. Why are you so adamant about this? You've never mentioned her. We've never seen her before." Brady nodded to Tom and then began to load the stretcher, pausing as Blair was up and into the rig and seated in a corner. "Blair?"

"I have to, Brady." He looked up, once more the unreadable expression in his eyes and on his face. "You see, I know her well. She's my fiancee."

His words stunned the four men, causing them to stare at each other, before they stared at Blair, who didn't see the looks, his eyes back on Devaney Daubney, who had disappeared from his life just as their college days ended, and before they had finalized the plans for their wedding. When had she come to Ontario from Alberta, he wondered? And why be on this road?

———

Barnabas Carey stood in the hospital corridor a number of hours later, his eyes on Blair as he paced, occasionally stopping to stare at the closed room door. He shook his head. Hadn't he just done this, Lord? Stood and watched one of his friends do almost the same thing? Was Blair to go through what Benen and Baird had? Please, Lord, protect him. Protect this lady he claims to know.

Branigan and Bradon flanked him, not sure what to say. They had relayed Blair's reaction and actions to Barnabas who had stared at them and then turned to study Blair.

"He said what?" Barnabas was not sure he had heard correctly.

"He told us she was his fiancee. I have never heard him mention her at all." Branigan shrugged, his thoughts muddled. "What has he gone and got involved in?"

"Another Baird. Another Benen." Bradon's droll comment brought brief smiles to the men's faces before Barnabas walked forward, the other two men keeping step with him.

"Blair?" Barnabas waited for Blair to respond. When he didn't, he deliberately stepped into his way, causing Blair to stop abruptly and stare at Barnabas.

"Barnabas? What are you doing here?" Blair was puzzled, his gaze going to the other two men, and then past them to Brady who was walking their way, his shift finished.

"I came to see a friend who needs me. Blair? Talk to me. Who is she?" Barnabas' hand on his arm drew Blair to a chair where he could still see the door.

"Devaney. We dated through college. We were to marry when we finished, but she just disappeared with no word, other than a note that said she had to do something and would be in touch. That's the last I heard. I've tried to find her." Blair rubbed at his hair and then his face, a hand resting for a moment on his cheek. "I don't think you knew. I was ready to tell you when you offered me the work here, but by that time, she was gone." His emotions were all over the place, he thought. Lord, I need to talk to her, but I am not sure what to say, or even if she'll want to see me.

"I knew something was up with you, but didn't know you well enough to ask." Barnabas studied his friend, close in age to himself. "It's been what? Six years or so?"

Blair nodded. "Almost that. She would have turned 29 last month." He shifted on the seat, uncomfortable at sitting when he wanted to be at her side. "Doc's the one who is treating her. He said he'd come get me."

"Was she hurt in the accident?" Branigan spoke up, his eyes first on Blair and then Brady, who was shaking his head.

"No, he said not. But she's not herself. I can see that. She's changed. And I want to know why and who did it."

His friends could hear the anger and worry in his voice. None of them knew quite how to respond to him. The four of his friends exchanged glances, not having seen Blair like this. They were not sure how to address him.

Brady had opened his mouth to speak when Doc approached, motioning for Blair to stay sitting. Doc sank down wearily. He had already worked a full shift and had been about to head for home when he was asked to stay. Some of the scheduled staff had not been able to get in with the weather, which was worsening. He didn't worry about Anna, knowing she was safe, but he worried about his young friends here, knowing they would want to leave as soon as they could.

He shook his head at Barnabas' questioning look before he searched Blair's face, frowning at what he saw there.

"Blair? Talk to me. How do you know this young lady?" Doc's voice was low and compassionate. All of the younger men living in the Foundation building were like sons to Anna and himself, and he cared deeply what was going on in their lives. He prayed for them daily, but right now, Blair was the focus of that prayer. He had called Anna earlier, just asking her to pray for Blair, without any details. Anna didn't need that, she had always maintained.

"Doc? How is she?" Blair refused to answer the question Doc had asked, worried about his lady.

"She's under treatment and has some imaging to undergo. She's not awake yet, if that's what you're asking." He sighed, knowing Blair was avoiding the question he had asked. "Blair? I need to know some things about your relationship with her before I can let you go see her. I know you told your friends she was your fiancee. You have never mentioned that to any of us, not in all the years we have known you."

Blair stared down at the floor, his eyes tracking the lines of the tiles, not sure how to respond, how much Devaney would want him to say. He finally looked up at Doc, not seeing the compassionate, caring looks on the faces of his friends.

"We've known each other for years. We ended up in the same foster home. She has always been in foster care. She never knew who her parents were. She was abandoned as a baby, with a birth certificate. When we tried to trace her parents, we didn't get very far. She's had a tough life, her foster experience not being great until she ended up in the one I was in. I ended up in that one when my mother disappeared. We tried to trace her as well, with no success. From what I can find out, my father died in an accident before I was born.

"Devaney and I went to the same college. We were friends, fell in love, and decided to marry once we were through college. We had most of our plans made, just needed to get the license, and we were going to do that right after graduation. I went to find her the next day after graduation and she was gone." Blair sighed, his head going back and his eyes closing, memories still sharp, brittle and hurting even after all those years.

"You tried to find her?" Doc's voice was certain on that.

"I did, Doc. I tried so hard. She hid herself well. I don't know where she went. I traced her to the bus station but I couldn't find out what bus she had taken or where she was heading. They wouldn't or couldn't tell me." He looked around at his friends, not sure what to expect. "I'm sorry, guys. I should have told you, but just couldn't."

———

"Not a problem, Blair." Brady spoke for the four. "We understand. You moved across the country right after that, not knowing where she was. That must have been hard."

Blair nodded. "It was. I felt like I had abandoned her. Our foster mother has kept in touch. She said she thought she saw her about six months ago, but couldn't be certain of that."

Doc looked up as a nurse approached and then rose, walking away for a moment, before he turned and watched Blair. He finally nodded, walking slowly back towards the younger man.

"Blair? You can come with me for a moment. I'll let you in to see her, but if she says you have to leave, you'll have to."

*Chapter 3*

Devaney Daubney roused, feeling warm for the first time in months, she thought, but disoriented. She cracked open her eyes, scanning quickly as she had become accustomed to doing, not seeing the man who had been haunting her for the last few years. She opened her eyes wider, taking in the cream of the walls and then the medical equipment around her, tracing the IV line from the bag to the back of her hand.

What did I do, she wondered? And just where am I? The last thing she remembered was desperately turning down a road, trying to lose the car that was tailing her. She didn't remember much after turning on to that road, where it led, she had no idea. She had felt the scrape and bang as her car had been sideswiped and, despite her best efforts, landed in the ditch. She had no memory of what had followed. Someone had come to her assistance, apparently, for her to be there.

She turned as she heard quiet footsteps approaching the bed and frowned at the older man who stood there, studying her, before he reached for her wrist and assessed her pulse.

"Now, young lady, how are you feeling?" Doc's eyes were kind, but shadowed, not knowing how she would react to Blair when he appeared.

Devaney shrugged, not quite sure if he was to be trusted. "Okay, I guess. Where am I?"

"In our local hospital. I know the police have been in. And I am told your car has been towed to a local garage." He watched her closely. "Where were you heading?"

She shrugged, wincing at the movement. "What did I do to myself?"

"Bumps. Bruises. You have a laceration on your shoulder, what from we're not sure. There are older bruises. You have some scars as well. From recent years, I would suspect." He shook his head as she refused to look at him. "You'll need a place to stay. I

———

367

have spoken with my wife about a young lady I met who needs a home. She wants you to come and stay with us."

"I can't do that! You don't know me!" She was shocked, but secretly pleased. Just maybe, she thought, I can find somewhere to hide and recover.

"Anna wants you to. She takes strays under her wing. You'll be able to leave in a while, once the IV is done. We'll make arrangements to get you to our home." He hesitated, then shook his head. Blair could explain, he thought. "We live in a building with a number of suites. You, in fact, were on the road to our place when you had the accident."

Devaney watched as he walked away before her head went back on the pillow and her eyes closed. Her head was aching and so was her heart. She wanted to see Blair, had in fact tracked him to this area, but she didn't know for sure where he was. She didn't want him to know she was here. He had been threatened years ago and that was part of the reason she had walked away. She was trying so hard to find the man or woman responsible for the threats against him and the accidents she herself had faced. But then, she didn't know if she wanted to see him again, not after what she had done.

Devaney heard footsteps approaching her, heavier footsteps, she thought. A man's. Probably a police officer back to question her again. She hadn't told much. She couldn't. She had no proof who had been in the car. She had hoped that she had lost her pursuer but wasn't sure. She didn't pray that she did. She no longer prayed, no longer trusted God like she had.

Blair stood by the side of Devaney's bed, his hands jammed into his jacket pockets, wanting to reach for her, but knowing he couldn't. Not yet. He wasn't sure if he ever would be able to.

Devaney sensed she knew the man standing there but refused to open her eyes. She didn't want to see Blair, if in fact that was him. She felt a hand rest on top of hers, the thumb circling near her own thumb. Then she felt a gentle hand brush down her hair before knuckles gently wiped at the tears she had not been aware she had cried. She heard the sound of the man's body as he turned slightly as other footsteps approached.

"Blair? Here's her knapsack. John brought it around for you. We'll be out in the waiting room when you're ready." Bradon's voice was quiet before his eyes searched the young lady's face. He nodded and turned away, not hearing Blair's soft words of thanks.

Blair turned back, his eyes on Devaney, before he sighed. She was not making it easy, and that was not the lady he remembered, the lady he loved.

"Devaney?"

His soft baritone voice washed through her mind, bringing back so many memories. She finally opened her eyes, to find him standing there, taller than she remembered, his hair cut somewhat shorter. She searched his face, seeing the lines time had started to work into it, the neatly trimmed beard and then she raised her eyes to his, finding his watchful, concerned, uncertain, caring, and full of the love he had always told her he had for her.

"Devaney? Talk to me, please? Why are you here? And just where have you been?" Blair waited, not sure how she would respond.

"Blair? You shouldn't be here. You shouldn't be around me." Devaney stared at him before she looked past him towards the door. "You need to leave."

"No, I'm not leaving. Not ever again. Not until you can explain to me fully and with the truth of why you walked away." Blair's hand tightened on hers, drawing her attention to that.

"I can't explain, Blair. I just can't." She refused to look up at him.

"Then, I'll take you to Doc and Anna's. You stay there, we'll talk." At his words, her eyes raised, startled. "Yes, I am friends with Doc Whitson, who was just in here."

With that, he dropped her knapsack on the bed and turned and walked away, Devaney's mouth open as she watched him just that. He's never done that before, she thought. What did I do to him?

Keeping Devaney's hand tight in his and her knapsack over one shoulder, Blair walked carefully towards Bradon's truck, where the two men waited for him, Branigan standing by the open doors, the sidewalks still icy and somewhat snow covered under the ice. Branigan searched Blair's face, seeing the shuttered look on it, before his gaze lowered to the lady beside Blair. So, this is the lady Blair loves. Lord, what do we do? How do we proceed?

Blair stood for a moment, his eyes on Bradon's truck, before Branigan spoke.

"Barnabas had Baird take your truck home."

"Thanks. I totally forgot about it until now." Blair grinned at his friend before he lifted Devaney into the truck and then slid onto the seat beside her. "Buckle up, Devaney."

She glared at him for a moment before she did that. She was confused, not knowing who the two men were that Blair seemed to know so well. She watched as best she could in the darkness of the night as Bradon drove away from town and then turned onto the same road she had taken.

Blair heard Devaney's breath be quickly indrawn and without thinking, reached for her hand, tightening his grip as she tried to pull away.

"This is the road you took, Devaney. It leads to The Barnabas Foundation. I work for that Foundation as do my two friends here." He watched her face in the dim light, seeing blankness on it. "Doc lives there as well. In fact, there are a number of us who are employed by the Foundation who work and live there."

Devaney felt the fear rising in her as she stared out the truck window, seeing where her car had dived into the ditch.

"Where did you find me?" She was certain Blair had been the one to find her.

"Brady found you off the road in the trees. He wouldn't let me near you. In fact, I didn't know it was you until they went to load you into the rig."

"You didn't?" She finally turned to him, her face lifted to study his. "Then, why?"

"Why? Why what, Dev?"

"Why were you there?" She was puzzled and not thinking straight, that much she knew. Time had taken a toll on her and she was exhausted, worn out in body and soul, her emotions shut down.

"Why? Because I was on my way home." He pointed ahead of them. "That's where I live." He shared a look with Branigan who had turned to study Devaney. "I couldn't not stop to help whoever it was. I don't think you realize just how your car was. It was nose down in the ditch. There is no way you could have gotten it out on your own. There was no sign of a driver. None of us could walk away and leave that person out there. We had no idea it was you. These two friends came looking for me at Anna's request, given the weather. We searched as did the emergency personnel. Our friend, Brady, is a paramedic. He was the one who was on duty, the team called to the accident."

Bradon pulled to a stop in front of the Foundation building, watching with amusement as Devaney's head twisted as she stared at it, her eyes tracing up the building's three floors.

Devaney clamped her mouth closed. This was not what she had expected, not at all. She sat, even after Blair opened her door, and then reached to undo her seatbelt. She felt his hand on hers, tugging her from the truck and then leading her to the doors. She stopped inside the door, her mouth dropping open as her eyes roamed the lobby.

"Not what you expected?" Blair grinned, knowing how she was seeing it for the first time. There were seating areas on either side, with comfortable chairs and couches, a gas fireplace on opposite walls. The floors were hardwood, something Barnabas had insisted on. A security desk sat off to one side, near the corridor leading to the office complex.

She shook her head, even as he tugged at her hand and led her to the elevators. "Not at all. What kind of place is this?"

"It's the headquarters for The Barnabas Foundation." He waited, seeing her processing what he had told her.

"I've heard of that. But that doesn't explain why you're here."

"Because I am employed by the Foundation and have been since I finished college." He saw the sadness that briefly flickered across her face. "I looked for you before I came east. I tried so hard to find you, Devaney."

She didn't say anything, just finally giving a brief nod. "I had to leave, Blair." She watched as the doors slid open and he once more led her from the elevator.

"I need to stop at my suite, and then I'll take you to Anna." He unlocked his door, his hand to her lower back as he directed her inside. "Take a look around. Have a seat. I just need to change." His work boots hit the tray in the hall cupboard and his jacket a hanger before he walked away, Devaney watching him.

Blair stood a few minutes later, his eyes on Devaney who had not moved from where she had stood. He shook his head and moved towards her, startling her. He frowned as she cringed back from him. Lord, what has happened to her?

Afraid to move, Devaney stood still, just letting her eyes roam what she could see of Blair's apartment.  She liked the rustic colours tones he had chosen, knowing those were the colours that he liked: brown, rust, orange, with some cream thrown in.  She heard his footsteps coming towards her and looked up, seeing the inscrutable look on his face and sighed to herself.  At some point, they would need to talk, and she was not ready to do that at all.

She stared down at the work sock clad feet of Blair before her eyes raised once more to his, a frown on her face as his mouth opened and then closed, his head shaking as he did so.

Blair reached for shoes, slipping into them, before he reached to take her backpack, not saying a word, not knowing what to say. Lord, this is hard.  What do we do?  Where do we go?  I still love her, always will, but I don't know how she feels towards me.  Not any more.

He motioned to the door, pulling it closed behind him before he reached for her hand, his warm on hers, leading her towards the stairs.

"If it's okay, I'd like to walk you down.  That way, you can get a feel for the building."

"And why would I want to do that?  I'm not staying."  She knew she sounded belligerent, not herself, not the lady he had known.

Blair shrugged. "If you don't, then you don't.  I know Doc and Anna would like you to.  If you have nowhere else, that is  If you do, once we can get back out, I'll take you there myself."

She stared up at him, tripping slightly as she took a step down, his hands out to catch her.

"We need to talk, Devaney. And soon. I'll grant you tonight or what's left of it. But then we talk."  Blair stared down at her as they stopped outside Doc's door, a gravity about him that she didn't recognize.

Devaney finally nodded. "Okay. We do need to." Her voice was low enough that he barely heard her

Doc stood for a moment, watching the two, not sure if he should speak. Blair looked up and spotted him.

"Devaney, you met Doc in the hospital. He was the physician treating you. He is also a good friend of mine as is his wife, Anna. Come. In we go." He left her little choice but to enter, her eyes searching Doc's face before she heard a gentle voice.

"And this is your lady, Blair? She's beautiful. Come, my dear. You've been through a lot in the last few hours. Let's get you settled into our guest suite and then you can sleep."

Anna's warm voice and the arm she wrapped around Devaney brought tears to the younger woman's eyes, tears she had not felt in years. She simply nodded, letting Anna guide her to the teal and cream bedroom.

"There's an attached bath. Take a shower or a bath or simply crawl into bed. Doc said you were tiny. He was right. I left some new pyjamas we had gotten for a granddaughter who's about your size. Use them tonight. They're our gift to you." Anna searched the younger woman's face before she kissed her cheek and then left.

She stood outside the bedroom, a troubled look on her face and a troubled feeling in her heart. Blair, my boy, she thought. She's hurting and I don't know why. I'm not sure she'll tell us or even tell you. We need to cover her with prayer.

Doc had watched the two women walk away before he pointed to the kitchen, reaching for the coffee pot and pouring mugs of coffee for both himself and Blair. He knew Blair would not be sleeping, not yet at any rate.

"Blair? Care to talk?" Doc's voice was low as he settled himself at the table.

Blair shrugged. "I'm not sure what to say, Doc. I lost that lady so many years ago. To have her here, like this? I have no words." He looked up, a bleak look on his face. "I don't know her anymore, Doc. I'm not sure if she'll even want to stay with me."

"But she still wears your ring, doesn't she?"

Blair nodded.  "She does, but it might just be out of habit."

Anna's arm came around his shoulders as she passed by him, stopping to hug him as she would her own son.

"I don't think so, Blair.  I caught a look on her face when you weren't watching her, when she looked back down the hall.  She still cares, but isn't sure what to do about it.  It's been a lot of years."

"It has, Anna, and I'm not sure we can overcome what happened."  Blair finally stood, swaying slightly, Doc on his feet, a hand on Blair's arm.

"Crash here, tonight, Blair.  There's the other spare room. Or take the couch.  It won't be the first time you've done that."

Her hand on the closed door the next morning, Devaney hesitated to reach for the knob. She glanced down at the clothes Anna had left for her, jeans, a nice sweater, heavy socks. It had been years since she had had nice clothes, had been able to buy anything new. She shopped at thrift shops, buying with distaste what others had donated. She hated that attitude, but she had had no choice. She sighed. Now, to face Blair. How did she do just that? She could tell he was hurt, was puzzled, but still wanted to hear her story. What could she tell him? She didn't want him near her. That, she thought, was why she had been run off the road. She had chosen the road to here, not realizing it led to Blair, but whoever was following her had known just that. Whoever it had been had chosen to run her off the road. She could have been killed or more seriously injured. She ached all over, she thought, not even the hot shower helping.

She stepped quietly down the hall, her eyes searching, not hearing many sounds, until she stopped in the kitchen doorway, Anna turning with a smile on her face.

"How did you sleep, Devaney? May I call you that?" Anna was across the kitchen, sweeping Devaney into a warm hug.

Devaney hesitated a moment before she hugged Anna back, tears prickling at her closed eyelids.

"I slept well. The best in a long time. But I shouldn't have slept so late." Devaney grimaced slightly from pain as she moved backwards.

"Doc said you'd be sore today. He left some medications for you." A frown crossed Anna's face as Devaney shook her head. "You need to, love. It's an over the counter one."

"I can't, Mrs. Whitson. I'm sorry. I've seen too many lives destroyed and lost."

"It's Anna, and it's okay. We'll get you better. Now, sit. Which do you prefer, coffee, tea, hot chocolate? If not those, we have water and juice."

Devaney remembered to shut her mouth.  She had not had such a choice in years, she thought.

"Tea would be nice."  She stood hesitating for a moment before she slid onto a chair, her hand coming out to feel the texture of the colourful placemats Anna had on the table, not seeing the compassionate look Anna was giving her.

Anna set a cup of tea in front of the younger woman and then paused, her hand in the air before she laid it on Devaney's head, feeling her flinch slightly.  What has she been through, Lord?  What does she need to heal from?  We need our Buckley to talk to her.  But will she talk to a minister?  I get the sense that she has walked away from You.  We need to bring her back.

Asked what she wanted to eat, Devaney had stared at Anna before she spluttered, her words not making sense.  Anna had simply laughed and then reached for food, finally setting a plate of French toast and a bowl of fruit in front of her.

Devaney ate, her thoughts not on the food, but on Blair. She wouldn't ask where he was, knowing he would be at work. He was that conscientious.  She shifted in her seat, uncomfortable at being inside for so long.  She had lived on the streets for months, seeking a room when she had work to provide funds for that.

Her head turned as she heard the outside door open and then male voices and laughter in the hallway.  She recognized Blair's as he protested in laughter at the teasing he was undergoing.  She sighed.  She did have to face him, but how?  How did she tell him why she walked away all those years ago?  How did she tell him about the threats against his life, the accusations she knew to be unfounded?  She had tried so hard to find the one responsible, tracking that person across the country, always just a step or two behind them.

The three younger men and Doc spilled into the kitchen, the younger men greeting Anna with a hug and kiss before they looked over the food supplies she had left on the counter, knowing they would be in shortly.  Blair gently moved Anna to one side, a grin on his face as he did so, a quiet comment that had her laughing at him, before he reached for the eggs and bread, soon plating French toast for the men.

Doc had drawn Anna to a side with a question before he nodded, heading for his office. Anna watched the bewilderment on Devaney's face before she took pity on her and sat beside her, an arm around her.

"They do this to me, Devaney. They walk in and take over, just like that." Anna watched the younger woman closely, seeing her nervousness and beginning agitation. A prayer rose for her.

Blair was watching Devaney as well, even as he worked away and joked with his two friends. Branigan's eyes moved between the young couple, a frown beginning on his face before he looked at the third man. Buckley Cullen, a close friend but also their minister, worked away side by side with Blair, a grin on his face as he accepted his fair share of teasing. Branigan placed the plates of food on the table as he was handed them, Buckley placing mugs of coffee and then startling Devaney as he set a fresh cup of tea in front of her, her eyes raising in fright before they shuttered.

Doc stood in the hallway where he could see but not be seen, his eyes on Blair, seeing the underlying tension in his friend before his eyes shifted to Devaney, a prayer rising from his heart as well, not sure where it was going but sensing Blair and Devaney were in danger, just as he had with Baird and Berneen and Benen and Cadee. Where does it end, Lord? Where does it end?

His eyes watchful, Blair slid into the seat beside Devaney, catching her slight jump as he did so. He sighed. How did he get to know her once more? He had not stopped loving her, never would, even if she walked away. She would take his heart with her, he knew, if she did so. They needed to get to know one another again. He reached for her hand as Doc led them in a blessing on their food, her hand fisting and then relaxing under his. His eyes opening once more, he watched from the corner of an eye, seeing her restlessness and anxiety.

Laughter spiced the conversation over the meal, the younger men taking the teasing Doc and Anna directed their way. Devaney kept her head down, seeming to study her mug, but her eyes watched closely through her lashes. She didn't see the looks Blair shot her way, even as his conversations with his friends continued. She jumped as his hand reached for her plate as the younger men cleared the kitchen, food stuffs away in their proper place, dishes in the dishwasher, the counter and stove wiped off, the mugs of coffee refilled as was her mug of tea.

Blair settled himself once more beside Devaney, his arm along the back of her chair, not quite touching her. He didn't watch her face but felt her jump as he did that. His eyes were on Doc.

"Buckley? Will you pray for us?" Blair's voice caused Devaney to turn to search his face, not sure why he was asking that. "Devaney, Buckley's a good friend. He is also our pastor."

Devaney stared at him and then at Buckley, gathering herself to push her chair backwards, unable to do so as Blair's arm laid across it. She felt trapped, unable to escape, and that was a feeling she hated. She had been trapped too many times over the last few years, just escaping death or a physical assault.

Buckley's head was down as he prayed, leading them to the throne of God, his words as simple as a child talking to his beloved Father, but deep enough that they were challenged. His heart broke for his friend, knowing the conflict he was undergoing.  These two had had a brief moment to speak earlier that day.

Doc studied the four younger people, his eyes lingering on Blair and then Devaney, seeing her discomfort at being in close contact with them.  What has she been through, Lord, that has led to this?

Devaney listened to the conversation that started after the prayer, not wanting to be there, not wanting to take part.

"Devaney?"  Blair's voice was close to her ear.  "Talk to us. Tell us why you were running."

She shook her head, not looking up, not wanting to see the anger and censure she was sure would be on their faces.

"Devaney?  Please?  Look at me."  When she refused, his hand came out and gently turned her face to him.  "Devaney, you will look at me and now."  His words lashed at her, not in anger, but with concern.

Her eyelashes raised and she studied him, seeing the man she had fallen in love with, his care, concern, compassion and love on his face.

"I can't."  Her voice was barely a whisper.

"You can, but you won't.  So, how be I take a guess at it? Remember, I know you well enough to read your face, even if you try to hide the truth."  He waited, and then sighed, his eyes searching the ones sitting, waiting for her to speak.

"Devaney, I don't know exactly why you ran, but it was something big that made you do that.  Someone you loved was threatened.  It had to be me.  You wouldn't have taken that step if it had been another friend or our foster family.  What was I threatened with?  Assault?  Injury?  Death?  Loss of my good name?  How close am I to the truth?"

Tears sparkled on her eyelashes as she first shook her head and then her face was buried in her folded arms on the table as silent sobs shook her body.  Blair's arm was around her, his head bent close to hers as he whispered gently and then began to pray, pray as he never had before.  His lady was hurting and he just wanted to make her better.

The other four watched silently before Buckley rose and came around the table, his hands reaching to lay softly on Blair's head and Devaney's as well. His prayer filled the room, stopping Devaney's sobs as she listened.

Blair finally raised his head once more, his eyes on her face as she refused to look at him.

"Devaney, please. Talk to us. No one blames you, least of all me. I, we, just want to help you. To help you find whoever it is that did this to you."

She finally nodded, her eyes on Branigan, a frown on her face. "I know you."

Branigan frowned, a puzzled look on his face. "We met last night."

"No." She shook her head. "I know you. Not from here."

Branigan shook his head again, and then paused. "Regina. You were in Regina. Your backpack had been stolen and I returned it to you. I never got your name, you were gone so quickly."

Devaney nodded. "Thank you. You were so kind. You made sure I was okay but I couldn't stay. He was watching me. He would have hurt you if I had stayed."

"Who would have hurt you, Devaney?" Branigan began to push, his employment as a security systems specialist coming to the forefront.

"I don't know his name. He was around before we finished college, Blair. I would find him watching you and then me. I found letters I think came from him, warning me against you. Telling me you were no good. That you were into crime. I knew he was wrong. I knew it because I knew you." Her voice shook with her emotions but her face remained shuttered.

"Devaney. Oh, why didn't you come to me or to our foster father?" Blair's heart hurt for his lady.

"I couldn't, Blair. The last photo I got was of you, walking towards me, but you had a red X through you." She stared at him. "He would have killed you, right then and there. I know he would have."

---

They had finally stood, the six of them, Devaney almost running to the bedroom she had used, the door closing quietly behind her.  She sank to the floor by the bed, unable to weep, unable to think, just unable to do anything.  She couldn't pray.  She had tried so hard the first year or so, to pray, to ask for guidance, for protection, but God didn't seem to hear or answer her.  She rubbed at her shoulder, at the scar from the knife attack that first year she was on the run.  They told her she was lucky, the medical people she had seen, that it could have killed her.  She just didn't understand why God hadn't stopped it.

Blair stood in the hallway, his eyes on her closed door, his thoughts muddled.  He didn't know which way to turn, which way to think, or what to do.  This had not been what he had expected to hear.  His thoughts raised in prayer, he turned as he felt a hand on his shoulder.  Branigan stood there, a frown of concern on his face.

"Blair?  What are you thinking?"  Branigan's voice was low, covered by the sounds of the conversation in the kitchen.

Blair shrugged.  "To tell you the truth, Branigan?  I don't know.  I never dreamed that was why she had disappeared.  I mean, I thought she had a line on her family and was trying to trace it, without worrying me.  That's what I thought the note meant."  His eyes grew more troubled, his heart heavier, his thoughts darker.  "I wish she had spoken to me.  I would have helped her."

"She didn't but we can now.  Let me have all the information you can think of.  Our guys will work on it.  Talk to your foster mother, see what she has to say."  Branigan's body shifted as he heard footsteps behind him, and Buckley appeared.  "Buckley?"

Buckley's look of concern stopped their words.  "Blair?  How strong a Christian was she?"

"One of the strongest I've known.  She had a rough life, shifted from home to home until she was about 12.  That's when she ended up in the home I was in.  Our foster parents were strong Christians and that helped her.  But, now?"  He shook his head, his eyes back on the door down the hall. "She tried to run when you went to pray. She's not open to God any more."

"No, she's not. She feels abandoned by Him. We'll pray that she finds her way back and soon." Buckley's hand rested lightly on Blair's shoulder before he excused himself and walked away, heading for the church office and the sermon he was working on for Sunday. He frowned as he did so, knowing that he had just changed his sermon. He paused, staring at the iciness the storm was still spreading and sighed. Guess I'm not going that way, am I, Lord? He turned as he heard footsteps heading his way and waited for Brady to catch up with him.

"Buckley? How's Blair? Have you seen him today?" Brady's voice held his concern for his friend.

"I did. We just had breakfast with Doc and Anna. Branigan's heading down to his office to do some research." Buckley paused and then motioned for Brady to go with him. "Come with me, Brady. We need to talk."

Brady sank into a chair in Buckley's office, not sure what to expect. He watched his friend closely, seeing how disturbed he was.

"Buckley? What can you share?" Brady waited, knowing Buckley would speak when he could and share what he was able to.

"Brady, it's bad. She's been on the run, trying to protect Blair. She's moved across the country, town by town, city by city. She doesn't know who, only that Blair was threatened. She admitted to Blair that just when they were graduating, she received a photo with an "X" through him. She felt she had no choice." Buckley stopped, unable to comprehend how she must have felt.

"And Blair feels guilty. He would. He would have asked her to let him help her, but she didn't or wouldn't or couldn't."

Buckley nodded. "That's how I imagine he is. He hasn't said, won't say. He wants to make it all better for her and can't. He's not even sure if she'll stay with him or move on. If she moves on, she'll take his heart with him."

"I thought that last night. I didn't know what to do, what to expect, when he said that. It's not what I thought he would say."

"None of us did.  It caught all of us off guard.  With Baird and Benen going through what they have, we didn't want anyone else to have that experience."  Buckley sat back, rubbing at his face, fatigue weighing him down.  He had not slept the night before, not when he heard what had happened.  He had been that burdened for his friend.

"Now what?"  Brady sat forward, reaching for a pad of paper and a pen.  He liked to make notes, needed them to help organize his thoughts.

"Now what?  We pray.  I think she'll try and run again, just to keep Blair safe.  He said she wanted to run when I prayed.  His arm around her was the only thing that kept her in her chair."

"Okay.  Number one - pray for her to come back to God.  Number two - pray for this guy, whoever he is, to be caught and caught quickly.  Next?"  Brady looked up, a frown on his face as Buckley didn't respond.  "Buckley?"

Buckley looked up, his eyes narrowed before he shook his head, clearing his thoughts, the frown on his face disappearing.  "She had met Branigan."

"Last night.  I know she did."  Brady continued to frown, his eyes watchful.  "What?"

Buckley was shaking his head.  "No.  She had met him before.  She questioned him.  Branigan remembered that he had run into her in Regina, that her backpack had been stolen and he returned it to her."  Buckley paused, a frown gathering once more on his face.  "She said if she had stayed, Branigan would have been hurt."

"So, whoever this guy is, he's staying very close to her.  She's afraid to get close to anyone, to ask anyone for help."

"We need to keep her here.  At least in the building, if not on the property."  Brady's head went back as his eyes slid closed.  "Not that it matters.  They managed to get to Berneen and Cadee both here on the property."  Brady had mentioned Baird's Berneen and Benen's Cadee, who had been endangered on the very property.

"That's my fear.  I'm sure it's Blair's as well.  He can't stay with her, not like Baird and Benen."  Buckley sighed.  "But I can see him wanting to take that step, to marry her, just to keep her close to him."

Brady nodded, his head turning as he heard a knock at the door. "I can see that as well."

*Chapter 9*

Cracking open the door, Breck peered in and then entered, the door closely behind him. His eyes searched Buckley's face before he sat, not saying a word, his thoughts muddled for once.

"Breck?" Brady's voice finally cut through his thoughts.

"Buckley? How's Blair?"

Buckley grinned. "Brady just asked me that not too long ago." He sobered. "He's hurting, Breck. For himself. For his lady. He's not sure where to turn or what to do."

Breck nodded. "I gathered that. How do we help him?"

"Prayer. Support." Buckley sighed. "He's not sure what he wants to do. He's waiting for Devaney to speak with him, and she's not. She's shut down and has been for a while." Buckley exchanged a glance with Brady, not sure what was going on with Breck. He was distracted, that much was obvious.

Breck was on his feet, pacing, before he turned, mouth open to speak, then shook his head and walked out of the office, leaving the two men staring after him.

"Did he just do that?" Brady stared at the closed door.

"He did. He wanted something but wasn't sure how to express it." Buckley studied his desk for a moment. "Pass the word, will you, Brady? Church is cancelled tomorrow. We'll meet here somewhere instead."

Brady nodded as he stood, his eyes on his fingers he was rubbing together. "What about Blair?"

Buckley sighed, sitting back in his chair, his eyes on Brady. "We'll have to leave that with God. There's not much we can do. The police will be investigating. Devaney isn't open to our meddling as Anna would say. Blair is quiet, too quiet."

Brady frowned, then grimaced. "I don't like it, Buckley. Not after what Baird and Benen went through. I don't want to see another one of us go through that."

———

386

Buckley nodded again. "And that's exactly what I think will happen."

Brady stood watching Baird, Benen, Bradon and Branigan as they talked in the lobby before he walked towards them, their circle opening up to include him.

"Brady?" Branigan shot a glance at the stairs.

Brady shrugged, a puzzled look on his face. "I don't get it, Branigan. How did she remember you?"

Branigan stared at him. "I don't know. I need to talk to her again, but I don't think she'll say more than she has." He turned as he heard footsteps approaching. "Blair?"

Blair just shook his head as he stopped. "Don't ask me, Branigan. I don't know how she remembered you. She always has been able to do that. It's scary." He looked around at his friends, knowing the other six of their friends were around the building somewhere. "Church tomorrow?"

"It's here." Brady looked around as well. "Will Devaney be with you?"

Blair shrugged, a puzzled look crossing his face for a moment. "I have no idea. I pray she is, but I can't guarantee anything." He paused and then turned and walked away, to stand at the front doors, staring out, leaving his friends to exchange glances.

Baird followed him. "Blair?"

Blair hesitated and then turned to Baird. "How did you ever do it, Baird?"

Baird shrugged. "I'm not sure I could even tell you other than God saw us through."

Blair nodded. "I know that. It's a given He does that. But emotionally, how did you manage?"

"It was tough, Blair. It was different for us. We were married, even though we didn't know one another. That was tough."

"I get that, Baird. I just don't know how you kept your head or your faith."

387

"Prayer from my friends. You all supported us. It was difficult and at times I really doubted." Baird stopped for a moment, gathering his thoughts. "Now, about you and Devaney."

Blair shrugged. "I am not sure there is an us anymore, Baird. I can't reach her, and I should be able to." He paused and then walked away, heading for the small chapel Barnabas had installed in the building, knowing that was where he needed to be. Please, God, bring her back to me. If not, please remove the love I have for her. I can't go on, not knowing, not loving her like I am and do.

———

# Chapter 10

Her arms wrapped around herself, Devaney stood the next morning in the small chapel, her eyes searching for something, anything. She did not want to be there, that was a given, she thought, but she felt she had too. Anna had asked if she was coming, taking for granted that she was. She felt a hand touch her back and shifted to look at who it was. Blair, of course, she thought. She was trying to avoid him but given the close quarters they were in at the moment, that didn't seem possible.

Blair watched the shuttered look on Devaney's face and sighed. This was not her, he thought. She was always so open, so interested in those around her. How do we get her back to that, Lord? He hesitated for a moment and then nudged her to a seat in the back row, sitting beside her. He caught the curious and compassionate looks of his friends before he saw Cadee and Benen sit beside them.

Devaney jumped as she felt a hand touch her arm. Carefully schooling her emotions, she looked to the side, a frown on her face for a moment. What had she walked into, she wondered?

Cadee waited for a moment before her eyes raised to Blair, whose own eyes were on Devaney, not realizing his emotions were out there for everyone else to read.

"This is Cadee Carroll, Devaney. And that's her husband, Benen, beside her. They have had an adventure that they need to tell you about." Blair waited for a reaction from Devaney, a frown once more on his face as she just quietly said hi and then shifted her glance to the front of the chapel.

Cadee shared a glance with Benen before she looked up at Blair, shaking her head.

"Devaney, would you like to join us for lunch?" Cadee's voice was soft, a question in it that Blair had never heard before.

Devaney's gaze shifted to her and then she turned to look at Blair. He waited, letting her make her own decision, knowing he would back her, to some extent, whatever it was.  She finally nodded, thinking it was easiest just to go and then she could leave. She prayed, as much as she did now, that the weather would be clear enough on the following day that she could leave.  She didn't want to be there.  Didn't want to be the one bringing danger to Blair or his friends and that she knew was a real possibility.

Buckley's voice caught her attention and she frowned once more as she studied him.  Her head tilted as she did so, catching Blair's attention.  This was not a man who she thought would be a minister.  Just how did he fit in here?  She studied all the other men, catching sight of another young woman around her own age, sitting beside Anna.  She had heard Doc had made his way back into town, just how, she wasn't sure.

Buckley's eyes found Blair's, who nodded.  He sighed to himself even as he led the hymns and choruses he had chosen for that day, Burney at the piano, Breck on guitar to accompany them.

He paused before he stared at his message, his thoughts muddled, fear for his friend and his lady uppermost in his mind. Lord, I have no idea what to say.  I have printed words in front of me but they just don't seem to fit today.  Lead here, Lord.  Please?

Buckley's hand reached for his papers and he literally tossed them over his shoulders, bringing a quick laugh from his friends, and a deeper frown from Devaney.

"Sorry, folks.  I had a message planned. Not what God wants this morning."  He moved to stand and lean on the pulpit.  "God is here.  He is always here.  Now, this morning, we share.  We pray. We talk.  God had isolated us at this time because of the weather. We can't be isolated from one another."  He looked around, seeing the understanding on the faces, his focus on Devaney's, not quite sure what was going on with her.

Barnabas began to pray, his voice echoing through the chapel, leading them to the throne of God. Other voices picked up. Devaney jumped as Blair's hand covered hers and she glanced up at him, seeing his eyes on her, reading in them his love for her, before his voice picked up the chain and he prayed for them all, and for whatever situation they found themselves in.

Devaney stood at the end of the time, her head already shifting away from what she had heard, but her heart had listened. It had started to crack the hardness she had developed over time. She followed Blair as he walked away, his hand on hers. She hesitated about that, but then shrugged. She would allow him that today. Tomorrow, she would be gone, once more. She couldn't stay near him. She just couldn't.

The weather had warmed up enough by the Monday morning that the ice had melted. Blair stood outside, his eyes on Devaney as she paced in front of him. She's going to run, he thought, and how do I see her from doing just that, Lord? I need to keep her safe, but I'm not sure she'll let me do just that. He walked towards her, finding her backing away from him.

"Blair?" She had a question in her voice, trying desperately not to let him see she wanted him to stop her from moving but knowing she had to stay away from him.

"Devaney? I won't let you run. Not again. We need to talk. We need to decide where we go."

She shook her head even as his hand on her arm stopped her movement. "We have nowhere to go, Blair. You need to stay away from me."

"I won't, my love. I just won't." He turned as he heard the sound of a motor revving and heard Devaney's scream, even as he reached to pull her towards him and then towards the other side of the parking lot, the truck heading for them at a higher speed than was usually seen. He could hear shouts from his friends but as he glanced over his shoulder and saw the truck looming behind them, he knew he would not make it in time. He wrapped Devaney in his arms and threw himself to one side, the truck fender glancing off him before it spun and sped away, mission accomplished.

Blair landed in a heap beside his truck and lay still, Devaney still in his arms. He didn't hear the shouts of the men as they ran towards him, Doc reaching him first. Hands reached to gently move Devaney away even as Doc's hands reached for Blair, feeling for a pulse, a moment of stillness as he found it, before he looked over at Devaney.

"Is she alive?" His words cut through the stillness.

"She is, Doc." Breck was on his knees beside her as was Branigan. "She is. Blair?"

"I don't know." He looked around. "The backboards and collars, guys. We need to get them out of here." He turned back to Blair, even as he heard sirens rising and falling in the distance and getting closer. "Never mind. Help is here."

The men stood back, watching as the two were worked on and then loaded into the ambulances, the red and blue lights of the emergency vehicles flickering across their faces. Barnabas had picked two of the men to go with Blair and Devaney, just staring down the paramedics until they nodded. He was afraid for Blair, afraid that he would not survive. He had read the look on Doc's face.

Berneen and Cadee had ran for Anna and then for one of their vehicles, following after the ambulances, knowing someone had to be there for their friends. Anna's face was taut, knowing from the look on Doc's face just how worried he was.

Barnabas turned as a patrol officer approached him.

"Barnabas? What happened?" Frank Wills looked around, a frown on his face as he watched the team of officers reconstructing as best they could what had happened.

"I'm not sure, Frank. I was in my office and Breck pulled me out here. I can't tell you who was around, but some of them were. That I know."

"Okay. Let me talk to them and see who knows what happened." Frank paused, then spoke again. "Who is the lady?"

"Devaney Daubney." Barnabas paused. "She was in an accident on Friday night, on our road. We found out at that time that she and Blair were engaged. I am not sure where that stands now."

Frank stared at him, knowing Blair from the garage he worked at. "Blair? Your Blair? Engaged?"

Barnabas nodded, even as he pulled his keys from his pocket, and stared at them. "I know. He never ever said. I'm not sure he ever would." He looked up, squinting in the sudden shaft of sunlight hitting his face. "If you don't need me any further, I'm off.'

"No, go ahead, Barnabas. I'll catch up with you. I will make sure Will knows where you are." He referenced the police chief, a good friend of Barnabas.

———

"Thanks, Frank. Let me know if you need anything further from me."

Barnabas stood an hour later, staring down at Blair as he lay on the hospital bed in the Emergency Department of their local hospital. He could see the scrapes and cuts and bruises that were already forming on his friend's arms and face. Why, Lord? Why Blair? Who did Devaney bring around him that endangered him? Who is after her, Lord? We need to find out and I am not sure she can even tell us.

He turned as he heard footsteps behind him. Doc stood there, his eyes on Barnabas before he walked to the end of the bed and studied Blair.

"Doc?" Barnabas was almost afraid to ask how Blair was.

"Barnabas, it's not pretty. He took a good hit from the truck. They'll be along shortly to take him for imaging but his lower right leg is broken. How bad yet, we don't know. I have an orthopaedic surgeon heading this way. Internal injuries we are still assessing. What was he thinking?"

"Thinking of saving Devaney more than likely." Barnabas turned to stare at the door behind him. "Who's with her?"

"Anna. We have no next of kin listed for her. She's been in the province long enough to register for insurance but she has nothing to say who to contact. Did Blair say anything?"

Barnabas shook his head. "No, he didn't but then we never really had a chance to talk. This has been such a surprise for us."

"That's what we thought. For now, I've talked to the Administration here. We are listing Blair and then Anna and myself or you for her. We need to do this. Someone has to take care of her."

"That's good." He turned once more, to study his friend and employee. "I'm going to track down Anna then." He stopped as Doc's hand came out to rest on his arm. "Doc?"

"Go find Devaney. She's in the room next door. She's still unconscious but she needs someone there."

Barnabas studied his friend. "What aren't you saying, Doc?"

Doc just shook his head.  "Nothing. It's just a burden I have for her.  Just like with Berneen and Cadee.  These two are not finished with what's going on. Not by a long shot."

A hand to her head, Devaney groaned as her eyes flickered open and closed. Where are I am, she questioned, and why do I hurt so much? What did I go and do now? She jumped as she felt a hand gently move her own hand back down.

Her eyes opening, she stared around, fear in her heart, at the hospital room she found herself in. I can't do this, Lord. I just can't do this again. What did he do now? Her eyes sought the person she could hear with her and frowned. Do I know you, she wondered?

"Devaney, dear, you are awake." Anna watched as Devaney frowned. "I know it's confusing but we have met. Just a couple of days ago. I am Anna, a friend of Blair's."

"I'm sorry. Blair? I haven't seen him in years." Devaney was confused.

"But you have, dear. You've seen him every day for the last three days. Don't you remember?"

Devaney shook her head and then her eyes closed as the pounding intensified in it. "I'm sorry."

"Don't be. Doc said you likely wouldn't remember. That's okay. We'll get you two back together soon."

"No, I can't. I can't see him." Devaney was becoming more agitated by the second, leading to a frown crossing Barnabas' face as he had entered the room.

"Devaney? Who is after you?" Barnabas' voice broke through her agitation and her eyes flew to him in fright. "I'm Barnabas. I employ Blair."

"You do? Where is he?" She looked past Barnabas towards the door. "I don't believe you that he's here. I want to see him."

Barnabas' hand on her shoulder kept her in place, a frown shared with Anna at her words.

"You can't.  Not right now.  He's in surgery."

"Surgery?"  Devaney sat upright, shoving Barnabas' hand to one side.  "Why?  What did he do to him?"

"Who?  Who did this, Devaney?  Do you know?"

"I don't know who.  I don't know his name.  He's been following me for years."  She looked up, fear in her eyes.  "Please?  Will you help me?  No one else will.  I can't let Blair be hurt."

Anna's arms came around the younger woman.  "Talk to us, Devaney.  We'll help you, but you need to let us know what you know."

Devaney nodded, a yawn catching her unawares before her eyes closed and she slept once more.  Anna glanced up at Barnabas, catching his eye and shaking her head.

"We won't get anything more from her for a while."  Anna sighed, her eyes back on the younger woman.  "Who did she mean?"

Barnabas shrugged.  "I have no idea.  Blair has never talked about her, not until now, and even now, he has not said much."  He shrugged, his eyes on Devaney.  "We'll have to wait, I guess.  I know Will wants to speak with them both."

"I'm sure he does."  Anna walked around the bed to hug Barnabas.  "I fear for these two, that they are just beginning something that has no end, at least not for a while."

Barnabas finally walked away, heading for the surgical waiting room, finding his men wandering the hallway, waiting for word on Blair that hadn't come yet.  He sighed.  Another one like Baird and Benen, he thought, and then had the horrible thought that maybe just all of them would go through something similar.  He prayed they didn't.

Blair stirred in the early morning hours, not quite sure where he was. Blinking, he tried to focus, staring around, his eyes finally settling on the cast on his leg. He frowned, not remembering having done anything to cause a cast to be placed. He reached for it, feeling the tug on his hand and then frowned at the IV that ran to his hand. His other hand felt at his head, finding a bandage on the side of it. He hurt all over, he thought, not quite sure what had happened. He shifted in the bed, squinting at the door before he reached for the IV and pulled it, a hand clamped over the spot for a moment, before he shoved at the blankets and pulled himself from the bed and then headed for the cupboard, knowing he'd find his clothes there.

It was awkward, he decided, to dress, balancing on the cast as he did so. He turned towards the door, finding Branigan standing there, a smile on his face.

"Breaking out, are you, Blair?"

Blair gave a grim nod. "I need to find Devaney. That was deliberate."

Branigan's hand came out to help steady Blair. "Here. Use your crutches. You do realize it's only four in the morning?"

"It is? Doesn't matter. Let's leave." Blair stared at Branigan's hand on his arm before his eyes raised and he searched his friend's face. "Branigan?"

"She's here in the hospital as well. You two were run down yesterday. You can't leave without permission, Blair."

Blair looked past him at Doc. "Doc's here. Is he my doctor?"

Doc just shook his head and handed over papers to him. "We figured you'd do this. Baird is waiting downstairs. Your lady is next door. Berneen is in with her, helping her get ready. We've all agreed to let you leave earlier than we should." He shook a finger at the younger man. "I'll put you in the infirmary if I have to, both of you, Blair. For now, Anna is waiting at home for you two. And no, you are not on your own for a few days.  If you insist on that, you'll not leave here."

Blair's gaze flickered between the two men before he nodded. "I can do that.  Now, find Devaney for me."

Doc watched him closly as he wielded his crutches and then shook his head.  "He's not giving up on her, is he?"

Branigan shook his own head.  "Not one bit, Doc.  I am afraid for him.  I talked to Barnabas earlier.  He said that Devaney didn't believe that she had seen him in the last few days and that someone was after Blair.  She doesn't want to be around him because whoever it is has threatened to kill him.  She doesn't know why."

Doc's hand rested briefly on Branigan's shoulder.  "He's hurting, Branigan.  Hurting physically and then in any other way you could think of.  His lady's back near him but doesn't want to be around him.  That's something he doesn't understand.  I'm not sure I even do."

"I'm not sure she'll stay or even let us know what is going on. I pray she does.  Yesterday was too scary and too close for Blair." Branigan stared down at the floor, searching for what he wasn't sure.

"He won't let her away from him.  Not this time."  Doc nodded towards Devaney's door.  "Go on, Branigan.  Get them home."

Blair studied Devaney for a moment before his eyes raised to Berneen.  "She's sleeping?"

Berneen nodded.  "She could barely stay awake to let me help her dress.  There is more going on with her, Blair, I fear, than just this."

Blair nodded, his eyes on Devaney.  "I know there is, Berneen. Thank you."  He looked around as the door opened and Branigan entered.  "Are we set?"

Branigan stopped for a moment, his eyes on Devaney, before he reached to scoop her into his arms.  "We are.  Let's get you two out of here."

Blair slid onto the truck seat beside Devaney, his eyes on her as he clipped his seatbelt on and then reached to cradle her close to him, hearing her faint sigh as she turned her face to him.  Branigan watched, a frown on his face, not sure what was going on.  His eyes rested on Blair's face, seeing the worry, concern but something else there.  Blair's thinking through this, he thought.  We need to sit down with him and work through it.

Blair stood in the doorway to Doc and Anna's living room, hands jammed into the sweatpants pockets he was wearing, the only thing he had that fit over the cast on his leg, crutches balanced under his arms. His eyes were on Devaney as she slept, fatigue and pain evident on her face. He turned his head slightly as he heard the outside door open and close and then felt a hand on his shoulder as Doc stood beside him.

"Has she awakened at all?"

Blair shook his head. "Not since we got her here. Berneen had trouble keeping her awake to get ready to leave the hospital." A frown covered his face. "Doc, what else is going on with her?"

Doc's face showed the compassion he felt at that moment, as he drew Blair to the kitchen and made him sit, reaching to prepare food for himself and then coffee for the both. He sat himself down, sighing as he did so. The last few days had been stressful in the Emergency Department and he had been on call to the local shelter as well.

"Doc?" Blair's voice was quiet, and when Doc didn't respond at first, he shifted in his chair to stare at the door.

"Blair, we need to talk, but let me eat first. It's been a long day." Doc watched Blair carefully, seeing underneath to where he was trying hard to stay strong, to trust in God, but knowing that his friend was suffering and doubting and struggling.

Blair nodded, knowing that Doc was right. He sighed to himself, his mind wandering back to when Devaney had walked away from him, just leaving him standing watching her, before he ran after her, a hand on her arm stopping her. She had refused to look at him, had stared straight ahead of her, a shuttered look similar to what she now wore on her face. His pleas and questions had not brought any further information from her. She had finally just moved away, almost on a run. He had run after her but she had disappeared. He had searched, had almost haunted her apartment complex but he couldn't find her. Friends had told him she was still in town, but when he went to the locations she was to be at, she wasn't.  He had finally had to leave and take his work with The Barnabas Foundation.  He had travelled back to the town a few times, searching for her, but never finding her.  He had finally had to lay that burden down at the foot of God's throne.

Now, he wondered, where do I go with her?  Lord, I just don't know.  I still love her so much but I can't read her.  Not like I used to.  And I don't want to let her go, not if I can help it.

Doc sat when he finished his meal, his heart raised in prayer for his young friend and his lady, watching the conflicting emotions crossing Blair's face without him knowing that was happening.

"Blair?" Doc's voice finally reached through to him and he looked quickly at the older man.  "Blair, let's pray.  Then we'll talk."

Blair nodded, his head bowing as he listened to Doc pray, before he raised his head again, his eyes on his mug of coffee.

"Blair?  Talk to me.  Tell me if she had any health issues that you know of."  Doc knew something was going on with Devaney, he wasn't sure what.

"She didn't have any, Doc.  Unless she has developed something in the last few years.  She was always so healthy."  Blair looked up, his eyes on the wall across from him.  "What is it you are asking me?"

"We ran some blood work.  It came back mostly normal.  But there are some factors I need to talk to her about.  I was just trying to see if it was longstanding."

"Is it serious, Doc?  Do I need to worry?"  Blair's eyes held his concern even as he tried to focus on what Doc was saying or rather what he was not saying.

Doc shook his head.  "No, it's not.  But I need to talk to her first."  He looked around as he heard a sound and Devaney appeared in the doorway.  "Devaney, come and sit, my dear.  Let me get you something to eat."

Devaney gave a brief nod as she sat, her eyes not quite staying open all the way.  "Just some water please."

"No, Devaney.  You will eat more than that." Doc's voice was firm.  He set a glass of juice in front of her and then reached for the pot of soup on the stove, ladling some into a bowl he also set before her.  "Eat, or I'll take you downstairs to the infirmary and hook you up to an IV.  Your choice."

Devaney looked up at him, assessing whether he really would do that, and then picked up her spoon, eating about half of what he had given her before she pushed the bowl away.

"You wanted to talk to me?"  Devaney refused to look back up, knowing what he would have to say.

"I do.  Do you need Blair to leave?"  His kindly compassionate gaze rested on her, Blair's quiet shift in his chair caught on the periphery of his vision.

She shrugged.  "I know what you are going to say.  Those values, the hemoglobin ones, have been low but likely rising.  I have been on iron, or at least I was.  I ran out and couldn't get any more."

Doc shook his head.  "You need to take that, Devaney.  If you can't afford it, we'll look after it for you."

She abruptly shoved away from the table and headed for the bedroom she had used.  She sank to the bed, arms wrapped around herself.  How did she do this?  How did she keep track of Blair but stay away from him?  Her gaze on the door, she shuddered, knowing that whatever danger she had been facing on her own just became the danger Blair would face.  She didn't want that for him.  She wanted him to stay safe and he just wouldn't. He wouldn't stay away from her.  Somehow, she needed to make that break and she knew it wouldn't happen.  Her eyes on the ceiling, she sighed.  Is this it, God?  Is this how it ends?  How do I find my way back to You?  I can't do it on my own.  She sat in silence, finding and feeling the peace she had not had for months, no, years, she thought.  Thank you, God.  Keep my Blair safe, that's all I ask.

## Chapter 15

Blair watched her walk away and then looked at Doc, a question on his face.

"Doc? How do we do this?"

Doc sighed, rubbing at his head. "We don't, Blair. We can't force her to do anything. She's free to do what she wants. She can even walk away from us and we can't stop her." His hand came up at the protest Blair voiced. "I know, Blair. You're engaged to her, but you haven't seen her in so many years. To her, you're a stranger. And the same for you. You don't know her anymore. You need to let her have her freedom and space. Get to know her again. God has brought her here. It may be you'll stay a couple and marry. It may be that she'll give back your ring and move on."

Blair buried his face in his hands, prayers rising from within him. He finally looked up and towards the hall, knowing that Doc had spoken the truth.

"I know, Doc. That scares me. I don't want to lose her again, not if I can help it." He finally rose from the table, hesitated, and then walked from the apartment, his crutches thudding as he did so. He knew he needed to give her space, he just didn't want to.

He stood in the lobby, staring out the windows, watching as the warming weather had drips coming from the eaves-trough on the building and creating puddles on the pavement. His thoughts were muddled. He could see no clear answers to the questions racing through his brain.

Bradon stood for a moment, Kade by his side, watching before he approached him.

"Blair?" When Blair didn't respond, he reached to touch his arm, causing Blair to shake his head and turn slightly. "What can we do for you? We are praying for you and Devaney. But, right now, what can we do?"

Blair finally turned to face him. "To tell you the truth, Bradon? I have no idea." His hand reached to rub at Kade's ears as the dog leaned into him. "I don't know. I know she'll try and run again. And I don't know if I can stop her, or even if I have the heart to."

"God knows, Blair. I know. It sounds like a repeated soft answer that doesn't convince or calm us of knowing that God is in control. But He is. He has placed you and she where you need to be right now." Bradon looked around, a frown on his face before it cleared. Devaney stood nearby, a questioning look on her face even as Kade moved to stand beside her, his nose nudging at her hand.

Devaney's eyes were on Blair, a question deep in them. She sighed to herself. She needed to walk away from him, but knew he would not let her. She wanted him to stay safe. Her hand rubbed at Kade, not even aware of what she was doing, before she walked forward, Kade keeping step with her, his eyes on her face. She stopped just short of Blair, knowing she needed to speak but hesitant to do that.

Blair watched her reflection in the window, not sure how to approach her. This is not me, Lord. I should know how to talk to her, but I don't. Not anymore. She has had experiences she can't or won't talk about. She had them on her own, without me. I can't share that part of her life. He finally turned to study her, finding her eyes showing her hurt and pain and something he just wasn't sure of. Her face was as shuttered as she could make it.

"Devaney?"

"Blair, you need to be sitting. Please?" Her voice held a plea for him to understand, but understand what he wasn't sure of either.

"Devaney, here you sit as well." He waited for her to slide down on the couch in front of one of the fireplaces in the lobby before he sat on the other end, motioning for Bradon to stay. Kade crowded close to Devaney, knowing there was something going on with her and wanting to bring comfort to her. Her hand rested on him.

Devaney had kept her eyes on Blair, not even seeing Bradon as he sat in one of the armchairs just out of her range of vision.

"Blair? You need to stay away from me."

"No, Devaney. Not anymore. It doesn't work that way. I have no idea what you have gone through, but God does. Whether you believe it or not, He is in control and has allowed this." His hand reached for hers, feeling the roughness of her skin, and sighed to himself. "How do I get through to you? I'm not running away from you. If you run, I will come after you. We need to talk, but I don't think you are ready for that."

She shook her head. "I'm not. Not yet. Maybe soon." She sighed, her head going back as she looked up before her eyes came back to meet his. "I'm not the same person I was, Blair. I've changed. I don't like who I have had to become to survive."

"I realize that, Devaney. Neither am I. We are not the people we were back then." He paused, his eyes on the dark hardwood floor, tracing the lines in the wood. "What I need to know is what happened to you all those years ago, who it was."

She shook for a moment, her eyes closing, her face turning white. "I can try, Blair, but it is not pretty."

"It never is. I get that, Devaney. We need to do this though. I, no we, need to be able to tell the police here what you went through and who caused it." His eyes raised as he heard quiet footsteps and saw Will Peters, the local police chief, sitting near them. "Our police chief is here, Devaney."

She shot a look at the older man, seeing for the first time Bradon sitting there. "Where did you come from?"

Bradon gave a quick grin. "That's my dog, Kade, who seems to think you need comfort. I can leave if you want."

Will shook his head at Bradon. "Devaney? May I call you that?" At her nod, he continued. "I am Will Peters. I want to help you solve this and get you back to the person you were and can be."

She finally nodded, her eyes going back to Blair. "I guess. I want this over." She stared down at the ring on her finger. "I need this over for Blair, so he can go on with his life."

———

Gathering her thoughts and her courage, Devaney kept her eyes on Blair, a frown in place before she spoke.

"Blair, what do you do?"

"What do you mean?  What do I do?"

"For a living.  I know you were training as a mechanic but I don't know what you do."

"I am a mechanic, Devaney.  Let me explain about the Barnabas Foundation.  This building is the headquarters.  We all have apartments here, as well as offices.  We are paid by the Foundation but employed by local firms.  That lets them hire more staff as they need to without having to worry about finances.  We also volunteer in the community.  I work with a local soccer club. Does that help?"

"It does but what is the Barnabas Foundation?  I didn't hear about you're going to work for them before this all happened."

"It came up just as you left.  The Barnabas Foundation was started by our employer and friend's father, who named it after his son, Barnabas, but also took it from the Barnabas in the Bible, to be encouragers to everyone we work with or meet."

She sighed.  "Then I did hear right."

"What did you hear?"  Will's question had her head flying around to look at him.

"That Blair was working for a charity of some kind.  But I know that's not what this is."

"It is.  Devaney, it is."  Blair's voice held a tone she had not heard from him.  "We are a charity.  Just not like what you would think of one.  Why would you say that?"

She shrugged.  "I don't know.  Just something I heard somewhere and I can't remember who."  Her face paled.  "It was him.  He was behind me in a bookstore where I had taken shelter from a rainstorm.  He talked about you and the Foundation, told me you were working for a company that was a coverup for illegal activities. I believed him. Blair, what did I do?"

He reached once more for her hand, his strong and tight on hers. "Tell us. Talk to us. Give us the details you can. Names if possible."

She nodded, a look of relief crossing her face. "I have carried this for so long." She struggled to continue. "But I know he's still out there. He threatened to kill Blair. Why I don't know."

"Talk to us, please, Devaney. Then we can sort it out. Will is going to take notes. So will Bradon. We'll get it figured out for you." Blair tightened his grasp on her hand, seeking to reassure her, even as Kade whined.

She searched the men's face and then nodded. "I will. I just don't know who he is or how he is connected to either one of us. I don't know that I have ever heard a name for him, although I have met people on the streets who know him and are terrified."

Shudders ran through her body. She wasn't quite sure where to start or even if the men would believe her. What she had gone through sounded like a bad movie or television series plot or a suspense novel that shouldn't have been written.

Her mind wandered back in time, to the last few days of college. She and Blair had been planning their wedding, knowing they were in love and wanted to spend the rest of their lives with one another. She had remembered hearing Blair vaguely speak of a job offer he was considering in another province, but she hadn't sat down with him as he had asked. That wasn't something she was worried about. It didn't matter where they lived, she thought.

She had moved through the days leading up to their graduation in a fog, she thought. She didn't know the man who had approached her, had not wanted to talk to him, but he had forced her too. She had run from him, not feeling safe.

Devaney found the envelope taped to her apartment door the next morning, not moving at first to take it down. She finally did, opening it and pulling out the folded paper. She had frowned as she read it, not understanding what the man was asking for. Blair, she knew, didn't have anything that this man wanted. What was it he was asking for?

The threats against Blair had intensified. Devaney grew afraid for him, but couldn't talk to him. That was something she just didn't know how to do, and they talked about everything. She knew he was wanted to talk to her about the job he was taking, how it would move them from their home province. She had walked away at one point, leaving him staring after her.

Graduation day had arrived and she knew that at some point she had to talk to him. They had planned their wedding for a few days after that, then planned on moving across the country. She just couldn't do it. She had been threatened and so had Blair. Devaney had no idea what the man was asking for.

Blair had stared at her the day after graduation, not sure if he had heard her right.

"Devaney, talk to me. What are you saying?"

"Just that I need a day or so. I have something I need to do." She watched his face, seeing his disturbance on it, knowing he just didn't understand.

She had run from him, leaving him standing, staring after her before he ran to catch up with her, a hand on her arm stopping her.

Devaney had stood, hearing his pleas for her to talk to him, feeling the eyes watching her, the evil around them. She had finally shaken off his hand and ran, disappearing in the crowd. Blair had run after her, not finding her, standing with a hand on his head, looking. He had haunted her apartment over the next few days, seeking to find her wherever he was.

Blair had finally had to pack and move east, Devaney standing in the shadows watching, sorrow in her heart, her eyes rising to see a shadowy form standing across from her.

She had searched their hometown, looking for what it was, before she had moved to another town. That town became another town, another city, another province as she moved slowly across the country, not at peace, feeling herself tracking Blair, knowing that the man was following her or had someone following her.

Devaney had finally arrived in Ontario, tracking Blair as best she could. She knew he had been offered work with The Barnabas Foundation and had researched it in the public libraries of the towns she had lived in. She had been homeless, on the streets, staying in shelters, finding a cheap apartment as she could.

She stood one day, watching as he walked away from a store, a man with him that she thought must be a friend. She didn't see the man watching her. Devaney had turned that day, knowing Blair was safe, but she was no closer to what she was to find. That disturbed her. How could she keep him safe if she had no idea what that monster as she termed him was looking for?

Devaney had looked up about a week later, seeing the men approaching her, knowing he had found her. She ran for her car, a cheap little second hand car, all she could afford, and sped away from town, knowing the men were after her. She drove in a wild circle, knowing they were following her. She finally turned down a road, the road sliding away from her as she hit the ditch. She shoved open her door, her eyes wild as she searched, hearing a vehicle approaching.  She ran for the side of the road and for the trees she could see, hearing the car stop and that voice once more.  She made herself run faster, not caring that she was getting wet with the rain that was turning to sleet.

Devaney's feet slid out from under her and she tumbled to the ground, hitting hard and laying still.  I'll just rest a moment, she thought, and then get up.  They won't find me.  I won't let them.

She didn't hear the other vehicles stopping or see the emergency lights.  She didn't feel the hands reaching for her, turning her over, or tending to her.  She didn't feel the men lifting her to a stretcher or the stretcher carried to the waiting ambulance.

Blair had stood, his eyes on her, walking forward to touch her.  She didn't know he was there or she would have tried to flee once more.  She didn't hear his words that claimed her.

Devaney came back to the present, her eyes on Blair, seeing the distress her words had caused.

"Devaney?"  His voice reached out to her.

"I'm sorry, Blair.  I can't do this."  She was on her feet, running from the room, Blair reaching for his crutches before Brandon stopped him.

"Let me to, Blair.  Let me talk to her."  Brandon followed her, catching up their jackets as he did so.

Brandon watched Devaney closely as she paced the lobby of the building, not sure if she was heading for the outdoors or not. He approached her, laying a hand on her arm, causing her to jump.

"Brandon, isn't it?" At his nod, she sighed. "Blair sent you, didn't he?"

"No, I volunteered. He was going to come, but I think you need to talk to someone other than him." He nodded towards the seats, reaching for the bottles of water the security agent handed him. "Let's sit, okay?"

She moved to one of the couches, slumping down on it, her eyes on the bottle of water he had extended to her before she took it, rolling in her hands. Her eyes were on him.

"So, you wanted to talk?"

He grinned at her. "Not really. I think you just needed a friend to sit with you."

Devaney just shook her heard. "This is too hard, Brandon. I can't be near him."

"And he doesn't want you away from him. You're torn. You want to stay with him but you don't want to be there in case he gets hurt again."

"That sums part of it up." She leaned forward, setting the bottle of water on the table. "I don't know his name. I have gotten rid of everything he has left me over the years. The letters, the packages, the photos. I just couldn't handle it. I couldn't keep it."

"We understand, Devaney." Brandon wasn't sure where to head with his comments. "You did what you had to survive. You're not the same person you were back then."

"No, I'm not. And I'm not sure Blair will understand." She had not seen Blair moving up behind her, pausing at her words. "And I don't know how to keep him safe."

Blair sat, his arm sliding around Devaney, causing her to jump, and her face to whiten. He sighed. This is not going good, Lord. How do I reach her?

Devaney turned to him, shaking her head, and then rising, walking away from him. I can't do this, Lord. I need to find somewhere away from here.

Blair watched her walk away, not liking it, but knowing he had to. Brandon watched him closely.

"Blair?"

"She never told me. She just wouldn't talk about it. I couldn't help her. I tried to find her but she was hidden. No one would tell me where she was." He rested his hand on his leg for a moment before reaching for his crutches. "She'll run, Brandon, just to keep me safe. I can't let her do that."

"And how do you stop her?"

"I have no idea." Blair thumped away on his crutches, not seeing Devaney watching him, a worried look on her face.

She approached Blair, finally, waiting until he had turned to her.

"Blair, you have to stay away from me."

"It doesn't work that way, Devaney. Not any more. You can be sure he knows you're here. Why do you think we were run down in the parking lot? That was him, wasn't it?" Blair had to tamp down his anger, praying for release from it.

She nodded. "I know it was. That was one thing he had threatened to do." She sighed, her arms wrapping around herself. "I need to get out in the air, to walk outside."

Blair nodded, squinting at the darkening sky. "Tomorrow, love. I'll get you out for a walk tomorrow."

Blair watched Devaney closely the next morning as she stood outside the building, her jacket open.  He could tell she was enjoying being outside.  He moved towards her, his crutches thumping as he did so, causing her to turn.

"Blair?  Are you sure about this?"

He shrugged.  "About as sure as I am about anything lately."  He nodded towards a path.  "We can take that one if you like.  It's not too long a path, leads to a little sitting area."

"Oh, really?  You didn't tell me that."

Blair grinned.  "Barnabas has set up lots of little areas like that.  He was planning ahead, knowing at some point we would need them.  He has a playground in the works now that Baird and Benen are married.  And the ice rink down near the road.  He'll let the town use it at times, but it's for us."

Devaney thought through what he was saying, even as she walked beside him.

"You like working here?"

"I don't work here on site, Devaney.  I work off site for a garage.  And I volunteer as well with the youth group at church, besides holding courses for ladies to learn about their cars."

"You do that?  You never liked to teach."

He shrugged.  "It's come with the territory.  I've changed, Devaney.  I'm not quite the man you fell in love with."

"We all do."  Devaney stopped at the end of the walk, her arms wrapping around herself.  "Blair, we need to go back.  Something's wrong."  Her scream was cut off by the hand around her mouth, even as she saw the men approaching Blair, shoving his crutches away from him, and dragging him to a van.  She was shoved inside, not allowed to touch him, her eyes huge with her fright.

Hours later, Brandon and Breck appeared at the sitting area, Brandon reaching for the crutches, both men searching for the tow, unable to find them.

"Brandon?"

"This is what Devaney feared. She didn't want to stay around Blair. That's what she told me. She was afraid he would be taken." He sighed. "Now we have to call in Will, don't we?"

Breck nodded, pointing back towards the building. "I know we do. Barnabas had a premonition of this, did you know?"

"No, I didn't but it's par for the course. This is what always happens, isn't it?"

They searched over the next few days, not finding their friends, not sure where they were. Three days after the two disappeared, an envelope appeared on the seat of the bench. Benen reached for it, searching the area, before he left on a run, heading for Barnabas.

"I found this, Barnabas. On the bench in that area." Benen breathed heavily, trying to regain his breath.

"You did?" Barnabas stared at it, seeing it addressed to himself. "This is strange, you know. Addressed to me."

"I know. Are you opening it?"

"I guess I have to, don't I?" He pulled out the flap and then the letter, seeing objects drop to the desk top. "What are these?"

"Barnabas, that's the pin from his college. He always wears it. I don't know why though, he's never said. And that's a ring I saw on Devaney." Benen was more worried than he let on.

"So they are." Barnabas unfolded the letter, a frown in place. "This doesn't say much, other than they have them. No ransom demands. No information as to when they'll be in touch."

"So, now what? You have to go to Will, don't you?"

"I should, but not today. There was no evidence there, was there?"

"No, other than that. No footprints, if that's what you're asking."

Barnabas nodded.  "Let's meet this afternoon, after everyone's back.  Bring all the research I know you have all be doing.  We'll see where we stand then."

Benen nodded, knowing there was little they could do, except wait.  The letter, he felt was bizarre to say the least.

———

The men milled around the conference room early that evening, concern for Blair uppermost in their mind. They wanted to head out to find him, but didn't know exactly where to look. They all turned as Barnabas entered, a sheaf of papers in his hand, before he looked up and nodded, each man finding a seat.

"Break up in groups, please. Let's spend time in prayer first." Barnabas looked over at Doc, who had entered with him, and motioned him over. "Doc?"

"We need to pray, Barnabas. I feel their very lives are in danger."

Three hours later, the men rose, not having made much progress in their search for the missing two. Talking quietly among themselves, they walked away, Breck watching carefully for signs of extreme stress or worry. He turned back to Doc and Barnabas.

"Doc? You're not saying much."

"There's not much I can say, Breck. I am worried about them but without knowing where they are, we can't go in and find them. I think that's the whole purpose of that letter. To drive up our anxiety and not give away any information."

"I think you're right, and it's succeeding." Barnabas reached to gather his papers, following the two men to the door, and switching off thc lights, cnsuring thc door was closcd and lockcd behind him. "I just want them back."

"We all do." Doc paused for a moment. "Devaney has struck a chord with Anna. She wants to mother that lady and can't. Devaney just won't let her."

"It comes from being on her own for so many years and living on the streets. I'm not sure how to reach her, if we even can." Breck walked away, leaving the other two men exchanging glances.

Buckley ran for Barnabas the next day, his phone out as he did so. He slid to a halt in the office door, not seeing Barnabas. Amy, his secretary, looked up in surprise.

"He's not here, Buckley. He had a meeting out of town."

"That's right. I did forget that." Buckley spun and was gone, leaving Amy staring after him before she shook her head and immersed herself back into her work

Buckley stood in the lobby, searching for who, he wasn't sure. Bradon approached, his head tilted to watch his friend.

"Buckley? You look lost."

Spinning, Buckley stared at Bradon, then waved his phone. "I have word. Come with me. I think I know where they're at."

"You do? How?" Bradon's step matched Buckley as they headed for Buckley's car.

"A friend, you might say. He told someone at the mission, who sent me word. We need to move, before they disappear again."

"Should we not have help?"

Buckley shook his head. "Not until I know for sure they're where he says. I don't want to raise hope."

The two men stared at the ramshackle building on the outskirt of a neighbouring village before they exchanged glances.

"They're here?"

Buckley nodded. "You can see the tracks of vehicles in and out. There shouldn't be." He opened his door, carefully closing it so as not to make a sound. Bradon followed, their steps quiet as they moved towards the building.

"There. I can see Blair's footsteps heading in but not out."

"And those would be Devaney's. This is bizarre, you know."

"I know." Buckley looked around, not seeing anyone or feeling like they were being watched. "Let's do this."

Bradon nodded, his hand reaching of the broken-down door and pulling it open.

———

They searched, keeping as quiet as they could, before Bradon's hand stopped Buckley and then he pointed. They moved forward, hands reaching for Blair and then Devaney, picking them up. They looked behind them as they drove away, a frown on both men's faces. It had been too easy, Bradon thought. Just too easy.

Doc watched closely as Devaney's head twisted on the pillow. He had assessed her and then let Anna help her to their spare room she had been using. He frowned, his thoughts puzzled, before he turned and walked away, heading for the other room where Blair was ensconced. Blair had roused when they reached the building, his head shaking when questioned.

"I don't know who they were. I don't think they were the ones after Devaney and then after me. It doesn't make sense." He looked up at Breck who had appeared in the kitchen. "It just doesn't make sense. They didn't question us, just left us. I think that last day, was it only yesterday, they drugged either our food or water."

Doc nodded at that. "I suspect that's what they did. Let's get you to bed, Blair. We can talk in the morning."

Barnabas had stood, his eyes watchful, as he listened. He sighed. He had spoken to Will earlier, letting him know they had the two, but he wanted it kept very quiet. Agreeing, Will had sent an officer out to search the building, who had found the two men searching for the missing couple and arrested them.

Breck turned to Barnabas. "What is going on? This does not make sense."

"No, it doesn't. I think Blair is right. There are two different parties at work here. Find the men. I think the chapel is the right place to meet."

Breck stared at him for a moment, and then nodded. "We need to talk to them. When's Will heading this way?"

"He's not, not tonight. He wants to see what they find in that building. I don't suspect they'll find much."

Breck shook his head. "I doubt it. Buckley seemed to think they were just dumped there." He looked around as he heard a noise, a frown appearing on his face. "Devaney?"

Devaney halted her steps, her eyes huge with fright. "Who are you? Where am I?"

"It's Breck and Barnabas, Devaney."

It took her a moment to understand and then she nodded, moving past them to open the fridge, reaching for a bottle of juice and then into the cupboard for a glass before she turned to stare at them.

"Where's Blair?"

"He's sleeping, Devaney." Breck pulled out a chair, motioning for her to sit. "Can you tell us what happened?"

She gave an unladylike snort, causing smiles to break out on the men's faces. "What happened? I went for a walk, Blair with me, and then someone's there. They took his crutches from him and then took us away." She sat back, lost in thought. "It's not the man after us. It was someone else. He told me he wanted that other man, and he would use us to bring him out." She looked up, fear on her face. "Does that make sense?

"It does, Devaney. We will need to talk more. Can you describe this man?"

She shook her head. "No, I can't, but I feel like I know him from out west. Does that even sound right?"

"It could. We'll need a list of men around his age from out there, if you can."

She nodded and then yawned, on her feet and moving away from them, leaving them to stare after her.

"Did she just do that?"

Barnabas laughed at Breck's comment. "She did. She's not used to being around friends and how to react or act anymore. She'll get there."

# Chapter 22

A week later, Devaney was on a search. She needed something and only going to town would work. She sighed. This is not right, Lord. I need my freedom and don't have it. She spun in a circle, before heading for the door. A walk might help, she decided, heading for the road and town, not realizing how far a walk it would be. She sank onto a bench at the edge of town, her eyes watchful, feeling someone monitoring her. She shuddered. Lord, I want this over and it doesn't appear that it will be any time soon.

Burnie paused in his walk back to his car and looked around. Yes, that was Devaney, and she was on her own. He changed directions, to come to a stop in front of her before he sat beside her, not saying a word.

"What? You're not telling me I shouldn't have done this?" She peeked at him, not sure of him. She hadn't gotten to know all the men to know how they'd react.

Burnie shrugged. "It's a free country. If you want to leave, you can. We would rather you didn't. Blair can't handle you leaving again."

She sighed. "I know. I needed to come to town and couldn't find anyone to bring me. I don't have my car back yet. Blair said they were working on it for me."

Burnie's hand stopped in its movement of running along his jeans. "You walked?" At her nod, he stared at her. "Do you know how far that is?"

"I do now." She stared towards town. "I have to get some stuff, but I think I'm too tired to walk that far."

"What do you need?"

"I have to get some clothes and some shampoo and toothpaste. I can't keep using Anna's. And I don't have many clothes." She was almost in tears.

Burnie stood, a hand reached out for her. "Come on. Pretend I'm Blair for a bit. I'll walk you down to the nearest store and you can shop. Then we'll head back for home."

She stopped, her body still as she heard his words, before she spoke. "Is that what it is, Burnie? Home?"

"I think it is. You've been running for so many years, Devaney, that I don't think you understand how welcome you are there." He looked around, feeling someone near him, but not seeing anyone. "How be we head off, and then I'll take you back to Blair?"

"Right. Blair. He'll tell me off, I just know it."

Burnie laughed. "Not Blair. He'll just look at you with that question on his face."

She gave a small smile. "I don't know him anymore, Burnie. I just don't know him. And right now, I need to stay away from him."

"He's not going to let you, you do know that, don't you?" He grinned down at her as he held the store door open. "Go on, get what you need." He paused. "If it's money stopping you from getting what you want, don't let it. We can work it out."

She stared at him for a moment, not sure on his words, before she moved away, quickly finding what she wanted and then standing in line, searching for the man who had haunted her for so many years. He was near, she knew. She looked through the people waiting to pay, seeing Burnie watching her and then looking around.

"Did you get what you wanted?" His quiet question broke into her thoughts as he reached for the bags in her hand.

"I think so." She sighed. "I'm not sure anymore on anything, Burnie. I feel that God has abandoned me. I don't trust that He's there with me. I used to know He was."

"He is, Devaney. He has never ever left you." He sighed to himself as he closed the car door, watching as she twisted to stare around her. Lord, why me? How do I get through to her?"

Blair stopped near Burnie's car, a question on his face, as Burnie slid from it before heading for the trunk. He watched as

Devaney took the bags she was handed, a quick glance at him, before she walked away, heading for Anna and Doc's apartment.

"Burnie?"

Burnie turned at the question in Blair's voice, not quite sure how to respond. He gathered his thoughts, hearing the chirping of the birds in the shrubs near the building.

"She walked to town, Blair."

"She did what?" Blair spun to stare after Devaney.

"She walked to town. She had to get some things, she said, and didn't know any other way to get there." He looked down, then back up, distress on his face. "Blair, she didn't ask for help. She just walked all that way on her own."

"And she could have disappeared, and we would never have known." Blair's eyes slid shut, before he turned back to Burnie. "How do we do this, Burnie?"

Burnie shrugged, a slight smile on his face. "That's something you'll have to figure out, Blair. We can't do that for you." He nodded towards the building. "She's been on her own for too long. She doesn't realize others will help her. And she says God isn't there anymore, that He's abandoned her." Burnie walked away, leaving Blair to stare after him, before his head slid back and his eyes closed.

God, please, help my lady. She needs to feel that touch from You, that healing from touching the garment. How do we do this?

Anna turned from the door the next day, her voice welcoming both Berneen and Cadee as they entered, heading for her kitchen.

"What can I get for you ladies?"

"Whatever you're having, Anna. You know us. We're not fancy." Berneen stood for a moment, watching as Devaney slumped on the couch. "Devaney?"

Devaney jumped, not having heard the ladies enter, her eyes huge.

Berneen slipped to a sitting position on the couch, her hand out to touch Devaney's. "I'm sorry. I didn't mean to frighten you."

"That's okay. I jump at everything. I have for years." She looked up as Anna handed her a mug. "You're here to visit Anna." She made a move to stand before Berneen's hand tightened on hers.

"We're here to visit Anna, yes. But we are here to visit you as well." Berneen exchanged a glance with Cadee, who nodded. "We haven't gotten to know you, but we would like to. You've seen us around. I'm Baird's Berneen, and that's Benen's Cadee. And we both have a story of an adventure to share with you. God spoke to both of us this morning, telling us we needed to come see you today."

Devaney stared at the two younger women before she turned to Anna, who was nodding.

"That's true, Devaney. They've come to my place, but you're the one they're here to see. They asked if you would be here today. It's up to you if you stay and visit with us. That is your choice. We really would like you to stay." Anna waited, a prayer in her heart that Devaney would do just that.

Devaney studied her and then turned to Berneen, searching her face before she did the same with Cadee. She finally shrugged, setting her mug on the coaster on the black walnut end table, and tucking the blanket she had over her closer around her. She wanted to visit with these ladies.  Devaney had not had an opportunity to do that since college, she thought.  I need this.  I can do this, can't I?

Berneen had been watching her face closely and saw when she decided to stay.  She breathed a sigh of relief.  God had impressed on her heart that morning that Devaney needed a friend, someone just to stand beside her.

"So, Anna, what verses do you have this morning?"  Cadee smiled at Devaney as she looked startled.  "Anna always has a verse for us, Devaney.  Today, I sense that it's one for you."

Anna just shook her head.  "Not yet, dear.  I'm still working through that."

Berneen nodded.  "That you do, Anna.  You don't know how many times I have needed those verses."  She turned to Devaney.  "Did Blair tell you about our adventure?"

Devaney shook her head.  "We haven't talked.  It's not likely that he will."  She frowned at the looks on the faces.  "What kind of adventure would you have had?  You're married, settled here."

Berneen and Cadee began to laugh, causing the other younger woman to stare at them and then turn to Anna.

"They did have adventures, my dear.  I don't know how they survived them."  Anna rose, heading for the kitchen, returned with a tray with a large teapot, cream, sugar and a plate of sandwiches and squares on it.  "We'll need this, I think."  She looked at Berneen. "You were the first, Berneen.  You can start."

Berneen nodded, a momentary look of pain crossing her face. "It wasn't fun, Devaney.  I had been kidnapped, held for months, and then Baird was kidnapped.  The guys came in and found him, he insisted I had to come.  We were kidnapped again the very next day, along with Buckley.  He was beaten to the point of almost dying. The only way to stop that was for me to marry him.  I did.  Do you know how hard that was?  Anyway, despite what they threw at us, and despite me having to raise my teenaged brother, Darby, we fell in love somewhere in there."  She looked up, seeing the shock on Devaney's face.  "It was brutal, I must admit.  God was there."

Cadee nodded.  "I know he was with us, Devaney.  Benen and I were old friends, losing touch.  My parents were missionaries in

South America. Dad had written to Benen to come visit and he did. I didn't know at the time that someone wanted me dead and the only way for me to get out of the country was a name change. Dad asked Benen to marry me, to provide that name change. Like Baird and Berneen, we had a lot of difficulty, almost losing one another at some point. But Benen is the love of my life. He always was. God was there for us as well. That I have no doubt of."

Devaney stared at the two women, her eyes huge, her mouth opening and closing. "There is no way you two went through that."

The three women with her laughed.

"But they did, Devaney." Anna's hand reached to lay on Devaney's head. "They did. All our guys became involved at some point or another, including Doc. When Berneen got here, she was very determined she had to leave. She needed to find her brother, who she had put into hiding. Once we had him here with her, she settled down. Well, sort of."

Berneen and Cadee laughed at Anna's phrasing.

"I did, Devaney." She shared a look with Cadee. "I know how Blair feels about you. If he hasn't said, he is still deeply in love with you. He wants the best for you. If it means letting you go, he will. He won't trap you into staying."

Devaney's eyes dropped to her hands, hands she had twisted into the blanket.

"I can't stay. I'm too dangerous for him to know." She blinked rapidly against the gathering tears.

Anna gave a small sound and then had Devaney wrapped in her arms, holding her as she finally wept. Wept for lost opportunities, for the danger she had been in, for the years she had lost. She wept for the danger she felt she had brought to Blair.

Anna looked up as she heard footsteps and saw Blair hesitating in the doorway before he was over to Devaney, taking Anna's spot, his beloved wrapped in his arms as she wept. His own tears wet her hair, as Anna and the other two ladies moved away, heading for the kitchen. Doc took one look at Anna and swept her into a hug.

"Whatever you said, you three, got through to her, I think." Doc watched the couple in the living room. "Thank you, ladies. Now, maybe we can figure out how to keep those two safe."

"We need to, Doc. We need to. I sense a growing cloud of danger overhanging them." Berneen reached to hug the older couple as did Cadee, before they walked away, the door closing softly behind them.

Blair stood later that night, staring out the living room window of his apartment, a hand resting on the glass, his eyes on the stars in the dark blue sky. His thoughts were muddled. How do I help her, Lord? How do I do this? How do I reach through to the lady I know and love?

He turned as he heard a tap at his door and frowned. It was late, he thought, for someone to be there. He walked through to open the door, not seeing anyone there. He stepped out, the boot case on his foot tapping loud on the tile floor and looked around. He shrugged, turning back to his door, frowning as he saw the envelope taped to it. Sighing, Blair reached for it, not recognizing the handwriting.

Dropping the envelope on his desk, he stared at it, not sure if he wanted to open it. He felt fear for a moment, not for himself as much as for Devaney. He finally reached to untuck the flap, pulling out the card in it.

Blair reached for a pen, using it to open the card. A sympathy card, he thought. This is bizarre. He read the threat printed inside, a threat against his lady. He had no idea what they wanted from him. He had nothing. Blair raised his head, his thoughts drifting back in years, to coming home from school as a young child, and not finding anyone home. He felt once more the fear he had felt that day, the anxiety, the stress. He had been thankful for his foster parents, but had longed for someone of his own. Was his mother somehow involved in this?

Rising early the next morning, Blair sought out Barnabas, handing him the card without a word. Barnabas read it, his eyes rising Blair.

"What do you make of this? And someone once more got in to the building."

"I have no idea, Barnabas. All I know is that my lady is threatened, and I don't like it."

---

"I didn't think you did.  Are you off to work this morning?"

Blair nodded.  "I am.  There are some things I can do, now that I'm not on crutches."  He paused, a grimace on his face.  "How do I leave her?  I need to talk to her but she won't talk to me."

"Let me.  Maybe I can get through to her.  Will was heading this way later this morning."  Barnabas studied Blair, reaching to lay a hand on his shoulder.  "Let me pray for you two.  I sense this is getting worse for you."

"It is.  And no matter what anyone thinks, we are not a couple. Not anymore.  I suspect she'll hand me back her ring and then disappear again."  Blair finally moved away, to where Bradon waited to drive him to the garage.

Devaney stood, shock on her face, as she had heard the words Blair had uttered.  Did he really think that?  She stood, sorrow on her face, not seeing Branigan watching her.  Barnabas and Branigan shared a look before Branigan moved towards her.

"Devaney?"

She jumped as she heard someone speak beside her and glared at Branigan.  "What is it with you guys?  Do you always sneak up on someone?"

Branigan laughed but the mirth didn't reach his eyes.  "Not always, but I would say you were deep in thought."  He reached to tuck her arm into his.  "Come with me, to my office.  We need to have a talk."

"That's all you guys want to do, is talk.  I want to find this guy, whoever it is"

"And we will."  Branigan unlocked his office, switching on the light and pointing to a chair, watching as Devaney sat before he sat in a chair beside her, watching her eyes skitter around the room, a frown still on her face.

"Branigan?  What?"  She stared at him, a puzzled look on her face.

Branigan shook his head.  "Nothing.  Now, about what you overheard?"

"I heard.  He's being threatened."

"Not him, Devaney. Not this time." He watched with compassion as she continued to stare at him, a puzzled look on her face before her eyes closed.

"It's me, isn't it?" She refused to look up. "I need to leave."

"If you leave, so will Blair. He was follow you, wherever you go. And that means he'll be hurt or killed, just to wreak revenge for something." Branigan paused, praying for the right words. "He still loves you deeply, Devaney. I am not sure that he would even stay if you left."

She nodded. "I think you are right. But how do we find this monster? I have talked to the police before. In different cities and towns. Blair doesn't know that that monster had me physically assaulted and beaten. I have a laceration on my shoulder that has just healed." She looked up at Branigan. "I want this over. I don't want to live like this anymore."

Her arms wrapped around herself, Devaney stood and began to pace, Branigan's eyes on her, a hand reaching for a pad of paper and a pen. She spun, staring at him, before she sat back down, her mouth opening and closing.

"What do you do, Branigan?"

"What do you mean?"

"Your occupation. Do you have an investigator on staff?"

He shook his head. "No, we don't. But I know of someone I can contact. As to me? I am a security systems specialist. I install or review security systems." His head tilted as she sighed and her eyes slid closed. "Devaney?"

"Then, you all do something different? Is that what you're saying?"

"We do. All of us have our own career or work. We also volunteer in our spare time."

"Do you have to volunteer?"

"No, it's not part of our contract, but it's part of who we are as one of the Barnabas Foundation people. The concept for the Foundation is to provide encouragement, and you can guess that comes in many ways. For me, I also teach self defence to teens."

———

"Okay.  Then, where do we start?"  She pointed to his pen. "You plan on writing this down?"

"That I do, Devaney.  And with your permission, I will pass it on to all of us.  That way, each of us will search and then combine our resources.  We also have friends we can pull in, if we need to."

She nodded. "Okay.  So.  Where do I begin?"

Her mind racing as she thought through the events in her past, Devaney leaned back in her chair, her hands rubbing against one another. Where do I start? Lord, this is so hard, but You've said You are with me. That if I seek You, I will find You. That's what I want, Lord. To find You once more.

Branigan waited, his eyes watchful, turning as he heard the door open, and Blair enter. He frowned. Blair was to be at work today.

Blair's head shook in the negative as he seated himself behind Devaney before his eyes sought her, a frown on his face. What was she up to now, he wondered? Barnabas had called him back from work, just stating he needed to be there, that Devaney needed him.

"Devaney?" Branigan's gentle voice broke into her thoughts, and she jumped.

"Branigan! I forgot you were here."

"I know you did. Now, can you give names, towns, events. I know we've done this, but this time I want you to really concentrate. Give me anything that comes to mind." He pointed his pen at her, a smile lighting his face. "It doesn't matter how minor or insignificant it is." He paused. "Blair's here."

"He is?" She spun, her eyes huge as she looked at him, despair on her face, but also the acknowledgement that he did need to be there. She waited as he drew his chair up beside her.

"Barnabas told me I needed to be here. Do I? I can leave if you'd rather."

She shook her head. "No, I think you should be here. I think, anyway." She blew out a breath, her eyes scrunching closed, as she tried to control her emotions.

He watched, before he reached to hug her, and then prayed for her. She relaxed in his arms, feeling that she had come home, that God really was with her.

Branigan waited when Blair finished, his eyes on Devaney, as she rubbed at her face before she looked at him.

"Okay, so, we should start."

"That would be good. How about you tell me what it was like when you were little? I know you were in foster care."

"I was. I don't remember being anywhere else, I don't think. I was shifted from home to home, I have no idea why. That made for a difficult childhood. I always felt the one left out, the fifth wheel, the unwanted one. That was until the last foster home. They made me feel like I was part of their family. I know they wanted to adopt me. They told me that. But they didn't, and I don't know why." She searched Blair's face to see if he had an answer for that, but he just shook his head. "That's where Blair and I met. I mean, it wasn't easy being a foster kid. It never is. Anyway, we made it through college. I studied business courses, but that really wasn't what I wanted to do. I'm not sure now why I did.

"But that last month or so, I could feel someone watching me. He finally started appearing behind me, leaving messages on my phone. I have no idea how he got that number. I would have letters in my box that were hand delivered. Photos. He threatened Blair, telling me Blair had something he wanted or needed him to do. He kept changing what he was saying. And no, I didn't keep any of them. I threw them away. I was so scared. When Blair asked me what was up, I couldn't tell him. I had to walk away. I wanted to find this man and stop the madness."

She paused, reaching for the bottle of water Blair handed her, sipping it, thoughts racing through her mind, before she capped the bottle again, rolling it in her hands.

Devaney finally started to speak again, her voice low and halting.

"He chased me across the country, from province to province, city to city. Here, Branigan, let me have your paper." She took it and began to write, turning over page after page before she sat back, drained, handing it back to Branigan. "This should help. I have listed everything I can think of." She turned as Blair reached for her, her face buried against him, a shuddering sigh drawn from her.

———

Branigan watched her for a moment, his eyes raising to Blair, watching him closely before he shook his head and his eyes dropped to the paper.  Reading through it, he drew in a deep breath, realizing just how vicious the man after Devaney had been, and just how close she had been to devastation or death.  They needed to find him, and find him soon.

They spoke for a while longer, before Blair, his arm around her, led Devaney away, desperate to find a place where she would be safe.  It didn't seem that she was safe here, not any better that Berneen and Cadee had been.  Lord, now what?  Where do we go from here?

Blair paced the walkways around the building, his cast thumping each time it hit the concrete, his mind on Devaney. How do we do this, Lord? I am at a loss. We need to find this person, and stop him. Devaney won't survive unless we do, or she'll run and I'll never find her again.

He turned as he felt someone near him, his mouth open to yell, before he snapped it closed, his hands going up into the air. Blair walked towards the man and then past him as the weapon held on him didn't waver. He knew he had to get away, but didn't see an opening to do just that. With his leg in a cast, he couldn't run, but he didn't think he could outrun a bullet. He walked towards the path that led deep into the forest, his eyes in constant movement to try and find a way to escape.

Slumping back against the truck seat, Blair's eyes held steady on the man beside him, the weapon still in evidence, even as he felt the truck move away from the building, away from safety. He had no idea who these men were, or what they wanted, just that they seemed to want him. He was pulled from the vehicle when it finally stopped in the town, pushed towards a factory building, and then up narrow metal stairs. The door opened and he was once more shoved forward, staggering to keep his feet, before he spun, hands up to defend himself. Blair frowned, his eyes on the man standing watching him.

The man pointed to a chair and Blair was shoved down into it, the man behind him holstering his weapon and then standing at the door. Blair waited, not sure what was going on, his eyes steady on the man walking towards him.

"Blair? This is not what you think. I wanted to speak with you but you just don't seem to be on your own."

"No, Timothy. I'm not. This is why." Blair stared at Timothy Meadows, a friend, he thought. "What do you want? Could you not have just picked up the phone? It would have been a lot simpler. This time, you'll be arrested for kidnapping."

Timothy sighed. "I know, Blair, I know. I just have to talk to you. Now that you're here, I'm not sure how to proceed."

"Just start talking, Timothy, or I'm leaving. Your men won't stop me." Blair felt anger rising in him and worked to tamp it down.

Timothy paced before he stopped in front of Blair. "I know your lady is in town. We've seen her around for a good month or more. She hasn't said anything but we've seen her watching you. You didn't know this, I gather. We have also seen men watching her, as well as a woman. Who they are, we're working on." He looked up at the man standing at the door, nodding. The man handed Blair a folder. "In this, Blair, are all the details we could find, as well as photos of them. I would take this to Will, but then I'd have to explain what I do on the side, and that I don't want to."

"And just what do you do on the side, Timothy? Tell me that."

Timothy sighed, his eyes raising to the ceiling as if seeking direction before he looked back at Blair. "I don't want to break a confidence but this is what I do. I am an agent for an organization that tracks people who are involved in national crimes. The ones after you are just such people. I know you are an orphan, Blair, that your father died and that your mother disappeared. We have looked into it." He paused once more, compassion on his face. "We have found her grave. I'm sorry."

Blair's hand rested heavily on the folder. "There is proof in here?" At Timothy's nod, he bowed his head, working to control his emotions. "But I don't understand how whoever it is, this monster as Devaney calls him, wants me. I have nothing that he would want. In fact, I have nothing other than what I have gathered over the last few years."

"That's what I thought." Timothy leaned towards him, tapping the paperwork. "Go through that. Have your friends go through it. I just ask that you don't give it to Will, not just yet. There is still something missing, and we're working on that for you." He looked up at the man near the door and nodded before he turned and walked away.

Blair sat, his eyes on Timothy, who he knew from church. How did this all come into play he wondered? He stood at the touch on his shoulder, finding the man who had been at the door standing there, an apologetic look on his face.

"We apologize, Blair.  We weren't sure if you would have come with us."

"I would have, if you had asked, and told me why.  Weapons weren't necessary.  Now, take me home.  Next time, if there is a next time, just ask."

Hands to her mouth, Devaney stared at Blair, not sure that she had heard him correctly.  She thought she had heard him say that he had been taken away at gunpoint, to meet someone he knew from church, who handed him the folder he now had in his hands, and then just let him walk away.

"That doesn't happen, Blair."

Blair gave a tired smile.  He was sore, the leg was hurting from being on his feet, and now his lady doubted his word.

"It really happened, Devaney."  His voice was weary and he turned from her to sit, seeing all of his friends standing there, Berneen and Cadee flanking Devaney.  He shook his head as he motioned to Barnabas.  "Here, take this.  Timothy said he's been doing some research.  He's included photos of the men and woman watching Devaney."  He drew a shuddering breath, his eyes sliding closed.  "He also said he found my Mom's grave."

Devaney was seated beside him, her arms around him, before he had finished, tears sparkling on her face.  She knew how much he had hoped his mother was still alive, that she would be back in his life.

"Did they say how?"  Breck's voice broke through the stunned silence.

Blair shrugged.  "I haven't read it yet.  I just got back."  He leaned forward, elbows on his knees, his face buried in his hands.  "I don't know how that relates to this, but it must.  In some way it must, or Timothy would not have included it."

He looked up as he heard footsteps.  "And there's Will.  I can't talk to him right now."  He was on his feet, disappearing up the stairs, Devaney beside him.

Will watched him walk away and sighed.  Another one running from me, Lord?  Why don't they just talk to me?

"Barnabas?  When did he get back?"

Barnabas shrugged, his eyes moving to each man and then the two ladies. "About an hour ago, I think. We were gathering to go looking for him and he walked in. He hasn't said much."

"Is he going to talk to me at all?" Will heard the footsteps of the men and two ladies as they walked away, leaving Barnabas standing alone with him.

"I don't know, Will. I honestly don't know. I hope he does. I pray that, but right now, he's hurting and so is Devaney."

Will nodded. "I do need to speak with her at some point over the next couple of days. I've been working on some of those names. They're nasty people, to put it mildly. She's in far graver danger than she realizes."

"She knows, Will. She knows. She's not in denial. Devaney is trying to come up with a way to lead them away from Blair but keep herself safe at the same time." Barnabas' hand rubbed against the folder. "Right now, I don't think she'll take off. But if she does, Blair will either go with her or track her down. And that worries me."

"It does me, too." Will squinted at his watch. "Tell them to call me tomorrow. I'm off but I'll be around home. Use my cell number." He looked back up, his eyes on his young friend. "Don't let them leave, Barnabas. No matter what you have to do. Keep them here."

"We'll do our best, but they are free agents, Will. We can't stop them if they want to walk away."

"Blair won't. He's too happy here." Will shook his head. "Let me rephrase that. He's happy here but he's not sure if Devaney will be. It hinges on her."

Barnabas nodded. "Berneen and Cadee spent time with her the other day. She was stunned to hear of their stories, and how they married the way they did. Anna said she was really thoughtful afterwards, and more softened towards them and she thought more softened towards God."

"That's our prayer, Barnabas. That she softens towards God. Once she's done that, she'll be more open to Blair."

———

Barnabas shook his head. "I don't see that. She's watching Blair to see how he's reacting to her. I can see her reaching out to him in a way she didn't when she was first here. She's worried he'll be hurt worse than he has been."

"That's true." Will pulled out his phone as he felt it vibrate, scanning the text. "We've got one of the men, Barnabas. He was just outside your property."

"I gathered they've been around there. Let's hope he talks. I want this over with."

Will nodded. "So do I. But what if this happens to everyone else? Have you given that a thought?"

Barnabas stared at him before he shook his head. "I pray it doesn't, but if it does, we'll go through it with God's help."

———

Pacing her bedroom that night, Devaney's heart was broken for Blair. She knew how much he had looked for his mother, waiting for her to come back, when he was young. She didn't imagine it had changed as an adult.

Devaney turned to watch the door, then watched the clock, sighing as she saw it was only five in the morning. She walked quietly to the kitchen, making a cup of tea, and then settling down on the couch, a blanket over her, her hand reaching for Anna's Bible. She idly turned the pages, stopping to read the verses Anna had underlined and the comments she had made. Her eyes stopped on one and she read and re-read it.

Is this still true, Lord? Will You be found of me? I used to think that but then life got in the way. I want that back, Lord, the sense that You are with me. Tears flowed down into her heart, her face dry, as she waited, listened and prayed.

Doc paused as he saw her before he headed for the kitchen himself. Making himself a coffee and reaching for a fresh cup of tea for Devaney, he sat in his favourite chair, a smile on his face as she looked up with a word of thanks.

"No thanks are necessary." He nodded towards the Bible. "Anna's?"

"It is. It is like reading her life story to go through it."

"That is it. She was told by her parents to never mark a Bible, but she said she had to. It was a love letter from her Father and her best friend. She had to respond."

Devaney's face grew more thoughtful. "That's how it should be, isn't it? I've missed that. I don't even have a Bible now. I lost it somewhere and just never had enough money to replace it. Or I guess, enough to replace something I didn't think was necessary any longer." She looked up at him, devastation on her face. "What did I do, Doc?"

"You didn't do anything. At some point, we all fail and fall. Just read David's psalms. The Good Lord is always with you, whether you feel Him or not. He has promised never to leave you or forsake you." He watched with compassion as her face crumpled, and she wept silently, finally sitting up and wiping at her face.

"Devaney, where do you go from here?" Doc waited, knowing he was asking something she might not be ready or willing to answer.

She shrugged. "I don't really know, Doc. We need to find the ones after Blair. I'm not sure where I stand with him or where I want to."

"He loves you deeply, Devaney. He has never dated, has shown no interest in any ladies here. There has been interest on their part, but he just moves through life, his focus on God and his work."

"That sounds like him." She frowned at Doc as her mind thought through what she had undergone over the years. "Doc, how do I figure out who it is?"

"What do you mean?"

"I need to figure out who it is. I think we know the person behind what's been going on. They seem to know things about us that strangers wouldn't."

Doc nodded slowly, before he rose, beckoning her to follow him.

"Sit. You do know how to use a computer word processing program?"

"I think I still do. I studied that at college." She stared at the screen. "A database, is what you're thinking."

"That's right. We list all the names you can think of. Their relationship to one another. Their relationship to either you or Blair. I'll leave you to get started. Anna's going to be up soon and she needs to be at a meeting by nine. I'm off to start breakfast. Call me if you need me."

Devaney shot him a quick glance as he walked away and then turned back to the computer, her fingers finding the keyboard. It was slow at first but then her fingers and mind began to work together.  Lord, is this You?  Are You doing this?  Help me to do this right, so that we can solve whatever it is and find whoever it is.

She finally sat back, her eyes on her work, before she rose, heading for the kitchen.  She stretched, stiff from sitting so long. Doc eyed her as she entered the kitchen before he reached for her cup of tea and pointed to the table for her to sit.

"You've not taken a break, Devaney."

She sighed, rubbing at her neck and shoulders.  "No, I didn't.  I used to get lost when I was doing this kind of stuff."  She looked up at him.  "I need to talk to someone."

"Who?"

"I need to talk to someone who does IT.  I need some advice."

Doc began to laugh.  "Benen and Cadee will be here shortly. In fact, Cadee and Anna are planning a meal for us.  Benen is in IT."

"Oh, wonderful.  Where is he?"  She went to rise, surprised to find hands on her shoulders stopping her from rising.

"He'll be here shortly.  He just had to stop at their apartment." Blair slid into a seat beside her.  "What have you been up to today?"

"Working on a database.  I need you to look it over."  Again, she went to rise, surprised to find Blair's hands holding hers and keeping her from rising.  "Blair?"

"Doc says he found you all day in that chair, sitting cross-legged I would suspect for most of it?"  Blair grinned at the look on her face.  "I'll take a look at it.  But you need a break.  Anna and Doc have asked us to stay for a meal.  I want that.  Benen will be here and he will take a look at it for you.  So will I.  We'll solve this, Devaney.  We will solve this."

Devaney looked around as she heard voices, seeing Anna, Benen, and Cadee appearing, Anna reaching for the meal in the oven, the younger men for the plates, Cadee for their beverages, coffee for most, tea for Devaney.

Sitting back finally to watch the others, Devaney was surprised as the two younger men cleared the round oak table, putting away the food, loading the dishwasher, wiping off the table before straightening the woven placemats, and then sat back down. A frown on her face, she studied Blair, finding him watching her.

"We pray after a meal here, Devaney. No pressure on anyone. But that is what Doc and Anna do."

She shrugged. "Ok. I'm fine with that." She didn't see the surprised looks on the faces around her as she bowed her head.

Devaney rose after a while and walked to the office, her mind already sifting through what she needed to do. Blair watched her and then turned to Benen.

"What has she done?"

"I would suspect set up a database. Let's find your lady and see what she has done."

Blair stood behind Devaney, his arms around her, as he stared at the monitor. "Care to explain what you've been doing?"

She spun, shoving him down into the chair, a grin crossing his face as he remembered how many times that she had done just that. "I need you to look this over. I have tried to think of everyone we knew, where we knew them from, how they might be related. That sort of thing. Please. Add to it." Turning to Benen, she stared at him for a moment. "When he's done, can you look it over? I need to start a search for anything that might be in common."

"I get you. I can do that." Benen watched as she paced before she abruptly left the room. He heard her footsteps heading for her bedroom and then sighed. Blair, this is not going to be easy. She's not letting anyone in, at least I don't think she is.

Cadee had been watching and followed Devaney, a tap at her open door before she walked in and sat with her.

"What? No words? Everyone needs to fill the silence, don't they?"

Cadee just smiled at the words. "No. No words. No platitudes. Just a friend sitting with a friend. Sometimes, that is all you need."

Devaney turned to her. "Is that what this is?"

"I would like to be your friend. You need us, and we need you."

"You do?" Devaney was surprised at her words.

"We do. Berneen and I would like to get to know you much better. Can we?" Cadee watched the other woman closely, finally seeing her nod. "But right now, you want silence. I can do that."

Blair finally stood, letting Benen have his place at the computer. Benen's fingers flew over the keyboard, before he sat back, a deep frown on his face before it cleared.

"Benen?"

"Blair, she's good. If she hasn't done this in a while, then she must have been really good at it once. We could use her where I work." He turned to look up and then rose. "It will take a while for this to work. She has made some interesting connections."

"I know she has. I don't see how." Blair paced before he turned to face Benen. "Will it help?"

"I'm sure it will. It certainly won't hurt." He paused, biting at his lip. "How are you really doing, Blair?"

Blair shrugged, not quite sure how to answer. "To tell you the truth, Benen, I am not sure. I have nothing to base what I'm feeling or seeing on."

Benen nodded. "The ladies do that to you. They get us all mixed up. That's a given with the ladies." He turned as he heard a chime from the computer. "It looks as if something has been found." He sat, bringing up the results, a frown on his face. "Blair?"

"What did you find?" Blair looked over his shoulder, surprise on his face. "Them?"

"Yeah. Them. I didn't know you knew them."

Blair shrugged. "I don't remember them. But Devaney has put them down for some reason."

Devaney spoke from beside him. "What did you find, Benen?"

He spun in the chair and then was on his feet, heading for the printer. "This. How do you know this couple?"

She stared at him and then at the paperwork. "Them? I'm not sure now. I just remembered their names and what they did." She paced, her eyes on the printed page, not hearing Blair speaking to her.

"Devaney?"

Devaney jumped as Blair's hand touched hers, and she looked up at him, fear in her face for a moment, causing him to frown and then sigh to himself. How do I do this, Lord? How do I approach her without scaring her?

"Blair? What is it?"

"Those names. I don't remember them. I'm not sure if I have even met them."

She shook her head. "I'm sure we did." She stared at him, her mind thinking back through the years. "At college. They were part of the leadership in the church, if I remember."

Blair's eyes slid closed. "They were, weren't they?" He turned to Benen. "We were part of a young adult group at church. We had, if I remember, four couples who sponsored us. This couple was one of them." He tapped the paper Devaney still held.

Devaney shoved the paper back at him. "Here, you take it. I don't want it anymore."

Blair grinned for a moment, passing the paper over to Benen. "Here, let Benen have it. He started it all."

Cadee began to laugh as Devaney and Blair stared at each other before their eyes turned to Benen, who stood, papers in his hand, his eyebrows raised, a look of almost shock on his face. He had not been prepared for Blair to do that. His eyes narrowed as he studied his friend and then his friend's lady before his eyes raised to his wife, causing Cadee to laugh even harder, bringing Doc and Anna to the door, questioning what was so funny.

Benen shook his head. "I'm getting blamed for this." He held up the papers. "Somehow, I don't think I did this." His eyes narrowed as he studied Devaney, seeing humour lurking in her eyes. "Devaney?"

She laughed. "Sorry, Benen. Blair does that. Didn't you know that?"

The others laughed as Blair protested that, saying it had only happened when he was a teenager, Devaney shaking her head at him.

―――

Blair was on a search that Saturday, not finding Devaney. He needed to talk to her. Will had been around, and Blair had given him the names they had come up with. He had looked at Blair, looked at the page, and then shook his head, asking why Devaney had started this, and did she not realize how much work she had just made for him? Blair had laughed, telling him he knew that, but did he know how much both he and Devaney wanted this over with? Will had shaken his head and told Blair to find Devaney. He wanted to speak with her.

Devaney raised her head from where she had it resting on her arm laying along the back of a bench. She had chosen to hide outside that day, the weather a bit warmer, but still cool. She didn't want Blair to find her, knowing right well he had questions for her. She had seen Will earlier and knew he had the same. She sighed to herself. Now what, Lord? I want to be free of this. I want to believe like I used to, to find You once more, but it just doesn't seem to be working.

Blair stood for a moment, his eyes on her, before he sat, an arm finally coming around her to pull her back against him. She waited, waited for what, she wasn't sure, but he didn't speak. His hand covered hers.

They sat, not speaking, the sounds of the morning in their ears. Devaney finally laid her head against Blair's arm, her free hand wrapping around his arm, before she spoke.

"Blair?"

"Yeah?" She could hear the hesitation in his voice, and shifted slightly in how she was sitting. His arm tightened around her before he spoke. "Will was looking for you."

"That doesn't sound good."

He laughed. "I gave him what we discovered. He said you made a lot of work for him."

She shook her head. "No, not really. If he looks at the ones we think are at fault, then it shouldn't be that much work."

Blair sat for a moment. "He'll look at them all. You know, I don't remember them."

"They were there, but I don't really remember much about them. Would our foster mom?"

"I sent her an email this morning. She's looking into finding a picture for us and any information that may help. She did say they are no longer there, that she had heard they moved east."

"Moved east? Like in where?" Devaney suddenly felt fear and turned more towards Blair. "Are they here? In this area?"

Blair shrugged. "Will said he'd look into that." His eyes raised at Bradon walked towards them.

"What does he want?" She sounded disgruntled, finding that she didn't want anyone else around them, she was content just to be held by Blair, with only his company.

Bradon sat at the other end of the bench, his eyes watching the birds as they fluttered around the feeders. Devaney kept her eyes on him, not realizing that Blair was watching her intently before his eyes raised to Bradon.

"Bradon? Shouldn't you be at work or volunteering or something?" Devaney finally spoke.

Bradon shook his head even as a grin broke out on his face. "It's Saturday, Devaney. I don't have anything on today."

She stared at him. "So, you just want to sit out here, in the cold, and watch us? Is that it?"

Bradon laughed before his attention was turned to the trees behind them, hearing a sound of footsteps that shouldn't be there.

"Devaney. Blair. Now. To the building."

Blair was on his feet, his hand pulling Devaney with him, as he ran towards the building, Bradon following. A sudden crack sounded through the air, and Devaney's hand flew to her head before she stumbled, her hand pulled for Blair's grip, and she tumbled to the ground.  Bradon tackled Blair, taking him down, before he slid towards Devaney, fear on his face as he saw the blood on her head.

"Bradon?"

"Stay down, Blair.  I'm not sure if they're done yet or not." He could see the men that were around exiting the building, running towards them.  He shoved at Blair, moving him towards Branigan and Breck, before he scooped Devaney into his arms, heading as quickly as he could for the infirmary, shouting for Brady or Doc, one of them to come, Devaney was hurt.

Brady reached for Devaney, helping to settle her on the bed, his eyes narrowing as he assessed the wound.

"What happened?"

"She was shot.  I heard something behind us, started them for the building, and then she was down."  Bradon was angry, angry that Devaney was hurt, angry that he couldn't have prevented it, angry that this was happening to one more of them.  God, where are You in this?  What's the reason?

Doc was there, his eyes on Blair before he motioned him from the room.  Blair fought them, not wanting to leave, his own eyes on Devaney, seeing just as Bradon had the blood on the side of her head.  Lord, please.  Don't take her from me now that I've found her again.  I can't do this.  He paced the hallway, Branigan keeping step with him, the other men mingling around them.

Barnabas stood and watched him, feeling like he had done this not too long ago.  Will stood beside him.

"This is hurting him even more, Barnabas."  Will's quiet comment barely broke the silence in the hallway.

"I know.  I don't know how to make it better for him."

"We can't.  Only God can.  And He has allowed this for some reason."  Will turned as an officer approached him.  "No sign of the shooter?"

The officer shook his head.  "Not much of a one.  He was in and out quickly, we can tell, but there's not a lot of evidence.  No shell casing.  Nothing." He was frustrated.

"Keep searching. Let me know if you find anything." Will turned back to see Blair standing in the doorway, his eyes glued to the room, his face white.

As Blair watched Doc and Brady, he could heard quiet, hurried words between them but was unable to make out what was being said. His eyes stayed focused on Devaney, not sure how she was. All he could see was blood, the bloody wipes they were using, the bandages they were pulling out. He could see they were rushing, but he just wished they would talk to him.

Baird pulled him to one side as he watched the paramedics coming down the hallway, almost on a run, the noise of the stretcher wheels loud in the silence surrounding them. He was afraid for his friend, for his friend's lady.

Branigan's hand was there to draw him away, to speak with Will. Will watched Blair closely, finally moving him away from the hallway and to the lobby.

"Blair? I know you want to be in there with her, but I need you to talk to me. What happened?"

Blair shook his head, his eyes focusing on Will. "I'm not really sure. We had been sitting out there. Bradon came out and then he was up and ordering us to run for the building. I didn't hear anything, just lost her hand as she fell. Bradon took me down and then the others were there, rushing me inside." He spun, his eyes towards the infirmary. "I need to get back there. I need to be with her."

Will's hand kept him in place. "They're working on her right now. She'll be heading into the hospital soon. We'll get you there." He paused, rubbing at his face. "Blair, I need your attention."

Blair's eyes focused on Will, a frown on his face. "My attention? Why?"

"That list? Could it be someone from it?"

Blair shrugged, his eyes studying Will. "Why would you think that?"

Will shrugged. "It just seems coincidental. That's all. We need to talk about that."

The younger man sighed, shoving his hands into his jacket pockets, his fingers on his keys as he rubbed at them. "How would they have know what we were working on? You didn't get it until this morning." He spun as he heard the stretcher heading his way and was gone before Will could stop him.

Barnabas shook his head, walking rapidly towards Blair, his eyes meeting Breck, who nodded, heading for the outdoors and a vehicle. He watched as Blair's hands reached for Devaney, his hand on hers as she was moved quickly towards the ambulance. His hand came out to stop him from climbing aboard.

"Breck will take you, Blair." He waited for Blair to respond, even as the doors were shut on the ambulance, and it raced away, leaving a white-faced devastated Blair standing, watching before he turned.

"What did you say?"

"Breck's here. He'll take you. Branigan's here as well. Go with them. We'll meet you there."

Blair finally nodded, his feet slow to move him forward towards the truck, Branigan's hand on his arm.

Will shook his head. "I'll have patrol follow them. There will be someone at the hospital when they get there." He sighed, his eyes searching the area. "Someone's out there, Barnabas."

"I know. I can feel them." He looked around. "Do you need any of us? They'll all want to go."

"Go ahead." He nodded towards the building. "Your security's here. We'll call you if we need to."

Blair paced the gray and white tiled floor in the Emergency Department waiting room, not see the various plants and pictures around the area. His sole focus was the door to the examination rooms, where Devaney was. He had no idea how she was, if she was even alive. His hands jammed into his pockets, he made tour after tour of the room, moving around those walking there and around the chairs and tables. He know his friends were there but he couldn't speak.  He didn't see Buckley pacing with him on one side and Baird on the other.

His friends exchanged glances as they gathered, Anna arriving with Cadee and Berneen, their voices hushed, their faces white and worried.  Doc had arrived, his feet carrying him to where Devaney was, his eyes assessing her, his hands reaching to help.  He followed as she was taken for imaging and X-rays, not willing to let her out of his sight.  He knew the staff, knew she was being taken care of.

He stepped back finally as the surgeon on call examined her, his thoughts muddled for a moment.  Devaney, for some reason, had taken a part of both his and Anna's hearts, without realizing she had done so.  He wanted her to be well, to walk out of there, but he knew she wouldn't.

The surgeon stepped back, his eyes assessing Devaney, before he turned to the physician treating her.

"Do you know a health history for her?"

Doc spoke up.  "She's a new friend to us, Tom.  But Blair may know something.  I did blood work a bit ago after she was found in the woods near our place.  She had been run off the road.  It showed she was somewhat anemic."

Tom Grafton's eyes studied Doc, before he nodded.  "And how is she related to Blair?  I thought he was an orphan."

"He is.  She was in the same foster home as he was out in Alberta.  Apparently they are engaged, but he never said a word. She's been making her way across the country by stages, from what she said."

"Let's get him in here.  He wasn't hurt?"

"Not this time."  Doc hesitated.  "They were run down a day or so after Devaney reappeared.  Blair had a broken tibia but it's healed."

Tom shook his head.  "What next!  Can't these young people find some other way to have fun?"

<hr>

Feeling a hand on his shoulder, Blair turned from where he was standing at the window, staring out at the parking lot, his hand coming out to brace himself against a pillar. Doc stood there, a closed look on his face, before he nodded at Tom.

"Blair, this is Tom Grafton. He's a surgeon called in to treat, Devaney."

"Dr. Grafton? How is she?" Blair was almost afraid to ask, as desperate as he was for word.

"We're still assessing her, Blair. There are imaging results to come." His hand reached for Blair's arm, turning him towards the examination rooms. "Come, let's get you into your lady. Before you go in, you understand that she was shot, the bullet creasing the side of her head. We are waiting to see if there are any fractures or bleeding in the brain. That we would need to treat."

Blair nodded, not quite understanding or hearing what they were saying to him. His whole focus was getting to Devaney. "She's alive?"

"She is, Blair. That she is. We'll have to wait until she awakes to fully assess her." Doc's hand on his shoulder guided him towards the cubicle she was in, Buckley's footsteps keeping pace with them.

Blair hesitated at the doorway, his eyes raised upwards as he prayed, his heart flooding with tears. He walked forward, Doc's arm on his shoulder for support, to stand, his eyes searching the equipment surrounding Devaney before they sought her face. He drew in a deep breath, seeing her pallor, the blood still evident where it had not been washed away, the beginning of bruising showing, the large white bandage that surrounded her head. He reached for a hand, finding hers cold and lifeless and limp. His heart tried to pray, but he had no words.

His eyes traced her beloved features, seeing the pain etched in them before his hand reached to touch her face. He looked up at Doc and then the surgeon.

"Doc?"

Doc shook his head. "I'm not the one treating her, Blair. Tom is and then there's the other emergency physician. They'll talk to you."

Blair nodded, his eyes back on his beloved Devaney, not hearing Buckley as he prayed for them and those treating her. He was finally moved back and to the waiting room, his head turning to watch her for as long as he could.

Will stood in front of him. "Blair?"

"Will, don't even ask another question." Blair walked away, anger on his face, his mind whirling with what had happened. He hit the exit door and paced the parking lot, finally realizing he wasn't alone.

Baird, Benen, Bradon, Brady and Branigan paced with him. He could see the other men watching from the sidewalk, Doc standing with them, Anna, Berneen and Cadee there as well.

"Why?"

"Why what?" Branigan answered his question with a question.

"Why her? Why shoot her? Where is God in this? How did He allow this?"

The men with him exchanged glances before studying his face even as they paced through the parking lot.

Baird finally spoke, his eyes searching the sky overhead for answers, watching the clouds scudding by. "He is here, Blair. She could be dead, but she's not. He has her in the hollow of His hand."

Blair shook his head. "I know that, Baird. I just want to know why. Why her? Who is it that's after her?"

Branigan shared a look with Benen, knowing what they had worked on the night before. "Can we get a list of the names you came up with? Benen said Devaney had set up a database and searched it."

Baird came to an abrupt halt, his hands scrubbing down his face. He finally nodded. "Doc or Anna can get it for you. Unless…". His words died away for a moment. "Benen, you took a copy?"

"I did. I'll pass it on to the guys. Will has it and said he was working through it." He gave a small smile that didn't reach his eyes. "He does need to talk to you, Blair. That's why he was out there this morning."

Blair sighed. "I know. I didn't want to talk to him. Nor did Devaney." He turned to study the hospital, not seeing Will standing hear him. "I have an email out to our foster parents about one of the couples. She was looking for more information for us, but she did say they had moved east. I wonder if they're in this province."

Will spoke, causing Blair's eyes to slide shut before he turned. "Which couple?"

Blair just shook his head, heading back inside, leaving them all standing and staring after him.

"Benen?"

Will's question brought his head around and Benen sighed. "I'm not sure which one. They were talking about three or four, I think."

"Can you remember which ones?"

Benen shook his head. "I would have to ask Blair, and I'm not prepared to do that right now." He walked away, leaving a frustrated Will behind him.

"Give them some time, Will. Blair needs that. So do the rest of the men." Doc stood beside him. "With what they've gone through with Baird and Benen, and now this, it makes them wonder which one of them will be next."

"That's what I am afraid of, Doc. That's it will be them all."

His eyes on the ICU doors, Blair stood, his hands jammed into his jeans pockets, not moving, waiting to be let into where Devaney lay. He heard the quiet conversations behind him. The men had all come to him, prayed for him and Devaney and then left. Other than Barnabas, Bradon and Buckley. He knew they wouldn't. Bradon had connected with Devaney for some reason, he thought, just as Branigan had. Benen had commented that he was going home to research the names, and just what ones did he want him to pass on to Will. Blair had stared at him and then just shrugged, stating he really didn't care at that point.

Doc watched him before he approached, just standing with him, no words necessary. He prayed for his young friends, knowing that Anna had contacted their church family, setting the prayer chain to work. He had receiving multiple texts from the men and women there, asking for updates as he could, just letting him know the young couple were prayed. for.

"Doc?" Blair's voice was broken and barely audible. "How is she? Really?"

"How is she? Lucky to be alive, Blair."

"I know that, Doc. But what are we facing? I can't lose her, not now. Not when I've just found her again."

Neither man saw the woman standing in the waiting room, her eyes full of hatred on Blair. She finally turned and walked away, her fingers busy on her phone, before a man appeared, standing where she had, watching Blair closely.

Blair finally moved forward, through the doors that swung closed quietly behind him, his eyes on the nurse who had come to find him. She smiled, pointing to a cubicle.

"In there, Blair. You can stay for a while. We'll be in and out. Dr. Grafton said he'd be around in a bit." She looked at Doc, who nodded.

Blair stood for a moment, before he entered the room, his thoughts muddled, knowing he needed to pray, but his mind just could not form the words.  Please, dear Lord?  He felt Doc's hand on his shoulder once more, heard his prayer, and then looked towards the bed.

He took in the medical equipment around Devaney, knowing it was necessary, but hating that hit had to be there.  He moved forward, his sneakers squeaking on the tiled floor, before he stood, his hands clenching and unclenching, tears flooding his eyes and blinding him for a moment before he blinked rapidly and turned to study his lady.

His hand reached for hers, holding it tightly, feeling it warmer than it had been.  His attention turned to her face and his free hand laid against her cheek, seeing her flinch at his touch, causing a frown to appear on his face.  He turned as he heard footsteps stop near the bed.

Dr. Grafton studied Blair before he moved up beside Devaney, assessing her, his eyes watching the monitors, before, a penlight in his hand, he checked her pupil reaction.

"Dr. Grafton?  How is she?"

"Lucky to be alive, Blair."  The surgeon stood, his hands on the bedrail, his eyes on Blair.  "I guess you could say God was watching for her today.  It could have been much worse."

"She could be dead."

Dr. Grafton nodded. "She could be.  Or the damage could be much worse.  We have the imaging studies back.  There is no fracture.  There is no brain bleed, and I don't expect there to be one.  However, she is far from out of the woods."

Blair nodded.  "I didn't think she was.  What are we facing? How long before she's awake?"

Dr. Grafton shook his head.  "At this point, I am not sure what we are facing with her.  As to that, we can't properly assess her until she's awake and coherent.  There was concern about her eyes, whether there was swelling around the optic nerves.  There isn't. But as to what she is facing when she awakes, we'll talk.  We'll talk about what she's facing and what you're facing with her."  He studied the younger man. "I am assuming you're not walking away from her."

Blair stood for a moment, shocked at the words, then shook his head. "I had too many years without her. I won't walk away from her, not ever. I don't know what I'd do if she did that to me again."

Doc shook his head at the other physician, knowing they'd talk, and he'd have to share what had transpired with the two in front of them.

His hand on Blair's arm once more, Doc led him from the room, back to where they could find chairs to sit. He sat, a sigh drawn from him, knowing that Blair would be back with Devaney as soon as he could. His eyes met Buckley's questioning ones before he shook his head.

"Blair?"

Blair finally looked around, his eyes shadowed. "Doc? What are her chances? Will she awake?"

"Right now, I don't know. I won't lie to you, Blair. You know me better than that. As for her chances, we can't fully assess her, as Tom explained, while she's unconscious. We can do limited testing, make educated guesses, give you those. But somehow, that's not what you want or what you're asking."

Blair shook his head, his eyes on his hands he was rubbing together. "It's not, Doc. It's not that. I just don't know what I'll face, or what she'll face. I don't even know if she'll stay with me. And I just want the person responsible to be found and face the consequences."

"We know you do, Blair. We all want that for you two." Buckley's voice had his head swinging that way. "We have you covered in prayer, Blair, both of you."

"Thank you, Buckley. I assume the prayer chain is at work."

"Anna's got it going. Benen was going over the list and was to speak with Will."

Blair nodded once more, his phone in his hand. "I just heard from my foster mom. That couple is in this area. How did they find me?  I didn't tell anyone other than my foster parents where I was moving to.”

“Then, we will need to give their names to Will.  He’ll need to look into them, just as a matter of course, you do know that, Blair.” Buckley’s eyes showed the sadness he was feeling for his friends.

“I know, Buckley.  I know.  I just wish it was different.”

Four days later, Blair stood once more beside Devaney, his hands on hers, as he watched her head begin to toss and turn, pain on her face as she started to rouse. He had been warned it would not be pretty when that happened, that he could expect her to rouse and then sleep.

He waited, a sigh rising within him, followed by prayers, as he watched her struggle to awaken, lose the battle, and then struggle again. It had been going on all day. He was fatigued, no, he thought, bone-deep weary, and he just wanted her to wake up, so he could tell her he loved her and didn't want to lose her, that he wanted her to be by his side for life.

Devaney's eyes finally stayed open, and she blinked, a frown appearing on her face, as she stared at the ceiling, not sure where she was or even why. She jumped as she felt a hand touch her hand and then her face. Her head turned and she blinked again, sighing as she saw Blair.

"Blair? Where am I?" She had to clear her throat to make the words audible.

"You're in the hospital, Devaney."

She continued to frown at him. "Blair, you don't look the same. You need to shave." Her eyes searched the room, a headache making it difficult to see. Her hand reached for her head, Blair's hand stopping it.

"Blair?" She questioned him, and then her eyes slid closed, and she slept, Blair's heart breaking for his lady.

Dr. Grafton had stopped in the doorway as he heard their voices before he walked forward.

"She's been awake?"

Blair nodded. "Just briefly. I don't think she knows exactly where she is. And I don't think she knows what year it is."

"Why would you say that?"

"Just the way she looked at me. She told me I didn't look the same. That tells me she's missing some years." He blinked rapidly, his heart breaking for his lady even as he prayed for recovery for her.

Dr. Grafton nodded. "We spoke of that, Blair, that she may have memory loss. Whether it's permanent or not, we will have to wait to see." He held up a hand, a small smile on his face, as he studied the younger man. "I know, Blair. You want her awake and the same as she was. That may never happen. You have been told that."

"I know. I do know that. It's just so hard, to see her like this, knowing someone tried to kill her and not know who or why."

"Will has not said anything?"

Blair shook his head. "I haven't talked to him since Devaney was admitted. I can't. He just says they're working on it."

Dr. Grafton's head turned as he heard footsteps and saw Will and a woman he knew to be a detective waiting at the door. "Will's here, Blair. Come. Let's get you out to speak with him. We need to assess your lady anyway."

Blair turned reluctantly before he turned back, bending to kiss Devaney's forehead, a hand resting on her cheek, a prayer rising for her complete healing. He blinked, not wanting the men to see him weep, before he raised her hand to kiss that, tucking it back under the blanket. He turned once more, straightened his shoulders and walked towards Will, knowing somehow that when Will spoke, it would change his life and that of his lady.

Will watched compassion in his eyes even as Bridget Green waited to speak with Blair. She was the detective assigned to his case and needed to question him and then bring him up to date on their findings. Will had already warned her that Blair would not like what she had found.

"Blair?" Will's voice was soft. "Have you eaten today?"

Blair stopped, not sure if he had. "I don't think I have, Will."

"Then, come. Let's find the cafeteria and get some food into you." He nodded towards Bridget. "This is Detective Bridget Green. She needs to speak with you. But first, we need to eat."

<hr>

His head bowed, Blair stared down at his tray of food, not really hungry but knowing Devaney would ask him to eat. He picked up his sandwich, laid it back down, and instead reached for the cup of coffee he had chosen. Will watched him closely, seeing the fatigue weighing his young friend down and knowing that when Bridget spoke to him, it would be even worse for him.

Will shook his head before he spoke. "Eat, Blair. Then, we'll talk. We do need to do that."

Blair nodded, reaching for his sandwich, his thoughts in the ICU with Devaney, before he finally pushed away his tray, not realizing he had eaten the meal he had on it. His hands wrapped around his mug, his eyes on Will.

"So, Will, where do we stand with this?"

Will nodded his head towards Bridget. "She'll update you. But I must say that the work Devaney did with her database was helpful."

"It was? We wondered if it would be. She was good at this at school."

Bridget spoke. "She has helped." She paused, not quite sure how to proceed, never having spoken to Blair before.

"Spit it out, Detective. I need to get back up to Devaney."

Bridget stared at him for a moment. "Okay. So, the couple you narrowed a list down to? We spoken to them. They are moving back to Alberta. They didn't know you were here."

Blair shook his head. "That's not happening. They can say what they want, but they knew. I've realized I've seen them here in town, found them watching me. So, go back to them and confront them. If I remember correctly, none of the young adults cared for them much. There were rumours about what they were involved in back there. Have you spoken to anyone there?"

"Not as yet. I didn't feel a need to." Bridget was becoming defensive.

Blair stood, his eyes on her, before he spoke. "I won't talk to her anymore, Will. I'll talk to you. I'll talk to another detective. To have this conversation? To have our concerns swept away, especially when someone just tried to kill my fiancee? Not happening again. And don't tell me it's our foster parents. I know that's what the thought is. It's not them. You wouldn't even consider it if you knew them." He turned as he heard his name called, his face whitening for a moment before he was across the room, hugging the older woman who stood there before hugging the man with her, turning to walk away with them.

Will shook his head at Bridget. "Did you not speak with anyone back in their home town?"

Bridget stared at him. "I didn't think I needed to. They were upfront with me."

Will sighed. "No, that's not how we do things. You know better. I am going to have to ask that you be removed from this. I need someone who can work with them. And Blair won't work with you, not after this. You don't have his trust in you, and you need that." He rose and walked away, leaving Bridget staring after him, before her phone was out and she was sending a text. She rose, walking away, not seeing an officer following her on Will's instructions. He waited as she met with a couple and then walked away. His own head shook as he recognized who they were. He just knew Will would not like this.

Blair turned from the window in the waiting room, his eyes searching for their foster mother. He had not expected the couple to leave their home and fly out here, but they had. Joseph and Ellen Liscombe had been there for both of them when they were teenagers. He had felt their prayers over the years, missing her hugs and words of encouragement each day, his words of well done and why can't you.

"Blair?" Ellen moved towards him. "How is Devaney?"

He shrugged. "We're not too sure as yet. I told you she was shot. She was awake earlier, but I'm not sure how well she is. She seems to have lost a few years."

"I'm sure she has." Joseph spoke from beside him. "It would be reasonable to expect that. Listen, can we get in to see her?"

Blair nodded. "Of course. She'll not expect you." He looked around. "Do you have somewhere to stay?"

Joseph shook his head. "That wasn't important for us. You and Devaney are."

Barnabas spoke from behind them, startling the older couple. "We have a guest suite you are welcome to use."

The older couple spun, their eyes on Barnabas, even as Blair smiled.

"This is my employer, Barnabas Carey. He's right. There is a suite you can use. Thanks, Barnabas."

Late that night, Blair stood at his window. Doc had made him come home, told him that he needed to, that Devaney would want him to. He hadn't liked that, but he knew Doc was thinking about him and worried about him.

Blair turned, a frown on his face. He was unsure about something, and just what that was, he didn't know. His frown deepened as he thought about the detective and realized that's what was puzzling him. She didn't seem to be doing the work she should have been doing, he thought. I need to talk to Will and see where the investigation really lies.

He pulled out his phone, reading the text from Will, knowing he would find him the next day. Walking through his apartment, he searched, looking for what he was not sure, but he knew he was looking for something. Finally stretching out on the couch, his eyes closed as he prayed and then slept, the early morning light awakening him. Sitting up, Blair rubbed at his eyes and then reached for his phone, afraid to check for any messages. There were none, especially not from the hospital, and that was good, he thought.

Showered, shaved, dressed in clean clothes, Blair drove away from the building, not noticing that Branigan and Baird stood watching him, before they were in Branigan's truck following him. They didn't want him on his own and had no way of knowing why. The two men stood in the waiting room, watching as Blair moved silently towards Devaney's room, eager to see his beloved.

Blair stood beside her bed, watching as she moved restlessly, not sure of anything anymore. He needed answers that weren't forthcoming. He frowned as he thought of his foster parents making the trip to be with them. That is not what he had expected. Now, that other couple? Where were they?

He watched Devaney closely, his hand on her cheek, as her eyelids fluttered and then she relaxed again. His hand was on hers, feeling hers turning to grip his.

"Blair? Is that you?" Her eyes finally opened, searching the room before she focused on him. "Where am I? My head hurts."

"You're in the hospital, love. You have been for a few days."

"I have? I don't remember. Where are we?"

"We're in a hospital in Ontario."

"Ontario? When did we come here? Aren't we supposed to be getting married on Saturday? Did I miss graduation?"

"No, you didn't miss it." He sighed, his hand tightened on hers. "We need to talk, Devaney. You're not remembering a few years."

"I'm not?  How come?"

"Because someone shot at you, trying to kill you.  You were hit in the head."

Her eyes were huge as she stared at him.  "Let me sit up."

"Not yet.  You can't. They want you laying flat for a few more days."

She pulled her hand from his, reaching for the controls, raising the head of the bed slightly.  "Now, why did I do that?"  Her head pounded for a few minutes until the pain subsided somewhat.

"That's what they didn't want."  Blair sat on the edge of the bed.  "What is the last you remember?"

"Us walking towards the library."  Her brow wrinkled.  "No, that's not it.  It's a building I don't recognize.  Why don't I?"

Blair's phone was out and he pulled up a picture of the Barnabas Foundation Building.  "Is this the one?"

She squinted at it.  "It is.  You said it's not Alberta."

"No, it's not.  You walked away from me back in Alberta.  I have work with the Barnabas Foundation.  Somehow you made your way across the country and found me, but it took years."

"Years?"  Her voice rose to a squeak.  "It can't have.  What year is it?"

When he told her, she frowned at him.  "It can't be."

"Sorry, my love.  It is.  We're in the middle of what we call an adventure.  We need to talk about that, but not right now."  Blair looked back at the door.  "Our foster parents are here."

"They are?  Why?"

"To see you.  I let them you know you were hurt.  You know how they are."

Devaney frowned before she looked up at him.  'They're not the ones, are they?"

"The ones, who?"

"The ones who have been following me. I know someone has been. I just don't know who. Why can't I remember?"

"Dr. Grafton, your surgeon, says you might not remember everything or you might. He wants to talk to you now that you're awake and coherent." He grinned at her frown. "You've lost some years. We don't know if you will ever get them back."

Her head went back on the pillow. "I can see someone standing watching me, Blair, but I don't know who. I should know him, but I can't remember. Why not?"

"You've buried everything deep in order to survive. I'll have Will, the police chief, come and talk to you." He frowned as he remembered the detective. "There was a detective, a Bridget Green, but she seemed to think our foster parents were the ones after you. We have figured out another couple, but she didn't think it was them. She said she spoke with them and was confident it wasn't."

"She didn't do her research, did she?"

"No, I don't think she did. She didn't contact anyone back there." He paused. "Do you remember the names we came up with?"

She shrugged. "Not that I know of." Her eyes slid closed and she slept, leaving Blair standing staring at her before he shook his head.

Devaney, what am I to do with you, he thought. How do we go on? You don't remember what happened, and I need you to.

He turned as he felt someone standing beside him. Will had appeared.

"She's been awake?"

Blair nodded. "She has. She doesn't remember much though. She thinks we're still just finishing college and then she's jumping to the present."

Will shrugged, concern on his face. "I suspect that's what she'll be doing." He turned to watch Blair. "I hear your foster parents are in town."

"They are.  They took vacation time to come east.  I would have told them not to."  Blair's head went down.  "And you want to talk to them."

Will shook his head. "I have already.  They approached me yesterday.  Barnabas put them in touch with me."

"And do you think they would do this?"

"No, I don't.  And now we can't find Bridget."

"Bridget?  What's her last name?"

Will spun as Devaney spoke.  "Green.  Why?"

"Because there was a Bridget Green in some of my classes.  Do you have a picture of her?"

"I can get one to you later.  Why would you say that?"

"Because she wasn't who she pretended to be."  Horror grew on her face.  "Blair!  That couple! She's related to them!"

———

Will walked back towards Blair as he sat in the waiting room, his eyes on Will. The older man sank to a seat, a sigh coming from him. Blair waited, knowing that Will would speak when he was ready.

"How's Devaney this afternoon?"

Blair shrugged. "A bit better. She's being moved from ICU tomorrow."

"And you'll be able to be with her during visiting hours only. I hear you, Blair."

"I know. Being engaged to her doesn't seem to make a difference."

"But being married would?" Will watched as Blair spun on his seat, his eyes on his friend.

"Just what are you suggesting?"

"That you marry Devaney. That way, you can stay all the time. We'll make those arrangements."

Blair sat back. "I've thought of that. I just don't know if she's ready to do that."

"She is. I've watched her. She's still in love with you, regardless of what she has said."

Blair finally nodded. "I need to talk to her." He looked up as Buckley sat beside him. "Buckley?"

"Don't wait. I heard what Will asked you. She's ready or rather, she was."

Blair nodded. "All we can say is to ask her. See what she says."

An hour later, Devaney stared at Blair, her mouth opening and closing. "You want to do what?"

"I asked if you would still marry me, today." He shoved his hands through his hair, pacing the room before he stood in front of her. "Forget it, Devaney. I know you're not ready, no matter what others say."

"Blair?" At her quiet voice, he paused in his walk away from her and came back, to stand, his eyes on her. "Maybe we should."

He shook his head. "I'm not sure, love. I don't want you to commit that way and then find out you made a mistake."

"It's no mistake, Blair. You said I ran from you all those years ago. Maybe, if I hadn't, I wouldn't be here in this hospital bed." She pointed at the door. "Get what you need. You say you have a minister friend?"

"I do. Buckley. He'll do the ceremony." Blair stood, his heart wanting to take this step, to keep his beloved safe, but he still wasn't sure. He prayed for peace, but didn't find it. At least, not the way he thought he would.

Devaney watched Blair walk out of the room, her head sinking back as her eyes closed. Lord, is this You? Are You leading us? Or are we rushing into something neither one of is sure we even want anymore? I know he still has my heart, he always will. He says he loves me, but he stays back from me, as if he's just saying the words, but isn't committed anymore. How do we do this? How do I do this? Lord, I know You're here. Please, Lord, give both us of peace about this.

Hearing the door open, she looked up to see Anna standing there before she walked over to stand beside her, reaching to hug the younger woman. Her head pounding as she moved, Devaney clung to the older woman.

"Devaney, what have you two gone and done?" Anna's quiet question finally broke the silence.

"We've decided to get married. Should we?" Devaney looked everywhere but at Anna.

Anna's arm rested around Devaney as she prayed for wisdom. "What does your heart say, Devaney?"

"It says to." She looked up, tears blinding her for a moment. "I asked Blair if I hadn't walked away all those years ago, would this have happened?"

"We don't know that, dear. It may have. It may not have. We have a young friend, who went through an adventure but his favourite saying is that God has a plan and purpose we don't know about yet."

"He's right, isn't he?" She looked up at Anna. "Oh, Anna, what did I do?"

"You did what you felt was right at the time. You were afraid for Blair." She hugged the younger woman and then stood back. "Now, we have to do something about this."

"About what?" Devaney looked around. "What is we have to do?"

"We need to get you all spruced up, as my father used to say. Let me call Cadee or Berneen. They'll help us."

———

Blair watched Devaney closely that evening knowing it had been an emotional day for her. He sighed. This is not how he had planned to marry her. Not with her in a hospital bed, recovering from a gunshot, her mind fading back and forth between years. He saw how she was playing with her rings, and reached for her hand, stopping her movement.

Devaney watched as Blair's hand reached for hers and then heard his prayer. She realized just how much she had missed that. She hesitated before she spoke.

"She was around today, wasn't she?"

"Who?"

"Bridget. I know she was. I thought I heard her voice outside the room this afternoon."

Blair stared down at her before he looked towards the door. "It's possible. Will said he hadn't been able to find her. And that worries him."

"Of course, it would. It always does, doesn't it? She'll come find us when we least expect her, take us somewhere we can't escape from, and put our friends in danger. That's how it always works in books and movies."

Blair gave a low laugh. "It does. Now, the nurses will be in to settle you for the night. I'll be in the waiting room. They won't let me stay for long. You're tired and need to rest."

Devaney's eyes were on his face, watching him intently. "I know, and so do you. Can't Doc just take me back to the building? He has an infirmary he could use."

"He's talked about that. Or having you stay with Anna and him. But now, you'll be staying with me." He bit at his lip. "I'm sorry, Devaney. I'm sorry you won't have the pictures and memories."

She carefully shook her head. "They're not important." She stopped. "Blair, is that what this is about? To stop us from getting married? Who hates us that much?"

Blair stared down at her, seeing the agitation in her face. "What makes you say that?"

She shrugged, her eyes on him. "We have nothing of value, except one another. What if someone wanted to break us up, make us turn to someone else? Did we even consider that?"

Blair groaned. "I didn't. I'm not sure anyone else did." His phone was out and he sent a swift text off to Branigan. "Let me ask the guys. I know they're trying to work through this, but we're missing a piece of information. You said Bridget Green was in some of your classes. I don't really remember her, but what if she's the one?"

"I think she is. Have our foster parents left yet?"

He nodded. "They flew back out tonight. We can call or email them about this. They may have an idea as well." He looked around as the door opened. "It's time for you to sleep, love. I'll be back in later."

Blair stood outside her door, wanting to stay there, but knowing he needed to be away from her, to think. Her question had puzzled him but made him realize that just maybe she had come to the right conclusion. He sank down into a chair, his eyes on the floor, not seeing the man sitting across from him, watching, a cruel look in his eyes.

His eyes finally closed as he slept, his sleep disturbed by dreams. He eventually rose midway through the night and made his way to Devaney's room, pulling a chair to the side of the bed and reaching for her hand, watching as she slept, his mind wandering to their conversation the evening before. He groaned as he thought through their friends. There had been one young man, he thought a friend of Bridget's, who had keep his eye on Devaney, a look on his face that had scared Blair. How had he forgotten him? And now he had to get the name to Will. No, he thought, I'll give it to Branigan. They'll search him out. I know they will.

Lord, can we end this and soon? I need my lady safe, and right now she isn't. I thank You that she's finding her way back to believing in You.  I know she always did, but she wandered, out in the desert for years.  Thank You that You never let her wander far from You.

He felt Devaney's hand tighten on his and he looked up, finding her still sleeping, but needing that touch with him.  He sighed.  Where do we go from here?  How do we keep her safe?  Has she been the target all along, or has it been me?  I can't get a clear grasp on that.

Blair looked up as he heard footsteps, and watched the nurse closely, watching that Devaney was not harmed, that she was taken care of.  He knew, somehow, that taking the step they had, they had placed themselves in more danger.  But he just didn't know from whom?  And just how could he protect his beloved if he didn't know who was out there?

———

Two days later, Blair carried Devaney into their apartment, hesitating as he watched her face, not sure where she wanted to be. Devaney was avoiding his look, staring around at what was now her home, not sure herself of where she wanted to be.

Blair sighed to himself. "Where would you like to be, love? The bedroom? The living room?"

She looked up at him and then stared down the hall, an uncertain look on her face. "What I would really like is a shower? Is that even possible?" She looked over his shoulder as a tap came at the door.

Anna entered, her eyes assessing first Blair and then Devaney. "I know exactly where you want to be. A shower. Blair? If you can help her to the bathroom, we'll get her cleaned up. And while we're doing that, she can decide where she wants to be. Your bandage is fine, Devaney. Doc will be along in a bit to change it for you."

Blair walked away, heading for the kitchen, reaching for the coffee carafe. He needed coffee and good coffee. The hospital coffee really didn't cut it, he thought. He then reached for the kettle, knowing Devaney would want her tea. At least, he thought she would.

Turning as he heard a voice, he stared at Doc and Will as they stood there, Branigan and Barnabas behind them.

"Coffee ready yet?" Doc grinned at him. "It's okay if it isn't. We can wait."

Blair nodded. "I just made it so it won't take long. What did you find out? You're all not here for my health, that I can tell. Doc, Devaney will need her bandage changed. Anna's helping her get cleaned up."

"Anna mentioned that. We'll look after it. But first, what can we do for you?" Doc's compassionate eyes watched Blair closely.

"Solve this. Let us figure out who it is. Will?"

Will pointed to a chair. "Sit, Blair. We'll pray and then talk. Perhaps by that time, Devaney will be out here and we can talk to you both together."

Devaney hesitated as she heard male voices and then turned to the living room, Anna at her side.

"I think I'll just stay here, Anna. I feel like I've run a marathon." Her hand was on her head, knowing she needed to take the pain pills she had been given but not wanting that. "Who is all here?"

"Doc, Will, Barnabas, Branigan. They're praying right now. They'll move here to talk to you. Have you remembered anything else?"

Devaney started to shake her head and stopped, not wanting the pain to worsen. "I don't know if I have."

Blair stood for a moment, a small tray in his hands with Devaney's tea and some toast, before he set it on the end table, and then shifted her over enough to sit beside her and then wrap her back into his arms, the blanket she was covered with pulled up over her. She tilted her head back to watch him, not aware of the looks they were garnering from the other five.

"Devaney?" Doc's voice brought her eyes to him. "I know I've changed your bandage, but you won't say how you're feeling."

"I'm not sure how I am to be. My head hurts. Someone is chasing either me or Blair or both of us. I want this over."

"We know you both do." Will set his mug of coffee down, pulling over a folder he had set down. "We've been looking into things. There is a new detective assigned to your case, and he's digging in backgrounds, including both of yours. It is standard that we do. From what we have seen, Bridget did not do that. We still can't find her."

"And if you can't find her, we are still at risk, aren't we?" Devaney's head went back on Blair's shoulder as he watched her closely. "When will this be over?"

"We're working on it, Devaney." Will searched her face before looking up at Blair. "We need to run some things by you.

And of course, by Blair, as well." He hesitated as he studied them, not knowing them well enough to know how they'd react.

"What do you have, Will?" Blair's head went back slightly as his eyes narrowed, sudden fatigue hitting him.

"First, let me preface it by saying how sorry I am it has taken all these years to come to light, Devaney. I know you felt you had no choice. That is always how the victims have felt. None of us fault you for what you did. This time, don't run, no matter how much you feel like it, and you will. Dallas, the detective, is working hard on tracking down these culprits. I have always told him he is like a terrier - never gives up on what he's after. You two need that. This had taken enough of your lives. I know why you did what you did, Blair, and why you felt you two had to marry so quickly. Well, maybe not so quickly." He paused to grin at the laughter his words brought.

He sipped his coffee, trying to organize his thoughts, without too much success. He opened the folder and then closed it, handing it over to Blair.

"What's this?" Blair was puzzled, studying the folder even as Devaney's hand came out to open it.

"It's where we stand right now. Dallas should be here to talk to you, but he's flown out to Alberta to follow up on some leads."

"He has?" Devaney shared a look with Blair and sighed, the sigh seemingly drawn from her toes upwards. "Then, we have more names for him to search into out there."

Will nodded. "I thought you might." He nodded towards the folder. "Look through that. Dallas is keeping me updated as he goes along. We are searching for that couple."

Devaney tilted her head back to look up at Blair, a frown on her face. "I think they are related somehow to Bridget? And there was a guy who hung around her. Do you remember him, Blair?"

"I do. Jerry Walsh."

Devaney wandered the apartment that evening, not ready to settle down, not ready to stay up. This is so unlike me, she thought, to be so unsettled. I guess I'm entitled, with all that I have gone through. I don't have to like it. She turned as she heard Blair behind her, to find him watching her, a shuttered look on his face.

"Blair?"

"We need to talk, Devaney, about what Will gave us. I know we've looked it over, but there is something missing there. I'm not sure what." He turned as he heard a tap at the door and looked over at the clock.

Benen and Branigan stood inside the door, sharing looks, before Benen spoke.

"That list you gave me? I had copied her database and continued to run it. I found more names as I expanded the parameters." He looked up as Devaney peeked around Blair at him.

"More names? Is Will going to like this?"

Benen grinned at her. "He has them. He didn't say anything, but I think he recognized one."

"He did? Who?" Blair turned Devaney back to the kitchen, making her sit and then reaching to make her a cup of tea, even as Branigan poured coffee for the men.

"Whiteside. Dixon."

Her eyes grew round. "Them? Why?"

"He didn't say, but he indicated he'd be talking to you two again and asked if you could please stop throwing names at him. He was going to call Dallas, I think he said, as well."

"Dallas is the new detective." Blair paced, his hand on his face, before Devaney's hand on his arm stopped him.

"Blair, sit. There's more that they want to say."

"There is, Devaney." Benen eyed her and then Blair. "Will said to warn you that he's had word Bridget is still in the area. She's with a man, but he didn't know who."

The young couple exchanged a glance, even as Devaney rubbed at her forehead, the headache making it difficult to think.

"She'll be with Jerry Walsh. He's one she hung around with when we were in college. I used to see him watching Blair at times."

"You did? You never said anything?" Blair's arm was around her.

"He wasn't there a lot. Not enough to be concerned about. I just didn't feel comfortable when he was. Neither was Bridget there a lot." She sighed. "I just don't get why."

"Burnie had a theory. You know him, Blair. Always coming up with plots and scenes for his work." Branigan took pity on Devaney. "He's an author, Devaney. I know you've met them all, but you haven't yet found out what all they do."

"No, I haven't. But what is his theory?"

Once more Branigan's eyes studied the couple. "He thinks Bridget wants you out of the way. She wants to be his wife. And for you, Blair? Walsh wants you out of the way to get to Devaney."

"What?" Devaney's chair shoved back, and she was on her feet, moving away from them.

Blair stood, watching, before he was seated again. "How serious is he about this?"

"As serious as I have ever seen him." Benen shook his head. "I have no idea where he comes up with this, but he could be right. This is personal, what has happened. The man watching Devaney all this years? Likely hired by Bridget to keep her from getting here."

"But I didn't know where she was. So, again, why?"

"That's what our guys have picked up on, and are working through it." Benen looked past him at the doorway. "Barnabas is sending Brody and Brennen to Alberta. No offence to Will, but he thinks we need to do this. He has connections out there they'll be in contact with. He's not leaving anything undone this time. Devaney could have easily been killed. Or it could have been meant for you and you killed, Devaney being in the wrong position at the time. Right now, we're not sure which one was the target."

Blair sighed, his hands scrubbing down his face. "I wondered that, you know. I wondered if I was the target and Devaney got in the way. How do we proceed?"

"Leave it with us. The guys are out there now, Barnabas sent them out earlier today in the company jet. We're not talking to Will yet. Barnabas has said not to. Not until we can find out anything. He'll verify what we have and then pass it on."

An hour later, Blair stood, his eyes on Devaney as she slept, seeing the pain and stress on her face, and then turned and walked away, heading for the living room and the couch. He had some thinking to do, heavy at that from what he had been told, and some time to spend with God. He needed that.

Three days later, Devaney took hesitant steps outside the building, fear rising within her. She didn't like that the violence had been brought there. Anyone could have been hurt, she decided, not seeing Cadee and Berneen watching her closely.

"It hurts, doesn't it?" Cadee's voice was quiet.

"It does. And we don't know which one of us was the target. That hurts even more." Devaney finally admitted her fear. "How did you two do this?"

"Prayer. Support from the team. Support from my brother for me. Support for her parents for Cadee." Berneen hugged Devaney. "It's different for you. You don't have family. Yes, you have your foster parents, but it's not the same." She studied the sky, seeing the grayness that had moved it. "How sure are you of them?"

Devaney shrugged. "I don't know. I think we're okay. I asked Benen to look into them. He said he would. I haven't heard that he found anything."

"Benen would tell you, but he would wait until he had proof." Cadee linked an arm with Devaney. "Now, what do we do with you? Doc says you can be outside but you have to take it easy."

Devaney shook her head. "I know what he said. I just can't not do anything." She looked up as well at the sky, a frown on her face before she rubbed at her forehead. "I hate this. I'm never sick."

They turned to head back into the building, finding seats in one of the sitting areas, Devaney's strength fading. Cadee and Berneen shared a glance before Cadee was off, back in short order with snacks and juice for them.

Devaney looked down at the bottle of juice she held, her thoughts muddled as she twisted at the cap. Her hand froze and her eyes slid closed. She had a sudden vision of doing the very same thing, only it wasn't juice that was in the bottle. She had thrown the bottle from her.

The two ladies with her watched as her face whitened and then Cadee reached for the bottle.

"Devaney? What did you remember?"

Devastated, she looked at the other women. "I remember doing this. Unscrewing a bottle cap. Only it wasn't juice. It wasn't water. It was poison. I could sense something off when I opened the cap. It didn't snap like it should have to be a new bottle. I threw it from me and ran as hard as I could."

"Where was this?" Cadee's arm was around her friend.

"In Winnipeg. He tracked me down in Winnipeg. Or she did. One of them did. Or was it someone else?" She looked up, a bleak look around her eyes. "How do I know who to trust? How do I keep Blair safe?"

Berneen watched her friend closely. "We'll work with this. Do you remember anything about it?"

"I'm trying but everything right now is so confusing. I'm getting glimpses of things, words, sentences, people. I just can't keep it all straight with the headaches I have."

"Then, this is what we do. We'll find you a notebook, and you'll right it all down. Does Blair have one?" Berneen's calm words reached through to Devaney.

"I'm not sure. I can look."

"Then, look we will." Cadee was on her feet, on a mission Benen would have said. "If he doesn't, I know we do."

Blair stood later that day, grubby from his work, needing to shower, but his concern was on Devaney, watching as she slept, stretched out on the couch, a soft blanket covering her. He smiled as he watched Anna's kitten curled up beside her, a tiny tongue grooming her paw. He knew how much Devaney loved her animals, and Anna must have shared. I don't know if you'll get your kitten back, Anna, but somehow I think you don't mind.

He finally moved back towards her, showered and in clean clothes, before he crouched down beside her, a hand on her face. Devaney stirred, her eyes blinking open and closed, even as a small smile emerged on her face.

"Have a good day, love?"  Blair waited.

"I did.  At least, I think I did.  How about you?  And what time is it?"

"Just after five."  His hand kept her still.  "Don't worry about getting up to get us dinner.  I hear someone has been through with a meal for us."

"Brady.  He dropped off lasagna.  I didn't know he cooked."

"He does.  He makes wonderful meals."  He reached to help her sit up, sitting beside her.  "What did you go and do?"

She shook her head.  "Brady set the timer for us to heat the lasagna.  It should be ready soon."  She leaned against him.  "Cadee and Berneen were here.  I started a journal of everything.  Berneen suggested it."  She looked up, fear and stress and another emotion he couldn't quite read on her face.  "I remembered something."

"What did you remember, my love?"  He watched, and waited. "Devaney?  What did you remember?  It's scared you, hasn't it?"

She nodded, a grimace on her face as the headache hit her hard for a moment.  "I remembered being in Winnipeg.  I had a bottle of something, but I didn't drink it.  I threw it away.  I think it was poison."  She looked back up at him as his arms tightened around her.  "Who does this?  Can't we find them and solve this?"

"We will, my love.  It's getting to that point.  Will wants to meet with us and the new detective in the morning.  It's Saturday, I know, so I'm home.  I told him it would depend on how you were."

"We need to, I guess, love. But not here.  I won't have them here."  She was becoming agitated, a frown on Blair's face as he studied her.

What is going on here, Lord?  Something has triggered this.

Mid-morning on the Saturday, Blair stepped back from the door, a frown on his face for a moment as Benen, Brody and Brandon entered. He sighed. I guess this means we don't meet with Will this morning. He reached to send a quick text off to Will to let him know they would be delayed.

"What's up, guys?" Blair pointed towards the kitchen. "Let me find Devaney."

"I'm right here." She peeked around Blair at the other three. "I don't like this. You've found something. Otherwise, you wouldn't be here."

"Sure, we would. We would come and see you." Benen grinned at her even as he accepted the mug of coffee and then pointed to the living room. "Can we sit in there? It will be more comfortable for Devaney."

Devaney sank to the couch, grateful that she could sit somewhere soft. She felt Blair's arm around her and then his words as he asked the men to pray. She knew they had found something, and whatever that something was, she would not like it.

Brody finally looked at the two, before he began to speak.

"As you know, Brandon and I headed west. That's beautiful country out there, guys."

"It is. I miss it at times, but Ontario does grow on you. Especially this part." Blair watched his friends intently, seeing the discomfort they were showing. "So, tell us. What did you find?"

The three men shared a look before Brody spoke up.

"We have talked with your foster parents. They had no idea what was going on. They wished you had talked to them, Devaney, but understand why you didn't. They were threatened as well, weren't they?" Brody gave a grim smile as she finally gave a small nod. "That's what we had thought. Now, as to what happened out there. We have talked with friends of yours, with your teachers from high school, your college professors. All claim not to have known what was going on, that you were imagining all this. That you had never really planned to marry Blair, but were simply leading him along and had planned to disappear all along."

Devaney stared at him, her mouth snapping closed. "Who said that? That's a lie."

"We know know it is. We have talked to many people who tell us that you and Blair were in love, that they knew you would marry, but they were saddened and shocked when you didn't and simply disappeared. You are loved and missed greatly, Devaney."

Brandon took over. "We've stopped in different towns, where we thought you may have been. In the small towns, you were remembered. The ones we talked to were helpful. They have given impressions and descriptions of the man and woman who watched you."

"People saw them? I didn't imagine them?"

"No, you didn't imagine them. There are occasions where these people have admitted to helping you escape, to finding ways to direct these two away from you, and helping you to escape." He paused for a moment, to gather his thoughts and his emotions. "I can't imagine living like you did. Running for your life at times. Not trusting that God was even there." He smiled as her eyes slid closed and a tear trickled down her face. "He was there, all along, protecting you, taking care of you, providing for you."

She nodded, her eyes closed as she tried to control her emotions, finally just turning into Blair's shoulder as he held her, his chin on her head.

"What else, guys?" Blair finally asked the question Devaney was unable to frame.

"We have spoken with the couple that you named. They are under arrest in Toronto. We can't say why but they did mean you two harm. Their words were along the line of you two deserved everything that happened to you. Investigators are tracking their steps and also their connection to Bridget and Jerry. There seems to be a connection but they haven't given us that information. They will be in touch with Will."

---

"So, I don't understand. What else did you find out?" Devaney sighed. "And we still have to meet with Will."

"He said this afternoon is fine. I got a text back from him." Blair's thoughts were puzzled. "I still don't see how they fit in."

Devaney's eyes slid closed. "I know why. When I was ten, Jerry was in the foster home I was at for a couple of hours. I think you'll find that out somehow and that he is connected to Bridget. I sort of remember comments that aren't clear, about a female cousin." She looked up at the men. "If I had remembered sooner, would this have not happened?"

Benen shook his head. "It would have. They seem determined to harm you in some way. We're taking steps to keep you two as safe as we can, but we can't be with you all the time." He looked over at Blair. "I heard you did some remembering yesterday."

"I did, thanks to your wife and Berneen." She pointed to the coffee table. "It's there. Everything I can remember and everything I didn't know I could. We looked through it last night. Take it with you. If you need to, talk to Will. I would rather he didn't have it yet."

"That we can do." Benen reached for it, flipping through it quickly, amazed at what she had been able to remember. "God is bringing up what you've buried."

"He is. Sometimes I wish He wouldn't."

Will studied the young couple as he directed them to an office, motioning for Dallas to come with them. The young detective had never met them but felt he knew them. He shook his head at the way Bridget had worked, knowing she was not what she had claimed to be. It was a shame, he thought. Devaney being shot may well have been avoided, if we could have found these people in time. And find them, he would. Dallas had a good idea that Blair's friends were working on something. He had been contacted by the Toronto investigators and had multiple contacts from police agencies across the country, all with information on what Devaney had faced and how worried they were about her.

Devaney sat, her hand reaching for Blair's, as both of them watched Will closely, before turning their attention to Dallas. Will introduced him and then sat, his thoughts becoming clearer.

"Devaney. Blair. We are finally making progress. I can't apologize enough for what you two went through."

"We know, Will. We know. We get that she was playing you." Blair paused, his eyes thoughtful. "Who else did she do this to?"

"No one that we can see. She was planted here, Blair, that much we know. They were watching Devaney move your way and were just waiting for you two to connect. We think she's the one who hired the man who ran you off the road." Dallas spoke, his voice full of confidence that he had the truth finally for them. He stared down at the folder on the table. "I have been out west, spoken with numerous people out there." He frowned for a moment. "There have been both positive and negative, though."

"About what we thought." Devaney spoke, her eyes steady on Dallas. "You'll find people will say I was a fake, that Blair was a fake, that we never planned to marry, it was all a hoax. That we were planning to rip people off. That Blair leaving was a sign of guilt. How am I doing?"

Dallas stared at her, then shook his head, smiling at her. "Just about right, I'd say."

"And then you'll have people who support us. If you look closely at the two groups, you'll find them divided as to who they support and who has gotten to them. Those that know us know the truth." Blair nodded towards the folder. "What else do you have for us? Devaney's been up for too long and needs to be sleeping."

Dallas nodded, understanding what Blair was not saying. "We have spoken with the police in Toronto about that couple. They have been arrested. Charges will be pending against them here as we have evidence they hired the gunmen. There were two, you understand. We working on determining just which one of you it was."

"It was likely both of us. We kept them from their plans, whatever they were. We needed to die." Devaney's head went down on Blair as she had difficulty keeping her eyes open. "What else?"

"We are talking to police agencies across the country, following your trail, Devaney. Do you realize how close you were at times to dying?" Will had been shocked, to say the least, when he found that out.

"I do know. I have the scars from some of those attempts. And I threw away a bottle likely containing poison in Winnipeg." She stood, her mouth open to speak, and then walked away, her steps faltering as her hand went to her head.

"Call me when you can, Dallas. Will." Blair walked away, stopping to sweep Devaney into his arms, before he headed for his vehicle, Branigan and Brady waiting for him. They had not let them come on their own.

Blair stared down at Devaney as he cradled her close to him, his thoughts muddled, but his heart praying before he looked up, his eyes on Brady who was driving.

"They don't know much more than what you've found out. Find these people, please? She can't take much more."

"No, she can't.  And neither can you.  It may mean putting you two away somewhere."  Branigan twisted enough in his seat to watch them.

"We won't go.  I know Devaney.  She'll be out there searching for them.  She's had enough.  And frankly, so have I."

"We'll find them.  I spoke with Burnie.  He has some new thoughts he's working through with Benen.  Those two are a scary team, you know."

Blair laughed.  "They are.  That they are."  He stepped down from the truck, reaching for his lady, carrying her through to their apartment, not seeing the compassionate eyes on them, the eyes that sought each other and then the men gathered in the boardroom, Devaney's notes in front of them, determination to solve that mystery surrounding their friends that day, if at all possible. Buckley led off in prayer and then Barnabas spoke words of encouragement to them all.

Pacing the boardroom the next afternoon, Devaney wrapped her arms around herself. She didn't like that they were working on Sunday. She sighed to herself as she remembered church that morning.

Blair had simply walked her in, her hand in his, and seated her near the back of the church. Berneen and Baird had sat on one side of them, Benen and Cadee on the other. She saw the speculative looks she was given and then the nods as her hand had raised to brush hair from her face, and they saw her rings. Blair's arm around her had tightened as he sensed her discomfort.

He had not let her stay long after the service, simply sweeping her away, leaving comments and questions in the air, ones that his friends had answered. Neither knew the support they had garnered from their church family, with offers to help flying at the men.

Blair watched as she paced, knowing she needed to do this, but also knowing it was wearing her down. How, Lord, do we stop this? How do we end this? What piece of the puzzle do we not have or don't know we have that would end this? Please, dear Lord, I need this over for my lady.

Breck paused beside Blair, his eyes on his friend.

"Blair, how are you?"

Blair shrugged. "I am no longer sure, Breck. I need this over for her and I just don't know where to turn to find that missing piece. It's like a big jigsaw puzzle we are putting together and the key piece we need is not there."

Devaney had paused as she listened to him before she turned, her eyes searching.

"Devaney?" Barnabas stood beside her. "What are you looking for? What do you need?"

"I need to visualize everything. Is there a large map of Canada we can put up on the wall? One that I can mark up?"

Bradon had looked up at her words and was away and then back with a large map that was attached to the wall, handing her a marker.

"I can't write on this. It's too nice."

"Write on it, Devaney. I can always get another one if I need to. Right now, you need this. Tell us what you want to write. We'll do it for you." He gently shoved her into a chair, taking back the marker.

An hour later, she walked past the map, her finger tracing her steps across the country, her face pale at how far she had travelled on her own for so many months and years. "Did I really do this?"

"You did. Fear drove you as did your love for Blair." Buckley grinned at her as she heard the murmurs of agreement from the men. "You tried to bury that, tried to hide it, deny it, but it's the catalyst that forced you to keep moving. You wanted him safe and you knew you had to find him."

"You're right." She paused, turning to find Blair. "He's right, Blair. I denied it, but he's right."

"I know you are, love." Blair's smile helped her to control her emotions, seeing his love and belief in her shining through. "Now, what do we do about that?" He pointed at the map.

Burnie walked up to him, his finger tracing her route. "There's something here, Devaney, something that you saw or heard or noticed that carried with you from Alberta. I would say that when you were attacked, that's when one of them was around you and decided you needed to pay for whatever it was."

"I think you're right." She studied the map and then him, before turning finding all eyes on her. "You all have a different occupation, right?" At their nods, she continued. "And different organizations you volunteer for?" Again there were nods. "So, how be if you look at this, look at what I've written, what Brandon and Brody discovered, and then note what you observe from your point of view. Not mine. Not theirs. Pull it apart as much as you can and then we'll fit it back together. Does that work?"

Brennen spoke up. "That's what we'll do, Devaney. I think you have just given us what we need to do. We will solve this, I promise you that.  We'll solve this and then you can get on with your life."

She nodded, seeing Anna approaching her.  "Anna?"

"Come with me for a bit, Devaney.  Let the men work.  If they have questions, they'll just write them down and then ask you.  I think doing this will let us finally work it all out for you."  She led Devaney from the room and to her apartment.  "Sit, dear.  I need to prepare some food for the men.  You need to rest."  She set a cup of tea in front of her before she sat.  "What can I do just for you?"

"For me?  You're doing so much all ready.  What more can you do?"

Anna shook her head at the questioning look she was given. "Devaney.  You are hurting in more ways than just physical.  You need to heal.  Doc can help you heal physically.  But in other ways, you need to heal.  I know you've renewed your faith. I can see that. Just reach out for that garment's hem, dear.  He is waiting for you to do just that."  Anna's arms were around Devaney as the younger woman wept, tears of healing spilling up and out, tears she could not control and made no effort to.

Looking for her later, Blair looked up as the door to the boardroom opened and the four ladies entered, trays in their hand. Doc followed with the large coffee urn that he set on a table and plugged in, quiet words to Cadee as she arranged mugs and creamer and sugar around it. A large teapot was added.

Barnabas rose, heading for Anna, taking her tray from her with a quiet word of thanks. He looked around, knowing they had made a lot of progress on their own. They now needed to combine their thoughts, ideas, and findings, but first they would take a break.

"Doc, lead us in prayer for the food, please." Doc nodded at Barnabas' words.

An hour later, Barnabas once more stood watching his men, the ladies with them, turning to watch Doc and Anna, and then finding Blair and Devaney. He could see the fatigue in them and wanted this over for them. How, Lord, how do we do this?

The men shared what they had each discovered or thought of, each one different. Doc had volunteered to be the scribe, writing everything down on paper taped to the wall. He drew arrows, lines, crossed out words, and added ideas and thoughts before he moved to a clean page and began to write facts called out from each man.

Blair watched, a growing conviction in his heart that they were on the right track. Devaney was tired, having trouble concentrating, before her head went down on her folded arms on the table and she slept, Blair's arm around her. Doc shook his head.

"She needs to be in bed, Blair. Not here."

"She won't leave, Doc. Not even if it destroys her health. She's mad, she tired, she's had enough. She wants this over. And frankly, so do I. We can't go on with our lives with this hanging over our heads."

"We know you can't. Will and Dallas are working as hard as they can. So are our guys." Doc studied the wall and the writing on the papers. "I would say they have made a good start. Someone will need to get this to Will or Dallas."

"Not yet. There's something missing." Blair looked down as Devaney mentioned a name, her eyes cracking open just a fraction of an inch. "Devaney? You're sure?"

"I am. Search and prove me right or wrong." Devaney slept again, her trust in Blair that he would do just that.

Benen frowned at the name. "They live here, don't they? How did she connect them?"

"That's what we'll have to look into. I would suspect somehow with Bridget." Blair sat back, deep in thought, looking up as Brendon spoke.

"She's right. That's our connection. They were originally from your hometown, Blair. And they are related to Bridget. And to Jerry."

Benen reached for the paperwork Brendon had printed. "That's how it is, then. Who gets to talk to Will?"

"I guess I do." Brendon sighed. "I can tomorrow. Let's condense this, finish off for the day, and let Blair and Devaney head home."

Will stared at Brendon the next day, his hand stopped in midair as he reached for the sheaf of papers Brendon was thrusting at him.

"You did what?"

"We worked through all this. Devaney asked us to look at it from each of our perspectives from work and volunteering. She was right to do that. We all saw something different that made a whole lot of sense." He thrust the paperwork into Will's hands. "This is the condensed version of it." He paused, biting at his lip. "She also gave us another name. They're related to both Bridget and Jerry."

"So she was right, wasn't she? I could use her on the force."

"I doubt that would ever happen. I have no idea what she wants to do. She hasn't had a chance to live freely in years. So I don't expect her to rush into anything."

———

Will shook his head. "I agree with you." He looked down at the paperwork. "I know you fellows are good. You'll have given us any links and websites that we need. All the information we can use to find these people. And we will find them. I can't tell you much, but Dallas is forging ahead on this." He sighed. "I wish he had been on it from the beginning. We not likely would be having this conversation."

Brendon shook his head. "I think we would have been having some form of it. We needed Devaney to start remembering, and to protect herself, she buried it very deep."

"That she did. If any of you come up with anything else, call me or Dallas."

"We'll do that." Brendon walked away, leaving Will staring after him before he searched for Dallas.

"Dallas? Barnabas' guys were busy. They've sent this for you."

Dallas turned from the copier, papers in his hand, as he stared at the papers in Will's hands. "What have they done?"

Will explained what Brendon had shared before Dallas took the paperwork, quickly flipping through it.

"This is good. It will help. But that's not all?" He eyed his chief closely.

"No, it's not." Will sighed, given the name of the couple and their likely relationship to Bridget and Jerry.

"That's what we had suspicions of. I'll prove it." Dallas walked away, knowing his work had increased, but he was determined to solve the problem or mystery or whatever you wanted to call it, he thought.

———

Standing near the lake the next morning, Devaney shivered, looking around her. She could feel the evil and suddenly turned and ran, heading for the building, sliding to a stop as a man appeared in her pathway. She turned and ran for the woods, finding a path to follow, praying it led her to safety. Hearing the heavy footsteps and cursing and yells behind her spurred her feet to a faster pace. She saw the building in front of her and ran harder, her breath coming in gasps as her chest heaved with the exertion.

Sliding to a stop just inside the doors, Devaney spun, her eyes searching for the man after her, hearing the security guard approaching her and then the man urging her away from the doors and windows. He followed her up to the apartment, admonishing her to lock the doors after her, and if she needed to go anywhere, to call him.

The man looked for Barnabas or Breck, letting them know how he had found Devaney. Grim looks covered their faces and were shared. The man or woman after Devaney was getting desperate, willing even to be on the property to try and kidnap her.

Blair's face paled as he listened to Breck that evening, before he almost ran for his wife, his shoes hitting the boot tray, the door locked behind him, as he searched, finding her in his office, asleep in his favourite chair there. He stood and watched, seeing new lines of stress on her face, the paleness of it, and the pain etched there.

He grew angry and determined. This would end and end now, he thought. But how? He moved away to change from his work clothes, coming back to scoop Devaney into his arms and sit, cradling her close to him. He gave a smile as he saw Anna's kitten sneaking through the room, to pounce up on the chair arm before she curled up on Devaney.

Devaney roused, for a moment fearful, then hearing Blair praying for them. She raised her head, studying him.

"Blair?" She was puzzled, confused as to time. Her head was hurting more today than it had and that scared her.

"Devaney?  Are you okay?  Breck told me what happened."

Her head went back down on his shoulder, even as her hands clenched together, her face pale and drawn.  "I don't feel good, Blair.  My head is really hurting."

He stared at her, then was on his feet, carrying her towards Doc's, knowing he was home.  Doc took one look at her and pointed back out the door, heading for the infirmary.

Blair stood and watched as Doc made his examination, then stood back.

"Doc?"

"We need to repeat the imaging, Blair, and now.  I'm sending her in by ambulance, asking that a CT scan be run stat.  I know she ran for her life today.  Whether that has triggered something or not, I don't know.  We need to find out."

Blair nodded, watching as the paramedics arrived and then headed out with Devaney, followed by Blair, who refused to let her out of his sight.  He didn't see the men who had gathered to watch, Cadee and Berneen heading for a vehicle to follow.

"Doc?"  Barnabas spoke from bedside him.

"She's hurting, Barnabas.  Just a precaution.  But her headaches should be easing."  He paused.  "Do you know if she's been taking her pain medication?"

"I'm not sure."  His phone was out, a quick text sent to Blair.  "He says she has but I wonder.  Doc, come with me.  Blair's told me to go in and find it and then bring it with me."

Doc looked at the bottle.  "It says what was prescribed."  Popping open the top, he dumped some out into his hand.  "No, this is wrong.  These are not them.  Someone's gotten to them."

Barnabas' face grew stern.  "So, either it was dispensed wrong, or someone has been in here."

"I would suspect someone has been in here.  And through the balcony."

Barnabas was across the room and scanning the door. "You're right.  Someone has jimmied it by the looks of it.  They wouldn't have caught it as they not likely have had the doors open."

Doc was out the door, Barnabas on his heels, a quick word to Breck, who stood, stunned, his eyes following them before he turned and ran for the security desk, questions flying from him.

Blair watched as Doc handed the medication bottle to the treating physician, their words too quiet to hear, before Doc walked towards him.

"Doc?"

"She wasn't taking the right medication, Blair.  We have to test to see what it is but it was not the pain medication prescribed for her."  He paused, not sure how to continue.  "Someone got in through your balcony doors."

Blair sighed, his head going back as his eyes closed, his hands jammed into his jacket pockets.  "She was right after all."

"What do you mean?"  Doc looked up as Will and Dallas stopped beside Blair.

"She said she thought someone had been in the apartment but we couldn't see any evidence of it.  She thought she was wrong."

"She wasn't, Blair."  He spun as Will spoke, not having heard him come towards him.  "She has instincts you don't see often."

"I know she does.  She always has had."  He watched as she slept, the pain easing from her face.  "How do we find these monsters?  We can't go on like this.  It will kill her."

Will nodded, his eyes on Dallas, who was lost in thought before he excused himself and walked away, his phone out to make a call.  "We know it's hard.  We know she was approached today."  He sighed, not knowing how to respond fully.

Blair paced the apartment the next night, knowing that Devaney had already retired and was asleep. This is so hard, he thought. At least her pain is better, and those pills didn't harm her, not that we know of. He spun, an idea running through his mind. Who could he talk to, he wondered?

His phone out, his finger scrolled through his contacts, finding one from years ago. He frowned. No, he thought, it couldn't be, could it? Blair sighed, knowing he had just added another name to the list, and sent a text off with it to both Will and Dallas.

Dallas' voice on the other end of the line startled him when he answered the call.

"Blair? How sure are you?"

"I'm not, but he's the only one who I've really kept in contact with over the years. Could it be him?"

"It could. His is one name that came up. Did you know he's related to that couple?"

"He is? And no, I didn't."

"He's a nephew of the wife. They have tried to say they have had no contact with one another but phone records show otherwise. We have tracked his records. He has been in the cities and towns where your wife was attacked."

Blair sank down to the floor, his head against the wall, his eyes sliding shut. "I've been the one, then."

"The one who?"

"The one driving this."

"No, I don't think you are. We're finding motives that aren't totally connected to either one of you, but there are motives connected to you both."

"Okay, then. How do we do this? What do we do?"

"You two do nothing. You go to work. Devaney works on healing. We will want you to be seen out and about. Take her out for a meal, a walk, shopping. As much as she can handle. Go about your daily walk. Does she work?"

Blair's eyes slid closed again. "No, she doesn't. She won't have to. I'm not sure if you are aware, but as we guys marry, an income is settled on the wives, so they don't have to work, or if they work, it's the same arrangement as us. Someone hires them, but the Foundation pays their wages."

"I see. So there is no motive there." Dallas' voice faded away for a moment, then came back stronger. Blair could hear papers rustling in the background.

"Dallas? You have a thought?"

"I did, but if her income comes from there, and not an inheritance or trust, then there's no motive that way."

"She has no inheritance or trust. We've looked into that."

"Okay." Dallas was silent for a moment. "I have an idea I need to think through. If you will be home tomorrow, I would like to stop by."

"Tomorrow night would work."

"Then, I'll see you tomorrow night. Get some rest, Blair. You need it."

"Thank you and you too."

Devaney turned from the doorway, knowing Blair had not heard her. She had listened to his side of the conversation, recognizing the name he had spoken, and knowing that the man named had not been a true friend of his. She had wanted to tell him but didn't know how.

The next night, Blair stood back from the door, watching as Dallas entered, greeting him and seeing him greet Devaney, a frown on his face. Something had changed in the last twenty four hours and that concerned him.

Blair and Devaney listened as Dallas spoke, their eyes meeting every once in a while.

"And how close are you to an arrest?" Blair was pushing, and they all knew it.

"Within the next forty-eight hours I suspect. We have just about all the evidence on everyone, including the name you gave me." He looked up, as Devaney made a sound. "Devaney?"

"It was him, all along. It was him. He's the one who threatened Branigan in Regina. He's the one who has been chasing me. He's been using Bridget and Jerry to do his work, but he's behind it. He's related to that couple and using them too."

Dallas shook his head. "How did you just do that?"

"Do what?" Devaney looked at him, before she shared a look with Blair

"Come to that conclusion so quick. It's taken us a lot of work and time."

"You have to have the evidence. I know them. That's how I did this." She burrowed against Blair, just needing to be held.

Blair nodded. "She does know them. She picks up on people in a way few I have seen can do."

"I can see that. We need her on the force."

Blair laughed at that even as he felt Devaney's head shaking. "She won't. I don't know what she wants to do, but policing is not it."

"No, not that. I don't know what I want to do. I have had so many jobs, all low paying, that I want to take some time. I've had to take them to survive. That's no way to live." She looked up as Blair shook his head. "Blair?"

"We need to talk, love, but you don't have to work. I explained to Dallas, but you and I need to talk. With the Foundation, you know it pays our wages, the guys?" When she nodded, he continued. "It is set up that when the guys marry, the Foundation pays their wives a wage. I'll let Barnabas explain it in detail to you as well as the amount you will receive, but you don't have to work. You have an income coming to you. You can work or you can volunteer or even go back to school to train in something new. It is your choice."

She stared at him, dumbfounded. "This is for real?"

"It is, love. It's how Barnabas and his father wanted it."

"Well, I don't know what to say. I didn't know that. It's not common knowledge?"

Blair shook his head. "No, it's not. It's confidential among us."

"Okay, so that's not why they were after me." She paused, a look of horror almost crossing her face. "Is it about Barnabas? Nothing started until you had been approached about working here."

Dallas and Blair shared a look, Dallas shaking his head at the new thought.

"We considered that, love, but we don't see that. No one knew Barnabas had approached me. He did it through a lawyer that knows the Foundation. We met privately. I hadn't made my decision until about two days before graduation."

She shrugged. "I know. It was just an idea, but who's to say that wasn't part of it?"

A week later, her hand tight in Blair's, Devaney walked the downtown of her new city, or town or village, she wasn't quite sure what to call it. She liked it. A small place, she thought, where you can know your neighbours.

Blair watched the flickering emotions cover her face, seeing the healing. He knew the headaches had greatly improved since they found the medication switch and had become much less frequent. He could see her heart healing as well, knowing from her prayers she had found her way back to God. He thanked the Lord for that, for the healing she had undergone.

"So, where is this store I just had to see?" She looked up at him, a quick grin on her face.

"Right here." He paused to open the door, waiting for her to walk through before following her. He nodded at Sam, the owner as he moved to the counter.

"Blair? This is a jewelry store."

"I know it is. I know you've worn my ring for years and now have a matching band. But I want to find something special for you."

She shook her head. "You don't have to. It's not necessary."

"But it is. I've missed out on years of bringing you jewelry. I plan to rectify that."

Devaney stared at him, recognizing what he was saying, without him having to put it into words, and nodded. She looked down at the simple engraved gold bracelet that he fastened on her wrist before he kissed her cheek.

They wandered the town, knowing they were being followed and watched. They had seen the man Blair had named and knew he was not alone. At this point, neither cared about that. They were ready to confront him and had given Dallas an ultimatum, which he had vigorously talked them out of. He needed them to let the police do their work.

Walking away from him, they had exchanged a glance, knowing that they would only allow so much time and then would put their plan into action. They had talked to no one, not even the men from the Foundation, knowing it would put them at risk.

Branigan and Bradon had followed the two, not being seen but watching the watchers as Bradon had half-laughing called them. They all knew the couple were ready to break loose and confront their enemies and wanted to be ready to help them.

Bradon pointed to Blair. "He's ready to run."

"I know he is. There he goes. Come on, Bradon. We need to keep him in sight." Branigan ran down the sidewalk, Bradon behind him, dodging pedestrians and benches and planter boxes. He slid to a halt. "Where did they go?"

"They've disappeared. I don't like this." He spun in a circle. "I think they were taken."

"I think you're right." Branigan's hand on Bradon pulled him in the direction they had last see the couple.

"They're not here. They can't have disappeared this quickly." Bradon's phone was out and he was quickly speaking with Barnabas. Sticking it away, he turned once more in a circle. "Barnabas is finding the guys and will be in. Where do we look for them?"

Barnabas stood and watched his friends before he moved forward. "No sign of them?"

"No. And no sign of the men we saw watching them. They were gone so quickly. I don't think this was their plan."

"No, I don't think it was. I spoke with both Will and Dallas. They're searching as well. Dallas said he was ready to make arrests and did I know how this complicated the situation?"

The two men with him gave grim smiles.

"We know that. And I am sure that Blair and Devaney didn't plan this. I know they were planning something in the next few days. But not today. That I know. Blair just wanted a day out with

Devaney. He said they needed that."   Bradon stood, his eyes searching.

"They did.   It was what whoever it was watching for." Branigan agreed.

Devaney's hand tight in his, Blair closely watched the two men who held weapons on them, his heart falling. This wasn't supposed to happen, not today. Today had been about getting Devaney out and about, falling more in love with her. Not about facing men with weapons. He felt her hand tighten on his. Yes, he thought, he knew these men. Lord, we need Your help to get out of this.

They walked forward as directed, entering the door that led to a second floor, turning as directed to sit in the chairs set just right for them. Devaney gave a small whimper as her hands were tied, the weapon against Blair's head keeping him from moving as his hands were tied as well.

Time passed as they waited. They watched the sun's rays grow longer and darkness appear before a light was turned on. Heavy drapes were pulled across the windows, leaving the night blocked from their sight.

Their gazes raised to the door as they heard it open and then glanced at one another. They had been right after all. Bridget and Jerry were connected to the Watsons. The four stood in front of them.

Devaney stared at them, then looked around them. "Where is he?"

"Where's who? There's no one else." Bridget sneered at her.

"But there is. Tony Watson. Where is he? You don't have the smarts, none of you, to have planned and carried out this." Devaney was defiant, knowing she had to draw them out in order to end it.

"What are you talking about? Of course, we've planned this." Jerry was arrogant, sure of his facts, he thought.

Blair shook his head. "No, not at all. I know you all. You're just doing what Tony has told you to."

They began to argue among themselves, drawing away and to another room. Devaney had worked at her bonds, finding them loosening. She shrugged them off, rising quietly and working on Blair's, finding his hand and drawing him away and out the door, moving swiftly to the back of the building and down. She opened the door, Blair's hand on her, and then ran from the building, heading for the police department and safety.

Dallas stared at her before he was on the move, heading for the building, officers with him, Will bringing them back to safety. He just shook his head at their words.

Devaney paced, Blair keeping step with her, until Dallas approached them. Hope sprang on their faces.

"We have them. We're still look for Tony."

"Of course, you do. He's a coward and will hide. That's a given." Devaney spun and walked away, Blair shrugging as he followed her.

"Devaney? It's not his fault."

"I know it's not. I just want this over. Where is God today. Blair?"

"He's here, love. He got us away from them."

She hugged him tight. "Take me home, please? Just take me home."

"I will. Except we need to walk to where my truck is. And it's dark."

Will stood there. "Come on, you two. I'll drive you home. Blair, let me have your keys. I'll have an officer follow me with it."

Will hit the brakes of his car as he saw the roadblock ahead of him, reaching for his radio, confirming there was nothing that should be there.

"Stay put you two. I need to look into this." He was from his car, the officer out of Blair's truck as they moved towards the road block, both men going down as they were shot at. Blair reached for the radio, frantically calling in that they needed help. He could hear the sirens in the distance before the door beside him was pulled open and he was yanked for the seat, hearing Devaney's small scream as she was pulled out as well.

They were shoved forward past Will and the officer, seeing movement from them, before they were roughly pushed down an embankment and up the other side, made to walk through debris until they reached a cabin. The door was pulled open roughly and they were propelled inside, barely keeping to their feet. They heard the door slammed shut and a lock snapped loudly shut.

Their eyes on one another, Blair drew Devaney to him, his arms tight around her, his heart raising in a prayer for safety and rescue.

"What was that?" Devaney's voice was low and shaky.

"I think that was Tony. He knew we were free. Somehow, I think there's a leak on the force. I pray not, but it's too obvious someone knows what we're doing."

"Someone who Grace has gotten to. Or maybe Tony." Devaney blew out a breath. "Where does this end?" She walked away from Blair before spinning and moving back. "Will? And that officer?"

"They were alive. I just don't know how hurt they were." Blair paced the cabin. "I know this place. It's on the Foundation property."

"Can you get us out of here?"

"I'm certainly going to try." He reached for the windows, shoving at them. "They've blocked them. They planned this. They let us get away tonight."

"That's what I wondered. It was too easy. Do they know they were set up?"

"Not likely." Blair stood, a hand on the door, searching the room, his eyes raising to the roof. "This cabin. It's the one with the leak. That means the roof is compromised."

He searched for a chair, dragging it over to a corner of the room, and standing on it. "We did some preliminary work here, just to mitigate the damage."

———

"My, my. What big words you're using?" Devaney grinned up at him for a moment, before she sobered. "Can we get out?"

"We'll make an effort. Just listen for anyone coming."

Devaney was by the door, her ear to it, her eyes on Blair as he worked away, finally seeing moon light through the ceiling, and was back at his side as he motioned her. His hands pulled her up beside him and then guided her to the roof, following quickly as he heard her drop down.

She stared at him. "Did we really just do that?"

"We did. Now, come on. Let's get you back to the building." His hand reached for hers as he ran from the clearing towards a path he knew would lead them to that very place.

Branigan stared at them as they entered through a back door, before he was with them, his hands motioning them towards an empty suite. Inside, he locked the door and then just stood and stared at them.

"Will said you had been taken captive again."

Blair gave a grim smile. "We were. They locked us into the white cabin."

"The one with the roof." Branigan was quick to understand. "Stay here. I'll get to Berneen or Cadee and get some clean clothes for you. We'll keep it quiet that you're here." He reached to hug them both, prayers of praise rising from him.

# Chapter 50

Will stared at Doc as he buttoned his shirt back up, finished with his assessment at Emergency. His chest hurt, but his vest had done its work, keeping him alive. The patrol officer had been hit in the arm but survived, and he was thankful God had spared their lives.

"What do you mean, Doc?"

Doc shook his head, pointing at the door. "I said, they're fine. We have them somewhere safe."

Will breathed a sigh of relief. "I won't ask, because I know you won't tell me. They're okay? They're not hurt?"

"Physically, no. I can't answer for any other way. That we'll have to look after once this is over."

"I know. Tell them to stay hidden. We're moving in on the last one but until we have him, they're not safe."

Doc nodded. "I know they're not. This was not what they planned. At least not today."

"I know. They did plan to put themselves out there. We're trying to prevent that. Today, that took everyone by surprise." Will paced the small area before he turned to study Doc. "Doc?"

Doc just shook his head. "Find them, Will. And soon. If you don't, then these two will be back out there." He paused, a frown on his face. "It just seems so bizarre. The way they could just walk out of there."

"That's what we think. The ones we have in custody aren't talking, but you know how I think. We've been friends for too many years, worked too many times together."

"And now you need to go. Go home, Will. Let your deputy chief take over for tonight. Those are medical orders."

Will sighed. "I knew you would say that. No talking you out of it?"

Doc grinned. "No. Your wife is waiting for you."

Doc turned from the door in the apartment late that night, his eyes on Blair, assessing his young friend before he nodded and headed for the kitchen. He needed a cup of coffee and he knew Blair would have some on. It had been a busy night, made worse by the shooting of the two officers. He thanked God they were safe, could go home to the families.

Blair slid into a chair, his head turning for a moment as he listened for Devaney, knowing it would be a night he would have little sleep. She would be up and down. That was a given, knowing what she had gone through in the past. The dreams and nightmares would drive their time that night.

"Doc? Will and the officer?"

"They're fine. Will's vest protected him. The officer was hit in the arm but is okay."

Blair's eyes shut. Thank you, Lord. "That scared Devaney. She thought they were dead when we were forced past them."

"I am sure she did. How is she?"

Blair shrugged. "She's sleeping but it will be a night of broken sleep for us both. It is what happens when the dreams and nightmares take over." He held up a hand as Doc went to speak. "She won't take anything. I've already tried that route. She is adamant she won't."

"No, I didn't think she would. What can we do for her?"

"I'm not sure what we can do. When it gets too bad, then I just hold her and pray."

"That's all you can do for now." Doc sipped at his coffee. "Will thinks they'll be able to arrest the man in the next day or so. They're closing in on his address."

"It can't be soon enough, but somehow I don't think they'll take him without a fight or without him finding us. He'll know we'd come back here."

"And the past has proven that they can get in and get to whoever it is they want." Doc was frustrated, knowing how hard it would be. "Has Barnabas been around?"

"No. We're trying to keep it quiet where we are. Branigan has been. He's relaying anything between us."

"That's good." Doc rose. "Call me if you need me, and I mean that, Blair. Anna's quite taken with your lady."

"Thanks, Doc. She needs Anna, whether she'll admit it or not. She's never had someone like that just for her. Even with our foster mother, she was busy with her own kids and whoever it was that came through from the system."

"Anna understands that. She's willing to be the mother Devaney needs. Her heart just expands to take another one in."

Blair laughed. "That's exactly what she does."

Locking the door after Doc, and turning out some lights, Blair sighed. This was not how he had planned their day, not one bit. He walked through the small suite, heading for the bedroom, turning out lights as he went. The mugs in the kitchen could wait until morning and then he detoured back to set the coffee for the morning and rinse out their mugs, setting them to dry. Blair stood, his hands resting on the countertop, his head hanging down. This needs to end, Lord, but how do we do just that?

Devaney paced the next morning, her arms folded around herself, her eyes avoiding Blair, knowing he wanted to talk with her. He sighed, finally just reaching to stop her and sweep her into a tight hug.

"Blair? Who was here last night? I thought I heard voices."

"It was Doc. Just came to check on us. He said Will and the officer are fine." He felt her relax at his words. "You were worried, weren't you?"

"I was. Enough people have been hurt by this monster. How do we stop him?"

"We don't. Will was adamant on that. We leave it to him and his department." He leaned back to study her. "We need to talk, but first we need to spend time in prayer."

She sighed, shoving away from him. "We do. This time, I am afraid. Really afraid. Before this, I was just mad. This monster could and would kill anyone who gets in his way."

"He will. That's why we leave it with Will and his people." He drew her down on the couch, his arm around her.

Later that morning, he looked out the peephole, then opened the door for Branigan.

"Branigan, you have word?"

Branigan nodded. "They found him. Where's Devaney?"

"Right here." Her arm went around Blair's waist. "What did you say?"

"They found him, Devaney. We think it's over"

"What did he have to say?"

Branigan was silent, his eyes on the floor, not wanting to be the one to tell them what had happened.

"Branigan?" Blair's voice brought his head up. "He's dead?"

"He is.  He tried to kill an officer.  They had no choice."

"No, they wouldn't.  But it doesn't answer the question of why."  Devaney leaned harder against Blair.

"No, but it might.  Dallas got word to us that there are many notebooks filled with information.  They have to work through it.  But until they're sure he was working on his own, they want you two to stay here in the building.  You can go back to your own home."

They spoke for a bit longer and then Branigan slipped away, leaving Blair and Devaney to stare at one another.  They finally walked away from the suite, heading for their own place.  Once there, Devaney stood for a moment and then walked through to the office, heading for Blair's computer.

"What are you thinking?"  He perched on the side of the desk.

"That he' married and now his wife will be coming after us."  She looked up at him, a bleak look around her eyes.  "We're here but we're still not safe.  And we are putting everyone else at risk."

Blair nodded.  "I know we are, but they will have it no other way, you know that.  Dallas is to report back to us later tonight."  He nodded at the computer.  "I am sure they will be looking for his wife."

She sat back, her eyes on him, before she looked at the computer monitor.  "I'm sure they will, but there is still something about all this.  I can't put my finger on it."

"Neither can I.  Come on, my love.  Let's find some food and then you need to sleep.  Your eyes are tired."

She sighed.  "I am tired.  I think I'll just go to bed.  Call me when Dallas calls."

He was on his feet hours later, running for the bedroom, hearing Devaney's whimpers and knowing she would be screaming next.  His arms around her, he rocked her back and forth, listening to her sobs and then the words she was saying.  His heart broke for his lady, knowing she had been in so much danger over the years, and he hadn't been there for him.

He rose finally, watching her as she slept, determination in his mind.  He would search for the one person who could end all this, putting his own life on the line to find her. And it was a woman, that much he was certain of. Devaney had named her and it was not who he had expected. Blair doubted that Devaney would remember in the morning what she had said. At least, he prayed that she didn't but then sighed, knowing he would have to speak with her.

Devaney rose the next morning, searching for Blair, finding him this time at the computer. She could tell he had been there for a while.

"Blair?"

Her voice cut through his thoughts and he looked up, an arm coming out to draw her down on his knee, both arms wrapping around her, a kiss on her forehead. She looked up at that, a frown on her face.

"Blair? What did you do?"

"I found the one who is behind all this. You said the name last night in your nightmares."

"I did? I don't remember." She turned her head, her eyes falling on the photo on the computer monitor, and she paled. "Her?"

"Her. She has the money to do this. None of the others do. They have been her lackies, shall we say, doing what they's been ordered. I sent the name on to Dallas and Will. They have promised to find her." He sighed, his arms tightening around her. "I also sent it to Barnabas and Breck. They're tightening up security here, to make sure she can't get through."

"I pray she doesn't but how do we know? She could change her looks, play the victim."

"Barnabas has thought of that. He has asked that we stay inside for the next few days. That will be so hard on you." He studied her face. "And no, we're not putting you out there."

"I know, but somehow I think that's what it will take. She'll stay hidden, and we'll have no life until she's found."

"Will mentioned that. If we are out, we have officers with us. Barnabas has brought in more security for here."

"He can't!"

"It's already done. Breck was by here earlier with Branigan. They'll all take as many precautions as they can. We'll end this." He looked over as his phone chimed and he tilted it to read the message. "Well, well. Dallas works fast. He's found her."

"He has? Wonderful!"

Devaney moved quickly through the book store, looking for a particular book, finding it and then heading for the cashier, ready to walk away. Her steps slowed as she approached, not seeing the woman. She turned and began to run for the back door, sliding to a stop at the appearance of a woman. She backed away, hitting a table behind her, unable to move any further away.

"Well, well. Who do we have here?" The woman's arm was extended, a pistol pointing at Devaney. "You'll not get away this time. All these years, I have been tracking you, finding you, only to have you get away from me. It's not happening this time. This time, you pay."

"I don't understand, Alice. Why?"

"Do I need a reason? You're why Jerry had to leave that foster home. I had him placed there, but they didn't keep him, sent him away after a couple of hours."

"How could that be my fault? I was only, what, ten?"

"They said they didn't have room for him. They should have let you go."

Devaney's horror grew. "You're the one."

"The one, what?"

"The one that caused their accident. That's why I had to leave."

"So what? No one will ever know. It's just you and me here." Alice Green moved forward again, stopping just a few feet away from Devaney.

Devaney edged sideways from the table, watching her closely. If I can get away from her, maybe I can run. The pistol moving to point at her head stopped her.

The two woman stood, neither moving, neither speaking. Afterwards, Devaney could not tell for how long that had been. She sensed movement behind Alice, not moving her eyes from the older woman, not willing to be shot for this woman. Devaney frowned, trying to piece together how Alice fit into it all.

She looked up a bit as she saw a shadow moving towards Alice, catching sight of the police officers, dropping to the floor at a motion from them, scrambling away under the table. Her hands covered her ears as she huddled down, not wanting to move. She heard the screams and curses and vile language spouting from Alice and shuddered, knowing just how close it had been. She didn't move as she heard footsteps around her, shifting away from the hands reaching for her, sobs rising within her, tears flowing down her face.

Will stood and watched, his heart breaking for Devaney, knowing they wouldn't reach her. He turned and walked to the door and then outside, his eyes searching before he walked to the police line.

"Will?" Blair was hardly able to speak.

"She's alive but shut down. We can't reach her. Come with me. It's an unusual set of circumstances but given what she's been through and what you both have been through, I need you to come with me. You'll be the only one to reach through to her."

Blair stood for a moment, his eyes on Will before they moved to the store, seeing Alice being led away in handcuffs, and then the store clerk helped out and to an ambulance. "Suzy?"

"She was knocked out. She wasn't out for long and heard what Alice said. That's good, in a way. We have an eyewitness so Alice is not going to be able to get off."

Blair's steps slowed as he approached the table, seeing the crumpled and huddled form of his wife. An word from Will had the officer stepping back that had stood guard, and Blair dropped to his feet, his hands reaching to gently move Devaney to him, sitting on the floor and cradling her.

Devaney fought the hands that reached for her, desperate to escape, until she heard Blair's voice praying for her. Her arms around his neck, she clung to him, even as sobs still wracked her body. She didn't know that tears flowed down his face as well before he was on his feet, Devaney cradled close to him.

He stood, once again, in the Emergency Department, his eyes on his wife as she was assessed. They had finally given her sedation just to settle her down. Blair hated that she had had to have that. His head turned as he heard footsteps and Branigan appeared.

"Blair?"

"She sleeping. They had to sedate her. That's the only way to settle her down. Is it over?"

"Was she hurt?"

"No, no physically. We'll need to see about counselling for her when she's ready."

"Buckley will do that, or he'll know someone she can talk to. Berneen and Cadee will talk with her."

Blair nodded. "I know they will. Is it really over this time? I can't go through this anymore."

"It's over, Blair." Branigan drew in a deep breath. "Dallas spoke with me on the way in. He's waiting to talk to Devaney but he said tomorrow would work. Will's posted an officer here for the night."

"Thank him for me." Blair paused, his hands rubbing together. "Thank all the guys, Berneen, Cadee, Doc, Anna, the security team, for me. I'll do it when I can, but please let them know we thank them and thank them for the prayers."

"I can do that. Listen, Bradon's going to stay. So is Burnie. Devaney has endeared herself to us all, but particularly to those two."

Blair gave a small grin. "I know she has. Now, to let her heal." He breathed an inaudible thanks to the Lord that he was standing in a hospital and not a funeral home. It could have gone either way, he understood.

A smile on his face, Will watched as Devaney mingled with the group from the Foundation, finally understanding that she was part of the family. He didn't think she had understood that fully before. Barnabas stood beside him, having arranged for the catered meal for them all, and the police officers who had helped. The officers had eaten, stayed for a while, and then left. Other than for Dallas. He and Will needed to finish off their conversation with Devaney and Blair.

Blair approached, his arm around Devaney, who smiled and then reached to hug both Will and Dallas, surprising Dallas as she did so.

"Blair. Devaney. All I can say is that I'm sorry we didn't know about her in time to spare you." Dallas was contrite, thinking he had failed them somehow.

"It's not your fault, Dallas. She hid herself well. I never knew her, but I always felt someone in the background." Devaney leaned back on Blair, his arms around her.

"She was always there. Jerry is her son, but she refused to raise him, to even acknowledge him until he was an adult and useful to her. That's so sad." Dallas paused for a moment. "She did have him placed in that home, Devaney, wanting him to stay there. She had something on that family, but we can't find out what it is. They don't know, and she's not talking. Jerry doesn't know, or won't say. And she did cause the accident they had. That's why you had to be moved. They couldn't look after foster children anymore, not with their injuries."

"That's so sad. They were wonderful people." Devaney reached to brush away a tear. "But what was her motivation towards us?"

"She wanted Bridget to marry Blair and you to marry Jerry, just as you figured. When you two became engaged, she searched for a way to break you up. She didn't know that Blair had accepted work here, not until later. She's the one who chased you across the country, arranging for you to be watched, and yes assaulted. She was behind the stabbing. That water bottle you threw away?"

Devaney nodded. "I wondered about that. Was it really poisoned?"

"It was. God led there. You sensed something wrong and didn't drink from it. She has indicated she put rat poison in it, enough that just a few sips would likely have made you really sick, and without knowing what you had ingested, you wouldn't have received the proper treatment."

Blair shuddered. "I am so thankful God protected Devaney. She could have been gone and I would never have known." He looked at Will and then at Dallas, seeing his friends standing nearby.

"That she could have been." Dallas finally walked away, shaking hands with the gathered men.

Will stood for a moment, his eyes on the younger couple, before he turned to Doc.

"Doc? She's okay now?"

"She's getting there. It will take some time but they're working together on it. They are two parts of a whole." Doc hesitated before he spoke. "You have answered everything?"

"We believe so. Alice was behind everything that happened, including Devaney's wreck that started this all off here, the truck that ran them down, the kidnappings, and then her own attempt at killing Devaney. She's a vicious piece of work."

"And I suspect that you'll find she's done a lot more than this." Barnabas spoke from beside him.

"I'm sure we will. We're reaching out to other forces and finding just that. There will be a lot of work. Those two will have to testify in court, unless she pleads and I don't think she will." Will walked away at long last, a glance back showing the men beginning to leave, Cadee and Berneen hugging Devaney.

———

Blair was on a hunt. He could not find Devaney anywhere. He was not afraid that she had been kidnapped again. That was in the past by about four months. Blair was thankful that she had not been hurt any worse than she had been, but he still was sad that she had to go through what she did.

He finally tracked her down in one of the gardens. Blair thought to himself he should have known. She liked her outdoors and her flowers. She had taken over the gardens, and Barnabas had willingly let her, knowing they brought healing to her.

Devaney looked up, surprised, then a smile growing on her face as she reached for her husband. She still couldn't believe that they were married. Not after what they had gone through. She knew the trials were still upcoming, only needing to face Alice. She had been told today that all the others had taken plea bargains. Devaney could see God's hand in that.

Blair laughed at her. "Playing in the dirt again, love?"

"Not this time. Just spending time in the garden with my Lord. Gardens have such a wonderful refreshing way with them."

Blair's arms tightened on her as he bent to kiss her. "They do. I think I like the fact that Christ prayed in the garden, and that He prayed for us."

Devaney leaned back to look up at him, seeing his gaze focused in the distance. "I forget that. I need you to remind me every once in a while that is what He did."

They walked for a while, arms around once another, no words necessary before he drew her down on a bench.

"What now, love?"

"What do you mean?" She tilted her head to look up at him.

"What are you planning on doing? I know you don't have to work, but you're not one to keep still."

"I'm not sure. I would like to volunteer somewhere, but I'm not too sure where. Buckley and Barnabas both said they have places and names, but they won't give them to me yet. They say I still need to heal."

"And you do. You've had years of abuse, and it was abuse, to heal from. Just be content where God has placed you at the moment. I know Cadee and Berneen enjoy your company."

"And so does Anna, even though her kitten won't go home." Devaney had a smirk on her face as she said that.

Blair laughed. "No, the little kitty won't go come. You do have to name her, you know."

"I know. I just haven't come up with one yet. I really thought she would be going home, you know."

Blair laughed again as his arms tightened on her, a prayer of thankfulness rising once more within him.

They sat for a while, not seeing the glances from their friends as they passed by, each one thankful that Blair had his love with him and that both had survived.

They finally rose, the sun setting behind them, heading for the building and the potluck meal that Anna had arranged. They would enjoy the meal and companionship of their friends. A question lurked in Devaney's mind, a question as to which one of them would be next and would adventures happen to them all? She prayed for the men's safety as they walked through the unknown future, that God would protect, and that He would bring each one a lady of his own to love and cherish.

Dear Readers

Thank you for picking up the story of Blair and his love, Devaney. This one took a long time to write. Neither Blair nor Devaney were willing to share their story with me until the last ten days or so. And even then, I had computer glitches that wiped out a good quantity of what I had written midway through the book.

We are told to seek the Lord and He would be found. Devaney had to relearn that. Her life through the years had driven her faith deep within her, needing Blair to help her find it again.

If that is where you are, feeling like you are wandering in the desert, know that God is with you, that He will be found when you seek Him. My father often spoke of wandering in the desert at times, needing to be refreshed in our walk with God.

God bless each one of you.

Ronna

# Bradon: Encouraged to Overcome

## The Barnabas Chronicles
### Book 4

By

Ronna M. Bacon

Deuteronomy 31:6 Be strong and of a good courage, fear not, nor be afraid of them: for the LORD your God, he it is that does go with you; he will not fail you, nor forsake you.

Psalm 9:9-10 The LORD also will be a refuge for the oppressed, a refuge in times of trouble. And they that know your name will put their trust in you: for you, LORD, have not forsaken them that seek you.

# *Table of Contents*

*Chapter 1*

With a light breeze blowing in his face, Bradon Cahill stood on the edge of a cliff, his deep blue eyes focused on Lake Erie, watching the roll of the waves crashing against the rocks. He drew in a deep breath, needing, he thought, to clear his lungs. He had been away from his home for the last couple of days, evaluating dogs for a security company. He missed his red merle Australian Shepherd, Kade, but had decided he needed to take a break on the way home. That's why he stood, overlooking the lake, feeling lonely for some reason. *Lord, I know You are with me, but seeing Baird, Benen, and Blair all finding their ladies, I wish I had my own lady. But You know best. Help me to be content.*

Turning, Bradon walked away from the cliff, shifting his pack to a more comfortable position, his eyes searching the area, not seeing anything wrong, but with a niggling feeling in the back of his neck, he knew something was about to happen, and he had no idea what.

He felt the wind picking up and turned to look back at the lake, seeing the dark clouds moving in from the other side. He shivered, knowing that rain would likely happen and he wasn't near his truck, not close enough if the rain happened soon.

Bradon paused, a frown on his face as he heard voices, one raised in anger. His head tilting, he listened and then began to run. *That's a female voice and I can hear fear in it,* he thought. *Lord, protect her. I'm not sure I can get there fast enough.*

He paused at a clearing, seeing a young person, he thought, struggling to escape from the hands that held her wrists tight. Without thinking, he was racing through the grass, launching himself at the man, and taking him to the ground. The three hit hard, before Bradon's fist met the man's chin and then he was on his feet, his hand reaching to pull the young person up and with him as he ran back the way he had come, his head turning to watch the man.

Turning back to pull on the hand he had tight in his, he caught a glimpse of dark brown eyes and blond hair. *She's beautiful and* my age, was his thought before she tugged at his hand, taking him down another path.

She finally slid to a halt, her hand to her throat, as she peered behind him, waving her other hand at him to keep quiet. She leaned against a tree, her breath coming in gasps, as she turned her attention to him.

"Thank you, I think."

"What do you mean, you think?" Bradon was astounded at her words. "Were you not just being assaulted?" His hand ran through his red-gold hair, ruffling the curls he tried to keep short.

"I guess. I'm sorry. I didn't mean it the way it sounded." She looked back up the path and down towards the end of it. "This will lead us out to the lake and then we can work our way around."

"I'm sorry? What did you just say?"

"I said we can go down there and get away." Her finger stabbed in the air as she pointed.

"That's what I thought you said." He looked around. "What was his problem?"

She shook her head. "You don't want to know." She studied him for a moment. "You're not from here."

"No, I'm not. I'm Bradon Cahill."

"I'm Ennis Dacre." She moved away, her head tilted to look up. "We need to move. There's a storm moving in and the area we need to cross floods with the lake tide."

Bradon shook his head as he followed her. "I still want to know what that man wanted."

Ennis spun, her mouth open to speak as the wind suddenly picked up. Bradon gave a yell, throwing himself at her, taking them to the ground, tucking Ennis under him as he heard a crack and saw the shadow of a fir tree heading their way. His arms covered their heads even as Ennis shoved at him, to get him to move. Bradon felt the thud of a branch against him and lost the battle to keep his eyes open.

———

He roused later, how much later he wasn't sure, and pushed at the ground, a groan escaping him at the pain in his shoulder. He squinted against the pain, before his eyes dropped to Ennis, finding her unconscious. Lord, what happened? Who was that she was fighting with?

His head dropped back as he heard low angry voices near him, one he was sure belonging to the man who had assaulted Ennis. What was that all about? His eyes closed as he lost the battle to stay focused and awake. He needed to get them out of there but couldn't.

Ennis stirred later, sometime after Bradon had dropped back into the well of blackness. She heard voices and twisted her body, trying to shove Bradon away from her and not succeeding. Her voice filled with pain, she answered the calls for her, bringing her brother and father towards the tree.

"Ennis? Are you under there?" Her brother, Evan, crouched down, carefully working through the smaller branches until he found her. "And who's this?"

"His name is Bradon. He saved me. We need to get him out of here."

"And we will. Here, can you move? Let me have your hand."

Reaching for her brother's hand, Ennis carefully crawled towards him, feeling Bradon's body falling to the ground behind her. She was out from under the tree and in her father's arms, before she spun, crouching down to watch as Evan carefully maneuvered Bradon from under the fir.

"Where's he hurt, son?" Ian Dacre's voice was quiet, his eyes studying the younger man.

"A shoulder, I think, Dad. He's got some blood on his head as well." Evan stared down at him and then up at his father. "I don't like to move him."

"We don't have much choice. There's more wind and rain moving in. Here, let's get him up and over your shoulders. Ennis, stand back. You're not hurt, lass?"

"I don't think so. I knocked myself out when I went down, I think. Likely, I'll have some bruises. But we need to get him out of here. Jason was around again, and Bradon saved me from him."

———

Ian and Evan exchanged a glance before Bradon was over Evan's shoulders and the four were moving out.  Ian stood for a moment as they neared the beach, his eyes looking backwards.  His heart was heavy for his daughter, knowing that the man who had haunted her steps for so many years was back.  How do we keep her safe, Lord?  We can't restrict her movements.  His eyes turned ahead to study his son, and then Bradon.  Is he the one, Lord?  Is he the one who will help her overcome what has happened in the past?  If so, thank you.  If not, guard both their hearts.

Ennis' hand came out to touch Bradon's face as Evan paused for a moment at the foot of the path.

"Go ahead, Ennis.  The truck just up ahead.  You'll need to sit in the back with him."  Evan watched her closely, a frown on his face, before he moved forward.

None of them saw the two men standing up on the cliff, watching intently as they moved away.  Nor could they hear the angry words exchanged between the two before the man called Jason followed along the cliff, just long enough to see Ennis disappear into her brother's truck.

*Chapter 2*

Ian had dug Bradon's keys out of his jacket pocket and then followed Evan home with his truck.  He shook his head.  Now, what?  Who is this young man and where is he from?  Questions raced through his mind, knowing they would have to wait until Bradon regained consciousness.

Evan gently dropped Bradon onto the antique maple wooden bed in the main floor guest room, and then stood back, breathing heavily for a moment, before his hands reached to remove Bradon's boots and set them neatly to one side.  His father had reached for Bradon's pack and dropped it to the arm chair before he eased the jacket from him and then his shirt.

"How bad is it, Dad?"  Evan watched carefully as Ennis stood by the bed, her arms wrapped around herself.  "Ennis.  You need to get cleaned up and into dry clothes.  Go.  We'll call you back when we're ready."  Evan's hands were gentle on his sister as he moved her from the room, a frown on his face at the look in her eyes before his head turned to watch Bradon.

Ennis stood for a moment before she ran for the room she was using at the moment in her parents' home.  She had just moved back home, accepting work in a town nearby as a medical office assistant.  She wasn't too sure about this, wanting her independence but knowing she needed time to accept the fact that she was back in her home area and knowing she needed to decide just where she would live.  She twisted her long hair into a clip as the final step to dry, clean clothes and gathered her wet things, throwing them into the washer on the way by back on the first floor, to head for the kitchen and something hot.  Ennis' hand rested on the kettle as her headed turned towards the hallway before she sighed.  No, she thought.  He can't be the knight on the white charger coming to my rescue, now can he?  Even though his truck is white?  Lord, why do I trust him to quickly?  It's not me to trust like that.

———

Her mother, Meg, stood for a moment, her eyes on her daughter before she swept her into a hug.

"This is not how we wanted you to come home."

"I know, Mom.  I thought I was safe out there today.  I was so careful.  Made sure no one followed me."  Ennis blinked back tears, tears she vowed would not fall.  She had shed enough tears over that man, now hadn't she, Lord?

"But who is this man that your Dad and brother are working on?  Your Dad just said they found you two under a fallen fir tree."  Meg drew her daughter down to a chair, placing their tea cups on the table and then reaching for a plate of homemade scones.

"I don't know, Mom.  Jason had me by the wrist and I was trying to get away.  In Mel's clearing.  Next thing I know, I'm on the ground and Bradon has knocked Jason out. He grabbed hold of me and we ran.  We were heading for Mel's beach when the wind picked up and brought down the tree."  She paused.  "Who is he, Mom?  And where did he come from?  There wasn't anyone else around, not that I saw."

Meg looked up as Ian paused in the doorway.  "When he's awake, we'll ask him.  Ian?"

Ennis raised her head as her father sat beside her, reaching to give her a hug.

"I am so glad he was there, Ennis.  I don't want to think of what might have happened."

"Has he been awake?"

Ian shrugged.  "Just briefly to ask if you were safe."

"How is he, Dad?  Do we need to take him to the hospital?"  Ennis rubbed her hands on her mug, her eyes on it, as she waited for her father to speak.

"No, I don't think so.  Evan has had a good look at him.  His shoulder is bruised and he won't be using that arm for a while.  The head has a bump on it, but not as bad as we had thought.  We'll wait and take him in when he awakens.  The rain is starting to pick up again as is the wind."

She nodded before she rose and walked away, leaving her parents to stare after her before they exchanged glances and then bowed their heads to pray for their girl and for the stranger they found in their home. Somehow, they both knew his coming would make a difference for her.

Ennis stood for a moment in the bedroom doorway before she approached the bed and sank into the chair her father had pulled close to it. She studied the man lying there, a frown on her face. She thought she knew him but that was impossible. She shook her head. There was no way she had met him before. Ennis didn't think she would have forgotten him. Her head bowed as she too prayed for him.

Bradon's eyes flickered open, and he frowned as he glanced around. This wasn't his bedroom. That much he knew. But where was he? His eyes stopped as they landed on Ennis, and his face softened. She's here, he thought. She's here and she's safe. Pulling his hand from beneath the blanket, he grimaced with the pain from his other shoulder. This is not good, he thought.

Ennis jumped as she felt a hand touch her, and her head raised rapidly, her eyes huge as she stared at the hand on hers and then at Bradon.

"You're awake?"

"I am. It's Ennis? I'm saying it right?"

"You are. How are you feeling?"

"Sore. What did I do to my shoulder?" He moved to raise himself up, a groan coming from him as he do, Ennis reaching to tuck pillows behind him.

"Evan thinks it's just bruised. He's a physiotherapist, in case you need one."

Bradon shot her a quick look, catching the sparkle of mischief in the brown eyes that he felt he could get lost in. "He is? Is he taking me to the hospital to verify that?"

"The weather's too bad. It's gotten really windy, and the rain is quite heavy. There are severe thunderstorm and tornado warnings out."

"Is that what hit the tree?"

She shook her head, her braid swaying with the movement. "No, just a heavy wind. That tree's been ready to fall for years."

"And it had to wait until we were under it, did it?" His head went back for a moment as his eyes closed. "Any chance for a shower? And are my clothes dry?"

"I'll get Evan to help you, if you need to. He's brought in your pack. Are there clothes in it?"

Bradon shook his head. "Is my truck here?"

"Dad brought it back for you. By the way, you're at my parents' place for now." She studied him, her head tilting to the side in a movement that fascinated him. "Do you have luggage in it?"

"There's a duffle bag in the back seat. It has some clean clothes." He groaned again and looked around.

"What do you need?" Ennis watched him closely.

"My phone. Did you see it?"

"We did. It's charging right now. Mom plugged it in out in the kitchen." She watched him closely for a moment and then walked away, Bradon watching her every move, something about her drawing him to her.

Now what, Lord? What did I do when I went to help her? And how do I keep her safe? He didn't see Evan watching him, his own heart praying for his sister, with a wish that just maybe someone had come into her life.

Evan watched later as Bradon sat in the kitchen, a quiet word of thanks to Meg for the cup of coffee and plate of toast that she slid in front of him, before his eyes raised to his sister, who was standing just out of Bradon's sight, her own eyes on the stranger in their house. He caught the wishful look of longing on her face and his heart broke for his sister, knowing that she had so much to give and had been chased from her own home for years, just to try and stay safe. Evan felt the anger beginning to grow in him and then felt his father's hand on his shoulder.

A few hours later, sitting in the living room, Ennis watched Bradon once more as he spoke with her parents, Evan beside her, a frown on his face. He felt he knew Bradon from somewhere but wasn't quite sure.

"Where do you work, Bradon?" Ian was curious, his eyes narrowing as he caught a glimpse of Ennis' face, and decided they needed to learn more about the young man.

"I work for K9 specialties. We evaluate and also train dogs for security companies and also for individuals that need one." Bradon looked down for a moment, biting at his lip, before he looked up, deciding he could trust this family with something that was not common knowledge. "I am actually employed by The Barnabas Foundation, which pays my wages. I work for K9S."

"The Barnabas Foundation? Barnabas Carey?" At Bradon's nod, Ian continued. "I know his father quite well. We've attended many men's conferences at the same time." He studied Bradon closer. "I heard some of your friends have had their adventures."

Bradon grinned, the smile lighting up his face. "That they have. First it was Baird and Berneen. Then Benen and Cadee. Blair and his Devaney just survived theirs a few months ago."

Ennis gave a soft laugh. "Three of your friends? What kind of adventures would they have?"

Bradon kept grinning, even as he shook his head. "No one believes us." He sobered. "It was so dangerous for them, and for those of us who got caught in it. Baird had been kidnapped, taken to where Berneen was being held. Some of us went in and rescued them, only to have them kidnapped again with our friend and pastor, Buckley. To save his life, Berneen agreed to marry him. They are such a wonderful couple. They faced some pretty tough and hard difficulties.

"Then, there's Benen and Cadee, friends for years. Her parents were missionaries. Long story short - there was a contract out on Cadee and the only way to get her out safely was a name change.  Benen agreed to marry her, brought her back from the country the mission was in.  Similar dangers to the first couple.

"And then there was Blair and Devaney.  They were in the same foster home, fell in love, decided to marry, and then Devaney walked away because someone threatened Blair's life.  She made her way across the country from Alberta, ending up here and reuniting with Blair."

"There is no way that happened!"  Ennis snapped her mouth shut. "It can't.  It doesn't happen in real life."

Bradon began to laugh, causing the others to stare at him. "I'm sorry.  Each of the ladies have said the same thing.  It can only happen on television or in books or movies."

Evan began to grin.  "And how many of you are there?"

"With Barnabas, there are fourteen of us who live in the Foundation Building.  Ian, I think you've likely seen it?"

Ian nodded.  "I have.  It's been years, but if I recall, it was set up to provide housing for all of you, as well as Doc and Anna?"

"Doc and Anna Whitson are still there.  She mothers us all. He's the father none of us can remember or haven't had for years." He sobered, realizing just how true that was for himself.  His parents had been killed in a home invasion when he was young and staying at a friend's overnight.  He had lived with his maternal grandparents until they both died just as he became an adult.

"I know Doc."  Evan spoke up.  "I can see him fulfilling that role."  He paused, his eyes on Ennis.  "Now what, Bradon?  You're not able to drive and I know you're anxious to get home."

Bradon nodded, his eyes catching a movement from Ennis that stopped his eyes on her face, a frown flitting across his.

"No, I can't drive, not a standard transmission.  I mean I could, but is someone volunteering?"

"Ennis will."  Evan just grinned at his sister as she spun on the couch, her mouth dropping open before she snapped it shut and then glared at him.  "She can drive standard.  In fact, she's the best of all of us at that."

———

"If you don't want to, Ennis, that's fine. I'll just one of the guys a call and they'll come get me. Or I can attempt the drive. I'm sure I can manage it."

She shook her head. "No, it's fine. Evan can follow us or I'll just load my bike on your truck."

Bradon stared at her. "Your bike? After what happened earlier today?"

Ennis nodded. "I don't let him control my life. If I want to bike, I will." She was on her feet, moving from the room, and they heard the back door shut quietly behind her.

Bradon's head went back. "What did I say I shouldn't have?"

"It's not what you said, Bradon." Meg spoke up, her eyes on Evan and his reaction to his sister's departure. "It's that she doesn't want to give him any more control over her life than he has had. She's lived away from here since she was twenty. That's eight years or so we missed out on the day to day interaction with her because of him. She has come home. Ennis is determined to stop him somehow and that makes us afraid for her. She will not let him win this time and drive her away."

Bradon had been watching Meg closely. "And she needs someone to step in? Someone not her family?"

Ian nodded. "That's exactly what she needs and what she refuses to ask for. We can only do so much. She is an adult and even though we worry about her, we have to let her live her life." He paused. "She's moving to your town, Bradon. I know it's only twenty miles from here but he will track her down."

Shaking his head, his eyes on Evan, Bradon hesitated to ask. "What is the issue? I don't want to misstep if I say something to her."

"We have all done that at some point, Bradon." Meg's hand rubbed about the arm of the chair she was seated in. "He had fixated on her, demanding that she date only him, intending her to be his possession is how she has phrased it. She has not told us everything that he has said, but I know it can't be pretty. She's been badly hurt by him and that has coloured her relationships with others and how she views herself at times.  Her faith is strong, but sometimes that just isn't enough in a young woman's life."

He shook his head. "That shouldn't happen."  He was on his feet, heading for the back door, searching for his shoes to slip them on, finding his jacket hanging up on the coat rack.  He slipped into it, his hand reaching for the door before he pulled it open and stood outside, the door closing behind him.

Ennis stood, her arm wrapped around a porch column.  He could see the dejection and fear in her stance.  Bradon moved to stand near her, not saying anything.

"Bradon?"

"It shouldn't have happened, Ennis.  He shouldn't have been allowed to treat you the way he has."

She shrugged.  "No one has been able to get through to him. And what you did?  You've made yourself an enemy.  He's brutal."

"Who all has he threatened?"

Ennis spun, her mouth dropping open.  "What do you mean?"

"He has threatened someone close to you.  Your parents? Evan?"  He watched her closely.  "He's threatened to physically harm you or worse, hasn't he?"

She nodded, tears clouding her eyes for a moment.  "Thank you."

"Thank you?  For what?"  Bradon's voice softened, even as he heard the sound of the rain thumping on the metal roof overhead and felt the faint spray hitting him when the wind blew it towards him.

"You're the first one who has verbalized that.  I couldn't say anything.  Evan would have been after him."

Bradon just reached for her.  "Come here, sweetheart."  He gathered her close, her arms around him, hugging him tight.  He could feel the shudders running through her.  "I won't let him hurt you. Not ever.  Not I can help it."

"But how?"  Her voice was hopeful, muffled as it was with her head buried against him.

"I'll stop him and I have thirteen friends who will help."

———

Ennis stared at him, her mouth dropping open at his words. He gave her a gentle smile as he tapped her chin, causing her to close her mouth.

"I have thirteen friends, one of them Barnabas Carey. The other twelve are employed by the Foundation. I also have a multitude of others I can call in. You will be safe."

She shook her head. "No, I won't. I haven't been in years."

He gave her a gentle smile. "You will be. I've found my lady, God willing, and I won't let anything happen to her." He dropped a kiss on her forehead and then, turning, walked back into the house, leaving her staring after him, a hand covering her mouth, tears sparkling on her cheeks she didn't know she was shedding.

Is he the one, Lord? Is he the knight I've dreamed about and begged You for?

——

The next afternoon, Branigan Clery and Benen Carroll, two of Bradon's friends, sat in one of the garden areas, idle conversation between them, Bradon's dog, Kade, stretched out at their feet.  They had fully expected Bradon back yesterday and were becoming concerned because no one had heard from him, unusual for their group of friends.

Kade's head raised as they heard a vehicle coming to a stop, and then, with a low bark, he was away, knowing he had heard Bradon's truck.  The two men shrugged and then rose, following him, anxious to know that Bradon was fine.

Their steps slowed as the driver's door opened, Kade stopping and then approaching the person who dropped down to the ground.

"That's not Bradon, but it's his truck."  Branigan walked forward as the passenger door opened and Bradon stepped down, his hand out to greet Kade, whose whole body was wriggling with excitement that his master was home, before he walked around to where Ennis stood, uncertainty in her stance, his free hand going out for hers.

"Are you sure this is okay?"  She was hesitant as he turned her towards the building.

"I'm sure."  His steps stopped as he saw his two friends. "Ennis, I want you to meet Branigan and Benen."

She gave a small smile, her hand tightening on his, as he made the introductions.

"Bradon?  What did you go and do?  Can't let you out of our sight, is that it?"  Branigan's voice broke through the short silence that ensued Bradon's introduction.

"I saved a lady in distress and then tangled with a fir tree.  It's just bruised.  I'll have Doc check it out."  He shook his head slightly at them.  "Is Barnabas around?"

"He will be later. We were wondering where you were. Kade was getting quite anxious."

Bradon laughed as he looked down at his dog, who by this time had plastered himself to Ennis' side, his eyes watchful, knowing somehow she was in danger. He nodded.

"I need to talk to him. Ennis here needs our help, and a place to stay that's safe."

"Another lady in distress?" Benen grinned. "I need to introduce you to Cadee."

"Cadee? She's the one from South America?" Ennis frowned as she tried to remember what Bradon had said.

"She was when I married her, but she's originally from my home town." Benen pointed towards the door. "How be we go in? I know she's around."

Ennis didn't move, her eyes now glued to Kade. Bradon could feel the shudders running through her and ducked his head to watch her face, seeing the fear, no terror, he thought, on her face before his eyes moved to Kade. A quiet word had Kade moving backwards and sitting, his eyes still on Ennis.

"Ennis?" Bradon's voice was quiet, a frown on his face, even as his two friends watched the pair closely. He didn't see Baird and Brady approaching, nor others of his friends gathering around, the three young ladies walking towards him. "Ennis? What is it?"

"Your dog."

"Yes, Kade's my dog. What about it?"

"I can't be near dogs. I'm sorry." She turned, her body ready to run, before his arm wrapped around her. "I'm sorry."

"What are you sorry about?" His eyes lifted to his friends, seeing their concern before they slid shut. "What did he do?"

"His dog. It attacked me. I can't do dogs." Her voice was thick with her tears. "I'm sorry. He looks like a nice dog."

"He is. He is very gentle. And he is worried about you. That's why he was so close to you. He won't attack." A small grin appeared on Bradon's face. "He'll protect you."

Branigan spoke up. "Bradon's right. Kade will protect you. He has seen you two together. He sees Bradon holding your hand. In Kade's mind, that makes you important to Bradon. That makes you his family, and he will protect his family. He did that to protect one of our ladies."

Ennis' eyes raised to his for a moment before they dropped back to Kade. "I'm sorry."

"Ennis?" Bradon's quiet question had her looking at him. "Where did you get bit? And what kind of dog?"

"A mastiff mix, I think. I'm not sure now. I've tried too hard to forget it. I wouldn't go with him, and he set the dog on me." Her face whitened even more at the memory.

"How many stitches? And where?"

"My right calf. About thirty or more, I think. I didn't want to know." Ennis' head turned back into Bradon's shoulder, not seeing the shock on his face or on the faces of those listening.

Bradon shook his head at his friends, turning Ennis to walk into the building, seeing Breck, the second in command at the Foundation, walking his way. A quick word and Bradon was leading Ennis into the building and to a suite near his. He knew someone would grab his duffle bag and backpack. He didn't have to ask.

Ennis finally looked up and around the suite, her mouth opening and closing at the comfortable look of the apartment. She walked slowly through, before she returned, to stand in front of Bradon, a question on her face.

"You can stay here, Ennis. Breck has okayed it."

"He did? I didn't meet him, did I?"

Bradon grinned as he shook his head. "Not yet, but he was out there. Now, about this guy?"

She nodded. "I need to talk to someone. I'm just not sure who. We have put in complaints. We tried to have him charged with his dog attacked me. All for nothing. The police officer wouldn't even take a statement from us. I have it all documented.

Medical records.  What have you.  It's all in writing.  No one in my family knows the extent of what I have been through."

"They know, sweetheart.  They have a pretty good idea.  Your father hasn't acted, not yet, but he will if this continues."

———

Looking for Bradon later that afternoon, Barnabas' feet slowed as he found Ennis in one of the gardens, Kade near her, but no Bradon. He had talked to Breck and then to Branigan, who had brought him up to date as much as they could. There were gaps they didn't know the answers to, and that he needed to speak with either Bradon or Ennis.

Ennis spun as she heard steps behind her, backing up and away from Barnabas, who paused in his forward walk to study her, Kade rising and coming to stand in front of her, eyes on Barnabas.

"I'm sorry. I didn't mean to frighten you." A grin broke through the grimness on Barnabas' face. "I'm Barnabas Carey."

"Dad knows you."

"Your father?"

"At least I think he does. He knows your father. My dad is Ian Dacre."

Barnabas nodded, the grin staying on his face. "He does indeed. Dad has mentioned him many times. But that doesn't explain why you are here."

Ennis shook her head. "I knew this was a bad idea. I'll leave as soon as I can get someone to take me home." She didn't see Bradon approaching her or the look on his face that said he didn't want her to do that.

"No, it's fine. Dad would want you to stay here. So do I. I understand you will be working in our town. This makes sense to have you here."

"But it doesn't mean I'll be safe, does it?" She brushed by him, hesitating as she saw Bradon, and then almost running for the building.

"Barnabas?" Bradon's voice had his friend turning.

"You're okay?"

Bradon shrugged, pain flickering across his face for a moment. "I talked to Doc. It's bruised from what he can tell. About Ennis?"

"Yes. About Ennis. Talk to me, Bradon. I know there's more than what you have said."

"There is." Bradon turned to walk back towards the building, anxious to find Ennis. He described what he had happened upon and what had happened to him, then went on to tell him what Ennis had confirmed about Jason.

"They did nothing?" Barnabas had to tamp down anger. "I'll talk to her parents, see what they can tell us."

Bradon shook his head. "I should be the one. Right now, she's not sure who she can trust. She's lived away for so long." He paused, his hand rubbing at his injured shoulder. "Breck said she could have the one suite."

"She can, for as long as she needs to. I understand from him that she's working here?"

"She is. I know she'll want her independence. And I can't say I fault her for that, but if needed, she can always catch a ride with one of us." He looked down at the sling. "And I have to talk to Rick."

"Yes, you do. But I know him. You'll be able to continue working, even in a sling." Barnabas gave a small wave as he moved away.

Ennis had stood just inside the building door, not seeing the lobby or the seating areas Barnabas had set up. The security guard on duty stood watching her, knowing that she was Bradon's lady in everyone's mind and that she was in trouble. She watched as Bradon walked her way, not seeing Kade standing as close to her as he could get.

"Bradon? Can you take me home?" Her heartbroken voice stopped him in his tracks.

He stared at her, then with a hand on her arm, directed her to a seating area, waiting for her to sit before he sat beside her.

"Why?" His voice was quiet.

"Why? Because I need to. I can't stay here."

"And why can't you?"

"Because I can't.  It puts you at risk."

"Actually, we've been there and done that."  He grinned at her and held up three fingers.  "Each of the ladies brought trouble here. We didn't let that stop us helping them, and it won't stop us helping you.  Barnabas has said you are to use the suite I showed you to. That's a given.  And if you're not comfortable driving back and forth, then one of us will take you.  We all work in town.  When we're not working, we volunteer."

"You volunteer?"  Her mind refused to take in that she had been offered a sanctuary.  "What do you volunteer at?"

"The community garden.  I find it a nice change of pace."  He grinned at the look on her face.  'Didn't see that coming, I guess?"

Ennis shook her head, leaning back on the couch, her hand rubbing at the leather.  "These are nice."  She looked up, surprise on her face, at the second seating area.  "This is quite the building."

"It is.  Barnabas and his father spent a lot of time designing it. They're expanding the facilities outside now."

"They are?"  Ennis grew quiet, not quite sure where she stood with Bradon or even his friends.  "Bradon?  If I'm to stay, I need my things."

"Your parents thought of that.  All you have to do is call them. They will gladly bring your things, as you call it, but they are sad that it has to come to this."

"I know.  He's taken so much."  Her eyes slid closed.  "I don't think he's working on his own.  That's the thing.  Someone is working with him."  She looked up at Bradon.  "And I don't know why he's fixated on me.  It doesn't make sense.  I had no contact with him before it all started."

"And how old were you?"  Bradon's arm swept her into a hug. "How old, sweetheart?"

"I never told anyone when it first started.  I thought it would go away.  I was like sixteen, almost seventeen."

Bradon's eyes slid closed.  So young, he thought, and to have had to carry that all these years, leaving home to protect her family and now that she's back, it will start up again.

*Chapter 6*

Ennis turned from the kitchen in her suite, a smile on her face as she listened to her father teasing her brother. I can do this, she thought, before she looked over at her mother, who stood, fridge door open, putting away the groceries they had brought for her.

"You didn't have to do that, Mom?"

Meg looked up, a smile on her face. "But we did. You know your father. He had to shop for you, to make sure you had enough to eat. Although, I do think he shopped for himself as well."

Ennis started to laugh, causing her mother to join in. "I'm sure he did. He can't hover, though, Mom. I can't have that."

"We know, dear, but you are his little girl. Always will be. Even when you marry, you'll still be that."

Ennis gave a snort, causing her mother to break out into fresh laughter. "I don't see that happening, Mom."

Meg just shook her head, her eyes on Bradon as he stood watching from the kitchen doorway, his heart in his eyes. Ennis wasn't ready for that, not just yet, she thought. Lord, protect these two. They are walking into something, and need that protection. Protect their hearts, please, dear Lord, and if she's the one for him and he for her, work it out for them.

Bradon moved towards the two ladies, his hands out to take the boxes from Ennis. "I'll get rid of these for you, unless you want to keep them?" Her head shook at his question. "All settled?"

"I think so." She looked around. "Where's your dog?"

Her question had her parents spinning and staring at her, knowing how she was so fearful of dogs.

"I left him in my suite. He's fine."

"No, it's not. He hasn't seen you in days. And I know he goes with you wherever you go here." She looked up, distressed. "I can't have you putting him away. I knew this was not such a good idea."

———

Her father's arm around her shoulder stopped her words. "I'm sure Bradon is comfortable with that. If he's not, he'll talk to you." Ian paused, not quite sure how to phrase his next sentence. "It has always distressed us that Jason took your love of dogs away. Maybe Bradon's dog will bring that back. I've met him. He's a beautiful dog, gentle in nature."

"That he is, Ian. And now that he's seen Ennis with me, he'll protect her."

Ennis was shaking her head. "He can't do that."

"But he will. It's in his nature to protect my friends." Bradon's hand gently touched her cheek. "Now, how be we head into town? You can show me where you work, and your parents and Evan can join us for a meal?"

"We can do that, I think." Ennis turned to her family, finding them nodding. "Well, okay, then."

Bradon watched her later as he drove back to the building. She had relaxed some but he could see she was still uncertain as to the wisdom of her move. She would relax, he prayed, knowing that once Berneen, Cadee, and Devaney spoke with her, she would find friends who would understand what she was going through. He knew it was tough on her parents to walk away, even though they lived close. Evan had made a point to speak with him, asking that Bradon keep him updated as to what was going on, and he would do the same. He had a friend, a private investigator, he would be speaking with, he stated. It didn't matter that Ennis had told him not to in the past. This time, they needed it over for her, he said.

Ennis' head turned as she watched the sky. "It's such a beautiful night."

"It is." Bradon's face held contentment for the moment. "We have a beach on the property. I'll show you tomorrow."

"Do you have bike trails?"

"Bike trails?" Bradon shot her a quick glance.

"Yes, bike trails. You know. Those trails you ride your bike on. I love to bike, and Dad brought mine."

"He did?  We do, but I would just ask that you let one of us know when you're heading out.  Even if it's just the security guard."

"About that.  Why have a security guard?"

"Just for protection.  The Barnabas Foundation is worth billions."  He grinned as her mouth dropped open.  "Barnabas' father insisted we have security.  Although the culprits can still get to our ladies when they want to."

"They can?  So, this security?  It's that good?"

Bradon had pulled into his parking spot by that time and at her words, shot her a look, his eyes narrowing at the gleam of mischief in hers.  "It's not their fault.  They do their best.  It's when the ladies are out and about that they seem to run into difficulty.  And that makes it hard for us guys to take care of our ladies."

"About that.  You keep calling me that.  And you have your friends doing the same."

"I do?  I guess they've picked up on something."  Bradon stared out the windshield, his hand rubbing at his arm.  Driving had put a stress on it, but he hadn't let Ennis drive that afternoon.  "I think of you as that, Ennis.  I know you're not ready, may never be ready for that."  He slipped from the truck, coming around to open her door, reaching for her hand to help her down and then not letting go.

"We do need to talk.  But right now, you need to rest your arm. You haven't and I can see the pain in your face."

*Chapter 7*

Spotting the white envelope under her windshield wiper, Ennis hesitated to approach her car after her work had ended for the day. *He's found me, hasn't he, Lord? And too soon. How do I stay safe and keep everyone around me safe?* She hesitated to touch it but finally reached to pull it out, her key fob out to unlock her car door. She was inside and the doors locked in just a few seconds.

Ennis stared at the envelope before dropping it onto the seat beside her. She didn't need to read it to know what he would say. She had brought danger to Bradon. And in doing so, she had brought danger to his friends.

Bradon was waiting for her, a frown on his face as he saw the disheartened look on hers.

"Ennis? What did he do?" He glanced at the envelope in her hand. "Where did you find it?"

"Under the wiper blade." She looked up at him, a shuttered look on her face. "I can't do this anymore, Bradon. I just can't."

His hand reaching for the envelope, he then swung his arm around her, directing her to the building. "We'll open this and then pass it on to whoever it needs to go to. I had a chance to talk to our police chief today. He's concerned. He'll want to talk to you at some point."

"What is the point of that? Nothing will get done."

"On the contrary, there will be."

A voice behind her had a small scream coming from her as she jumped and spun. Will Peters stood there, waiting for Bradon to introduce them.

"Ennis, this is our police chief and good friend, Will Peters." Bradon made the introductions, then handed Will the envelope. "She found this just a bit ago, Will. We haven't opened it."

Will nodded, his eyes on the envelope before he looked up. "Can we head for your office, Bradon? Ennis? Do you need to change or anything before we talk?"

She finally nodded. "If I could. I always change when I come home. Where's your office, Bradon?"

He grinned. "I'll wait here for you."

Ennis stared at him for a moment before she was off, almost on a run. Will and Bradon watched her go before Will spoke.

"I talked to her father today after we spoke. He called me. When he told me the name of the officer, I can see why it didn't go anywhere. It's not common knowledge, but he is connected to this man."

"And he was let investigate?"

Will nodded. "I have spoken with the chief there. He wasn't aware of the connection at the time or it would never have happened. That officer has been dismissed from the force. He had too many complaints such as hers to let him stay on."

Bradon sighed. "And if he hadn't been the one, this could have never gotten to this point."

"We don't know that. From what I understand, it likely would have. I have asked Dallas to take a look at what we have and decide from there where we go."

"Dallas. That's good. We'll need to connect with him at some point." Bradon reached for Ennis' hand as she stopped once more beside him. "Kade's in my office. Is that okay?"

She shrugged. "I guess. Just don't let him near me."

Will frowned. "There's a problem with Kade?"

"Not with Kade, per se. But with dogs. This monster let his dog attack her years ago, and she ended up with multiple stitches."

Will shook his head. "We'll stop him, Ennis."

"Before or after he kills someone? He's quite capable of that."

Will sank into a chair in Bradon's office, his eyes on Kade for a moment as he rubbed the dog's head. "I get that, Ennis. That's what we want to avoid."

"And can we do that?"

"We will do our best to prevent that. You're an important part of our family now, Ennis." Will watched Bradon as he spoke, the younger man's head nodding at the words. "Now, about this envelope?"

"Yes, that. Please? Just make him go away. You have no idea how much I have prayed for just that."

"I have a good idea on that, Ennis. Before I open this, what all has he done? How many times have you had something like this?"

Ennis shrugged. "About two dozen I would say. None when I was living away from home, but I would find evidence I was being watched. Footprints in the garden around the house. The odd photo that showed up. He was really bad before I left."

"And just what did he do?" Will had his notebook and pen out, taking notes.

"He threatened to hurt me. He threatened to hurt my family, even threatening to kill them. But nothing that said why he was. And I found that strange. He would approach me at times, trying to make me go with him. His dog, he set him on me once." She shook with fear at that memory, not realizing that Kade had approached her and laid his chin on her knee, his eyes on her face. Her hand laid on his head without her knowing she had done that, finding comfort in touching him.

"That dog attack? It was reported?"

Ennis nodded. "We did but he had hidden the dog, said it was a stray that attacked me. It was his word against mine. I ended up with the stitches, a scar, and having to take rabies shots."

"That shouldn't have happened. I have spoken with the police chief in your town. The responding officer is not on the force anymore. The chief sends his apologies, although that cannot change the fact that this was mishandled and mishandled badly."

"It's what I expected.  I figured that officer was a friend of Jason's."  She sank back in her chair, her eyes focusing on Kade as he sat near her, his chin still on her knee.  "Bradon?  Your dog?"

Bradon grinned at her.  "He does that when he thinks someone is upset.  It's his way of comforting that person.  You're not the first lady he's approached like that."

She nodded, her fear of dogs starting to rise within her, before she sighed and then prayed for that to be over as well.

"What's in the envelope, Will?"  Bradon's question had Will fingering the envelope.

Will pulled latex gloves onto his hands before he opened the envelope.  A single photo dropped out.  "When did you two go to the restaurant?"

"Last Saturday.  We were with my parents and brother. Why?"

He held up the photo.  "This is taken there, as you are leaving. He's following you, Ennis."

"Of course he is.  Isn't that what they always do?"

*Chapter 8*

Will had spoken to the young couple for close to an hour, Ennis being as honest as she could with everything. He had frowned as he heard how young she had been when it started, and that no one had stepped up to stop it for her. He would need to speak with Dallas. He wanted this stopped before it went any further, but he knew that would not happen.

Ennis had paced Bradon's office as she heard the two men discussing what to do, Kade keeping pace with her, his eyes on her face. She had stared down at him, not quite sure if she could trust him, but seeing the calm and steady look in his eyes, she had rested her hand on his head, a low whine coming from him as he pressed closer to her. Ennis didn't see Bradon's eyes on her at that point, his heart warming more towards her as he saw Kade's desperate attempt to make friends and to comfort her.

Bradon walked Will out and then returned to his office, leaning against a doorway, watching Ennis as she just stood, her arms wrapped around herself.

"Ennis?"

She spun, not having heard him return. "Bradon! You scared me! I didn't hear you."

"No, you didn't, but Kade did. If I had been a stranger, he would have been in front of you, pushing you backwards."

"Why?"

"Why? To protect you. He has decided you need his protection. I have seen that once or twice with him, but not to this extent."

"Branigan, I think it was, said it was because he saw you with me and that he decided I was family."

Bradon laughed. "That would be about it. Now, what do we do with you?"

"It's not just me anymore, Bradon. He's fixated on you as well."

He nodded. "I know he has. We'll not let him win. I can guarantee you that." He looked behind him. "Listen, tonight's when we have our weekly potluck."

"A weekly potluck? As in everyone in the building?" She stared at him, not quite sure she had heard him correctly.

"That's right. All of us. Anna and Doc started it just after we all moved here. And we are all from different parts of the country. And did we tell you we are all orphans?"

"No, you didn't. What's with that?"

Bradon shrugged. "It's what Barnabas felt led to to. We're all orphans. And we share initials."

"What? All of you?"

He laughed again. "All fourteen of us."

Ennis shook her head. "I don't see how he managed to accomplish that feat."

"He says it was God, and I must admit, I have to agree."

She just stared at him and then walked past him, his hand coming out to stop her.

"We won't keep you here, if you really do want to move somewhere else." His words were quiet.

She waited, before she looked at him, nodding. "I know that, Bradon. I feel safe here, probably for the first time in years. Even when I moved away, I wasn't safe. I just worry about Mom and Dad and Evan, what he'll do to them when he can't get to me."

"I talked to Barnabas, who talked to his father. They both met with your parents and Evan. There are plans in place for all of them."

"There are? Thank you." She moved away from him, heading for her own apartment, leaving him staring after her, a hand on Kade's head to keep him beside him, a low whine coming from the dog.

---

"I know, Kade.  I know.  You want to protect my lady, but she's not sure how she feels towards you.  Give her time.  She'll get there."

## Chapter 9

A couple of hours later, Ennis stood, her eyes huge, as she watched the men mill around a board room, their voices teasing as they spoke with Anna and then Doc. She saw the three younger wives helping to set up the meal and suddenly felt out of place. Bradon was watching her from where he stood talking with Brady and Burnie before he excused himself and walked towards her.

"Ennis? Are you okay?"

His voice brought her head around and she stared at him, before she shook her head.

"No, I'm not. I don't belong here." She was gone before he could stop her, his feet carrying him after her.

"Ennis? Wait?" His hand stopped her forward movement. "If you don't want to stay, that's fine. At least come back and fill a plate. You can take it with you."

She stood, her arms wrapped around herself. "I can't, Bradon. I just can't." Tears clogged her throat and she ran, her apartment door closing behind her before she slid down and sat on the floor, her back to the door, tears raining down her face. Why, Lord? Why can't I stay? What do I fear so much? I could feel the fear intensifying in there, and I don't understand why.

Doc stood for a moment beside Bradon, before his hand rested on the younger man's shoulder and he prayed for his friend.

"I suspect she felt overwhelmed. Until you get to know us all, we can have that effect."

"I know, Doc. I know that, but there's something else. She found a picture of the two on us on her car today, and then we spoke with Will. I think she's just too tired to do this. I shouldn't have pushed her." Bradon stood, not sure if he should go after her or not.

"Let her have some time, then, Bradon." Doc looked behind him, seeing Anna standing there. "Anna will go talk with her, take her some food. Come on. Back in here with you. You need to eat too."

Anna watched as Bradon finally nodded and returned to the room, dishing up a plate, but not eating much. She sighed. Why, Lord? Why do these young men go through this with their ladies? She spoke quietly to Doc before fixing a plate and heading to find Ennis.

Ennis stood for a moment, studying Anna before she stepped back enough for Anna to enter. Anna's hands set the plate down in the kitchen before her arms swept Ennis into a hug, surprising her.

"Ennis? What can I do for you?" Anna stepped back, her eyes on the younger woman.

"End this? I really don't know, Anna. I'm sorry. I shouldn't have left."

"No, you should have. They all understand. They've all been there. Except that Berneen and Cadee were married, and Devaney was engaged, although she tried hard to not remember that."

"They belong. I don't. I'm only here until that monster is caught." Ennis turned to the counter, pulling the plastic wrap from the plate, and then just standing, staring down at it.

Anna sighed. Well, Lord, I guess it's up to You and I, isn't it?

"Ennis, I don't think you've picked up on something from Bradon, or if you have, whether you're ready to hear what he has to say. He has never done this before. He has shown no interest in any young lady, and there has been interest on their part. He has taken a step with you that we never thought to see him take. He wants to keep you safe. And I would gather once you are, he'll be speaking with you. I can see the interest he has in you, as a special young lady."

Ennis shook her head. "He shouldn't. He'll get hurt." She sighed, her eyes sliding closed. "He already has been. This monster is brutal. He'll go after Bradon. I know that."

"That's what he's done all along, isn't it? You've never been able to date, to see if one of the men in your circle of friends might be God's plan for you."

"You understand, Anna.  How could I?"

Anna's arm was there, drawing Ennis to the living room and down on the couch, her voice raised in prayer for the younger woman.  When she was finished, she sat, her eyes closed for a few minutes before she looked at Ennis.

"Draw your strength from the Lord, Ennis.  Even when you go through the battle you are just entering, He is there, every step of the way.  He does not wish for you to be beaten down.  He wants you to overcome through His strength."

Looking up from his desk at the canine compound he worked at, Bradon frowned as he heard footsteps heading his way. He was to have been on his own, Kade in a kennel in the training room, and he was sure he had locked the door. He didn't recognize the steps and rose, heading for the door, stopping suddenly as he saw the two men standing just outside his door.

"How can I help you two fellows?" Bradon's arms were crossed against his chest. "And perhaps you can explain how you got in, when the door was locked?"

Jason Lloyd stared at him, a scornful look on his face. "Doesn't matter. Just leave her be. Let her go home."

"Who would that be?"

"You know. That woman. Ennis. She's mine, not yours. Let her go back home."

Bradon shook his head. "You see, there's the issue. She doesn't belong to you. Never has. Never will. And as far as telling her where she is to live, I leave that decision to her. She's made her own plans. And they don't include you."

He didn't see the sudden movement of the second man until he felt the man's fist drive deep into his abdomen, doubling him over. He barely felt the blows that followed, leaving him in a crumpled heap on the floor before the two men walked away. He didn't hear Kade frantically trying to get out of his kennel to get to Bradon.

Dallas had met up with Branigan and concerned enough, they had set out to find Bradon. Touching the door to the building, Branigan frowned.

"Bradon said he'd be here on his own. The door is always locked if there is only one person here." Branigan pulled it open, heading for where he could hear Kade. "Something's up for Kade to be that upset. What's wrong, boy?" He reached to unfasten the kennel, Kade shoving against the door and then racing for Bradon's office, the two men staring after him before they followed on a run.

Kade was down on his belly, his nose and tongue frantically moving to try and rouse Bradon. Branigan's voice pulled him back from his owner and Dallas dropped to his knees, before he spun.

"He's been beaten, Branigan, and badly. Call it in, and then stay with him." Dallas was on his feet, his eyes searching for anything. "How long would he have been on his own?"

"It's hard to say. I would have to speak with Rick, his employer."

"Let me have the number and I'll call. It's officially our investigation now." Dallas watched as the paramedics worked on Bradon before he turned to the patrol officers who were searching the area. "Branigan? Where would we find Ennis?"

Branigan shrugged as he glanced at his watch. "She's usually done about this time. Bradon's been driving her back and forth." He groaned. "And he can't today, and she'll be frantic."

"Head over and bring her to the hospital. She needs to be there." Dallas had turned before he saw the look on Branigan's face.

Ennis stood on the sidewalk in front of her work, her hands covering her mouth, as she stared at Branigan before he had her tucked into his truck.

"How bad?" She could barely get the words out.

"I don't know. They were still working on him when Dallas sent me to find you." He pulled to a stop outside the Emergency Department. "Ennis, wait. You can't just walk in there."

Ennis stared through the windshield, knowing Branigan was right. "I know, Branigan. But he's likely hurt because of me." She spun on the seat, a horrible thought coming to her mind. "Kade?"

"He was in a kennel, so not harmed." Branigan sighed. "We'll have to deal with him."

"I'll take him." Her words were fierce, even as her brows lowered. "I'll take him. He knows me. He needs me." She blinked rapidly to clear her eyes of tears. "And God help me, I need him."

Branigan nodded, his eyes on her. "Let's get you in. Doc's working today, so maybe that might help."

———

He slipped from the truck, walking around to open her door, his hand reaching for hers as they walked in. Sitting where she could see the doors, Ennis ignored the foot traffic around her, instead concentrating on calming herself. Branigan watched her closely before he pulled out his phone, turning it over and over, not wanting to call Barnabas. No, Breck, he thought. Barnabas was away for a couple of days with his parents.

"Breck?" Branigan could hear the sound of waves in the background and knew that Breck was on their beach. "It's Bradon."

"Bradon? What happened?" Breck walked quickly back towards the building, knowing something had happened.

"I'm not too sure what happened. Dallas and I went to meet him. We found him beaten and unconscious."

"He's still out?"

"He is. Kade was in his kennel but frantic to get to him."

"I see." Breck waved Blair over, his hand covering his phone for a moment as he explained what was going on. Blair nodded, heading on a run for the building. This is when the guys all came together, Breck thought. "He's in Emergency?"

"He is. Dallas sent me for Ennis. She's almost as frantic as Kade."

"Kade? Yes, Kade. Which one of us takes him?" Breck waved at Brady as he saw the men heading for their vehicles, the four women with them.

"Ennis."

"I'm sorry. I must have heard you wrong. I thought you said Ennis would." Breck's foot on the accelerator keep the truck at the speed limit on the highway until he slowed to turn into town.

"I did. Ennis has said she will take him. She is adamant on that, Breck, said he needed her." Branigan paused in his pacing, his eyes on Ennis. "She made an interesting comment."

"And that would be?" Breck threw his truck transmission into park and slipped from the seat, the doors locked after himself as he headed for the hospital door

“She said she needed him.”

“She did.”  Breck watched as Branigan turned towards him, pocketing his phone.  “Any word?”

“Not yet.  It’s been about thirty minutes.”

“Doc’s here?”

“He is.”  Branigan pointed to the chairs beside Ennis, sitting there, startling her.

“Branigan?  Any word?”  She was desperate to hear that Bradon would be walking out, but she knew better.

“Not yet.”  Branigan exchanged a glance with Breck.  “They’ll come find us.”

“Kade?”

“Dallas said a patrol officer would take him to the Foundation building.  The security guys will watch him until we can get you to him, or him to you.”

She nodded, her eyes back on the door, her thoughts muddled, even as her hands clenched and unclenched against one another.

Bradon's friends milled about the waiting room and then outside and back inside, worried about their friend. No one had heard anything yet. Compassionate eyes sought and found Ennis, sitting huddled into a chair, her eyes glued to the door to the examination rooms. Anna sat on her one side, Meg on the other. Blair had called her parents. Her brother and father were around somewhere, they knew.

Will watched her for a moment before he spoke quietly to Dallas, heading for the examination rooms. They needed to talk to Bradon, but from what Dallas had said, Will knew that would have to wait. They had pulled security video feed but it hadn't helped in their investigation.

Doc stepped back from the stretcher, his eyes on Bradon. I prayed that he would not be hurt, Lord, but he is. How bad, we're not even sure yet. He turned as he heard footsteps and found Will and Dallas beside him, wincing at the bruising and blood they hadn't had a chance to clean away.

"Doc?" Will's voice was low, his eyes troubled.

"I can't give you much yet, Will. Dallas. But I would say whoever did this knew what they were doing. He not likely had a chance to defend himself."

"No defensive wounds then?"

Doc shook his head at Dallas' question. "None that I can see. His hands are clean. There is some bruising and at least one finger is fractured, but nothing to indicate he defended himself."

"Sucker punched." Dallas drew in a deep breath. "What can you tell us?"

"We're sending him for imaging studies. We'll know more then." Doc turned, a frown on his face, his mouth opening and then closing. "We know there are internal injuries. His abdomen is very tender. The ribs may be fractured. Imaging will show that."

"You're looking at surgery?" Will shook his head, knowing that was a real possibility.

"We may be. The surgeon on call is heading this way. He'll let us know. At the very least, we suspect a pneumothorax, a collapsed lung. That means a chest tube." Doc turned back. "Ennis?"

"She's in the waiting room. Both Anna and her mom are with her." Will shook his head, a small smile cracking through the grimness on his face. "She is insisting on taking Kade."

"She is? That's interesting. I wouldn't have thought that." Doc pointed to the door. "Who do I talk to? I know Barnabas is away."

"I've spoken with him. He said he'd fax authorization through to let you talk to Ennis." Will pushed through the doors, pausing as he saw Ennis on her feet, heading his way, desperation in her movement.

"Doc?" She hugged him back as he swept her into a hug. "Bradon?"

"He is still unconscious." Doc's arm tightened on her as he turned her back to her chair. "We're still assessing him, taking imaging pictures. The surgeon on call is on his way in."

Ennis sank into her chair, watching as he sat beside her, Anna moving to let him. She didn't feel her mother's arm around her. "All that? I didn't know it would be that bad." She looked up at Will. "Who did this?"

Will shook his head, pointing to Dallas. "He's the one working on it. He'll keep you updated." He glanced at his watch. "I'm sorry, Ennis. I have a meeting I need to get to. We'll speak."

Her eyes were back on Doc. She was desperate to see Bradon. Needed to, she thought.

"Can I see him?"

Doc watched her, knowing that Barnabas would have made that same decision, and sent through authorization for just that contingency. "Barnabas is his next of kin. Don't worry, Ennis. He'll let you in."

———

"But he's not here!  How can he?"  She was becoming frantic and then was on her feet, pushing through the men, heading for the outside.  She needed to be away from everyone.  She didn't see Jason waiting just outside the door, his hands reaching to stop her before he pulled them back, his angry eyes on Brady and Brennen as they moved in on either side of her.

Ennis paced, the two men keeping step with her, others of the men standing around, their eyes watchful.  Dallas stood as well, his eyes not on Ennis but on Jason as he ran from the area.

"That's him!"  Dallas' voice broke through Branigan's thoughts.  "That's the man we want."

Dallas was running after him, Branigan on his heels as he took in what had been said.  They slid to a stop, not finding him, before, frustration evident, they walked back towards Ennis, finding her just standing still, tears on her cheeks, Buckley standing in front of her.

Branigan frowned before he motioned to Brady, who walked slowly towards him.

"Brady?"  He studied first Brady and then Ennis.

"They're taking him to surgery, Branigan.  The surgeon sent Doc out to talk to her.  They need to stop some bleeding and then put in a chest tube.  He has a collapsed lung."

Branigan's eyes slid shut.  It was what he had expected but had hoped he had been wrong.  "They'll get Ennis in to see him?"

"They don't have time.  Doc said he was being rushed up there as he was out here speaking with us."  He looked past Branigan towards the edge of the parking lot.  "What was that all about?"

"That monster, as Bradon puts it, was here.  If you two hadn't been with her, she'd have been gone."

Brady paled.  "He was that close?"

"He was.  Dallas spotted him.  I'll make sure we all get photos of him and anyone who is known to associate with him.  I pray we can keep her safe."

Brady nodded as he watched Ennis move back inside, Doc's hand under her arm.  "She's taking it hard.  Where do they stand?"

Branigan shrugged, even as he studied the men gathering around them.  "I don't think she knows yet.  Bradon?  I would say he's found his lady."

"That's exactly how he's acting."  Brendon spoke quietly.  "I'm heading for the chapel.  I know, Buckley, you've set the prayer chain to work."

"I have.  I'll be there shortly."  Buckley stood for a moment, watching his friends walk away, before his eyes raised to the sky.  "Lord, we could use Your healing powers for these two.  Bradon's spoken to me, a bit, about what Ennis has gone through.  She needs that touch of the garment, to help her overcome what is in her past, before she can move forward.  Thank you for opening her heart to Kade.  None of us saw that coming, but You did."

———

Ennis paced the surgical floor waiting room, not willing to sit, not willing to leave, her thoughts muddled as to what Bradon actually meant to her. She had become accustomed to his being in her life. She had a good idea, she thought, of where he wanted to take their friendship, but she had been hesitant, not willing for him to be hurt. Sighing, Ennis acknowledged to herself that Bradon had become important to her. She was afraid for him right now, afraid that he wouldn't come back to her, that his life would be drastically altered because of the beating he had taken at the hands of that monster. She refused to call him by name. That gave him too much importance, and Ennis decided then and there she would bring him down, somehow, somewhere. Her life had been consumed by him for too long.

Meg watched as her daughter paced, knowing Ian and Evan were around somewhere, Ian likely in the chapel. Evan, she had last seen with Baird and Berneen and Berneen's brother, Darby. Where they had ended up, she had no idea. She rose, her arm around her daughter, drawing her down to a chair, a prayer raising in her heart for how much she was hurting.

"Mom? Why?"

"Why what, dear?"

"Why is he like he is? Can't he just leave me alone?" Ennis blinked rapidly, tears too near the surface, tears she refused to shed.

"Who? Jason? It's the sin in him that drives him. He knows no other way." Meg's head tilted as she saw Ian sit beside Ennis. "Your father has been doing some research, as he put it, into Jason's family."

Ennis jumped as she heard her father's voice and turned to face him. "Dad?"

"I wish I had done this years ago, lass. Maybe we won't be sitting here having this conversation. But then again, maybe we would be. Only the good Lord knows that for sure." He sighed, his eyes sliding closed for a moment. It was late evening by now, and they were still awaiting word on Bradon. "I've spoken with Will and that detective, Dallas. I've found information on him that was shoved under the carpet and hidden."

"Did you, Dad? Will this stop him?" Ennis' voice was low, cautious, hopeful, but doubt filled her that they could stop him.

"It's much worse than we ever knew, Ennis. The Lord has protected you in a way I never imagined. I won't go into details right now, but we will talk. I want Will or Dallas in on it. And likely Barnabas."

Her face whitening even more, Ennis could feel the fear rising within her. "Dad?"

"It's that bad and worse, Ennis. I can see how God protected you, even moving you away. Why you returned at this particular point in time? Only He knows, but we do need to take steps to keep you safe."

"Work?"

Ian nodded. "Your work. You can't be out and about right now." He shared a look with Meg. "Branigan talked to me earlier. Jason was here. When you went outside and the two fellows walked with you, he was ready to take you then."

Ennis drew in a deep breath. Her parents didn't think she could pale anymore than she had but she did. "I guess I won't be working then." She blinked rapidly once more, refusing to cry. "I'll have to call the office in the morning." She looked up at a sound from her father. "Dad? What did you do?"

"I didn't. It was that young detective. He's way ahead of me in this. He spoke with your employer, explained the situation. He agreed your safety was more important than you come in. He said he valued you as a trusted employee and wanted you to stay safe so you could come back to work."

She nodded. "I know I can't be there. It brings too much danger to them as well." Her eyes strayed to the door to the operating suite. "When will we hear about Bradon?"

Ian and Meg exchanged another look, Meg's look helpless even as Ian drew in a deep breath.

<hr>

"Ennis?" He waited until she looked at him. "I'm going to ask you a question that I want you to think seriously about. And pray about. Bradon has stepped in as a friend and defender. I can see how he looks at you, just from the little time we've spent with him. I would hazard a guess he feels strongly he has found his lady, his heart, the one he wants to spend his life with." He paused, knowing that this was a conversation the younger couple should be having, without his interference, but given the danger they both found themselves in, he felt he had to step in. To counsel his beloved daughter. To ensure that she thought through and prayed over what decisions she would need to make. "I know you, lass. I see the stress and worry you're under. If he is the one that God has led to complete your life, we welcome him. If he's not, then we pray God protects your hearts, both of you."

Ennis nodded. When she spoke, her voice was barely audible. "Thank you, Dad, Mom. I know you have been praying over this, and that you won't have spoken, Dad, unless you felt strongly that God meant you to." She looked up at the ceiling, gathering her thoughts, as much as she could. "I don't know how I feel. I mean, I'm so grateful he has stepped in. I hurt because he was hurt on my behalf. As to the future, I don't see it clearly enough to answer."

Ian nodded. "That's what I was picking up, then, lass. Pray over it. I know Bradon is waiting for you to do that. It may come that he will speak to you before this is over. All we ask is that you listen and then pray. Seek counsel where you need to. With your Mom. With me. With Anna or Doc. With Buckley as your pastor. And better yet, with those three young ladies I see waiting for you to open up to them. I understand they have been through something similar. They will have counsel and advice for you."

———

On her feet, Ennis moved towards the surgeon as he walked her way.  He studied her and nodded.  Doc was right.  She's invested in Bradon.  And I know Bradon from church.  He would be doing his best to protect her.

"Doctor?"  Ennis could barely speak, seeing the fatigue and grim look on the surgeon's face.

"Let's sit, Ennis.  I'm Dr. Walter Wilson.  I've just finished with your young man.  I stayed in Recovery with him until we transferred him to an ICU bed."  He sank down, grateful to be sitting.

"Doctor?  How is he?"

"He's alive.  God had his hand on him, Ennis, make no doubt about that.  He could very easily have died.  Dallas and Branigan found him in time."  He watched her face closely.  "I spoke with Barnabas.  He asked that I add you to Bradon's medical records as next of kin."  He smiled at her look of surprise.  "Bradon thinks of you that way, I'm told."

She shrugged, her eyes looking everywhere but at Walter.  "I guess.  I don't know him well enough to know what he thinks."

Walter grinned at her.  "I know Bradon.  He thinks that way.  I've been told a bit of what he did.  He's interested in you.  Explore your friendship with him."  He sighed.  "As to his injuries?"

Ennis searched his face.  "Doctor?"

"Call me Walter.  We share a church, so no formality.  Now, as to his injuries.  He has two broken fingers on his right hand.  Fractured ribs.  One of them did puncture the lung.  I would say he was kicked there.  We've inserted a chest tube to aid that.  He had bleeding internally.  He has lost his spleen.  The kidneys were bruised.  The liver had a laceration.  We've fixed him up as best we can.  He's in God's hands, Ennis."  He stood, reaching for her hand and drawing her to her feet.  "Come.  Let's get you to your fellow.  Once you've seen him, I want you to go home and get some sleep."

He nodded towards the waiting room. "There will be some of the fellows here all night. But they have all spoken to Doc. They want you safe and that means back at the building."

She sighed. "In other words, I just accumulated more guardians. Two weren't enough?"

Walter laughed as he led her towards Bradon. "Just keep in mind there is a lot of equipment and lines running to his body. He is sedated. We had to do that."

Ennis nodded, knowing what he wasn't saying. "I get that. Can I see him, please?"

She stood, her hands covering her mouth, seeing the deepening colouring of the bruising against his white face, the shadow of a beard there. She reached to touch his face, tears flowing that she angrily swiped at. Ennis prayed for his healing and that Jason would be found before anyone else was hurt. She knew him well enough to know that would happen. He was like that.

Finally turning away at a touch on her arm, she was wrapped in her father's arms, silent sobs shaking her body before he led her from the room and to his vehicle, heading for her home. He knew Breck had ensured someone from the Foundation was with them. He just didn't know that all of the men were there, their vehicles surrounding his, to ensure that Bradon's lady was safe before some headed back for the ICU, intent on taking turns to be there for their friend.

Ennis stood inside her door, her eyes on Kade, who stood, waiting for her to speak. Dropping to her knees, she swept him into a hug, his tongue licking at her face before he looked past her, searching for Bradon.

Early the next morning, Ennis had finally stretched out to sleep, her sleep broken by dreams. Kade had stood, his chin on the bed, his eyes on her before he cautiously crept up beside her, tight to her back, his chin on her neck, knowing he wasn't allowed on the bed, but this time, he just had to. His master's lady needed comfort and he couldn't do that from the floor.

———

Two days later, Ennis stood at Bradon's bedside, watching as he moved restlessly.  He had been moved to a regular hospital bed, and that encouraged her, but also frightened her.  It would be so much easier for someone to get to him here, she thought, even though she knew there was a police officer stationed outside his door for now, just until Dallas could talk to him.

Ennis wanted him to wake up, to ensure her that he was recovering, and that he didn't blame her.  On the other hand, she didn't want him to wake, to blame her, to tell her to leave, that he didn't want to see her again.  That was her fear, she decided, and then took that fear to the Lord.  Whatever is Your will, she thought.

She finally walked away, knowing she needed to, nodding at Evan as he rose from his seat in the waiting room, his arm out to hug his sister.  She didn't see Dallas waiting to speak with her, her eyes blinded with tears.  Dallas stared at her and then towards Bradon's room, moving that way, nodding at the officer on guard before he pushed open the door, his feet taking him to stand where Ennis had just been standing.  He didn't believe in God, but seeing how much trust these new friends of his had in God, he was starting to question that.

Dallas stood, watching as Bradon roused and searched the room.  He's looking for Ennis, he thought, and she's not here.

"Bradon?"

Bradon's head shot around, and his eyes closed as the vertigo hit.  His stomach roiled before he could control it.  His eyes opened to see a contrite Dallas watching him, his hand on the call button.

"Dallas?  Is that you?"  Bradon's voice was rough.

"It is.  I called your nurse."

"Why?"

"Why what?"

"Why would you call me a nurse?  Where am I?"

"You're in the hospital, Bradon. We need to talk." Dallas stepped to one side as the nurse approached. "Sylvie?"

"Yes, Detective? I see he's awake. That's good." She assessed him, taking his vitals, and then standing watching him. "Bradon?"

Bradon carefully moved his head to look at her. "The room's spinning. I don't think it should be."

"Vertigo. Dr. Wilson was afraid of that. I'll put a call in to him. He's somewhere here in the hospital."

Bradon watched her walk away, before his attention turned to Dallas. "What did I go and do? And please, don't move. Stay in one spot."

Dallas gave a low laugh. "I can do that." He set his portfolio down and reached for a chair. "How's this?"

"That's better." Bradon's eyes closed. "Tell me. What happened?" His eyes popped open. "Ennis?"

"She's fine, Bradon. In fact, she left not too long ago. We've had to make her leave. Barnabas has been adamant about that." He grinned. "Besides, she has to look after Kade, did you know that?"

"What?" Bradon stared at him. "She doesn't like dogs. Why would she be looking after Kade?"

Dallas shrugged. "She was adamant that she took Kade. Said he needed her." He frowned. "She also said she needed him. Does that make sense?"

The other man frowned in turn, and then laid his head back. "It does make sense. She's terrified of dogs, but Kade is just moving in on her, not letting her back away. I would say she's made a connection with him, and he with her."

"That happens, does it?" Dallas stared at Bradon for a moment before he reached for his note pad. "We need to get your statement, Bradon, before anyone else talks to you. Can you tell me what happened?"

"Jason did. He and another man appeared in the building. The door was locked, so I have no idea how they made it in. I was focused on Jason, telling him that they needed to leave when I was sucker punched. I don't remember anything after hitting the floor." He sighed and then grimaced with pain, finding it difficult to draw a deep breath. His hand hit the chest tube and he frowned once more.

"The other man beat you up. Did a good job on it. Walter went in and repaired the damage. He'll be around to talk to you." Dallas looked down at his notes and then back at Bradon. "You won't be working for a while, I can tell you that. And Ennis is not working, either. Jason was waiting outside the doors to the Emergency Department. If two of your friends hadn't been there, she would be gone." He looked back at the door. "And her father has been doing some digging into this man. He's provided information that should have been found before."

Bradon stared at the IV dripping through the line to the back of his hand. "I was getting some stuff on him. He's not a nice person." He turned to Dallas, his eyes closing until the vertigo eased. "How do we do this? How do we keep her safe? He'll be watching her. When she comes here. When she goes home. Around our building. And that can be a problem, around the building. They can get in there as well."

"We know that, Bradon. Breck and I have talked, as have Branigan and I. We're working on keeping her safe. All your friends have come to me at some point, volunteering to help. Anna and the three younger ladies have been adamant they won't be left out. And then we have her family."

"And that's going to be a problem. If he can't get to her, he'll go after one of them. I would suspect her mother, but her father or even Evan will be targeted." Bradon's voice died away as he thought it through. "Kade can't stay with her all the time. I need to find a dog for her."

"She won't take one." Dallas grinned at the frown on Bradon's face. "She has already told me that. I asked her."

Bradon sighed. "There goes that idea. What ideas do you have?" He stared at Dallas when he stated his preference. "That's not happening."

———

584

Bradon stared at the thirteen men, no, fourteen, he corrected himself as Evan slipped into the room, three days later as they stood, arms folded across their chest, grim looks on their faces.

"I can so leave." Bradon didn't shake his head, knowing the vertigo would be there. "I have my discharge papers."

"That may well be. But, where do you go? You can't stay on your own for a few days. Anna and Doc are away. The rest of us are working." Breck spoke for the group.

"He can come stay with us." They all turned as a group as Evan spoke up. "That's why I'm here. Ennis sent me. She wants Bradon to go stay with Mom and Dad."

Breck pulled his mouth down as his head bobbed from side to side, a small smile lurking in his eyes. He met the eyes of all the other men, seeing their relief and agreement.

"Okay, so you're off to stay with Meg and Ian." Barnabas nodded. "That's good. You won't get away with trying too much too soon."

Bradon stared first at Barnabas, then at Evan, frowning as he saw the faint hint of mischief on Evan's face. "Does Ennis know?"

"Does Ennis know what?"

His eyes slid closed as Ennis made her way through the group of men, who parted to let her in.

"Bradon? Do I know what?" When he didn't answer, she spun to study each man, stopping with her eyes on her brother. The men watched in fascination at the silent battle of wills between the siblings, Evan with a grin on his face.

"Mom asked that Bradon stay with them for a few days. He can't be on his own, and Doc said he and Anna were away on a planned holiday." Evan reached for his sister, drawing her into a hug. He kept his voice low enough so only she could hear when he spoke. "It's okay, sis. If you don't want that to happen, I can stay with him at his place.  Mom just thought it might be easier for him to be with them.”

She nodded as she hugged him back.  “I wondered if she would.  It’s fine.”  She stepped back, her eyes on his face, before she spoke.  “Bradon, Mom has spoken.  She does want you to stay with them.  In case you missed it the other time, she’s a retired nurse.”

“That’s perfect.”  Brady spoke, a grin on his face.  “Then we don’t have to worry about him.”

“You do.”  Evan laughed at their looks and the glare from Bradon.  “Her cooking is excellent.  We can’t let him eat much.”  Then a look of horror crossed his face.  “I forgot.”

“You forgot what?”  When Evan remained silent, Brennen spoke again.  “What did you forget?”

“Kade.  Ennis doesn’t like dogs.”

Ennis watched with amusement the looks of consternation on the men’s faces as they frantically tried to come up with a different plan, her eyes finally settling on Bradon, who sat in the wheelchair, fully dressed and ready to leave, seeing the smile lurking in his eyes.

“Who?  Kade?  Of course he comes.  He’s not a dog.”  Ennis reached to push the chair forward, leaving stunned silence in her wake.

“What did she just say?”  Benen walked after her.

“That Kade wasn’t a dog?”  Blair followed, as they did other men.

“Guys?”  When they turned, Evan spoke.  “She’s made her peace with Kade.  He’s won her over, proving that dogs can be gentle.  She will still fear other dogs, but not him.”

They shared a look and then nodded.  Evan had stated just what Ennis had shown them.

An hour later, Bradon sank down with relief into a wing back chair, his eyes closing for a moment as his head spun.  He jumped slightly as he felt a cool hand on his forehead, and then hands tucking a blanket around him.  He slept, no seeing Meg standing watching him, her arm around Ennis before she turned her daughter to the kitchen.

"I know this isn't what you wanted or planned, dear." She moved around the kitchen, making tea for them, checking on her meal in the oven, before she sat, her hand reaching to still her daughter's restless one.

"No, it's not, Mom." Ennis stopped, her emotions in a roil. "He could have been killed, and it would have been my fault."

"Not your fault, Ennis. Never your fault. And he would not and will not walk away from you. That is a given, as you say." Meg watched her daughter closely, seeing how emotional she was. "It's not easy, dear. Not when you fall in love and aren't sure if the other person feels that way."

"How do I do this, Mom? I can't let him see that." Ennis buried her face in her hands.

"You go on as you have. Taking care of him. Taking care of yourself. And taking care of Kade." Meg smiled down as Kade stood with his chin on Ennis' lap. "Kade has made you his duty, you know."

"I know he has. He was like this before Bradon was hurt." Ennis' hand rubbed at Kade's head. "But how do we end this?"

"Dallas is working on it, Will said. He can't say what has been found or what evidence they have. He did say Dallas wanted to talk to you two when Bradon was able to." She rose as she heard a tap at the door and returned, Barnabas behind her.

"Barnabas? Why are you here? What happened?" Ennis was beginning to panic.

"It's okay, Ennis. I just stopped by to make sure you two were fine and to offer any help we can. The guys are working through what happened. I think you'll find they'll dig up information even Dallas can't."

"They are? They will? But that's not what they do."

"It's what they do for their friends, and they consider you a friend." Barnabas' look was compassionate. "They see how Bradon is with you and how you are with him. They want to do this for you two." He paused, his eyes on Ian as he entered through the back door. "Branigan and Brendon want to talk to you. Benen is searching for whatever information he can find on the internet. The others are talking to your friends, Bradon's friends, searching for this person."

"But how do they know who my friends are? I never told them." Ennis was puzzled at his words.

"All they had to do was come to your town, ask a couple of questions, and the list of people wanting to talk to them just grew on its own."

"It did? Okay, I guess. I just pray they find him and soon. He's taken enough of my life." Ennis was on her feet, moving for the living room, Kade pacing at her side, his head turned up to watch her.

"One would never have known she is scared of dogs, seeing her and Kade." Ian's voice was quiet as he spoke.

"No, you won't. Kade has done wonders for her." Meg rose, pulling her meal from the oven. "Barnabas, you'll stay for a meal?"

"I will and thank you, Meg."

A week later, Bradon sat carefully into his chair in his office at the building, sighing as he did so. He felt better, but also worse, if that made any sense. Kade was pacing restlessly, and he watched him, a smile coming to his face. *He's missing Ennis, isn't he? Lord, I don't know where I'm going with this lady, or where this adventure will take us. All I know is I love her, and want her to stay in my life for as long as You allow. But this has to be from You. I can't run ahead of you.*

He looked towards the door as he heard a tap and then Branigan entered, followed by Baird, Benen, Blair and Brady. *My team,* he thought, aware of how Barnabas had divided the men into two teams of six, thinking this worked for fostering their growth in God and sometimes when he needed to send men into a situation.

The men seated themselves, passing around their coffee, before Bradon spoke.

"I take it you're here for prayer and then a conference."

They all grinned and nodded. They broke up into twos, spending time in prayer, before they gathered once more.

Bradon searched his friends' faces, knowing that they would support him in whatever it was he decided to do. Just what that was, though, he was uncertain of.

"What are your plans?" Baird spoke first.

"My plans? Right now, I don't have any other than not falling over when I stand up." Bradon's hand rubbed at his temple. "Did that even make any sense?"

"It does." Brady spoke up, the paramedic in the group. "You took a hard few blows, Bradon. We know you had a concussion. That beating could have killed you, but didn't. You'll live with the vertigo and learn how to handle it."

"That's what I'm afraid of.  That I have to live with it.  It can affect my work."  His eyes slid closed as he tried to imagine not doing what he had always done.

"Doc said he talked to a chiropractor friend who is willing to see you.  He's had good success treating conditions like yours."  Brady continued to watch his friend, concern on his face.

"Now, what about Ennis?  And what's going on with her?"  Bradon searched his friends' faces once more, seeing the concern but also the determination to solve this mystery.  "How close are we to finding him?"

"That we don't know, but he's a nasty bit of work, from all that we're finding out."  Benen held up a folder.  "I have given a copy of everything we've managed to track down, including the names of other victims."

"Other victims?"  Bradon's voice stopped, horror in his heart.  "There have been other victims?"

Blair nodded, a grim look on his face.  "There have been.  Young ladies.  Teenagers."  He paused, his eyes on Bradon as Bradon made the connection.  "You're right in what you're thinking.  Human trafficking.  As to what he wants with Ennis, we think it has now turned to revenge.  She escaped him, and no one does that.  That's what we're hearing on the street."

"And I can gather, she won't be walking away from him if he gets his hands on her."  Bradon sat back, his hand idly rubbing at Kade's ears.  "How do we keep her safe?"

"That's what we been discussing.  We didn't mean to behind your back, Bradon."  Branigan spoke up.  "We've been able to talk to other ladies who escaped him.  Between us all, we spoken to probably a dozen.  What they have in common is that they have a significant other, a boyfriend, a husband.  You catch the drift?"

Bradon's eyes were on Branigan, the leader of their group.  "I do.  Once someone takes over their protection, he backs away.  But I don't think he will with her."

"No, I don't think he will.  He's proven that when he came after you.  You two are not a couple, at least as far as we know.  All that has happened is that you have been seen with her.  That was enough to set him off.  If your relationship deepens, it will only get worse for you."

"That's what we're afraid of.  We talked over the last week, on our own, with Evan, with her parents.  Barnabas.  Will.  Dallas.  We just didn't talk to you guys, but I have a pretty good idea what you're thinking."  He smirked at the looks on their faces.  "I mean, after all, three of us have married.  But I won't do that to Ennis.  Not unless it's a last ditch effort.  She's not ready for that.  I don't know that she ever will be."

"She's interested, Bradon."  Benen spoke up.  "She's interested but she won't say anything.  Not until you do.  And even then, if this is not resolved, she'll walk away.  She doesn't want you hurt anymore than you have been."

"That's right."  Branigan eyed his friend.  "No one else saw her when I went to get her that day.  It almost destroyed her, Bradon, to think that a friend had been hurt because of her."

Bradon nodded.  "I know.  She's talked to me about that."  He didn't see the looks of surprise on the others' faces.  "She's been upfront with me.  We're talking about where we want to go."  He paused, biting at his lower lip, not quite sure how much to say.

Pacing her apartment, Ennis was growing tired of feeling like a captive. She sighed, knowing that she had to stay safe and right now that meant staying inside. But that wasn't her. She wanted to be out on her bike, to be running, to even walk the grounds. She grabbed her keys and headed for the lobby, standing staring outside.

She didn't see Bradon approaching her and jumped when he spoke from beside her. Turning, she studied him, seeing he was staring out the window, not looking at her. Kade nudged at her hand, and she laid it on his head.

"Feeling like you're a captive or in prison, sweetheart?"

"I am, Bradon. But I know if I go out there, it could mean my death or the death of someone with me. When does it end?" Ennis could feel the despair rising in her.

"Soon, I pray. But, for now, we can go out, as long as we stay close to the building. There are gardens with seats or paths we can walk." He reached for her hand, tugging her to the door and outside, Kade keeping pace.

Ennis walked beside him, watching him carefully.

"How are you feeling now, Bradon?"

"Better, thanks. The vertigo is getting less. I just need to be careful how I move. The chiropractor is working wonders with that."

"I'm so glad." She shivered. "When I first saw you, when Will took me in, I didn't think you would live. It was pretty brutal."

"That's what I'm told." He felt at his face, knowing the bruising was turning yellow and green. "I can live with what happened. But can you?"

She stopped, her hand rubbing at her face. "That I'm not sure of. Not anymore." She looked around, tugging him to a bench, and sitting, her eyes on the building in front of her. "I really hate him for this."

"I know you do. It's to be expected. It's our humanness that comes through in situations like this. It's how we let it affect us. That's what we need to take to God. I have had to."

"And what answers have you gotten? I know he's not done. I am sure he's here somewhere watching us or has someone watching us. How do we go about our normal lives?" She shifted on the bench so she could see his face. "How do you go back to your work?"

Bradon shrugged. He had talked to his employer, and they were working on a schedule for him. He knew he wouldn't be travelling for a while, and he could accept that. It was the training that would be affected. Right at present, he wasn't able to. That distressed him. They had both agreed he'd do assessments on buildings and people and have the dogs they needed to assess brought to them. He would work on that when Rick was in the building.

"Rick and I have talked. We're working it out. I just don't get to travel. That's all." He watched her closely. "That's what I had done, you know. I had been away assessing dogs and stopped for a break that day."

"And if you hadn't, who knows where I would have been. Or even if I would still be alive." She wrapped her arms around herself, distress on her face. "I know what he does. He told me. That's what drove me away the first time. I had to stay safe to be able to stay here."

"He told you?" Anger grew in Bradon. "When?"

She shrugged. "When he first started all this. He told me he would sell me to someone."

Bradon's arms came around her, holding her as she wept. "I'm sorry, sweetheart. That shouldn't have happened." He paused, getting his anger under control, praying that God would stop this monster. "I'm sorry you've had to live with that."

She shrugged. "It's him. He's the one driving this." She paused, a thought running through her mind. "Can we use that to catch him?"

"What do you mean?" Bradon wasn't sure what she was saying.

"I mean, can we use his words to trap him? I know he has had to have help from the authorities. That's the only way he's been able to get away with this." She lifted her head, her eyes staring into the distance. "There has to be someone else involved, someone behind him. He doesn't have the smarts or the ability or the contacts to do what he's done." She sighed, sorrow on her face. "How many has he done this to? How many have disappeared, had their lives destroyed?"

"Dallas has said the same thing. He's digging into that and he has other police services doing the same. It's not a pretty picture they're finding." Bradon's arms tightened on her.

"I didn't think it would be. I just want this over."

"Me, too. But if it hadn't happened, I would not have met you." Bradon waited as she thought about his words and then turned to him. "I would not have wanted to miss having you in my life, Ennis. Not at all. We need to talk at some point. I'm not sure you're ready for that conversation yet."

She shrugged, her eyes telling him she was, her words asking for space. "I'm not sure, Bradon. I'm just not sure."

Brady was on a search two days later. He had been handed a letter as he came out of a local business, the young boy running away before he could stop him. He had stared down at it, seeing Bradon's name printed in bold black letters.

Bradon turned at Brady's call, catching his balance as he shifted his weight, Kade leaning tight into him. Kade was torn, Bradon thought, amused for a moment at the distress that was causing Ennis. She didn't want him with her, stating he was Bradon's dog and needed to be with him, but at the same time, welcoming his attention.

"Brady? What's the rush?"

Brady waved the letter. "This. I was handed it by a young boy as I came out of the book shop. They are looking for you but can't get to you." He handed over the envelope. "I called Dallas. He wants you to wait to open it. He's on his way out."

"And Ennis will need to be here. She's with the other three ladies today. Something about baking or some such thing."

"Baking?" Brady's face lit up. "Will they share?"

"Of course, we will." Ennis' voice behind him had him jumping and then spinning, catching the grin she was trying to hide, and then his eyes dropped to the container she kept shoving at him. "These are yours. I was headed for your place when I saw you pull in and head for Bradon."

"Thank you, Ennis. I'll catch up with the others later." Brady's face lit up with a smile before he sobered. "I was looking for Bradon, yes. And here's Dallas."

Dallas grinned at them. "And here I am. Brady, you have baking!"

"I do, and I'm not sharing." Brady laughed at the glum look on Dallas face.

"I have some set aside for you and Will, Dallas." Ennis took pity on him. "We ladies wanted to say thanks. I'll grab it when we're through." She shivered as she looked around. "Can we go inside? I can feel him somewhere out there."

Bradon's arm was around her as he turned her towards the building. "We can. How be we head for your apartment? That way, Dallas can grab his goodies when he leaves."

Ennis made sure the men had their coffee before she excused herself, heading for her spare room and the paperwork she had dug up from years ago. She had hidden it away, making a trip home the day before to find it. Evan had found her staring down at it, an arm coming around her, his prayer in her ear before he asked what he could do. She had simply shaken her head, knowing he was talking to people, finding information he was passing on.

She stood just back from the kitchen doorway, watching the three men as they interacted, knowing they were waiting for her to return, but also knowing she was hesitant to. Something told her this day would change her life. She just wasn't sure how. Her eyes dropped to the folders, some of them thick. Evan had simply handed her his investigations and asked that she pass them on to either Dallas or Will.

Bradon's eyes raised as he sensed her near him and rose, coming to stand in front of her, shielding her from the others.

"Ennis?"

"This is hard, Bradon. This is so hard." She held up the folders. "I had stuffed some of these away, never wanting to look at them. I deliberately kept from remembering what I had. Maybe if I hadn't, you wouldn't have been hurt. And Evan has been busy as well."

"We'll let Dallas take this. He or someone he works with will go through it. They'll talk to you and Evan, I'm sure." His head bent to hers as he prayed, knowing his lady was hurting.

Dallas eyed the stack of folders that Ennis slid across the table at him. "This is what you've been doing lately."

"Some is Evan's work. He's been working the last few weeks on it." She sighed, a bleak look on her face, even as her face whitened. Brady watched her closely. "Some of it goes back to when it all started. I had forgotten what I had. I think I was shoving it all away, not wanting to see it. Not wanting to have to deal with him. And that has gotten us to this point." She poked at the letter Dallas had set down. "Aren't you going to open that?"

"We will, sweetheart. But first, you know what we do." He waited until she nodded. "Brady?"

"Of course." Brady's head bowed as he prayed for them, for what they would find, that it would advance the investigation to the point they could arrest Jason and whoever it was he was working for.

Dallas paused as he reached for latex gloves, his eyes on Ennis and then Bradon. When I open this, there is no going back. We don't know what this man is planning but my experience tells me it isn't good.

He slit open the envelope and pulled out the folded piece of paper, hesitating before he unfolded it, his eyes going to first Ennis and then Bradon before they stopped on Brady. He glanced down to read it, his face growing grim as he did so, taking in the words. He folded the paper back up and inserted it into the envelope again, no words coming from him.

Bradon and Ennis exchanged a glance before Bradon spoke.

"Dallas?"

Shaking his head, Dallas looked at him and then Ennis. "I can't or even won't show it to you. It's ugly. Bradon, your life has been threatened once more. You don't want to know what he's planning for you. We need to take even more steps to keep you safe. Ennis, we need you to stay here, in the building as much as you can. I know. I know. You want to be outside. Just make sure you have some of the men with you when you do. You can't be out there on your own or with just the ladies. He's made it very clear he intends to take you. He hasn't said what he plans, but the threat is there that you don't live."

Ennis, her face pale, had nodded. "That's what he's done along. Threatened that." She paused, biting at her upper lip. "What is triggering it now? It's not just because I'm home. He could have taken me when I was away."

"I think that you'll find it's partly you coming back to where he's been defeated." Brady studied her closely. "And you did defeat him. You managed to escape and make a life for yourself. Coming back here has triggered his anger towards you."

"I would say Brady is correct, Ennis. He likely feels that you are the one who got away and you did. He needs to rectify that. Seeing you with Bradon has triggered a deep-rooted anger in him. He wants both of you to pay. Bradon, you helped her escape and are keeping her safe. Ennis, you have escaped him many times on many levels. He can't accept that you have done so." Dallas paused to gather his thoughts. "He may also be getting pressure from whomever it is he is working for."

"I would think he would be." Ennis stood, pacing. "So, how do we do this? How do we catch them, but keep us safe? I don't want Bradon hurt again."

*Chapter 19*

Locking up after the men had left, Ennis cleaned the kitchen, her hand resting for a moment on the chair back where Bradon had sat, his hand reaching at times for her. She was beginning to depend on him in a way that she didn't depend on anyone and that scared her. Her heart lifted in prayer, asking for wisdom and guidance, before she headed for her computer.

She had signed up for a college course, planning on working on it in her spare time. She snorted. That's all she seemed to have, she thought. Spare time. Working in a medical office had been what she had thought she wanted to do. Now, she wasn't so sure. She had some money saved that would get her by until she was back at work, but she was torn. She didn't think she could go back.

Ennis stared at the computer monitor before she shut the computer back down. This wasn't what she wanted to do. Just what that was, she wasn't even sure. She just knew she was at loose ends and didn't like that feeling. She had never been like that.

Her phone chiming caught her attention and she reached to swipe her finger across the screen to wake it up. Pulling up her text messaging app, a soft smile covered her face. Bradon! Now, she wondered, how did he know she was feeling like she was?

Her fingers flying across the phone, she sent off an answer, and waited for his response. A soft laugh came from her as she saw the photo of Kade staring intently into the camera and then read the accompanying text. I miss you, too, Kade, and I miss Bradon. How did that happen? How did he become such a part of my life?

She thought through what she had given Dallas and sighed. He had a lot of work to do to confirm what she had noted, and she knew he would do his best. But would his best be good enough? Would he find Jason and his backer in time? Ennis knew that she was on borrowed time, that she would be found. She just prayed that Bradon was not with her when she was.

Bradon turned out his bedside light as he pulled the covers up over him, waiting for the spinning sensation in his head to stop.

———

That always happened when he laid down or sat up, and he was getting frustrated. His thoughts too turned to the conversation they had had with Dallas and Brady. He wanted this over. Bradon wanted to explore the relationship with Ennis that was developing. He had covered it in prayer and felt confident enough to move forward.

He turned to his side, his hand reaching for Kade, knowing Kade was not to be on the bed, but Kade had had plans of his own, crawling up beside him to lie tight to him. Bradon frowned, and then smiled, knowing this is how Kade had reacted with Ennis. He didn't have the heart to tell Kade no, but he would have to at some point.

The next morning, Bradon walked back into his work, Kade pacing beside him, his face white and stern. He didn't find it easy coming back to where he had been assaulted, and his physicians had acknowledged to him, almost killed. That he was alive was God's hands, they told him.

Rick watched as Bradon moved through the building, Kade beside him, before he approached him.

"Bradon?"

"Rick? How do we stand for training?" Bradon went right to the point.

"We're good. I can use you in the office, sorting through our applications and security requirements. That you are good at, better than any of us. Just don't over do it." He looked down at Kade. "How's Kade?"

Bradon began to laugh, bringing a puzzled look to Rick's face. "Now, Kade. He's in love and doesn't want to leave his lady. It's Ennis. He's become her protector, wants to be with her."

Rick grinned. "Well then, do something about it." He walked away at Bradon's protest.

His protest dying in the air, Bradon looked down at Kade. "And I could, you know. I could ask her to marry me. I just don't think she's ready for something like that." He sighed, his hand reaching to rest on Kade. "Come on, boy. Let's find Sandy and see how much paperwork she has for us. I know it will be lots. And I can't work a full day. Not yet, anyway. But I could take some home and work from there, keeping Ennis with me. Now, there's a thought."

Ennis looked up as she heard her name, rising from the bench at the front of the building as Doc approached.

"Ennis. I haven't talked to you in a few days. How are you?" He reached to hug the younger woman.

"I have no idea, Doc. Everyone asks me that. I always say I don't know. Maybe I should come up with a new line." She grinned as he laughed.

"Now, there's the spirit. Just keep saying that. All our guys and ladies here understand. Your parents and brother as well. By the way, where is your brother?"

"Evan? I heard from him this morning. He was catching a flight to the Yukon. A trip he has planned for years."

"That's good. He's safe there?"

Ennis shrugged. "I have no idea. Are any of us safe right now?"

Doc studied her, seeing the fine lines that the stress and danger were working in her face. "I would pray that we are, but God may have other ideas for us and allow us to go through hard times. He has with you. I can see you working with the ladies and girls at the shelter. Have you thought about that?"

She stared at him. "How did you do that?"

"Do what?" Doc was puzzled.

"Give me a new line of work. I was looking for something." She sat back, her hands rubbing down her legs. "I have my psychology degree, but decided I didn't want to use it. I wanted to be out in the medical office."

"And now, you're not sure you want to continue with that. All I can say is pray, Ennis. Ask God to show you. This may be why you've gone through what you have. We don't always know the plans God has for us, not until He is ready to show us."

She nodded. "I will do that, Doc. I was looking at a course I had signed up for. A business course and suddenly found I wasn't interested in it. I have resigned from it." She looked up at him. "How do you know the words to say? I've seen you do it with the others."

He shrugged. "God, Ennis. He gives me the words I need when I need them. That is how I have always prayed, you know. For Him to lead me as He will, that I might encourage someone else."

"Just like Barnabas encouraged Paul." She sat for a moment, her face thoughtful. "That's what Barnabas does, isn't it? He found the men God wanted here, to use them in the community, to do just that."

Doc smiled. "And you have gotten exactly what Barnabas and his father planned. Not many do until it is explained. They think it was just named after Barnabas."

Ennis shook her head. "God chose the name when Barnabas was born, and then led them on this journey. He has been needed greatly." She looked up at Doc again. "But where's his lady? He needs someone to encourage him."

"He has never said, Ennis. And I won't pry. If he wants you to know something, he tells you." Doc sat back, confident that Ennis really did understand his words.

Ennis sat for a moment before she rose, her thoughts muddled. She needed to speak with her mother, but then again she couldn't. She looked up to see Kade standing in front of her, eager for her attention, before she raised her eyes to Bradon, seeing a similar eagerness on his face, and walked towards him, into his arms and his hug. I have come home, she thought. I have come home to someone who loves me.

Chapter 20

Bradon watched Ennis closely as they walked back towards the building, her hand in his. Today, he sensed a change in her, she just seemed more open to him. Lord, I don't know what's going on, but You do. Thank you for this lady.

"Bradon?" Her voice caught at his attention, there was such a difference note to it.

"Yes, sweetheart?"

"Doc had an interesting comment." Her feet stopped, as she bit at her lip, Kade nudging her to move. "He said maybe I went through this, so I could help others. Would God do that?"

Bradon shrugged. "He could and He would. Depends on the person and where God wants them. But I can see that happening for you."

"You can? That's what Doc has said. I'm not sure on that." She moved forward, blowing out a breath, Bradon's eyes on her, a puzzled look on his face. "I guess I should tell you I have my psychology degree. I didn't want to use it. Didn't like that thought. But now, is that what God wants?"

"He will tell you when you're ready for that step. I'm guessing you don't want to work in the medical office again."

She shook her head. "I thought I did, but now I'm finding I don't like it. It's not what I want to do." She stopped just inside the doors, her toe rubbing against the hardwood floor. "How do I tell my parents?"

"I think you'll find they understand and are expecting this." Bradon's arm around her drew her to one of the seating arrangements, Kade's chin on her knee as soon as she sat. "Your Dad mentioned that you really didn't fit the office, and why would you have chosen to do that?"

She looked up, surprise on her face. "Dad said that? He's never questioned me on it."

"And you'll find he wouldn't, not unless he really had to. And it's not to that point as yet." He looked around. "Now that you're not working, and I can't, what do we do to put in time?"

"Research. And more research. And road trips. We need to find this monster. He's not hiding, at least not very well. The last I heard from

———

Evan before his flight took off was that Jason was seen in our hometown, right out in the open.”

“And he will be. Legally at least. But morally? That is done to put the pressure on you, to make you afraid. He’s hoping you make a mistake and he can grab you.” Bradon’s arm tightened around her. “And I don’t want that to happen. I would miss you greatly if you disappeared. And so would Kade.”

“Kade? He would?” She reached down to rub at Kade’s back, a blissful expression on the dog’s face at her touch. “He’s something else, you know. I am afraid of dogs, but he just walked right in and took over.”

Bradon laughed at her comment, even as he saw Branigan and Brendon heading their way. “He knew you needed him, sweetheart. And he needs you. But I don’t want to lose my dog.”

She spun on the seat, seeing something in his eyes and face that had her face softening. “You don’t? And what makes you think you would?”

“Kade.” He looked up as the two men sat. “Afternoon, gentleman. To what do we owe the pleasure?”

Ennis spun back around, her eyes on the men, surprise and then worry and then fear appearing on her face. “Branigan? Brendon? What now?”

“We need to talk to you both. We have new information.” Branigan hated to spoil their day but knew the information he had been given could not wait.

“Branigan?” Bradon’s gaze shifted between the two. “What do you have?”

“We have received a new threat. Dallas is aware of it and has someone tracing it.” Brendon spoke, his voice tight. “This time, it’s worse, he says. There is a contract out of you, Bradon. You’re to be taken out of the way so this man can get to Ennis. Apparently, he thinks you’re the reason he hasn’t nabbed her.”

Bradon snorted. “As if that were the case. It may be. What else did he say? I know there was more. I can see it in your face.”

Branigan sighed. “There was. Your family has been threatened as well, Ennis. We have your parents here and safe. They wanted that. Your brother, on the other hand, we’re trying to track him down.”

“He’s up north.” She pulled out her phone as it chimed. “It’s Evan. He’s safe but says he was met by an RCMP officer and put somewhere safe. This is not how he was to be spending his vacation.”

"No, it's not how any of you want to live, but at present, you must. When Evan comes back, some of us will head up there and come back with him." Branigan's hand went up at her protest. "Barnabas has talked to him, so he is prepared."

She was on her feet, her eyes on them, before she shook her head and walked away, heading for the elevator. Bradon had risen when she did, watching carefully as she entered the elevator and disappeared before he sat back down. His eyes still focused that way, he spoke.

"What didn't you say?"

Branigan and Brendon exchanged looks. "He's gone past just wanting her, Bradon. He has threatened to kill her once he finds her. How do we do this with you two?"

Fearing the worst, Bradon was on a hunt two days later. Dallas had called. He was on his way out, and where were the two of them? He had word that Jason had been seen around the building. Bradon's feet took him towards the lake, fear rising in his heart. She hadn't, had she? He knew Ennis was getting restless and wanting to be outdoors, but did she really head for the lakeshore, despite the numerous conversations they had all had with her?

Bradon's feet paused as he heard a voice, his head tilting. He was sure it was the same male voice he had heard before. His feet dug into the sand and he raced towards Ennis, who he could see once more struggling with the man he now knew as Jason. He didn't see the man running towards him until he was tackled and taken down into the cool waters of the lake.

Struggling to get away, hearing Ennis' calls to stop and for help, he just couldn't get free. He felt the man's hand on his head, holding him down below the surface, even as he tried to escape. His vision blurred, and he heard Ennis' calls coming softer and softer until his body just floated in the water, not moving except from the waves washing against him. He didn't see the man wading through the water, then stopping, hands in the air as Bradon's friends ran their way. His assailant was down on the ground and Blair and Benen were into the water, pulling him free of its greedy grasp and carrying him to safety. Depositing him on higher grass, the two men went to work, rushing to save their friend, their glances towards where Ennis now lay still, Brady on his knees beside her.

Ennis had been simply walking, she thought, out for some fresh air when she had stopped, her feet freezing in place, as she looked up to see Jason standing in front of her, a gloating expression on his face.

"Well, well. Who do we have here? Ennis, my dear. And on your own. How convenient." Jason's hand had reached for her, even as she backed away from him, her hands hitting at him to leave her alone. "Not happening, my dear. You're coming with me."

Ennis screamed as she scrambled backwards, her hands hitting at his as he tried to grab her. She heard Bradon's voice and called for him and then for him to get away. He was behind her, she thought, and then heard nothing more from him. She saw the gleeful look that crossed Jason's face before he stopped, his hands rising before one dropped. A knife appeared and she screamed once more, hearing running footsteps behind her and her name being called.  His hand was back, and the knife thrown before Bradon's friends had reached her.

Brady had her in his arms and to safety before laying her gently down, a grim look on his face as he saw the knife, sending Brendon and Burnie for the supplies he needed.  He knew Branigan had tackled Jason and even now had pulled the man's belt to bind his hands.  Branigan's chest heaved as he shoved Jason forward, to stop near Brady.

"Brady?"  Branigan's voice was quiet.

Brady shot him a look and shook his head.  "We need an ambulance, Branigan.  I'm not at all sure she'll make it."  He shot a look at Bradon, seeing him on his side, moving slightly as the two men spoke with him.  "Bradon?"

"He's good for now.  We'll get them there, somehow."

Brady looked up again as Doc dropped to his knees, his hands reaching to help.

"How long?"

"Five minutes, maybe?  Ten at the most.  I didn't pull the knife."  Brady's hands were reaching for the packing material being pulled from packaging for him.

"No, we don't want that."  Doc's hands were there, reaching to wrap bandages around the knife and then around Ennis.  "We need to keep it as steady as possible."  Doc looked around.  "We need the backboard and collar."

Burnie reached for the backboard, sliding it to the ground beside her.  "We thought you would, Doc.  We tried to think of everything you might need."

"Good.  Now, gentle as we roll her, Brady.  Burnie, at her feet.  Buckley, good, you're at her knees."  He shot a glance towards Bradon.  "Bradon?"

"They tried to drown him, Doc.  The guys got to him in time.  They're not letting him up until we have help."

Doc nodded, his focus back on Ennis, hearing the sirens coming their way.  "Someone go find the men and bring them here.  Brady, you ride with Bradon.  I'm not leaving Ennis."

Doc paced the corridor outside the two cubicles, looking up to see Walter walking his way, once more.

"Doc?  Someone was knifed?"

"Ennis. It was deliberate from what I understand." Doc sighed as he followed Walter. "And then someone tried to drown Bradon."

Walter paused, his head shooting around to stare at Doc. "What did you just say?"

"I said, Ennis was stabbed. Bradon drowned." Doc nodded at Ennis. "We kept the knife in. Brady was there and took charge."

"That's good. He's got a good head on his shoulders. How long would you say?"

"Thirty minutes at the most. It's not looking good, Walter."

Walter paused and studied Ennis before he reached to pull bandages away, Doc's hands now gloved and helping. "I thought you were done for the day, Doc."

"I was. Thank God I was. With the two of them, Brady was torn as to who to look after. If I had needed him to, he could have taken over Bradon's care."

"This was done on purpose?" Walter winced as he carefully touched the knife. "Deb, we'll need imagining and then call the OR. We'll be taking her there within a short time."

"Already done, Walter. Imaging is expecting you. A CT is what you wanted?"

"Did we do a chest X-ray?"

"We did, as soon as she arrived. Images are up now for you." Deb stepped aside as the team moved into take the stretcher. "How long, ladies?"

"Ten to fifteen minutes." The nurse glanced over at Walter. "Back here or upstairs?"

"Upstairs, I think. Page me when the images are ready." He stared at Ennis as her stretcher moved away and then at Doc. "No, on second thought. I'm coming too. I want to see exacting what is going on."

<hr>

Doc stood back, his heart breaking for Ennis. He knew her parents were there and were waiting for someone to come and talk to them. He moved across the corridor, to stand watching the activity around Bradon, hearing his rough voice. His head shaking, Doc turned and walked away, his heart heavy, his body slumping, before a hand on his shoulder stopped him. Barnabas and Buckley stood beside him.

"Doc? What's the word?" Barnabas was almost afraid to ask.

"Bradon's talking. I suspect he'll be moved to a room soon. I haven't talked to anyone. That you'll need to do."

"Ennis? Brady said it was bad."

Doc sighed, his eyes on his young friends. "It is. Walter's with her in the CT area. He's taking her to surgery. I just don't know if we'll be able to save her."

Barnabas' face hardened. "But we have him, don't we?"

"We do, I saw. But that doesn't mean he'll stay in jail." Doc's hands ran through his graying hair. "She's not safe, if she even survives."

"Why was she on her own?" Buckley's puzzled question had the two men shaking their heads.

"She's needing to be out. She likely thought she was safe." Doc looked up at Dallas spoke from in front of him. "She was backing away from him, that much we can tell. Bradon must have realized she was missing. We're assuming his are the tracks we see running for the lake." Dallas looked around. "Has anyone spoken to her parents?"

"Not yet. I will." Walter appeared beside him, his finger beckoning for Buckley to follow him.

Walter paused, his eyes on the couple he knew had to be Ennis' parents. "How well do you know them, Buckley?"

"Not well. They've been in our building now for a few days. I've met and talked with them over the last few weeks, since Ennis has been involved with Bradon."

Walter nodded. "That's what I thought. They're believers?"

"They are and strong ones. I just don't know if they're strong enough for what you have to say."

"God will provide that strength, thank goodness." Walter walked towards the couple, Ian on his feet, his face strained and white, Meg's hand tight in his.

"Buckley?" Meg's voice held hope and despair as she spoke.

Walter shook their hands and then sat, after introducing himself. "What have you been told?"

Ian and Meg shared a glance.

"Branigan told us she had been stabbed but not how bad." Ian was desperate to hear his daughter was not as harmed as he envisioned.

"She was. She was stabbed in the chest. I have just viewed the imaging. She's upstairs right now, being prepped for surgery. I'm expecting to be in there for a while." He paused, assessing the couple. "I have to be blunt with you. I can't be anything else. I don't know that she will come through the surgery. At this point, we have not removed the knife. And it is a good thing Doc and Brady made that decision. We would not be having this conversation if they had." He watched with compassion as Ian's arm came around Meg. "Leaving it in helped to stop the blood flow. That we can deal with in the operating room." He looked up as he was paged. "There's my call. Buckley will take you up to the waiting room. I'll send out word as I can."

His head back against his pillow, Bradon watched from under lowered eyelids as Barnabas paced his hospital room, Branigan and Brady leaning against a wall. He had no idea where the rest were, but he assumed somewhere nearby. Dallas had been in, taken his statement and then left before he could ask any questions.

"Barnabas, what aren't you saying? And just where is Ennis?" He waited and then paled at the looks on their faces. "Guys? What about Ennis?" He raised up, pushing at the blankets before he sank back against the pillows. He didn't have the strength to rise. "What aren't you telling me?"

"Bradon, you were almost killed. Don't you understand that?" Barnabas' voice was stern, covering his emotions.

Bradon stared at him, not quite sure. He could vaguely remember coming to, being rolled to his side, and Benen's hand on his side, holding him steady as he coughed and gagged and spewed water. He had heard Blair's voice as well. He couldn't remember seeing Ennis and that scared him. Coming to again in the Emergency Department had not been pleasant, he decided. Still coughing and gagging to some extent, he had barely been aware of his treatment, and then being moved to a room. His glance moved from Barnabas to Branigan and then stopped at Brady. Brady's face was closed, but Bradon knew his friend well enough to know he was extremely upset and worried.

"Brady? What happened to Ennis? I can remember running that way, hearing her screaming, but I don't remember much after that."

"Benen and Blair pulled you from the lake, Bradon. They had to revive you. Do you get that?" Brady's words had a bite to them. At Bradon's nod, he sighed. "Ennis was hurt. That man stabbed her, Bradon. Doc and I worked on her until the paramedics got there."

"How bad?" When none answered, his gaze hardened as it shifted from man to man. "How bad? If you don't tell me, I'll be out of here and searching for her."

Brady walked towards the bed, his hand out to still Bradon's movements, a prayer raising in his heart for his friend's lady. "It's bad, Bradon. We didn't think we'd get her here. Doc stayed with her all the way. His friend, Walter, is the surgeon. Right now, she's in surgery."

Bradon's eyes slid closed. This was what he had feared the most. "She's alive?"

"She is, Bradon. But I talked to Ian and Meg. Walter didn't give them a lot of hope." Barnabas voice was filled with all the emotions he was going through at the moment. "Ian said Walter told them that Doc and Brady wouldn't remove the knife. They left it in. If they had removed it, she wouldn't have made it."

Bradon's eyes were on Brady, seeing the confirmation of Barnabas' statement on his face.

"Thank you." Bradon's voice was hushed. "How long?"

"It's been a while. I'm not sure how long she's been in there." Branigan began to pace. "How did he know she'd be there?"

"He's watching that close. Have we searched for any cameras?"

"We're doing that now, Bradon, not that it's any consolation. He seems to have set up somewhere to watch for her. With her going to the beach on her own, that gave him a perfect opportunity. And the man who tried to drown you? That was the police officer Dallas said they were looking for."

Bradon's head shook as he pulled at the plastic identification bracelet on his wrist. "Brady? Find out what you can? Please?" He watched as Brady nodded and then walked away, not knowing what he would find out.

Brady stood for a moment, staring down at his clothes. He had managed to scrub away the blood from his hands and arms, but his clothes were still stained. He looked up as he felt a hand on his shoulder. Breck stood there, compassion on his face, as he handed over a pack.

"Go get changed, Brady. You need to."

Brady sighed. "I do." He hesitated before he looked back up. "We've just told Bradon."

Breck nodded. "I thought so, just by the look on your face. Go. Change. I'll be in the waiting room. Ian and Meg are still in the surgical one. I'm planning on heading that way. They want to speak with you."

Brady nodded, his eyes dropping to the floor, staring at his stained shoes. "How do we get Bradon through this, Breck? If Ennis doesn't survive, how do we do this with him? This is worse than it was for the others."

"It is, Brady." Breck paused, drawing a deep breath. "I heard from Dallas. Jason ended up in a fight in jail."

Brady's head went back. "He's dead, isn't he? No justice there. And no end in sight for Ennis. Who was he working for?"

"That's what I asked. Dallas is clearing off names he's been given, but still hasn't come to the one in charge."

———

Their eyes glued to the door to the operating room, Ian and Meg sat, hands clasping one another, just waiting for word. They knew that Anna was around, she had stopped and prayed with them. And the three younger women had been in and out, ensuring they were taken care of. Barnabas had sat with them, prayed with them, walked away to find Buckley to send to them. A nurse had been out not long before, letting them know that Ennis was still alive, that they were working on her but Walter expected it to be a while yet.

"Meg?"

She turned at Ian's voice. "Ian? Have we talked to Evan?"

"I did. Barnabas has sent a couple of his guys up there, to bring him back. He said they were taking the Foundation plane."

"Oh, okay. That's good. He'll want to be here." She sighed as her head went down on his shoulder. "Why Ennis? What did he want from her that badly that he had to try to kill her?"

"I don't know, love. Dallas said they were working on something. Breck said Bradon's friends were as well."

Breck hesitated for a moment before he sat beside Meg, his eyes on her and then Ian. Buckley sat beside Ian, his heart praying for his friend, his lady and her family.

"Breck?" Ian's voice was quiet. "You have word on Bradon?"

"He's awake. Not happy we won't let him up." Breck gave a tight smile. "He was adamant he was coming up here, Branigan said, until he fell asleep."

"That's what he needs. But you have something else weighing you down." Meg studied the younger man.

"I do. Dallas got word to me that Jason has been killed in jail."

"Of course, he would be. That's what would happen. Now, how do we find the others?" Meg's acceptance of Jason's death and its implications stunned the two men until they looked at Ian's face and then nodded.

"Dallas said he was working through what he had and making progress. Just not the kind of progress he wants. He'll need to talk to both of them again at some point." Breck sighed, the day long and not over yet.

"That he will." Ian's eyes rose as he heard footsteps and then he was on his feet, his hand extended to shake Walter's. "Walter?"

"Sit, Ian." Buckley moved so Walter could have his seat, a frown on his face as he watched the looks exchanged between the two men.

"Walter?" Meg's voice was hesitant.

"She's still alive, Meg. God was there, directing every movement we made." His eyes closed for a moment, fatigue hitting at him. "We managed to stop the bleeding. It was as I suspected. If the knife had been removed before, she would have died. We had a time controlling the bleeding. But we did. I stayed with her through Recovery and until we could get her to an ICU bed." He sighed. "This is getting old, you young people getting hurt."

Breck gave a quick grin. "We know that. We've told everyone else this is not to happen. They've just shrugged."

"Can we see her?" Ian reached to wrap an arm around his wife. "We need that."

"I know you do. We're just getting everything settled and set. She's unconscious, as you can imagine, and will be kept that way. Part so she doesn't undo our work. Part for pain control. Suzy will be out shortly to get you. Evan?"

"He's on his way back or will be shortly. Our guys have gone to get him." Breck spoke.

"Good. He needs to be here and Ennis needs him as well." He shared a look with Breck. "How's Bradon?"

"Hurting. He wanted to go find her but fell asleep before he could get up. We'll have a struggle to keep him away from her." Breck walked beside Walter as he moved away towards the exit doors. "What didn't you say, Walter? I know you."

"She still may not make it, Breck. The knife went deep. We've tried to do our best. Only God knows if we've succeeded. Get Bradon up here when you can. They need each other."

"They do, Walter. I have no idea how serious they are, although it was looking that way." Breck sighed. "Only justice won't be done for her. The man was killed tonight in a jail riot, which he instigated from what Dallas said."

"Of course, he would be.  But find whoever it is that was behind him.  Until you do, she's not safe.  And I would hazard a guess that Bradon won't be either."

Breck watched Walter walk away, fatigue weighting his body down before he turned, finding Barnabas standing beside him, holding out a cup of coffee."

"That bad?"

Breck nodded.  "From what Walter said, yeah, it was."

Two days later, Bradon stood, his hands wrapped around the bed rail, his eyes on Ennis as she slept, a drugged sleep, he thought. His heart was raised in praise that she was still alive, but he knew that might change at any moment. Her parents had both spoken with him, and at their request, so had Walter. Bradon understood only too well what the outcome could be.

He studied the monitors, and then shook his head. He couldn't understand them. That's not what he did. When he had returned home the previous evening, Kade had been wild with delight but Bradon could see he was looking for Ennis. He had spoken with Rick, and was to go back to work the next day, working from his office in the building, but he had no real desire to do that, and that concerned him. Where had his drive to work and succeed at doing what he did go?

He felt a hand on his back, and turned slightly, finding Meg there. She had taken him under her wing, she said. He needed her, and she needed him. Evan had been around, compassion on his face as Bradon apologized for not being able to prevent Ennis getting hurt.

"You can't blame yourself, Bradon. She made the decision to go there, on her own. She would have felt she couldn't bother one of you men."

Bradon sighed. "I know. It doesn't make it any easier, you know."

"No, it doesn't. But he would have attacked her then even if one of you had been with her. Look what they did to you."

"They were brutal. I wanted to face him, you know, to ask why." Bradon blinked rapidly, to hide the tears, to keep them from falling, his eyes on Ennis.

"We all wanted that. The other man, the one who attacked you, he's not talking. We think he's afraid of someone."

"He would be. He's a coward."

"He is, but you're not. You have proven that." Bradon turned slightly as he heard Ian speaking from behind him. "Ennis hasn't said, but we can see how she looks at you. You have her heart, Bradon. That much we know."

Bradon nodded, his eyes back on Ennis, his hand resting on her cheek. "And she has mine, but we can't do anything about it. Not yet. It's not fair to her. She has not had the time to be free from that monster, to enjoy life without that hanging over her, and she needs to."

"But if she says no, she doesn't want that? What would you say?" Ian's hand rested on Bradon's shoulder. "Don't let that stop a commitment from you." Ian walked away, his footsteps heavy, not knowing if his daughter would ever get that chance. He had spoken with Walter just moments earlier, unknown to Meg, and the word had not been good. Walter was still concerned that they hadn't been able to stabilize her as much as they should have. He told Ian the knife had missed the heart, had missed the lungs, but had still done damages to the blood vessels.

Meg watched him walk away, praying for him and for her daughter, and for the young man standing with her. She hugged him, leaving him standing beside the bed, his eyes still on Ennis.

"Oh, Ennis, what are we to do? Lord, heal my lady. I'm not ready to let her go. Nor is her family. Lead Dallas and the others to a quick end to the investigation. Ennis can't do this again. It will kill her next time." His head bowed and he didn't even try to control the tears that flowed, not hearing Brady approach, not feeling his hand on his shoulder, but hearing his prayer. He thanked God that he had praying friends. That would help to get them through what they faced.

"Bradon? What's the word today?" Brady spoke quietly, hesitant to ask.

Bradon shrugged. "About what Walter said yesterday. I know he's concerned. He doesn't have to say that."

"No, he doesn't. We've seen too much at times. Barnabas said to tell you that Rick dropped off some paperwork for you. Kade is looking for you as well. He's searching the building and the grounds. We think he's looking for Ennis."

"I think he will be. He's taken with her, sensing her need. And considering she's afraid of dogs, that has to be God that did that."

"God does use our animals, doesn't he? You've seen that many times. I've seen it with patients." Brady pulled up a chair, shoving Bradon down. "You need to rest, Bradon. They'll be sending you away soon. I'll be in the waiting room when you're ready to go."

Bradon gave an abrupt nod, his eyes on Ennis as she had started to move restlessly, pain on her face. He looked up as the nurse approached, reaching to take Ennis' vitals and then assess her wound.

"Nurse?"

She looked over at him. "You're Bradon?" At his nod, she smiled. "Just checking her over. Making sure everything is fine."

"She's restless. I didn't think she would be."

"It happens. Sometimes before the next dose of medication is due, they can get like that. And yes, she can feel pain, and that can make her restless. Dr. Wilson will be by later." She looked at the clock. "But we do need to ask you to leave."

Bradon stood, nodding, understanding that he did really have to leave, bending to kiss Ennis' cheek before he walked away, away from his lady, uncertainty in his mind as to what he would find when he returned in a few hours. No, he thought. Not until tomorrow. Her family has to have the time with her.

Brady stood, his eyes on Bradon as he walked towards him.

"All set?"

Bradon nodded at the question, turning so he could look behind him

"I am, Brady, but I'm not wanting to leave. Something tells me she's in trouble again."

"She's in good hands here, Bradon. You know that."

"I do, but it doesn't make it any easier." He slanted a glance at Brady. "How much digging have the guys done?"

Brady laughed. "You know us too well. We're digging and digging. Dallas is almost ready to tell us to stop sending him material, but he wants this over for you two. That's what he has said."

"And he's not the only one."

Ennis could hear her mother's voice, calling her to wake up. She couldn't. Her eyes just would not open. She slipped back to the place she felt safe, knowing that if she did open her eyes, she might not like where she was. Moving restlessly with the pain, Ennis slept once more. It had been a week since her attack, a week of ups and downs. Walter had taken her back to surgery at one point, finding a small area that was still bleeding and repaired it. Since then, her condition had improved.

Meg stood beside her, her hand on her daughter's face, a frown on her own. Ennis just wouldn't awaken properly. They had told her she should be but she wasn't. Meg was afraid, afraid that they could still lose her, that the man behind Jason would appear and Ennis would just disappear.

Dallas had spoken to them, updated them as much as he could with the investigation. She knew it wasn't where he wanted it. Ian said Dallas was waiting for a name or a piece of information that would open up the investigation. She prayed it would be soon.

She turned as she heard footsteps. Bradon and Evan stood there, watching her and then Bradon moved to Ennis' other side. For the first time, Meg noticed that Kade was with him and frowned.

"It's okay, Mom. We talked to Walter. He said to bring Kade in. Maybe that would be what Ennis needed." Evan looked down at Kade. "We know that Kade needs her. I think Bradon has lost a dog."

Bradon just grinned, knowing that wasn't true, but he had decided in the wee small hours of the darkened night that he wouldn't mind losing Kade, if it meant keeping Ennis in his life. Kade tilted his head to look up at Bradon before he stood up at the bed, his nose finding Ennis' hand. Not satisfied with just touching her hand, he leapt for the bed and settled down beside her, his chin on her shoulder, a tongue reaching out to lick at her face.

"Kade, stop. I don't need you licking my face." The hoarse whisper stilled them all and brought their eyes to one another. Ennis had spoken from her sleep.

"Ennis?" Meg bent over her daughter. "Are you waking up?"

"No, I'm sleeping. Is that Kade?" Ennis shifted on the bed, her eyes flickering open and closed.

"It is, dear. Bradon and Evan are here too."

"They are? Where am I? And why does it hurt?"

"You're in the hospital, Ennis." Meg looked around as she heard Walter's voice. "She's awake, Walter, or has been."

Walter nodded, his eyes on Kade. "It took a dog to wake her up? Why didn't we try this before?"

"Because it not likely would have worked, Walter." Bradon reached for Kade, who shifted away from his hand, his eyes still on Ennis. "Kade. Now. Off the bed."

Kade jumped down, his very attitude saying he didn't want to and why would they make him? Bradon watched, a smile lurking on his face, before he looked up at the door. He was away from the bedside, following the man who had been standing there, his phone out to take a photo before the man disappeared. He didn't know him and wondered at the look of hatred on his face directed at Ennis.

Dallas pulled out his phone, sighing at its chiming again. He had not had a break, he didn't think, all day. He studied the photo Bradon had sent, a chill running through him. He knew that man, knew the danger Ennis was in if he had been at her doorway. Dallas ran for Will, had a few moments of conversation with him, before he headed for his desk, his computer programs up. He needed to find this man and find him quickly. Will looked up as Dallas appeared in his doorway, his phone extended towards him.

"Do you know this man?"

Will shook his head. "Not offhand, I would say. Why?"

"Because Bradon just took his picture in the doorway to Ennis' room. The man walked away and disappeared when Bradon approached him."

"That's interesting. Run with it, Dallas, and see what you come up with." Will stared at him for a moment. "You are taking time off, aren't you?"

Dallas nodded. "I'm out of here by six if possible, not working Sunday for sure. But it's a difficult task, balancing the investigations."

"It is. And I know you well enough to know you don't want this to go cold."

———

"No, I don't." He looked down at his phone and frowned. "Now, Barnabas is calling me." He walked away, phone to his ear, not liking what he was hearing from Barnabas.

Will watched him go and then studied his own desk, rising from it and walking through the department, stopping to speak with the officers and then moving towards the outside, heading for his vehicle. He had to speak with someone and that someone was an hour away.

Bradon had turned back to the room, finding Evan's eyes on him, a question in them that Bradon shook his head at. He walked back towards Ennis, finding her asleep again, Kade huddled down beside her, not looking at his master. Evan gave a snicker at the look on Bradon's face.

"He waited until you turned your back, and then was up there. Ennis was talking to him again before she fell asleep,"

Meg nodded. "That he did. Now, have you heard with the investigation is?"

"Not today, not yet anyway. Dallas did say he was waiting for some information or something." Bradon's arm came around Meg's shoulder. "You've been in here for a while, Meg. Let me take you to the cafeteria and find you something to eat."

Meg looked up at him, wondering why all the men in her life were so tall. She had hoped that when Ennis found her fellow, he wouldn't be quite so tall.

"I can do that. Evan? You're staying?"

"I am. Someone has to. Kade might just kidnap her and disappear somewhere."

Bradon's steps stopped before he spun, a narrowed look on his face before he shook his head. "He just might."

*Chapter 27*

A week later, Ennis sank down onto the couch in her parents' home. She had needed to be there. Her mother had asked and she did not the heart at that point to say no. Kade stood for a moment before he was up beside her, curling up with his head on her knee. His eyes shifted between her and to where he could hear Bradon. Her hand rested on him even as her eyes closed. She was exhausted, Walter had warned her about that, but she didn't realize just how bad it would be. She contemplated the stairs to the bedrooms and sighed. There was no way she could do them.

Hands on her shoulders shifted her over until the person sat, and then arms wrapped around her, drawing her to him and her head to his shoulder. What was she to do with Bradon, Ennis wondered, and then decided she just didn't know. His actions spoke of his love for her, but he had not said anything. His eyes spoke and she was afraid that hers were answering the question he was asking. Ennis just wasn't sure she was ready for anything else to change in her life. Not at this point.

Bradon watched her, his head tilting so he could see her face, then looking past her at Kade. He just shook his head. Kade was very protective of Ennis, almost too much, Bradon thought, but he didn't have the heart to stop him. Ennis needed someone right now and that someone was Kade. He reached to pull a blanket over her, earning himself a quiet thank you.

"Ennis? How are you doing?"

She gave a small shrug, her head burrowing into his shoulder even more. "I hurt. I'm tired, exhausted. I don't want to be here." She raised her head slightly. "And I have to climb stairs to get to the bedrooms. I just can't do that."

Bradon could hear the trace of tears in her voice, but didn't hear Meg's soft steps that stopped at her words. Meg was away, hunting for Ian or Evan. Ennis would not be climbing the stairs, she thought. There was a full bathroom down here, Ian putting it in for the men's convenience when they came in dirty or muddy. They could set up a bed in Ian's office very easily. Bradon watched her walk away, praying that somehow she had heard and would solve Ennis' difficulties. If she couldn't, he was prepared to wrap Ennis into his arms, take her to Anna, and then stay there himself.

"Bradon? Have they found them yet?"

———

He shook his head. "Not yet. Dallas wants to talk to us, as does Will. He did say they weren't much further ahead."

"That's what I'm afraid of. That they can't or won't find him and whoever it is appears again."

"I will do everything in my power to make sure that doesn't happen." Bradon had been adamant about that when his friends had spoken to him. He knew they were searching still, but whoever it was seemed to be hiding.

"But I don't want you to be hurt again. That can happen." She yawned, fatigue weighting down her body.

"I know, sweetheart. I know. But I would do it all over again for you."

Bradon wasn't aware that she had cornered the men the day before, finding out exactly what had happened. No one had told her and she just had to know. Horror had flooded her when she heard that Bradon had been drowned but brought back by his two friends. Fear flowed in her that he would be hurt again, and she just couldn't have that. But she couldn't or was that wouldn't make him stay away from her.

"About your dog."

"Kade?'

"Kade. Why won't he leave me alone? I don't like dogs."

"Kade knows you're hurting and need him. He's wired that way. Always has been. He's chosen to make you part of his life. I can't keep him away. He frets and stresses when he can't be near you."

"But he's your dog."

"I know, sweetheart. I know. But dogs are funny creatures. You can own a dog, but the dog will choose who they want. He's done that with you." Bradon bit at his lip before he continued, his voice barely audible. "And he's not the only one."

Ennis shifted until she could look up at him, brushing back at her hair until the blanket was tucked around her once more. "Bradon? What are you saying?"

"That I want you to stay in my life. This is not the time nor how I wanted to tell you. I love you more than anything. I want to explore our friendship, see where we head."

She sighed. "Thank you, Bradon. I was afraid it was all one sided. I love you, too. But I don't want you to be hurt, and that could happen."

———

"It could happen at any time or in any place. We can't let that stop us, sweetheart." He watched her face closely, seeing when she accepted his words. "So, are we a couple or not?"

Ennis shook her head, her hand clutching at his shirt. "I guess we are. Wake me in an hour." She slept, his arm tight around her, his head on hers, curled up against him, Kade crowding in as close as he could get.

Meg stood for a moment, watching her daughter, seeing contentment in her face even with the pain and tiredness. They've decided something, haven't they, Lord? They are so suited to one another.

Bradon looked up at Meg. "Meg?"

She shook her head. "Ian and Evan are bringing a bed down for her. We've set up in his office for her for now. She doesn't have the strength to climb up and down the stairs."

"Thank you. I hoped that's what you were doing. I was ready to take her to Anna."

"I know you were." Meg dropped a kiss on the top of his head, just as she would with Evan. "Thank you, Bradon. She trusts you like she doesn't many people. And for her to accept Kade that way? That's a God moment, I would say. She needs you to stay in her life." Her head tilted. "And I think you need her to stay in yours. I know Kade does."

Bradon grinned as Meg finished and then walked away, not telling her that's the conclusion they had come to. Telling them? That would come, at some point. Right now, he was content, holding the woman he loved in his arms, his dog close to him. He pulled out his phone, to scroll through the messages he had received, stopping on the one from Rick, a frown on his face. Who was tracking him to there? He sent a quick reply, asking Rick to contact Dallas or Will, and also Barnabas. This just opened up the investigation a whole lot wider, he thought.

———

Shaking his head, Bradon stared at Dallas a couple of days later. He had dropped into the police department, wanting to talk with him about the man who had showed up at his work, and found Dallas deep into their investigation.

"There is no way that person is involved. They're too prominent in that community." Bradon was adamant that the name given was wrong.

"I'm sorry, Bradon, but they are. We're finding out more and more information on them. And it's not good. I can't say for sure they're the ones behind it, but they could easily be. We see it all the time, Bradon. Now, about that man who showed up at your work?"

"That's right. He appeared today. I wasn't scheduled to be there, but I had to talk to Rick about some problems I was seeing with one of our dog recruits." Bradon sat back in his chair, a puzzled look on his face. "I had Rick pull some video and stills for you." He handed over a thumb drive. "They're on there. But that man? I know him from somewhere, and it wasn't good. I just don't know from where."

Dallas listened as he brought up the photos. "Do you know who this is?"

Bradon shook his head. "I have no idea. I was hoping you did."

Dallas sat back, blowing out a breath and drawing in one deeply. "This is Tim Russell. He's a bodyguard for the mayor of our town."

"He is? That's where I've seen him then. But why would he be around, asking all sorts of questions about me?" Bradon shook his head. "I've never spoken to him, barely seen him." His eyes narrowed. "Russell, did you say? We had trouble with someone named Russell a year or so ago. I wonder if they're related." His head went back as he groaned. "He lives in Ennis' town." He glared at Dallas. "Now, you're going to tell me he was involved with that Jason."

Dallas grinned at the look. "We'll not say that. I suspect he was. That means both of you are on their radar." He sat back, his pen tapping on the papers on his desk. "You both have to be so careful right now."

"We know that." Bradon sighed before he stood. "Ennis is hurting so much, part of that being my being hurt because of her. We need this over, Dallas, before she can heal. Both of us want that, I know. Her family is hurting."

"And so are your friends."

"That they are. Let me know what you find out. I'll be heading towards Ennis later today. She wants to move back here."

"She does, does she? Can't stay away from Kade, I gather?" Dallas just grinned at the look thrown him before Bradon disappeared. He sobered at he stared at his computer screen, before reaching to print the photos. He needed to talk to some of the older detectives and he needed to talk to Will.

Will stared at the photos, before looking up at Dallas. "Bradon brought these?"

"He did. I'm heading out to see what I can find out on the streets, but the streets are being very quiet. I know if he tells his friends, they'll be searching as well."

"And you can be sure he will. Be careful, Dallas. If I remember correctly, there are a lot of rumours about this man, and they're not good. I don't know how he's managed to stay working for the mayor."

"Unless the mayor is involved." Dallas and Will stared at each other before Will nodded.

"There are those persistent rumours, Dallas. Run with this. Keep it as quiet as you can for now."

Later that afternoon, Will stood and watched as Bradon and Ennis made their way towards the building and towards himself. He had come out, wanting to see how they were, but also to talk to them. Dallas was on his way as well. They both were concerned enough about the investigation they were ready to find a safe house for the couple, only Will knew Bradon would never leave, and that his friends would do their best to keep them safe and alive.

Ennis looked up as she saw him, a smile lighting her face as she stopped, Bradon's hand holding hers tight, Kade tight to her other side. "Will? You're here? Good news for us?"

Will smiled as Bradon just shook his head. "How are you feeling now, Ennis?"

"Cooped up. Sore. Wanting to get my life back. Protected. Too much at times." She grinned up at Bradon who was watching her closely. "But you're not here with good news, are you?"

———

"No, unfortunately, I'm not. Here, let me grab the door. Which suite?"

"Mine, I think, Will." Bradon spoke. "I have more information to give you. The guys have been busy, you know."

"I am sure they have been. I've talked to Barnabas and so has Dallas. Your friends are good."

"That they are." He assisted Ennis to a seat on the couch, shaking his head as Kade jumped up beside her. "Have either of you eaten? I know Anna had set something in the oven for us."

"No, and thank you." Will looked around as Dallas appeared, his briefcase hitting the floor as he reached to help Bradon.

Ennis watched the three men closely, trying to hide the pain she was feeling. She thought Bradon was picking up on it, but wasn't sure. All she knew was that she wanted this over with, and to go on with her life. Bradon had made it clear he was not walking away, that he wanted her in his life, and she felt the same. Moving her foot slightly, it touched Kade, who was snuggled as close to her chair as he could get. Ennis felt guilty about that.

Bradon pointed to the living room. "We can meet in there, or in my office."

"Let's try your office, Bradon. Is there a couch there that Ennis can lay on? She's about done in." Will reached to support her as she stood, receiving her nod of thanks.

"There is. And I left a blanket there for her."

Dallas watched the young couple before he looked up at Will, who was watching him.

"Dallas? What have you to share?" Bradon got right to the point. "Here. This is for you, and this for you, Will. It's what the guys have come up with. I'm not sure how much you already know."

The two men flipped through the information, Dallas with a frown on his face.

"How did they come up with so much in such a short time?"

"They can concentrate on that only, and I know the ladies have been working when they can. You don't have the resources to do that." Bradon pointed to the paperwork. "They also have sources that won't talk to the police but have provided valuable, at least we think it is, information that may help break this case wide open. We want it over. It's taken too much from Ennis."

Unable to keep her eyes open, Ennis dozed at the men discussed the findings, not hearing Will's exclamation.

"Will?" Bradon waited for him to respond, speaking again when he didn't.

"Bradon, where did Brody find this information?" Dallas had been drawn to a conclusion, the same one he suspected Will had discovered.

Bradon shrugged. "He's the paralegal on the team. I have no idea where that came from, but he did say for you to call him. He expects that."

"And I will. He has picked up on something we may have overlooked, or not found yet in the investigation." Dallas finally sat back, his eyes straying to Ennis. "She's asleep."

"She is. She crashes early since her injury." Bradon reached to wake her, stopping as Dallas shook his head.

"It's okay, Bradon. We just wanted to touch base with you two, to see how you're doing, to see if you had any other thoughts or idea. We'll need to work through what you've given us."

The men spoke for a while before Will and Dallas left, leaving Bradon to clean his kitchen, and then head back to the office, a cup of tea for Ennis and his own cup of coffee in his hands. He sighed as he watched her sleep. He needed to wake her but it hurt his heart to do that.

Ennis roused, sitting up to take the cup of tea with a quiet thanks. She looked around through blurry eyes.

"Will and Dallas? Where are they?"

"They've left. You slept through them talking to me."

"I did? What did they have to say?"

"First, let me tell you there was a man who appeared today at my work. They've identified him at Tim Russell."

"Russell? As in bodyguard Russell? As in muscle for hire?"

Bradon's head tilted as he studied her face, watching as she pushed her hair away from it.

"That would be him. Do you know him?"

"Everyone in my town knows him. He's always been known for that. Doesn't he work for the mayor here? Or is it is wife he works for?" Ennis looked up, a thought hovering in her mind. "Did you know Jason is related to her?"

"He is? Did we overlook that?" His phone was out as he sent a quick text off to Branigan. "I'll let Branigan look into that. They may have discovered that." He stared at the text message he had just received. "Branigan says they found that out and passed it along in the documentation to Dallas and Will. I didn't know the man until today. I don't know how they came up with that, but they had some reason for finding it."

"Your friends are good." She stared at him for a moment, before looking down at Kade. "I'm sorry, Bradon."

"You're sorry? For what?" Bradon was puzzled.

"For involving you in this. You shouldn't have been. And I'm sorry Kade is sticking so close to me. He shouldn't when he's your dog."

Bradon just grinned at her. "Kade is doing what he's been trained, in part, to do. He works with me during the day. In his off time, he's spending time with a friend. And if he spends time with this friend, then I get to as well." He paused, gathering his thoughts, which became dark as he thought of what she had been through. "I'm not sorry I got involved. I wouldn't have met my lady if I hadn't."

"Do you really mean that, Bradon? You're just not saying that to appease me? Make me accept Kade when you know how scared I am of dogs?" She was desperate to know exactly how he felt, but wouldn't come right out and ask him.

"I mean every word and more. You are my love, sweetheart, the one I've been waiting for. Let's find these people who are after you, and then we can decide where we want to go."

"That's not fair to you. It may take ages to find them." Ennis rose and walked away from him.

Before he could rise to his feet, he heard the click of the outside door and knew she had left. His head went back on his chair as his eyes closed and his heart hurt for his lady, praying that she would find peace somehow in all this, and that this would be over soon. That was his feeling, Bradon decided. That it wouldn't go on for long, not with Russell tracking him down as he did.

He looked down as his phone chimed. Rick? What now? He read the text message and groaned. No going into the building for him then, he decided, not if there were cars and people moving around there the security feed had captured. Rick would bring him the work he needed to do, the text read. And then Rick asked how he was, how Ennis was, and what could he do for them?

*Chapter 30*

A week later, Ennis was on a hunt, once more. Only this time, she didn't quite know what or who she was looking for. She had driven herself back to her hometown, sending Bradon a text message that she was there. Ennis wandered the downtown area, greeting friends, before she finally entered a shop. An antique shop she decided would be just the place to hide contraband. She didn't think it was all about her. Now, Jason might well have been involved in things she didn't want to even imagine, and she prayed she was wrong, that ladies and girls hadn't really disappeared under his drive to money, but she could see that. He had stalked her for so many years, and she had run from him. That hurt, she decided, that she had lost time with her family and friends that she would never get back.

Ennis searched the store, finally focusing on the old books, which she handled with care. A lump rose in her throat as she picked up one. This was what she was looking for, and didn't know. She walked quickly to the cash desk, paid for the book, and walked away, her eyes searching for anyone watching her.

She almost ran for her car, sliding into it, and locking the doors, her eyes on her purchase. There had to be an answer here, she thought, but how do I find out? Her phone chiming startled her, and she glanced down at it, her breath coming in sharp gasps.

"Ennis? Where are you?" Bradon's voice came through and she could hear the worry.

"I'm at home. I'm heading back your way. Can you stay on the phone with me, if I leave it on speaker?" She was worried, more worried than she had been in years. She thought she could feel someone watching her but looking around, she didn't really see someone.

Bradon was waiting in the parking lot for her, pacing, worried more than he wanted to show. Breck paused on his way through and then detoured to talk to him.

"Bradon?"

"Breck? Don't you have a meeting or something?"

"I do. Just wanted to make sure you were okay. You seem to be pacing."

———

632

Bradon grinned. "Is that what this is called?" He sobered. "Ennis went back to her hometown this morning. She's on her way back. We were on a call, but the call dropped."

"And you don't know if she's safe or not." Breck nodded, turning as he heard a vehicle. "I would say she is."

Bradon spun, then almost ran for her car, stopping short as he watched Ennis through the window. She looked out at him, and he drew in a deep breath at the raw fear he saw. Wrenching open her door, he reached for her even as her seatbelt released.

"Ennis?"

"Bradon? He followed me. I am not sure who he is, but I managed to grab a photo of him and his vehicle." She clung to him, and he could feel the shudders running through her.

"That's good. Here, let me have your phone. I'll pass it on." He glanced up at Breck, who was nodding, before he walked away. Bradon knew that the search would commence, even though Breck had a commitment he had to be at.

"Wait, Bradon. I found this." Ennis reached for the book and then her purse. "This was in an antique store in town. I think it might have some information we need."

"That's good." Bradon took the book, and then wrapping an arm around her, led her to the building. "You didn't want company this morning?"

She shook her head. "I wasn't really sure what I was looking for. But when I saw the old books, a memory triggered. Jason had said something one time about that book. I just ignored it and shoved that memory away."

"You've remembered now." Bradon swung her around to walk towards the building. "Do you know what is so important about it?"

She shook her head. "Not really." She stared down at his, her eyes puzzled, before she groaned. "It's a family history, Bradon. About the Russells. Was Jason related?"

"I can't remember, but we will figure it out. That I can guarantee you." He held the door for her, and then followed her in, his eyes meeting Blair as he walked towards them. "Here's Blair. I know Devaney's home today. How be we go see them?"

"We can't just drop in on them. That's just not acceptable." She was horrified at the thought.

Bradon grinned at her. "It's okay, sweetheart. Blair's right here."

"He is? Where did he come from? I didn't know he was here." She looked at Blair and then down at the book, suddenly thrusting it at him, almost dropping it in her haste to be rid of it. "Here, you take it. I don't like it. I don't want it anymore."

"If you don't like it, why do you have it?" Blair was puzzled, even as his smile still lit his face.

"I have no idea. I saw it and just knew you needed it. Will it help?"

Blair glanced through it. "It might. You took a chance bringing this back, didn't you."

Bradon nodded. "She was followed. I sent a photo and license plate over to Breck and also Dallas." He paused, his eye on Ennis. "Is Devaney at home?"

"She is. In fact, she had sent me to find you two. To see if you would like to join us for lunch?"

"Food? Did you say food?" Ennis was almost running for the stairs. "I didn't eat this morning. I'm starved."

Bradon stared after her, remembering to snap his mouth closed. "Did she just do that? And she's not supposed to be running."

Blair was laughing at his friend. "She did, and no, she isn't. I think the idea of food was uppermost in her mind, not her safety." He paused, sobering. "How is she really doing, Bradon? We can't get a reading on her."

Bradon shrugged. "I have the same trouble. She's learned to hide a lot of what she's feeling and thinking. Her Mom says that's not her. She should be very vocal."

Blair stared to laugh once more. "You will have your hands full, my friend. Let's find our ladies before Ennis eats our portion of the lunch."

Devaney watched Ennis closely, see how tight to the edge she was and then shook her head. Ennis was getting ready to run and when she did, Devaney feared she would never return, and either take Bradon with her or leave him behind, devastated.

Blair sat as well, his eyes assessing Bradon before turning to Ennis. He nodded to himself. It was coming to a conclusion, soon, he thought, but how did he and Bradon's friends force that. He finally rose, returning to the table with the book, and sat back down near Ennis. Ennis shuddered as she saw the book, not sure why. She felt Bradon's arm come around her and leaned back against him.

"Blair? We need to pray first, I think." Bradon spoke, his eyes on her. "Ennis needs that."

"You both do." Blair stared at his friend before he did just what Bradon had asked, for the couple and then for their friends and then the police officers work on their case.

Ennis looked up with the men had finished, thankful she had praying friends. She studied the book and then poked at it, afraid of what they would or would not find when it was opened.

"Ennis?" Blair's laughing voice brought her head up. "Would you like to open it?"

She glared at him even as she shook her head. She was exhausted to her very bones, she thought, and wanted this over. Bradon needed to get on with his life, and then she could too. She really didn't believe that he meant what he said. Bradon's arms tightened on her, letting her know through his touch that he cared. She leaned back on him before she spoke.

"We do need to open that. I don't know why I was led to it. I've never seen it before."

"And you are afraid people will think you planted it." Devaney's soft voice broke through the silence that ensued after Ennis' words.

"I am. That's exactly what I am afraid of." Ennis looked up at her friend. "How did you ever do it, Devaney?"

"With a lot of prayer. Support from our friends. Support for and from each other. It was the same for Baird and Berneen and for Benen and Cadee." She suddenly grinned, startling them. "I already feel like I have a laundry list of friends this has happened to.  Do you think it will affect each one of you?"

Blair just shook his head at his wife, even as Bradon laughed, and then answered her.  "With the rate we're going, more than likely.  I mean, after all, how are they to find their ladies, unless they come to their rescue in the ladies' distress?"

Ennis stared at him for a moment before a small smile lit her face.  "Thank you, Blair.  Now.  This book."

"This book.  I understand you had someone following you today."

"I did.  Bradon said he sent the picture to Breck and also to Dallas."  She shifted until she could turn her face to him, to find him watching her with his head tilted to see her face.  "Bradon?  You did, didn't you?"

"I did.  Breck had it before he left for his meeting.  Dallas let me know he had it and had someone working on a name.  He'll let us know as soon as he can."

Ennis nodded, reaching for the book, hesitating as she did so, a sudden fear running through her.  She clenched and then unclenched her hands, knowing she needed to open the book, but not wanting to.

"Ennis?  Do you want me to open it for you?"  Bradon's voice was soft in her ear, his breath blowing at her hair.

She shook her head, blinking rapidly.  "No, I think I need to.  I'm just afraid of what I'll find, of what I'll open up.  Does that make sense?"

"Perfect sense."  Devaney's voice was equally quiet.  "If you can't today, you could leave it for another day."

Ennis shook her head.  "No, I need to do it today.  God help me, please.  I just don't know."

She slowly opened the cover on the hardback book, a frown on her face.  "This is a diary, I think."  She looked up at Bradon, whose hand rested on hers.

"It is, Ennis.  That's what it is, I think.  A diary.  But why would it be the store?  Shouldn't family members have it?"

"That's what I don't understand."  She looked around.

"What do you need?"  Bradon watched her closely before glancing up to see Blair shaking his head.

"My phone.  Did I give it to you?"

"You did. I never got it back to you." Bradon handed it over. "Why?"

"Because I need to call Mom or Dad. Ask them about the Russells. They know them, not well, but they will have an insight we might need." Ennis sat back, her eyes on the book. "I'm sorry, Blair, Devaney. This will take a lot of time and you two have commitments in the morning."

"Actually, we don't. It's Saturday." Devaney shook her head at her friend. "You've been through so much. Our actual worry is that this will be too much for you,"

Ennis stared at her and then at Bradon. "We need this over for Bradon. He should never have been involved." She turned her attention to her phone, not seeing the brief look of sorrow and another emotion his friends couldn't read that crept across his face.

The next morning, Ennis stopped short in the doorway to the boardroom, snapping her mouth closed. All the men are here, she thought, already at work. She saw the three younger ladies around a table to the side and noted the coffee, tea, and food on that. They've prepared for a long haul, haven't they, Lord. Her eyes raised to the walls and she frowned.

Bradon was watching her closely, seeing the emotions that were fluttering across her face, and saw the exact moment she caught on to what his friends were doing.

"Just like in the movies, Ennis, only we have to use paper and our boardroom walls."

"They've been busy. This can't be just from this morning."

Barnabas shook his head as he came to a stop in front of her, his eyes doing his own assessment of her. Doc had asked that of him. "No, they've been working for the last week or so on this. They have made some progress, and that information has been sent on to Dallas. He was quite impressed with how they worked on it for Blair and Devaney."

"So, we're not the first?" Ennis made a move to the side, to study the whole room, before she felt Bradon's arms around her.

"We're not. We've told you that. And no, I pray that we don't go through everyone else." He laughed at the look on Barnabas' face. "It was commented on last night that we still have a number of friends for this to go through." He gave a quick look behind him and then moved Ennis to the side so Dallas could enter.

"Your guys are just too good, Barnabas. How do they discover this stuff?" Dallas, a grin on his face, held up a thick folder.

"Probably because they don't think like you do." Ennis' comment caught them by surprise. She didn't see the startled look thrown at her.

"What do you mean, Ennis?" Dallas was curious, never having had that comment made to him before.

"You think like the police. They think like ordinary people trying to solve a puzzle." She looked up, a spark of mischief playing across her face. "And this is what it is, a huge puzzle that I want solved." She moved away from the men, leaving them staring after her.

"She's right, you know. Now, how do we solve this puzzle?" Bradon moved away, intent on finding out what was happening and what more information had been discovered.

Barnabas snickered at the look on Dallas' face. "Can we do that? Solve this?"

Dallas shook his head, an answering grin on his face. "I hope we can. At least, I mean, I pray we can."

Barnabas' hand on his arm kept him from moving forward. "Dallas? Care to explain?"

Dallas shook his head. "It's you. It's your friends. Their ladies. Doc and Anna. Will. Even going through what Blair and Devaney did and now what Bradon and Ennis are facing, and seeing their faith not wavering, I had to search. Even though Bradon was technically dead and Ennis so close at times, I had to search. Someone kept them alive."

"And that Someone is God, is that what you're saying?" Barnabas' eyes raised to Will, who stood behind Dallas, a surprised look on his face, that changed to happiness.

"I guess I am. I just wonder why I never did that before."

"Because you weren't ready for it. God has used my two friends, and when you tell them that, they will be overjoyed."

Dallas shook his head. "Surely, He could have used an easier method."

"Not all the time. Besides, they went through what they did and are at present to bring someone to justice."

"And there's that." Dallas walked away, towards Burnie who was beckoning to him.

"Did you suspect that, Will?" Barnabas' voice was low.

"I wondered. He has changed, become more settled. I talked to his girlfriend. Katie's a believer, knew she shouldn't be dating him, but did. She is overjoyed that he is now a believer."

"That's good. Now, about this."

"Yes, about this. Dallas showed me the photo Ennis managed to snag. Do you know who that is?"

Barnabas shook his head. "No. I haven't seen it." He took Will's phone, staring down at the photo. "It's not, is it?"

Will nodded. "It is. He's related to Jason, to the Russells, our good mayor's wife. How far does it go?"

"I fear for my friends, Will. These people are brutal and will stop at nothing." Barnabas walked away himself, heading for Doc, who stood watching closely.

Will shook his own head and headed for Ennis. He needed to talk to her, to see how she was. He saw the fatigue in her face, the paleness of it, the stress that had caused fine lines. He turned to find Bradon beside him.

"She's not sleeping?"

Bradon shrugged. "She won't say. Kade doesn't want to leave her side if he's around her. I've never seen him like that."

"But then he's never seen you interested in a lady."

Bradon grinned. "And there's that. Where do we really stand, Will?"

"Dallas knows better than I do. He's planning on updating you two and I gather all your friends today. He has found some interesting tidbits, as he calls them." Will studied each man before he spoke again. "This is where it gets very dangerous, Bradon. Your friends will need to take care, as will the ladies. Dallas was able to identify the man in the photo."

"And that, I take it, is not good."

"No, it's not. It opens up a whole new line of investigations."

―――

Dallas stood beside Burnie, his head tilted as he listened to him. Burnie was an author, and as such, had been handed the diary for the first look-through. He had scanned it quickly and then sat back, worry in his mind for his friends. This was not just an ordinary diary, he thought. Looking around, he had caught Dallas' eye and beckoned him over.

"Burnie? What do you have? It's not good, that much I can tell." Dallas perched on the side of the table, a foot swinging idly.

"Not, it's not, Dallas. How did she ever get ahold of it?"

Dallas shrugged. "From what Bradon said, she was in her hometown, went into an antiques store and was looking around. She felt drawn to the books and found that." He stabbed a finger at it. "What can you tell me? Or can you already?"

Burnie nodded. "It's not just a diary. It's actual a step-by-step history of the Russells, and how deep they were into crime. How did they ever let it go?"

"We'll ask them that. How much can you tell me already?"

"Not a lot, not until I go through it more thoroughly. But it is frightening. It names Ennis' parents."

Dallas sat upright more. "It does. But why?"

"That's what I'll need to dig through." Burnie took a better look at the book. "It's not really that old, I would say, and not that thick. How be I make a copy, let you have the original for your team to go over, and I'll work from the copy. That way, I can mark it up all I want."

"That sounds like a plan." Dallas looked around. "Do you have to leave here to do that?"

Burnie grinned. "Not at all. Barnabas has the rooms all stocked with whatever equipment we need, and that includes a photocopier. I'll be right back." He was on his feet and away to the other side of the room, Ennis' eyes watching him before she turned back to Buckley.

"How do we pray for you, Ennis?" Buckley pulled out a chair beside her and sat, his eyes watchful, catching Bradon moving around on the edge of his line of sight.

"I don't know, Buckley." She sat back, her brow furrowing as she thought. "I guess. I don't know. I guess, safety for my family, for Bradon, for all of you. For all of this to be over. That way Bradon can go on with his life."

Buckley nodded. "But that's not quite what I wanted to hear."

"It's not? What did you think you would hear? Pleas for me?" She shook her head. "I don't do that, Buckley. I don't ask prayer for myself."

"And in this case, you should. You need it." Buckley prayed hard as he watched her. "How be we pray like this? We pray for what you've asked for. But we also pray for you, as Ennis, as an individual."

"And what would you pray for?"

"I would pray like this. For your peace. For your safety. For wisdom. For strength. For courage. For your family. For your friends. For Bradon."

She watched him closely as he paused. "We need to pray for you. You bear a heavy burden at any time. But now? You are bearing much more of one."

Buckley smiled at her. "You understand, don't you? This is when I remember that we were prayed for in the Garden. And that all we need to do is touch the Master's garment. Just the very edge of a hem, and we can be healed."

"That has gotten me through so much." Ennis looked around, her eyes narrowing on Burnie. "How is Burnie making out with the diary? I know he was handed it."

"I have no idea. Shall we go over there and ask him?" Buckley grinned at her as his eyes raised to Bradon standing behind her. "Maybe Bradon knows."

"Bradon doesn't know. Burnie has not said, although he has passed the original on to Dallas, Ennis. He kept copies of it. That way, he says he can mark them up." Bradon paused, biting at his lip. "Dallas would like to speak with you."

"But do I want to speak with him?" Ennis sighed as she rose, heading for the door, and away from Dallas. "You talk to him. Any questions he has? Write them down and get them to me. Right now? I'm crashing and need to sleep."

Ennis was out of the door before Bradon could stop her, a nod coming from Brennen as he followed her.

———

"Ennis?" Brennen voice stopped her in her tracks. "Are you okay?"

He watched as her shoulders shook with sobs, before he walked up and just hugged her. "Do I need to get Bradon for you?" He felt her head shaking.

"No, I don't want him hurt again, and I am just so afraid that's what will happen." She pushed away from him. "How do I get him to stay away from me?"

"That won't happen, Ennis. I can tell you that. No matter what or who you face, he will be there or he'll find a way to get to you. That's a given. We can all see how he feels about you." His voice compassionate, he continued. "And I would say that's how you feel about him." He wrapped an arm around her and steered her for the lobby and then to one of the couches, pushing her down and sitting on the coffee table in front of her. "So, tell me. Let me ask once again. What do we do for you?"

She shrugged, her eyes on the floor, hiding or so she thought her emotions. "I don't know. I have asked my family to stay away, and God help me, I need them. I can't have them near me."

"We get that and so do they. But they'll be here if you need them. That's a guarantee. But what do we do for you?"

She shrugged, startled as a cup appeared in her vision as Cadee handed her a cup of tea. Brennen took his mug of coffee with thanks. Cadee moved to step away when Ennis caught her hand.

"Please? Cadee? Stay? Brennen was just asking what you all can do for me."

"Other than the obvious?" At Ennis' nod, Cadee settled back on the couch, a leg tucked up under her, her own cup balanced on her leg. "That's a tough one, Ennis. We all know what we want for you, what Bradon likely wants, what your parents and your brother want. I saw Buckley talking to you and I have a pretty good idea of what kind of pep talk he handed you. He's good at reading people." She considered what she should say. "For you? I would say, first we need to end this. But before that, we need to get you well." Ennis stared at her, dumbfounded at how she narrowed in on that.

"How did you know?" Ennis' voice was barely above a whisper, fatigue washing through her as did relief that someone understood.

"Because to a certain extent, we've been there. We've never told you our story but when Benen and I were running for the aircraft, I was shot with a small dart. That dart was poisoned. I almost died that night,

———

643

just like you, and if Benen hadn't mentioned that I said I thought I had been stung by a bug, it would have been overlooked."

Ennis' eyes were huge as Cadee finished. "That happened to you?"

"It did and much more. Some day, I'll tell you the rest of our story. Some of it is down right ugly. Now, you and Bradon. Do you know what happened to him that day?" Cadee felt led to share what had gone on that day.

"No, and I wish someone would tell me. All Bradon does is shrug it off, says it's in the past, and that he's more concerned about me."

"It is all that, but more, Ennis." Cadee reached for Ennis' cup, setting it past her on the table by the couch. "If you don't put that down, you'll spill it. Apparently, Bradon went looking for you, heard you yelling, tried to get to you and was tackled. He was held down in the lake." Cadee watched with compassion as Ennis' face whitened.

"He wasn't, was he?" Ennis felt the tears in the back of her throat and swallowed hard, her eyes focusing on the turning leaves on the trees surrounding the building. "He wasn't hurt that bad, was he?" When neither one of her companions responded, she turned back. "Cadee? Brennen?"

"For all intents and purposes, Ennis, Bradon died that day. He was drowned. Blair was one of the ones who reached him quickly and worked on him." Brennen knew he would never forget his friends racing for the water and then lifting his eyes to what they were running for and that he never would forget the sight of Bradon's lifeless body being carried from the water, seeing him laid on his back, and the two friends working frantically to clear his lungs and bring him back. He remembered the relief that had surged through him when Bradon finally started coughing and hacking, being rolled to his side to help with that.

Her hand covering her mouth, Ennis stared at Brennen in horror. She had not known that what was had happened to Bradon. He had brushed it off, not wanting to talk about it, more concerned about her.

"Brennen?" Her voice was barely audible. "Is that what happened?"

Brennen nodded, his eyes on her, sorrow in them. "It is, Ennis. He never wanted you to know. He refused to tell you and didn't want us to, either. But you needed to know. He almost lost his life coming to save you. That's how much he loves you."

Cadee's arms were around Ennis in a hard hug. "That is so true, Ennis. We almost lost you too, then."

Ennis nodded. "I know. Walter talked to me. I made him. Mom and Dad didn't want me to know how bad it was, not right away. But it's my body. I needed to know that." She sank back, reaching for her cup to take a sip. "But where do we go from now? I mean, with the investigation. Dallas talked to me last night."

"He did? And?" Brennen leaned forward, his arms resting on his thighs. "What did he say?"

"That I was right. That Jason was related to the Russells, on his mother's side, I think he said. And they found evidence that he won't talk about, that showed Jason had been stalking me for years. We're just not sure why. Dallas said he had an idea, but he had more work and thought to put into it before he would talk with me. I don't like that, but I have accepted it." She looked up as she felt hands shifting her over and then someone sitting beside her, arms wrapping around her pulling her back against a body.

Bradon had been standing out of her line of sight as Brennen had spoken. He had shaken his head. He had never wanted her to know that, at least not yet. He didn't want her turning to him out of gratitude, them making a commitment to one another, and then Ennis walking away from him. He could not handle that, he thought.

Ennis shifted enough she could look up at him, a frown on her face. "Bradon?"

"I'm okay, sweetheart. I'm okay. It happened. And I would do it all over again to save you." He watched as she sat, a puzzled look on her face.

"Who did it?"

"What do you mean?"

"Who held you down like that?"

"The one who had been with the police. I'm not sure how much you remember."

"Not a lot. I can remember walking out towards the lake. I needed some freedom, some space. I had told security where I was heading, but I gather they didn't get to tell you?" She watched as Bradon shook his head. She sighed. "Somehow, he found me. I don't know how. He threatened me, tried to drag me away. I can remember screaming and fighting and seeing the other man run away. Then, I don't remember anything."

Bradon nodded before his chin rested on the top of her head. "That's how we cope. God provides us the needed ability to forget some things. This is one of those times, sweetheart."

"But, Bradon, you didn't tell me about you." She was dismayed but also angry to a point that he had hidden something from her.

"No, I didn't. I wanted you to heal more first, but you did need to know. I didn't want to tell you though."

"It involved me. Don't ever hide anything from me again."

"I won't." Bradon shared a look with Brennen. "That's a promise. Now, about the investigation."

"What about it?" She was disgruntled and it came through loud and clear.

"Dallas has had to leave. You didn't see him go?"

"I did. He waved on the way by. He'll be in touch. That much I know." She twisted to look up at him. "What did your friends come up with?"

"A lot, actually. They've been working on it off and on since you were first hurt. They upped their time working on it."

"They shouldn't. They have their own lives to live."

Brennen shook his head, catching her attention. "It's what we do, Ennis. We work together as a team, two teams actually. I don't think it has ever been explained to you that we're divided into two teams, along the lines of what we do.  Barnabas would need to explain his reasonings to you.  He's the one best to do that.  But we do step outside of what we do and how we volunteer when we need to.  And this time, it's for you and Bradon.  Not one of our begrudges the time we've had to take.  We realize it could be one of us.  Three of us have already gone through it.  So, don't apologize.  And don't run.  If Bradon's not around and you need someone to help you, each one has said that."

She finally nodded, finally getting it that she had become part of that family Bradon belonged to, a family drawn together by choice and not blood.  She knew she had a lot yet to overcome, Jason had seen to that.  She shifted how she was sitting, drawing up her legs, her head going down on Bradon's shoulder as she slept, feeling safe, secure, and loved.

Brennen watched her closely, nodding as Cadee rose and gathered their mugs, her comment softly spoken that she had an errand to run.  Bradon's eyes were on Ennis, his love for her not shuttered for a moment.

"Bradon?  What did Dallas really say?"

Bradon gave a soft sigh as he looked up.  "He's afraid it's going cold.  Any lead they have that looks promising dies out.  If he doesn't get something soon, he'll have to put our investigation to the side."

"That's what we're afraid of.  Ennis can't continue to live like this.  Nor can you."

Bradon shrugged.  "It is what it is.  We'll deal with whatever happens."  He looked down as Ennis stirred, her eyes opening slowly as she looked around, finally focusing on him.

"Bradon?  Is it over yet?"

"Not yet.  We're working on it, sweetheart."

"Oh, okay.  I dreamt it was all over.  I was so hoping it was."  Her head snuggled down on his shoulder again, before she looked up, lifting her face enough to kiss his cheek, stilling his motions.  "Wake me when it is, please?  I love you."  The two men stared at each other, wonder on Bradon's face, mirth on Brennen's at the look on Bradon's.  "Marry me?"

Bradon stared down at her for a moment, then kissed the top of her head.  "In a heartbeat, sweetheart."

"Okay.  Today, then?"  Ennis was asleep again before Bradon could respond.

An hour later, Ennis sat upright on the couch, shock and disbelief on her face, as she shook her head. Bradon and Brennen had talked, had prayed, and then Brennen had left, to return with fresh mugs of coffee for them and a bottle of juice for Ennis.

"I did no such thing!" Ennis was adamant that she had not asked Bradon to marry her.

"But, you did. Brennen heard you. And you asked to have the wedding today."

"No, I didn't!" She stared at him as he continued to shake his head, before she turned to appeal to Brennen. "Tell me I didn't, Brennen."

"Sorry, Ennis. You did. You took Bradon aback, I think. He wasn't expecting that." Brennen was having great difficulty containing his mirth.

Her head back, Ennis groaned. "And I can't take it back, can I?"

Bradon was laughing himself at this point. "No, you can't. And I accept. So, I guess we're engaged." He laughed harder at the glare she shot him. "It's okay, Ennis. I'll let you off the hook, if that's what you want."

Brennen shook his head at the two, seeing the concern lurking in Bradon's eyes before he glanced at Ennis. His head tilted as he studied her, seeing something on her face that didn't go with their conversation at present.

"Ennis?" When she didn't respond, Brennen spoke again, raising his voice just slightly.

Ennis jumped, then stared at Brennen. "Brennen?"

"Ennis? Where were you just now? You weren't here in the lobby with us."

"No, I wasn't. I was…." Her voice died away. "I'm not sure. I can remember seeing Jason heading my way and I ran and hid. He searched for me. Now, where was it?" She shifted in Bradon's arm, her hands clutching at his. "I can see him so clearly. See the hatred and malice on his face. Why did he hate me? That's what I don't get."

"I would say it's because you kept escaping him and then ran, staying as far away from him as you could. You kept your family safe by doing so." Breck sat down into another chair, drawing all their eyes to him as he spoke.

"Is that why? I always wondered. I thought it was me."

"In a sense, it was. He wanted you, for reasons that Dallas and his team are just uncovering. No, I'll let him tell you. All he said was that it wasn't pretty, and he was glad the man was dead. But we still have to watch you carefully, until we find the ones behind him."

"He wasn't working on his own?" Ennis spoke quietly, a frown on her face. "How do the Russells fit in them? He's related to them. I spoke with Mom and she confirmed that."

"Dallas has managed to get that. What else has your mother indicated?" Breck was searching for any little thing that could solve this mystery.

"She didn't say much." Ennis stared at Breck. "I just wish I had lived in another town."

"That didn't happen. Now, what did you just remember?" Breck grinned at her.

"I'm not sure if it's something I actually remember that happened or have been told." She paused, her hands rubbing together. "It's Tim Russell. Did you know there are three? Tim, Tom and Tam. They all look a lot alike. I think it was Tam that hung around with Jason. They were close to an age. Jason was about five years older than me. What did they do?"

Breck shook his head. "I didn't know that. I'm not sure that Dallas has made that connection." Breck has his phone out and was sending a text off to Dallas. He stared down at his phone before he looked up at Ennis. "He didn't have that connection. How do you do this?"

"Do what? Make the connections? It's called living in a small town all my life." She sighed as she leaned back. "What else can I tell you? The rumours were there that the three lived life on the edge of right and wrong. Tom actually is in prison right now, convicted of manslaughter in a drug deal gone wrong. Tim is working for the mayor here, but I doubt he got that on his own. He was known to do a little blackmailing." She sighed. "The mayor's wife? Connected to the Russells. We were all surprised that he got in as mayor, given her history."

"That bad?" At her nod, Brennen shared a look with the other two men. "That gives us a new line to trace. And I think one of the guys already had that thought."

"You're ahead of me, then. Thank you for that. I wish I had more information."

"We've talked to your parents, to Evan, to others in your town. There is a lot of fear out there, but what happened to you? And to Bradon? That has changed how the people feel about them. They are tired of living in fear, of not being free to go about their lives. They wanted us to thank you."

Ennis nodded once more, watching as Breck stood and excused himself. She studied Brennen.

"Don't you have to be somewhere?"

Brennen and Bradon grinned at her even as Brennen shook his head.

"Not right at the moment. I'm waiting to hear the wedding plans."

Ennis groaned and buried her head against Bradon. "I'll never live that down, now will I?"

Bradon just hugged her tighter, his mirth-filled eyes on Brennen, before they raised past him, and his arms tightened on Ennis, even as Brennen caught his look and moved to rise, his body flying forward to lie on the floor, sent there by the vicious blow to the back of his head.

Ennis screamed, her scream echoing through the lobby, even as Bradon rose and pulled her with him away from the men. He stopped suddenly as he felt the gun barrel poking him in the back, not letting go of Ennis. She shook, fear for Bradon coursing through her, even as she glanced down at Brennen.

Please, Lord, let him be alive. Get Bradon out of here somehow. I don't care about me. She screamed again as she was torn from Bradon's arms, a hard grip on her wrist pulling her away from him. She struggled to escape, managing to do that, hearing Bradon's shout for her to run. She ran, her feet slipping on the hardwood floor, before she was tackled and taken to the same floor. She struggled once more, a flying hand catching her assailant in the face and releasing her. She scrambled to her feet, running from the area until a hard blow to her knee sent her facedown to the floor, her hand reaching for the area, sobs of fear and pain forced from her.

Ennis didn't hear the struggle that Bradon was putting up, seeking to release himself, and get to her. She didn't see him forced from the building and into a waiting vehicle, the doors slamming behind him, and then the vehicle racing away.

The men who had been in the boardroom looked up, startled, as they heard Ennis scream and then, on their feet, ran for the door, wrenching it open and racing towards the lobby. Brady and Doc were on their knees beside Ennis, even as some of the others ran for the outside. Brady was on his feet, moving towards Brennen as Blair called for him.

"What happened here?" Barnabas stood, staring between the two, and then looking around. "Where's Bradon?"

Doc shot him a glance. "Ennis said men appeared, knocked Brennen down, and then Bradon told her to run. She doesn't know what hit her or where he is."

Burnie's sudden yell from the security desk had Barnabas heading that way. He stared down at the security guard, and then up at the destroyed equipment.

"They did a number on that stuff, Barnabas. Mick's alive but he needs help."

“I can see that.” Barnabas sighed as he pulled out his phone. “We just can’t catch a break, can we?” He walked back towards Brennen, finding him sitting up, as Brady looked him over. “Brady, Mick needs you. He’s down.”

Brady shot him a glance and then nodded. “Brennen seems to be fine, but we’ll know more once he’s assessed. Any word on Bradon?”

Buckley spoke. “It seems they took him with them. No sign of him around. We can see scuff marks on the sidewalk where it looks as if he was struggling to get away.” He looked around. “How did they do it?”

“They took out Mick, and the security equipment at the same time. I would suspect Bradon or Brennen saw them coming and tried to intervene.”

“I would say Bradon. Brennen was sitting with his back to the hallways when I walked by thirty minutes ago.” Buckley rubbed at his face, his eyes going to Ennis. “How is she?”

Doc had approached, leaving Ennis in the care of Benen and Baird for a moment, as he looked towards Benen. “Her knee is damaged. How, I’m not sure? She’s in too much pain to think clearly. Why did this have to happen? Hasn’t she had enough? And I have no idea how bad it is.”

“I know, Doc. We all know that.” Breck spoke from beside him, his hand on the older man’s shoulder. “Ride with her when they go. Brady’s gone to assess Mick.”

“Mick?” Doc spun, held in place by Breck’s hand.

“They knocked him out, surprised him, I would think.” Breck’s hand dropped from Doc’s shoulder as he moved towards the security desk.

“Okay, Barnabas. Who goes with who?” Breck looked around at the gathering men, the ladies watching from near the elevators, their arms around one another.

“Brady with Mick. Doc with Ennis. Some of you can head in. The rest, I want working on this. Call your employers. For now, you’re here, in this building, or out searching. We meet for prayer at seven in the morning and again at seven in the evening.” He turned, searching. “Buckley, tomorrow’s Sunday, but get the prayer chain working.”

Buckley nodded and was away to the other side of the lobby, watching as the emergency vehicles approached. He sighed to himself. No one needed this right now, did they, Lord? But You are in control. We just need to remember that. Keep our friend, Bradon, safe, and heal both Ennis and Mick and Brennen. This is hurting our guys, Lord. This isn’t the first time one of them have been taken from this very land, but not from inside the building itself.  These people are getting bolder and bolder all the time.

Later that day, Meg stood at her daughter's bedside, once more, watching as Ennis moved restlessly. She knew Ian and Evan were around. They had been in with her but left to find Barnabas or Breck or Dallas or even Will. They wanted to know exactly what had happened to Ennis. And just where was Bradon? She had been looking for him to find Ennis, but he had not appeared.

Meg turned as she heard the door, to find Ian walking towards her, a stern, shuttered look on his face.

"Ian?'' When he didn't answer, she reached to grip his arm, even as his eyes studied his daughter and then the equipment surrounding her.

"Meg? How is she?"

"Lucky. There was some damage. Doc explained it as tears to the cartilage and tendons. They're waiting to do surgery, wanting to see how the knee repairs itself." She shot a glance back at the door before turning Ian to face her. "Ian? What's going on? How did this happen? And where's Bradon?"

"Bradon? They're not sure." Ian's hand reached out to touch his daughter's, stilling her movement.

"What do you mean? They're not sure? Isn't he here?" Meg spun to stare at the door.

"No, he's not. He's disappeared. At the time Ennis was hurt."

"And just how was she hurt? I can't get anyone to tell me."

"She was running from some men who appeared in the building lobby. I guess she and Bradon and Brennen were talking. Brennen was knocked out, Bradon yelled for her to run. She had a bit of a scuffle with her attacker and in trying to get away was hurt. Bradon seems to have been kidnapped."

"Kidnapped?" Meg's voice rose as she said the word, her mouth clamping closed as she finished. "Brennen? Is he okay?"

"He has a headache and is very angry. Somehow, the men who appeared took down Mick, the security person on duty today, destroyed the equipment, and then made their escape." He looked back down at Ennis, before turning to Meg, sweeping her into a hug, feeling the sobs shaking her body, a prayer rising within him, a prayers without words that he knew would be heard.

Evan stood for a moment, watching his parents, his heart hurting for them. He walked quietly to stand at the foot of the bed, watching Ennis, seeing her eyes flickering before he moved up beside her.

"Evan?"  His mother's voice brought his head around and he reached to hug her.

"Mom?  What's the word?"

"No surgery as yet.  They're waiting to see how it does.  Surgery is a possibility, but she'll not be bearing weight on that foot for months."  Meg watched Evan closely, seeing a small smile he couldn't hide.  "Evan?"

"They didn't tell you?"

"Who didn't tell us what?"  Meg shared a look with Ian, worry in her heart.

"Apparently, Ennis asked Bradon to marry her.  And today.  But then, again, she was almost asleep when she did that."

"She didn't, did she?"  Her mother was dismayed.  "Not another one of her almost asleep requests.  We should have warned Bradon."

Evan just shook his head.  "Apparently, he agreed.  These two are in love, Mom.  I just don't know how much they know that, or where they're heading."

Ian sighed, having had a heart to heart talk with Bradon.  "Bradon loves her, he's told me that, but he won't go any further with it until this is over, and she's had a chance to live as a free woman, he said.  He seems to think she needs some time just to be her, without something hanging over her head."

"And that she does."

Ennis roused as she heard her family, her eyes finally staying open, groaning as she moved.  "Mom?  Dad?  Evan?  Where am I?"

"You've been hurt, Ennis.  You're in the hospital."  Meg's hand rested on her daughter's head.

"I am?  What did I do?  Never mind.  I don't want to know."  She slept again, leaving her brother with a grin on his face, that changed to a frown as he saw Dallas and Barnabas approaching through the opened door.

"Barnabas? Dallas?" Ian turned, watching them closely. "You're here. Something is up."

"Yes, there is." Dallas paused, assessing them and then Ennis. "How is she?"

"She was awake briefly, but is out again." Ian studied them. "You're not here for just that."

Dallas sighed, his eyes meeting Barnabas. "No, we're not. We have to put all of you under protection now. Barnabas has suggested his building." Dallas' hand went up. "We know. It was breached today, but for the foreseeable future, all doors will be locked, and he has brought in more security. That team is hurting, not just because one of their men was hurt, but because Ennis and Brennen were as well and because Bradon disappeared."

Ian nodded. "It makes sense, but Evan and I still have to work. We can't just walk away from that."

"We know. We're making arrangements to transport you both back and forth. In fact, one of the teams will take you back, Ian, to your place, and Evan to yours to gather some belongings for you all." He nodded at Ennis. "Doc has agreed that she should be in the infirmary there. It will work. He's taking a leave from here for now and Anna is a retired nurse. We'll make do."

"We need to do more than that, Dallas. This is twice Ennis has been hurt this bad. And Bradon? Is he still alive even?"

"He will be, Ian." Barnabas spoke up. "They want him alive to get to her. They took him with that thought in mind, more than likely. We'll receive a ransom note, of sorts, directed at her, that will want to make an exchange."

"Exchange?" Ian was puzzled for a moment. "You mean, Bradon for Ennis?"

"That is exactly what I mean." Dallas stared at the floor for a moment, before he looked up, a bleak look on his face. "I can't tell you how sorry I am this happened. I was out there this morning, talking to them all, finding out what information they had I could use. Will was there. Whoever it has been, had to have been watching. We have officers searching the area right now."

"You won't find him out there." Evan walked over to stand in front of Dallas. "I have an idea."

"You do? Care to share?"

Evan shot a look back at his sister. "Sure. Just not in here. I don't want Ennis to wake up and hear us."

Dallas nodded, even as he followed Evan out of the room, listening closely as Evan spoke, shaking his head at times, before he turned and walked away, walking back rapidly, his hand out to pull Evan with him, beckoning to Breck and Brady as they watched the two men.

His head spinning from the blows he had taken, Bradon lost his balance, his hands and knees hitting the floor of the room he had been shoved into. He had stayed like that for a few moments, his head hanging down, trying to get his balance back, before he raised his head and then sat back on his heels. He looked around, surprised at the cleanliness and tidiness of the room.

Rising to his feet, Bradon searched the room, not finding anything he could use to protect himself, but also finding the door to the hall locked. He paced, opening the doors, finding a huge walk-in closet and then an ensuite. He stopped there to reach for a cloth he wrung out under warm water and swiped across his face.

He turned from there to feel along the windows, staring out them at the well manicured lawns, the tidy buildings around the yard, the neat driveway that wound through the area. Where was he?

Bradon refused to turn as he heard the door open and then the sounds of a tray being set down. He peeked at his watch, surprised to see how late it had gotten to be. They must have driven him around for ages, but for how long, he wasn't sure. He turned to contemplate the door and then walked over to study the tray. Supper, he decided, lifting the cover off the plate, surprise at the meal set there. He sighed, before he reached for a chair. Bradon decided he needed to eat, needed to keep his strength up.

Bradon finally rose, walking back to stare out the window again, seeing the sun setting, throwing out the pink and purple and red shafts of light. He finally drew the drapes and turned to the bed, sitting on the side of it before laying down, and pulling the blankets over him. His eyes closed, as he prayed. He had no idea where Ennis was, how she was. He had heard her scream and then sobs of pain before the men had wrestled him out of the door and into the vehicle, where he was shoved to the floor and a blanket thrown over him. Bradon worried about Brennen, not sure how hurt he had been.

He was puzzled. How did the men get into the lobby? They should not have make it past Mick. Then, he sighed, knowing that Mick must have been hurt. He prayed for his friends, but also for his lady, a slight smile cracking through the grimness on his face as he remembered her request and then her denial. Ennis, we really do need to talk, don't we, sweetheart?

Bradon slept, not hearing the door open or the tray removed after the man had entered on silent feet and stood over him, nodding that the sedative in the food had worked. He hadn't liked that when he was told it had been done. He knew the man lying in front of him. Bradon. He worked for Barnabas, he knew. The man's gaze lifted as he stared in front of him and then glanced back at the door before looking down at Bradon. He had heard bits and pieces of the conversation around him, being ignored as he usually was. Somehow, he had to get Bradon out of there and he would.

A week passed like this for Bradon, alone in the room, only seeing the man's shadow as he brought in and then removed the trays of food. He felt sleepy all the time, almost groggy, not realizing he was being sedated. Bradon wondered when he would be asked the questions he thought he should be, or be taken out and killed. That he knew was a real possibility. He prayed for his love, for her family, for his friends. He didn't really care about himself anymore. He didn't think he would be walking away alive.

His hands on the window frame, Bradon stood one afternoon, once more watching the dusk coming in, swaying as he stood, unsteady on his feet. He turned to head for the bed, knowing he needed to lie down, but his eyes closed and he slipped to the floor, not hearing the thud his body made, not feeling as his head hit hard on the rug overlaying the hardwood floor.

The man dropped the tray to the table and hurried to Bradon's side, his hands feeling for a pulse. He sat back on his heels, his eyes on Bradon, before he turned to the open door. He was alone that late afternoon. Now was the time to make his escape and take Bradon with him. He had nothing of his own that he really cared about. What little he did care about, he carried in his pocket. He pulled Bradon to his feet, and over his shoulder, heading for the stairs and the outside. Unlocking his vehicle, he gently set Bradon on the seat, securing the seatbelt before he rushed to slide into the driver's seat, carefully searching for anyone watching. He would head out the back way, he thought. That was how the hired people always came and went. They would not be able to track him, at least, he didn't think so.

They were not there to hear the curses and blame when the owner of the house found the empty room, the forgotten tray sitting on the table by the door. The man spun, orders flying from his mouth along with the spittle of his rage. The employees or hirelings or whatever you wanted to call them ran to do his bidding. Some ran, just to escape. They had had enough. The talk among those few was that he was mad, that he would hurt Ennis even more that she had been.  They hadn't liked the fact they were now accessories to kidnapping.  They had all agreed that they would find some way to escape his clutches and make their way to the authorities.  Now seemed to be the right time to do that.

The birds and night creatures gradually crept forth from their hiding spaces, filling the night with their sound, covering the thundering footsteps and curses from inside the house.  He was on his own for the moment and rage filled him.  She would pay, he declared, and so would he.

Ennis shifted on the couch she was sitting on. She was back in her suite at the building, Doc having moved her to the infirmary for a few days before he let her move home. She knew Anna was around somewhere. Ennis had told Anna she could manage, that her Mom would help, but Anna had just given her a look and continued to take care of her. She was grateful, she thought, but she felt like she was putting so many of her friends at risk.

Ian had talked with her, had told her what had happened as far as they could determine. She had watched him, nodded, said it was about what she had expected, and then thumped away on her crutches, leaving her father staring after her, not sure if she really understand what risk she was still at, or if she even cared.

Evan had approached her that morning, sitting with her, not saying anything. Ennis appreciated that about her brother, that he could be quiet with her when she needed that.

He had finally turned to her, a twinkle in his eye. "Did you really ask Bradon that?"

Her brow furrowed as she tried to remember. "Ask him what? Evan, what are you talking about?"

"Brennen said you were almost asleep and then suddenly just asked Bradon to marry you. When he agreed, you asked it be that day." Evan was openly grinning at his sister by this point.

"I did no such thing!" She stared at her brother, horrified at what he was saying. "Evan! I didn't do that!"

Evan kept grinning at her even as he shook his head. "But, you see, you did. Brennen heard you. And Bradon agreed."

Ennis' head went back as she stared at the ceiling, before her eyes slid shut. "I did it again, didn't I? Almost asleep and making a request. How many times have I done that over the years?"

Evan simply shook his head. "I have no idea. Usually it's something simple or something easy for us to get for you. This is a tough one, you know."

Ennis nodded. "I know. I have no idea what I was thinking."

"That you love him and that you know he loves you. You are a couple, whether you agree or not, sis." Evan sat forward, his eyes on his clasped hands. "Did you really mean that?"

"Mean what?" Ennis watched her brother. "Oh! That! Asking him to marry me?" She shrugged. "I guess. I usually do when I make those requests. I haven't done that in a long time."

"No, you haven't. In fact, I don't think you've done that since before you moved away. It's usually when you are under stress that this happens. Ennis, what aren't you telling us?" Evan twisted his neck so he could watch his sister. "What is it, sis? There has to be something."

Ennis sighed. "I think there is. Did you see that old briefcase I used to use in high school?"

"I did." Evan was on his feet, moving quickly to where she had set up her office, and then was back, the briefcase in his hands to give to her. He watched as she sat, her own hands resting on its soft sides. "Ennis? What is it? Come on, tell me. You used to tell me a lot, but not everything. I would have stopped this monster."

"I know. That's why I didn't tell you. He would have killed you or had his friends do that." She studied her brother. "I couldn't let them do that to you."

"I wish you had told me." He watched her closely for a moment, before he nodded at the briefcase. "What's in there?"

"I can't rightly remember. I think....I don't know." She reached to open it, stopping as Evan's hands covered her, not seeing Branigan and Baird coming in and sitting silently near her, or Dallas stepping in behind. Barnabas had stopped in the kitchen to have a word with Ian.

"We need to pray first, sis. Let's pray. I fear for you and what you have in there." Evan watched as her face whitened and then hardened into resolve.

"Please, Evan. Please pray that this is over and Bradon is back with his friends, unharmed."

She jumped as she heard the other men take up the prayer, followed by her father. She hadn't realized so many had gathered around her. She had felt her mother's arm around her as Evan had prayed. Ennis looked up, tears sparkling in her eyes as they finished, a silent thank you on her lips.

Ennis stared down once more at the briefcase before she spoke. "Dallas? Any word?"

"No, I'm sorry, Ennis. We have a lead we are tracking but nothing yet. I wish I did have news for you."

She simply nodded as she reached to unbuckle the briefcase, pausing before she folded back the flap, and then she opened the briefcase, staring inside, pausing once more before she continued to reach her hand inside, pulling out the papers inside before her hand felt around inside. She pulled out the small packet that had hidden itself in the lining, a frown on her face, before it cleared.

Ennis looked up at Barnabas. "I'm sorry, Barnabas. I'm so sorry."

He frowned. "Why are you apologizing, Ennis?"

She held up the packet. "I had this. I had forgotten about it. It is proof, I think, of what Jason had been involved in. I think it also lists people he worked with. I'm sorry. If I had remembered, then maybe Bradon wouldn't have been hurt."

"I don't think it would have mattered, Ennis." Dallas spoke up. "There is just so much we are uncovering about him. All I can say is I am thankful God kept you out of his hands."

Ennis nodded. "I know only too well what he intended. He told me, many times. I had forgotten some of it, burying it deep inside me. I never wanted Mom and Dad to know. And Evan?" She turned to her brother, tears on her cheeks. "He would have killed you if you had gone after him."

"You told me that, sis. And I have no doubt he would have tried." Evan reached to grip her hand, finding hers ice cold. "What is in that packet?"

She turned it over and over and then handed it to him. "Here. You can open it." She gathered up the papers and turned to Branigan. "Here, you take these. Copy them for Dallas. I tried to document everything I knew, every time he approached me, every time I got a card or a letter or a photo."

Branigan studied her carefully before he looked down at the sheaf of papers, covered in her tidy handwriting. "All this?"

She nodded. "All that. Maybe, there is something in there." She sat back, Meg's arm around her, even as they heard a noise at the door, Barnabas rising to answer it, a surprised tone to his voice that brought the men to their feet.

Barnabas reached out a hand, gripping Bradon's upper arm in his hand, even as he stared past him at the man standing there. He frowned, thinking that he knew the man, before Dallas was there beside him. The man was ushered in, hesitation in his manner, even as Barnabas led Bradon to the living room, finding Ennis' eyes on Bradon, shock on her face.

Ennis stood, her eyes on Bradon as he wavered in the living room door way, her brother's arm helping her to balance. Somehow, Bradon found her, gathering her close, before Evan shoved them both down onto the couch. Bradon landed heavily, taking Ennis with him, not hearing her muffled groan of pain as the movement jarred her knee. Evan watched with sympathy before he helped her to shift her body to a more comfortable position, her legs up on the couch, a pillow tucked under her injured one.

Quiet conversation surrounded them before Dallas sat near them, his mouth open to speak, snapping it closed. He turned to Barnabas, catching the look on his face before he settled back. Ennis had her head turned, watching Bradon, seeing how difficult a time he had been through, just by his face.

Dallas finally spoke, after studying Bradon, watching as he took the mug of coffee with thanks. Ennis frowned, her eyes tracking between Bradon, Dallas, and the man who had returned Bradon to her. She caught the man's slight shake of his head before she sighed to herself. Okay, now what, Lord, she thought. Obviously, something is going on here I don't know or understand. But You do.

His eyes on Ennis, Barnabas spoke. "Bradon? Talk to us. Tell us what happened."

Bradon just shook his head, his eyes heavy. "I really don't know, Barnabas. All I can remember is trying to get back to Ennis before I was dragged outside and shoved down into a vehicle. A blanket covered me. They drove around for ages, I suspect, because when I was shoved into a room, it was late afternoon or early evening." He paused, gathering his thoughts, fatigue making his thought processes difficult to understand. "They never took me from that room, never asked for anything. Absolutely nothing. I got my meals, but the supper meal must have been drugged. I barely remember finishing those meals before I collapsed and slept." His eyes raised to the man who had freed him. "Thank you. You don't seem to fit with them."

The man shook his head. "I don't. I was put there for a reason, God only knows that it must have been for you. I don't know much about what they were up to. I was only the low man in the group. They talked some around me, but not a whole lot. I never saw the owner of the house, but I would say he's someone with money."

Bradon nodded, then wondered why he had done that, the headache spreading behind his eyes. "I think you're right. The room I was in was decorated tastefully, shall we say?" His head went down on Ennis' and he slept, not hearing Doc approach, or hear the men moving away.

Meg gently tucked a blanket over Bradon, waiting as Ennis moved to sit up, Bradon's arm tightening around her. Ennis turned her head to study him, seeing his face relaxing as he slept, knowing he was free once more.

"Mom?"

"He's not letting you go, is he, dear?" Meg's voice held amusement. "You two need to come to an understanding." She turned as she heard a snicker from Evan.

Ennis tried to hold back her groan. "I think we already did, Mom. I just didn't know it." She glared at her brother. "Evan, shut up."

Meg stared at Evan, and then turned back to Ennis, seeing her daughter burying her head in her hands. A trace of humour showed in her voice as she spoke.

"Ennis? What did you do?" She waited, not hearing Ennis speak, but hearing the snickers from Evan. "Ennis? You didn't?"

Ennis nodded, her eyes on Bradon. "Apparently, I did, Mom, and don't remember. Apparently, he said yes."

"Oh, Ennis! Not another of your requests when you're almost asleep?"

"It was, Mom." She turned back to her mother. "And I wanted to marry him that day, from what I'm told."

"Ennis, my dear!" Meg sat on the coffee table, reaching for her daughter's hands. "You have not done that in years. It only comes out when you are really stressed." Her head bowed and she prayed for her daughter.

Shaking his head, Ian pointed to the outside door, beckoning Dallas and Barnabas with him, nodding at Doc as he passed them to enter the apartment. He stood, a hand rubbing at his face, his thoughts on his daughter's words and then Meg's.

"Is that true?" Dallas' voice held a bit of awe at Ennis' admission.

Ian nodded. "More than likely. Evan talked to me. Apparently, she asked Bradon to marry her, when he said yes, asked that it be that day. She doesn't remember doing that." He sighed, his arms crossing over his chest. "She has a history of doing that, of asking things just as she's almost asleep. Although, it's always been small things and things we can easily accommodate for her. This, this is something new."

"Stress will have done it. Bradon makes her feel safe, I would gather." Barnabas shook his head, a small grin on his face. "Brennen had mentioned it to me."

"He did? I didn't realize he had heard." Ian was surprised.

"He was there. Now, where do we go, Dallas?"

Dallas had been listening to the two men, but his attention had been directed at the apartment door. "First, I take Bradon's rescuer down town and have a talk with him. Bradon's in no condition right now to give more of a statement than he has." He looked up as the door opened and Doc appeared.

"Doc?" Barnabas' voice was quiet but they could hear the concern in it.

"He's still sleeping. He likely will for a while. From what the man said, the cook always put a drug in his supper. Bradon may not have realized what was happening, or else he didn't care."

"Probably both, Doc. I don't think he expected to come home." Barnabas turned and walked away, deep in thought, heading for the boardroom and the men gathered there. They needed to find these people and fast, he thought. It will not go well for Bradon just to have disappeared. And how did they keep his presence quiet? He sighed at that, knowing Bradon would not be agreeable to just that plan.

The men were scattered through the room, deep in their work, all looking up as Barnabas entered, closing the door behind him, and just standing, his eyes on the floor.

"Barnabas?" Burnie spoke for them, their eyes meeting in puzzlement. "What's going on?"

Barnabas looked up. "Bradon's home. One of his captors just walked in with him." He waited as the men reacted, sounds of surprise and joy in the room, before he continued. "Thing is, he was sedated, we think, the whole time. He doesn't remember a lot."

"And now we need to hide him? Is that what you're saying?" Brandon spoke up.

"He'll never go for that." This from Brennen. "Where is he?"

"Right now, he's sound asleep on Ennis' couch."

"And not letting go of her, I suspect?" Brennen grinned. "Do we have a wedding to arrange?"

Barnabas' grin cracked through the grimness on his face. "I have no idea. It's up to them to tell us. Right now, we just need to solve this. Where do we stand? Dallas has taken Bradon's rescuer down town to talk to."

"How did he get here?" Brady spoke from where he stood at the printer.

"His rescuer said he just walked out with him and drove away. They were the only ones at the house at that particular time."

"God!" Buckley's smile lit up his face.

"That's it, Buckley. God brought him back. Now, God will lead us to the answers." Burnie buried himself back into the notes from the diary, wanting to finish that day. He had found a trace of something, and had pulled Ennis' notes she had handed Branigan to compare.

Breck walked over to stand beside Barnabas, his shoulder against the wall, watching the men as they once more buried themselves into their work.

"How is he really, Barnabas? What kind of help will we need to find for him?"

Barnabas shrugged, his eyes on the floor, deep in thought. "Right now, Doc has looked him over. He'll do a better assessment when he's awake. Dallas will be back around, and I'm sure Will may make it out at some point.  I would like to see him talk to someone, but I doubt he'll remember a lot.  For now, he's where he needs to be, with Ennis."

"And how is Ennis?"

Barnabas shook his head.  "I have no idea.  Did you know she had a habit of making requests like that?  Apparently she hasn't in a while, and nothing that major."

Breck stared at him for a moment before he smiled.  "And this is a major one.  I can see Bradon teasing her about that for years to come."

"So can I.  The thing of it is?  I don't know if they'll stay together."  Barnabas sighed.  "Didn't we just go through this with Blair and Devaney?"

"We did, but theirs was totally different from this."  Breck turned to the door.  "I'll head up there, and then talk to security to see what we need to do."  He stopped, his hand on the doorknob.  "And I can tell you this.  Neither one will want to be hidden away.  They'll be out there, on their own if necessary, to draw out the culprits."

"That's what I'm afraid of, Breck.  That they will do just that."

———

Staring at Ian, Bradon finally just shook his head. He could not just marry Ennis, even though she had asked him, and he had agreed. He turned his head to stare towards the living room before he walked across the kitchen, his socked feet quiet on the floor, and reached for the coffee pot, to stand hands resting against the counter, not quite sure what he wanted.

Ian watched with compassion as Bradon moved in almost slow motion before he reached out a hand, tugging him from the kitchen, and hand on his back, directing to the bathroom.

"Get cleaned up, Bradon. I know you'll welcome a shower. Breck was through your place and brought some clean clothes for you. For some reason, he didn't think you would want to leave my daughter's side." He had a grin on his face that reminded Bradon of Evan.

Bradon shook his head. "A shower and clean clothes sound good. There was a shower where I was but I refused to use it. I guess I was stupid not to." He swayed for a moment, grabbing ahold of the door to keep his balance.

"No, I don't expect you did." Ian watched Bradon closely. "Are we needing to have a chat, Bradon?"

Bradon turned carefully, his eyes on the older man, before he sighed and nodded. "I guess we do. I love Ennis more than I thought I could love anyone." He grinned suddenly, the sternness and fatigue disappearing. "I guess you heard what she asked of me."

Ian gave a low laugh. "I did. Evan has kept it quiet, but I am sure the men all know. They won't tell a soul, I know that much. She'll be teased but it will be without malice." He paused, his eyes on the floor for a moment, before he raised them to study Bradon. "Go. Get cleaned up. I'll make you some breakfast and then you'll need to sleep again. Ennis finally headed to bed early this morning. We had to make her leave you."

"You did?" Bradon shook his head. "Thank you, Ian. You have raised a fine daughter who is caring and compassionate. I want this over for her and for you." He closed the door, standing with hands on the vanity, staring at his image in the mirror. Lord, I know what I want. But it's what You want that matters. Help us to help her overcome what she's faced for years.

Bradon finally pushed away his plate, thanking Ian for the food, before he cradled his mug in his hands. He felt somewhat more awake but was still groggy to some extent. Whatever they had given him over the past week was still affecting him. He knew from Ian that Dallas planned to stop by that morning, as early as he could, to get his statement. He also knew from Breck that the men were still hard at work, pulling information from the copy of Jason's diary and from the notes Ennis had handed them. It would take time, but he was reassured that they were making progress, and that progress was being passed on to Dallas, who just stood and stared at them whenever they handed him something new.

Ian stood for a moment as he heard movement from down the hall, watching as Ennis headed his way, her crutches thumping along the floor as she did. His heart was saddened for his girl, knowing that the injury may curtail what she loved best, to bike, to run, or just go for a long walk. He had talked with Doc in general and that talk had not gone the way he would have liked.

"Dad?" Ennis paused for a moment. "You're here?"

"Your Mom and I have been all night. She's gone home to get some sleep. I'll do that when she's back." He tilted his head to watch the emotions playing across her face. His next words were quiet enough that only she could hear him. "Ennis? What are you thinking?"

She shrugged. "I have no idea, Dad, other than being thankful Bradon is back, angry that he was taken, angry that I'm hurt, and anxious about what is happening." She gave a small smile. "Is that enough?"

Ian shook his head. "It is for now." He pointed at the kitchen. "Bradon's up, had a shower, and has eaten. We've talked, the two of us. He loves you, you do know that?"

Ennis nodded. "I do, Dad. I thought I had ruined it asking what I did."

Her father grinned at her. "Not at all. He just wishes it had been him doing the asking, but he wasn't sure enough of you to do that. He's still learning how to read you."

"Is that what you call it?" Balancing the crutches against her, she reached to hug her father. "And what decision did the two of you make for me?"

"None. It's your decision, Ennis. Yours and Bradon's." He gave a low laugh. "I hear tell the fellows are thinking an early wedding."

Ennis shook her head. "Not with this hanging over us, Dad. And Bradon wants me to have some time where I can enjoy life like that, to experience life as a young woman shoul.  At least, that's what he has said to me."

"And he's right.  You're overcoming this.  I can see that.  God is blessing you with many new friends, all of whom want to help you."  He stepped back, pointing to the kitchen.  "Go on.  Find your fellow.  He's waiting for you."

Bradon stood as she entered, his eyes searching her face, before he just swept her close to him.  They finally sat, quiet conversation between them, not talking of what had happened, talking instead of what their hopes and dreams had been as youths and what they were now.  Their talk drifted to different scripture verses they loved, surprised to find they shared so many.

Dallas stopped to watch them before he approached the table, his portfolio going down on the wooden table top.  He reached to pour himself a cup of coffee before he sat, his eyes studying the two, finding them watching him.

"Dallas?"  Bradon finally spoke.

"Bradon?  We'll need to get your statement today.  Now, if possible.  Then, we'll need to talk."

Bradon shrugged.  "Okay."  He watched as Ennis stood, reached for her crutches, and walked away.

"Did she just do that?"  He asked of Dallas.

"She did.  She needed to.  She can't be here when you give your statement."  Dallas reached to open his laptop, setting up a video camera, and then nodding at Bradon.  "Whenever you're ready, we'll start."

———

Dallas finally sat back, his eyes thoughtful, before he reached to print Bradon's statement, handing it to him with instructions to read it over, make any changes, initial them and then sign it. He waited, seeing the fatigue weighing Bradon down and then rose, heading to find Ennis.

She was standing, balancing on her crutches, as she stared out the living room window. She turned, her eyes going past Dallas to the kitchen, before she looked at him.

"Dallas?"

"He's done. Just proofreading it for me." Dallas' head tilted as he studied Ennis. "How are you, Ennis?"

She shrugged. "I have no idea. Everyone keeps asking me that."

"And they will. They're concerned." He hesitated, then spoke. "I need to talk with you both. Can you come back to the kitchen, or no." He pointed to the couch. "Sit. Doc tells me that you need to elevate that leg as much as possible." He watched as she seated herself, helping to settle the pillow under her knee. "Now, Bradon and I will be right back."

Bradon appeared in the doorway, before he headed for Ennis, shifting her enough that he could sit beside her, then reaching to hand her the mug of tea he had made. Dallas returned with his notes and his own refreshed cup of coffee before he sat, his eyes down, a prayer in his heart.

"Okay, Dallas?" Ennis' voice was soft, hesitant, not like hers at all. "Where do we stand? I know you and your fellow detectives have been busy with our case as well as many others. Will has stressed that. And I know Bradon's friends have been busy as well."

"That we have, Ennis. That we have." His eyes found hers, a look in his that she could not read. "I can only say how sorry I am you had to face him on your own."

She shrugged. "It's in the past. He can't hurt me anymore. But his friends and whoever it is that was behind him can."

"Talk to me, Ennis. I know there are things that you have not said to anyone."

Staring at him, Ennis finally nodded. "There are. He was a brutal, vindictive, sadistic man. No one knows what he threatened me with. How he threatened my family.  How he threatened to harm anyone if I sought help." Her face had whitened at the memories.

"Why don't you just talk, Ennis?  I'll make notes.  Then, when you're ready, we'll discuss them.  I don't think you'll say anything that will surprise me." His eyes lifted to watch Bradon, whose own eyes were on Ennis. "Now, do you want Bradon to leave?"

Ennis' face turned to Bradon, seeing in his eyes his love for her, his acceptance of what she might say, his trust and confidence in her, and shook her head. "No, he can stay.  This is just so hard."

Bradon's voice broke through the silence that ensued, raising a prayer for strength and courage for his lady, wisdom for Dallas, and an end to it all finally for her.

Ennis' hands tightened on Bradon's.  "It's hard, you know.  I've buried it so deep, that it hurts to bring it out.  But I know I need to.  And the hurt will heal, but I'll never be the one I was before this all started.

"It started, I guess, when I was around sixteen, seventeen.  I didn't know he was watching me until he approached me one day.  I ran from him, but he kept coming after me.  I tried to make sure I was never alone, but he somehow managed that at times.  The things he would tell me?  No teenage girl should ever hear them."  She paused, shudders of horror wracking her body, the almost silent tick of the grandfather clock the only thing breaking the silence.

"He tried to get me to do drugs.  When that didn't work, he tried alcohol.  I refused, telling him to leave me alone.  I told him I was going to my parents and to the authorities.  He just laughed, said that wouldn't work, that he would kill them."  She paused, blinking rapidly to clear the tears threatening to overflow.

She looked up at Dallas.  "Do you really want to know what he said?"  At his nod, she sighed.  "I thought you would.  He threatened to make me into a drug addict.  If that didn't work, then he threatened to make me an alcoholic.  He threatened to kidnap me and traffic me.  If that didn't work, he threatened to kill me.  He had all sorts of scenarios on how to do that, including taking me up in a friend's plane and shoving me out."  She bit at her lip, drawing blood at how hard she did that.  "Why would he do that?"

"Evil.  Malice.  Not getting what he wanted."  Dallas looked down for a moment.  "It wasn't you, actually, that he wanted, Ennis.  He told you that but there are deeper reasons.  One of them was revenge on Evan."

"Evan? Why?" Ennis was shocked, and she felt Bradon's arms tighten around her. She raised her head to stare at Dallas and then looked up at Bradon, seeing his love and compassion for her on his face. "I don't understand."

"I talked to Evan. I didn't tell him what I just told you. Apparently, Evan and his friends would make sure the young ladies were safe. He never told you that, I gather. His friends didn't tell him how bad it was for you because they knew he would go after Jason. They didn't want that. I gather they have told him some of it now. I've talked to them. Jason was all what you said and more. We are just so thankful God protected you. You have a lot of memories and feelings and whatnot to overcome, but you are doing just that. Bradon is helping you."

"I will continue to do that, Ennis, no matter what happens. I hope you understand that."

"I do, Bradon. But Dallas, there has to be more than what you're saying."

"There is, Ennis. A lot more." He stood, reaching for their cups. "I'm going to make myself to home, Ennis, and make fresh coffee. We're going to need that. What can I get you?" He walked away, leaving Ennis staring after him before she looked up at Bradon.

"Bradon?"

Bradon's arms tightened around his lady. "That's a lot to take in, Ennis. I thought it would be bad, but nothing like this. You should never have had to live with that."

"I know, but it happened. Now, what do we do? Where do we go with this?"

Dallas stood for a moment, his eyes watching his friends, letting them talk quietly between themselves for a moment.  Lord, this is just so hard.  And how do we keep Evan from feeling as guilty as I know he will?  He loves his sister deeply and would do just about anything, I suspect, to protect her.

Ennis watched Dallas as he walked back into the living room, accepting with a quiet word of thanks the cup of tea he handed her.  Her eyes moved around the room, taking in the soft green of the walls, the light hardwood floors, the colourful rug, the dark brown of the furniture.  She had set some of her knickknacks around, but it still didn't feel like home, she didn't think.  She refused to look at Bradon, even thought she knew he was studying her.

Finally turning back to Dallas, she opened her mouth and then snapped it closed.  She had no idea what she wanted to ask him, and she didn't think she could just come right out and ask who he suspected.  She knew the Russells were involved somehow, just how, she wasn't sure.

"Dallas?  What can you tell us?"  Bradon finally broke the silence, his head tilting as he heard the door open, and then frowned as he saw his friends filing in.  "Guys?"

Branigan shook his head.  "We knew Dallas would be here.  We wanted to sit in on what he has to say, if that's okay with you both."  He watched as Kade moved among the men, heading for Ennis, barely acknowledging Bradon.  He's got a problem there, doesn't he, Lord?  He has to reclaim his dog and I don't know that he will.  Do I see another dog in the family?

"That's fine with me, Branigan."  Ennis frowned at Dallas.  "Okay, Dallas.  Talk.  Tell us where we stand."

There was a moment of shocked silence before the men laughed, knowing Ennis had done that on purpose to try and relieve the stress they were all under.

Dallas shook his head, a smile on his face.  He caught the look on Bradon's face and sensed that Bradon knew what might be coming.

"Ennis?  How well did you know Paul Baker?"

"Paul Baker?  I don't think I know him.  Should I?"

Dallas nodded. "We have found evidence that he was also tracking you. Not for Jason. but for the Russells."

"Why?"

Brandon spoke up, "That is something we wanted to talk to you both about."

"I don't get it." Ennis frowned before her brow cleared and she nodded. "I can remember him. I just forgot or wanted to forget,". She sighed. "Another cousin, I think."

"That's correct, Ennis." Dallas opened the folder he had dropped to the table when he entered. His eyes rested on the photo before he handed it to her. "Do you know who this is?"

Bradon watched as she took the photo, a frown on her face as she looked down and then froze.

"I know this man. I don't know his name. He was always in the background when Jason approached me. Who is he?" She looked up at Dallas, her face white and drawn. "Is he the one behind it all? He looks about our age."

"He is, Ennis." Dallas paused, biting his lip, uncertainly in his manner. He didn't know how to tell Ennis who this was.

"Dallas?" Bradon's voice caught at his attention, and he looked over at him, seeing the concern on his face. "Who is it?"

Ennis was shaking enough that the other men were concerned. She didn't know her parents and Anna were standing just inside the kitchen doorway, their eyes on the group scattered  throughout the living room. Meg wanted to go to her daughter, but knew Ennis would not want that. Ian's face was drawn into grim lines. Branigan and Breck had approached him the night before with what they had found. He knew it likely matched what Dallas had, just by what he had said.

Finally raising her head, Ennis looked up at Bradon. "I'm sorry, Bradon. I'm so sorry. I didn't know. I didn't realize he was there all the time."

"Who?" Bradon waited before he asked again. "Who is it, Ennis?"

"A third cousin of mine. I never knew." She didn't hear the gasp from her mother as she turned to Ian, who nodded. "I wish I had. I never liked to be around him. I guess this is why." She studied the men, seeing their compassion and caring for her on their faces. "That's Jack Dixon."

———

Dallas nodded. "We have enough evidence to arrest him and will do just that. Ennis, it is imperative that you stay safe. You can't be out and about until we find him."

Ennis shook her head. "I can't stay locked away. I never could." She struggled to rise, kept in her place by Bradon's arms around her. "Bradon?"

"Just listen, sweetheart. That's all we ask. And if you are going to be out and about, one of the guys will be with us."

"You need to stay away from me. I just know he's the one who did this to you."

She heard the murmuring of agreement from the men and then leaned back on Bradon, her eyes on Dallas.

"I want this over with, Dallas. How much time do you need?"

Dallas looked up from his phone. "I just got word. He was found, Ennis, about an hour ago."

"Good. Then you can talk to him and this will be over for me." She didn't catch the look on Dallas' face.

"Ennis, sweetheart, I don't think it's over." Bradon could hear the mutters coming from his friends, who had picked up on what Dallas hadn't said yet.

"Bradon?" She looked up at him before her eyes swung back to Dallas. "Dallas? You found him? You've arrested him?" When he shook his head, her eyes slid closed. "He's dead, isn't he? Then, how do we find the ones responsible?"

"That is where we come in, Ennis. Bradon." Barnabas spoke, sharing a look with the other men. "We have done a lot of research and, Dallas, we have copies of it all for you. Some or I guess a lot of it has been verified by other police forces as they were investigating as well."

Dallas nodded. "That's great. We'll certainly take a look at it and add it to our investigations. Are you sure you're not detectives?"

The men laughed at him before sobering.

"We're not, Dallas, but we want this over for these two." Burnie spoke up. "If we find more, we will certainly pass it on to you."

Ennis watched the men closely, seeing the soberness they were trying hard to hide. This is it, isn't it, Lord? We are not there yet, as Evan would say. When will we be? I need to move on, to overcome what I've lived with for so many years. And when I can move on, so can Bradon.

Just, dear Lord, keep him and his friends safe. Give us the peace and courage we need to face what's upcoming, and I know it's going to be big and going to hurt in so many ways.

Two days later, Bradon stood by his truck door, a hand out to steady Ennis as she slid from the seat and then balanced the crutches under her arms.  She had wanted to come to town, needed to, she told him.  He had shaken his head and then helped her out to his truck.

Bradon raised his head, searching, feeling watched but not seeing who it was.  He knew some of his friends would be there, he just wasn't sure who.  His eyes dropped to Ennis, seeing the strain in her face, the fatigue, the pain caused not just by her physical injuries but by the emotional and mental, and yes, spiritual, pain that she had endured for so long.

"Where to?"  His question brought Ennis' eyes to him.

"I'm not sure."  She sighed, holding up one of her crutches.  "I'm not walking too far, I suspect.  Maybe, just maybe, this wasn't such a great idea."

"We'll make do.  We'll look around here.  Then, back in the truck you go, and we move down the street."  He grinned at the frown she threw him.

Ennis sighed.  "This is so hard, you know.  And the doctor said he can't guarantee this will work.  I still might face surgery because of them."

"If you do, we'll all be there for you.  None of us are walking away from you."  Bradon held the door open to a small diner, watching closely as she stood for a moment, lost in thought, before she shook her head and then looked up at him, a look in her eyes that gave him hope she returned his feelings.

Branigan studied the area around the diner, looking for someone who was out of place, but not seeing anyone.  He could feel the prickles on the back of his neck, and knew someone was out there, but who and where?  Brennen spoke from beside him.

"Someone is out here.  But where?"  He spun in a slow circle, his eyes narrowed as he searched.

"I know there is."  Branigan nodded towards the diner.  "We may as well go in and watch from there.  Did you know that this was where he was heading?"

Brennen shrugged. "He asked her about going out for a meal. I'm not sure this is what she had in mind coming into town, but it gets her out. She's starting to wear thin."

"She is. She's had this over her head since she was, what fifteen or sixteen?"

"Something like that. Baird and I talked to Evan. He's devastated with what Dallas told him. He had no idea it was that bad or that his friends had picked up for him without telling him. They all think of Ennis as a younger sister."

"I thought it would be bad for him." Branigan slid into a chair at a table where he could watch the door and also Bradon and Ennis. "I never thought, when we hired on with Barnabas, that it would come to this."

"I don't think any of us did. For four of us to go through this, it makes you wonder if your own turn is next."

Branigan nodded as he accepted the menu, laying it down to the wooden table top, moving his utensils to one side to do so. "It does, but then, God is in control here, isn't He? He has let each of us to gain the knowledge we need to help one another." He looked around. "Someone is in here that's watching them."

"I know. I can feel them, but I can't see who."

Ennis looked up, catching Branigan's eye, and then looked across the booth at Bradon.

"Branigan and Brennen are here. Did you know they were following us?"

Bradon gave a grim smile even as he nodded. "I knew someone would. That's what they've told me they would do. Dallas has said if they don't, he has volunteers from the force to do just that."

"Volunteers? Like police officers?"

"Just like that. On their own time at that." He suddenly smiled, the smile lighting up his face. "So, here we are. On a date. What would you like?"

"A date is it?" It took Ennis a moment to shift her thoughts. "I don't know. I don't think this was that great an idea." She chewed at her lip even as her eyes dropped to the menu. "I don't know what I want. Just order something for me."

"Ennis?" Bradon's hand reached to still the hand she was rubbing on the table top. "If you don't want to eat, we'll leave. Find something else to do. Go home. But you need to get out, restricted as it is for you."

She studied him and then beckoned for the waitress, a frown on Bradon's face as she did so.

"So, tell me, what is the best thing here on the menu to eat?"

The waitress smiled. "That would be the fish and chips. The best in town."

"Then, that's what we'll both have. He has coffee and what kind of teas do you have? An Irish one by chance?"

"We do." The waitress gathered their menus and headed away, leaving Bradon staring at Ennis, mouth open, as she smirked at him.

Later, they stopped beside Branigan and Brennen, who both watched closely around them.

"Brennen? I think we're heading back to the building. Ennis is tired enough she's almost asleep on me." Bradon watched her as she teased Branigan, a smile on her face that didn't quite reach her eyes.

"She is. Head out. We'll be right behind you." He looked around. "There is someone here, Bradon. Take all the precautions you can. Both Branigan and I felt the presence in the diner, but couldn't pick out just one person."

"And you won't. Whoever it is, that person is known to you. You won't suspect who it is." Ennis had caught Brennen's words.

Bradon headed for the road home, not thinking of the route he was driving, his thoughts instead on Ennis. She is so special, Lord. She's the lady I've been looking for, but didn't know. Only thing is, she has so much to overcome. I don't want to rush her, but I don't want to lose her. He felt peace flow through his heart and almost the touch of a hand on his head. He knew God had heard and would honour his request, if that was His will for them both.

He slammed on the brakes suddenly, a car appearing across the road. He frantically looked around, shoving the truck into reverse, seeing Brennen doing the same before Brennen came to an abrupt halt. They were boxed in, with nowhere to go. He heard the soft cry from Ennis and turned, seeing a masked man appearing at her door, a weapon raised and pointed directly at her.

Reaching for her hand, Bradon watched Ennis carefully before he heard the tap on his own window and sighed. This is it, isn't it, Lord? He slid from the truck, ignoring the motions to move away and walked around to help Ennis out and get balanced on her crutches.

Bradon stood, watching as Branigan and Brennen were shoved towards them, reluctance on their part. None of their assailants could be identified, masks covering their faces. His arm around her, he stood, waiting for what he wasn't sure. The men made no effort to force them away. It's almost as if they are waiting for someone to arrive, Bradon thought. He felt Ennis shift under his arm and looked down at her, seeing first a frown and then dawning understanding on her face.

"Ennis?" Bradon kept his voice low.

"That one behind Branigan? That's the Russell they've been looking at. I would suspect these are his sons and nephews. They all have similar builds and stances and looks on their faces." Ennis leaned into him, her leg aching, part from the stress she knew. "I just wonder when his boss will show up."

"You really expect that?" Bradon's hold tightened on her as his friends were forced over to stand beside him.

"Bradon?" Branigan's voice was low as well, barely audible. The noises from the surrounding trees and pond that had halted as the vehicles stopped, started up once more.

The men knew just how close they were to home. Brennen had managed to get off a text to Barnabas before he was forced from the truck. They just prayed Barnabas had received it and would appear to rescue them. At the moment, they held little hope out that that would happen.

Ennis frowned as she stared at the man she suspected was the eldest, the leader of the six men, and Bradon felt her move slightly.

"Ennis?"

"It's okay, Bradon. I know who this is. And I know who he'll be expecting." Ennis shifted to watch Branigan and Brennen, finding them watching the men in front of them. "There's no one behind us, is there?"

Bradon shook his head. "No, there isn't. But we can't get away that way. You can't run."

---

"I know that." Ennis was frustrated. "I just wanted to make sure they were all in front of us, with no one behind us. That's all. It makes it easier to watch them." She looked around. "What would you suggest?"

Branigan shook his head at her. "We can't do anything, Ennis. They have guns, in case you missed that."

"I know that. It's just we won't be surprised if someone walks up behind us." She looked around. "And I know that someone else is on the way here. They would have moved us away if not. What they are planning? For your friends to find our bodies here."

Brennen stared at her before he looked at the men. "I suspect that's their plan. Who would have thought of us being ambushed here."

"I would."

Bradon looked around. "What is here that they would want? Or need? Or desire to take us to?"

"There's the old cave, isn't there?" Brennen spoke up.

"No, not that. Is there a quarry, or a deep hole, or something like that?" Ennis was running scenarios through her mind, desperate to find some way to get the men away from her and to safety.

Branigan stared at her and then groaned. "There is. There's an old pit that is deep with steep sides. We wouldn't survive very well, if at all, if we were shoved down it."

"And that's their plan. Make us disappear. Take the trucks like to a scrap yard and trash them. No one would ever find us, now would they?" Ennis heard a faint rustle behind her and stiffened. Not that, Lord. Please, no one behind us. She looked up to see men rising up behind their captors, and shook her head slightly to halt their progress. She could feel the tension but relief in the way Bradon was holding her.

"Tim Russell! I know that's you. I know these are your sons and nephews. So stop hiding." Ennis's voice ringing out in accusation startled them at first. "Why did you do it?"

Tim Russell stepped forward, the mask dropping from his face. "Because of you. You stood in our way."

"And just how did I do that?" Ennis' anger showed in the way she spat out her words. "I didn't know you. I had nothing to do with you, or your sons. In fact, I ran as far from them as I could. So did all my friends and anyone else we warned." She paused, a sudden thought drawing a deep breath from her.

"And I would say that is it, Ennis." Bradon's arm tightened on her as he heard low mutters from his two friends. "You prevented something and didn't even realize it."

"And you did. You don't know how many times the ones we were after disappeared from our grasp or were only seen in a group. It was because of you. You wrecked a network we had set up." Tim's anger at Ennis had his body shaking, and the loudness of his voice stilled the sounds around them once more. "You have to pay."

Ennis shook her head. "I don't think so. Not this time. You've taken enough from me. Years I should have enjoyed as a teenager and a young lady. That, I can never get back. God have mercy on your souls, Tim, because I sure don't. You have ruined how many lives? Look at your own family? Your sons are following in your footsteps. Did they really want that? What about your daughters? I've seen them around town. They are beaten down, unhappy, and afraid. You've done that to them.

"And how many people have you done that to in your line of work? Is that why witnesses to crimes disappear and aren't seen again? You threaten them. I would even say at times you've stooped to murder. How close am I?"

Ennis was taunting him, hoping to break his silence. She knew one of Bradon's friends was recording it. She wasn't sure who from the camouflage they had on, but he had waved his phone at her.

Tim spun, his eyes on the men with him, not seeing the men standing back from him, or seeing the police officers moving in behind them. He spun back to face her, charging at her, to miss her as Bradon pulled her to one side, her crutches clattering to the ground as she dropped them. Tim lost his balance, falling heavily to the ground, where he lay, the breath knocked out of him. He didn't hear the words for his family to drop their weapons, or their rights being read to them. He felt his hands pulled behind him and cuffs around his wrists before he was pulled to his feet.

Dallas watched the activity closely before he approached the four, his head tilting to study Ennis even as Brennen handed her the crutches she had dropped.

"Ennis?"

"Dallas? Is it over?" Ennis had hope in her heart but doubted that it was

"It is.  We stopped and arrested the mayor's assistant.  Brady sent us a text as to what was going on and kept us updated as we arrived.  It was a brave thing you did."

Ennis shrugged.  "It had to be done.  God chose me to do it.  I just wish He hadn't.  I wish this had never happened."  She clumped away from them on her crutches, heading for the building she knew was up ahead.  Bradon watched, not moving to follow her, surprise on his friends' faces.

"Bradon?  Aren't you going after her?"

Bradon shook his head.  "I can't.  I have to let her have time to absorb this, to heal.  If I don't, at some point, she'll resent me and walk away for good."  He turned and walked from them, heading for his truck, where he slid behind the wheel and just sat, his eyes watching Ennis as she struggled to walk, until Burnie approached her and stopped her, then led her to a vehicle.

Is this it, Lord?  Does she walk away for good?  Or will she be back?  I hope You know she's taking my heart with her.  There will never be another one for me.  But I need to let her have this time.  Protect and heal her, please, Dear Lord?

A month later, Bradon sat on a rock near the lakeshore, watching the waves crashing up.  It was a windy, damp day and he knew better than to just sit but he had no desire to do anything.  He had been back to work and back to his volunteer duties, but his heart wasn't in it.

He felt the nudge of Kade's nose and absentmindedly rubbed at the dog's head, knowing how Kade felt.  He felt the same.

"You miss her, don't you, boy?  I know.  So do I.  I pray she comes back, but I don't think she will.  It's just you and me again, fellow."  He heard the deep sigh Kade gave, almost as if he understood his words.

Kade wandered the lakeshore, not even barking at the seagulls that tormented him.  His head turned suddenly as he caught a familiar scent and he was away across the sand and the rocks, heading for a person he now saw walking towards them.

Bradon had missed Kade's flight, his thoughts deep and dark.  He jumped as he felt a hand on his shoulder, not expecting anyone to be there.  He rose, wonder in his eyes and on his face, as he stared down at Ennis.

"Ennis?  You're here?"

"Bradon?  Forgive me for walking away.  It was just too much."  Ennis stood, eyes raised to him, hope on her face, but hesitation and the fear that he would reject her in her bearing.

Bradon simply shook his head, swept her into his arms, and held her tightly, his tears wetting her hair, feeling her tears on his shirt and felt her arms around him.  They stood, Kade watching, head tilting before he gave a bark.  As far as he was concerned, his lady was back and with his master.  That made life good for him.  He finally laid down, nose on his paws, eyes raised to his people.

Ennis finally shoved back a bit, her eyes on Bradon, seeing the emotions roiling on his face, but uppermost, she saw his love for her.  *I didn't lose it after all, did I, Lord?  Thank you.*

"Ennis?  You're okay?"  He pulled her down to the rock he had been sitting on, an arm tight around her, her head on his shoulder.

"I'm getting there.  I had to leave you that day, Bradon.  I was a broken mess of humanity.  I have been in counselling with a friend, had it out with Mom and Dad and Evan, found some friends I thought I had lost. Buckley has kept in touch."

"He has? That doesn't surprise me. That's who he is." He paused, just content to hold his love. "Has Dallas spoken to you?"

"He has. We've met a number of times, in fact. He told me Tim Russell hasn't confessed, so he'll be going to trial. His sons and nephews have, and they're facing what they need to." She paused. "Did you suspect the assistant at all?"

Bradon shook his head. "Not one bit. Did you?"

She nodded. "I did. I know her. She's always been a bit shady, as they say. She's not saying a word, Dallas tells me, but the wealth on information and evidence means she'll be facing a long prison term. It makes me sick to think of the lives they've ruined, the people lost to their families forever."

"It is a sick world, sweetheart. But we have God and that makes it bearable for us. All we can do is pray for them."

"That's all we can do. It was a struggle for me to get to that point, but I have found forgiveness for them. If I couldn't, then they would have won. I would never have overcome the obstacles I faced all my life."

"Those obstacles have made you who you are. The lady I love dearly and would like to spend the rest of my life with. Besides, Kade is moping. We can't have that." He smirked at her before he added. "Besides you asked and I said yes."

Ennis stared at him, her mouth open for a moment, before she laughed and then hugged him. "I did do that, didn't I? You know that's what you'll face. Me asking something as I drop off to sleep."

"I know, sweetheart, I know. I will delight in those very requests." He drew her to her feet, and taking her hand, led her back towards the building. "We need to make some plans. First, I talked to your Dad weeks ago. He didn't say anything, just looked thoughtful, and told me I had to take it up with you."

"He did? I guess he knew what had happened." She shook a finger at him as he laughed. "So, when will we set a wedding date?"

"Soon, I hope, sweetheart. We've lost time to those men."

"We did, dearest, but God was there. He knew what He was allowing. We needed to face my past before we could move to our present and our tomorrow."

———

"And just so you are aware, when we marry, the Foundation provides a salary for you." He watched her eyes grow round and a stunned look cross her face.

"They do that?"

Bradon nodded. "They do. They think a wife is valuable not only to her husband, but to God's work. By paying a salary, she can devote herself to her family and what she chooses to do. You don't have to work. You could volunteer. The choice is yours. And if you do decide to work, you are hired by a company at no charge to them."

Ennis shook her head, stunned at the revelation, and then a beautiful smile crossed her face. "God is so good to us, isn't He? He had this planned for us, all along."

"That He did, my love. That He did."

Two weeks later, Ennis stood, her hand tucked into her father's elbow, a sheaf of peach roses in her hands, her eyes fastened on the door ahead of her. Bradon and she had decided they didn't want to wait long, that too much time had already been lost to them.

Ian watched his daughter closely, thankful beyond words that she was finally safe. He could see the changes in her, changes that her trials had wrought, but that had brought her to who she was. Lord, bless this couple. You planned this. You brought Bradon here from Alberta all those years ago. Your plans have come to fruition for these two. We welcome Bradon as another son.

Bradon turned later that afternoon, searching for Ennis, seeing her talking with Berneen, Cadee and Devaney. He was glad these four were friends. They would be a source of comfort and strength and joy for each other. He turned his head as he heard footsteps stop beside him.

"Bradon? You're okay?" Barnabas' voice was low. He was one who always checked to ensure his friends were healthy, happy and safe. With him, it went beyond mere employer and employee.

"I am, Barnabas. Thanks for asking. You're okay taking Kade for me?"

Barnabas laughed. "I am, but I don't think Kade is all that impressed. He thinks he needs to go with his lady."

Bradon joined him in laughter. "She is that. I don't know how we're going to work this, but we will. Kade has been like that all along with Ennis."

"He knew she was in danger. He also knew somehow that she would be important to you."

"That he did." Bradon reached to wrap Ennis in his arms, a quick kiss dropped on her mouth. He didn't hear Barnabas walk away.

Ennis had watched him. "Bradon, what's Barnabas' story?"

"His story? I'm sorry, I'm not sure what you mean."

"Has he never had a lady in his life?"

"Not that we've ever seen. And he keeps that close to himself. I sometimes wonder if there had been and he was hurt."

Bradon turned her to face the lake, watching the sun as it set, sending out the beautiful coloured rays it always did on days like this.

"I love you deeply, Ennis. Never doubt that."

She looked up at him, eyes shining with love and happiness. "I know, and I love you deeply as well. I know we'll have our struggles, our differences, sickness, whatever God allows. But He has already overcome those for us, hasn't He?"

Bradon continued to stare at the sky, his thoughts sifting through her words. He finally stared down at her upturned face. "You have said it so well. He is truly in everything with us, and has already given us the victory over it. We just need to trust Him."


Dear Readers


Thank you for picking up the story of Bradon and Ennis. Once more, I had no idea where they were heading or the ride they would take me, as the author, and you, as the readers, on as they never tell me until the words are actually appearing in the manuscript.

What do you have to overcome today? I pray that you will just place your hand in God's and know that He desires only the best for you. Sometimes He lets us go through struggles of many kinds in order to be refined to the person He desires us to be.

During the writing of this, we were still dealing with the COVID-19 lockdown. It has been tough but necessary. Once more, I can say, God has been in control, even though it seems He isn't. He could have stopped it, could have changed it, could have not allowed it in the first place. But He did. That's where trust and faith come in.

God bless each one of you.


Ronna

# Brady: Encouraged to Heal

## The Barnabas Chronicles
## Book 5

By

Ronna M. Bacon

Exodus 15:26

If you diligently heed the voice of the Lord your God and do what is right in His sight, give ear to His commandments and keep all His statutes, I will put none of the diseases on you which I have brought on the Egyptians. For I am the Lord who heals you.  NKJV

*Table of Contents*

# Chapter 1

Drawing in a deep breath of fresh air, Brady Coghlan stood for a moment, his eyes on the distance hill he could see through the trees and underbrush. This was what he needed, he thought, to be away from everyone, to be on his own. Brady had gone to his employer and friend, Barnabas Carey of The Barnabas Foundation, asking for some time. It had been a rough few months in his work as a paramedic, to say nothing of the assaults and abduction and whatnot that his four friends had just gone through, even though they had found their ladies to love and adore in that all.

He was beaten up, beaten down, and soul weary. Almost losing his friend, Bradon, to a drowning and Bradon's lady, Ennis, to a knife attack, he felt the need to walk away, to be refreshed, to spend some time healing in God's presence. Barnabas had taken one look at him and nodded, just asking that he keep in touch, and how much time did he need?

Brady had taken a leave of two weeks from his work as a paramedic, knowing he would be covered. That's what his friends on the EMS teams did. He didn't know if he would be able to continue, but he would sort that out, he prayed, over the next couple of weeks.

Coming to a sudden halt, he searched the area he was in, trying to find the source of the stench. He recognized it only too well. Over the course of the years he had been a paramedic, they had had calls to places where corpses were found, even though there was nothing they could do. He hated that part of his work, knowing someone was dead and he couldn't help them. He saw the pile of clothing and groaned. Not what he needed to be finding on his vacation.

Backing away, Brady reached for his phone, hoping he had service. He wasn't quite sure of the location, but gave it as best he could to the dispatcher, who seemed to know where he was.

Two hours later, Brady stood, leaning against a police cruiser, arms crossed against his chest, watching the activity that surrounded the area. He knew the coroner was on the scene, but he frowned as he studied the older man, wondering why the delay, why they weren't moving the body. He shrugged.

The police officer approached Brady carefully, not sure of the man standing in front of him. He had asked for information on him, surprised to find out who his employer was. It still didn't explain why he was out in the wild of Northern Ontario.

"Mr. Coghlan?"

Brady turned as the officer spoke. "It's Brady. Do you have all you need from me?"

The officer nodded. "I do, but I would ask that you stay in the area for now, in case we have more questions." He looked down at his notes. "You're not from here."

"No, I'm not. I'm from Nova Scotia but have lived in Southern Ontario, near Lake Erie, for years." Brady sighed. "If I can't leave, I guess I'll be needing to find somewhere to stay."

The officer grinned. "I'm Eric Thomas. I know where you can stay. My aunt has a B&B and I'm sure she'll find a room for you."

Brady nodded, his black hair reflecting blue highlights in the sun, his deep gray eyes watchful.

"That sounds good. How soon can I leave? My truck's in the parking lot down below."

Eric grinned. "We know it is and right now, it's blocked in. If you can leave your keys, I'll have it brought to you." He took Bradon's keys even as he glanced down at his watch. "I'm about finished here and can give you a lift."

Brady's eyes lifted as he heard the sound of a vehicle and saw a small white van stop and then the door opening. He frowned as he studied the young woman who dropped from the seat and walked around to open the side door. He watched as she pulled on the white coveralls and a mask, picked up booties and her kits and walked towards the coroner, who had approached her.

Eric shook his head. "I thought Dan would call in Fynn. It's not a nice line of work she's in." He pointed to the trail. "Let's head

---

out. I have to stop by the detachment and then I can take you to my aunt's. I'm sorry you can't take your truck."

Two hours later, Brady sat in a local diner with Eric and some of Eric's friends. He listened to their talk, but wondered at the empty chair next to him. Eric sat on the other side of it, his arm laying across the back as he waited for their food.

Brady jumped as he felt a hand touch his shoulder before the chair beside him slid back and the young lady he had seen in the woods sat beside him, her head shaking at something Eric had asked in a quiet voice. Eric looked past her and then introduced her.

"Brady? This is Fynn Daley. She's the one that was out there today." He paused, knowing Fynn was always hesitant to give her occupation.

Fynn turned, her curious aqua eyes with the flecks of green, blue and brown focusing on him.

"Hi." Her voice was quiet, her gaze assessing in a professional manner. "You're the one?"

"The one?" He studied her, thinking that her short cap of curls reminded him of the copper pots his grandmother had had.

"The one who found the body."

"That would be me." He wondered that she didn't say or ask anything more, just turning to answer a question from Eric.

Later, he walked beside her as she headed for the sidewalk, obviously not having a vehicle.

"Wait? You're walking?" Brady's hand on her arm stopped her.

"I am. I usually walk when I can." She paused, her eyes raised to his, thinking how tall he was, six four likely. She found it odd having to look up at a man, being tall for a woman herself.

"Let me give you a lift." He grinned, the grin lighting up his face. "I just can't let a lady walk on her own."

She snorted, causing him to stare at her, and then laugh. "My friends know better."

———

699

"Well, then, consider me a friend who won't let a friend out on her own."

She shook her head again. "I go into places most men wouldn't go in to. I have to for my work."

Fynn turned as she heard running footsteps approaching them, finding Brady shoving her behind him before he was tackled and taken down. A swift blow to his temple knocked him unconscious even as Fynn scrambled backwards, trying to find her feet to flee, unable to before her wrist was grasped and she was pulled away from Brady.

She fought her assailant, finally scraping her fingernails across his face, bringing a cry of pain from him before she was shoved violently to the ground, her face scraping in the gravel. The man knelt with a knee in her back, his mouth close to her ear.

"Don't go any further with your investigation. Let it drop."

"I can't do that."

"Do it and you live. Don't and you die. And he dies too." A hard shove from the knee drove the breath from her before she heard running footsteps heading away from her and then footsteps running towards them.

Eric reached to help her up, frowning at her face, before he questioned her.

"Who was that?"

"I have no idea, Eric. Other than I was told to drop the investigation from today, or I died and so would Brady." She stalked towards Brady, who by this time was sitting up, being assessed by a paramedic friend of Eric's. "Just who are you?"

He looked up, pain flickering across his face. "What do you mean? Just who am I? I am a paramedic from southern Ontario. I work for The Barnabas Foundation. I have never been here before and I have no idea who I found." He glared at her, not seeing the amused looks on the men around them. "And just what do you do, anyway?"

"I'm a forensic entomologist. And why would I be told to drop the case or we both died? Who did you anger?"

"Me?" Brady shot to his feet, a hand to his head as it throbbed with pain. "I didn't anger anyone. Did you?"

Fynn shot him a dark look before she spun on her heel and stalked away, leaving Brady to stare after her, the men around him trying to hide their smiles.

The next day, Brady wandered the town he found himself in, not willing to move on, not willing to stay. Eric had contacted him that morning and told him that he was free to move on if he wanted to, but there was an underlying tone of humour in his voice that Brady didn't understand. He finally settled himself into a booth at the diner where he had eaten at the night before, reaching for the menu, and then just laying it down, tapping at it idly. Having no idea why he was so restless, Brady sighed. He needed to go home but didn't want to.

Hearing footsteps stop beside him, he glanced up and then slid from the booth, staring at Fynn as she stood there, hesitant to disturb him, his eyes finding Eric right behind her.

"Fynn?"

"Brady, I need to apologize for last night." She slid into the seat he had risen from, Eric sliding into the one across from her.

Brady frowned at Eric for a moment, who just grinned at him, and then slid down beside Fynn, watching as she played with the menu he had just sat down on the tabletop. His hand finally reached to still hers, bringing her eyes up to him. She's haunted by something, isn't she, Lord? And how do I help her?

"Who scared you, Fynn?"

She stared at him, disbelief on her face, but knowledge in her eyes that he was right. "I'm not sure what you mean." She waved at the waitress to place her order, avoiding Eric's frown and look and certainly not looking at Brady.

"I repeat myself." Brady spoke after the waitress had moved away. "Who has scared you that badly? It's not just from last night."

Fynn once more avoided his eyes, finding Eric watching her closely, before her glance moved to the window. A shuttered look covered her face.

"That's okay, Fynn. I'm prying. I don't really need to know, but I will pray for you." His eyes were on his folded hands, not seeing when she turned her gaze to him. "It's just that I hate to see any lady afraid. The wives of four of my friends have gone through some pretty bad stuff. I've seen it on my job. So, again, if you don't mind my asking, who scared you?" At this point, he looked up, to find her watching him closely.

Fynn sighed. "I'm not sure, Brady. I have felt like I have been watched, followed, things have been moved around in the lab where I work." She shivered, not from cold, but from the fear that was growing within her.

"Have you reported this?"

She shook her head, hearing Eric's low murmur. "I'm sorry, Eric. I had no proof other than a gut feeling. I did talk to my supervisor at work, and we've upped the security there, but someone is still getting in."

Eric nodded. "And without proof, you weren't sure anyone would believe you. I get that, Fynn. But, please, tell me next time?"

She shook her head at her cousin. The only children in their family, they had grown up almost like siblings, fighting with one another but having each other's backs as needed. "I can't promise that, Eric. I just can't."

Brady moved his arms back for the plates to be set down in front of them, staring down at his own meal, hearing Eric ask the blessing on their food, and then the two cousins talking quietly. He was searching through his memories to see what he could offer her, and then sighed to himself. He wasn't close enough to do that. He just wanted to make it better for her, and knew the thirteen others who lived in his building would want the same.

Fynn laid her hand on Brady's arm, causing him to look up at her, a frown on his face that disappeared as he studied her. This is a lady I would like to get to know better, Lord, but I just don't see how that's possible. I don't want to move from where I am. It's too much of a home for me, and the guys and their ladies are family. And she has work here that she won't leave.

Fynn stood later that day, her eyes on her work, but her mind on Brady. What was it about him that made her feel safe and cherished, Lord?  Is he the one I've been praying for, the one who will help me solve what's happening?  Is he the one that I'm missing in my heart?  I've hurt so much for years that I just don't know where to begin to heal.  She sighed, reaching for one of the vials in front of her, no longer so eager to press ahead in her line of work. What is causing this discontent, Lord?

A week later, Fynn stared at the vials and containers on the lab desk, her mind once more wandering to Brady. They had spent time together over the last week, and she had to admit, he was wriggling his way into her heart. She despaired of what she would do when he left the next day. Brady had sighed as he told her that, that he had to head home, but he really didn't want to leave her here when she was facing something

She studied her work, knowing she had just finished the task from the previous week and at the moment, had nothing pending. A growing conviction and desire in her heart had her looking up, before nodding. She hung up her lab coat, threw away her gloves, and headed for her supervisor, letter in hand. Fynn had prayed hard about her decision and knew she was making the right one. She just didn't know how her parents would react, but she didn't think it would matter too much to them. She had always felt an outsider in her home, but welcomed at Eric's. She wondered at that.

Her supervisor stared at her and then at the letter of resignation in his hand, not sure if Fynn was really quitting.

"Fynn?"

"I am sorry, Joe. I just can't do this anymore. I need a break." She paused, biting at her lip. "I have everything up to date. Nothing is outstanding or pending. I have never taken holidays except for the odd day here and there. With my accrued vacation and sick time, this brings it well past the time I have set for my resignation."

Joe sighed, knowing he had lost the best one in his office. "Okay, then, I guess. You will be missed." He peered closely at her, seeing the fine lines that were beginning to show. "If you change your mind?"

She simply shook her head and walked away, finding a box to pack her personal belongings from her office, noting that she really didn't have that much. Her pass and keys were handed off to the security guard, who stared at her in disbelief, and then she walked to her car, placing the box into the trunk, and then just standing, her hand on the trunk lid, blinking back tears as she realized that she had just cut her ties with her family, her friends, and her work. Where now, Lord?

Brady watched her closely as she stood in front of him, not looking at him. They had spent a lot of time together during the last week, and he cherished the friendship that she offered him. Eric had taken him to one side, told him that she didn't offer friendship that freely, and he was to make sure he didn't hurt her. Brady had nodded, his eyes watching Fynn from where he stood, and sighed to himself, thinking that was exactly what he would be doing.

Fynn stood, hesitation in her that was not normal, before she looked up at Brady, taking the hand he reached out for her. These two had had deep conversations over the last week, finding out how much they thought alike, but also had had spirited discussions.

"Fynn?" Brady's voice had held concern as they walked along the riverside paths.

"I don't know if I made a right decision today, Brady." She sighed, worry niggling at her mind. She no longer had employment, but maybe, just maybe, she thought, she could make a break from here.

"And that would be?" Brady's voice held confidence in her decision.

"I quit my job. I am now at loose ends." She looked up again, seeing his eyes watching her as he stopped their steps.

"You did? Okay. So, now where do you go?'

She shrugged. "I have no idea. I'm thinking of leaving town."

Brady turned as he heard running footsteps and swept Fynn into his arms, pulling her away from the area. "Where can we go, Fynn?"

She looked around. "No where. This is a dead end area of the path." She spun to face the man standing in front of her. "You again? What part of I don't know what you want is it that you can't understand?"

The man gave a twisted smile, evil showing in his eyes, as he studied her before he looked up at Brady. "You know what I want. Drop the case."

Fynn snorted. "I don't have any cases and I certainly wouldn't drop on your say so. So, get lost." She looked past him, not seeing his sudden charge towards her, taking her to the ground, Brady hitting the area beside her, before the man was up and away.

Brady lay still for a moment, his head turning to watch Fynn, before he sat up, reaching to help her to a sitting position, before he just wrapped her into his arms and held her. Eric stood for a moment, watching them. He had been following the man, determined to stop him from attacking Fynn again, but had lost sight of him. That was, until he heard Fynn's voice raised in anger.

Brady raised his eyes to look at Eric before shaking his head. Fynn was distraught, to say the least, and he hated that for her. Eric nodded and then headed past them, searching for their assailant, but knowing he would not find him. He stood, drawing in a deep breath, his eyes raised to the sky. This is it, isn't it, Lord? My best friend and almost sister is moving away. Sadness wafted through his heart. He could not keep, would not keep her here, not if she needed to move on. And it certainly seemed that way. Maybe, he thought, just maybe if she leaves town, this will stop, but he had no guarantees that it would.

Fynn finally raised her head and then stood, embarrassed for a moment, before she spun, her mouth opening to speak. Brady just shook his head and reached to wrap her into a hug. He didn't say anything for a moment.

"Where were you thinking of moving to?" He felt her shrug. "Would you consider moving my way?"

Fynn tilted her head back to look up at him. "I might. But you've never really told me about this foundation you work for."

Brady shook his head, his eyes on Eric heading their way. "Why don't we go find somewhere we can get a coffee. Eric looks as if he wants to talk to you too."

She looked over at her cousin, seeing the realization in his eyes that she was moving and sighed. This was not how she meant to do this. She felt her phone vibrating and from force of habit, pulled it up, checking the text message.  She paled as she read it, causing the two men to exchange a glance before Eric reached for her phone. His face grew stern as he read it.

"Fynn?  Your home?"

She nodded, tears near the surface.  "Someone broke into it.  I can't do this, Eric.  I just can't."

Brady watched Fynn closely as she moved through her house later that night, picking things up, putting them back down, moving aimlessly, he thought. He finally approached her, hands on her arms to stop her, causing her to raise her eyes to him.

"Fynn? What is it you really want to do? Stay here tonight? Go to the B&B?" He watched her face shift with her thoughts.

"What do I really want to do? Leave town? Right at this moment." She shrugged away from him, disturbed that he had been able to read her so well. *Lord, where do I go? I feel anchorless right now.*

"Then, move my way. I'm sure you could find work or even set up your own business, if that's what you want. I know Barnabas would help. That's what they do."

Fynn spun at his words, hope on her face for the first time in days, he thought. "He'd do that?"

"More than likely. If he won't fund you, then he knows plenty of people who will."

She walked back towards him. "Okay. So. He would?"

Brady laughed, his phone out, sending off a text to Barnabas. "I'll ask him. I don't think I explained how we work. Each one of the guys is employed by the Foundation, who pay their wages, but we work for different employers in town. This way, they can hire as they need to without feeling the pinch of finding extra cash to do so. We also volunteer our time to different organizations."

Fynn stood her mouth open in surprise, not seeing Eric standing behind her. "How can he do that?"

"Relax, Fynn. The Foundation is worth a lot of money, more than Barnabas or his father could ever spend. They do a lot with just the interest from the money." He felt his phone vibrate and looking down, saw Barnabas was calling him. He excused himself to take the call.

---

"Brady?" Barnabas' voice held concern. "I got your text. What's up?"

"Barnabas, I didn't expect you to call back so soon."

"Branigan was here, asking about you. Can I put you on speaker? That way, we can all be part of the discussion."

"Yeah. Sure. I guess."

"Okay, tell me about this." Brady could hear the creak in Barnabas' chair and knew he was sitting back, his elbows on the arms of the chair, head tilted as he listened.

"Fynn Daley is a forensics entomologist. I met her when I found that body. She has been attacked twice in the last week, being ordered to stop her investigation. She has no idea what that would be. She has also indicated that she thinks her lab and office have been searched." Brady paused, turning so he could watch her and Eric as they picked up the pieces of her life that had been strewn around the living room. "Her home was broken into tonight and tossed. She has also quit her job here. Fynn wants to move away. What can we do to help her?"

Branigan and Barnabas exchanged glances. They could hear the same tone in his voice that the other four had had when their ladies were going through things. They just shook their heads.

"If she's quit her work, where is she planning on living?" Barnabas had a good guess as to where Brady would like her.

"I have no idea." Brady had turned away for a moment and the turned back to watch Fynn and Eric as they stood, her eyes on Brady, Eric watching Fynn. "She seems to be wanting to leave this area."

"If she does and wants to head this way, I'll talk to her." Barnabas asked a few more questions, some that Brady could answer and some that he couldn't.

Fynn studied him as he pocketed his phone, standing for a moment staring into space, before his eyes turned to her. Brady walked towards her, stopping just short of her, his head ducking so he could stare at her face before he looked past her at Eric, seeing how torn he was for his cousin.

"Brady?" Fynn's voice was hopeful, but her heart was heavy. She just didn't think anyone would help her out. They hadn't in the past when she had needed someone. Well, other than Eric, and he didn't know the full reason she had chosen her profession.

"Barnabas asked where you were planning on moving to." He watched carefully as she stared at him before turning to Eric.

"I don't know, Brady. I just don't know. I can't stay here. But if I move, does he follow me?"

Eric spoke from behind her as he wrapped her into a hug, pulling her back against him.

"Don't let fear rule your life, cuz. If you need to move on, move on. It's not like you can't." He paused, biting at his lip before he continued. "I know your parents do love you, but they are just so complete in one another, you have taken the backseat all these years. Mom has mentioned that on more than one occasion."

She nodded. "I know." Her voice was sad but resigned. "I know that, Eric." She turned to look at him. "I just don't like leaving you. You're more than a cousin. You're my big brother."

Eric smiled. "As you are my sister. But God has opened this door so unexpectedly for you." He paused, biting at his lip. "Besides, I'm moving as well."

"You are?"

Eric nodded. "I am. I have found a little town on Lake Erie that needs an investigator. I didn't want to tell you, but it seems we're heading in the same direction."

Brady had been watching, his eyes narrowing before he nodded. He knew the town. It was Bradon's wife's, Ennis', town. That was good. It was close to the Foundation Building where he lived and where he hoped Fynn would take up residence, at least for a while.

———

*Chapter 5*

Standing outside Fynn's home early the next morning, listening as the early morning chatter of nature was starting, Brady looked around, a frown on his face. He sensed someone out there, just couldn't see anyone. It wasn't light enough, he thought. He turned back as he heard footsteps approaching.

Fynn studied the man in front of her for a moment, wondering why she trusted him so quickly. It must be a God thing, she thought, something her aunt always had her looking for. She watched as his smile lit up for her and he reached for the bags she had in her hand, quickly stuffing them into the back seat of his truck, and then opening the door for her, a hand out to help her up to the seat.

Brady waited as she did up her seatbelt before he closed the door, watching her for a moment before he walked around and slide behind the wheel, his fingers tapping quietly on it before he started the truck, and then surprised her by reaching for her hand.

"I always pray before I travel, Fynn." He watched the relief that flooded her face

"Do you? So do I. I don't know of many others who do, except for Eric and his parents."

"Where is Eric this morning? I thought he would be here."

"He was. He was headed into work. I wouldn't let him stay long." Fynn stared out the window at her hometown, watching a familiar buildings and scenes passed by, knowing she would never move back here, if she ever even came to visit, she thought.

Four hours later, Brady pulled off the road into a little eating area, his eyes searching. He felt followed but he couldn't see what vehicle. He turned to Fynn, a smile on his face as he watched her sleeping, reaching behind him for a pillow he tucked under her head, and then a blanket he tucked around her, his hand lingering for a few seconds on her face. His heart raised in prayer for his new friend, knowing already he didn't want her to disappear.

———

712

She's the one, isn't she, Lord?  Is she the one who is my helpmeet, the other half to my heart, my cherished one?  He turned back to stare out of the windshield, his thoughts muddled for a change, before he shook his head and pulled back on to the highway. There were still miles to go, he thought.  I will be glad to be home.

Fynn had stirred slightly as she felt Brady's hand on her face and then drifted back to sleep, her mind not active for a change, she thought.  Usually she couldn't sleep, her mind too active.  What was it about Brady that calmed her enough that she could?

Brady finally pulled to a stop in his town, jumping down from the truck, and stretching.  He needed a break before he drove the last few miles to home.  Turning, he watched as Fynn still slept and wondered if she would even sleep that night.  Lord, heal my lady. Bring strength to her.  I fear we are just starting something, like the other four guys.  I don't want to see her go through what they did, particularly Ennis.  Bradon almost lost her that day, Lord.  I can see how he watches her at times, when he knows she's not aware of it.

Returning to the truck with the few fresh groceries he knew he needed and some for Fynn as well, Brady stood for a moment, feeling a prickling in the back of his neck.  Someone had followed them, that much he knew.  But he also knew he would never see them.  Not unless they wanted him to and he doubted that very much.

He turned on to the highway leading towards his home.  It was late afternoon, and he was tired.  Brady twisted his neck to relieve some tension, and then looked in horror at the truck racing his way, in his lane.  He twisted the wheel to go around it but the truck moved back towards him.  Lord, where do I go?

He spun the wheel to turn the truck back into his own lane, his heart in his mouth as the tires hit the gravel and then his control was gone.  He could only hold on and pray they both survived the crash. His head hit the window and as his consciousness faded, he prayed for safety for Fynn, not for himself.  Brady didn't hear the scream that came from Fynn as she roused and saw the ground rushing towards her as the truck rolled, before landing back on its wheels, dust sifting through the air as silence once more reigned.

———

The creatures that had fled at the noise and at the large object heading their way finally made their paths back out, standing to stare at the truck before moving on.  They scattered once more as they heard and saw the truck that suddenly stopped and the doors on it popping open, to let two men out who ran for Brady's vehicle.

Branigan Clery and Brennen Connolly had been in town earlier, heading home not long after Brady had left town. Their conversation was quiet, sparked with laughter, before Brennen frowned.

"Branigan, those look like skid marks."

Branigan agreed, his foot easing off the accelerator even as his eyes searched the area. "Whoever it was hit the gravel. Do you see anyone?"

Brennen was searching and then pointed. "There. Oh no!"

Branigan shot him a glance and then turned his eyes to the truck. "Brady?"

"I think so." Brennen barely waited for Branigan to stop the vehicle before he was out and racing for the truck, Branigan on his heels.

Brennen tugged hard at Brady's door, then leaned in to the window, his hands framing his face. "It's Brady, but he's not alone." He looked around at Branigan. "I can't get this door open." He reached for the back door, with the same results.

"He's rolled it at least once." Branigan ran for the passenger side. "Call it in, Brennen. This is not Brady, to do this."

"No, it's not." His phone in his hand, Brennen ran for Branigan's truck, searching for the tire iron and returning with it. "They're on their way. Ten minutes or less." He looked down at the tire iron and shook his head. "This isn't going to work."

Branigan shot him a glance and then agreed. "The frame is jammed. I can't get this door open either." He looked up as he heard a vehicle. "There's Barnabas?"

Brennen was off, stopping to drop the tire iron back into the truck before he ran towards Barnabas.

"Brennen? Is that Brady?" Barnabas ran towards the truck even as he heard the sounds of sirens rising and falling as they approached.

"It is. He's rolled it. I'm not sure how, though." Brennen slid to a stop, a hand out to stop Barnabas just short of the truck. "He has a lady with him. Do you know anything about that?"

Barnabas nodded, his face grim as he assessed the truck. "Did he hit the gravel?"

Branigan nodded. "It looks like it. But I can't figure out how."

"His dash camera may help." Barnabas stepped back as he watched the firefighters approaching, gear in hand. "What was that you said about a lady?"

"She's in the passenger seat." Branigan turned to stare at the truck. "What's that about?"

"Fynn." The two other men turned to stare at Barnabas. "Fynn Daley. She's moving this way. We talked to Brady late yesterday about her, Branigan. He sent me a text early this morning that she would be with him."

"That we did." Branigan turned to watch the activity around the truck, seeing the paramedics arriving. "Brady was due back at work on Monday."

"He was?" Barnabas turned away for a moment, hearing his name called. "Will? You're here?"

Will Peters, police chief in the nearby town that covered the area the Foundation Building was in, stood beside them, studying the scene.

"I heard it was Brady."

Barnabas nodded. "It is. He was almost home from his vacation. I am not sure what happened."

They looked towards the truck as they heard the screeching and groaning of the metal as the equipment pulled it away from the two in the cab, and then watched the hurried movements of the paramedics and firefighters as they worked to free the two.

The two working on Brady stood for a few seconds, their eyes on their friend, seeing him slumped forward against the seatbelt before they worked to stabilize him.  A neck collar was in place before the older of the two slid into the back seat of the truck and steadied Brady as he was moved backwards.  A quickly indrawn breath from the younger paramedic sounded loud in the silence.

Brady groaned, his eyes flickering as he woke, not sure what had happened or even where he was.  Dried blood showed in a trickle below one nostril, and still dripped from a small cut over his eyebrow, down across his eyelid and cheek.

"Brady?  Can you hear us?"

Another groan came from Brady as he answered, his voice gruff with pain.  "I can, Travis.  Where am I?"

"You're still in your truck.  Looks like you rolled it somehow.  Do you remember what happened?"

Brady shook his head, his face tightening in pain at the movement.  "No, I don't.  Am I home?"

"You are.  You don't remember?"

"No, I don't."  Brady's voice faded as he lost his grip on consciousness.

Travis shared a look with David before he shook his head, his attention going momentarily to the team working on Fynn.

"Let's get him out of here and to help.  Doc's working today?"

"He is.  He's on the afternoon shift.  I'm glad."  David reached for Brady, the hands helping gentle as they shifted him to a backboard and then to the stretcher, which was then wheeled hurriedly to the waiting ambulance.  Travis stood for a moment, eyeing Brady, before he turned to watch the activity at the truck.  Who did this, he wondered?  Brady's too careful a driver to have this happen to.  And I wonder who the lady is.  He wasn't dating anyone when he left for vacation.  He slammed the doors shut and then heading for the driver's seat, his mind running scenarios before he shook his head, at a loss to explain anything other than a good friend was hurt.

The officer watching as the other paramedic team worked on Fynn took the wallet he was handed, his eyes on her before he opened it, a surprised look crossing his face.

"How is she?" His voice sounded loud in the sudden silence.

"Not sure. She's battered, that's for sure." Carol turned back to the other lady, reaching to undo the seatbelt, her partner, Ted, in the back seat, helping to stop Fynn for falling forward. They had found her slumped against the door.

The officer nodded, his eyes once more on the identification he held. He turned to study the truck and then walked towards Will, a puzzled look on his face.

Will reached for the wallet, assessing the look on the officer's face, before he looked down at the license.

"Fynn Daley?"

"Yes, sir. I thought she lived up north."

"She does. What is she doing here and with Brady?" He turned at a sound from Barnabas. "Barnabas, do you know why?"

Barnabas exchanged a look with his two friends before he nodded. "I do. Brady met her when he was up there on vacation. Long story short is that she was ready to move, on the run you might say, and he suggested she might like to move this way. Apparently she agreed. I knew they were heading this way. Just didn't expect this."

"I will need to talk to her employer." Will watched as Barnabas moved slightly. "Barnabas?"

Barnabas sighed. "She doesn't work there now. She resigned and decided to move this way. That's why she was with Brady."

"I see." Will handed the officer back Fynn's wallet. "Follow her in, Justin. I'll be by later." He watched as the paramedics settled Fynn onto a stretcher, did what they needed to and then wheeled it to the waiting ambulance, Justin following and then hopping up into the back, to settle into a corner where he could watch Fynn.

Justin was puzzled. He knew of Fynn's work, that as Dr. Fynn Daley, she was well known and respected in her field, even at her young age. He figured she must have hit college around age 16 and then graduated with her master's at age 20. He shook his head. There is no way he would have done that.

Doc Adams looked around as he heard his name called before his eyes dropped to the stretcher being wheeled towards him and gave an inaudible sound.

"Brady? Travis, what happened?" He walked quickly that way, pointing to an examination room, before he was at Brady's side, his eyes watchful, before he glanced up at Travis.

"Car accident. Somehow, he rolled his truck on the highway near your place."

"Rolled his truck? That's not Brady."

"No, it's not. He was awake for a few seconds. Didn't remember doing that."

Doc nodded, his hands already at work assessing his young friend. "Sue, we'll need imaging. Blood work." Doc paused for a moment, his face thoughtful, before he shook his head. He had a thought that just maybe Brady was going to go through what his other four young friends had, and that he feared. Each one had been through enough violence.

Brady stirred, the familiar odours of antiseptic and sickness in his nostrils. His eyes blinked open, and he stared around before he groaned. What did he do, he wondered?

"Brady? Can you look at me?" Doc's voice was soft but firm and Brady did just what he had been asked to do.

"Doc?"

"You were in an accident, Brady. No, don't move. You're not getting up yet." Doc's hand on Brady's chest kept him still. "Do you remember anything about the accident?"

"Accident?  What accident?"  Brady's eyes flickered open and closed, before he focused on Doc.

"You were in an accident.  Do you remember?"

"No, I don't."  He looked around almost in a frantic manner.  "Fynn?"

"Fynn?  Who's that?"

"She was with me.  I need to find her.  She's in danger."  Brady pushed at Doc's hands and then the blankets, before his head fell back and he faded away from them.

Doc looked around as he heard footsteps and Will and Barnabas stood beside him.

"Has he been awake?"  Will's voice was quiet as he spoke.

"He was.  He was asking for a Fynn."

"Fynn Daley.  She was with him."  Barnabas shook his head.  "Why Brady?"

"Who is this woman?"

"Dr. Fynn Daley.  She's a forensic entomologist.  Apparently, Brady convinced her to move this way."

"He did?  That doesn't sound like our Brady."  Doc eyed the two men before he shook his head.  "Don't tell me.  He's set for an adventure just like the other four."

"Looks that way.  How is he, Doc?"  Barnabas was concerned enough that he didn't leave when the stretcher bearing Brady was taken to the imaging department.

"We'll know more when I see the scans, but I don't think there's much damage done.  He'll be bruised and sore.  The cut on his forehead is minor.  It won't need stitches.  It's a concussion I'm worried about."

———

*Chapter 8*

Her head turning restlessly, Fynn roused in the early morning hours, her eyes opening. She groaned softly, her hand raising to feel at the side of her head. It hurt, she decided, and I have no idea why. And why am I in a hospital bed? She reached for the controls, raising the head of the bed, and then settling back, feeling better that she was sitting more upright. She hated lying flat on her back, always had. Lord, I don't remember where I am, but I don't think I'm at home. I know You're here, but I'm scared. I hurt in more ways than one, not just physical. I need to heal, Lord, but I have no idea just how to do that.

Her eyes slid closed as she listened to the quiet sounds of the late night hospital activity. She heard the soft tread of rubber-soled feet as they approached her bed and just kept from jumping in fear as a hand touched her wrist, feeling for a pulse and then the stethoscope as it was placed for the physician to listen to her heart. She heard the quiet words spoken and breathed a sigh of relief. No real damage, she thought. Just bumps. And bruises. A lump on her head that hurt. She wanted to touch it but didn't want whoever was in the room with her to know she was awake. Fynn listened as the steps moved away from her before she cracked open one eye and then popped open the other one.

Where is Brady, she questioned? Is he okay or even alive? Fynn pushed at the blankets and sat up, waiting for the spinning in her head to stop. What had happened? She knew the truck had rolled. She remembered the sight of the ground outside her window. It didn't seem like Brady to have done that, she thought. Her feet hit the floor and she moved towards the cupboard, finding her clothes and then heading for the bathroom, dressing quickly, the hospital gown abandoned on the floor. Her purse over her shoulder, she crept out of the door and then searched, finding Brady sitting in the waiting room, head back, eyes closed.

Brady had awakened not long before that, on his feet and dressed, heading for where he would find Fynn. He had already made an excursion her way that night, finding her sleeping, and

———

being sent back to his own bed by the charge nurse, who frowned at him, but had smiled to herself at Brady's actions. Brady was well liked by the hospital staff, having won a place in their hearts by his compassion and caring for not only his patients but for everyone he met. She shook her head and walked back to the desk, her mind already on the multitude of tasks she had to perform that day.

He jumped as he felt a hand touch his before it gently touched his face. His eyes opened and he studied Fynn who sat beside him.

"Brady?"

"I'm okay, Fynn. Shaken. Battered." He watched as her eyes closed and a single tear crept down her cheek before his finger was on it, wiping it away.

"I'm so glad. I was scared."

Her admission told him much. He knew she went into areas most people would not. For her to admit she was scared both worried and touched him.

"Fynn? You're okay?"

"I am." She looked around, shivering with fear as she did so. "Can we leave?"

Brady grinned at her. "You want to leave this establishment?" He looked up and past her as he heard footsteps. "We do have a ride. Fynn, this is a friend of mine. Baird? What are you doing here?"

"Doc sent me. He figured you two would be making a break for it about this time." He grinned. "It's good to finally meet you, Fynn. Let's go before we're stopped." Baird looked up as he felt eyes on him and nodded at the charge nurse, who simply smiled and nodded.

Fynn frowned at him, not sure what he meant, before she turned to Brady, finding him watching her, a look on his face that gave her pause, but almost made her feel loved and cherished.

"All set?" Brady stood, hesitating as his head cleared before he wrapped a hand around Fynn's and led her down the stairs and out of the Emergency entrance. "Where are you parked, Baird? And just how did you get chosen?"

Baird just grinned as he pointed towards his vehicle. "Over there. Doc didn't say. He just walked up to me last night, asked me to be here about this time as he just knew you two would be making a break for it, as he put it."

"We can't just walk away!" Fynn dug in her heels, refusing to move forward. "We don't have our discharge papers." Her mouth opened as Baird held up a folder. "No way! That can't be them!"

"It is, Fynn." Brady almost shoved her into the truck and then slid in beside her. "Buckle up. Doc would have made arrangements for this. He knows me well."

She stared at him and then at Baird, who was nodding.

"Four of us have gone through stuff, Fynn. We have an infirmary in the building. Well stocked, I might add. I know. I spent time in it not too long ago."

"You did? Why?" Fynn's curiosity was getting the better of her.

"Let's just say I had an adventure and was hurt. The guys found me and also Berneen, my wife, and brought us to safety. Someday, we'll tell you our story."

Fynn frowned at him, disgruntled that he didn't say more. "I'll hold you to that. Later today will be our talk." Her eyes closed and her head went down on Brady's shoulder as she slept. He watched her for a moment, before his eyes raised, staring out the side window, not catching Baird's look at him.

Fynn stared around the suite she had just been ushered into, remembering to snap her mouth closed.

"Brady? This can't be right. It's too nice for a guest suite."

"It's not a guest suite. It's a regular everyday apartment and for you, yours to use. Barnabas had your belongings brought here when they cleaned out my truck. I'm just across the hall from you."

She shook her head. "This is too nice for me. I'm not used to that."

Baird studied her, seeing the fear, no terror, he thought, underlying her words and actions. He then studied Brady, noting that he had seen the same things and sighed. Knowing Brady, he will want to step in and make it all better, just like we all do. This time, I don't know that he can. Lord, please. Protect his heart. Protect Fynn's heart. Heal her from whatever it is she is running from. Lead her to run to You.

Baird stepped away quietly, moving back towards his own apartment. All the men had a suite in the building, with offices for each one on the main floor. Doc Whitson and his wife, Anna, also had an apartment on the main floor, beside Barnabas.

Berneen looked up as Baird entered, before moving into his hug.

"They're home?"

"They are. Both are hurting, I can tell you that much."

"What's she like?" Berneen leaned back to watch her husband's face.

"Different. She's hurting, love. Really hurting. And running. Why, I don't know." He sighed. "She's young, Berneen. I would say a bit younger than you."

"How can that be?" Berneen was puzzled.

"She hit college at age 16, or university rather. She graduated with her doctorate degree at age 20 and went right to work. She needs a break but I don't know if she'll get it."

"Doesn't she have a position? Why is she here?" Berneen was trying to understand but felt too tired to make a start on that.

"Branigan told us that she quit her position and moved this way. Brady's happy, he said, that she did. I suspect he's more than a little interested in her." He turned her around. "Time to sleep, love. It's an early day for us in the morning."

"That it is." Berneen stopped. "I'll go see her later."

"Go on your own for now. The other ladies will want to meet her, but she's looking very overwhelmed right now."

Later that morning, Fynn stood, the refrigerator door open, staring open mouthed into it. Someone had stocked it with fresh fruit and veggies, she thought. Her mind wandered to Brady. No, it hadn't been him. He hadn't been able to. Her face softened as she thought through what she knew of his friends and knew that one of the men or the ladies had done that. She hadn't had anyone treat her like that in years, she thought, other than Eric and his parents. Her own mother would have had to be asked to do that, and likely would have grumbled at doing it. Fynn frowned. Now, why would I think that? It's just so bizarre, how I am finding out what Mom and Dad would do and not do. Why? Lord, I could sure use some help here about now. I'm so confused. I hurt in more ways than one.

Hearing a tap at the door, Fynn moved that way, standing with her hand on the open door, watching the lady about her age who stood there, holding up a basket of muffins.

"I'm not sure if you've had breakfast, but I wanted to bring you these." Berneen tilted her head to study the other woman. Baird, you are so right. She is hurting in many ways. "I'm Berneen, Baird's wife."

"Berneen! Of course. Come on in. I'm sorry. Everything is such a struggle this morning." Fynn walked back into the kitchen. "Coffee? Or tea?"

"Water's fine." Berneen set the basket down and then surprised Fynn by reaching to hug her. "You've been through a lot, thrown into a building overrun with caring overprotective men and you're lost."

Fynn started laughing. "I don't know how you managed to sum it up so perfectly, but yes, that's about it."

Berneen grinned. "This is mild to what I have seen and what I went through." She pointed to the chair. "Can we sit? I need to tell you our story."

---

Fynn finally sat back, her eyes huge. "You did not go through all that?" She stared at her new friend as Berneen nodded.

"We did. I was held captive, Baird was taken captive. We were freed, kidnapped again and Buckley was forced to marry us to save Baird's life."

Fynn stared at her. "That doesn't happen in real life."

Berneen grinned at her. "For us, it did. Just like for Benen and Cadee. They married so she could get out of a South American country alive. Blair and Devaney were engaged years ago but she left him to try and save his life. Bradon and Ennis. Theirs is quite the story. Both almost died at the same time."

Fynn shook her head. "Brady didn't warn me. He should have." She jumped as she felt an arm come around her shoulder and turned her head.

Brady just grinned at her before he moved to fill a mug with coffee, returning to sit beside her. She stared at him and then past him at the two men filling their own mugs. Baird she recognized, sort of, from the night before. The other one, she shook her head. No, she didn't know him but she felt she should.

"How are you this morning?" Baird merely grinned at her as he sat beside his wife. "That good, huh?"

She shook her head at his half-smile. "I have no idea how I am to feel. I have never been in an accident before. Certainly not one where the driver couldn't control his vehicle."

The others laughed at the look on Brady's face and his protest.

"I didn't do it on purpose. Someone ran me off the road."

"That's your story. I didn't see another vehicle." She smirked at him as she said it.

His eyes narrowed as he caught the glint of mischief in her eyes. "How could you? You were sleeping."

"And I notice that you didn't wake me up to verify your story." She jumped as her phone chimed. She knew it was Eric and just let it go to voice mail.

The eyes of the other three kept bobbing between the two before Barnabas spoke.

"Do you remember what happened, Brady?"

Brady shrugged. "I can sort of remember a vehicle in my lane and trying to avoid it. I couldn't. It was done deliberately. I couldn't avoid him. I tried."

"We know you did, Brady." Barnabas watched him closely, Doc having spoken to him. "Dr. Daley, I am Barnabas Carey. We were to talk, but not like this."

She studied him for a moment before she spoke. "Please, it's Fynn. I think I left the doctor part behind. At least for now, I have. And we were?"

Barnabas smiled at her. "We were. Brady asked me to. I was going to let you get settled in, but it seems as if that isn't to be the case."

Fynn shook her head. "I have no idea what the case was to be." She groaned. "I thought I left all that behind me. I guess I haven't."

"Fynn, Brady said you were threatened."

Fynn slowly nodded. "I guess you could say I was. The thing is I have no idea who or why. I know others older than me were upset that I received the employment offer I did at my age. It is usually someone well experienced and older that gets them."

"We understand. So it could be someone from your work, someone who lost out of a position, or someone from your past." Barnabas had pulled out his pen, holding it posed above his notepad as he listened to her.

She sighed. "I suspect all three. If there are three after me, why go after Brady?"

"Will Peters, our police chief, has a detective looking into that as well. The detective will be out tomorrow to talk to you. No, wait, tomorrow's Sunday. He'll be out on Monday."

Fynn nodded, a question on her face as she turned to Brady, to find him watching her intently.

He gave a gentle smile.  "We haven't introduced you yet.  This is Barnabas Carey.  He's the one you were going to speak to."

Her eyes shot back to Barnabas, before a frown settled on her face.  "I'm not sure this is such a good idea after all."

"What isn't?"  Barnabas had a good idea of what she was thinking, but waited for her to verbalized her thoughts.

"Moving here.  Brady could have been killed yesterday,  Did whoever it is follow me?"

"Or was I the one whoever it is was after?"  Brady shook his head at her look.  "That's a possibility.  I have made enemies over the years without knowing it.  I have been warned by the police about that."

"But it doesn't make sense that they would wait until now."

## Chapter 10

Barnabas watched Brady closely, knowing he would be thinking the same thing.

"Who is after you then, Dr. Daley?  Who wants to hurt you that bad?"

Fynn's eyes had flown to him as he spoke and then she sighed, her head dropping.

"Please, call me Fynn.  I want to leave the doctor bit behind for now, if I even can."  She shifted in her chair, not seeing the concern on the others' faces.  "I don't know.  I know my office was searched.  Security couldn't figure out how it was done.   My home was tossed as they say.  I know I have been followed at times."  She sighed once more.  "I know there was one student who was really jealous of me in high school.  A senior.  He resented the fact that I was in the same grade and three years younger than him."

"I see.  If you have names, please let us know.  Branigan will look into them before we hand them over to Will Peters, our police chief."

Baird spoke, his eyes on Berneen, who was closely watching the couple across from her.  "Not just Branigan.  We'll all research.  We've done it before."

"You have?  How?"  Fynn's mind took off on the possibilities, and they all realized they had just lost her.  Brady was watching her, a grin on his face before he looked up.

"You lost her, Baird.  She'll be thinking through how you do that.  She may come up with an answer before you do."  He watched as she reached for her phone, to scroll through her messages, before her fingers were flying over the keys.

Fynn sat back, knowing that Eric would head her way.  He was in town, that much she knew.

"My cousin, Eric, he's in town. He's heading this way." She looked up, an apology on her face. "I'm sorry. I shouldn't have asked him to come."

"Fynn, let me say this once and only once." Barnabas waited until he had her attention. "This is your home. Yes, it is the Foundation building, but it is home to us all first and foremost. If your cousin is here, he is welcome to stay."

Brady spoke, knowing Fynn wouldn't say what she was thinking. "Eric is a police officer. He has just taken the empty detective spot on the force in Ennis' town."

She nodded. "I didn't know that he was moving, not until I said I was leaving town." She looked around at the four with her. "He's my cousin, but he's more like a big brother to me. I am an only child." Her voice died away. "No, I'm not an only child. God, please, don't let it be true." Her head went down on her folded arms.

Brady shot the others a look before his arm enveloped her and his head rested next to hers as she sobbed.

Berneen was on her feet, coming around to sit beside Fynn, her arms around her as Brady stood and moved away, anger showing on his face. Baird and Barnabas moved with him.

"Brady?"

"What?" Brady spun, the anger that had flared subsiding. "Sorry. I hate to see her like this. She doesn't open up to anyone, not this way."

"She's past her limit, Brady." Baird turned to watch the two ladies. "Coming here. The accident. Finding people who cared about her without knowing her." He looked back at Brady. "What did she mean?

"Mean what?" Brady shifted so he could see Fynn's face as she raised it, tears covering it, his heart breaking for her.

"When she said she wasn't an only child?"

Brady shrugged. "I have no idea."

"I'm not. I had an older brother, who just disappeared when I was about two. I had forgotten him. He was about four years older than me.  No one ever talks about him."  Fynn stood beside Brady.  "Why?"

"They never talked to you, Fynn?"

Fynn spun as she heard Eric's voice.  "Eric?  What do you know?"

He shrugged.  "No one seems to talk much about it but I did some research over the last few years.  Your brother just seems to have disappeared when he was six.  They could never find him.  It's still an open case."

"That's so weird.  Why would all his pictures disappear?"

"They have?  I didn't know that.  I know Mom has some.  I'll get her to email me a couple and then we can look into it."  He looked up at Brady, catching his look, and nodding, before he was introduced to the others.

"Brady?  Have a moment?"  Eric's voice was low, his eyes on Fynn.

'Sure.  What's up?"

"I don't like that Fynn was never told.  I don't know why she just remembered, but it could be dangerous for her.  Mom said her parents received death threats against them and against Fynn.  Fynn is smart.  She's thrown herself into her studies and then her work, trying to please her parents."

"But she never could because she wasn't her brother."  Brady's eyes slid closed as he sighed.  "That's why they seem so distant to her, isn't it?"

"I would suspect so.  I can't do much right now, but we can't let this lie.  If her brother is  still alive, where is he?  And is he the one behind all this?"

"That's my fear, now that I know.  How do we keep her safe?  She's going to want to wander out in the forests and the fields, researching her creepy-crawlies."  Brady grinned at the frown directed his way as Fynn moved into his space.

*Chapter 11*

Her mind not on where she was stepping, Fynn tripped over a small fallen branch in her way, just catching herself from hitting the ground.  It had been four days since Eric had appeared, confirming that she was not an only child.  He had passed on some photos from his mother but she didn't recognize her brother.  Flannery, they said his name was.  She didn't remember.  Fynn had been just too young at the time.

She sighed, knowing that Brady would be looking for her.  He had gone back to work the day before, insisting he was able to, but she had her doubts.  She had seen the fatigue and pain in his face the night before and insisted that he just go to bed, not spending the time with her that he had planned.  Brady had hesitated, wanting to be with her, before he sighed, nodded, gave her a tight hug and walked away.

Fynn stooped, her eyes on the creepy-crawlies Brady teased her about, not hearing the footsteps stealthily approaching from behind her.  A scream that rose in her throat was cut off by the hand wrapped around her face even as an arm wrapped around her waist, trapping her own to her sides.  She struggled, trying desperately to escape, her feet kicking at the legs of the man who held her.  Fynn didn't hear the muttered words between the two men before she was carried at a rapid pace from the area and then through the shallow water to a waiting cabin cruiser.  She was shoved roughly down the stairs and into a cabin, the door swung shut behind her and locked before she could regain her feet.

Propelled across the room, her legs struck the edge of the bunk and she fell forward, her arms out to stop herself.  She spun and was on her feet, her hand on the door handle, twisting and yanking at it before she pounded at the door, calling for the men to let her go, to free her, that they must have the wrong person.  Hearing no response, she stood, hand on the door handle, the other hand flat on the door itself as she twisted to study the room.

No, Fynn thought, there is no escape from here.  I can't get out of the windows or whatever they are called on a boat.  The locked

———

door had trapped her. She finally slumped onto the bunk, her eyes studying the room, a calmness settling over her. Who were the men, she wondered, and why me?

She shuddered from sudden fear, a fear she had never known before. She willed the tears welling in her eyes back down before she blinked rapidly, rising to her feet to systematically search the cabin and attached bathroom, finding nothing that she could use for a weapon. Fynn paused for a moment, her eyes on the spray bottle of cleaning solution. If necessary, she would use that to protect herself.

Lord, why? Couldn't You have gotten my attention in some other way? For now, it's just You and me. I guess this is when I need to trust, isn't it? Lord, I need to heal. I have been hurting and struggling for so long, I don't know when I felt free. Help me to trust You, to lean on You. I have no idea what I am facing but You do.

Hours passed before she heard the door unlock and open. Fynn had refused to put on a light, sitting in the dimness of the dying day, her mind focusing on the verses that she could remember on trusting in danger, of peace, of God's protection in all things. She looked up through her lashes to see a tray set on the table near the door before the man, or youth, she thought, watched her as he backed away, the door shut and locked behind him. Fynn finally rose and walked over to study the tray, turning away, knowing that anything on it could harm her. The sandwich and fruit looked harmless, but she was taking no chances.

Fynn searched for a pen and paper, finding some stuck away deep in a drawer and sat back on the bunk, switching on a light overhead. She tapped the pen idly against her mouth before she back to jot notes and then scribble furiously as her thoughts flew. Who was it, she wondered? Someone she knew? Someone she didn't know but who knew her? Someone from one of the cases she had worked on?

She settled back against the pillows, her legs drawn up as she curled up on her side and finally slept. Her last thought was for Brady, praying for his healing from their accident and for protection. She had no idea if her captors would go after him, but she suspected that they would, if she couldn't or wouldn't tell them what they wanted. And just what that was she had no idea. Maybe tomorrow

---

they would tell her.  She slept, not feeling the gentle swaying of the boat as the waves rocked it in the night.

Mid-morning, she turned from where she had been watching the water, trying to determine if the boat was still in the same spot. She thought it was, but wasn't quite sure.  She watched as a man entered, an older man, stooped, his hair unkempt, a straggly beard on his face.  He paced towards her and then back towards the door, his hands to his sides, clenched into fists.

"Where is he?"  When Fynn didn't respond, he stalked towards her, stopping just short of touching her.  "I said, where is he?"

"Where's who?"  Fynn's head tilted to the side, her eyes looking past the man at the youth standing just outside the door. He's the one from last night, she thought.  Who is he?

"You know who I mean.  Where is he?"

Fynn shrugged.  "I have no idea who you mean.  And just where am I?  I would like to go home, if you don't mind."

"Not yet.  Not until you tell me where he is."  The man lumbered away, an unkempt smell lingering in the air after him that roiled Fynn's stomach, and that took a lot to do, given the situations she found herself in.  She watched as the door was closed and heard the lock sound before she sighed and then sat carefully on the edge of the bunk.

She had discovered that there were loose boards on the bunk, and she had hidden one under the thin mattress with the hopes that she just might be able to use it to escape.  Fynn's thoughts turned to Brady, wishing she could see him, needing to feel his strength of character to help her through what she was facing.

She sighed to herself, not knowing who the man was that she had been asked about.  Her brow furrowed as a thought passed through her mind before she shook her head.  It couldn't be her brother, the one she had forgotten about.  That would be just too strange.

Fatigue weighing his body down, Brady slid from his truck seat and shut the door, leaning back on it to close his eyes. He hurt worse today than he did yesterday, if that was possible. He shook his head, regretting it as the headache that had lingered behind his eyes all day came out in full force. He shifted the duffle bag he carried to his other hand and reached for his keys as he headed for the building and his apartment. He didn't see Breck watching him closely before he followed him, concern on his face at the slowness of Brady's walk.

Brady eyed the stairs to the second floor and then headed for an elevator, not up to the climb that night. He paused as he exited the elevator, his eyes tracing down the hall to the apartment Fynn had been assigned, but shook his head once more. He needed to clean up before he sought her company.

His heavy work boots hit the tray in the hall closet before he detoured through the kitchen to flick on the coffeemaker he had left ready to start that morning. He dropped his duffle bag in the laundry room before heading for a shower.

Refreshed to some degree, he gathered his dirty clothes and headed back for the laundry, dropping them and the contents of his bag into the washer and setting it. He reached for the coffee carafe to pour a cup of coffee before he opened the fridge door, staring in and then closing it. He wasn't ready to eat, not just yet.

Brady headed for the door of Fynn's apartment, puzzled when she didn't answer. He shrugged, figuring she was outside somewhere and headed that way himself, searching through the seating areas before standing at the building entrance, a hand on his head, his eyes narrowing as she searched. He jumped as he felt a hand come down on his shoulder.

"Brady? How are you feeling today?" Blair stood there, the other men gathering around them.

"Sore." He searched the faces to his friends, his heart sinking at the grim looks on their faces. "Guys? What's up?" When no one answered, he turned to Blair.  "Blair?  What's going on?  I don't like the looks on your faces."

"And we don't like what we have to tell you.  Fynn has disappeared.  Bradon and Kade tracked her for a while until Kade lost her scent."

"Disappeared?  How?  When?"

"We think sometime early this afternoon.  Berneen had met her for lunch and then Fynn told her she wanted to be outdoors, to look for her creepy-crawlies as you call them."

"I thought so."  Brady's shoulders slumped.  "I tried to reach her around two and didn't get an answer.  But then she tends to leave her phone on mute."  He looked around at his friends, seeing Barnabas walking his way accompanied by Will.  "You've reported it?"

"We have.  Given her profession and the threats from her hometown, Will has made it a matter of importance right now.  There are officers out there searching.  We need to go through her apartment."  Blair looked around.  "What about her cousin?"

"I spoke with him this morning.  He's had to go back north to finalize his move here.  He's on the road somewhere, I think.  I'll call him in a bit."  Brady straightened, his eyes on Will.  "Will?  Any word?"

Will studied his young friend, his heart hurting for him. "Nothing yet.  Our own K-9 teams have tracked where they could, same as Bradon and Kade.  They lose her scent."

"And that means she wasn't walking then, doesn't it?"  Brady paced away from them, not willing to let them see how upset he was, not knowing that they knew.  His four friends who had already faced something like this exchanged glances.  Brady paced back towards Barnabas.  "Has anyone checked her apartment?"

Barnabas nodded.  "Breck did earlier.  Anna went with him. Fynn's phone was on the kitchen table.  There were no signs that she had been back and then left again."

"So, where is she?"  Brady walked away, pausing to turn. "Where was she?"

"Near the lake, and you can't go that way yet, Brady." Will's words stopped Brady as he turned. "There's a crime scene there we are processing." He shook his head at the look on Brady's face. "It is a crime scene, Brady. You know that."

"I know." Brady walked past his friends, to slump down onto one of the couches in the foyer, Branigan sitting beside him, just waiting.

Buckley watched from the chair he had chosen to sit in for a few moments before he began to pray. Brady's heart quieted as he listened.

He's right, Lord, Brady prayed. You are in control of this. You do have Fynn in the hollow of Your hand. I just want her here with me. Yes, she is becoming that important to me. I never believed in love at first sight, but that's what happened. Is she the one You've chosen for me? Please, dear Lord, bring her home.

His mind drifting, Brady tuned out the quiet conversation between the two men, concentrating on the verses of protection and healing that he could think of. He knew Fynn needed to heal, in just so many ways. He hurt that she was gone, that he didn't know where she was.

Finally, Brady stood, a thought crossing his mind and he walked towards the stairs, leaving his friends staring after him before they exchanged glances and then shrugged. He shut his apartment door quietly, standing for a moment leaning against it, his head back and his eyes closed. He knew God was in control, that He was leading him with that thought. He reached for his phone as he walked towards his office, sliding down into the leather chair with a sigh. He hurt too much to sit but he had to. He needed to research.

"Eric?" Brady could hear the quiet conversation that surrounded Eric coming faintly through the phone.

"Brady? Why are you calling me? Hold on a sec."

Brady heard Eric asking for his bill and then his quiet thanks as he paid it.

"Okay, I'm in my vehicle. What's up?"

"Fynn."

"Fynn?  Isn't she with you?  That's what she said this morning, that she would be spending the evening with you.  Her words were along the line that Brady would occupy her evening with a walk and quiet conversation."  Eric waited, not hearing Brady reply.  "Brady?  Where is Fynn?"

"That we don't know, Eric.  She's disappeared.  Sometime this afternoon.  We're looking for her but haven't found her.  It's like she disappeared into thin air."  Brady waited, hearing the silence on the other end of the phone

"I'm on my way back."

"No, finish what you need to.  If anything, Barnabas will send Andy up with the plane and have one of our security guards come too so he can drive your vehicle back."

Eric was torn, wanting to be in on the search for Fynn but knowing he had to be in his hometown on the next day.  "Okay, I'll finish what I need to quickly and head back down.  I should be able to be on the road before noon.  Call me, please?"

"I will.  Pray, Eric.  Just pray for her to come home."  Brady set his phone down, staring at it, before he pulled up a search engine on his computer and starting searching, hunting for what he didn't know.  He didn't hear Branigan and Baird enter, followed by Benen.

"Brady?  What are you up to?"

Benen's voice caused Brady to spin, surprise on his face.  "I'm trying to research her brother.  Does that make sense?"

"It does.  It seems to come back to him."  Benen motioned him.  "Let me.  I might have more resources that you do."

Brady stood, his hand extended to his chair.  "Be my guest."  He began to pace, stopping in surprise as a mug appeared in front of his face.  He took it with a quiet thanks to Baird, before he found a chair and slumped down into it, pain evident on his face.  He needed to take something but couldn't, he thought.  He started to shake his head as the medication bottle appeared in front of him and then nodded, reaching for it and shaking out two pills before he swallowed them, his eyes going back to Benen.  Please, Lord, let us solve this.  Let my lady come back home.

Every day, Brady walked the woods surrounding the building, searching.  Searching for anything that would help them find Fynn.  Sometimes one of his friends was with him, quite often Bradon with his dog, Kade.  He didn't want to show it, but he was becoming discouraged and downhearted that he would find her.  His heart weighed heavy.  He knew his friends and Dallas, the detective assigned to the case, were searching, trying to come up with a culprit or a suspect, and Benen and Eric, he knew, were searching for any word on her brother.  No one had said anything to Brady, and he found that odd.

Brady sighed.  He looked up, searching the sky for answers, seeing the heavy rain clouds moving in.  He prayed for her return, but so far, God had not answered, or maybe He had and Brady had missed it.  He turned for home, not finding peace that day, feeling agitated more and more.  He was unable to really eat, but Anna had insisted that he take his meals with Doc and herself, mothering her as she did them all.  Barnabas had been quiet, not saying much, but he kept a watch on Brady.

His phone ringing startled him and he paused, staring at the number for a moment before he answered.  A quick conversation and he was off on a run.  He was needed at work, to replace a coworker who had been injured.  He couldn't say no, now could he?

Breck watched as he pulled away, a hand rubbing at his face.  He had wanted to talk to Brady, to bring him up to date on their investigations.  He would have to wait, he thought, before turning as he heard his name called.

"Breck?  Have you seen Brady?"  Burnie walked towards him at a rapid pace.  "I just got off the phone with someone, and I need to talk to him."

Breck nodded towards the road.  "He's off.  I suspect he's heading in to work.  I heard one of the paramedics was hurt today."

"Oh, no.  That's not good."  Burnie turned in a circle.  "I can feel someone watching us."

———

"There is. Security has mentioned that they have found traces of that, but no one is around when they find those traces. We've passed it on to Dallas, and he had a crime scene team come up and look around. They haven't said much about what they found."

"I don't think they will. Listen, Blair and I are heading down to the lake to search. We've seen the same cabin cruiser anchored off shore for the last few days."

Breck spun, his eyes on Burnie. "For how long?"

Burnie paused, his face paling before growing stern. "For as long as Fynn has been missing. You don't think?"

"I do think. Come on. I'm with you. Let's see what we can find. I would love to be able to give Brady good news tonight. It's going to be a hard enough day for him as it is."

"That it will." Burnie paced towards where Blair waited and took the backpack he was offered. "Breck's with us."

"Sure. I thought he would be." Blair grinned as he handed over a pack to Breck. "Here you go. Devaney gave me three, although at the time I questioned why. Now, I know. She would just tell me God told her to."

"And she would be right." Breck followed after Burnie. "Before we go too far, let's pray. I just have a feeling about today."

"You and me both." Burnie paused and turned, nodding at Blair to pray.

Blair's prayer lifted Fynn up to God, pleading that she would come home and that they would find her that day. He lifted his head as his eyes opened, a confidence in his look that said God would answer their prayers that very day.

The three men searched together, then moved a ways apart, their eyes watchful, looking for any sign of Fynn or her abductors. Burnie paused for a moment, a water bottle raised to his lips, before he lowered it and capped it, a frown on his face before he was running forward, startling the two men with him, who followed, puzzled glances exchanged between them.

Burnie paused, his head tilted as he listened, his hand raised to still the question on Blair's lips, before he was off again. The other two men followed, seeing him drop to his knees in the longer grass, before they heard quiet murmurs coming from him. They ran after him, fighting their way through the grass that attempted to entangle itself around their legs and ankles and trip them. They paused, wonder on their face, before praises were raised.

Burnie had dropped to his knees, his eyes on Fynn, watching as she lay in a huddled heap, her head burrowed under an arm. His hand was tentative as he reached for her, feeling for a pulse and then he sat back on his heels.

"Burnie?" Breck's quiet question had Burnie raising his head and looking up, nodding. Breck's eyes slid closed in an inaudible prayer.

"She's alive, but bad she's hurt, I don't know." He reached for her again, finding her shifting away from him and sitting up, fear on her face as she stared at him before looking up at the other two.

Fynn's gaze stopped on Blair, and she studied him, her mouth opening and closing before she spoke in a hoarse whisper.

"I know you. Don't I know you?" She shifted backwards as Blair crouched in front of her.

"You do, Fynn. I'm a friend."

"You are? What's your name?"

"I'm Blair. I'm a friend of Brady's."

"Brady? Who's he?" She studied Blair before looking at the other two men, confusion in her gaze.

"He's a friend of yours." Blair extended his hand. "Can you stand and walk? We can take you to him."

She shook her head. "I can't. I can't go near him."

"Why not?" Breck's question had her head spinning his way, her hand to it as her eyes slid closed and she crumpled once more to the ground.

Blair watched for a moment before he stood and gathered her into his arms, her arms around his neck in an unconscious movement. "Hold on, Fynn. I'll carry you. You don't seem too steady on your feet." He looked around at Burnie's indrawn breath.

———

"She can't walk, Blair. Not on those feet." Burnie gently raised one, his hand grasping her ankle as she tried to pull back. "She has no shoes, but it looks as if she's done some walking, and that over some rough ground."

Breck nodded. "If she came up from the lake, and I suspect she did, it's really rough with shoes on. I don't know how she made it this far." He turned. "Let's get her to the infirmary. Doc was home when we left. He said he had planned to catch up on some reading. Anna and Amy are away from the day. Barnabas had told Amy to take the day off."

Reaching the building, Blair headed for the corridor that led to the infirmary, the security guard running ahead to unlock it. Burnie headed to find Doc, Breck following Blair. He watched as Blair gently laid Fynn on the bed and then moved back to stand beside him.

"Did she say anything at all?" Breck's question was low.

"Not a word. Nothing since those few sentences." His phone was out. "I need to let Dallas and Will know." He paused. "We need to call Eric. What time will Brady be out?"

"I don't know but it was only a part shift he picked up." Breck eyed his watch. "Likely soon. We'll need to watch for him." His head turned as he heard rapid footsteps coming his way. "Here's Doc."

"It's Fynn?" Doc's voice was hopeful.

"It is, Doc. She was awake for a bit before she passed out again. We found her about a mile from the lake."

"The lake? The boat that's been there?"

Breck nodded. "That's what we think. Which one of the ladies do you want?"

"Cadee, I think. She's helped in the clinic at the mission. Though Berneen seems to have made contact with Fynn that the others haven't."

"I'll go find Cadee then. Berneen, Devaney and Ennis were away this afternoon. Cadee wasn't able to go." Blair turned, to find Cadee standing beside him. "Cadee? How did you know?"

---

"Burnie. He came and found me. He's rounding up the others, he said, and they'll watch for Brady."

"Good. Call us if you need us, Doc." Blair stepped back from the room, his hand pulling the door closed behind him, his eyes seeing the others waiting. "Don't ask how she is, guys. I really don't know at this point."

His eyes on Fynn, Doc hesitated a moment to pray, as he always did before he assessed a patient, before he moved towards her. Cadee stood on the other side of the bed, her hand on Fynn's, staring in disbelief.

"How, Doc?"

Doc shrugged. "I don't know, other than God. The three of them went searching and Burnie found her. She was out of it, his words, when they found her, roused for a few minutes, and then passed out again." Even as he spoke, Doc was at work, in physician mode now, assessing her. "Cadee, Burnie said her feet were hurt."

Cadee moved to look. "Oh, my, Doc. They are. She has no shoes on, did you know that?"

Doc shook his head. "No, I didn't. I'll take a look in a moment. We'll need the saline to rinse them off." He looked up. "Are you up for that?"

Cadee snorted, bringing a grin to Doc's face. "You should have seen what I had to help with. This is nothing. But I've never had to work on a close friend before."

"Is that what she is, Cadee? A close friend?"

"I know it's only a few days, but I would like to think that, Doc. She needs us." Cadee blinked back tears as she spoke, before she turned, hunting for the saline solution and then the cloths, bandages and basin that Doc needed, without being told what to find.

Doc watched her for a moment, before he nodded. He would need to talk to Benen, but Cadee was a natural nurse. If she had training, then he could use her here and perhaps at the mission where he volunteered. He knew she was looking for something, had been for a while now, not quite sure what she wanted to do.

"Doc?" He looked up at Cadee's quiet question. "Does Brady know?"

"I'm not sure. He had been called in to relieve someone this afternoon." His head turned as he heard scuffling in the hallway and the sound of a louder voice than had been heard. "I would say Brady's out there right now, and not happy he can't come in."

"That's what I wondered. Fynn hasn't said anything but I see how she watches him, without him knowing. She's in love with him, Doc."

"That may be, Cadee, but it's a discussion those two need to have. All we can do is pray for them."

Cadee sighed, knowing Doc was right, but wanting Brady and, yes, Fynn, to find the happiness she and Benen had found.

Doc worked away, his mouth in a tight, grim line as he treated Fynn's feet, finding wrapping them and then stepping back, a hand wiping at his face. He headed for the cabinets to pull out a bag of intravenous solution and the tubing and needle before he paused, then nodded. God, You did protect her. Thank you. He returned to Fynn's side to start the IV drip before he once more stood to watch her.

"Brady will want to come in, you know." Cadee grinned at Doc.

"I know he will. But first, I want to keep her here tonight. Can you stay for a bit? Anna will be back soon and she'll be here all night."

"I can. Doc, her feet?"

"I know, Cadee. She'll not be walking for a bit, that's a given. How she managed to get to where they found her, I'll never know. She's cut the one quite severely. Bruises, scrapes and minor nicks on both."

"But how, Doc? Wasn't she wearing shoes?"

Doc shook his head at Cadee's question. "No. She didn't have any on when I got here and Burnie said she wasn't wearing any."

"So, what happened to them? It's not like Fynn to wander around outside in her bare feet, at least, not out there." Cadee was puzzled, as she stared at her friend.

———

"No, it's not.  That's something Will and Dallas will have to discover."  Doc reached for his stethoscope once more before he stepped back again.

"Doc?"

"Hmm?"  He looked around at Cadee before he smiled.  "She's in good shape overall.  Now, let's see about getting Brady in here."

His feet dragging as he walked towards the back entrance of the building, Brady paused before he entered, his eyes drifting towards the lake. I'll search there tonight, Lord. I might even make my way out to that cabin cruiser and see what is up with it. It's been anchored there for so long, it makes me think it has something to do with Fynn's disappearance. Closing his apartment door behind him, his boots hit the tray in closet and he headed for the kitchen. It had been a stressful day, and he had already been worn out before he had headed into work.

He reached for clean jeans and a favourite T-shirt after his shower and shave before going back to the kitchen, reaching for his coffee and then for the sandwich he had made earlier but hadn't eaten. He had just taken a sip of coffee and bit into the sandwich when a knock came at his door. Brady stood, sandwich in one hand, his other hand of the door as he studied Blair standing there, puzzled at the look on his friend's face.

"Brady? You just get in? We were watching for you." Blair stepped inside as Brady moved back towards the kitchen.

"I came in the back way. Just wanted to grab a bite to eat before I head for the lake." Brady spun to face Blair. "I want to check out that cabin cruiser. It's been hanging around there for too long."

"Brady, before you go out, we need to talk." Blair sighed in frustration as Brady ignored him to finish his sandwich, take a last swig of his coffee, clicking off the coffeemaker and then reaching for a water bottle from the fridge. "Brady? Can you stop for a moment?"

Brady turned, surprised at the frustration evident in Blair's tone. "I can, but I do want to head that way. What's your problem?" He headed away from Blair, intent on finding his sneakers and shoving his feet into them.

"We found her, Brady." Blair waited, finally shaking his head, and stalking over to stand in front of the door, stopping Brady in his tracks.

Brady stood, a frown on his face. "Blair? What is it?"

"Fynn. We found her. She's here in the infirmary." Blair watched as Brady turned away from him. He saw the exact moment he understood his words.

Brady spun back, surprise and then hope on his face. "What did you say?"

"Fynn. Burnie, Breck and I found her. She's downstairs." Blair's hand came out to stop Brady's forward motion. "Doc and Cadee are with her. Dallas and Will are on their way out. They will need to talk to her first. If she's awake, that is."

"She's alive?" Brady didn't dare breathe, waiting for Blair to answer. "Blair? Please? How is she?"

"She's hurt, but I am not sure how bad. I haven't talked to Doc yet. She was unconscious when Burnie found her, talked for a bit, and then slipped away again. Her feet are torn up. Doc can tell you more." Blair's hand on Brady's chest kept him from moving forward and through the door, he was that anxious to find his lady. "Before you go, let's pray, Brady. She didn't remember who we were."

Brady nodded. "Given what she's been through, she'll have shut down to some extent. She'll remember us."

Blair snorted. "Remember you, you mean. Don't deny it, Brady. She's your lady."

Brady reached to brush away Blair's hand, not answering his unspoken question, before he was out of the door and heading for the stairs at a rapid pace. Blair swung the door closed behind him and was on Brady's heels, a hand out again to stop him.

"Brady, wait. We need to pray. We didn't."

Brady stopped, his head dropping forward, his eyes closing. He had forgotten. He had been in such a rush to get to Fynn, he had forgotten Blair had asked to pray.

"I'm sorry, Blair. You're right. Please?"

———

Blair nodded, his prayer quiet, raising Fynn up to God for healing, for Brady as he struggled to work, for the couple who were such new friends but had made a connection. He prayed for swift resolution of the mystery surrounding Fynn's disappearance, for protection for the two, and for wisdom for the police services as they sought to understand and then arrest the ones involved.

Brady raised his head, a thought crossing his mind. "Does Eric know?"

"I'm not sure. Will was reaching out to the chief in Ennis' town."

The two walked down the stairs, Brady's thoughts muddled as he approached the infirmary, heading for the door before he was stopped. He glared at Baird standing in his way, before he tried to shove by him. Hands reached to stop him and pull him backwards. Brady hit the wall and then tried to escape the hands holding him there. This was the scuffle Doc had heard and smiled at.

Will smiled and shook his head before nodding to Dallas to proceed to the infirmary. Will stood in front of Brady, his eyes searching the younger man, before he nodded. Will's wife had been correct in her assessment. Brady cared deeply for Fynn, he could see. The devastation and stress had taken a toll on Brady, he could see it in his face and in the lost weight. Brady had never been heavy, Will knew that, but the few pounds he had lost over the last week showed. Fynn's disappearance and the pain from his accident were all part of that, Will knew from experience.

Dallas tapped at the door before cracking it open and peeking around it, seeing Doc motioning him to enter.

"Doc? Talk to me. How is she?"

Doc shook his head. "To tell you the truth, other than her feet, she's in good shape."

"Her feet?" Dallas frowned, a pen and notepad in hand, as he waited.

"Her feet. They're torn up, but that would be from her walk up through the rocks and then the woods. She was on her way here, but I'm not sure she remembers that. She didn't have any shoes on her feet by the looks of it."

Dallas nodded.  "Any other injuries?"

Doc nodded.  "When we raised the head of the bed a bit ago, she was in pain.  Her back is bruised, I would say from falling against something.  It doesn't look like she has been abused or beaten.  She's dehydrated, has lost weight.  She doesn't give the appearance of having been drugged, but I drew blood and sent it in to the lab to verify that."

"Good."  Dallas shot a look back at the door.  "Now, is she awake that I can talk to?"

Doc shook his head, his eyes of Cadee as she pulled the sheet and light blanket up higher on Fynn's shoulders.  "She's been drifting in and out, but she sleeping now.  I have no idea how long she'll sleep for."

Dallas tucked away his pen and notepad.  "About what I figured you'd say.  I'll talk to the three who found her.  Will sent a team out to where she was, but I don't think we'll find anything."  He paused.  "Interestingly, that cabin cruiser has disappeared."

"That's where she'll have been then, on it.  So close yet so far away."  Doc turned to Dallas.  "Find out who did this before either one of them is hurt again."

Looking up as his captain sat in a chair by his desk, Eric drew a deep breath.  He had been burning the candle, he thought, at both ends, working the cases he had been assigned and trying to make good doing that, and then searching for Fynn and researching for any information he could find on Flannery.

"Eric?  How is it going for you?  Fitting in okay?"  Captain Walters had taken the call from Will and was relieved for his new detective.  It would mean one load of stress would be lifted from Eric's shoulders, but another added, as the detectives searched for Fynn's abductors.

"I am.  The group is great, sharing tips and helping out.  Not what I had expected, given the experience I had on my old force.  There was always a reluctance to share information."  Eric's gaze dropped to the report he had just finished and printed.  He had closed the case of the armed robbery at a local convenience store, but still had cases that were open and needing his attention.  He looked back up, catching a look on his Captain's face that he frowned at.  "Captain?"

"Please, call me Jim.  The others do.  We're part of the same church family, as well."  Jim paused, his eyes on the fingers he was rubbing together.  "I received a call from Chief Peters a bit ago."

Eric straightened up in his chair, his eyes not moving from Jim's face.  "And?"

"Three of Brady's friends went searching this afternoon."  Jim shook his head.  "It had to be God, that's all we can say."

"Fynn?"  Eric's voice was barely above a whisper.  He had talked to his mother that morning, who had called, concerned.  He frowned as he remembered her words that Fynn's parents had left on a planned vacation three days earlier, without waiting to find out if Fynn was safe or not.

"She's safe. They found her."  Jim watched with compassion as Eric tried to control his emotions.   He knew from his conversations with Eric how important Fynn was to him, that he considered her the sister he never had.

"Thank God." Eric looked up. "And, how is she?"

"In good shape." Jim pointed at the desk. "Where are you with your work? At a point you can leave it?"

"I just finished the report on the armed robbery, but I was to interview the bank teller." Eric was torn, wanting to head for Fynn, but wanting to prove himself.

"Do your interview and then head out. I've put Leslie on call. He came and volunteered, hearing the rumours that Fynn was found."

"He did? He didn't have to." Eric was surprised but thankful. He enjoyed the crew of detectives he was paired with.

"No, he didn't, but that's what we do here, Eric. We share the burdens of all our people, not just our own. Head out when you're ready. Call me if you think you need tomorrow."

Eric's head was down as he prayed, not watching Jim walk away. He was so grateful that Fynn was alive and safe. He reached for the file that was waiting and rose, heading for the interview room and the bank teller.

His thoughts on Eric and wondering if he had been called, Brady's head went back against the wall. He had struggled with his friends to get to the door but had been held back. He finally nodded to them and their hands dropped away, even as concern for both he and Fynn coloured their faces. He couldn't pray, didn't know how to frame his words, but he knew God understood, that at this time was when the Holy Spirit prayed for him. He looked up to see Will in front of him.

"Brady?" Will's voice held a question he didn't ask, that he wanted to know how Brady really was.

"I'm okay, Will. The guys would say otherwise, but I am okay." He gave a quick grin at the comments and quiet laughter that reached his ears. "How is she?"

"I haven't talked to Doc. That's Dallas' job. I am here for you, my friend." Will's heart uttered a prayer as he saw Brady taking in his words before he nodded. "And yes, Eric will have been told. I talked to his Captain earlier. It depends on what Eric has on his desk that he has to deal with today before he can head over."

"Thanks, Will." Brady's gaze went past him as the door opened and Dallas approached him, stopping just short of where Will stood, a shuttered look on his face. Brady's heart sank.

"Go on in, Brady. She's sleeping right now. I'll talk with her later." Dallas shared a glance with Will, who nodded, knowing that Dallas would not leave that building until he had had that talk with her.

Brady shoved away from the wall, his legs feeling weak for a moment, before he walked towards the door, his hand resting on it for a moment before he shoved it open. He knew his friends would hang around for a while before they headed for their own places, or perhaps the chapel. He knew Buckley would stay around close, ready to be his pastor instead of just his friend. That he was grateful for. A sudden thought crossed his mind. How did people who had no faith manage situations like this? He knew he wouldn't have handled it as well if it had not been for his own faith and trust in God.

Dallas watched as the other men lingered for a while and then left before he turned to Will. Barnabas had not left, standing watching Dallas closely

"Will? What do we know of Brady's past? Could it be part of this?"

Will shrugged and turned to Barnabas. "Barnabas?"

"Brady is from Nova Scotia. I found him just as he graduated from high school and offered him a position here. It was his decision to become a paramedic. He said his father had been one and had died on the job, working a flood when Brady was around ten. His mother never got over it, he said, dying from what Brady termed as a broken heart when he was seventeen. He was in foster care until he graduated high school. I can have the guys look into it for you."

"I have been, Barnabas." Dallas frowned, then grimaced. "I hate going behind his back."

"He understands that you would have been looking into him as well.  He mentioned that last night, in fact."  Barnabas shook his head.  "I just want this over for him and Fynn and something tells me it isn't."

"Not yet.  Not until we find her abductors and solve that."

Letting the door close quietly behind him, Brady stood, his eyes on Doc, who nodded at him to approach, then on Cadee, who gave him a gentle smile before she too pointed at the bed. His eyes dropped to Fynn, watching for a moment before he walked forward, hesitation in his steps. He stood, one hand clutching tightly to the bed rail, before he reached to touch her hair, one curl tucking between his fingers and wrapping around one. He waited for her to rouse but she lay still.

Brady studied her face, seeing the lines and shadows and hollows in it that were new. He sighed. Lord, why? Why Fynn? Who did she anger so much that this happened to her? I pray for healing for her.

He reached for her free hand, tucked near her cheek. She tightened her grip on his even as she sighed and shifted to her side, to face him, her grip tightening even more as he tried to free his own. Doc just shook his head, knowing these two were in love with one another, whether they had acknowledged it or not.

Brady prayed as he hadn't before. He needed Fynn to wake up. Yes, he acknowledged to himself that he needed her in his life. He prayed that she would be agreeable. The last week had been no difficult, not having her there. He had missed her, her dry sense of humour, her teasing, but also the deep thoughts she brought forth, thoughts she said she never shared with anyone else not even Eric. He did that to her, she accused, a smile on her face as she said it. Brady knew that she made him think, to delve back into the Bible to prove or disprove her thoughts.

Fynn stirred, a hand wiping at the hair on her forehead, brushing it back, even as her eyes opened. She stared at the navy T-shirt in her line of sight and frowned. Who was that? It was too tall for Eric, and her father wouldn't have been there, not in a hospital room, and that was where she was convinced she was. She gave a soft moan as she moved, the bruising on her back painful but the pain and soreness of her feet stronger than that.

"Fynn? Darlin'? You awake?" Brady's voice was low enough that only Fynn could hear him. He didn't realize he had slipped in an endearment, he was that focused on her opening eyes.

"Go away." Fynn's tone was disgruntled.

"Sorry, darlin'. No happening. Come on, love. Wake up." Brady's face held a small smile, but underneath it was the concern and worry he was trying so hard to hide.

"I'm sorry. Do I know you?" Fynn rolled slightly to look up, way up, she thought, at Brady, not realizing that he still held her hand. That was something she never allowed. No one held her hand, but Brady made her feel safe.

"You do. I'm Brady. We met a few weeks ago when I found a body and you were brought in. I've missed you the last week. We haven't been out to look for your creepy-crawlies." He grinned as she frowned at him.

"Creepy-crawlies? Really?" She gave a soft sigh. "I remember. You're the reason I moved, did you know that?" She frowned as he grinned at her. "It's not funny."

"No, it's not. How are you feeling?" He bent closer, a hand reaching to cup her cheek.

She gripped that hand, her mind working to remember. "I think I'm okay. But I don't know where I am, other than not on that boat."

"You're in the Foundation Building. Barnabas had set up an infirmary for it. That's where you are. And likely will be overnight, if I know Doc." Brady's head turned slightly as he heard Doc moving closer.

"Doc? Do I know him?" Fynn turned her head slightly, her eyes sliding closed at the sudden onset of a headache. "My head hurts."

"Of course it does. You're dehydrated. That would do it." Doc reached for her wrist, all the while watching her face. "I'll keep you here overnight. Anna will be alone shortly, but for now, Cadee is here. But now that you're awake, we need to get Dallas in here to talk to you." He paused, a smile on his face at her frown. "He's the detective who has your case, as they say."

"And before you ask, Eric will be here shortly.  At least I think he will."

"Real definite there, buster."  Fynn's eyes closed as she swallowed hard.  "Did they find them?"

"Find who?"  Dallas spoke from where he stood at the end of the bed.

"The men."  Fynn frowned at him.  "I don't know you, but I pray you're the detective I can tell my story too and then I need to sleep. I haven't slept in a week."

"Let me take your statement, and then I'll disappear.  We'll find the men, Fynn.  We will find them.  We're searching.  Brady's friends are searching.  Your cousin and the men and women on that force are searching.  The police chief from your hometown has been in touch, wanting to know what they can do to help."  He held up a hand at her protest.  "It's what we do for anyone, Fynn.  But you're one of us, whether or not you are still doing your forensics stuff, as Baird calls it."

Fynn nodded, her eyes on him.  "I guess that means Brady and Doc and Cadee have to leave."

"Doc stays.  Brady and Cadee need to step outside for now.  I want Doc here to monitor you and to tell you to stop if you. need to."  Dallas nodded as Brady took a reluctant step away, his eyes on Fynn's face before he walked to the door, holding it open for Cadee, and then stepping through himself, the door closing almost on his heels.

His pen poised over his notepad, his computer set to record her voice, Dallas waited, watching as Doc spoke quietly to her and then handed her a glass of water to drink. Fynn's hand shook as she took it, Doc's hand reaching to help her bring the glass to her mouth and drink. She nodded when she was finished, her eyes on her now-clasped hands.

"Where do I start, Dallas, is it?" Her voice was low, taut, shaky as she strove to control her emotions.

"Talk to me about that day. What did you do, what you had planned." He nodded at her look. "It's okay. It can be part of the statement." He watched as she swallowed and sighed to himself. It's never easy when you're the professional who has to be on the other side of the coin.

Fynn looked up at him, knowing that there were things she would never tell him. She suspected he knew that. "Okay. I guess I can. This is not easy. I never knew how the victims would feel. I never talk to the families. I stay in the background."

Fynn reached for the glass, sipping slowly as she thought through what she needed to say. She shuddered at the remembered feel on the man's hand around her mouth.

"I had had lunch with the ladies here and then went out. I was just walking, taking a look around, getting to know the area. I wanted to start a study on the bugs and insects indiginent to the area, just in case I do go back to my work. I had headed towards the lake. As I remember it, I was bent over or crouching down when I felt a hand come around my face, over my mouth, and another arm wrapping around me, trapping my arms to my sides. I fought. How I fought to get free, but I couldn't. I was carried away towards the lake. I thought I was going to be drowned but instead I was dumped into a small rowboat. I tried to jump out, but the man grabbed my arm and held a knife out towards me. He forced me up a ladder, across the deck and then down some stairs before he shoved me hard enough into a cabin that I landed on a bunk. I tried to get out but the door was locked.

"I didn't sleep well, couldn't in fact. I searched for a way out but there was none. Twice a day a youth, an older teenager I think, would bring in a tray and take away the one he had left. I refused to eat." Fynn paused to catch her breath. "I had water from the small washroom, I wouldn't touch what was on the tray."

She blinked rapidly, her eyes unfocused for a moment as a puzzled look crossed her face. "Every morning and then again in the afternoon, the man who threatened me appeared. He didn't stay for long, just kept asking where someone was. Where is he, was what he asked. He didn't give a name at all. Never in all the times he questioned me. I found that odd. I had to say I didn't know. I didn't. It was just so bizarre."

She looked up at Dallas, finding him watching her intently. "That last morning, the youth left the tray. I was by the window, port, porthole, whatever it is called, not looking back at him. I had tried to make my way out of it, but it was too small. When he left, I waited for the door to lock. I still don't know if he left it open on purpose or just forgot. I waited for about an hour and then approached it, not sure what I would find. The door was, as I suspected, unlocked. I went out, watching for the men, but didn't see them. Not even on the deck. The cruiser was deserted. I climbed down the ladder and then had to swim for shore. I was so afraid. I had heard of tides in the area that took unsuspecting swimmers away from the shore

"Once on shore, I walked towards the rocks, forgetting I had no shoes. The man who questioned me took them from me on the second day. I fought him to keep them. That's when he shoved me back against the corner of the wall, and I hit it hard with my back. I couldn't stop him from leaving."

Fynn blinked rapidly once more, her thoughts on the trek she had made. "I walked as fast as I could, stumbling over debris, my feet hitting rocks and stones. I think that's when I cut my foot. I remember a sharp pain and dropping down, wrapping my hand on my foot and seeing blood. I couldn't find anything to stop the bleeding. I had to keep moving. I didn't know when the men would come back and find me. I don't remember the walk towards the building, but I prayed, prayed that God would lead me where I needed to go, to where I would be safe. The last thing I remember is walking into long grass and thinking I can't go on. That I couldn't walk any further. I don't remember anything until I woke up here." She looked up at him and nodded.

"That's good, Fynn. Now, can you describe the men?"

"I can. If you can find me a pad of paper and a pen, I can do a sketch of them."

Dallas held up his hand. "I'll have a police artist come out tomorrow. She'll do the sketch for you."

"Of course. I wasn't thinking, now was I?" Fynn was angry, angry that she had been hurt, angry that she had lost a week of time when she wanted to be doing something else, angry that she had been taken captive and threatened. "He threatened me, threatened Brady, threatened the men and ladies here. How do I stay, Dallas?

"You stay because this is where you will be safe, as long as you stay close to the building. You stay because this is your home. You stay because a certain male I know wants you to."

"Male?" Her brow wrinkled as she puzzled that out. "Eric doesn't live here. He would want me to stay but he would leave the decision to me."

"It's not Eric that I'm thinking of. It's Brady. It went hard with him this week when you were gone."

She frowned again. "Brady? He shouldn't have been like that. I'm not that important to him. I mean, he's a friend and all that." Her words died away as Dallas simply smiled and shook his head. "Dallas?"

"It's more than that with him, Fynn. In case you missed it, he cares deeply for you. He would spend hours searching for you, praying to find you. You're the most important person in his life, I would suspect."

"I can't be." Her voice was barely above a whisper, even as hope rose in her heart, that just maybe God had been behind this all, that God had provided her the knight she had prayed for all her life. The knight that was never wove into bedtime stories just because her mother or father never told her bedtime stories. Those were reserved for the times she spent staying overnight at her aunt's. Those were the cherished memories she had.

"He's your knight." Dallas almost seemed to read her mind. "And his new truck is white." He didn't look up at her as he packed away his laptop, a smile hidden from her, but he heard her gasp and then her quiet prayer, a prayer he didn't think that she realized she was breathing aloud. "I'm out of here. I'll have more questions over the next few days for you. If you think of anything, call me or call Will. He can send someone out to talk with you."

Dallas paused outside her door, his eyes on the floor, his heart heavy knowing that he was no further ahead in the search. The man she described as her captor? They had found a body matching his description this morning in the downtown area. The responding officers had informed Dallas that the man had been described as being intoxicated and because of that had lost his balance on a balcony and fallen to his death. He would find a picture of him and show it to her, he thought. Now, the youth? What was that about, he wondered?

Brady moved closed to Dallas, his head tilted at he studied his friend.

"Dallas?"

Dallas shook his head to clear his thoughts, even as he raised it to answer Brady. "You can go back in. She's given me her statement. I'll need to have her read it over and sign it in the next hour or so. Don't be asking her any questions or letting her talk about it."

"I won't. Thank you." Brady moved past him, the door closing behind him even as Cadee walked towards Dallas.

"Dallas?"

"She's hurting, Cadee. Brady will help, but you four ladies? You have experienced something similar. Talk to her. Be honest with her. I know you and Benen were married when you went through what you did." Dallas paused, his head turning so that he could eye the door. "Somehow, I think those two will marry before this is all over."

“I think you may be right, Dallas.  Only time and God will tell us.”

*Chapter 19*

A week later, Fynn stared at Brady, in shock at his words, before she spun and ran from him, her hands hitting the lobby door and flying open from the force of her shove. She stopped and stared over her shoulder before she turned, heading for the garden that had become her favourite, the ones with all the daisies, columbines, and coneflowers. She loved to sit and watch the butterflies and bees as they hovered over the flowers. Fynn dropped to a bench, her face covered with her hands as she willed back the tears, a few falling that she could not stop. Brady was hovering and she couldn't have that. In fact, she wasn't used to it, and while she could see and understand his concern, she didn't like feeling trapped. Not unless there was a deeper meaning to his concern, and that he had not said.

Brady stared after her, his hands clasped on the top of his head. He hadn't mean to scare her or chase her away with his words. He had simply asked her to go out to dinner with him, and that he wanted to talk to her about where they were headed, if they were heading anywhere at all as a couple. He headed after her almost on a run, but stopped short, almost knocking Buckley down as he appeared in his path.

"Brady?" Buckley's voice held a touch of amusement. "Chasing someone down, are you?"

Brady smirked. "I was, until someone jumped into my way. Buckley?"

"Do I need to talk to her for you? I can, you know." Buckley's hand on Brady's shoulder moved him forward. "I gather you're trying to talk to her, and she didn't like it."

"No, I don't think that's it." Brady sighed, his hands scrubbing down his cheeks. He had come home from work, a long, hot, heartbreaking day with fatalities in the accidents they had responded to, and after he had cleaned up, the only thing he had any desire to do was to take Fynn out to dinner and for a long walk along the boardwalk that ran the shoreline in the town.

"She's scared, Brady. We've talked, her and I. She didn't have that great an upbringing. She told me her parents were distant, that she could never please them no matter how hard she tried or what she accomplished or won. She didn't understand it growing up, but now that she has remembered her brother and after speaking with her aunt and uncle, she thinks that her parents withdrew because of that."

"I think she's right, but it doesn't help now." Brady's steps slowed as he watched Fynn, huddled over, her face still buried in her hands. "How do I reach her, Buckley? How do I help her to heal?"

"By being there for her. By praying for her. By encouraging her. Barnabas would say that is crucial to your relationship, you encouraging her. That's what this Foundation is about. You've watched us all at times doing this, particularly our four friends who are now married. She needs to heal, and a big part of helping that is for you to do just what I said. Encourage her to talk, to seek help when she needs it. She's rootless right now. Her work was her life, and she has stepped back from that."

"It was, and she has. She told me she wants to set up a lab somewhere to study the insects here more fully, but she doesn't have the money to do that. She understands that the Foundation would help her, as her research would and could be used in fighting crime."

"That it would." Buckley watched as Fynn's head raised as she realized she was not on her own. "She knows you're here, Brady. I'll let you two talk."

Brady's hand on his arm stopped Buckley in his tracks. "No, please stay. I need to ask Fynn some questions and I would like our pastor to be in on that." He gave a small smile. "And as a friend, but mostly as our pastor. I need guidance and advice."

Buckley nodded, having a feeling in his heart where this was going. "First, has Dallas said if they are any further ahead in their investigation?"

Brady shrugged, at a loss in that. "He said the vagrant they found dead was the man who abducted her. They have tied him to Tyler Oakes."

"Tyler? He's the one, then. The youth she talked about. I've worried about him. He's always been hard, but he has a good heart underneath.  If we can find him before he comes of age, maybe we can reach him.”

“I think you have, Buckley.  I have watched him study you and try to do what you’re doing.”

“He has?  I’ll put the word out that I need to talk to him.  Don’t worry.  I won’t push him.”

Fynn watched as Brady and Buckley stood talking before she rose and approached him, ducking under the arm Brady raised to draw her to his side

“Guys?  You seem deep in conversation.  I don’t want to intrude.”

“Never intruding.  I’m here as your pastor and friend, Fynn. Brady tells me that he needs to talk with you.”  Buckley grinned at the glare tossed his way.

“I do, Fynn.  I really wanted to take you out to dinner and for a walk, but let’s sit.  I need to explain myself better.  I’m not good with words the way Burnie, our author, is.”

Fynn sat, Brady’s arm still around her to tuck her close to him. “Okay.  You wanted to talk?”

“First, Brady, Fynn.  Let’s pray.  God is here but we need to ask for His guidance in this conversation.”  Buckley’s head went down and he was praying before either one of the others could respond.

Brady gave a quiet word of thanks when Buckley finished.  He knew that whatever Fynn was facing was not over, not by a long shot as his father would have said.  He studied the ground, his shoe moving over the grass.  He felt Fynn’s hand on his, her grasp light but reassuring.

Looking up, Brady studied the beautiful lady in front of him, thankful for her and how she challenged him, grateful for the courage she showed, but unsure how to really say what he needed to say.  His mouth opened and closed a few times before he caught the gleam of mischief and teasing in Fynn’s eyes.

“Fynn.  We haven’t known each other that long, but I feel that I know you better than anyone I’ve known for years.”  He groaned as she laughed at him. "That's not how I meant to say that. What I mean is that I love you, love you more than I ever thought I could. I want to explore our friendship, to see where it goes, to see if you would be willing to be the missing part of my heart, the helpmeet God has sent for me."

"Explore our friendship, you say?" Fynn was enjoying herself teasing him, seeing him tense at her words. "Brady?" When he didn't look at her, her hand reached to his face, to turn it towards her. "Don't you see? Others have. You are the missing part of my heart, the one I didn't know I needed. I love you as well." She turned as she heard a choked sound from Buckley, her puzzlement turning to a glare. "Buckley, behave yourself."

"I'm sorry. It's just that we've all seen this since you arrived, Fynn. We just couldn't figure out how you two were missing this." His grin said he was enjoying himself, even as he prayed for them.

"We weren't missing it, Buckley. God hadn't prepared our hearts yet. But now He has." Fynn turned back, missing Buckley's nod at her wisdom. "So, Brady, what do you say? Will you marry me? Grow old with me? Serve God as He would direct us?"

His heart pounding and his whole body shaking, Brady stared at Fynn, not quite sure that she was serious, but he could see she was. He saw the glimmer of tears in her eyes and knew that she had put herself out of her comfort zone to ask him that very question. He reached to draw her close, his arms wrapping around her, his head down on hers. He didn't hear Buckley's quiet words of prayer for them.

He leaned back, his eyes meeting Fynn's before he grinned. "What will we tell our children, darlin'? That you asked me to marry you?'

"Brady!" Fynn's cry of disbelief hit him in his heart.

"I agree, darlin'. I will marry you. Buckley, be quiet."

Buckley had begun to laugh, although he had tried to choke it back. "You two are just too funny for words, did you know that? I would be pleased to explain it to your children, if God so blesses. Let me pray for you, and then I'll disappear. This moment is for you two alone. Come see me to set a day, although I do have this Saturday available."

The couple could hear Buckley's chuckle as he waved as he walked away, before they turned to each other.

"Did I really ask that?" Fynn was dismayed. It should have been Brady.

"You did. Now, let me ask you a question. Will you be mine, Fynn, mine to cherish and love and grow old with, to serve God as we should, to be that blessing to others that He would have us be?"

She nodded before she was swept into his arms. When she could breathe again, she looked up at him, content for the moment, but still worried.

"But what about the men after me? What happens with them?"

"We can worry about the all we want, but it won't find them. We'll leave it for Dallas and his teammates to find them." He sat back, his arms around his love. "When?"

Fynn began to giggle, something he had not heard from her before. "Buckley did say he had time this Saturday, didn't he?" When Brady began to laugh, she smirked. "I don't want to rush it, but I don't want to wait too long." She sighed, bringing his eyes to her. "Mom and Dad are away for a month. I'll send them a text, but I don't think they'll care."

"We will wait if they want us to. If not, we can do a virtual ceremony with them, if they want."

Fynn nodded, rising when Brady stood, taking the hand he held out for her, a shiver running through her as she feared for his life. She remembered the threats that had been lodged against him. How did she do it, Lord? How do I do it? How do I keep him safe? She searched the area around them as they walked slowly back towards the building, not seeing the youth who had been her captor standing in the shadows, watchful, his eyes searching for anyone who would find him. He finally turned and walked away, his shoulders slumped. To see them together had not been what he had hoped for. He knew Buckley was wanting to speak with him and he had a good idea what it was about. He had been avoiding him and would continue to do that. He would also need to avoid the men who had hired him. Suddenly, Toronto or even Ottawa or the Maritimes seemed like a wonderful place to live.

Brady stopped suddenly, a hand rubbing at his face. Fynn stared up at him, not sure what had happened.

"We need to talk, Fynn. I don't think that it has been explained to you what happens when we fellows marry."

She nodded. "The ladies did. I would expect to receive a salary, wouldn't I?"

Brady nodded, his eyes searching her. "You will. But more than that. Barnabas caught me when I got home today. He's wanting to speak with you. He's talked to his Dad and the other board members. They want to offer you the funds to set up a research facility for your bugs and insects. He's hoping you will say yes. He's looking far into the future, but his Dad mentioned that you could become a training facility for entomologists, using your forensics experience that way.”

Fynn stared at him, her eyes huge, her mouth in a circle. “How did they know?” Her voice was barely audible.

“Know what, darlin’?”  Brady hugged her, waiting for her to speak.

“That’s my dream, you know.  I had a vision of myself doing just that before I graduated.  Thank you.”

“No, the thanks go to Barnabas and the board.  Now, let’s head into town.  I want to take my sweetheart out for a meal.”

Neither saw Barnabas standing in the parking lot, his hand raised to flag them down.  Buckley stood beside him, a smirk on his face.

“They only have eyes for each other tonight, you know”

“I can see that.  Know something you want to share?” Barnabas grinned at him.

“Nope.  It’s theirs for the telling.”

“Like that, is it?  I can wait.  If you see Brady or Fynn, let them know I want to talk to them, sooner rather than later.”

“I will.  Listen, I talked to Dallas today.  He was looking for the youth.”

“And?”  Barnabas waited, his eyes on the keys he held in his hand.

“They can’t find him but the word on the street is that someone is looking for Fynn and means to find her.  Knowing she’s connected here, the street people are staying silent.”

“That’s good.  Send out word that meals and what they need will be available through the shelter or the diner.”  Barnabas walked away, his words echoing in Buckley’s ears.  It wasn’t the first time the Foundation had done that.

“I will, Barnabas.  I will.  But I fear for Fynn and now for Brady.  It’s not over for them, not by a long shot.”  Buckley stared towards the road before he too turned and walked away, not seeing

Blair and Devaney watching him before they exchanged glances and both shrugged.

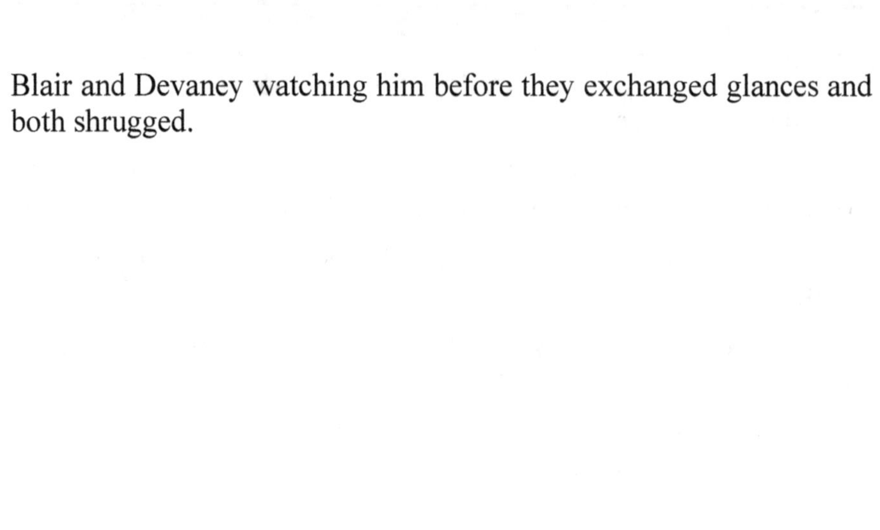

A week later, Fynn shoved her feet into her hiking boots, tied them, and then stood, her hand reaching for the cotton shirt she had set ready to don. She was heading out to research the area, but fear held her back. She shrugged. What can happen that hasn't already happened, she thought. I can do this. I have to, don't I, Lord? I can't hide or live in fear. I just ask that You protect Brady. I can't live with myself if he is hurt once more. Fynn paused, a thought crossing her mind. Was someone different after Brady? Was it connected to her only or to him as well? She shrugged, her hand reaching for the backpack she had left handy.

Shutting and locking her door, Fynn headed for the lobby, stopping in surprise as she saw Brady as well as Bradon and Ennis waiting for her, all dressed in casual clothing that said they were ready for a hike.

"Brady?" Fynn walked slowly towards him, a puzzled look on her face at his grin.

"I had the day off. Unexpected. To make up for some shifts I've picked up. Bradon and Ennis were free as well. We would like to join you on your hike, if we may. If you say no, we'll just head in the same direction but stay behind you." He continued to grin at her frown, hearing Bradon's chuckle and Ennis' laughing comment to behave himself.

Fynn shrugged. "I guess. It's not exciting for anyone else. Most people don't like my creepy-crawlies."

"I, for one, would enjoy it greatly. I have always been fascinated with certain bugs, but have had no one to talk to me about them." Ennis linked her arm through Fynn's and drew her outside. "So, tell me. How do we go about this? Do you gather them into containers or just watch them?

Fynn laughed, her heart suddenly free of the restrictions she had always felt. She had been an anomaly in her family. She knew her mother didn't like her line of work at all and her father had bluntly told her to find something else to do. She had stared at him that day, watched him walk away from her in anger, and knew in her heart that she just would never please them, no matter what she did.

"I plan on doing both. You can help."

"Great!" Ennis' smile lit up her face. "Talk to me, Fynn. Tell me about your work."

Fynn did just that, explaining how she took samples of eggs, larvae, and bugs or insects from a crime scene and then analyzed them, determining their ages and if they were resident to the area.

"Wow! I didn't realize it was so involved." Bradon's voice had Fynn's head snapping around, surprise on her face. "I'm sorry. I wasn't meaning to eavesdrop but this is fascinating. Have you ever considered lecturing on this?"

Fynn shrugged. "At one point, I had been asked to but refused. I couldn't face the people in my hometown with this. They would have shrugged it off as an obsession I have had since a child."

"An obsession?" Brady shared a look with Bradon before he spoke again. "Not an obsession, Fynn. Not in the way they would mean. You have done a lot of good and brought healing to many through your work. I know you don't think of it that way, but God has given you knowledge and a talent that is rare to find."

Fynn blushed at his praise, not used to words such as his. "Thank you, love. Now, here's where I was hoping to work today."

Brady's hand on her arm stopped her. "Are you sure?"

She nodded, looking around the small meadow where she had been found. "I need to take this area back, Brady. If I don't, I can't heal and move on. I certainly would never be able to come this way again."

Brady nodded. "Then, that's what we do. We take it back for you. Bradon, a prayer to start, if you don't mind."

Hours later, flushed with laughter, Fynn sat back on the log she had found for a perch, a water bottle in her hand. She had never had so much fun, she thought. She had never taken time to make friends, to just be herself, the way Ennis was drawing her out. She missed Brady's speculative glance at her before he nodded.

"So, Fynn, now that we have been crawling around on our hands and knees chasing fast moving creatures, what do you do with them?" Bradon grinned at her as she made a face at him. He had come to appreciate the fine, dry sense of humour she had, dark at times, but he knew that came from her line of work. He saw it in Doc and Anna and in Brady.

"I take them home and preserve them. They will become the foundation of my work." She looked up suddenly, unsure of herself. "I just don't know if I can do this."

Brady's arm drew her close to him. "You can, darlin'. You can. This has been a dream of yours for years, hasn't it? Barnabas is wanting to talk to you again, didn't you say? He seems to have found land and an architect already."

"I know, and the speed of that scares me."

Ennis laughed. "Barnabas is a mover. He makes things happen. He doesn't throw his wealth around, asking for favouritism. People know that when he asks for something, it has been thought through thoroughly, and that he is ready to move. He has many friends and acquaintances who know him, know his character, know that the causes he picks up are near and dear to his heart, and that these are usually ones that will educate or enhance or bring about a change in someone's life, or in other words, bring change that is wanted or needed."

Brady nodded. "Ennis has said it well. That's what Barnabas wants. Even more, he wants to encourage people. He strives to be like Paul's companion, Barnabas. That's why he searched the country for men like us. He wanted to find ones who were on their own, that needed the encouragement he could offer. He also has said he was driven to find men with the same initials as his."

"Right there, that's what I don't get." Fynn sat forward, absentmindedly recapping her water bottle. "How did he find you all?"

Bradon shrugged, his thoughts going back to how he had been found by Barnabas, his heart grateful to the man who had become a good friend. "God. That's what he always says. He had investigators searching, presenting names. Barnabas would track us down, observe us, talk to people, and then offer us the position with the Foundation.  His father has backed him all the way.  Some of the board questioned at first what he was doing but they have all come around to thinking the same as he does."  Bradon paused, his eyes on Ennis.  "Even though we have gone through some pretty horrible things, he has stood beside us, not moving until we were safe. That's who he is."

Fynn nodded, a thoughtful look on her face.  "I can see that, for the short time I have known him.  Brady, we're not done yet.  I talked to Dallas yesterday.  He needs to sit down with us both in the next couple of days."

Dallas studied the young couple in front of him, his eyes assessing them, not liking the strain that showed in both their faces. Lord, can we end this? They need this over. Fynn has healing to do that she can't while this is hanging over her head. They don't have to say anything but I know they have reached an agreement of some kind. They will tell us when they are ready, if and when he corrected himself.

"Dallas? Where do we stand in the investigation? It's seems to have gone on for so long." Fynn shook her head. "That's not fair. I know they things take time. I just so want this over."

"We do too, Fynn, for both your sakes." Dallas paused in his speech, looking down at his notes. "The man who abducted you? We are tracing him back, to your hometown in fact."

"That doesn't surprise me. Who is he connected to?" Fynn sat forward in her chair, intent on understanding what Dallas was or was not saying, depending on how you looked at it, she thought.

Brady watched her closely, seeing another side to her that he hadn't seen before, except so briefly that first day. "Fynn? What are you thinking? Or rather, who would you suspect?"

"The one you would suspect the least. Now, it could be the one you would suspect the most and set aside as being too obvious."

Dallas stared at her, amazed at how she had gotten right to the point.

"The latter, I think, Fynn. How well did you know the town treasurer?"

"Ted Langley? We went to school together but he was older than me. That was a given. I think he had failed a grade or two at the beginning of his school life. We could never figure out how he became the town treasurer. He was never good with math or numbers." Fynn rubbed at her temples, a headache starting to burn. "Are you saying that he's the one?"

Dallas shrugged. "We're looking at him. What else can you tell me about him? I have to make a trip up that way, but I would like to have more information on him. The townspeople I've talked to haven't been really forthcoming."

Fynn snorted, bringing a grin to Brady's sober face. "And they won't. The ones you would need to talk to won't talk to a stranger. They might talk to me, but I'm not the investigator. I don't think that they would talk with Eric even." Fynn rubbed at her face, distress showing. "Who can I send you to?"

"How about Eric's mother or his aunt?"

Fynn nodded, her eyes lighting up. "Perfect. His aunt has a B&B that you could stay at. That would be the perfect cover for you."

Dallas began to laugh. "You're reading too many cop novels, Fynn."

She stopped in her movement of raising her glass to her mouth to take a drink of juice, her eyes narrowing at him. "No, I don't read those. I don't read a lot, not any more, and I should. I need to go back to that." She set her glass down and moved away from the table, pacing before she was out of the room and then back, shoving one of her high school yearbooks at him. "Senior class. Read what he wrote about his life ambitions. I had forgotten what he had wrote." She shivered as she sat back down, her chair moved closer to Brady, who reached out to draw her close to him.

"Fynn?" Dallas raised his eyes. "Did he really say that? That he wanted to live life to the fullest and he really didn't care how he got to that?"

"He did. He was like that in school. We suspected he was behind the drugs and alcohol that used to appear at the parties. I never went but I heard rumours and stories. We think he was doing more that providing that."

"What are you thinking?" Dallas watched her closely as she shrugged.

"I am not really sure. There is someone else." She stared at the wall, a frown on her face, before the two men exchanged glances and then shrugged.

Dallas finally rose, taking Fynn's yearbook with him at her request. "Thanks for the information, Fynn. I'll be in touch."

Brady watched him walk away before he rose, gathering their dishes and washing them, waiting for Fynn to speak. When she didn't, he turned to lean against the counter, drying his hands on the small towel she kept draped over the over door handle.

"Fynn?" When she looked up, he drew in a deep breath at the devastation of her face. He was across the room, back in his chair, his arms reaching for her. "Fynn? What didn't you say?

"I couldn't. I have no proof."

"Who, Fynn? Who do you suspect?"

She buried her face against him, and he felt the sobs shaking her body. His head rested on hers as he prayed for her, bringing her to the throne, asking for healing for her.

Fynn finally just rested against him. "I don't have proof."

"And you don't want to accuse anyone without it. But, who, Fynn?" He waited before he finally spoke a name.

Fynn stilled even more. "How did you guess?"

Brady shrugged. "It just makes sense. Now, we have to prove it. I know the guys will want in on it."

Fynn sat back, her eyes on him. "I have a contact I can reach out to. She's good at what she does. She'll look into it without anyone knowing. I have no idea how she does what she does but she is so good at it. She has resources even the biggest police department doesn't have."

"Okay, let's do that. But for now, where's your Bible? We need to find verses to live by."

She rose, a hand reaching out for his, and headed to the living room, curling up on the couch as Brady lifted her Bible from the end table where she had left it. She listened as he read through numerous verses, her heartache easing, her mind beginning to slow. Thank you, Lord, she breathed, for. bringing Brady into my life. He's what I need, and You knew and planned for it.

Barnabas hesitated the next day as he walked towards his vehicle, a frown on his face for a moment. I should know this couple, but I'm not sure that I do. The lady, and it was a lady, he decided, not just a woman, walked towards him.

"Good morning. Do you know where I can find Fynn? I need to speak with her." Her voice was low and melodious.

The man with her reached for Barnabas' outstretched hand. "You are Barnabas Carey. We met years ago."

The name finally came to Barnabas.

"Abe Finlay. And this must be Emma."

"That would be me." Emma looked past him, before she moved away, without excusing herself.

Abe grinned. "Sorry. She can have a one-track mind at times. I would suspect that she has found Fynn."

Barnabas spun. "And she has. And all my guys as well." Barnabas grinned at Abe. "Where are your guys?"

"They all wanted to come. Don't be surprised if they all show up at some point. They know of Fynn. Know her work. She helped solve a case for a friend of ours back a couple of years. They have not forgotten that. They said to tell you that they will help in any way they can."

The two men approached Emma and Fynn, Brady standing with an arm around her, the other twelve men and the four ladies circling them. Emma and Fynn were in deep discussion.

Abe looked around, feeling uncomfortable.

"Can we go somewhere inside, Barnabas? Someone's out here."

Barnabas nodded and then spoke to the group, directing them inside. "Thanks, Abe. I think we'll need to have a talk with Fynn.

She has no fear, or hides it well. She's out and about, without any concern for her safety."

"No, she's concerned. She's hiding her fear and concern from you. She doesn't want to worry any of you and certainly does not want to put any of you in danger. But she has, just by doing that very thing."

Barnabas stared at him for a moment, not quite sure Abe had read Fynn right. He turned as he heard a throat clearing beside him.

Brady stood there, his eyes on Fynn as she moved away with Emma, the other four ladies with them, his friends following, their eyes watchful.

"Abe's right, Barnabas. She tries to hide how she's feeling. She has felt for years that no one listens to her, that no one really cares what happens to her. Eric, now there, she has been freer with him than with others and with her aunt and uncle. But that's because Eric pushes her. I've heard their discussions, full voice at times." He grinned at the astonished look on Barnabas' face. "Didn't expect that, did you?" He paused, a thoughtful look on his face. "What she went through when she was abducted? That is changing her. Coming here, away from her hometown? She is uncertain if she should have. She's trying to find her way, to heal from the past and whatever hurts she has not yet shared with me."

Abe's hand was in the air as he waved it to stop Brady's words. "Just a moment. Did you say she was abducted?"

"She was. She was gone for a week. She made her way back towards here. The only thing they asked of her was where a man was. She has no idea who." Brady paused, his face hardening. "Did you know that she has a brother who disappeared when she was two?"

Abe stared at him before he spun to stare after Emma. "That must be what she meant." He walked rapidly towards the building.

"What who meant?" Brady ran to catch up with him, Barnabas torn between where he needed to be and where he wanted to be before he headed to his vehicle and drove away. He would catch up with them later.

"Emma.  She was muttered something about a man named Flannery."

Brady held the door open for Abe and then pointed towards a hallway.  "They'll be in the conference room.  And yes, Flannery is Fynn's brother.  She had forgotten him, driven her childhood memories deep inside.  She's tried so hard over her lifetime to please her parents, but hasn't been able to reach through to them."

"A friend of ours who is a psychologist would say that she did that to protect herself.  Repressing her memories."  Abe sighed as he stood just inside the conference room doorway, his eyes wandering over all the people in there, watching as they had scattered to work. Emma stood beside Benen, deep in conference.  "The man Emma's talking to?"

"Benen?  He's an IT guy."

"She finds them, somehow.  She has her employees working on this.  She wants this over for Fynn."

"How did they meet?"  Brady watched his lady, seeing her ruffled curls where she had drawn her hands through them, her attention focused on Brendon as he spoke with her.

"Fynn was instrumental in solving a case that involved close friends of ours.  The man had disappeared and we searched for him. Fynn was brought in as an expert witness, having done what she does best, finding the evidence that proved when he was killed.  It saved his son from being charged."

"Wow!  I knew she was good."

Abe grinned.  "And when's the wedding?"  He laughed as Brady stared at him, finally remembering to snap his mouth closed. "All my guys on my team, Emma and I, and a number of close friends have had what we call adventures, sometimes to the point of being life threatening."

"Sounds like four of my friends.  We almost lost Bradon and Ennis."  Brady finally walked towards Fynn, his hands resting on her shoulders.

Fynn tilted her head to look up at him, silent communication between them, before she went back to the papers in front of her.

———

"Fynn?  Talk to me."  Brady slid into a chair beside her, exchanging a look with Brendon.

Fynn looked up, a devastated look on her face.  "This!  How did Emma ever find this?"

Finally, Emma rose from the computer she had been using, her eyes on Abe as he nodded. She approached Fynn, sitting beside her, an arm around her.

"Fynn. We need to be leaving. We'll come back if you need us to. Call me. I'll send what I have found to the detective, Dallas, is it?"

Fynn nodded, a sad look on her face. "Thank you, my friend. I am glad you have found Flannery. Or at least, I think you have. He's nearby, isn't he?"

Emma nodded. "That's what we have determined. He is likely watching for you. We have found his foster parents. He was never adopted, and no one knows why. He would be able to tell you. Jace has traced his travels in the last few months. He has been back to your hometown."

"He has? Is he the one I've felt watching me?" Hope rose in Fynn's heart. She desperately wanted to meet the brother that she could only vaguely remember.

"We suspect so. Call me, Fynn, even if you just need to talk. You know my story."

"I do." She looked past Emma at Brady, who stood nearby, deep in conversation with Burnie. "May I share it with Brady?"

"That you can. If you need to talk to any one of us ladies, call us. The guys are worried about you. If they hadn't had to be training today, they would have all come."

Fynn started to laugh, Emma grinning with her. "I can see that. Other than the seven, how many others would have come?"

Emma laughed. "You know us too well. Listen, when you get your facility up and running, call us. We want a tour. And I know Joseph will want to do your security system."

Fynn shook her head. "Tell him Brady has a friend, Branigan, who is as good as he is. A little healthy competition there won't hurt."

Emma laughed. "You know them well." She rose, a final hug given and then she walked away.

Brady stood for a moment before he approached Fynn.

"You okay?" He enveloped her in his arms, his chin on the top of her head.

"I am, thank you." She moved so she could look up at him. "Emma says Flannery was back in our hometown."

"I am sure he has been. He's trying to figure out how to approach you, without putting you in danger. Or any more danger than you have been in."

"Do you think so?" Fynn sighed, the sigh seemingly drawn up from the very tips of her toes.

"Now what, Fynn? Are you at a point you can leave it for today?"

Fynn leaned past him to study the table, seeing the untidy mess of papers, and frowned. "I don't work like that. I don't have messy piles of papers." She turned as she heard laughter.

Bradon was grinning at her even as Baird was laughing.

"I would say you did this time. Let me tidy it up for you and then we can lock it away in the safe. We'll let you set your own combination and then you can access it whenever you want. I feel like I'm going to tell you something you already know, but don't bury yourself in here or under the paperwork. Understand, please, that we all will be working on it. Dallas has copies, I just spoke with him. You need to keep your strength up, Fynn, and I suspect you won't do that unless we set boundaries on you."

She frowned at him, anger flaring for a moment, her mouth opening to speak before Brady's arms tightened around her.

She nodded. "I know that, Bradon. I really do. It's just that......"Her voice died away before she broke away from Brady and ran, tears that she wasn't even aware she was shedding glistening on her cheeks.

———

Brady stood for a moment, his eyes following her, his hand rubbing at his face. He finally turned to his two friends, not seeing the others gathering around them.

"I'm sorry, Bradon. I don't know what to say."

Bradon shrugged. "It's okay. She's been due to break. I thought it would have happened earlier."

Brady shook his head, finally seeing his friends surrounding him. "It's just that Emma confirmed her brother has been here in town, likely looking for her, and then back in her hometown." He listened to the murmurs from the men. "She doesn't remember him, and that hurts her. It hurts her too how her parents are reacting and haven't even been in touch since she moved down here." He could feel anger building and struggled to control it. "Do you know that they left town when she was abducted, sometime during that week. They never bothered to even call Eric to see what they could do, or to see if Fynn had been found. That cuts deep. It just gives her more to heal from. And how do I encourage her to heal with that hanging over us?" He stopped speaking, his mouth opening as if he wanted to say something else before he shook his head and walked away rapidly, heading in the opposite direction that Fynn had. He needed air and a chance to clear his mind and let his emotions settle. He did need to talk to Barnabas but that would wait until the next day.

Shutting his apartment door, Brady walked towards his office, sinking down in the chair, his head going down on his hands as his elbows rested on the desk. He was discouraged, down in the dumps, he thought, to use a phrase of his mother's. Lord, I am not sure anymore. Not sure where I'm heading. I love my career, my volunteer work at the shelter, my life here. Even now with Fynn, Lord, how I love that lady, but it seems that I am waiting for something, something that's about to happen, and I have to admit that scares me.

He raised his head, a bleak look on his face as he stared across the room. He ignored the vibrating of his phone. He needed to, he thought, before he rose, heading for the outdoors, his head bent as he walked, hands shoved into his jeans' pockets. He didn't see Brennen watching him and then following after him, concern colouring his face.

Brady finally stopped at the lake, his feet sinking into the sand, before he walked towards a rock pile, perching himself on one and staring out at the lake. He was watching the waves moving towards the shore, nor the seagulls wheeling in the air. He ignored their harsh calls.

He finally stood, his head down for a moment before he raised it, determination on it and in his walk as he headed back for the building. He paused as he saw a man standing in his way, a younger man he thought, around his own age. His steps slowed before he finally paused.

"Can I help you? You are on private property."

The man nodded. "I know. You're Brady? If you are, we need to talk."

"Maybe. I need to know who you are. Let's see some identifications."

The other man gave a quick grin before he pulled out his wallet and tossed it at Brady, whose hands came up instinctively to catch it.

Brady watched the man closely before he glanced down at the wallet, opening it and pulling out the driver's license. Shock waved through him and he glanced up quickly, to find the man nodding.

"Please, don't say my name out loud." He paused as his hand reached for the wallet. "I just wanted to find you, to let you know I am around." He spun on his heel and was gone before Brady could speak.

Finding Barnabas on the patio at the back of the building, Breck approached, to drop down in the chair beside him, his head going back as his eyes slid shut. He breathed deeply, feeling that he needed to clear both his mind and his lungs. He felt the warmth from the rays of the setting sun on him and heard the sounds of dusk, the daytime creatures settling down as the nighttime creatures were awakening. It was a favourite time of day for him, a time just to sit and meditate, letting his favourite Scriptures run through his mind before he bowed his head to pray. That wasn't happening tonight.

"Breck?" Barnabas' voice finally broke through the silence between them. "You're burdened heavily tonight."

Breck nodded, without opening his eyes, a look of concern and then sorrow crossing his face. "I am. I think of Fynn and how her family have treated her. That would make good fodder for a psychiatrist."

"It would. Unfortunately, all we can do is pray for that.. But there is more." Barnabas watched his friend closely, knowing that Breck, who the men affectionately called the boss' stand-in, took his responsibilities seriously, and prayerfully. If he is that burdened, Lord, there is something there that we have missed or thought of lesser importance.

Breck raised his head, his eyes opening before he turned to his friend. "There is. There is something off about this whole thing. I think Fynn knows who is behind it and is denying it. I want to look closer at that lab she worked in. I know it's well thought of but there is something not ringing true."

"Abe mentioned that. He said Emma was looking into all of the men and women who worked there. If Fynn had found her lab and office searched, then someone wanted something from her or was doing it to scare her."

"That's my take." Breck looked up, one eye closing against the sunset, to find Brady and Burnie standing in front of them. "Brady? I don't like the look on your face."

Brady gave a grim nod even as he sat on the bench in front of the two, Burnie dropping down beside him. "I'm not happy. I am more worried about Fynn than before." He exchanged a look with Burnie. "I went for a walk to the lake. On my way back, I was approached by a man. I have no idea where he came from or disappeared to, but he showed me his identification." He paused, still not quite sure of who he had met.

"And?" When Brady didn't answer Breck's question, he asked again. "Brady? What aren't you telling us?"

"It was Fynn's brother. He didn't say what he wanted or even where he is staying. He stated he simply wanted to find me."

"That's bizarre. What did he actually want?" Barnabas leaned forward, his gaze moving between the two men.

"He didn't say." Burnie spoke. "I was near enough to hear the conversation. It's just as Brady said."

"We'll need to search the woods. Brady, you'll need to keep an eye out as you work. Whoever it is that seems to be after Flannery will be watching you as well, hoping you will lead them to him. He took a chance, meeting you like that."

Brady shrugged and then nodded. "I suppose. But who's after him and why? Why go after Fynn?"

"That's what we're working on. The guys have all said they're taking time, just like they did with Bradon, to work on this. Brody said Emma was sending him a lot of information. In fact, she told him she'd be back in a couple of days."

"And bringing all those people with her?" Brady had to grin as he remembered the look on Fynn's face. "I don't know that Fynn could handle that."

———

The other three laughed, and then conversation turned to a new topic, the series of messages that Buckley was bringing, on how to be a blessing to others.

Bradon was on a search. Ennis had heard from her father, that someone had been in their town, looking for Fynn, and had asked them to warn her. He would, he thought, if he could find her. He stood for a moment, eyeing the path to the lake, and then shook his head, searching instead through the parking lot before nodding. Her car was missing. But where was she? He ran for his own, heading into town, knowing he needed to find her, but not sure that he could.

Driving through the town he called home, he finally spotted Fynn's car. He pulled in and parked beside her, his eyes on the library. Was she there, Lord, or am I on a mission for nothing? He locked his door behind him, then paused. He should be talking to Brady, but Brady was on duty. Bradon shook his head, heading for the library, holding the door open for the two little children who scurried through and then held up the picture books they had in their hands, excitement emanating from them, their faces glowing. He grinned at them and then at their mother, who tried to apologize.

"Don't apologize." Bradon's words brought a smile to her own face. "I'm glad to see kids excited about reading."

He searched the library without finding Fynn. Where is she, Lord? Her car's here but she's not. I am not sure if she would have left it here and walked through the town. I don't know her well enough to make that kind of assessment.

Bradon turned as he heard his name call. Dallas was running towards him, a worried look on his face.

"Bradon? Where's Brady?"

"On duty. He's to be done at three but he figured it would go later. Why?"

Dallas held up a photo. "Do you know this man?"

Bradon took it, his eyes on Dallas before he looked down. "No, I'm not familiar with him. Should I be?"

Dallas shrugged. "His name has come up in our investigation. I need to speak with Fynn and Brady."

"I have a bad feeling, Dallas. I've been looking for Fynn and can't find her." Bradon turned, pointing to Fynn's car. "Her car's here but she's not in the library."

Dallas shot him a glance and then approached the vehicle. His hand on Bradon's chest stopped him in his tracks.

"Dallas?" Bradon's voice held confusion. He couldn't see the driver's side of the car, but Dallas could.

"Bradon, I need you to step back." Dallas' voice was grim as he spoke, a shuttered look coming over his face.

"Dallas, I can. But what's up?"

"What's up? There's blood on the side of her car, and I suspect that's her purse there."

Bradon's eyes slid shut as his heart fell. "She's been taken again. Is that what you're saying?"

Dallas nodded. "That's my fear." He turned, pointing to the bench under the spreading red oak tree on the library lawn. "Sit over there. I'll need to talk to you."

It was only noon when Dallas finally approached Bradon, sinking down with a sigh. He was weary, he thought, too many cases and not enough time. He thought coming on the force here and then moving up so quickly to detective would be an easier life for him. It hadn't happened that way.

"Dallas?" Bradon's voice broke into his thoughts.

"Whoever it was, they've been injured. We're not sure if it's Fynn, but with her purse there, we suspect it was." He looked down at the photo he had retrieved. "The word we had was that this man was looking for her. I pray he didn't find her." His head raised as he heard a yell and then he was up and running towards the officer heading his way, Bradon on his heels.

"Dallas? Someone saw Dr. Daley shoved into a vehicle and managed to snap a photo of the vehicle and the plate. We've found the vehicle, abandoned in the woods near the Foundation building."

The officer paused to catch his breath. "Will is sending a team out there now."

Dallas spun, heading for his own vehicle. "Bradon, after me. Head for the Foundation. The guys who are there right now will want to know. But we can't have you out there, not yet. Not until we know for sure that's where she's likely to be."

Bradon nodded. "On my way. I pray it's not Brady who gets the call."

Dallas spun, horror briefly on his face before he shuttered it. "Pray that way, but it's a toss up if he does or not."

Dallas approached the vehicle shortly thereafter, a frown on his face. He remembered seeing the vehicle around town, the out-of-province license plate a giveaway that whoever it was didn't belong there. He turned as an officer approached.

"We've run the plates, Dallas. It was stolen three weeks ago from British Columbia."

"Three weeks? Any sense of who?"

The officer shook his head. "No, there isn't. Not surprisingly." He turned, looking towards the trees. "We're searching. The K-9s are here and headed in. Will's pulled in whoever he can to search."

Dallas nodded, walking towards the vehicle. "I've seen this car around town but never got a good look at the driver. I wish I had. I had no reason to suspect it wasn't on the up and up."

"None of us did. Dr. Daley? Is that who you suspect is involved?"

"I think so." Dallas ducked to look through the driver's window. "Her purse was found beside her car and there is some blood on the door. Look, there are folders and what looks like documents on the seat. Whoever it is was either sloppy or planned to return. Find some officers and start searching for the man."

"Man?"

"I would suspect so. Fynn wouldn't go with a woman, not if she could help it. I see a man's jacket and hat on the backseat."

———

Dallas turned as he heard running footsteps and then ran towards the path, meeting a female officer running his way.

"Alice?"

"We found her, but we're not approaching her. Something is off. Will is there. He's asked for the ERT and bomb squads."

"ERT? Bomb squad?" Dallas paled, his face growing stern, before he was past Alice and on the run for Will.

"Dallas?" Will turned partway to speak.

"Fynn? Alice said they found her."

Will was grim. "They have but we need to send in the right people. I have a call in for the paramedics as well."

"Let's pray it's not Brady, but those teams have been extra busy for some reason today."

Will nodded. "That was my request, but dispatch said they'd send whoever was free, even if it was Brady. What's your sense of what's going on with those two?"

"I would say they're engaged or close to it."

They waited, stress building as first the ERT and then the bomb squad members passed them. Finally the ERT leader returned, his face pale, sweat beading his forehead.

"Will? We have a huge problem."

"Robert? Explain, please."

"It's Dr. Daley but we can't move her right now. She's alive, has a knife wound on her side, but that's not the issue."

"And the issue would be?" Will waited for a moment as Robert composed himself.

"She said she's laying on something and that if she moves, it will inject her with a drug of some kind."

"What?" Will's exclamation expelled from. "Now what?"

"Theodore's working on a solution, but it's Dr. Daley. It's like she has given up and is resigned to dying."

That morning, Fynn had risen early, just as the sun was rising, and grabbing her Bible, had headed for the balcony of her apartment. She had spent time searching for verses that would encourage her. She was discouraged, she thought, and that was not her. She could usually look on the bright side of life, but the last few months, work had drained her. She had been driven from her home by someone unknown, she had left the only town she had ever really gotten to know. Fynn sighed as she thought of her parents. Where are they, Lord? Why is there no contact? I just need my Mom and she's not there for me. I can't go to my aunt, not and endanger her. Eric is near but our relationship is changing, now that I'm dating. He's stepping back as my protector, letting Brady take over.

Fynn's face softened and her eyes grew wistful as she thought of Brady. I know he's the one, Lord, the one You mean for me, but I don't want him hurt. Buckley would tell me to trust, we've had some good talks, he and I, but it's so hard when I feel something hanging over me, something that may well endanger my love.

She grinned to herself as she remembered the look on Brady's face the night she proposed and then the look on his face as he proposed to her himself. He has such a dry sense of humour. I'm glad he takes pleasure in what he does.

She finally rose, setting her Bible back on the end table in the living room before she reached for her purse. She needed to get out, to get to know her town. A stop at the library was in order, she decided, a place she could lose herself for hours if she knew herself.

Fynn walked towards her car a couple of hours later, keys in her hand, her thoughts on the welcome she had found in the building behind her. She smiled, knowing that she had found somewhere she could live and work and yes, marry and raise a family, if that was God's will for her. She didn't see the man approaching her until she was shoved against her car, a small scream torn from her, her keys and purse falling to the pavement. She felt the slice of the knife as it hit her side.

"Dr. Daley. You're a hard person to find on your own. This must be my lucky day." The man's voice was hoarse, a smoker, she decided, and wheezy.

"Please? Let me go. I don't have anything you want."

Fynn was afraid as she slumped against the car, her hand on her side, eyes wide as she studied the man in front of her. It was difficult to see his face, the hood on his sweatshirt pulled up and as far forward as he could get it. She didn't think she knew him, but she feared. She was in his hands, literally as he roughly pulled her away from her own vehicle, her bloodied hand brushing against the door, and shoved her towards his own vehicle. The trunk was popped open, and after glancing around, he shoved her into it, binding her hands.

Darkness descended as the lid slammed shut. Where are You, Lord, she murmured. Do You know where I am? Do You care? Her unspoken prayer was one of desperation and despair.

She felt the car moving, picking up speed for a bit before it slowed and she felt it turning, the ride becoming bumpy. The car stopped and she felt it shift as the man slid out. Fynn prayed, fear rising within her, in a lady who really didn't fear. This was out of what she had ever expected she'd ever face. In her work, she had gone into scenes and sites that made men cringe, but she had always felt safe, knowing there were officers around. This time, she was on her own.

The trunk lid opened and she was pulled out as roughly as she was shoved into it. She took a moment to find her balance, wanting to reach for her side, but prevented from doing so. The man muttered to himself before he dragged her away from the car, turned her to face the woods, and then hand on her back, shoved her forward. She stumbled as she walked, unable to find the balance that she needed, knowing that the fear and pain was driving that from her.

A hand on her arm stopped Fynn's forward step. She stared around the small clearing, fear once more rising harder and higher.

"Over there." The man pointed with his knife and Fynn cringed back, not moving. He muttered something, cursed and then dragged her forward, stopping in the centre of the clearing, his eyes on the ground and then searching the area around. He had scoped out that very clearing for the task he had been given. That it was a woman he had been tasked to kill made no difference to him. It would not be the first time he had done that very deed.

"On the ground." His harsh voice thundered at her.

Fynn froze, her eyes on him and then the ground, her head beginning to shake even as she tried to move away from him.

"On the ground." He shoved her forward and then down.

The pain from hitting her side with the stab wound rushed through her and Fynn bit at her lip to stop her cries from sounding. She felt his hands on her, positioning her on her side, even as blackness welled in front of her. She blinked, watching as the knife approached and then sliced at the bond holding her hands together.

Fynn shuddered, not knowing what was coming. The man stood and watched her, finally speaking.

"Don't move, unless you want to die."

"What?" Fynn's voice was getting weak. "What do you mean?"

"I mean, little lady, that you don't move. You're are laying on a container that if you move, a syringe will pop up and inject you with a drug. Enough drug to kill you quickly." He cackled as he saw the look of horror cross her face and her lips trembling before she bit at them.

"Like I said, don't move. I'll just leave you here. I am sure the bugs you study will find you."

He cackled once more, pulled out a cigarette, looked at it before he stuffed it into his mouth, and then spun on his heel to walk away, leaving Fynn on the ground, terror on her face, tears she didn't know she was shedding dripping from her cheek to land on the ground.

Fynn had no doubt that he had meant what he said, but she wasn't sure. She also wasn't ready to take a chance on moving, not yet. She just didn't know what to do or think. Her mind slipped to prayer as she stared ahead, watching the grass and weeds and flowers blow in the light breeze, hearing the calls of the birds return once more as did the chatter of the animals and the sounds of the insects.  She shuddered, knowing exactly what he had meant, that if no one found her and she could not move herself, the insects would find the stab wound.

How much later it was, Fynn was never able to fully say. She had closed her eyes once more, her body still tense, her muscles aching from the strain of laying still. She heard the sounds of the grass moving from legs swishing through it and heard the silence that descended at the disturbance. She felt rather than heard someone drop to a knee beside her, a hand on her shoulder. She caught herself before she jumped in fright, her eyes opening and turning to stare at the man in uniform who knelt beside her.

"Dr. Daley?" Robert, the ERT leader, tilted his head to watch Fynn's reaction, seeing first relief and then fear. "Are you okay? Let's get you on your feet."

Fynn didn't dare shake her head, and her voice was very low as she spoke.

"No, I can't. I can't move."

"You can't move or you won't move."

She gave a small cry as Robert's hand reached to gently grasp her arm, ready to help her sit up. He paused at the look on her face, raising his eyes to his second-in-command who stood watching.

"I can't. I don't want to die." Fynn had forgotten momentarily that she was a professional in her career, well thought of in that, and became just a frightened young woman, afraid of what might happen if she did move.

Robert's voice was calming as he spoke. "Is there a particular reason that you can't?"

Fynn gave a small sigh, hardly daring to breath in case she moved when she shouldn't. The man had cut her bonds and she had one arm tucked her her head, the other hand flat on the ground beside her.

"I can't. If I move, I'm dead." Her eyes shifted to watch the other four ERT members surround them, backs to her, their eyes searching for her assailant. "He made me lie like this. He said I was laying on something, that if I moved, a needle would inject me and I would die."

Robert's hand rested gently on her shoulder as he stared at her, not quite sure he had heard her correctly. He raised his eyes once more to Patrick, who was staring at Fynn, shock on his face.

"Patrick, send someone to find the bomb squad. I want Theodore here. He'll have an idea of what we can do." His head turned as he heard a voice. "Alice? What did you say?"

"I said, when we found her, that's what she said. That's why you were asked to come in and also Theodore and his squad." She looked behind him. "There's Theodore now."

"Fynn? I'll be right back. I just need to speak Theodore. He's our bomb squad leader. I think he'll have an idea on how to get you back on your feet again."

Robert rose, approaching Theodore, a tall lanky man dressed in his gear.

"Robert? What do we have?"

"Dr. Daley was kidnapped earlier and brought here. She states she is laying on something, that if she moves, a needle will inject her with a deadly dose of a drug."

Theodore shook his head. "That's a new one. What do you need from us?"

"First, I need you to take a look and see what you can find."

Theodore nodded before he turned, sending one of his team running for their rig, to bring the shovel he decided they needed.

"We can dig down around her and see what we can find. I'll need your men to help stabilize her if we have to take out too much dirt." He pointed to the other side of Fynn. "Right there, Stuart. You have the shovel. Dig carefully around on the other side. We're looking for a box or something that is underneath her." Theodore paced around Fynn, his eyes assessing the ground under her. He finally pointed to an area near her back and hip. "I would suspect right there. The ground seems to have been disturbed."

The officer dug carefully, his eyes on Fynn at times, before his shovel hit a metal object. He stopped, drawing in a deep breath,

———

waiting for Theodore to approach. Bending down, his hands reaching to dig away the dirt, Theodore paused for a moment, his eyes on the box before he looked at Fynn.

"Dr. Daley? Exactly what did he tell you?"

She sighed, her eyes drifting closed as she thought back, trying to focus, but having difficulty doing just that. "He said I was on a box. If I move, it would make a lid slid back or something like that and then I would be injected with a lethal amount of drug. He didn't say what drug." She frowned, before her eyes turned up to Robert. "That didn't make sense. Usually they tell you what drug it is."

"Not all the time." Robert's hand gripped her shoulder gently. "Theodore?"

Robert stood and moved away with Theodore, who had sent one of the men back to their rig to retrieve a thin metal plate.

"We need to slid the plate under her before we move her. It will be tricky. I can't assess like I want to. I don't want to dig down too much further in case it shifts."

Robert nodded, his eyes on the ground around Fynn. "If I can raise her body just a fraction of an inch, you may be able to slide it under her. When that happens, I'll grab her and run." He studied the plate Theodore had been handed. "Good. It's long enough that once we feed it under her, we can have one of our men on each end."

"That's my thoughts. Okay, let's do this. I have no idea how long she's been out here but she needs to be seen." Theodore looked up as Alice approached. "Alice?"

Alice shook her head. "It's the paramedic team. It's Brady and his partner."

"And that is a problem how?" Robert had a suspicion of why, but he needed to know for sure.

"Brady and Dr. Daley are a couple. How close, I'm not sure. I know others from the Foundation are down there, waiting."

"Then, let's go, Theodore." Robert walked back to crouch beside Fynn, assessing her and seeing the fear and stress on her face.

Fynn watched as Robert dropped down near her, wanting to know what his plans were but afraid that it would mean she would be hurt. *Lord, please? Let Brady know how much I love him, please? I know I needed to come here, I needed to heal, but it doesn't seem as if I'm going to even get that chance.*

"Fynn?" Robert's hand rested gently on her arm. "Here's our plan. Theodore has that metal plate that we're going to slide under you. He has the box unburied on one side. I'll lift you just a bit to let him work it under you. We need you to trust me, to let me move you. We don't want you moving on your own. Just relax and let us do all the work."

She frowned at him before grumbling. "That's easy for you to say. You're not the one laying here on a box, just waiting to be stuck with a needle and die."

Robert grinned for a moment and then nodded at Theodore. Moving carefully and in tandem, Theodore and Robert worked away to slid the metal plate underneath Fynn. Robert felt her tensing as his arms slid under her back and knees, but she closed her eyes and resolutely remained as still as she could. Finally, Theodore nodded at him.

Robert waited for a moment, knowing that if they had guessed wrong, it could be Fynn who paid for their mistake. He took a deep breath, his eyes back on Fynn before he quickly moved, pulling her up and away from the ground, hands on the back of his vest to pull him up and back. He stumbled for a moment as the same hands helped to steady him on his feet, his eyes on Fynn. He realized that her body had gone limp and decided that was no surprise. He turned, heading for the road and to the paramedics, the others on his team surrounding them, Alice keeping step with him.

Will approached as he saw Robert and his burden, fear in his heart before Robert looked up.

"She's fainted, Will. I doubt that's like her, but given what she just went through, it's normal."

"The weapon, and it is a weapon?"

"Theodore and his squad are looking after it. He'll want the techs to move in before he takes it away. So far, we have it stabilized under a metal plate." Theodore looked towards the paramedics. "I hear Brady's here?"

"He is. I'm not happy about that, but he was the one who took the call."

"The luck of the draw." Robert shot a glance behind him. "I think you'll want to take a look at whatever it is that Theodore has found." He walked away, leaving Will staring after him before he walked back the way Robert had just come.

Brady stood, his heart in his mouth, watching as Robert approached. He didn't like it that his lady had been kidnapped again. He didn't understand why she was out here or why Robert was carrying her.

Brady reached for his stethoscope, watching closely as Robert placed Fynn on the stretcher, tucking her hands close to her body.

"She's had a knife wound, Brady. I'm not sure how long it has been, but she was laying with that side down in the dirt." Robert watched as Brady looked up in shock before he nodded. "Deliberate, Brady. We weren't supposed to find her. Not yet."

Brady nodded before he turned to confer with his partner, Fred, who nodded even as he reached to start an IV and then carefully cut away Fynn's T-shirt to reveal the wound. All three men drew in a breath at the look of it.

Finally lifting the stretcher into the rig, Brady slid in beside her, Robert following.

"I'm not leaving her, Brady. I promised to get her safe. I want to make sure that happens."

Brady walked behind the stretcher into the Emergency Department, his eyes finding Doc heading his way. Thank you, Lord. Doc's here. Just the one we need. Fynn is going to just disappear on me, if this keeps happening, and I would lose part of me. I want to marry her so quickly, but she needs this time. I just ask that she gets a chance to enjoy life without any more difficulty, but somehow, Lord, I don't see that happening.

———

"Brady? It's Fynn?"

"It is, Doc. Long story short, she was left with the wound in the dirt. I haven't heard all the circumstances surrounding it, but from what Robert said, she was afraid to move. He didn't say why."

Doc nodded, pointing to one of the exam rooms, a nurse following closely. "Give me your report, and then head out. If you weren't on duty, I would let you stay."

Brady nodded, devastation flickering across his face as he and Fred wheeled the stretcher into the room and then carefully lifted Fynn to the bed. His report given, he stood for a moment, his hand on Fynn's face before he moved away, Fred hesitating as he watched him.

"Talk to Robert, Doc. There's more than what we were told. It was a few hours she was like that from what I gather."

Doc shot him a keen glance, before he looked past him and frowned. Why was that man back here, he wondered, before he nodded to a security guard to approach him. The man was gone but not before shooting a look of hatred at Fynn.

Fred caught up with Brady as he stood near their rig, eyes on the horizon.

"Brady?"

"Yeah?" Brady shook his head, his own eyes finding the man now watching him. He pulled out his phone on a pretext and snapped a photo of him, sending it onto to both Dallas and Eric. "Sorry, Fred. Not a good day."

"It's been a bad day all around. Listen, I talked to Sam. He's made arrangements for Colin to come in early and take the rest of your shift."

"He has? That's great." Brady walked around the rig and stood for a moment before he opened the door and slid in. "Heading back to headquarters, are we?"

"We are. I'm sorry about your lady."

"Thanks." Brady stared out of the side window, his eyes not on the passing scenery as his thoughts shifted to Fynn. "I want whoever it was."

“We all do, Brady.  For your sake and for hers.”  Fred shot him a glance, before he shook his head.  “Doc will take good care of her.”

“I know, but it hurts to see her hurting.”

———

Fynn's eyes flickered open and she frowned as she glanced around before she sighed. The hospital. That's right, she thought. Here I am, back in the hospital and I have no idea why or how or even who did it. She tried to roll to her side and stopped as a swift shaft of pain stopped her. Now, what did I do? I must have been pretty clumsy, she thought. God, are You there? Do You even care that I am hurt? I guess in my head I know that You do. It's the heart that's having trouble understanding that. Guess that's where my trust comes in. She didn't have her phone, she realized, not knowing where it was.

Footsteps approached her bed and then stopped. She heard soft breathing and muttered words before a hand reached to smooth her hair. She leaned into it before she looked up.

"Brady? What are you doing here? Aren't you working?" She frowned again, seeing that he wasn't in his uniform. "You were working today. What time is it?"

"Just after four. Sam had someone come in and cover for me. He somehow decided that I needed to be with you."

"And why would he think that?" Fynn sounded grumpy, she knew, and then spoke quietly. "I'm sorry. I'm not great company right now."

"Not a problem." Brady leaned his arms on the bed rail, his hands clasped as he studied them. "Fynn? We need to talk."

"About what? I don't remember what happened, other than I was laying on the ground and someone in a monster suit found me and then brought in a whole bunch more men in monster suits." Robert and Theodore were standing behind Brady, grins on their faces at her grumbling.

"And glad we are that you are safe." Robert moved to the end of the bed. "How are you now, Fynn?"

"Grateful to you and Theodore, is it? I don't remember leaving there."

---

"You fainted." Robert laughed at the disbelieving look on her face. "You really did. Doc says it was expected, that your body had to relax once you were out of danger. No problem, Fynn. We won't stay for long. We just wanted to ensure you were safe and on the mend."

"Safe? Now, that's an interesting word to use." Fynn shared a look with Brady. "I don't think that I'm all that safe, not yet. Dallas was by and said they hadn't found the man, but that he had been seen here. Know anything about that, Brady?"

Brady shook his head even as he grinned. "You caught me. I found the man watching me, snapped a quick photo and sent it on to Dallas and, yes, even on to Eric."

"Great! Now, Eric will be locking me away somewhere and throwing away the key." Fynn knew she was out of sorts but felt that she had every right to be, before she shook her head. "I'm sorry. That was uncalled for. Please, forgive me?"

"No apologies needed. Eric won't do that. He'll leave that up to me." Brady's grin widened as her eyes narrowed and she glared at him.

Fynn waved as Robert and Theodore left, knowing that she had to talk to Brady, but how did she do that? She loved him with all her heart but she felt she was bringing danger closer to him every day.

"Before you say a word, I'm not leaving." Brady shook his head. "Not one inch. You mean too much to me, Fynn darlin'."

"What have they told you, Brady? He grabbed me at the library, shoved me into the trunk of his car, and then drove around before he forced me to walk to that clearing and then shoved me down. He wanted me to die. I wasn't to be found, you know. He told me that the insects would find me before anyone else."

"You can thank Bradon for the quick find. He was looking for you, found your car at the library and then Dallas found him. Long story short? They were able to find the vehicle, which was from out of province and stolen, and then find you. I wasn't supposed to take that call. Will had asked that I not, but God knew I needed to be there."

Fynn's face softened. "He did. The verse that I kept hearing was "I am the God that heals you". Is that what God is doing in all this?" Her head went back. "One of Abe's men has a saying that we don't know the plans and purposes God has for us. That is just too true."

"It is." Brady snagged a chair with his toe and pulled it over, slumping down in it, fatigue running through him. "Doc said you could go home tonight."

"I can?" Fynn looked around. "Brady, where can I go where they won't find me? They're getting bold. I am afraid that your friends or the ladies will get hurt."

Brady watched her for a moment, his thoughts tumbling over one another. "They know the risk. It's what we do, Fynn. We have each other's backs. That's a given. Now that you're part of our family, they will watch for you as well." Brady gave a groan.

"Brady?"

He shook his head, a slight smile on his face. "It's just that we never talked about something. When the guys marry, their wives automatically became employees of the Foundation and receive a salary." He held up a hand at her protest. "It's how Barnabas and his father and then the board wanted to do it. That frees the ladies up to work the same way we guys do, or volunteer, or even go back to school. It is not mandated that they have to work. The board is fine with that."

"Wow! I don't think I've ever heard of that before." Fynn sat up, swinging her legs off the side of the bed, pulling the scrub top that she had been given to wear into a more comfortable position. "How come?"

"How come?" Brady shrugged. "Each one of us questioned Barnabas when we came on board and he said that the way they felt about it was that they wanted to encourage the couples, not make it more difficult for them. Expanding the options available for the couples makes it easer in some ways and more difficult."

She finally nodded. "That sounds like something Paul would have suggested, I think. He had a great encourager for himself in Barnabas." Her voice died away as her head tilted so she could look up at the ceiling, her hands clasping in her lap. "He's a wonderful man. I want to meet his parents."

"They've been around but I don't think that it's been when you have. We're to have the monthly potluck this Sunday and I heard that they would be there." Brady's voice stopped as he watched Fynn, having heard the door open and close behind him. When no one approached them, Brady started to turn, stopping as he felt the muzzle of a revolver on his neck. His eyes were on Fynn as she paled even more and he could see the shadows of fear in her eyes.

Fynn froze as she saw the man. It was him, once more, she thought. I thought he had disappeared. Lord, now what? Where will we end up? I know it won't be good, wherever it is.

"So, little lady, you didn't die after all. Such a shame! You've made it difficult for me, you know." The man's hoarse voice sounded loud in the room. "Here's what we are going to do. You and your boyfriend here are going to walk out of here, right ahead of me. No tricks, young man, or she dies. And the same for you, little lady." He motioned with his revolver.

Fynn's eyes turned to Brady, who gave a slight shake of his head. They had not choice, he thought, and Lord, we need You to step in somehow. He rose, his hand reaching for Fynn's, leading her from her hospital room and then down the stairs, hitting the panic bar on the steel door at the bottom of the stairs and walking out into the darkness. A hand shoved him forward as Fynn gave a small scream, quickly subdued as a man appeared in front of them, a weapon in his hand as well.

"To the van. Move it!"

They were shoved forward and then into the van, Fynn's hand tight in Brady's again, as blindfolds were wrapped around their heads and then Fynn's hand was torn from Brady's and rough rope was wound around her wrists and pulled tight. She bit back a whimper. She had more backbone than this, she thought. She could feel Brady's arm agains hers and wanted so much to feel it around her, to feel his protection, but knew that would not happen. Not yet.

Brady felt the van shift as it left the hospital grounds, not stopping at the barrier, the wood breaking as it was hit at a high rate of speed. He could hear yells from the security guards. Please, Lord, let them find us quickly. I fear for Fynn.

He tried to follow the twists and turns of the speeding van, but was unable to. He sighed to himself, trying to come up with a plan but unable to. He was determined to protect his lady, no matter what happened.

Thirty minutes later, Branigan and Burnie stood in Fynn's hospital room, surprise on their faces at not finding either one. They turned as they heard footsteps and the nurse appeared, paperwork in her hand.

"Why? Where is Dr. Daley?" She looked around, not seeing her or Brady. "Brady was here with her. She didn't leave, did she?"

"Brady would not have let her go without that." Branigan pointed to the paperwork. "He's a stickler for that, you know." He looked around before heading for the door and then the stairs, looking for a security guard. A quick word with one and he was following the guard to their control room, watching as the video stream for the past hour outside of Fynn's door was pulled up.

"There. Who's that?"

The guard took a look. "You know, he's been hanging around here today. One of our guys approached him and he took off almost on a run. We reported it. You don't think he's responsible?"

"Given what happened earlier to Fynn, I would say it's a good chance that he is." Branigan paused, lost in thought. "Can we pull up any from outside the building? I would think the back, where there is less traffic." He watched again. "There. Brady and Fynn. They're not going on their own. What! The van drove right through the barrier. We'll never catch them."

"We didn't know. I'm sorry. We thought it was someone who didn't want to pay for parking." The guard was contrite.

"Not your fault. You didn't know." He paused again, before turning to leave. "Dallas from the police will be speaking with you all. We need to find them. This is the second time today Fynn has been kidnapped."

The guard spun in his chair, mouth open, as he stared at Branigan in shock, unable to say anything.

Burnie met Branigan at the bottom of the stairs, his eyes watching his friend closely.

"Branigan?"

"Yeah?" Branigan finally looked up, a frown on his face. "Sorry. She's been kidnapped again, along with Brady. There were two.  One forced them outside where another one was waiting.  The guard says it was likely the van they were in that tore through the barriers at the gate.  That was reported, but I'm not sure if they got a plate number or not."

"That's not good."  Burnie spun, almost running down the hallway.  "We need to find the rest of the guys.  We have a lot of work to do."

"That we do."  Branigan pulled his phone out as it chimed.  "Emma's sent something."  He tossed his keys to Burnie.  "You drive.  I want to see what Emma has to say.  If she's up at this hour working, it must be important."

"Fynn says she's like that.  If it involves a friend or a child, she won't sleep until Abe makes her or their son needs her."

Barnabas watched the men as they mingled in the conference room, shock on their faces and in their voices. They spoke quietly before they found seats, pulling up programs on the computers, reaching for pen and paper, brainstorming.

Breck stood beside him before he moved away, heading for where Branigan stood, his eyes on the wall, not moving. His phone was in his hand as he thought through the information that Emma had forwarded on to him. I have no idea how she has found this. Fynn's brother has been here. That must have been who Brady spoke to on the way back from the lake. He never did tell us, did he? Lord, please? Protect them. Put a hedge around them. Bring them back safely to us. I know they are making plans, I am just not sure what they are

"Branigan?" Breck's voice broke into his revery and he jumped slightly, meeting Breck's quick grin as he turned. "Sorry. I didn't mean to startle you. You were deep in thought?"

"I was. Emma sent some interesting information to me. We need to look at it. I've sent it to the printer, enough copies for us all and Will and Dallas. I suspect Eric will want copies as well."

"Has anyone spoken to Eric?"

"I think Burnie was going to." He turned, searching the room for Burnie. "Eric's here. I didn't see him arrive."

Breck gave another grin. "I think we should just offer him an apartment here. He's here enough." He paused, a thought rising. "Does Eric remember Fynn's brother?"

Branigan shrugged as he heard a voice from beside him and turned to find Dallas standing there.

"I asked him that very question. They're around the same age. He says he does to a certain extent but he was only five when the brother disappeared. He has heard his mother and father speak of him. But that was too many years ago for Eric to be certain what are his memories and what are theirs." He looked up as he heard Buckley's voice.

Buckley had risen from his chair, his eyes on Barnabas before he looked around.

"Let's pray, my friends. Like we normally do. We have one extra, no, Doc's here. We can break up into twos. Brady and his lady need our prayers. We have no idea where they are or if they've been hurt. God needs to be in control."

"God is in control, Buckley. We just don't see it." Doc nodded at Dallas. "You're with me, Dallas. Let's find some seats."

Thirty minutes later, they all shifted in their chairs, looking up in surprise as the four younger ladies, Berneen's brother, Darby, and Anna entered, trays of food in their hands. This is needed, Brendon thought. Thank you, Lord, for these ladies. Now, open our eyes. Help us to find our friends.

Barnabas turned away, his emotions overcoming him for a moment. He had grown to appreciate Fynn's understated sense of humour, as morbid and dark as it was at times. She had laughed at him once when he had commented on that, just saying that when you worked in a medical field, you used black humour sometimes to cope. He could appreciate that. He walked away, his phone in his hand. He just needed to speak with his father, to hear his thoughts and then his prayers, to hear the verses his mother would draw from her memory for him. They were away right now, and he knew that. It still didn't stop him from wanting to talk to them.

He returned to find the group staring at Burnie, who stood, his hand up, distress on his face.

"Burnie?"

Burnie spun as he heard Barnabas' voice and then walked rapidly towards him, pointing out the door.

"Burnie?"

"I just caught a call from Will. He's on his way to the bluffs. Someone reported a van going over them." Burnie could barely get the words out.

———

Barnabas froze, his hand half raised to rub at his face before he dropped it. "Where?"

"The bluffs. Near our end, he said."

Barnabas spun. "Come with me, Burnie. We can be spared. Let's head that way and see what Will can tell us."

Behind the wheel of his vehicle, Barnabas paused before he shoved the gear stick into drive and took off, a little faster than his normal speed. "What have we discovered so far?"

"Not much on our part. Emma's sent through a lot on both Eric and Fynn's brother. They called him Flannery but that wasn't his name. Eric couldn't explain why he was called that. His legal name is Farr."

Barnabas shot him a look, before he pulled to a stop behind Will's police vehicle, shoving the transmission into park. "I have met a Farr. A few years ago. He works in town here, as a paralegal." He sighed, a hand rubbing at his chin. "That's who she looks like."

"Say what?" Burnie studied his friend.

"Fynn. She looks like Farr. I never made the connection, just wondered who it was." He shoved open his door, his attention moving to Will, who stood watching them. "Will?"

"Barnabas. Burnie. I didn't expect you to be here, but I should have. Any word?"

Barnabas shook his head. "None, but we know who her brother is."

"You do? Who?" Will turned as he heard the heavy sound of a Diesel engine and moved to one side for the tow truck to approach. "I'm praying, guys, but it's tough. I thought I told your men that I didn't want any more adventures like the four had."

Barnabas shook his head. "I told them that, too. Brennen's response was that if only four had adventures, that left the rest of us not finding our ladies."

Will laughed. "So, he's saying that in order to find your ladies, you have adventures. Not like Bradon's, please. It was too close a call for him."

---

Barnabas' attention shifted to the activity near the edge of the bluffs. "What can you tell us, Will?"

"Not a lot yet. It was empty, but it looks as if it was deliberately sent over. The team will take at quick look here and then go over it with a fine tooth comb once they get it back to the yard. It does match the description of the van from the hospital." Will excused himself as he heard his name called.

"Alice?" He stood for a moment, peering over the edge at the activity below him.

"They're not there. From the looks of it, it was left in drive and then shoved forward. We've found footprints."

Will nodded, his eyes rising to meet Barnabas'. "Keep me informed. I'll be at the Foundation Building."

"Of course. The techs should have a preliminary report shortly."

Three days had passed, with no sign of the two. Will had been around, his keen eyes on their friends, but not saying much of what he knew. Dallas had been called away due to the sudden illness of a close relative but was due back the next day. Barnabas had been putting out feelers, but not getting any response, which both surprised and perplexed him. He had confided in Breck that must mean the two were not in town.

The men had all taken leave from their work to dedicate their time to their research, but even at that, they were not finding out too much. Branigan had gone on a search, accompanied by Burnie, looking for Farr. A source had told him that Fynn's brother was still around but had taken to hiding and wearing a disguise. Breck had sighed. That meant he knew he was being sought and not by Fynn.

Berneen had taken Cadee with her and gone on a search through town, almost to every home and business. Darby had sought out his friends and searched in the surrounding woods and parks and down by the beach. He had even been seen at the marina, checking out any boats that might be hiding the two.

Buckley had spent his time divided, part with his friends, the other part with his congregants, leading in the hourly prayer groups that were set up. Everyone was on a search, but no one had found them. Nor heard a word.

Brody and Brandon had taken Doc with them that day, heading for a larger centre, hoping that they could find someone who had seen them. Brenden was deep in research, Eric helping as he could. They were all puzzled that not a sign of the two had been found. There had been no communication from their kidnappers.

Barnabas turned from his computer, rubbing at his eyes. He was disheartened, he thought, and then took that burden to the Lord. Lord, where are they? We're looking but not finding them. And that I don't understand. Please, Lord? Where do we search? He rose and walked towards the large map Darby had taped to the wall, marking off where they had searched. His finger traced along the shoreline, stopping at the spot where the van had been dumped. Barnabas frowned. Now, what was it about the particular area of the bluffs that bothered him?

Ennis watched for a moment, Bradon beside her, before she walked over, her head tilting as she ran her finger along the map, much like Barnabas had just done. Her finger stopped, and she tapped at a spot.

"There's an abandoned farm right here, Barnabas. Do you remember? I know we used to go there, as teens, just to look around. The guys used to try and scare us with ghost stories."

Barnabas' body stilled before he nodded. "It's close to where they dumped the van. I don't want to say anything to Will. Come on, you two. Let's go take a look." He turned and almost on a run, headed for his vehicle, Ennis and Bradon right behind him.

Barnabas stopped his vehicle at the end of the overgrown lane and ducked his head to see through the windshield, his fingers tapping on the steering wheel.

"Someone's been through here."

Bradon leaned forward, an arm resting on the seat back, as he too scoured the area for any signs of the culprits.

"And recently too. More than once, I would say."

Ennis nodded. "There's a second entrance that not many people know of. Not unless they know the property."

Barnabas snapped his fingers. "You're right. I had forgotten."

Quickly backing up, he drove away and then turned onto a gravel road. He could tell it had not been travelled much, at least not in the last couple of days. He pulled off the road and then shifted to look at Ennis and then Bradon.

"Well? Do we go in?"

Ennis nodded and reached for the door handle, Bradon's hand coming to rest on her shoulder.

"We need to pray and pray hard. I have this feeling that we need to find them today and now."

"You and me, both." Barnabas prayed and then slid from his vehicle, Ennis and Bradon following.

Ennis took the lead, walking rapidly, her hands reaching to push branches, weeds, and long grass from her path. Coming to a stop, she studied the buildings. The barn, she noted, had collapsed almost totally. Not surprising, she thought.

Bradon gave a low whistle. "Wow! You said it was abandoned. I certainly didn't expect to see this."

Barnabas shook his head. "It's been a few years since I was out here. Let's head for the house."

Ennis shook her head. "No. That would be too obvious." She tapped her mouth with a long forefinger, the pale peach nail polish reflecting the sun. "There's a root cellar and a storm cellar. Between the house and the barn." She went to move forward but a sudden noise stopped her in her tracks and then the three stepped backwards into shelter, watching as a ramshackle truck that was more rust than blue drove in and a man jumped down, grabbing a plastic shopping bag and heading for the house. They waited, not able to see if he had entered the house or not. An hour later, he returned to his truck and drove away.

Ennis looked around and then ran quickly for the house, heading for the back, the two men on her heels before Bradon's hand stopped her

"Let one of us go ahead, Ennis. I don't want to answer to your parents or brother if something happens to you."

She nodded, impatient to be searching. Barnabas studied the building before he spoke in a low voice.

"Where are the cellars?"

She pointed. "The root cellar is there. The storm cellar is closer to the barn."

The men nodded before moving out, Ennis' hand on Bradon's back.

They paused as they reached the root cellar, seeing the shiny new hasp on it, and the open padlock. Glances were exchanged before Bradon reached for the lock, removed in and then shoved the door open.  Barnabas entered, climbing down the rickety few wooden steps, brushing away the cobwebs, his eyes searching.  He could see debris left over from years ago.  The musty, mouldy smell hit him as did the dust he had stirred up.  Shadows briefly blocked the sun before he turned and climbed back out.

"It's been disturbed, but I can't tell if it was Brady or Fynn or just some animal."  He looked around as he brushed at his hair.  "The storm cellar?"

"This way."  Ennis headed towards the barn, almost on a run and then detoured to her left, stopping short of the cellar, hidden for a moment by the overgrown brush.  "It's here."  She glanced around, nervous, feeling as if she was being watched.  "Someone's out here."

"I feel it, too."  Bradon brushed by her, heading for the door, pausing as he saw, once more, the hasp and this time a closed padlock.  "There's a lock here.  Someone wants either to keep people out or keep people in."

"I would say to keep them in."  Barnabas looked around.  "We need to break it open.  The wood is likely rotten, but it seems to have been repaired to some extent."

Bradon agreed, looking around for a long rock, stopping short at the metal pipe waving near his face.  He gave a quick grin at the smirk Ennis threw him.  "Thank you, love."

"Where did you find that?"  Barnabas studied it before he turned to her.

"Right there.  I have no idea why it's there, but it's not rusted."

"No, you're right.  It's not."  Bradon paused.  "Barnabas, pray please.  I think we've found them, but I'm afraid of the condition that we'll find them in."

"I know.  I keep thinking of how close it was to losing you two."

Once more, Bradon reached for the lock, this time prying at it with the metal bar.  A snap and the hasp separated from the door and the door opened slightly.  The three paused, staring at each other, hesitant to move forward but knowing they needed to.

A tap at his door had Will raising his head from his paperwork, a sigh stifled quickly as he saw Alice standing there, hesitant it seemed to disturb him, her glance shifting between his office and back down the hallway.

"Alice? Is there something you wanted?"

Her head whipped around as Will spoke and she nodded. "There is. There's a man here who wants to speak with you."

"There is?" When she didn't continue, he rose and walked towards her. "And does this man have a name?"

She nodded. "Farr McIntosh."

"Farr McIntosh?" Will puzzled at the name before his brow cleared. "Farr, is it? And I would gather he is here about Fynn."

"I think so. Where would you like me to put him for you?"

Will raised a hand. "Let me get a glimpse of him first. Then, we'll see." Will followed Alice back down the hall, standing just out of sight of the front desk and reception, his eyes on the man standing with his back towards him, watching out the window. He's nervous, and I wonder why. "Bring him back to my office. Give me five minutes. I want to grab a coffee and I'm sure he could use a coffee or tea. Ask him as you bring him back. I want you nearby."

"Sure, Will."

Will sat back at his desk, his coffee mug nearby, as he stared down at the budget he was to be working on. He sighed. It would have to wait, he thought. Fynn and Brady came first. He looked up as Alice tapped at his door and then stood, assessing the younger man who stood, hesitant, shifting slightly from foot to foot as he watched Will.

"Farr McIntosh?" At the man's nod, Will pointed to a chair. "Alice got you a coffee?"

Farr nodded, his eyes dropping to the mug he held, his hand shaking slightly before he reached to set the mug on the table beside his chair. He looked up, and Will saw the resemblance to Fynn, although his hair was a deeper red than Fynn's copper locks and his eyes a dark enough brown to be almost black.

Will sat in the chair beside him, his own mug in his hand, and waited, knowing that Farr was there for a reason. He had time, he thought, to wait.

"Chief Peters?" Farr finally looked around, settling back in his chair. "I understand you know Fynn Daley?"

"I do. She's dating a young friend of mine. Why?"

Farr sighed. "This is so hard." His face became buried in his hands. "I have no idea where to start."

"The beginning is usually a good spot." Will grinned as Farr's head shot up and he stared at him dumbfounded. "Take your time."

Farr nodded. "It usually is, but I can't start at the very beginning. I am only just remembering things. One of those things is that I have a sister. A sister named Fynn. And she is in great danger."

Will nodded. "I understand. Tell me your story."

Farr's eyes grew distant as he began to tell his story, a story that Will had already partly determined.

"I am sure you are aware from Fynn that I disappeared from my parents when I was about six. Maybe Eric, I am beginning to remember him as well, would have said something. I didn't remember them. Honest." He looked up at Will, tears in his eyes for a moment. "I have no idea why I was taken or why I was kept from them. The couple who took me drove that memory down inside me. They were abusive at first and then began to ignore me. I had what I needed to survive and nothing more. I found a church when I was a teenager and became involved, eventually realizing I was a sinner and accepting Christ's sacrifice for me. I know I need to heal, but I am not sure how.

"Anyway, the couple are involved in white collar crime. I would hear them talking sometimes when they didn't think I was around. I finally began to write everything down. That notebook is in a safety deposit box in town.  They are from this town.  I will tell you their names but I need to get through this first.

"McIntosh is not the name I was raised under.  I was never adopted.  They told me I wasn't worth the time or money to do that. I still don't understand, but they seemed to have something on my biological father or mother, which one I am not sure."

"We can sort it out.  But what brings you here today?"  Will was watchful, his mind racing at the possibilities of who it could be before he nodded.  He had a good idea who the couple was.  In fact, he was sure he had seen Farr with them around town over the years. "Go on."

"I had to come forward.  A few weeks ago, I heard them talking about a Dr. Daley.  That they had sent a man to find her and kill her for some reason.  That reason, I don't know.  They never came out and said."  He looked up, tears momentarily blinding him. "I need to save her, Chief Peters, but I don't know how.  I've tried to find her the last couple of days but haven't been able to.  I did speak with the man that I have seen her with, but he didn't say anything. Do you know where she is?"

Will sat back, knowing he would have to put Farr somewhere he would be safe, but not quite sure if he was on the up and up.

"She's missing, Farr.  She and Brady disappeared about three days ago."

"Oh, no!  They have them!"  Farr shot to his feet, agitation in his body, and began to pace.  "Where would they put them?"

"That's what we are working on.  I want you to talk to the detective, Dallas, who is in charge of the case but first, we need to put you somewhere."  Will stood, reaching for his keys and pointing to the door.  "We'll go out back.  The Foundation Building is the best spot for now"

"I can't go there!"  Farr stopped dead in his tracks, horror mingled with hope on his face.  "They'll blame me."

"To the contrary, no.  All of us have been trying to find you. They want that for Fynn."

"You have?  They do?"  Hope sprung to his eyes.  "What can I do to help find her?"

"Right now, the best thing is to come with me and then stay in the building.  There's security there.  Breck will set you up in a suite."

"Thank you, Chief.  I don't know what to say."

"It's Will.  It looks as if we are going to be friends."  Will grew stern.  "And if this is a ploy to harm either one of them, you'll answer to many men."

"It's not, Chief, I mean, Will.  It's not.  I lost so many years with my sister."

"And your sister with you."  Will's hand raised to wave at the guard at the gate before he spoke again.  "She only has just remembered having a brother.  She buried it deep.  I should give a bit of history.  Your sister pushed her way through school, graduating at 20 as an entomologist.  But like you, she didn't have the parental love and caring that she needed.  She has found love and acceptance with all of us.  I think she and Brady have come to terms and a wedding is in the offing. But we need to find them first."

A short while later, Will watched as Farr spoke with Doc and Anna, Breck at his side.

"You say he just walked in and asked for you?"

Will nodded.  "He did. I'll fill you in on what I know, but there are some names I need Dallas to research."

Breck studied Farr for a moment.  "I've seen him around town. I think I know who you mean."  He grinned suddenly.  "Let's see who finds out the information first.  Say, did he ever change his name?"

"No, and that's part of the puzzle."  Will looked around, seeing the intensity the men were working under.  "Any word?"

"No.  Barnabas, Bradon and Ennis took off a while ago.  They had been looking at the map and then disappeared without saying where they were heading."

Will hesitated before he turned.  "Keep me updated.  I'm praying we find them."  He glanced down at his phone.  "Breck? The loading dock?"

———

Breck stared at him before he left the conference room on the run, waving at the security guard to follow, Will on his heels. They slid to a halt, watching as the door opened and Barnabas drove in, hearing the exhaust fans kick in to clear the air of fumes, before the overhead door slid down and Barnabas' vehicle door flew open.

Barnabas stood for a moment, watching inside the vehicle, before he turned, relief on his face as he nodded.

"We have them. We need the stretchers from the infirmary."

The security guard spun and left on a run, his hand on his mike to call for help.

Barnabas stood for a moment, his eyes on Will, before he turned back to the vehicle, his hands reaching for Fynn and carrying her to the stretcher quickly wheeled towards him. He could hear muttered protests coming from Brady, and Bradon's laughter-filled voice commenting. Ennis walked beside Brady, a hand out to help balance him before he was swung up on the other stretcher. The three stood back, Breck and Will approaching them.

"Barnabas? You found them? How?" Will's voice was quiet before Barnabas nodded.

"Let me put my vehicle back outside." He turned, finding one of the security team beside him, hand stretched out for the keys. With a quiet word of thanks, he handed them over and then pointed towards the hallway. "Let's walk. Ennis, go find your ladies. We'll need to meet, but I think we'll need a meal first. Let's find out what Doc has to say."

Will paced beside Barnabas, Bradon keeping up with them, stopping as they came to the infirmary. Doc nodded as he brushed past them, Anna with him. He had used Brady's help in situations similar to this, not liking it that Brady was one of the ones he had to treat. He stopped by his stretcher, assessing him, letting Anna go on to Fynn's room. Anna was back in short order, her hand on Doc's arm, rushing him to Fynn.

The three men watched, concern on their faces, before Will turned to Barnabas.

"We need to talk."

Barnabas nodded. "We do. Let's head to my office. I want to talk to you first before I talk to the others. You'll need to send a team out to the old Miller farm."

"The Miller farm? Why? It's been abandoned for years. They can't sell it, it's in such bad shape."

"Exactly. That's where they were."

Will held up a finger, his phone out as he made the call. He was thoughtful as he pocketed it. "They'll head out that way. Alice is already making her way there. Something had been said to her that she felt she needed to investigate."

"Good." Barnabas sank down onto his couch, his eyes closing for a moment. Fatigue washed over him, the stress releasing. He jerked as he felt a hand on his shoulder and looked up, finding Breck standing beside him, a mug of coffee held out.

"Okay, my friend, talk."

Bradon's mind drifted back to the moment they had shoved the door open, Barnabas' voice fading as he spoke. The door had creaked open, dust mites and flies circling in the shafts of sunlight before they had stepped down, missing the broken steps as they did so. Their eyes were drawn to the rough shelving with debris on it. They could see the evidence of animals on them. An exclamation from Ennis drew their eyes downwards and they sprang forward, dropping to their knees, Bradon beside Brady, Barnabas beside Fynn. Their hearts were in their mouths as they reached for the wrists, their heads nodding at Ennis's question.

Bradon gently rolled Brady over, a groan coming from his friend. He heard Ennis' quickly indrawn breath at the bruises on his face.

"Brady? Can you hear me, buddy?" Bradon's voice, though low, sounded loud in the area.

"I can. I don't want to go to school today, Dad. Let me sleep. I'm sick." He tried to roll to his side, but a hand on his chest kept him on his back. "My chest hurts. I'm sick." He drifted off again, leaving Ennis and Bradon to exchange worried glances before Ennis moved to Fynn.

"Barnabas?"

"She's alive, Ennis, but sick. She's running a fever. I don't want to look at her wound. Not here. Not in this dirty place. Bradon?"

"Let's go. I don't like that we're here, not when someone could return shortly."

"I agree. Can you manage Brady?"

"Yeah, I think to.  Help me get him up and outside and I'll swing him over my shoulder.  Ennis?  Stay back behind us until we're in the clear.  I don't like having to walk across the yard."

Barnabas stood for a moment staring around the yard before he was back into the root cellar, gathering Fynn into his arms, her body limp, her head drooping over his arm until Ennis turned it into his shoulder.

"There's a path behind here that should lead us back to other side of the yard.  I think I can find it."

"That's what I was trying to remember.  Lead on, Ennis.  I feel like we're running out of time."

"I think we are."  She was off, finding the overgrown path and heading down it, watching carefully for the two men and their burdens.  She opened the doors for the men and then slid in beside Fynn, her arm reaching to wrap around her friend.

"She's so hot, guys.  Hurry!"

"I know she is.  How's Brady?"  Barnabas keyed the motor to life and drove off as quickly as he could.

"Still out of it.  Who would do this?"

"That's what Dallas and Will are working on.  Any word from our guys?"

Bradon pulled out his phone.  "Brenden.  He says they have found some information that they need to talk to us about.  He's been trying to reach you."

"I felt my phone vibrate but we had other things to do.  Anything else?"  Silence greeted his question and his head turned for a moment, seeing the look of surprise on Bradon's face.  "Bradon?"

Bradon shook his head as he felt Ennis' hand on his shoulder.  "It's Breck.  He said Will's at the building.  And he has brought out Fynn's brother, Farr."

"Her brother?"  Ennis's voice held surprise.  "How did he find him?"

"It was the other way around, Breck said.  Farr walked into the police department looking for Will."

"Good. They need each other. God has been in this so far. Both of them are alive. We'll catch up once we have these two safe." Barnabas pulled abruptly to the side of the road, his fingers tapping at the gearstick.

"Barnabas?" Ennis leaned past Bradon to search his face. "Why are you stopping?"

"I'm thinking. We can't take them to the hospital in town. Given their condition, their kidnappers will look for them there."

"Take them to Doc. He'll decide where they need to be. If he can treat them and have Anna stay with them, that may work." Ennis had full confidence in Doc and Anna. The older couple had become good friends of hers, almost as if they were a second set of parents, which they were to all of the younger people in the building.

"I agree." Bradon shifted to look into the back seat. "Fynn needs help. I don't like the fever she's running."

"Nor do I." Barnabas pulled away, finally drawing up in front of the building, his eyes searching around. "I feel like someone is out there, watching us."

"They are. Security has seen evidence of that even though they have not found anyone."

"I know." Barnabas sat, sorting through scenarios before he sighed. "I guess we'll have to take a chance."

"The loading dock." Ennis finally spoke up, stating what she felt was so obvious. "Go around to the loading dock, open the door, drive in, and close the door behind you. The windows on your vehicle are dark enough, and it's getting close enough to dusk, that they can't see in, whoever it is that's out there."

Bradon laughed at the expression of Barnabas' face even as his friend shook his head.

"Too obvious, wasn't it? I didn't even think of that. I was just trying to figure out how to get them from here to the door. Smart lady, you have there, Bradon."

Bradon grinned as he looked back at his wife. "She is. I keep telling her that. She just says it's God who is telling her these things."

———

"Well, it is." Ennis sounded disgruntled. "Well? What are you waiting for? Sitting here doesn't get them to Doc and Anna."

The men laughed as Barnabas did exactly as she had requested, the door closing behind them, even as Bradon sent a text to Breck. They looked up to see the security guard, Will and Breck heading their way.

Doc finally stood up, his eyes on Fynn, his hand reaching for her wrist. Her pulse was still thready, he thought, before he walked to the medication cabinet and unlocked it. He kept it stocked with what he felt he would need and prayed that the antibiotics he would choose would work. Fynn had been upfront with him one day when they were talking, giving him her medical history, knowing that he wasn't asking just for curiosity. No allergies to medications. That was good, he said.

An hour later, he stood back, once more assessing her. He didn't like the high fever she was running but prayed that the cooling blanket and the antibiotics and pain medications would kick in. He had agreed with Will when the police chief had popped in. They didn't want to hospitalize her if they could help it. If Doc needed anything, Will had agreed to find it for him.

Anna stood for a moment, her eyes on her husband, before her arm was around him.

"Doc?

"I pray what I have done will work. Her wound looked good, all things considered."

"It did. When Bradon said where she was found, I was worried."

"You and me both." He turned. "Brady?"

"He's been awake and had some broth and water. He's sleeping. Naturally, I would say. It will take time for him to recover. Worrying about Fynn won't help."

"No, it won't. We'll need to get him in to see her for a few moments when we can." Doc paused, his eyes on his wife, praising God that He had given him such a helpmeet. "What's the story with those two?"

Anna smiled. "Brady let it slip that they are engaged. I gather from what he said she asked first and then he asked her. Buckley was there when Fynn asked."

"He was, and he wouldn't say a word, now would he?"

"Absolutely not. Barnabas was looking for you. He's hoping you can give an update on these two to everyone. Go. I'll send someone if I need you. And you need to call the centre. You're not going there today, I know that."

"No, I'm not. Thanks, love." Doc paused at the doorway, his eyes turning back to Fynn before he moved to stand in Brady's doorway. He sighed. What is it with these young people, Lord? Can't they find love in the normal way, like Anna and I did? I know, You're in control. I just hate to see them hurt. He turned to find Breck watching, waiting for him to walk towards him.

"Doc?"

"Brady's sleeping naturally, Anna says. We need to pray for Fynn. She's in rough shape. High fever. The wound seems fine but I have debrided it. I'll be watching it. They're waiting for me, Anna says."

Breck grinned. "They are, if you can spare the time. The ladies have brought in sandwiches and salads and fruit for us. They informed us we were working too hard and needed a break."

"They are right on both counts."

"I know, Doc. I know. But we want this over for Brady and Fynn."

"That we know. And we will. Just don't forget that God is leading in this. There is a reason for what they are going through. Fynn needs to heal from her past and so does her brother."

"Brady too. I don't know that he's ever really reconciled to his parents' deaths."

Doc's steps slowed before he nodded, having reached the conference room door. "I suspect you're correct, Breck. We all have things we need to heal from. That's where we come in for him. We need to encourage him to do just that. Fynn too. That's where the ladies come in. What they have been through will help. They all have a different perspective on life now. She needs to hear those.”

“She has, Doc. I know she has. She told me she had and was working through what she was told and how she could apply those lessons to her life. She’s hurting way deep inside. It will take time.”

“That it will.” Doc moved away, heading for the food and then sitting himself down at a table, his eyes watching his young friends as they mingled and then sat to eat. His gaze lingered on Barnabas for some reason, a prayer rising for the leader of these men. Something told him that in the not too distant future, Barnabas would be going through a fight for his own life and that frightened Doc.

———

Will finally stood and walked away from the room, his phone out, turning to search the room to focus on Farr. He spoke quietly before he dialled another number.

"Dallas? Where are you right about now?"

At the urgency in Will's voice, Dallas stared at his phone for a moment before he answered. "Just getting up. I got in about nine this morning after driving all night. Why?"

"Because we have had a major turn in the investigation. Alice says she tried to reach you but got your voice mail. I'm at the Foundation. Fynn's brother walked into the detachment this morning, and I talked with him. Farr's here. It's a nasty piece of work that has been done."

"I can only imagine." Dallas swung his house door closed, checked it was locked and then ran for his car. "I''m on my way. I'm putting you on speaker."

"Good. Here's what we have. I haven't talked to the fellows here yet to find out what they have, but Alice said that someone called Tracker has been calling for you and then sending information by courier. Apparently you have a number of packages on your desk."

"Tracker? That's Emma. Didn't you know that?"

Will drew in his breath. "No, but I gather from what I've heard she keeps her identity hidden. It goes no further."

"No, sir. I'll stop by my office and grab what's there. I'll find a spot there to work."

"Good. Breck said he had a desk and computer set up that you could use, with its own printer. He anticipated that you would want to work here for a while before heading back into the office. For now, this has become part of our detachment, just so nothing can be said."

Dallas paused as he stepped into his office, a frown on his face. "That bad, Will?"

"That bad. The ones we are looking at have ties to the town council."

"Oh, great. Just what we needed." Dallas stared at his desk. "How much information did Emma send me?"

Will laughed. "That bad?" He hung up on Dallas' grumbling.

Barnabas walked towards him. "Will, we'll give you our statements if you like. Then, that's over with."

"Hold that thought. Dallas is on his way out. He'll take them."

"Sure, whatever." Barnabas didn't sound like himself. "There's something about that place that is bothering me."

"And that would be?"

Barnabas shrugged. "I'm not sure. Something different about it. I know it's been years since I've been out there as a teenager and I know it's decrepit, but something was off. I'll think of what it is at some point." He turned to stare back at the room. "What do you make of Farr?"

"Now, that's someone who is difficult to read. He's hiding something, but I can't pinpoint what it is."

"I know he is. I pray he doesn't hurt Fynn or Brady."

"No, I don't think he will. I think that he doesn't know us or trust us enough, given his history." Bradon stood beside them. "I've talked to him. He really didn't remember. The abuse he suffered drove it down so deep. It was when he heard the couple talking about a Dr. Fynn Daley that he began to research her and when he found her picture, the memories started to come back. Selective amnesia, maybe?"

"And the man Brady found is somehow connected to the couple. That's what Brennen and Baird are working on."

"Okay. What else do we need to do?"

———

"Find the Evans' family. They're involved. Their son was one of our kidnappers. I recognized his voice even though his face was covered." Brady stood beside them, shaky, but upright.

"Should you even be up, Brady?" Will's hand reached to steady him as concern flickered across the faces of the three men.

"I need to be. We need to solve this, find whoever it is. There is a deadline, guys. By Friday. They told me Fynn had to agree to something or find something by this Friday. If she didn't, she would die." He looked at them, distress and despair on his face. "I can't let them hurt her. I just can't."

"We won't, Brady. We're working hard on that. Emma's sending us information to help." Breck drew Brady into the room and to a seat, the room growing in silence as his friends stood and approached him, each with words of their own for him.

Brady looked around. "Where do we stand? And what can I do?"

"First, you give Dallas your statement. He's right here. Then, you talk to us. You tell us what you know. Hopefully we can get Fynn's side of the story."

Brady shook his head. "You won't. She won't tell it, not unless she has changed her mind. Whatever they said to her, it hurt her and drove her down. It broke her." Tears brimmed in his eyes and then overflowed, but he was not ashamed. His heart hurt too much for his lady. "She whispered to me that she had given up, that she just couldn't go on, not when she found out that someone at the lab was involved."

"That's what we thought. Did she say who?" Will had sat beside Brady, an arm leaning on the table.

Brady shook his head. "No, but she dropped enough hints that I think we can figure it out." His head dropped to his arms, causing the ones around him to exchange glances. "Where's Dallas? I want to give my statement, and then get in on the hunt." He stood as he heard a voice behind him.

Fynn sat there in a wheelchair, the only way Anna would let her up. Her face was pale, her hair a mess, and her eyes fever bright.

"Will? Can we talk? Can you take my statement?"

————

Will approached her, to crouch down in front of her. "I can do that. But you shouldn't be up."

"I have to be. Everyone here was threatened. I need to tell you who it is. And, God forgive me, I brought this to you." Her voice died away as she stared past Will. "Who? Is that? It can't be?" Her hand covered her trembling mouth as her emotions tried to overwhelm her. "Farr?"

"It is. But before you talk to him, you talk to me. I don't want anyone to come back on us to say the statements are contaminated and have the charges thrown out." Will reached for the handles on her chair, turning it and wheeling her away, following Breck as he headed for his office, knowing that Dallas and Brady were heading for Barnabas' office.

Her head spinning as she sat upright, hardly able to keep her eyes open, Fynn struggled to find the words that she needed, to tell her story

"Okay, so. We were taken from the hospital. The man who forced us out is the man who left me in the field. I don't know how he knew where I was. He must have been watching. We were forced into a vehicle and then driven around for a long time. I lost track of the turns and stops, but I know we did go over railroad tracks many times. I think they were just driving around in circles. Or that's how it seemed."

Her mind traced back to that late afternoon into the evening. Brady had shown up in her hospital room, refusing to leave, just grinning at her as she tried to send him back to work. He was done work for the day, he informed her, Sam calling in someone to cover for him so he could be with his lady.

She frowned at him before she shook her head. "Is that what I am, Brady?"

"You are." He stood for a moment before he carefully gathered her close. "You're the one I've been waiting for. I thought I made that clear."

She sighed, her head on his shoulder, feeling his strength yet gentleness in how he held her. "You did. It's just that I've never had this before. Had someone tell me that they love me and really mean it."

Brady's heart broke for her. At that point, he was ready to sweep her out of the hospital room, find Buckley and a license and marry her right then and there. They spoke quietly for a while before her eyes looked past him. He saw the fear on her face and how it paled. Before he could turn, he felt the revolver pressed against him. No amount of protesting stopped the man from forcing them from the room and down the stairs, no staff or visitors in the hallway to see them or stop them.

Fynn stifled a scream as she saw the second man approaching them, his face covered with a bandanna and his sweatshirt hood pulled up over his face as far as as it could be. Forced into a van, she had clung to Brady's hand until she was forced to drop it and her wrists bound and a blindfold slapped ruthlessly around her head. She so wanted Brady's arm around her, not just touching her, but knew that wouldn't happen. She felt his arm moving and then his hands were gripping hers, stilling the trembling of hers with his strength.

After who knew how long, the van picked up speed and she twisted her head, listening. They had headed out of town for a while before the van slowed and then she felt the roughness of the ride pick up. A gravel road, she thought, and paled even further. The pain from her side had her growing faint. Then, she felt the van slow even more and turn once again, this time to drive slowly up a rutted path, rocking from side to side. Brady's hands tightened on hers and she heard him muttering something, not quite catching what he was saying.

The van stopped and she felt the movement as the two men dropped down out of it, an argument ensuing. The door slid open and she felt Brady pulled from the seat and then hands reached to pull her out. She dropped to her knees, her bound hands finding her side as pain shot through it before a hand dragged her to her feet and then shoved her over rough ground. Fynn was barely able to keep to her feet before she was shoved forward, losing her balance and falling down. She hit the packed dirt and lay still, not hearing the door pulled closed on creaky hinges and a lock snapped closed. Her eyes shuts as waves of pain rocked through her body and she felt the nausea beginning. Please, Lord, don't let me be sick. I can't handle that. Please, Lord. Her eyes closed as she fought against the nausea and pain and then, she lost consciousness, not hearing the man return and stare down at her before he roughly shoved her over to her back with a booted foot and then reach to cut through the ropes binding her. He shrugged. It's wasn't his worry that she didn't stay awake. He had been tasked with finding her and bringing her here. His work was finished.

Brady tilted his head, listening as Fynn was moved away, and then began to fight the hand holding him, trying to get to her. A blow to his jaw sent him to the ground, his vision whirling in front of him as black spots danced in it.  He felt hands dragging him up and across the ground, unable to get his feet working before he too was shoved down some stairs, hitting his hands and knees.  A hand on the back of his neck kept him still before he was dragged to his knees, his bonds cut and then a shove forward on his back sending him down to his hands and knees again.  He waited, hearing the muffled sounds around him, knowing that the door had closed as the light vanished and he heard the loud snick of a lock closing.

He finally reached for the blindfold, dragging it from his head, blinking in the half light that was gradually growing dimmer.  Brady stood, his hand reaching to the rough dirt wall to steady himself.  A root cellar?  He turned abruptly, his head spinning as he did so, and he made his way up the ramshackle stairs, his foot catching on the broken step near the top, and he shoved at the door and then pulled at it, finally giving up and turning around, one hand resting on it, the other rubbing at his face.  Fynn?  Where are you?  Are you okay?  Please, Lord, save my lady for me.  I don't know who, but you do.

Two days had passed since they had been taken.  Food and water had been brought to each one, the man silent as he did so, his face covered so they couldn't identify him.  They were given only so long to eat before he returned, gathering up what they hadn't and taking the water bottles with them.  Brady sank back against the floor that afternoon, thoughts whirling through his mind.  Somehow, he had to get free, to get to Fynn.  He had searched for a weapon, finding none in the root cellar, just as he had thought.  He had pulled and pried at the door without success.  His head tilting, he heard footsteps sounding across the ground and the door flew open.  The man beckoned him up.  Brady refused, knowing this might be his only chance to escape.  He fought with the man, finally managing to knock him down, and running for the stairs and up.  He paused, his eyes searching, not seeing the second man until he was tackled and taken down.

A booted foot hit his face as he was going down and he tumbled over and over before he lay still, face down, arms spread out above his head.  The men broke out into an argument, each blaming the other for what had happened before the first man reached to flip Brady to his back and then grabbed his wrists, dragging him away from the root cellar and towards the storm cellar that Fynn was captive in.  They needed him to take care of her, they had decided, knowing that he was a paramedic. They had brought in supplies for him.

The argument grew louder and louder after Brady was dumped on the packed dirt among the debris that littered it and the men had taken themselves back outside. There was a sudden pop and the second man stared in shock at the first man, a hand raising to his chest before he fell backwards and lay still. The first man stared down at him dispassionately before he looked around and then dragged him to the abandoned barn and dumped his body there. He didn't think he would be found for days. There would be nothing to connect them, he thought. Both of them were from out of town.

Brady roused during the night, laying still, hearing the rustle of the night critters, the call of the night birds and insects and then shifted, a hand going to his face. It hurt. He wiggled his jaw. At least, it's not broken. That's a good thing, isn't it, Lord? He rolled to his side, frowning, before he crawled towards the soft sounds he heard. A hand found a body and he felt for the face. Fynn, he thought. You're here. You're alive. He couldn't assess her, he realized, not in the dark. He sighed before he stretched out near her, a hand on hers, not finding that she even stirred or roused when he did so. This is not good, he thought. He reached to feel her face, finding it burning hot and dry. Oh, Fynn, his heart cried. I need to get you out of here, but I can't. His own head pounding as he laid it back down, his eyes closed and he slept. Neither roused in the early morning as the door opened and the man stood there.

Dropping the food, he stood over them before he spun and ran up the stairs, heading for his ramshackle rusty truck and speeding away as fast as he could. He would find supplies, he thought. That paramedic could do his job then, fix her up and have her ready when his boss appeared late that afternoon. He knew his own life was on the line if they were awake when that happened.

———

Brady roused slightly late that afternoon as he felt hands on him before he was raised carefully to his feet and directed up the stairs, the same hands holding him upright. He vaguely remembered stating that he was sick, that he had told his father he didn't feel well and didn't want to go to school. His heart clenched at the thought. That had been the last words he had said to his father that day. His father had laughed, felt his head, and agreed that he could stay home, that he was sick.

Brady roused again as he felt hands pulling him from the vehicle, protesting at being awakened again before he felt what he thought was a bed under him. He roused later as he felt a hand on his wrist and jerked, his eyes springing open to find Anna watching him.

He had to clear his throat before he could speak, his voice husky. "Anna? Where am I?"

"In our infirmary. Doc's been around. Here. I have some broth for you and some cool water. Drink both." Anna helped hold the cup to his mouth, his hands too shaky to do it on his own. She watched as his head went back on the pillow and he slept, this time just sleep. Pulling the light blanket up on him, her hand rested on his head as she prayed for him, her head turning to watch the door, knowing she had to go find out how Fynn was.

Doc watched Fynn closely before he felt Anna's arm around him. Quiet words about the two and then Doc walked away, heading to find Will and Barnabas.

Dallas studied Brady, knowing him well enough to know he had given all the information that he could.

"The two men? Can you describe them?"

Brady shook his head and regretted it. "Not really. I think you'd get a better picture off the security feed in the hospital.'"

"I understand Branigan did just that. Now, Fynn? How is she?"

Brady shrugged. "I have no idea." He was on his feet, heading for the conference room before Dallas could stop him.

Dallas sighed, looked down at the signed statement and tucked it away in his locked briefcase. He studied the piles of courier envelopes before reaching for the first one. Emma, what have you sent? He was soon lost in his work, not seeing Alice appear in the doorway until she spoke.

Alice finally walked away, heading for her car and home. It had been a long day, she thought. Dallas is deep into the investigation. She thought through the scenario that they had found, including the body. She didn't think the couple knew about that. That was something for Dallas or Will to discuss with them.

Dallas stood watching Brady, seeing his concentration on Farr, was it? He walked towards Breck, who stood studying the map on the wall, Darby beside him.

"Breck? Is that really Fynn's brother?"

Breck nodded, his concentration not really on Dallas. "It is. Fynn doesn't know that he's here, I don't think. Brady's not too sure of how to approach him."

"I can see that. Have you talked with him at all?"

Breck finally turned. "I have and so has Will. It's not pretty how he's been raised or not raised. We suspect he was taken because of their parents. And we can't reach their parents at all. Eric has been in contact with his. Apparently, they have not come home at all. And that is puzzling to them. They never don't come home from vacation."

"I see. Do we know where they were?"

Breck nodded. "We do. Barnabas has sent Brendon and Brandon out to Saskatoon to look into it. Barnabas has talked to the police chief out there as has Will."

"Okay. Listen, I have to run. I have their statements so they are free to talk." He looked around. "Where's Fynn?"

"Back in the infirmary. She's still really sick, Doc says, and shouldn't have been up."

"Okay, then. I know you all have been working hard. Send me anything you have that might help."

Breck grinned as Darby appeared back beside him, a file box in his hand. "This is what we have. Burnie has sorted through it with Brennen and put it into order for you, he says."

Dallas stared at the box. "Thanks, I think. Catch you later."

Brady finally approached Farr, who stood, feeling lost and lonely, watching the activity and how well the men worked together. He had watched as well as the young wives had come and gone, bringing food, including him. He had liked that they all were friends. That was what he had been missing his whole life, he decided. He needed to change that. Once he made sure Fynn was on her feet and well again, he would leave. He was too dangerous to be around her.

"Don't you leave her."

Farr spun at the harsh words from beside him and stared up at Brady. "I'm sorry?"

"I said, don't leave your sister. I won't let her grieve for you again."

"You must be Brady."

"I am. And you are Farr. You look like your sister. I've seen you around town. I didn't know Fynn had a brother here in town. In fact, Fynn had forgotten you."

"And I had forgotten her. We were torn apart and because of our parents." Anger and bitterness coloured Farr's words. "Look, you need to be sitting down. You're going to fall over if you don't."

Brady nodded, fatigue weighing even that down. "I do. Sit with me." He looked up with a word of thanks as Cadee handed him a mug of coffee. "Thanks, Cadee."

She hugged him and then turned away quickly, blinking back the tears that threatened. Her heart raised in prayer for her friends. Lord, heal them. They need that. So does Farr. We need to bring him into our group, but I am not sure we can.

A week later, Fynn moved around her apartment, Eric leaning against the kitchen doorframe watching her. She has been too quiet, he thought. He had talked to Dallas, passing on information he had been handed by an informant in his town. Dallas had looked at it, nodded, and thanked him, stating that would help to tie up some of the loose ends. And there were many, he had been warned.

"Fynn?" When she didn't respond, he walked directly into her path and made her.

Fynn glared at her cousin and went to move around him, his hand on her wrist stopping her. He felt her flinch as he did that and dropped his hand. She had more healing to do than he had thought.

"Eric? Have they told you anything? I feel like I am walking around, something hanging over my head ready to drop on me and kill me. Brady feels the same way." Before he could respond, he heard her phone and saw her pale.

"Fynn?"

"That's Dad's ringtone. He hasn't call me in months. Why now?"

"He hasn't? Longer than they have been away?"

She nodded. "Yes. Like in six months and that was only an order that I had to be at a dinner they were giving. I couldn't go. I was on call that night and had been called out to another district. He doesn't understand."

"No and he should. It's been explained to him enough times. You know that body Brady found?"

"Yes, that one. I know. It's tied to here somehow. Dallas said he was an employee of the couple they are looking at. He can't say much, he said, other than that the investigation is moving rapidly. He's worried about Farr."

"Farr, yes. Have you and he talked?"

Fynn nodded, tears momentarily blinding her. "We have. Eric, it was too cruel. I lost a brother growing up, he a sister. I know you've stepped in but it's not the same.'

Eric reached to hug her, his eyes on the door as it opened and Brady appeared, still in his uniform. "I know, Fynn. That I know. I did the best I could as a cousin."

She nodded, hearing Brady's boots hit the tray she left by the door for them. "Brady's here. He shouldn't be. He's not to be done work yet."

"Fynn?" Brady's hands reached to turn her, his eyes looking up at Eric, who nodded. "I had to come. Will asked me to."

"Brady? Why? I don't like this. You're too sober." She reaching to hug him. "Who is it? Who's dead? Please, not Farr. Not Eric's people."

"No, it's not them." An arm around her, he directed her to the couch, holding her close to him when they were seated. A prayer rose in his heart, knowing he would hurt the one that he loved and that he had no choice. "It's your parents."

"My parents? What about other?" She leaned back, studying his face, seeing the sorrow there. "They're dead?"

"I'm sorry. Brendon and Brandon called Barnabas, who found me. I don't have all the details, but they told him that it was a drive by shooting."

"Deliberate. They were followed and then taken out, as they say." She sat in silence, in shock, before she looked at Eric. "You knew?"

"Not for sure. Barnabas had asked me to be with you until he could spring Brady to come home."

She nodded and rose, disappearing, her bedroom door closing quietly behind her. "This is it, isn't it, Lord? Now, I'll never know how to reach them or why they were so distant. I think it has to do with Farr, but I'm not sure. Please, dear Lord, Farr and I will need You. Brady is here, but he didn't know my parents. They refused to meet him." She frowned before she was running for Brady, finding him standing waiting for her, his arms open to sweep her to his heart.

<hr>

"Brady, they didn't want to meet you.  How come?"

"I never knew that.  Did you, Eric?"

Eric shrugged.  "I just thought it was them being them.  They really didn't care what Fynn did or who she hung around with. I don't know that they met many of your friends."

"They didn't.  Now, how does all this tie to here?  I don't remember them ever talking about this town."

"Dallas is looking into that.  He had a lead he was following." Eric's eyes dropped for a moment before he raised them.  "I need to run, Fynn.  I am so sorry."  He reached to hug his cousin and then set her back from him, his hands on her shoulders before he looked up at Brady and nodded, turning to walk away, sorrow and yes anger in his heart towards his aunt and uncle.  A sudden thought had him stopping in his tracks before he ran down the stairs towards his vehicle and headed for Dallas.  Dallas just stared at him before he nodded, having had the same thoughts.

Another week had passed. Fynn was growing stronger, but still angered by what had happened to her. She knew she needed to let it go but was having difficulty with that very deed. Brady had talked to her. Buckley had talked to her. Berneen had finally pulled her aside one day, sat her down, went through the Scriptures with her and then prayed with her, leaving her with her thoughts and a hug. She didn't know where Farr stood with God and that bothered her. He had been around, staying in the building as he was, but not as much as she would have liked. They had talked some, but he had become distant and withdrawn. She really didn't know how to deal with that.

Barnabas found her as she stood, staring out of the lobby windows, wanting desperately to be outside but not sure if it was even safe. He shook his head after a moment and approached her.

"Fynn? Do you have some time? The building is at the point that they need some more input from you."

"It is? How did it get ahead that fast?"

Barnabas laughed. "Because it's for you. Once the contractor heard who it was, he put everyone on it. He said you had helped a family friend solve a death years ago."

"I did? I have worked on so many. I'm tired of that, Barnabas. Burnt out. Beaten down."

He nodded, sympathy on his face. "Of course, you are. You've done this for so many years. You pushed your way through, trying to please your parents. You never had a chance to be a teenager, a young lady. Brady realizes that, you know. That's why he's not pushing you any harder than he is. It's the rest of us that want to see you two settle down together."

Fynn blinked at him, before she hugged him. "Thank you. Very few people get that. Are we safe to go?"

"We are. I spoke with Dallas. Alice is here to provide an escort for us. Our security team has a car as well to follow us."

"Wow! Not taking any chances, are you?" Fynn felt life beginning to stir within her once more.

She stood in what would be her office, looking around, knowing she would need to make decisions as to what she wanted for decor and furnishings. Just for the moment, though, she paused, thankful for the friends that Brady had brought into her life and thankful that God had spared her life.

She walked back through the building, the contractor approaching her. Lost in their conversation, Fynn didn't see Barnabas and Brady approaching her, a grin on Brady's face as he saw her excitement. She squealed as his arms surrounded her from behind.

"Happy, love?"

She nodded, a mouthed word of thanks to Barnabas. "I am. This is so me. What I have dreamed about. Does God let us fulfill dreams this way?"

The contractor grinned at her. "He does. He uses people like me to do that. That happiness in your voice? It wasn't there when we spoke last week. It is today. That gives me all the thanks I need. We'll be speaking again, Fynn."

Fynn watched as he walked away before she turned to Barnabas. "Okay, spill. You have news."

Brady began to laugh at the comical look that crossed his friend's face. "You don't get away with much with her, my friend."

"That I can see. You have a handful there, Brady." He grinned at her squeal of outrage. "I do have word. Dallas is meeting us after supper at the building. He can't make it before. Right now, how be we head home? I hear tell Anna and the other ladies have arranged a potluck."

"They have? They didn't tell me. I don't have anything to bring."

"Fynn." When she looked up at him, Brady just smiled. "You don't need to. There will be plenty and you will have opportunities in the future to share."

She shrugged. "It's just not right. That's all I can say. What does he want?"

"That he didn't say. Just asked if you two would be around. I promised him that I would make sure you were."

"Planning our lives, are you?" She walked away, leaving Brady laughing, Barnabas staring after her.

"Did she just do that?"

"She did. She's right. It sounds as if you were planning our lives." Brady ran to catch up with her, an arm around her. "Okay, love?"

She nodded. "Getting there. I'm angry, Brady, and have told God that. I have yelled at Him, been repentant, sobbed out my feelings, been as emotional as I ever have been. I want this over. We need to make plans."

"I know." He looked back as Barnabas walked towards them. "How about we set a date? We can announce it tonight."

"Really? We can do that?" She reached to hug him, holding him tight before she stepped back. "Then, two weeks from Saturday. Buckley stopped me this morning, questioned if we had set a day, and told me that he was free that day, would it do?"

Brady shouted with laughter, unable to resist at the smirk she sent his way, simply shaking his head at Barnabas.

Brady stood after their meal, his hands on Fynn's shoulders, as he waited for his friends to notice. Quiet finally moved through the room as their eyes watched him and then dropped to Fynn.

"We have an announcement to make, my friends." Brady's eyes dropped to the copper hair in front of him. Thank you, Lord, that You have sent Fynn into my life. We're still in for a rough ride, but You are there. She has brought joy and fun into my life in a way that I didn't know I missed. "We have set a day. Buckley, I understand you are free two weeks from Saturday. Will that do?"

Buckley shouted with laughter as his words came back to him. "It will and I am. Congratulations, you two." His eyes moved past the couple to rest on Dallas, who stood, Alice and Will with him, just inside the doorway. This is not good, he thought. Not at all.

Dallas shook his head. This was always the difficult part, so near the conclusion of the investigation but so dangerous for the victims. And that was what they were, victims. He searched and saw Farr sitting beside Blair, deep in conversation. He looked down as he felt something touch his hand and then reached to pet Kade, Bradon's Australian Shepherd.

"Dallas? You have what you need to give an update?" Will's voice was quiet.

"I do. I needed both of you here as you have information to pass on. Alice, I haven't heard. Did they identify the body Brady found?"

"They did. It was a family member to the couple. From what I understand, he was sent up there to take out Fynn. How he got put in the woods, we don't know, but we suspect her father did the deed."

"That makes cruel sense, you know." Dallas walked towards the young couple, Fynn's eyes meeting his, the sparkle of happiness fading a bit.

"Dallas. Alice. You're here. You need to hear our news." Fynn struggled for a moment, finding her happiness once more. "We've set a date and you both need to come."

"You have? You hadn't the last time we spoke." Alice slipped into a chair beside Fynn. They were become close friends, sharing a faith but also a connection through their occupations.

"We have. Buckley told me he was free two weeks from Saturday. Will this all be wrapped up by then?"

Dallas grinned at her for a moment, knowing exactly what she was doing, pushing him to clear it all off his desk in two weeks. "We will do our best. We have some updates to give you and the rest. Do you have time now? You're finished your meal?"

"We have except to clear the remains away. And that won't take long." She was on her feet, moving away from them, a hand to her side for a moment as the healing muscles pulled.

"Does she ever stop?"

"Sometimes but not for long." Brady turned to face Dallas. "Is it good news you have to share?"

"To some extent."

Dallas finally stood, his eyes wandering over each face that was there, lingering on Farr as he sat beside Fynn, who was sandwiched between Brady and himself. He nodded. They will take care of her. Eric sat beside Farr, his eyes on his cousins, a desperation in his heart that it would be over for them and they could all heal. Yes, he thought, even me, Lord, and my parents. We need to heal as well, and only You can provide that.

Dallas cleared his throat, his thoughts scrambled for a moment, so unlike him. He hated this part of it, when he had most of the information to share, but not the culprits. They had gone underground and the search was on. Information was trickling in to the detachment in a steady stream, picking up more and more as each hour went by. The street people knew Brady. They knew he worked for the Foundation and that the Foundation had and would provide for them, what they needed and sometimes even what they wished for.

Will watched as well, his focus on Farr, a frown on his face. Something was off about him that night, he thought, but what? What did they really know about him, other than what he had told them? He spoke quietly to Alice, who nodded.

"I looked into him, Will. He's clear. I don't know what is going on tonight, but he's not involved in her kidnapping. He hasn't had contact with the men we've picked up. They deny knowing him, but I am sure that they have to."

"I'm sure that they do."

Dallas began to speak, drawing all eyes to him.

"Fynn. Brady. Farr. First, Fynn and Farr, your parents. They were targeted, that has been determined by the police in Saskatoon. They didn't have a chance. We haven't been able to determine if they were there for any other reason than what they said, a holiday. The authorities are just waiting for word from you two as to where to return their remains.'

Fynn and Farr exchanged glances before Fynn spoke. "As far as I am concerned, they can be buried out there. I have no reason to visit their graves. They made sure of that." She sighed in the silence. "I know. That's not the attitude I should have. I'm sorry. They had shown all my life that I was an encumbrance to them, a nuisance. No matter what I did, I couldn't reach them."

Benen spoke up. "We understand, Fynn, probably better than you think. We have seen the change in you since you moved here. We stand with you in your decision. Farr?"

Farr shrugged. "I don't remember them all that well. For me to go to their grave? It would be going to a stranger's grave. So, I guess I would agree with Fynn."

"Okay, that's about what I thought you'd say. I'll relay that to the authorities out there. Any expenses I have been told that are not met by their insurances will be picked up by the Foundation. Is that correct, Barnabas?"

"It is, Dallas. It's what we do, Fynn, Farr. We take care of our family and both of you are that." Barnabas nodded at the gratitude on Brady's face.

"Brady, we need to go back to that body you found. It was the son of the couple we are looking for. Farr, did you know that they had a son?"

Farr looked surprised and then shook his head. "No, I didn't and I should have. Where was he?"

"Away at boarding school and camps for all his life, until he became an adult. Then, they groomed him to fit into their business. And by grooming, it was not good. He became their exterminator, to be in one way. Fynn, he was there to kill you. Did you know that?"

Fynn paled. "No, but is he the one that I felt watching me, who went through my home and office?"

Dallas shook his head. "He's the one who had been watching you, but not the one who went through your home and office. I'm sorry. We have confirmation that your father was the one. He was looking for any evidence you might have against him and your mother."

Fynn nodded, having already reached that conclusion. "That doesn't surprise me at all. He used to search my room every day and I know he tried to get into my locker at school. Why?"

"He was involved in white collar crime. He was an accountant, was he not? He used to launder money for the mob, and the couple who took you, Farr, were part of it. They apparently took you to keep him silent, only it didn't work. He really didn't care if you lived or died. I'm sorry. I wish both of you had had better lives."

Farr shrugged. "It is what it is. God protected us, gave us experiences we can use to help others. What else do you have?"

"We have determined, with the help of the police in your hometown, that your father is the one who murdered him. He made arrangements to meet him there. You weren't to be the one called in, Fynn. He had hoped that the body would never be discovered. This we have determined from detailed notes found in his safe."

"That safe!" Fynn leaned forward. "What all was in it? Or can you tell me?"

"I can give only generalities. It is part of the investigation that won't be released yet. There were financial records, thousands of dollars in cash, and a safety deposit box key. That box has been turned over to the authorities. They may be contacting you."

She shrugged. "I don't know anything about it." She looked up at Brady for a moment, finding his trust and confidence in her showing on his face. "Farr wouldn't either, would he?"

Farr was shaking his head. "No. And I know nothing about the people who raised me. Like Fynn, I was barely tolerated,"

"That's the word we have. Now, your kidnappers. We have the one in custody who took you the first time and then from the hospital. He is not talking but won't make bail as yet. He is facing murder and kidnapping charges relating to your case but he is a person of interest in numerous others."

"Murder?" Brady watched as Fynn's face paled before he spoke again. "Who did he murder?"

———

"The second kidnapper. We found his body in the barn."

Fynn's cmotions overwhelmed her for a moment and she turned her face into Brady. "How sad! I mean, they did that to us and likely others, but that is no way to end your life."

"We understand that, Fynn. We really do." Dallas paused, taking the bottle of water Berneen handed him as she moved around the room with Cadee and Ennis, handing out beverages to all of them.

"Where do we stand now, Dallas? Do you have the couple in custody?" Farr was anxious to hear that they were. He had been contacted by a friend, who had indicated that his parents or so-called parents were looking for him, and that he had been told it was not for his good. In fact his friend had asked him to leave town, his very life depended on it.

"No, we haven't yet, Farr. We are going to ask that you and Fynn not leave the building or the immediate surrounding area." He held up a hand at Fynn's protest. "We know, Fynn. We know. You don't want to be restricted in that way but we need to. Sources on the street have told us that there are contracts out on both of you and on Brady as well. Brady, Will took the liberty of talking to your supervisor. For now, you're off on sick leave."

Brady nodded, already having come to that conclusion. "I don't need to go off on sick leave. I spoke with him earlier today, I think after Will did. I have taken a leave of absence for now, which is fine. It's an agreement we all have with our employers."

Dallas was not surprised, having already been warned by Barnabas how the men were employed. "That's good. I can't stress enough that you three stay safe. They are still in the area. That much we know." He turned to Ennis. "Ennis, how did you come up with that farm?"

Ennis shrugged, her eyes on Barnabas. "I have no idea. God, I guess. We used to come to it when we were teenagers. Drawn to the haunted farm. Barnabas used to do the same. When I saw him pointing to where the van went over the bluffs, I remembered how close it was. It was just too convenient."

"Very convenient, I would say. I am just so thankful that Brady and Fynn weren't in it. We would not be having this conversation if they had been."

Two weeks later, on the Friday night, Fynn stood in a room in the church building, her eyes on her brother as he paced.

"Farr? What's wrong?"

He turned, hesitated, and then came to hug her, standing back with his hands resting on her upper arms. "I'm sorry we lost all these years, Fynn. You are a beautiful, talented, Godly woman I would have loved to have grown up with."

"Thank you. God had a reason, Farr, that we don't know about. We may never here on earth. I am taking my experiences and putting them to use as a volunteer. My building is almost ready and I can start my collections and studies. I already have the schools approaching me about teaching from there."

"That's great." His eyes lifted to the door. "Brady's a great guy. He loves you deeply."

"I know, just as I do him. Now, you need to find someone." She caught the grin he tried to hide. "Let me guess. Alice."

His grin broadened. "Alice but we won't date, not yet. Not until this is done."

"I am so glad, Farr. She's a wonderful friend." She turned as she heard footsteps.

Doc stood there, his heart happy for his young friends, but concern weighed him down. This wasn't over, not by a long shot. Precautions were being taken, but it was safe to say that until the couple were in custody, Fynn, Brady and Farr were not safe.

"We're ready for you, Fynn. Farr, you're the one escorting her to Brady?"

Farr grinned, his likeness to his sister evident. "I am. Let's go, Fynn. By this time tomorrow, it will be over and you'll be with the love of your life."

"I like that thought, mister." Fynn grew lighthearted, determined to set the trouble aside for the next few days. She didn't tell Farr that she and Brady were planning on disappearing for a few days, not going too far, but to a cottage of some friends of Doc's. They hoped to avoid being spotted.

The next afternoon, Brady turned from where he stood beside Blair, his eyes on his bride, amazed that the beautiful lady was his. Buckley watched the couple, amusement lurking in his eyes as he remembered how Fynn had asked the question Brady should have. They will never live that down, now will they, Lord?

A week later, Fynn moved through Brady's apartment, settling in, her hands reaching to move things around to add things of her own. Not that she had a lot, she thought. Most of what she had belonged in her office at her building. And that Brady had promised to help her with tomorrow. She understand clearly that they would have security with them, that the couple still had not been found. That worried her. She knew Brady was anxious to get back to work, but won't go, not wanting to put his fellow workers at risk.

Brady stood for a moment, his hand behind his back holding the peach coloured roses that Benen had brought him at his request. He was content, he thought. Thank you, Lord, for your protection over the past week. Fynn needed that, to feel she was safe and just be normal.

Fynn turned, her eyes on Brady. "What are you hiding behind your back?" Her face lit up as she saw the roses. Brady groaned to himself, realizing he had missed out on something. He should have been doing this all along.

The next morning, they headed for her office, his truck filled with boxes, Blair and Bradon following with another truckload. She had apologized but the men had grinned at her, saying it was nothing and just where did she want her things?

Fynn wandered her building, smelling the freshness of the paint and stain, the newness of it. She had a lot to be grateful, she thought.

Brady finally tracked her down, watching as she sat at her desk, her hands flat on the top, her head turning as she studied the room.

---

"Get everything settled the way you want?"

She gave a quick grin. "Pretty much. Things will get moved around, but you have to work in an office or a building to know the bones and how it feels before you can really settle in. Are we ready to go?"

"We are. Blair and Bradon have gone. Just the security team waiting for us." He paused as he heard a door open and close. "They weren't planning on coming in."

Fynn froze before she rose and headed for the door. "I don't like this." Her walk towards the front of the building halted suddenly as she stared at the couple standing in front of her. "Well, well, well. Who do we have here?"

The man sneered at her, a weapon held up and pointing towards Brady. "You know who it is. You two are coming with us. You've cost us plenty."

"Brady, I would like you to meet Duane and Eva Woolley. Friends or so-called friends of my parents. But you weren't really, now were you?"

"Shut up and move this way." The weapon wavered between the two of them.

"I don't think so, Duane." Fynn had seen the door open silently and close behind Dallas, Alice and some other officers. "We're not going anywhere. But you can explain something. Why did you kidnap Farr?"

"It wasn't supposed to be Farr. It was supposed to be you. The man who took him couldn't find you. He took your brother instead." Eva sneered at her in turn. "Let's just say, he'll never make that mistake again."

Fynn paled even as she shifted closer to Brady. "You killed him?"

"Not us, but it happened. He was working for too many bosses and that screwup was the last straw. Now, walk this way. We're going to go for a nice little drive, end up near the quarry, take you two for a little stroll. Only you won't be coming back."

Eva gave a scream as her wrist was caught and pulled behind her, the snap of handcuffs loud in the air. Duane made to turn, his weapon on Brady as he felt a weapon jab his back.

"I would drop that, if I were you. Duane Woolley. You are under arrest for kidnapping, attempted murder, murder, and whatever else we can come up with."

"I want my lawyer." Duane's whine sounded loud in the silence.

"And you will have. Okay, off you go with my friends here. They'll take you two for a nice little car ride of your own to a nice large building with cells in them. We have a lot of information on you two. Today? That's the icing on the cake." He watched as the pair were led away before he turned to Fynn and Brady.

"You two okay?"

Fynn have a huge breath. "We are, finally. This is it? They're the last ones?"

"We believe so. I'll have to ask you two to stay safe for another few days, but this should wrap it up. I'm glad for you two and for Farr."

"And for Alice." Fynn grinned at Alice who looked surprised before she too grinned.

"Alice?"

Brady began to laugh, having heard from Fynn Farr's story. "Now that this is over, Farr and Alice can begin dating. Another wonderful couple, I must say." He looked down at Fynn with a smile, crooked his arm and then led her away when she looped her arm through his.

Dallas stood and watched them, a bit of shock on his face causing Alice to laugh. He twisted his head to watch her. "You and Farr?"

"Me and Farr. Now, let's blow this joint, as my Dad would say. Fynn wants to lock up. They have some celebrating to do."

"That they do. By the grace of God, they do."

Brady was on a hunt through Fynn's building, not finding her. He paused, his hand on his head before he nodded, and headed out the back door, towards the flower beds she had worked up and planted with multiple kinds of perennials. He could hear the bees from the hives a beekeeper had been glad to bring over.

He stood, his eyes on her as she knelt on the ground, bent over looking at something before he walked towards her, kneeling beside her.

"What are we watching, love?"

She looked up, a grin on her face. "The ants. They are such busy creatures. God made them. He even directs us to consider them, to watch how them work and store away for winter. It struck me as I was watching them that is what I need to do. I need to store His words away in my heart. I didn't have enough when I needed them."

"You had the ones He wanted you to have and He made sure you had just the right amount." His hand took her to pull her to her feet before he led her to the arbour she had wanted. "This is nice. But going back to your thoughts, He planned for all this."

Fynn's head went down on Brady's shoulder. "He did. It has been, what two months? It feels like forever and yet still like yesterday. The guys and the ladies have been so gracious."

Brady nodded. "It's who they are. I know we're not done, not by a long shot, not with our adventures as we term them. I had a long talk with Abe the other day, about how he coped."

"They have quite the story, don't they? Married, torn apart by greed with Abe thinking she didn't want him and Emma thinking he was dead. And all their guys and so many of their friends." She looked up at Brady. "God protects us. But He also heals. I have turned so much to the story of the woman who touched Christ's garment and fpund peace."

"I also do but I also find peace in knowing that God is the God who heals us. He takes our brokenness and brings something new and refined from it."

"That he does." Fynn sighed, content for the moment. "Brady, thank you for being who you are."

"And you as well, love."

They finally rose as twilight was descending, Brady locking up her building before wrapping her in his arms and kissing her. She was the helpmeet God had planned for him. Lord, help me to be worthy of the woman whose price is far above rubies. I know there will be times I screw up but help us to be open with one another and build the marriage You have planned for us.

Dear Readers:

Thank you for once more picking up one of my novels, this time the story of Brady and his Fynn. I had fun with this one, insects fascinating me for years. Back in the 1960's my father worked for a lumber company, building homes and cottages. There were many times he would bring something home to show my sister and myself, whether it was a leaf in the fall or an insect. One time he even brought us a pony for Christmas.

Forensics entomology fascinates me, being able to determine the age of eggs, larvae and insects to help solve a crime. Perhaps, if I had chosen differently, I might have done that. Being a paramedic is a difficult work. I have had exposure to them with my Mom's sudden passing and with my Dad who had health issues. Wonderful people who had a difficult task.

It was not planned that Fynn would have a brother who had disappeared on her. Characters have a way of just walking into the stories, usually dragged in by another one. I call the characters in my books unruly, as they don't let me write the story I planned but take over as soon as I set fingers to the keyboard, take off and as an author friend has said, don't let me have a road map or a GPS unit to know where I'm headed. But I love them. Bringing in Abe and Emma brought back beloved characters from the *His Guardians Series*. Their story is the last one in that series, *His Protector*.

God is a God who heals. He does not want us to be broken. I have attempted to show that in Fynn and Farr and even with Brady. They had to learn to trust Him in a way that we don't think we can. A favourite passage of Scripture is the woman with the issue, who touched just the hem of Christ's garment. I have used this in another book, *A Touch of His Garment*, involving close friends of Abe and Emma. (Do I like the town of Riverville and its characters much? I do and miss them.)

God bless each one of you. Reach out to touch the hem of the garment. He provides not just physical healing but any healing.

Ronna

# Branigan: Encouraged to Hope

## The Barnabas Chronicles
## Book 6

By

Ronna M. Bacon

Psalm 119:114 You are my hiding place and my shield; I hope in Your word. NKJV

864

# Table of Contents

## *Chapter 1*

Reaching into the backseat of the small SUV he preferred to drive, Branigan Clery caught the handle of his briefcase, and then paused, his hand on the car door, looking around the small building lot that he had parked in. He shook his head. Why me, Lord? Are there not others who could have been called in to set up the security system for this small trucking company? A brand new building and likely not wired for this. I know, Lord, I know. It's my calling first and foremost, but just for once I would love an easy job. Something tells me this one is going to try my patience well past what I can handle right now. Having my friends go through what they did has worn us all out. None of us were prepared for any of it.

Closing the car door, he paced through the gravel parking lot, to stand for a moment staring at the small office building and then stepping back to stare at the larger building, the garage for the company, to hold the mechanics shop and warehouse. He wondered at the two buildings and then shrugged. It didn't matter to him, or at least, it shouldn't. He reached for the door and walked through, the green steel door with a window closing quietly behind him. He frowned. Nothing to indicate he had entered.

He stood for a moment at the reception counter before placing his briefcase on it and then wandering around the small waiting room, studying the windows and then the door, looking at it from a security standpoint. He nodded to himself, pleased with what he saw. Someone had done their homework, he thought.

He spun as he heard footsteps behind him, his heart pounding for a moment. He was jumpy, he admitted, and prayed for that to leave. It wouldn't do to show that, not when he was here to set up a security system. His employer, Barnabas Carey, of the Barnabas Foundation, had asked him to. The client was a board member of the Foundation and also a fellow church member, although Branigan had to admit he didn't know him that well.

"Branigan. Thanks for coming. It's going to be good to get the security set up. I've been on edge ever since we moved out to this location." Brett Danby grinned as he extended his hand for Branigan to shake. "I know. I know. I should have had you involved from the beginning, but you were helping out your friends, and I didn't want to intrude."

"Brett. It would not have been an intrusion. I don't think this will take that many days. I'll need to go over your buildings and then sit down with you to have a chat about what you want. By the way, I didn't hear any chime to let you know I had arrived."

Brett grinned. "No, you wouldn't. Guenivere has trouble with chimes, always has had for some reason. So the electrician wired up a light for us that indicates when someone enters. I would like to keep that but connect it to a video feed if we can. A monitor set up in my office and in the break room, as well as in the warehouse would suit me just fine."

"Shouldn't be a problem." Branigan reached for his briefcase. "Let's start with a tour. I didn't realize you had moved out this far."

"We needed the extra room, now that the business has grown. Guenivere has some ideas that she wants to try, and I must say, she is usually right with her thoughts."

Branigan finally settled down in the office Brett had taken him to, his notes spread out around him, his computer open to the program he used to plan his projects. He heard movement out in the hallway as well as quiet conversation. He tilted his head. That must be Guenivere, he thought. He didn't think that she had been around much, he hadn't noticed her at church. Soon, lost in his thoughts, he ignored the activity outside the office.

A loud, coarse laugh brought his head up, and his dark gray eyes narrowed. That was not Brett, he thought. He rose and quietly moved to stand in the hallway, his eyes searching for the commotion, and commotion it was. He could hear a young woman's voice raised in protest and he walked forward, his very stance stating he would not tolerate any nonsense towards her.

Guenivere Danby faced the man standing across the counter from her, her curiously coloured aqua eyes holding the fright she was trying to tamp down, without much success, she thought. Her father had had to leave, and she felt all alone, forgetting the younger man her father had said was working in the extra office.

868

"No, you can't tour the warehouse. Only employees do." She straightened up as tall as she could, trying to bluff him.

He laughed again. "Oh, but I can. And you are going to show me. I intend to become a partner of your father's. We'll play nice, won't we?" He reached for her hand, his eyes suddenly rising to stare behind her.

Guenivere gave a muffled shriek as arms encircled her and pulled her back against a tall strong body.

"Guenivere, hon. Do you need some help out here? I'm sorry I didn't hear the door. I was involved in that task for your Dad." Branigan did not hesitate to intrude.

"I can use some help. This gentleman was on his way out. Only he can't seem to find the door." Her hands had risen to grip Branigan's, and he wondered at the tightness of her hold.

His head tilted slightly so he could watch her face before one hand came up to tuck the long blond hair behind one ear. Then he glanced over at the man standing there, hatred and evil emanating from him. He frowned once more. What is this all about, Lord? You knew I was needed here today.

Branigan walked around Guenivere and tucked her behind him. In a low voice, he muttered, "If I say run, run to somewhere you can lock yourself away. Don't even question me." He felt her head nodding against his back and bit back a grin. She had buried her face against him.

"Now, you sir. The door is behind you. I would suggest you leave and don't return."

The man sneered. "I don't think so. You can't tell me what to do."

Branigan moved suddenly, around the counter and with the man's arm twisted behind his back, before anyone could realize what he was doing.

"I do believe you were asked to leave. Let me escort you to your vehicle. If you do not leave, we will certainly call for the authorities to come on out and escort you to their building for a tour there. Somehow, I don't think you'll like that tour."

Branigan shoved the man forward, directly to his car, wrenching open the door and shoving him into it.

"Now, sir, you will leave. You will not return. If you do, they will call for help."

Slamming his door shut, a look of hatred still aimed at Branigan, the man sped away. Branigan watched for a moment before he heard a soft voice from beside him.

"He's gone?" Guenivere had appeared, not content to wait in the office.

"He has, and you should not be out here." Branigan stared at her in disbelief.

Guenivere stared up at him, her eyes narrowing as she took in the dark brown hair and gray eyes. Lord, he looks just like the image Mom always wove into my bedtime stories. I can't do this right now. Or at least I don't think I can.

"I know, but I was afraid he would hurt you."

Branigan swung her around, his hand to her lower back to direct her back into the office. "He wouldn't have. Not in the open like this. He's a bully and they work best from undercover." His head tilted as he heard a sound and then he was shoving Guenivere towards the building. "Run, Guenivere. Run."

She took off, fright welling up as she heard the sound of a racing motor. She prayed for that they would make it in time. She heard the sound of gravel spraying as the car raced back into the lot and then slowed somewhat. The next sound she heard was the sickening sound of a body hit by the car and then landing on the ground. She stopped suddenly and spun, hands to her mouth as she saw Branigan sprawled on the ground, the car near him, and the man who had accosted her standing with his arm leaning on the open door.

His eyes raised to hers and he smirked an evil grin at her. "Next time, it will be you. I'll be in touch. I will be a part owner of this company. Just you wait."

She stared in horror as the gravel sprayed from his tires as he took off before she was running towards Branigan, to drop to her knees, a hand to his chest as he sprawled on his back. Tears gathered in her eyes, and she angrily brushed at them. This is no time to cry, girl. He needs help, only I don't want to leave him. She heard her name called and looked up to see the mechanic racing towards her.

"Douglas, we need an ambulance and the police. Branigan was just run down."

Douglas nodded. "I called. They're on their way. What was his problem?"

"I don't know for sure." She stared down at Branigan. "He made him leave but he came back. Dad wasn't here." She looked up, such fright in her eyes that Douglas drew in a breath. "What would have happened if Branigan hadn't have been?"

Douglas dropped down beside her. "God had you, Guenivere. That He did. Run and get  a blanket for me. We'll try and keep him comfortable."

She ran, flinging open the door and racing for the break room, reaching for the blanket her mother had left there before she turned. Something was off in there, she thought, and shrugged, her thoughts going back to the man laying out in their parking lot, unconscious and all because of her.

———

Chapter 2

Running back through the building, Guenivere tripped over a package dropped near the door, landing on her hands and knees, shock and pain hitting her before she was on her feet again, the blanket in her arms, heading for Branigan.

Douglas looked up as she approached, standing for a moment, his hand out to stop her before he reached for the blanket, to shake it out and cover Branigan.

"Douglas? Has he been awake?" Guenivere stared up at him with hope in her eyes, that died away when he shook his head. She was on her knees, Branigan's wrist in her hand as she felt for a pulse. "It's weak, Douglas. Where are they?"

"They are their way." He could faintly hear the sounds of the sirens approaching. "I can hear them."

She nodded, her hand out to touch Branigan's face, trying to brush away the small bits of debris that's covered one cheek. "Why? All he had to do was leave and not come back."

"What did he want?" Douglas paced. "We've never had any trouble. Not like this."

Guenivere looked up, shaking her head. "I don't really know. He never said." She turned as she heard a heavy motor and the paramedic rig appeared behind the police cruiser that slid to a stop near the building. She didn't let go on Branigan's hand, feeling that she had to hold on to it, that for some reason he needed her to. She just knew he was going to affect her life and that she didn't understand or really know if she wanted that.

Alice stood for a moment, studying the three, before she approached, her breath indrawn for a moment as she recognized Branigan.

———

"What happened?" Alice stared between Douglas and Guenivere, waiting for one of them to speak. "I asked, what happened?"

Douglas drew Guenivere to her feet and away from Branigan, almost fighting to do so. He frowned. This was not the young lady he had watched grow from a toddler. He was a long-time friend of her father's.

"I'm not sure, Alice. I was working away and heard the commotion out here. By the time I got to here, he was on the ground and Guenivere beside him on her knees."

Guenivere nodded, and then shuddered. "He was here again. I've seen him lurking around. But he has never come into the building. Why would he want a tour? Why would he say he was going to be a partner with Dad? That won't happen."

Alice's pen paused above her notepad, as she studied the younger woman. "He said that. Walk me through from the beginning. Then, I'll have to have you come in and give a formal statement."

Guenivere talked, giving what information she could, her eyes not leaving Branigan. The paramedics had hesitated for a few seconds as they recognized him, before they were down beside him, assessing him, reaching for a neck collar and backboard before shifting him to a stretcher and then heading for the rig. Guenivere broke away from Alice and ran after them.

"Please, let me go with him? He was hurt saving me." She didn't give them a chance to respond before she hopped up into the rig and huddled into a corner, the two men exchanging glances and a shrug.

Branigan stirred for a moment, his eyes flickering open and closed, a groan rising from him as the pain hit. He only had one thought. Guenivere. Was she safe?

"Guenivere?" His voice was rough with pain. "Is she okay?"

Pat, the paramedic riding in the back, shook his head, his eyes on Guenivere.

"She's fine, buddy. She's right here."

---

"She is? Where?" Branigan tried to rise, the straps around him keeping him flat on his back. "What are these? I need to get up and find her."

Guenivere had slid closer, Pat's finger beckoning to her, before her hand touched Branigan's face.

"I'm here. Right here."

"You are?" Branigan blinked as he tried to twist to see her. "You're okay? He didn't hurt you?"

"No, you made me run. Now, lie still. We don't know how hurt you are."

Branigan's hand found hers, the clasp tight enough that she couldn't remove her hand. She stared at Pat, who shook his head as he bit back a snicker. *Lady, he just claimed you, whether you realize it or not. This is not what Branigan does.*

Guenivere felt the rig backing up the hospital entrance and she ducked her head to look out the back door before she turned back to Branigan. He had not let go of her hand, no matter how she had twisted hers. Pat had just shaken his head.

"He's not letting go, you do know that?" He grinned at the look she threw him. "I don't think he'll let go even when we lower the stretcher. So, here's what we do. If you can stand up a bit and walk down the rig, once we get to the point we're lowering the legs, we'll lift you down. You can stay with him for now."

Guenivere nodded, a sudden fear in her heart. What if he didn't recover? What if he was really hurt? How would she ever live with herself? She followed Pat's instructions, not seeing the amused look shared between the two paramedics, once more trying to release her hand.

Doc Whitson, friend to all the men who were employed by Barnabas Foundation and father figure to them, watched, a frown on his face before he saw Pat shaking his head. He'd find out what was going on with Branigan. This was not him, Doc knew, and then had a sudden sense that Branigan too had found his lady in the midst of an adventure as the younger men liked to say.

He reached for his stethoscope as he listened to Pat's report, quiet words spoken among them. Doc turned, reaching for the requisitions needed to order bloodwork, imaging studies, as he kept turning to watch Guenivere. She stood, her hand still tight in Branigan's, her other hand lightly touching his hair, not aware of how disheveled she looked.

"Guenivere?" Doc finally stood beside her, a light of amusement showing in his eyes. "How well do you know Branigan?"

Her head flipped around, her mouth rounded in surprise and her eyes huge.

"I don't. I didn't meet him until today when he stepped in to help me. Dad had him out at the buildings to see about a security system." Her face darkened. "Now, look at him."

"We know, Guenivere. I just wondered seeing as he won't let go of you. Pat said you both tried."

"We did." Guenivere looked back at Branigan, not realizing her face had softened.

Doc nodded. Another one, Lord. What will these two go through?

Doc had finally managed to loosen Branigan's hand enough that Guenivere could pull her free, and she rubbed at it as she paced the waiting room. She had had to leave, much against her wishes, as he was further assessed.

Hearing her name, she spun, catching her balance with a hand against the nearby wall. Her father was walking towards her, accompanied by Alice, and then she frowned. The man who had accosted her and then run down Branigan was standing in the doorway, a smirk on his face. She grew angry and then stomped towards him, Alice spinning before she followed behind her.

"Why are you here? You're not wanted here or on our property."

"Too bad, little lady. Get used to me being around." He took a look past her at Alice heading his way, her hand resting on the weapon on her belt, before he looked down at Guenivere with a sneer. "I'm gone. We'll talk again, little lady. A nice quiet dinner, just you and me." He spun and was gone, Alice on his heels, her hand catching his arm and stopping him.

Brett stood with his arm around a now-trembling Guenivere.

"Lass? Who was that?"

Guenivere struggled to speak, tears of fear choking her. "That's him, Dad. He's the one who said he would be your partner." She looked up at her father. "Do you know him?"

Brett shook his head. "No, I don't. And you know I don't plan on taking on a partner. "I'm sorry, Guenivere. I would not have left had I known."

"But you had to. You had no choice. You left Branigan with me." She spun, heading back for the exam rooms, as her father caught her arm and stopped her. "Dad?" She turned her head, a frown in place.

"You can't go back there, lass. Not yet. You're not next of kin, no matter how tightly he held your hand." He grinned at his daughter, looking young and carefree for a moment. "I hear tell he claimed you."

"He did what?" Guenivere's voice rose as she finished. "No, he didn't." Her head was shaking in the negative as she stared at her father. "No, he didn't, Dad. He couldn't have." When her father didn't respond, she sighed. "Pat muttered something along those lines. I don't see it."

Brett's arm came around his daughter as he drew her to seats where they could see the doors, his heart and mind in a turmoil as he prayed, trying to find the words he needed. Lena, you need to be here. You should be the one explaining this, but God seems to think I should be.

"Dad?" Guenivere's voice held a tone he had not heard before, a mixture of despair, hope, longing and denial..

Brett sighed. "I know of Branigan just from being around Barnabas. He has a good heart, lass. He has never dated, has never shown interest in any lady. Not until today. Whether it was because you were in danger or not, I would have to ask him that. But don't block his friendship from your heart. Pray that God will show you His will. I see the spark of interest you have. You are a beautiful, compassionate Godly young woman. I have seen the interest in the young men who cross your path, but you haven't shown any interest in anyone. Not until today."

She leaned her head on her father's shoulder. "I know, Dad. I didn't want to put out false hope or ruin a friendship. I just never felt God was leading that way with any of them." She looked down at the hands she was rubbing together. "I don't know what it was about Branigan. He just appeared behind me, called me hon, and then shoved me behind him to protect me." She paused, at a loss for words. "He made me feel safe and cherished at the same time. Does that make sense?"

"Perfect sense, Guenivere. It's what you've been raised with." Her mother's arm came around her.

"Mom? You're here? You're supposed to be in school, teaching!" Guenivere stared at her mother, dismay on her face.

———

"You needed me. Will Peters stopped by and asked me to come." She grinned, looking so much like her daughter.

"He did? Then, I guess it's okay." She looked past her mother as she heard footsteps and then was on her feet, almost running for Doc as he approached.

Barnabas Carey stood for a moment, assessing the situation, seeing Doc's nod at him. Breck, who worked directly with him, as his second in command, stood beside him, a small grin on his face.

"I didn't see that coming, did you?"

"What coming?" Barnabas had a good idea where Breck was heading with his words, but hid his grin.

"Branigan and Guenivere. I wouldn't have put those two together."

"Danger does that. We know that from the other five who went through their adventures, shall we say?" Barnabas paused, his mind racing. "But, yeah, I can see it. Guenivere seems quiet but she has a side to her that she doesn't show many. Branigan would bring it out. And she would bring the stability he needs."

"That she would." Breck watched as Doc led Guenivere away before he headed for Brett, greeting the older couple. "Any word?"

"Not to us. Now, to our daughter, I would say that there has been." Brett grinned. "I hear tell Branigan claimed her."

Barnabas grinned. "That's what Will said when he called. I'll head back in a bit, talk to Doc, see what paperwork I need to sign as his next of kin." He leaned back against the wall. He felt old, worn out and tired. He knew why. It always hit him about this time of year, and he refused to admit it or talk to anyone.

## Chapter 4

His head tossing restlessly, Branigan fought against the nausea that welled in his stomach, not sure why he felt like he did. His hand reached for the sore spot in his head, before a hand gently lowered it back to his chest. His hand flipped to grasp that hand. A lady's hand, he thought. It wouldn't be one of my friend's ladies. It's a left hand and has no rings on it.

Guenivere watched with concern as Branigan moved restlessly. It was her fault, she thought, that he was in this situation. She didn't like it. Alice and Will had been around, assuring her that the man who had accosted her was in jail, and would be for a while. He had a number of police departments very anxious to speak with him.

The door opened quietly and Guenivere had footsteps approaching her. She tried not to let her sudden fear overwhelm but found it difficult. She looked up at the man, just older than her, she thought, who had stopped at the other side of the bed, his eyes on Branigan before he looked up. A grin crossed his face.

"And you are Guenivere? I have seen you around town and church, but have never had the pleasure of meeting you. Not until Branigan claimed you." His grin widened as her eyes narrowed and her mouth opened and closed. "I'm Baird, a good friend of Branigan. Thank you for what you did."

"For what I did? I didn't do anything. He's the one who got hurt, saving me." She blinked rapidly for a moment, before she looked back up at him. "I've seen you at church. With your wife and it is her brother?"

"Berneen and Darby. Yes. She has commented in the past she would like to get to know you, but you have disappeared so quickly."

Guenivere nodded. "I have. I don't always do well with crowds and then too I volunteer in a small chapel outside of town."

"I have heard that." Baird studied her, seeing the strain she had been under, but also steel that had been tried and strengthened running through her. "Has he been awake?'

"Not really. Just rousing a bit." She felt a tug on her hand and looked down, to find Branigan watching her, his eyes clear. "Branigan? You're awake. Your friend is here so I can leave."

Branigan's hand tightened even more on hers. "No, I need you to stay. Please?" His head turned slightly at the snicker Baird couldn't contain. He frowned, bringing on a headache. "Baird? Why did you make me go and do that? What are you doing here?" He craned his neck to look around him. "Berneen?"

"She's in the waiting room, didn't want to disturb you. Besides we were told only two visitors and you already have one." He smirked again at Guenivere as she gasped at his audacity.

"Give it a rest. Help me up. I need to get out of here." He raised his head and then let it flop back on the pillow, his eyes closing against the pain, not seeing the look of horror and concern that flooded Guenivere's face.

"Branigan, you need to lie still. That's what you were told."

"I don't remember. I want to go home. I hate hospitals." His eyes closed and he slept again, pain flickering across his face.

"Guenivere?" When she looked up at him, Baird smiled. "Now, are you okay? I heard you had quite the time today."

"I did." She frowned. "Why go after us? That I don't understand." She sighed. "If Dad had not asked Branigan to take a look at our security, he wouldn't be in this hospital bed right now."

"On the contrary, he is glad to be there, knowing he saved you. Have you even considered what might have happened to you, had he not been there?" Baird tamped down his frustration and, yes, anger as Guenivere stared at him, a blank look on his face. "Guenivere. I've talked to Alice. That man, the one who appeared in your office? He's wanted by many forces, for kidnapping, assault and murder. He would have taken you, hid you somewhere, and then used you against your Dad."

Guenivere was horrified. Her hand covered her mouth as she fought against her emotions. "That can't be true!" At Brady's nod, she looked up, her eyes clouded with tears of fear and anger. "He would have, wouldn't he? He was reaching for me when Branigan spoke up. How do I repay him?"

"He won't want that, Guenivere. All he wants is to know you are safe." Baird stared down at his friend for a moment, his thoughts muddled as he tried to sort through them. "He has staked a claim to you, whether you accept it or not. He will not walk away from you." He looked up to see her shaking her head. "I repeat, he will not walk away from you. For now, consider that you two are a couple, and that you have a boyfriend. That's how he'll want to play it out. For his sake and for yours, as well as your parents', think about it. With Branigan, you have the backing of us all from the Foundation."

"And there are so many of you." Guenivere paused. "What did he mean, when he said something to Dad about being paid by the Foundation? Doesn't he work for a company?"

"He doesn't. He works for Barnabas, who sources out the companies, businesses and individuals that needs security set up." Baird paused, trying to think of how to phrase what he needed to say. "For us all, we are paid through the Foundation. We are hired on as employees by businesses and companies, but they don't pay us. That way, they are free to hire someone else without worrying where the money needs to come from. That's how the Foundation was set up. Barnabas and his father wanted to encourage others, just like Barnabas in the Bible. I'm sorry. I've startled you with that." He looked back down at Branigan before looking up. "I think that should have been a conversation you had with our friend."

"No, it's okay. This isn't going to go anywhere." She gently extricated her hand, laying it for a moment against Branigan's cheek, feeling the end-of-day stubble there, before she walked away without another word, the door swishing closed behind her

Baird watched her walk away, before he turned back to his friend, a prayer for healing rising in his heart. Branigan, she's your heart. You show that by your actions. Please, dear Lord? Help them. Keep them safe. I don't want them to go through what five of us have, but I fear that is exactly what will happen.

*Chapter 5*

Glaring at first Brady and then Brennen, Branigan slumped back onto the hospital bed. It was two days later, and he was fighting to be released, wanting to be home, but wanting to be with Guenivere. That didn't make sense to him, but the other men had laughed when he had asked where she was and if she was okay. He really couldn't remember much of what had happened since the early morning of the day he had been run down.

"Take it easy, Branigan. The physician said you could be released. We're just waiting for your paperwork." Brady and Brennen exchanged glances, knowing that Branigan would want to head to only one place and that would be where he could find Guenivere.

"I need out of here. I left all my work at the trucking company. They need that security set up yesterday." He stood, a hand on the bed rail to balance himself before he turned to his friends. "Either you help me or I walk out of here on my own. Doc said he'd see me at home but I can't go there. Not yet."

"We know that, Branigan. Give us a few minutes to round up your paperwork and then we'll take you to your lady." Brennen smirked at the glare sent his way before he turned as the door opened.

Guenivere stood for a moment, her eyes on the three men before she headed for Branigan, a sheaf of paperwork in her hand.

"Branigan? What are you doing?"

He paused, taking in her beauty, before he grinned. "Looking for you, I think." He ignored the smothered laughter that sounded. "Forget these two jokers. Can you spring me?"

Hiding her own smile but her eyes brimming with laughter and mischief, Guenivere tapped at her chin before she nodded. "I can. I have your paperwork right here. Mom said that seeing as you were hurt on our property, you are to come and stay with us for the next week. And yes, Doc has agreed to that. In fact, he encouraged it." She frowned as she recalled the eagerness with which Doc had responded to her question. "And yes, all of your friends are welcome to come and visit. The more the merrier, Mom said, although she will limit them if there are too many, just for the first two days."

Brady and Brennen had been listening with interest to the conversation before they exchanged a glance, seeing Branigan had given in and was waiting as he saw the nurse approaching with the wheelchair. This was unusual for him. He was usually the one who was stubborn and ready to head into a fight, not sitting back and letting himself heal.

Watching as Guenivere drove carefully away, Brennen's head turned as he heard footsteps stop beside him. Barnabas stood there as did Buckley, their friend and minister.

"I thought you were bringing Branigan back to the building." Barnabas was puzzled.

"That was the plan. Doc had other ideas, it would seem. I gather he talked to Lena Danby and Branigan has been taken in there for the week. Guenivere stated it was because he was hurt on their property, but I think there's more."

"She feels responsible for him being hurt, seeing as he was trying to protect her." Buckley just shook his head. "Are we allowed to visit or are we banned from the house?"

"Guenivere has graciously told us we can visit but we have to limit the number at a time." Brennen shook his head as he remembered the feisty, determined look on her face. "I wouldn't want to cross her."

Barnabas looked surprised. "I wouldn't have thought that."

"They're a couple, Barnabas, whether they acknowledge it or not. They will do what they can to protect one another. It's up to us to back them and help." Brady walked away, leaving the others staring after him before staring at one another.

"He's right. That's what he did with Fynn." Brennen looked around, and then spoke. "I saw the two together. It's not something

I've seen, not even with the other five. There's a spark there that didn't come from the problem the other day."

"No, Branigan has been searching, I know, for the helpmeet God planned for him." Barnabas halted his words, not wanting to destroy a confidence from Branigan.

"I think we all are, Barnabas." Brennen walked away as well, heading after Brady, to catch a ride home with him.

Buckley snickered, drawing Barnabas' eyes to his face before Barnabas laughed as well.

"I guess we got told." Buckley laughed out loud. "And he's right."

"I know he is. It doesn't make it any easier if the rest of us have to face what they did." Barnabas pulled out his keys. "Let's go. No use us hanging around here when they've already left."

"I'll stop in later to see how he's doing." Buckley paused, his eyes raised, searching. He could feel eyes on them, but why? Branigan was not there.

Guenivere stood for a moment, a few hours later, in the doorway to her parents' living room, her eyes on Branigan as he lay, stretched out on the couch, seemingly asleep, one arm flung over his eyes. She knew he was hurting, but didn't know how to make it better for him. That she couldn't do. Only God would heal him.

She felt hope rising within her. Hope that what had terrified her, terrorized her and suppressed her would be over. God, is Branigan the one to help with that? I need hope, to feel that I can finally live as I should, for You, for myself.

Branigan stirred as he felt her hand on his forehead, his hand reaching for hers, and pulling her down to sit beside him as he sat up. His free hand rubbed at his temple for a moment as he watched her and the emotions flickering across her face. She's hurting a lot harder than just from this. How do I help her?

"Guenivere? Want to talk?"

She shrugged, her eyes on his face. "I'm not sure. How are you feeling?" She chose a safe topic of conversation or so she hoped.

———

884

He grinned, knowing she was deflecting his question. "Better. The headache is there but not as bad. I know I am battered and bruised. The gravel did a number on me even through my clothing. The shower helped. But that's not what I asked."

She looked down at their hands, not even trying to pull hers free. She had given up on that, realizing that Branigan would not let go of it unless he wanted to, and it certainly didn't appear as if he did.

"I know. I just don't know how to express what I need to say." She looked up, longing in her eyes to do just that. "You are the first one who has ever asked me that, in the way you meant. You're digging deep."

He nodded. "I know I am. I have to. I lost my parents to a hit and run accident. They were gone before I could even say goodbye. I was only twelve, with no siblings and no other relatives. Being raised in foster care isn't always the easiest or the best. I had good foster parents, who raised me to continue to believe and trust in God. They asked the hard questions, waited, and then asked again until I was ready to talk. It helped. I want the same for you. It will free you to be who God meant you to be."

She felt hope rising within her once more, hope that she had not felt for years. She hadn't been able to talk to her parents, to tell them of the threat that she had encountered when she was a young teenager. It had reflected on her life and in a negative way, she realized, not letting her live her life as she should have.

Branigan paused in the garden area of the Danby yard early the next morning. He had not slept all that well, his mind not wanting to shut down and let him. He was worried about Guenivere, more worried than he wanted to admit. He felt that what had happened, the man who had appeared, was not working on his own. He couldn't use a computer, Doc had warned him not to, and he needed to. He had research to do. Branigan sighed. This is not how he had planned to spend the weekend, he thought. He had had plans to go away on the Friday night and come back early on the Monday morning, to find a little cabin he could hide in. He was tired. Having gone through their adventures with his five friends, he wasn't willing or ready to face it himself.

Turning as he heard footsteps approaching, Branigan reached for the mug of coffee handed to him. Brett watched him closely, mindful of what Doc had said.

"Branigan, I or rather we will never be able to thank you for what you did yesterday." His hand went up at Branigan's protest. "I know, Branigan. You did what you feel anyone would have done. It scared me when Guenivere told me what had happened. She's fearless to a point, but there is a depth to her where she keeps things hidden that she never shows to anyone. I know there was something in the past that has affected her. She has never said. I have asked her friends and they either don't know or won't say, not wanting to break a confidence."

Branigan nodded, sitting in one of the deck chairs on the back patio, his mug of coffee going onto the table beside it. He didn't know quite how to approach Brett.

"Brett? What happened all those years ago? It has to have been when she was young."

Brett nodded. "Something did and we have no idea what. We've watched her. Been careful with her. She won't let us smother her." He pointed a finger at Branigan even as he grinned.

"You holding her hand? That's unusual. She usually shuns any contact with the young men of her acquaintance, content just to be part of a group. For her to give in and let you? That tells me you have made a connection with her that others haven't."

Branigan nodded. "I guess. I'm not like that. I don't push. I haven't been dating." He sat back, reaching for the mug of coffee to sip at it, the early morning nature sounds ringing in his ears. He hesitated before speaking, not quite sure how to word what he needed to say. "You have a beautiful, caring, compassionate daughter, Brett. I would like to spend time with her, to get to know her. Her friendship is one I treasure already." He looked over at the older man, finding him studying him closely. "I have no idea where this will go or how your daughter feels."

Brett nodded, confident that Branigan had showed his heart. His head bowed and an audible prayer rose. Branigan stared at him for a moment before his own eyes closed.

"Branigan, all I can say is watch her heart and yours. If you don't believe this will go anywhere, then stop where you are right now." Brett rose, his eyes in the distance, hearing the sounds of a neighbour's car door closing before it drove away. The normal everyday sounds of his neighbourhood. He looked back down at Branigan. "But somehow, some way, Lena and I believe that you have been brought into Guenivere's life and that you will be the one to help her." He walked away, heading back into the house, leaving the younger man staring after him before Branigan's eyes closed and he prayed.

Guenivere stood for a moment, eyes closed, breathing in the scents from the last summer roses near the house. She slipped silently into the chair her father had vacated, her eyes on Branigan as he prayed, knowing that some how he was praying for her.

Branigan stirred finally, feeling refreshed in his heart and soul, knowing that he had lifted up his burdens and hopes and dreams and that God heard and understood. If Guenivere was the one for him, God would lead. If not, he had asked that their hearts be protected.

"Hi!"

<hr>

His head whipped around, and he closed his eyes for a moment as the headache pounded behind his eyes. He squinted, seeing Guenivere with her hands to her mouth, a look of horror on her face.

"I'm sorry. I didn't mean you to do that."

He reached for her hand, fascinated with the neatness of the nails and the slenderness of her fingers. "It's not your fault. I forgot and moved too quickly." He grinned suddenly. "So, what are we up to today? Do you go into work? And can I come?"

She stared at him for a moment before her mouth snapped closed. "No, I'm not working today. Dad wants me to work from home for the next couple of days. He has your plans for the security system and Barnabas called in a friend of Fynn's, I think he said, to help."

"Joseph. Yes, he's a friend of Fynn. Do you know her?"

Guenivere shook her head. "No, I can't say that I have met the ladies from the Foundation." She sighed, knowing she would be bearing her heart to him with her next words. "I would like to get to know her and the others. I have a couple of friends but they are more interested in things that don't interest me. I'm not one for dating anyone and everyone. I don't like movies. I don't travel well." She looked up at his snicker and then glared at him. "What did I say that was so funny?"

"You could be describing me to some extent. Since I moved here from PEI, I have pretty much stayed in the area. The guys and I have travelled some. I had planned on heading up north just a bit, up the peninsula to a small cabin this weekend, just to get away. I'm sure you are aware of what has transpired with five of my friends."

She leaned forward, her eyes intent on him. "That. That's what I don't get. Why did God let them go through that?"

Branigan shrugged. "I don't really understand it myself but each of the couples said they had to, to resolve past issues, to find the ones responsible for evil, to begin to become the people God meant them to be." He hesitated, not sure how to express himself. "I'm not sure I'm saying it right."

"You are. God allowed what happened to bring them into a closer walk with Him and to use them in ways we don't understand."

———

Branigan nodded. "That's it. Exactly. What I was trying to say." He groaned. "No, that's not how I wanted to word that." He looked at her, his face straight but mischief gleaming in his eyes. "I lose my train of thoughts and can't put a sentence together when I'm around you."

Guenivere's head whipped up and she stared at him, her mouth open until he gently tapped under her chin, causing it to close.

"I've surprised you, I see." He reached for one of her hand, finding her fingers curling around his. "I want to date you, Guenivere. Explore our friendship. I know from your Dad that you don't date. Nor do I."

She sighed. "Dad's been talking." When he shook his head, she frowned. "He must of. There's no way you would ask this on your own."

"Who did this to you, Guenivere? Who beat you down so you don't even recognize your own beauty and worth. Yes, your Dad mentioned that you kept to home, didn't seem to be interested in the men of your acquaintance, but he did not, and I repeat, he did not ask me to date you. I had that idea all on my own. I did ask his approval, if you want to call it that."

Hope began to rise in Guenivere's heart. Was he the one, Lord? Would he be the one she could trust enough to help her find the teen who was now a man somewhere in the area who had beaten her down in her spirit all those years ago, made her feel ugly to the core, even though she wasn't? And just why had she let him?

"Branigan? You do need to rest." She sat back, her eyes watchful. "And yes, I would like to go out with you." Her hand raised as his mouth opened to speak, a light in his eyes that startled her. "First, you heal. Then we talk."

———

Hearing his name called, Barnabas paused in his walk through town and turned. Breck was running towards him.

"Breck? I thought you had to be in court for that case this morning."

"He took a plea deal just as the court was about to begin." Breck pointed towards a local cafe. "Do you have time for coffee? We need to talk."

Breck slid into the booth across from Barnabas, his eyes on his friend and employer. Something was going on with him and it wasn't what had happened to Branigan.

"Breck? You tracked me down for a reason, other than to stop me from hitting the bookstore."

"You still can. I figured that was where you were heading. Amy told me you had come to town."

Barnabas grinned. Amy was his secretary and like Doc's wife and her sister, Anna, she tended to mother all fourteen of the men who resided in the Foundation building and now mothered the five ladies who had become part of the family

"She keeps track of me, I must say."

"She does, but not overboard on it. She's concerned about Branigan, she said." Breck looked up with a quick word of thanks as a plate of food slid in front of him. He was not surprised that he didn't have to order. They ate there enough the owner had memorized what they usually had.

"Me, too. It was typical of him to do what he did. All of us would have." Barnabas sipped at his coffee before continuing. "But that's not why you tracked me down."

"No, I talked to Alice and then Dallas. There was a package left on the doorstep of Brett's office building. Brett found it this morning on Guenivere's desk. I guess the responding officers placed it there. After what had happened, he didn't open it but called in Alice." He paused, his face growing stern. "It contained dead roses and a photo of Guenivere and her mom from the day before. Brett is ready to lock them away."

"A threat, but why? How does it have to do with what happened?"

"That's what Will wants to know. He's going to have Dallas or Alice talk with Guenivere. Brett said something happened years ago that affected Guenivere. She never said what and when they asked, she just shook her head and walked away."

"I got the sense from her that she is hiding something way down deep." Barnabas sighed. "All the ladies did or tried to."

"They don't want to worry us. That's a given." Breck paused, a slice of toast in his hand that he was staring at. "Why did I have toast?"

Barnabas began to laugh. "You could have said no, but you wouldn't, not wanting to offend." He sobered. "What are we to do? Did Will ask anything of us?"

"Not of us. Branigan. He's made a connection with her that her father says she has never had with any of the young men of her acquaintance. She just hadn't wanted to go out with them or be seen with them other than in a group and that not very often. He told Alice that for Branigan to be able to hold her hand and for her not to break their contact was not his daughter. But he was glad to see her reaching out. He said at times she seems to have no hope."

Barnabas nodded, a frown appearing on his face as he stared at the man sitting down the cafe from him, who seemed to be focused on him. Just why, he had no idea. He didn't recognize him. He sighed as he pulled out his phone, snapping a quick picture and sending it on to Dallas before he glanced at the text message that had arrived. He paled.

Breck looked up at the muttered exclamation from Barnabas and then stood, the bill in his hand as he walked through the cafe on Barnabas' heels.

"Barnabas?"

Breck's voice stopped Barnabas who stood, his eyes back on the text message.

"It's Brett. He just received a death threat. This time aimed at Lena and himself." Barnabas looked around. "Someone is out here, Breck. They're watching us. Why?"

"It has to with Branigan?" Breck shook his head. "Listen, I'll head that way and then to find Branigan."

Barnabas nodded, his eyes searching his friend's face. "I agree. The bookstore doesn't need my money today. I'm heading back to the office. I'll see what I can find out." He was away before Breck could say anything or do anything other than to just stand and watch his friend stride rapidly away from him.

$$Chapter\ 8$$

Lena stood back from their front door, pointing to the living room as Breck stood outside. He had not wanted to come, had not wanted to tell them what had been found, but Brett had asked him to.

"Lena? It's been a while. How are you?"

She sighed, and he could see the fine lines of strain in her face. "I have been better. Come on into the kitchen. There's a fresh pot of coffee and it's near lunchtime. You'll stay, of course." She headed down the hallway, hesitating for a moment at the living room doorway, her eyes on her daughter.

Guenivere had brought out her laptop, plunked herself down in her favourite chair and started to answer office emails. But now she sat, her hands idle on the closed laptop, her eyes on Branigan as he slept once more. She had risen at one point and covered him with the afghan her mother kept in a chest under one window before she sat back down. Her hand had brushed his hair back into place and had lingered for a moment on his cheek, a prayer rising for healing from him.

Breck watched as well, before he shook his head. He knew Branigan, knew his heart, about as well as he had let anyone in. He had driven himself to help solve the mysteries surrounding their five friends, working long hours on it. He had worn himself out, Breck supposed, before he moved on to the kitchen, to reach for the mug of coffee he was handed and then taking a seat at the round oak table.

Rising once more, he reached for the tray Lena had in her hands, heading for Guenivere. He set the tray on the coffee table, turning to find Guenivere watching him, a puzzled look on her face.

"I'm sorry. I didn't mean to startle you." He grinned at the look she shot him.

"No, that's okay. I have it happen all the time." She sighed. "Nothing is easy anymore, and I dislike that."

"Something I can do to help?"

She shook her head. "Not unless you can trace some emails for me. They're threatening somewhat in nature. I don't want to go to Dad. He'll lock me away somewhere." Guenivere was grumbling and she knew it.

Breck perched himself on a chair near her. "I can but so can one of our friends who is an IT specialist."

"He is? Oh wonderful." She thrust the laptop at him. "Here. Take this. The password is Truck."

"Truck?" He grinned at that.

"Yes. Truck. Too obvious I know, but it is what it is."

"Breck? When did you get here?'

Neither of his companions in the room had realized that Branigan was awake and had been listening to the conversation, a frown on his face despite the headache or because of it, he couldn't decide. Good, he thought. She's reaching out. That's what I want to see.

"Branigan! How are you feeling?" Breck shifted to look around at him, finding Branigan watching Guenivere, who had suddenly discovered something interesting on her hands and was refusing to look at him. Breck bit back his grin. Here we go again, Lord. Only this time, please? We don't want to almost lose either one of them. It's been too close with all of them.

"Like I was run over by a car. How am I supposed to feel?" He shook his head slightly, finding the headache better. "What are you doing here?"

"I'm supposed to be having lunch here. Or at least, I was asked." He pointed at the tray. "Lena sent that in for you."

Branigan sat up and then stood, reaching for the tray. "We'll eat in the kitchen. We don't need to make more work for her." He walked away, not hearing the muted sound from Guenivere.

Breck spun back, his eyes narrowed as he watched her. "Go. Tell him not to make decisions for you. You can make your own."

———

She shook her own head. "No, he's right. Mom shouldn't have." She made to rise, stopped when Breck's hand was laid on her arm.

"No. It was your decision where you ate. If you want to eat out there, fine. If you had wanted to eat in here, that would have been okay. Find your voice. Tell him how you feel." He laughed at the look on her face, a look of shock and disbelief. "Trust me. He can take it. We've all had conversations with him at some point or other, sometimes at the top of our voices. Surprised you with that, didn't I? He cares about us and that's why he's like he is. I can see he's concerned about you. How far it will go, only God knows. Trust Him to lead you two. But don't be afraid to speak up."

Once more, Guenivere felt hope rising in her. "You're right, Breck, but I don't want to hurt his feelings or get him mad at me." She jumped as she felt an arm around her shoulders and then Branigan perched on the arm of her chair, a thank you mouthed to Breck.

"Is that what happened, love? Someone got extremely angry with you and put you down?" He waited until a hesitant nod came. "I'm not like that. Breck's right. I sometimes step in where I shouldn't and take over. Don't let me. I don't care if you yell at me. Scream at me. Shove me. Hit me. I can take it all." His arm tightened, his only thought in how to make her understand.

None of the three saw Lena hovering in the shadows of the hallway just outside the door, a hand to her mouth, blinking rapidly to clear away the tears. All this time, Lord, and we never knew. She just refused to tell us. Lord, help us to help her. Don't let her get put down again. Not like that. I sense that Your leading here, bringing Branigan and the rest of the Foundation guys as we call them into her life. I pray that she can make friends with their ladies. They can help her in ways that I or her father can't.

*Chapter 9*

A week later, Branigan had moved back to his apartment, albeit it very reluctantly.  He knew he would be unable to have the contact with Guenivere that he had had, that he had come to enjoy.  He would make a point of seeing her every day,  he decided.  Just how that would work out, he wasn't sure.

He turned as he heard footsteps and his friends, Baird and Blair, approached.  Blair pointed towards the sitting area at one side of the lobby.  The Foundation Building housed the men, Doc and Anna, and also had offices for each one, as well as a well-stocked infirmary.  The lobby was larger than most buildings, and had a sitting area on each side of the door, with gas fireplaces facing one another.

Branigan sat, relieved to be off his feet.  He had been on the run all day, he thought, catching up on the tasks and security plans that had sat on his desk for the last few days.  He still had some to work through, but he felt better about what was there.

"Branigan?  How are you feeling now you're home and back to work?"  Baird watched him closely, seeing something different about his friend.

Branigan shrugged.  "All right, I guess.  I've made a dent into the work on my desk."  He paused, not sure how to continue.  "Have you heard anything from Will or Alice?"

Blair shook his head.  "Not a thing.  They won't unless they need to talk to us."  He shared a look with Baird, the two men and their wives, Berneen and Devaney having spoken about Branigan and Guenivere.  "How's Guenivere?"

Branigan shrugged.  "I haven't talked to her today, so I am not sure.  I plan on calling her later.  Why?"  He looked between the two, eyes narrowing as he tried to determine what they were up to, and they were up to something, they had that look about them.

———

"Berneen asked if she would be willing to come for dinner one night.  She's seen her around church, is in the same evening Bible study group with her, and has wanted to get to know her better. With you involved with her, she thinks it's a perfect opportunity."

"Devancy feels the same, Branigan."  Blair held up a hand as Branigan went to protest. "We're not prying or interfering in your life.  It's just that Devaney has picked up on something with Guenivere.  You know how her instincts are after having lived on the streets for so long.  She's worried about her."

Branigan sat back, his eyes on the dark hardwood floor and then nodded.  "There is something, but she hasn't shared it all with me. I'm getting bits and pieces.  It's not just what happened to us. There's something else, something I don't feel right sharing until I've talked to her and had her permission to bring you in on it.  And that I would like to do. We work together well as a team, all of us, ladies included, and I think that's what is going to be needed.  I fear for her.  For her life.  For her sanity." He groaned. "Did I really say that?"

"You did.  I gather she has had something happen that has affected her in ways she has hidden.  We all do that."  Blair stood, seeing Devaney hesitating near the doorway. "I have to run, but talk to your lady.  Let her know we'd like to have her for dinner.  Either just you two or some of the rest of us.  Maybe ask her to our potluck on Sunday."

Branigan stared after him as he walked away, hearing Baird snickering near him. "Not funny, Baird."

"Actually, it is.  Now you know how we felt."

Branigan dropped his head to hide his smile.  "Yeah, I guess I do.  Sort of.  How did you do it, Baird.  You and Berneen married under duress but you survived everything, growing to love her so deeply.  How?"

"God.  That's the only way, Branigan.  Berneen had been beaten down just by being held captive.  She has often told me she was afraid she would never be free, but when she saw me, she knew God had sent someone.  When you dragged her away with me, she fought you, but down deep inside, she was glad we had."

Branigan sat back, mulling over what Baird had said, his hand absentmindedly rubbing at his cheek, touching a fading bruise. "I can see that. She had Darby to worry about as well." He paused, gathering his thoughts, knowing that what he would say would go no further. "Did you hear about the parcel that had been left that day? Dead roses and picture of Guenivere and her mom. Who does that?"

"I would suspect it's related to the man who was there. I heard from Barnabas that he's been taken to another district where he's facing murder charges. God had His hand on you two that day."

"He did." Branigan looked up as he heard the door open and then was on his feet, moving towards it. Guenivere had appeared, and he could tell she was distraught.

Guenivere paused inside the doorway, her mouth dropping open as she took in the welcoming foyer, searching for a board that would show where Branigan's apartment was. Not seeing one, she looked further, finding the security desk tucked away unobtrusively near the elevators. She had taken a couple of steps that way when arms swept around her and pulled her into a tight hug. Branigan, she thought. She turned, her own arms around him as she tried to compose herself.

"Guenivere? You're here?" Branigan turned her back towards where he had been sitting. Baird had stood, watching them closely. "Here. Sit. What's wrong?"

Guenivere sank down, grateful to be off her feet, grateful for Branigan's arm around her.

"I had to come." She thrust her phone at him. "Swipe it and then take a look at the picture." Tears welled in her eyes, tears she refused to let fall.

Branigan reached for her phone, his eyes not leaving her, hearing Baird muttering something. He heard footsteps approaching, that stopped short of where they were.

He finally looked down at her phone, staring at the picture. "It's us, from that day. Someone else was there."

"There was. I didn't see anyone but someone had to leave that parcel. It wasn't that man. I watched him walk up to the door. He didn't have anything."

"So, someone left the parcel when you weren't in the reception area?" Baird had spoken up, startling Guenivere, who shrank back against Branigan for a moment.

"They have to have. I was working in the one office for a while and was back and forth. They could have left it at any time that morning." She sighed. "We'll never know, now will we?"

Branigan looked past her to see Buckley and Benen standing there before they approached and sat as well. Guenivere stared at them, not sure if she wanted them there or not. But, after all, Buckley was their pastor or minister or whatever you wanted to call him. She guessed to herself that if she and Branigan really were dating that she would have to get to know his friends. Suddenly she felt alive, wanted, loved, and ready to face whatever it was.

"Guenivere? Can we talk with the others? Can I tell them what you have shared? If you say no, that's fine. I'll work on it, but having the others take a look at it will help."

She shrugged, her face turning to him, seeing the concern on his face as well as something just for her alone in his eyes. She nodded. "I think so, Branigan. It's time. It may all be related somehow."

"That's what I was going to suggest." Benen spoke up. "Listen, it's near supper time. I know Cadee has planned a barbecue for us. Join us, Guenivere." He laughed at the look she threw Branigan. "Yeah, he can tag along, if he really must." He laughed harder as Branigan spluttered out some unintelligible words. "Buckley, you're free, you said."

"I can't put her to all that work." Guenivere was horrified at the thought.

"Trust me. She loves doing this. In case you had forgotten, she worked on a mission field with her parents. They were used to putting on big meals. She has told me she misses that." He looked past her. "And there she is. Cadee? Have you met Guenivere?"

"I have." Cadee reached to hug Guenivere, pulling her to her feet. "You're staying for supper. I won't take no for an answer. And then we will talk. I want to know what it is that's been going on with you. I can sense you're having an adventure. All of us like to tag along on those." Her arm linked with Guenivere, she led her away, leaving the men staring after her before Buckley started to laugh.

"Well, I guess that settles it. What do we need to do to help?"

"If I know Cadee, likely not much." Benen rose, following after the two ladies, leaving Branigan lost in thought.

"Branigan?"

Buckley's quiet voice broke through to the other man and he turned, a sudden look of understanding on his face.

"I think I know where this is going. I have a feeling I know who. I've seen him watching her, not realizing what was going on."

"Do you have a name?" Buckley's eyes widened as Branigan spoke again rapidly. "We'll need to prove that. You'll need to find out from Guenivere if that is indeed who it is. I suspect you are correct in your surmising. I have seen him around town. All the girls and younger ladies avoid him."

"They do? I missed that." Branigan was quiet as they headed for Benen's apartment, Buckley tapping at the door and then opening it, hearing Cadee and Guenivere's laughter spilling out towards them.

"I haven't heard her laugh like that. Thank you, Cadee. And thank you, Lord. She needs friends like these ladies."

Cadee finally turned to Guenivere, their meal over and the remnants put away. The two ladies had taken over the couch, one on each end, their feet under them, laughing at the nonsense that Buckley was coming up with. His comments were getting more outrageous the more they laughed.

Finally, Benen bought into the conversation, watching Cadee for a moment before she nodded.

"Buckley, can we spend some time in prayer? We are going to need all the wisdom and protection that the Good Lord can provide. I just have that feeling."

Buckley nodded, seeing the consent from the others and bowing his head, led them to the throne of God, his words bringing peace and soothing to Guenivere's sore, troubled heart.

Guenivere looked around at the four gathered with her, her eyes resting on Cadee, who was nodding, a smile of encouragement on her face.  She turned suddenly, looking for Branigan who rose, came towards her and shifted her over on the couch so that he could take her spot and just wrapped her in his arms.  The strength and trust in her that she felt gave her courage to speak.

Guenivere kept her eyes on her hands, seeing Branigan's wrapped around hers. She tried to sort through her thoughts but wasn't very successful at that. She bit at her lip, not sure where to start.

"Start at the beginning, love. Start where is all started. You told me you were young, what 12 or so?" Branigan's quiet voice in her ear had her looking up at him before she nodded.

"I was 12. There was a group of us youth from the church that hung around together. A lot of them have left town now, finding a life elsewhere. There are still three or four around, but we don't talk much now. He destroyed that."

"Who, Guenivere? Who destroyed this group?" Benen leaned forward, his forearms resting on his knees as he intently watched her.

She shook her head, paused, and then shook it again. "I need to tell you what happened. I am almost sure that you'll be able to guess. He's made it that obvious."

"Jason Lang." Cadee's quiet voice had Guenivere's head whipping around to stare at her, even as her face paled.

"You're not from here. How did you know?"

Cadee shrugged. "Sometimes God does that. He speaks a name. I know of a lady, the wife of a police chief, who God always spoke to when their friends were going through things. She was always right. She would rather He had used someone else. I guess that what He's done here. I've seen him around. Seen him watching you when you didn't know he was there. He has an evilness about him that I can sense."

"Thank you, Cadee. No one else has ever picked up on that so quickly. He hides what he does." She paused, biting at her lip, feeling Branigan's hand on hers, squeezing lightly. "I have to go back to when I was 12, almost 13. Jason used to come to the church every once in a while, but not on a regular enough basis that we wanted him in our group. He resented that. He wanted to come in and take over, and we just wouldn't let him. I know the guys chased him away many times. The girls were all afraid of him. I have no idea what he did or didn't do or say to any of them. We never talked about it and we should have. I guess we were ashamed or something like that.

"I was riding my bike home one day from my grandparents. I usually cut through the park in town, feeling it was safe enough to do so. He was waiting for me. He must have followed me. I didn't see the wire he had strung across the path until my front wheel hit is and I flew off my bike, landing in a small pond. As I tried to drag myself up, Jason was there, his hands on my shoulders. He kept shoving me down into the water. I pleaded with him to let me go. I know I was crying. He just didn't listen.

"Jason told me that I was no good, that I was ugly, that no one would ever want to marry me. He kept repeating this every time he shoved me down into the water, until finally he made me agree with him. He shoved me back down once more and then disappeared. I crawled up the embankment and just laid there until I could get my breath back. I think I was crying but I couldn't tell, my face was so wet and muddy. All I could think of was what Mom would say when she saw me. I finally got up, found my bike and wheeled it home. The front tire was bent. I knew I had to fix it before Dad saw it or he would question me on what happened. Neither of them were home. I showered, got into some clean clothes, and threw my dirty ones in the washer, hoping to have them done before Mom got home and questioned me.

"They were late getting home that night, having been delayed by some road construction on the way. I have often wondered, if they had gotten home earlier, if I would have told them. I really don't know." She turned her face to look at Branigan, seeing a shuttered look on his face before he smiled at her. "Anyway, I drove it all down inside, as deep as I could. I couldn't talk about it. He had threatened to do something to Dad's truck or car. He also threatened to burn our house down. He said he wouldn't do anything if I kept quiet."

———

Cadee slid over, her arms around her new friend, holding her as the healing tears began to fall, Branigan's hand resting on her back for a moment before he rose, nodding with his head towards the balcony.

"Branigan? Did you suspect this?" Buckley's voice was quiet, they were all in shock at what she had said. "She was too young."

"She was. She has let some things slip. I had a suspicion that's who it was." He sighed, running his hands through his hair, and then gripping the balcony railing tight enough they turned white. "I want him. I want him for what he did to Guenivere. Who knows what all he's done to the others."

"Makes me wonder if that's why they moved away. He hasn't." Benen looked back through the patio doors. "Cadee will talk with her, find out anything more she can, and then ask permission to share it with us. We need to get him, Branigan, for her sake and for the others."

"That man who ran you down? How is he connected to Lang?" Buckley's question had the men stopping any motion before they stared at one another.

"I wonder. I need to talk to Alice or Dallas or Will. I know we can't do anything about the past. But I want this cleared up. Guenivere deserves to live the life that she should have had and didn't." He paused, sorrow flickering across his face. "Brett and Lena will be devastated when they hear, and hear they must. Whoever it was behind that man hasn't stopped. I have seen evidence on their security system that someone matching his description has been lurking around the building."

"But I thought he had been taken to another town?" Benen was puzzled.

"He was. Will called me late this afternoon. He escaped custody somehow and they think he headed back this way. That was three days ago." Branigan turned to the doors, ready to race to Guenivere's side but knowing she needed the time with Cadee. "They think he's come back here, ready to seek revenge."

"And that puts you in danger, do you know that?" Buckley's hand on Branigan's shoulder stopped his forward motion. "We need to bathe you two in prayer. It's going to get ugly, uglier than it has already."

Later that night, Branigan followed Guenivere as she drove home, not willing to let her go on her own. He parked on the street and was at her car door before she could open it, his hand reached out for hers.

"Branigan, I'm sorry. I shouldn't have talked." She was contrite, ashamed at what she had said.

His finger under her chin raising it so he could see it clearly in the streetlight, Branigan shook his head.

"No, the time is right for this to be settled. You have lived too much of your life in the shame and shadows of his words and actions. You did nothing to deserve that treatment. I want to see the bright, vibrant, beautiful lady that I care a lot for live her life as she should and as God would want her to."

She reached to hug him before she stepped back. "Do you think we'll catch him?"

Branigan nodded. "I can guarantee you we will. All the guys will be working on this. Ennis', Bradon's wife, cousin is a detective in the next town. He'll want to be involved. We need to talk to Will or Dallas or Alice, I think. What he has done continues to affect the town. We don't know who all he's gone after."

"That's my fear, Branigan. I had a friend commit suicide when we were 16. I know she was really afraid of him, would go out of her way to avoid him. I don't know that we can prove he was behind that or not."

"Let me have her name, and we'll look into it." He wrapped her into a hug again. "Come on. Let's get you inside. I don't like you out here."

She nodded as they walked to the door, his arm still around her. *Thank You, Lord. You heard my pleas and begging and* brought someone in who is strong enough to stand up to him. Just don't let him get hurt any more than he was.

Branigan watched the house, waiting for the lights to go out, his fingers tapping at the steering wheel, his phone on the seat beside him. He had called Will, letting him know he wanted to speak with him. Would tomorrow do? Will had asked him to come over that night, even late, knowing that Branigan would not be calling him and asking for that if it wasn't serious.

Will sat across from Branigan at his kitchen table, his hand wrapped around a mug, waiting for Branigan to speak. When he had, Will sat back, nodding.

"That explains a lot we could never understand. Why did so many of that group leave town. I know who she means about the friend committing suicide. She's not the only one, unfortunately. There have been at least three others that we know of, but we were never satisfied they killed themselves."

"You think he did it and made it look like they did." Branigan sat back, his thoughts muddled for a moment. "That makes me worry even more for Guenivere."

"Let me ask you a question, Branigan. You don't have to answer if you don't want to. I know it would have been a question your father would be asking."

Branigan nodded once more, his thoughts drifting to his father. His mother had died in childbirth, his baby sister not living past a few days. His father had been the one to raise him on his own, before kidney disease had struck and taken him too soon and too young. Branigan had just finished high school in his hometown in PEI. He had been at loose ends for a few months, finally enrolling in college. When he had been approached by Barnabas and offered employment with the Foundation, he had jumped at the chance, eager to get away from the memories that haunted him.

"Go ahead."

"I have seen you two together. You make each other whole. She is your heart, Branigan, whether you realize it yet or not. I have seen her watch you, seeing the hope in her eyes. She trusts you in a way I have never seen her trust anyone before. Watch her heart. That's all I ask."

Branigan nodded. "You're right, Will. She is all that. We've talked. She's been reluctant to go forward with our friendship, I think because of Lang. She has more she hasn't said about what happened and what he told her. You'll likely find he has threatened her family, her friends and any boyfriend she might have." He paused, groaning as his phone chimed, excusing himself to pull it out. It was late, after ten o'clock, and he didn't know of anyone who would be calling him.

Guenivere's voice flooded over his phone, her words mingling together in a manner that he couldn't understand. He was on his feet, heading for the door, Will at his heels.

"It's Guenivere. I can't make out what's wrong."

Will pointed to his car. "I'll drive. We'll get your car later." His phone was out and he was calling for backup at the Danby's, not sure what they would find.

Guenivere stood, her arms wrapped around herself, giving her statement, when she saw Branigan standing, waiting for her. She flew across the yard into his arms, as fast as her feet would take her, sobs shaking her body.

Will stood for a moment before he turned to the responding officer, trying to determine what had transpired. He frowned when he heard, his eyes finding Branigan and nodding.

Branigan's arms tightened on Guenivere before he led her to Will's car, lifting her up to sit on the trunk, leaning against it himself, his back to the house.

"Guenivere? What happened? I couldn't make out what you were saying."

She was still shaking. "He was in the house. I don't know how, but I heard him moving around downstairs. I called you instead of the police. I'm sorry. I shouldn't have done that."

"No, you did right. I was with Will, discussing something, when you called. He called it in on our way here. Did Lang find you?"

Guenivere shook her head. "No, he didn't make it up the stairs. I heard the sirens and then heard the front door slam." She looked back at the house. "Mom and Dad are away for the next few days. I don't want to stay here. Not on my own. That's something else he's taken from me." She could feel the anger growing within her.

"I'll take you out to the Foundation building. There are suites there you can use for now. We have security on site, so he won't get to you in the building."

Will stood listening, nodding as he heard Branigan's words. "That's a good idea, Guenivere. Your father would agree."

She sighed. "I know he would." She glanced past him at the house. "I have to get some things. Can I go in?"

"Give us about twenty minutes. I want you to walk through with me. And yes, Branigan can go with you." He grinned at the look she threw him.

Branigan laughed at her muttered comment that everyone seemed to be making them a couple, did he know that?

"I would like that, Guenivere. I would like that a lot. But we have time. We'll talk." He reached to brush the hair back from her cheek, her eyes on his, hope in them, he thought. "We'll talk and figure it out. Right now, we need to get you safe. I came with Will. He'll take us back to his place and I'll grab my car. He'll have someone follow us, that I know without him saying a word."

Two weeks later, Guenivere rose from her desk in the office building, heading for the work building as it was called, intent on finding Douglas. She had an invoice for work on a vehicle that she didn't recognize

"Douglas?"

"Right here, Guenivere. What's up? You look like you're on a mission." Douglas grinned at her, wiping his hands on a rag he stuffed into his back pocket. "What do you have there?"

"This. An invoice for work. I don't recognize the vehicle. It's not one of ours, but it says you worked on it."

"Let's see." Douglas frowned. "No, that's not one of ours. And I didn't work on it. I would have signed off on it, and it isn't signed. Now, who?"

"Lang. It has to be him."

"Jason Lang?" When Guenivere nodded, Douglas sighed. "I've seen him hanging around here at times. Whenever I approached, he ran. Your Dad knows he's been here. I talked to Alice and she was going to talk to Will, to see what they could do."

"There's not much we can do. I just don't understand how the invoice ended up on my desk. It wasn't there yesterday and I pulled these first thing this morning. It was there then."

Douglas shook his head. "We need to talk to that boyfriend of yours and see if he can find out if the security system has been tampered with. I suspect it was."

"My boyfriend?" She turned to face him. "Just who do you mean?"

"Branigan. Isn't he your beau?"

She groaned. "You, too? What is it with everybody?"

Douglas stopped her before hugging her. "I've seen the two of you together. You make a couple, cute couple at that. We're glad for you, Guenivere. That's all."

"Thank you, Douglas. Now to track him down and talk to him."

Branigan stood later that day, his eyes on the security feed from overnight. Then he saw the man approaching the building, a key in his hand, reaching to turn off the security system before he was back resetting everything and then locking the door behind him. Brett stood beside him, shock on his face.

"How did he get a key and the security code?"

Branigan strode over to the panel, a grim look on his face, before he pried off the cover.

"Here. This is not part of the control panel." He pointed towards what seemed to be a small camera. "He's placed this sometime the office was empty. It wouldn't have taken long. I can almost guarantee you it leads to a computer somewhere."

"I'm sure it does." Brett turned. "Guenivere, call it in, please. Branigan, it's not your fault. We'll need to replace that, I gather, and also the locks."

"You do. I'll have to slip away and grab another control panel. Stay safe."

Two hours later, Branigan stood, watching as both Brett and Guenivere changed their passcodes. He had talked to Will, who had sent out a crime scene tech. Together they had searched the office and warehouse, finding a number of cameras hidden away. They had also found some hidden outside. That worried Branigan. He didn't think it was Lang that had done that, but who? He had put in a call to Baird, asking if he would set up a meeting for the men at the building that night. He needed their help.

Guenivere stepped away from the control panel, fear running through her. She jumped as she felt arms coming around her and then leaned back against Branigan. He made her feel safe, she decided, and that was what she needed at that very moment.

Brett watched the two closely, a frown on his face as he looked past them. Douglas stood at the door, beckoning him. He walked towards him, the office door closing quietly behind him. Brett took a look at the new lock and smiled to himself. Branigan had been adamant that they get a high quality lock with a keypad.

"Douglas?" Brett walked towards the picnic table under the nearby trees. "Something's wrong?"

Douglas sat, rubbing at the back of his head. "There is, and I don't know what. Did Guenivere tell you about the invoice? Of course, she did. That's why the activity." He drifted off in deep thought for a moment. "Do you remember that company that tried to become partners with you?"

"The Grayson Trucks. I do. They seemed to disappear from the area." Brett paused. "You're telling me that they're back?"

"I found out from a cousin that they never left the area. They went underground. He said the rumour at the time was they wanted to come in with you and use your company as a cover for their activities. For some reason, he has connected Jason Lang to them."

"It all comes back to him, doesn't it?" Brett sighed, his hands rubbing together. "Guenivere has finally told us what happened all those years ago. I wish she had told us then, but as a young teenager, she was scared. He played on that. She said he had threatened everyone she knew."

"He did, Dad." The men looked up to see the young couple standing near them. "I found dead animals on my way to school or the library or to a friend's. He made sure I knew it was from him."

"Guenivere, I wish you had told us, but I can understand why you didn't." Brett watched Branigan closely. "Branigan, this is out of our league, Douglas and I. We can watch to a certain extent when Guenivere's here on site, but we can't be with her all the time."

"I know. I have a meeting set up with my friends for tonight. We'll do some brainstorming and see what we can come up with." He looked down at Guenivere. "Barnabas called me when I was out getting the new control panel. He has offered Guenivere an apartment in the building until this is over."

Guenivere twisted to look up at him. "He did?" She looked over at her father, seeing the relief on his face. "Dad? Do you think I should?"

"Perhaps.  I would like to see you stay safe and at home but if going there means you do stay safe, then your mother and I would agree with Barnabas."

Douglas had been listening intently. "It would help, Guenivere, but it may also make it worse.  If he can't get to you, then he may go after your parents."

"Barnabas thought of that.  He'll be talking to you, Brett, but he has offered some of the security men and ladies that we have on site.  One to be with you.  One of the ladies to be with Lena."

Brett breathed a sigh of relief.  "That would work.  I know Lena would be agreeable."  He looked down, his heart sorrowing for his daughter, but also praying through what they needed to do.

Guenivere slipped to the seat beside her father, her arm wrapping around his, her head leaning against it.

"I don't know what to do, Dad.  I want you and Mom to stay safe.  Does that mean I don't work for now?"

Douglas again spoke up.  "It may be what it takes, Guenivere.  We have you set up to work remotely.  We can do that.  If your Dad's not in the office, we just leave a sign on the door to look for me.  I can handle it.  I'm sure we can set up a fax machine to forward what you need."

Guenivere looked relieved, feeling Branigan's hands resting on her shoulders.  She felt the first ray of hope once again, that she hadn't felt in a long time."

"Okay.  Let's do this.  I heard what you said about that company, Dad.  Didn't you know they were still around?"

Brett looked surprised at her question.  "No, I didn't. Did you?"

"I did.  I've seen their vehicles.  They're only around late at night or early in the morning, before there's much traffic."  She paused, her face paling.  "I just remember.  Jason is related to one of them, I just can't remember how."

*Chapter 13*

Late that same afternoon, Guenivere walked the apartment that Branigan had led her to, her bare feet whispering against the oak hardwood floor, her eyes taking in the comfortable, inviting furnishings.  She studied the walls, liking the butter cream colour of them and then looking upwards to study the lighter cream crown molding and ceilings.  She turned, a smile on her face, to find Branigan watching her, leaning against the doorframe of the living room, arms folded across his chest, one leg tucked over the other, the toes of that foot resting on the floor.  His smile drew her to him and as he opened his arms, she walked in and hugged him.

"Thank you."

"Thank me?  For what?"

"For this.  For caring.  For watching out for me."  She leaned back to look up at him, seeing once more that look in his eyes that said she was special to him.

Branigan's smile widened.  "It's what I do, my love.  You deserve this and so much more."  He dropped a kiss on her forehead.  "Now, about supper.  Are you hungry?"

"I didn't think I was, but I am.  But I don't know that I have food here."

Branigan's hand on her arm stopped her.  "You do.  Cadee and Ennis took care of that for you.  But Doc and Anna have asked if we would join them.  Anna says she knows you well from the toddlers' class at church."

Guenivere began to laugh, her eyes lighting up with amusement.  "Oh, we do.  We have such fun with them.  Have you ever tried to carry on a conversation with a two year old?"

Branigan laughed as well, as taking her hand, he led her from her apartment, locking the door and handing her the key.  "I can't say that I have.  It will have to go on my bucket list."

"You would be good in that age group." She laughed even harder. "Although, with you being so tall, I don't know that you would fit into one of their chairs."

He grinned at her lightheartedness. "I can always sit on the floor. What do I need to become part of your team?"

She stopped short in Doc and Anna's hallway to stare up at him. "You're serious, aren't you? Talk to Buckley. He'll walk you through what you need to do." She looked around to find Anna standing near her. "I just found a new recruit for our class, Anna."

"You have? Wonderful. Now, come. The roast and the fixings are all ready to eat."

The next morning, Guenivere looked around the office she had set up, a mug of tea in her hand as she studied the office in the apartment. Whoever designed these had put a lot of thought into them, she thought, raising the mug to her mouth to sip from it. She grinned suddenly, thinking of what had happened earlier.

Barnabas had dropped in, just to welcome her to the building he said, and to make sure she felt safe and secure, and had everything that she needed. He had dropped a set of keys on the desk, telling her that they were for the gym, if she wanted that. She had nodded eagerly. She was a runner and cyclist, and knew that going outdoors to do that would be a foolish risk. He had stayed for a few minutes, finally walking away, calling back that he welcomed her to the family. He had just laughed at her cry of disbelief and closed the door behind him.

Guenivere shook her head. Just maybe she would be part of the family one day. She felt that was where it was heading with Branigan, but she wasn't sure. She had been beaten down for so long, she didn't really trust her instincts where men were concerned. Although Branigan was certainly changing that for her, she thought, Branigan and his friends.

She reached for her phone as it chimed, answering her mother's call. Lena had hidden her real feelings when Guenivere had told her the plans, but she was glad that her daughter was safe, at least for now. She had parted the sheer curtains on their front window that morning to see the same vehicle parked across the street, the man obviously watching their house.  Alice had been by and taken down the information, promising to deal with it.

Late that afternoon, Guenivere opened up the last work email she had planned to deal with, her hand freezing as she read it, her face growing white.  She shoved violently backwards from her desk, her chair clattering to the floor as she fell with it.  She lay still for a moment, horror growing within her.  The knock at the door had her spinning and then on her feet, racing for it, throwing it open and then throwing herself into Branigan's arms.

Branigan's arms closed around his lady as he stared down at her head before he looked sideways at Benen and Cadee.  Something had happened and he wanted to find out, but first he had to calm his sweetheart down, and that was exactly what she had become.  His sweetheart.

"Guenivere?  What happened?"  He moved her gently into the apartment, the door closing behind Benen and Cadee.

Benen strode through, looking for something, anything that would explain her reaction.  He paused in the office as he saw the overturned chair.  He reached to right it, his eyes stopping at the computer monitor.  Not wanting to intrude or read something that was business related, he hesitated.

Guenivere stood in the doorway.  "Read it.  I can't."

Benen glanced over at her, seeing her nod and then turned back to read the email.  His face grew grim as he read it, nodding to Branigan who had walked over.

"This is brutal, Branigan.  Who is this guy?"  Benen had heard some of the story but not what had happened the previous day.

"He's stalking her for some reason.  I had to swap out the security system control panel yesterday.  He had managed to get into the office.  Will sent out a tech and during the sweep we found cameras in both buildings and outside as well.  He had even managed to get a key cut."

"He did what?"  Benen's voice exploded in anger, although he kept it low.  He shot a glance back towards the doorway.  "Cadee's has her in another room.  What do we do?"

"We find him. But Guenivere remembered that he was cousins or something like that to a trucking company that tried to become partners when she was young." He paused. "I wonder if it was around the same time that she was attacked." His phone out, he was quickly dialling through to Brett.

"The timing for that company?" Brett had difficulty following Branigan's words. "Slow down, Branigan. I'm having trouble following you."

"I wondered how old Guenivere was when they tried to buy into yours."

"Guenivere? About 11 or so. That's right, it was about four months before she turned 12." Brett's voice died away. "That's why."

"To get you to come to terms? Possibly. Listen. Guenivere pulled up an email just before I got here. It's brutal, to say the least. It threatens your buildings, your trucks, you and Lena. Doesn't say anything about threatening Guenivere." Branigan listened for a moment before he nodded. "That's my plan. I'll send it on to Dallas and Will. Let them look at it. They'll be around more than likely to talk with you." He pocketed his phone, his face thoughtful.

"We didn't get to meet last night, Branigan. The guys are assembling after supper in the conference room. You know the one. Where we always meet to figure out the adventures."

"Right, we didn't." He reached to print the email, before sending it on as he had promised Brett. "I want to show them this. I don't know how much information we have, but we'll work through it and see where we go."

"Cadee offered to stay with Guenivere if she likes. The other ladies are around as well."

"That's good." Branigan turned for the doorway. "She needs that. She needs to hear their stories and know that she's not on her own." He paused, his phone out. "There is one person I think may be more than able to help us."

"Emma?" At Branigan's nod, Benen agreed. "Send on what you can. I know she'll help. She told me that when Brady and Fynn were going through what they were."

Her eyes huge, Guenivere stared around at the five ladies seated in her living room, not really believing what they had said.

"There is no way on earth you have gone through this. You couldn't have."

The ladies laughed before Berneen spoke up.

"We did. God got us through that. We have had to learn to trust Him in ways we never would have. I think that's what you are learning."

Guenivere nodded. "I am. Having heard what happened to you five, it gives me confidence that God really does listen."

"He does." This from Ennis. "I know He does." She looked around at the other ladies. "We need to meet on a weekly basis, I think, for prayer, if only for prayer. I would like to start a Bible study, but for now, we need to support one another and really support Guenivere and Branigan. They are a cute couple, you know."

The ladies laughed even as Guenivere blushed. That was what she was thinking of them as, but with Lang hanging over her, she just didn't see how it would work out, not without Branigan getting hurt again.

A hand gripped hers and a soft voice spoke. "Leave it with God, Guenivere. I know it's hard, but trust Him."

Guenivere looked up at Fynn. "It is hard. It's hard to trust in someone you can't see, isn't it?"

They all agreed before six heads bowed and they raised up each other to God's throne. They left shortly after they had finished, Guenivere wandering through her apartment, to pull open the French door to the balcony and finding a chair to sit in, to watch the setting of the sun over the lake. She felt at peace, the first time in weeks, no years, she thought.  No matter what happened, she would trust and leave her hand in God's.

She rose when she heard the doorbell, opening it find Branigan standing there, arms open to enfold her.  Breck stood beside him as did Burnie, another friend of Branigan's.

"Can we come in, my love?  We need to talk to you." Branigan's voice was sober as he asked, eyes searching her face.

"Sure.  Can I get you anything?"

"No, we're fine, Guenivere.  We just need to go over something with you.  I'm not sure if you have met Burnie yet."

"I have.  His books ship through Dad's company."

"Nice to see you out here, Guenivere.  I wish the circumstances were different." Burnie's voice was soft as he spoke, finding a seat in a chair in the living room.

"They aren't, are they?  But I know God has allowed this.  We just have to wait on Him, I guess."  She turned to Breck.  "You said you needed to talk to me?

"We do.  We have had a long discussion on what it going on.  We know it's only going to get worse, as I am sure you have surmised.  We're pulling names and dates and addresses and whatever we can find on that company and on Lang.  He is a cousin to one of the owners.  Branigan talked to your Dad earlier, asking when the trucking company tried to buy into his.  It was about four months before you turned 12."

They watched as her face paled and understanding dawned on her.  "It was because of them?  All along?  That's why he did it?  To get Dad to come to terms.  Only I never said anything, and they had to wait."  She stared past Breck for a moment before her eyes turned back to him, determination beginning to colour her face.  "Of course. That would be why.  But now?  Why come back?  Why break in and set up what they did?  And the man who showed up that day?  How is he involved?"

"That's what we working on."  Branigan's hand tightened on the one of hers he was holding.  "Fynn has a friend who is really good at finding things.  I took the liberty of contacting her and asking her to research it."

---

Guenivere stared at him for a moment before her brow cleared. "Emma?"

"Yes, Emma.  You know her?"

She nodded. "I have met her.  It's Leah that I know better.  Our fathers connected through the Christian trucking company organization.  In fact, Branigan, her husband, Joseph, was the one who came in and set up the security system."  She frowned.  "He is as good as you are.  How did it get hacked?"

"That's what we want to know.  I'm not sure we have that information yet."  Breck spoke up.  "I called him in.  I'll talk to him tomorrow."  He stood as did Burnie.  "Let us know if you get anything more, not matter how minor.  Sometimes that is all it takes."

"That's what Will said.  He had a detective, Dallas, come out and talk to me.  Right now, there's not a lot they can do."

"No, there isn't.  We have to connect the dots for them.  Trust me, we will."  Burnie said good night at that point, walking away with Breck, leaving Branigan to wrap Guenivere in his arms.

"Are you okay?"

She shrugged.  "I'm not sure how to feel, to tell you the truth."

"Sounds about normal to me."

Branigan stood inside his doorway a short time later.  He hadn't stayed as long as he would have liked to, seeing the fatigue on his lady's face.  His head went back against the door as he first prayed, and then thought through what had happened.  A grim determination filled him.  He would track down Lang and bring him in, on his own if he had to.  This needed to be over for Guenivere, he thought.  It's gone on too long.

———

Two days later, Branigan stood in the shadows of a building, watching intently as the man he had been following stopped in front of a business before he entered. His phone out, Branigan took a quick picture of the place and sent it on to Brennen and Brandon, knowing they were home and could work on discovering more about it.

He watched as the man left and walked past him before he stepped out and followed, his eyes searching for anyone following him. He could see the arrogance of the man in front of him just by how he was walking. He heard the sound of a motor and stepped back into a doorway, noting the unmarked cruiser pull up in front of the man and halt his footsteps. Alice stepped out from the passenger's side as the officer stepped out from the other, hands on their police issue weapons. Alice spoke with the man, and Branigan could see the anger flying at them from him. A sudden move towards his pocket had the male officer shoving him against the cruiser as a knife clattered to the grounds. Handcuffs snapped around his wrists and he was shoved into the back seat through the door Alice had opened. Branigan continued to watch from the shadows, seeing Alice looking around, almost as if she knew he was there.

Branigan waited until they left before he headed back towards his truck, his phone out to call Brennen.

"Brennen? How is it going? You have. Wonderful! What's that?" He scanned the street both ways before he ran across it, his key fob in his hand to unlock the door. He slid onto the seat, the door closing behind him, and he reached to lock it. "Who contacted you? Oh, Jace from Emma's. That's good. They have? Okay, I have a couple of stops to make. I should be there by about four." He laughed as Brennen commented that Guenivere had shown up that morning, determined to help them as best she could. "She will do that. She wants this over, and frankly, so do I. We need to find something to give her hope, and I might just have that.  See you in a while."

He drove away, scanning the area around him, not seeing the delivery vehicle that had pulled out behind him and was following him.  The men argued with one another as they followed Branigan through his day.  They needed to find somewhere to ambush him, but they never found that opportunity.  They lost sight of him mid-afternoon as the traffic picked up in town, not knowing that Branigan had finally spied them and had headed for the police department, watching for them, and then finally heading his truck for home.  He was anxious to find out what his friends had discovered, but he was more anxious to find his lady and see how her day had been.

Guenivere felt an arm come around her and leaned into Branigan as he pulled a chair over with his foot and sat beside her, his eyes assessing her.  She was more relaxed, feeling better about herself and where she was heading after having spent time that day with Cadee and Fynn and then spending time searching through stacks of papers she had been handed.  She had stared at them and then up at Brennen, who grinned at her.

"How are you, my love?"  Branigan's voice was low enough so only she could hear him.

"Okay.  I think."  She sat back in her chair, before she leaned against him.  "Your friends are helping.  They have kept me busy today."  She looked around him to see Brandon watching, a grin on his face.  "And Cadee and Fynn rescued me for a while.  They are such fun people."

"They are.  They have been through a lot on their own and then with each other.  I'm happy to hear they're tracking you down.  You need them.  And they need you."

"And how is that?"  She was puzzled at his words.

Branigan paused, realizing she didn't understand.  "They need to be valued for themselves.  They want to help others, to be the encouragement that person needs.  Right at this moment, that person is you.  Because your Dad's on the board, you know that the basis for the Foundation is to be encouragement to others.  They can do that for you, and you can do that for them."

She frowned as she thought through his words before her face cleared and she nodded. "That's a wonderful thought, Branigan. The Foundation has done that for so many. Like with you all. I know you are all orphans and come from all over Canada, that Barnabas sought you out and offered you work. He didn't do that without a lot of prayer and I would gather seeking counsel. Just because all his friends had to have the same initials." She smirked as he broke out into a laugh, causing the others to raise their heads and then smile at them.

"So, my love, where do we stand?"

"I have no idea. I thought we were still sitting."

Branigan stared at her again, seeing the straight face she wore but the mischief in her eyes. He grinned. "Got me on that one. Where is the investigation at this point?"

She pointed to Brendon. "Talk to him. He and Brady and Bradon are working on something, and they won't share what they've found." Her voice was pitched at a level that the men heard and began laughing. They had been the victims of her sense of humour all day, appreciating how she could see the sunny side of life even with what she had been through.

"Okay, so, we'll talk to them." Branigan raised his voice slightly. "Guys, just an update. Alice picked up Jason Lang around noon. She doesn't know that I saw it."

"Following him, were you?" Benen grinned at him. "Let's pray he stays there or is transferred elsewhere. I found out just about ten minutes ago that he's wanted for murder in Ottawa, and they are sending a team to take him back there."

"That's good news. It will remove at least one of the players." Baird stood, stretching, before he headed for the door. He was back in short order, followed by the ladies who carried trays of food. "Supper's here. Let's take a break and then go back at it for a while. Buckley?"

Buckley rose from where he had been sitting, a prayer for their meal rising, and then a prayer for each one in the room, specific to what they needed. Each had asked Buckley over time how he knew what to pray for them. He just shrugged and said God told him.

———

Finally, Barnabas rose. He had walked in just as they had started eating. He looked around at the men, thankful for each one, thankful for the ladies who were one by one joining the family, and making the men's hearts complete. His gaze rested on Branigan and Guenivere, knowing it was far from over for them, but not knowing how bad or dangerous it would get. He prayed for their safety, not knowing his prayers would be needed just a few days later.

*Chapter 16*

Waiting for Branigan to run back towards her after parking his truck, Guenivere shuddered, looking around, feeling something evil near her. Who or what is it, she wondered, her hand going out to grip the one Branigan extended to her. She caught his glimpse at her before he held the restaurant door open for her. It was Saturday afternoon, and he had begged her to come out for a meal with him. He promised to behave himself, a grin in place as she snorted at that idea, telling him he had no idea how to.

Finishing their meal, they lingered at the table, quiet conversation between them before Branigan rose and took her hand, tucking her tight to him as they walked back towards the truck. He settled her on the front seat and closed the door, his hand lingering for a moment on it as he watched her before he turned to walk around to his side.

The sound of running feet behind him had him turning, but not soon enough to prevent himself from slamming into the side of the truck. The breath driven from him, he stayed there as a hand shoved against his back. He couldn't see Guenivere but he had heard a sound from her.

Pulled back abruptly and then shoved into his back seat, a heavyset man following him, his assailant grabbed up the keys that had fallen and ran for the driver's side, pulling away almost before he had seated himself. Guenivere stared at him in horror, afraid to look back at Branigan. From where Branigan had been shoved, he could see her face and saw just when she determined she would not become a victim again. Just be careful, Guenivere, was his thought. They mean business. Don't do anything that would cause harm to come to you.

Branigan was with growing horror as the truck pulled to a stop in front of a locked gate. The man beside him slid out, unlocking the gate and shoving it open, shoving it closed again and setting the lock after the truck drove through, sliding back in beside him.

———

925

Branigan and Guenivere were forced from the truck this time, pushed forward towards the old mill and then up to the second floor. Branigan sought for a way out as they plodded up the steep stone steps and didn't see an opportunity to escape. He was shoved down on the floor, back to the wall and his hands bound behind him. He heard the whimper of fear from Guenivere as the same was done to her, prevented from rising by the man's hand on his head. He watched as she bent her knees and buried her head against them. Lord, we need Your help. No one will know where we are.

Guenivere felt the time passing in the coolness of the twilight that seeped into the building, causing her to shiver slightly, and by the lowering rays of the sun that she could glimpse through the broken and dirty windows, the overgrown trees helping to block the light. She heard the men arguing and knew they had stepped outside of the room, hearing the crunch of their feet on the debris and garbage that littered the stair landing and had tripped her as she stepped up. Branigan, she knew was near her. She could hear his breathing and his struggles, however quiet, to free his hands.

Branigan's hands twisted in their bonds, desperation in his movements to escape. He had to get Guenivere free, that was a given, he thought. But how? He had watched the men pace outside the room before one had thundered down the stairs. He heard the sound of his truck starting up and moving away. He knew the mill, knew how close to home he was, and knew the path back there better than most. Branigan had walked it many times, sometimes in anger, sometimes just in solitude, sometimes when he had heavy thinking to do, and other times just to find the peace from God that he only found in nature. He felt something touch his arm and jumped, looking down, finding that Guenivere had moved closer to him and rested her head against his arm.

"Are you okay?" He kept his voice as low as he could.

She nodded, her hair brushing against his chin. "I am. I know this place. It belongs to the Langs."

"It does? I've walked this way many times. I never knew."

"You wouldn't. They likely have it buried into a numbered company by now." She frowned, her eyes on the doorway. "There's only one out there now. We should be able to get away."

"We're tied up, remember?"  Branigan jumped as he felt her hands on his wrists, working to release the rope.  He rubbed at them when the rope dropped away before he rose and crept towards the door, eying it and the debris around it.  The second kidnappers had disappeared down the stairs.

"I think if we shut the door, we can block it."  Guenivere had followed him, her hand on his back.  "There's another way down that not many people know about.  We used to explore here when teens, partly to irritate Jason, partly because it was always good for ghost stories."

Branigan stared at her in disbelief.  "Ghost stories?"

She nodded, a quick grin on her face.  "Did you not do that?"

"No.  I had a paper route after school and spent other time mowing grass or shovelling snow.  Dad didn't want me sitting idle.  He wanted me to learn to help others."

"He did right.  Now, find something we can block the door with."  She reached past him to grab at the door, working it inch by inch to close it.  She stood against it when she was finished, watching as Branigan approached with a large branch.

"This should do, but we can move some other debris close to it.  There are some larger rocks I'll grab.  You go find the other entrance and make sure we can get down it."  He paused, his eyes on her face, before he reached to give her a quick kiss, then moving away from her, leaving Guenivere standing, staring after him, her hand on her mouth.

Waiting across the room for Branigan, Guenivere searched for anything they could use to defend themselves, finding an iron pipe about three feet long.  Her hand reached for it, and then paused, her face growing white as she backed away, right into Branigan, whose hands came up to balance her.  She spun, her hand grabbing for his as she pulled him away from the area and then to the secret door. She shoved him through, pulled the door closed behind her, even as she heard pounding at the room door.  Her hand pushed him down the broken stone steps and then out into the open where they were hidden by the overgrown shrubs and grass.  She pointed towards the Foundation building.

"That way.  We need to leave."

———

Branigan grabbed for her hand once more and pulled her with him, moving as silently and as rapidly as was possible until he reached the well-worn path he liked to walk. He slowed his steps, looking back over his shoulder before he looked down at her

"What was that all about? I saw you reach for the pipe and back away."

Guenivere nodded, her throat moving as she swallowed hard. "I had to. There were bones there, Branigan. And they were human."

He stopped suddenly, looking back once more before he wrapped her into a hug. "Bones? Come on. Let's run, if you can. I'm glad you're wear flat-soled shoes."

"I hadn't planned on running for our lives when I got dressed this morning. I thought a nice quiet lunch, a walk along the river or lakeshore. Not getting dumped in an old haunted mill and then finding a dead body and then running for our lives. Not once did I expect this." She was grumbling, she knew, seeing Branigan trying to hide his smile, and felt entitled to do just that.

"It's okay, my love. We're almost at the building now. About ten minutes or so." He stopped as she pulled at his hand, a question on her face.

"Branigan? What you did?" She looked up at him, her heart in her eyes for him to see.

He sighed, looking past her, biting at his lip, before he nodded. "I know. I shouldn't have kissed you. I couldn't resist."

Her hand on his cheek turned her to him. "It's okay. I just never expected it. Is that what I'm in for with you? The unexpected?"

He grinned, satisfied that she held no grudges against him doing that. "Yeah. Probably. More than likely."

"Real definite there, buster. Make up your mind." She spun and walked forward, leaving him staring after her, his mouth open before he grinned and ran to catch up with her, his hand reaching for hers, finding hers nestling into his.

———

I could get used to this, Lord, he thought.  Is she the one?  Is she the one Dad prayed for all those years?  The one he wove into stories for me at bedtime as a young boy?  The one he said would be my Proverbs 31 lady, my helpmeet?

Breck stared at Branigan's truck and then back towards where he saw Branigan and Guenivere emerging from the woods and shook his head. Now why, he thought, are they walking and from there? He walked rapidly towards them, as Branigan looked up and waved.

"Branigan? What on earth? You two are filthy!" Breck's voice held concern and a touch of amusement for a moment until he had a closer look at their faces and sobered. "What happened?"

"We were kidnapped, dumped in the old Lang mill, found skeletal remains, and then walked back here. Isn't that enough adventure for the day?" Guenivere was frustrated and scared at the same time. She brushed past Breck and headed for the back door of the building, intent on getting cleaned up. Branigan's hand stopped her.

"Just a sec, my love. I'll walk you in." His head turned as he eyed Breck. "She's right in what she said. We need to meet, all of us. And I would like to have Will or Dallas here, if Will lets him." He pointed to his truck. "He'll need a crime scene team to go over that. Did anyone see it drive in?"

"I have no idea. I just saw it as I saw you two walking back here." Breck shook his head, his phone out as he held up a hand for them to wait. A few minutes' conversation with Will and he approached them. "Will wants you to change but put your clothes into a clean garbage bag. Your shoes as well. He'll be out here in twenty."

"Twenty? As in twenty minutes? That doesn't leave a girl much time to get cleaned up, now does it?" Guenivere broke free from Branigan and ran for the building, leaving him staring after her in frustration.

"She's terrified, Branigan, frustrated, hurt." Breck's voice caught his ear as he walked away.

Branigan spun, his hand up. "I know. I know. I just wish it was different. Sometimes I really don't know how to help her, to give her the hope she needs."

"Only God can. Pray for her. Be there for her. I sense both of you have feelings for each other, and no, I'm not prying into that. You are prayed for, you and your lady, my friend. Go. Get cleaned up. We'll meet in the conference room. I think some of the guys are already in there." Breck watched as Branigan nodded before he too headed for the building and to clean up.

Watching Will later from where he stood leaning against the wall in the conference room, Branigan kept his arm tight around Guenivere. She had sought him out, tears in her eyes as she clutched the garbage bag holding her clothes. He had taken it from her, handed it to Alice who had approached and shaking his head at her, swept Guenivere into his arms and away to a corner of the room where it was quieter.

Guenivere finally turned, her eyes on Will as he approached, sighing to herself. Now, comes the fun.

"Guenivere? I know you've given your statement as has Branigan. Tell me."

She shook hard enough that her hair trembled before she gained control of herself. "I was looking for something to defend us. I had found that pipe. My hand was on it when I saw the bones." She stared in horror at her hand, Will watching her closely, before he looked around and beckoned Brady over.

Brady studied her and then Branigan, whose eyes were on his lady.

"Guenivere?" When she looked up at Brady, he gave her a grin. "Will's worried about you. He thinks you're shaking because you're afraid of him." As a paramedic, Brady had found that humour sometimes helped.

She glared at him for a moment before looking at Will. "No, it's that's place and that body. We used to go there as teens. It was our haunted house where we told ghost stories. I guess we shouldn't have but you know teenagers."

"I do, Guenivere. I do. Been out there a time or two myself in the last few years and felt the evil there. And that's what is there, evil. I just wanted to make sure you hadn't remembered anything else."

Guenivere's head shook as she frowned in concentration. "I don't think so. Branigan was piling stuff against the door to keep it closed and I had headed for the secret staircase. We had found it as kids and couldn't figure out why it was there."

"The mill's been there for years. Rumour had it that it was part of the Canadian route of the Underground Railway from the States."

Branigan nodded. "That would make sense. Bring them in after dark and then take them out again before it became light." He paused, a thought turning in his mind. "But who is that we found?

"Alice and Dallas are looking through missing persons' reports from here. If there is nothing there, they'll expand out to the other forces nearby. It will take a while, likely, to identify who it is. And the coroner thinks it's a male."

Guenivere paled even more. "Lang's father. He just disappeared a few years ago. No one could find him." She raised startled eyes. "Is that him?"

"That's a possibility we'll be looking at. We have a lot of footwork and investigations to do. Now, you two? Can you please stay out of trouble?" A grin covered his face for a moment before he walked away.

*Chapter 18*

A week later, Guenivere walked into her father's office, a sheaf of papers in her hand. She had started working out of the office again, shrugging when the protest went up. She simply stated that she was done running, that they could find her anywhere they wanted to, and had. So, why should she hide? Her mother had protested but she saw the glint of admiration in her father's eye. She knew she was scared of what could happen, but she refused to live her life in fear any more. Buckley had spent time with her over the past week, bringing up verses for her to study about trust, protection and hope. He said he had to add hope. That God had told him he had to.

Guenivere had smiled at Buckley, taken the list of verses, and had been drawn deep into a study of them. Branigan had joined her as he could, but he was run off his feet, working long hours on security systems. He had laughed but also grumbled that the jobs were cutting into their time together.

Branigan had stood silent when she told him that her decision was not to hide but to be out in the open, working back in the office. He had simply hugged her without a word, but his attitude had told her he trusted her instincts and that he would back her all the way.

Brett looked up as his daughter entered, momentarily frowning, before he reached for the papers.

"What do we have here?"

"Someone wants to set up a new contract. I'm not comfortable for some reason with them."

"Sit. Let's have a look." Brett read through the paperwork before he dropped it to his desk and sat back, studying his daughter. When did she grow up, Lord? It happened far too quickly, I think. "We'll have Branigan look into this. I agree. There is something off about it."

———

Guenivere nodded, before she groaned. "I know why it's so familiar. Leah called me the other day. She was putting out a warning to all of the trucking companies in the area, big and small. Her father had been approached and refused to take the contract."

"And it was this company?"

"I think so. I mean, the name is a little different than what she gave, but that's what they'd do, isn't it?"

"Change the name enough that we couldn't connect the two?" Brett looked up as he heard footsteps and Branigan appeared in the doorway, entering as Brett motioned him in. "That's exactly what they would do. Here, Branigan. You can look into this."

Branigan took the paperwork handed him, glancing through it briefly. "I would suggest you not take on this company for deliveries. We came across it actually last night when we were doing some research. Brendon red-flagged it for further investigation. What he had discovered was that the Langs are somehow involved with it."

"It all comes back to them, doesn't it? But who is behind them? None of them had the smarts to think this up." Guenivere was lost in thought as soon as she had spoken, her mind tracing the family and what friends she knew they had.

Branigan read back through the material, slower this time, his pen out to make notes before he looked up at Brett, who had gone back to his own paperwork.

"Brett? I think I know who this is. We've had dealings with someone who talks like this. I need to speak with Barnabas to be sure."

Brett nodded, pointing to the papers. "Take that with you. Now, you two. Off with you. We're closing up for the day." He rose, tidying away his work, and then following the young couple through the office, securing the door after setting the security system. "Don't come in tomorrow, Guenivere. I've closed the office for the day. Mom and I are going to that conference for the weekend. Douglas will handle the men in the warehouse."

"I can come in, Dad." She paused as he shook his head. "Okay, I'll work from home. I'll send Douglas anything that he may need."

The next afternoon, Guenivere wandered the gardens around the building, finally settling down in a seat near the rose garden. She looked around, feeling safe for a moment, but then feeling she was being watched. She rose, spinning around, and running for the building, hearing footsteps behind her that spurred her to run faster, reaching the back door, wrenching it open and then pulling it closed behind her before she ran for the stairs, heading for her own apartment. She heard the door open cautiously behind her and peeked over the railings, seeing the tallest of their kidnappers standing there, searching for her.

She covered her mouth to control her gasp before she sped on silent feet the rest of the way to her apartment, struggling to find the lock and then shutting the door and locking it behind her. She heard movement in the hall and peeked out the peephole, seeing the man trying the doors as he walked along. Her door rattled, even as her hand rested on the lock, as she drew in a deep breath, desperate to control her sobs. She slid to the floor, her head buried on her knees until she could control herself and then rose, determination in her stride and headed for the office.

Will hung up the phone, disturbed by his conversation with Guenivere, and then rose, heading to find Dallas, who was nowhere in the building. He finally sighed, reached for his keys and walked out, heading for the building to talk in person with Guenivere. He knew he should wait for Dallas, but it was too urgent.

Barnabas met him in the lobby, a frown on his face.

"Will? What's this I hear?"

Will nodded. "He followed her into the building and then went along the hallways, trying the doors. She just made it in to her own in time by the sounds of it."

"I don't like that, not one bit. Listen, the guys are gathering tonight for prayer and then to work on this. Brady heard from Emma and she was sending stuff by courier, which I think had just arrived. Can you stay?"

Will shook his head.  "I wish I could.  Call Dallas.  He's been assigned to this case.  Give him what you can, unless Emma's already sent it on to him."

"She has. Not as much as before, but she's still working on it, she said.  She's put Jace, I think she called him, on it full time."

"Good. Now I need to find Guenivere and have a chat with her, then direct her to Dallas.  This is getting old, you know."

Barnabas grinned for a moment as Will walked away before he looked around and saw Branigan standing near him, puzzlement on his face.

"Barnabas?  Will is here?"

"He is."  Barnabas pointed to the chairs near the one fireplace. "Let's have a seat.  Will wants to talk to Guenivere before you do."

"What happened today?"  Branigan was torn.  He wanted to hear what happened, but he wanted to find his lady and ensure that she was okay.

"Apparently, Guenivere went wandering in the gardens and found the ladies' favourite bench near the rose garden.  She says she felt someone watching her and ran for the building, hearing footsteps behind her.  It was the tallest of your kidnappers."  Barnabas paused, anger growing in him.  "He followed her into the building through the back door.  He went along the hallways, checking for an unlocked door.  She could have disappeared and no one would have known."

Branigan sat back, his face stern and sober, as he mulled over what he had been told.  "We can't lock her away.  She needs to have some freedom.  And no one can be with her all the time."  He sighed. "Now, what do we do?"

"We meet tonight and come up with some plans.  Hopefully, your lady will be agreeable."

"She might but she is also finding her voice as she brings hope back into her life.  Be prepared to have a battle or two over this."

Branigan looked up that evening, from the paperwork he had been studying, the schematics of the system he had designed for Brett. They were his plans, Joseph had followed them, but somehow, someone had tampered with them. He suspected someone in the company. He rose, heading for Benen and with a quiet word, asked if he would investigate a name for him. Benen looked startled and then nodded.

Branigan stood back, watching his friends, from all over the country, and thought how well God had chosen each one to become part of the Foundation family. He paused to pray for each individual man, knowing some faced danger every day in their employment. He paused as he came to Barnabas, for some reason a heavier burden weighing him down for his friend and employer. Why, he had no idea, he only knew he had to pray for him.

Breck watched Branigan closely. He did that with the men, assessing who needed time away, who needed someone to talk to, who just needed someone to stand with them. This time, Branigan needed that, to have someone just standing with him, not saying a word.

Branigan looked up as Breck's hand rested briefly on his shoulder.

"Branigan, how are you doing in all this? Do you need to talk to someone?"

"Actually, Breck, I'm doing okay. Burnie and I have talked, thanks." He looked around. "A lot of activity going on, isn't there?"

"There is. It seems to get busier each time one of us goes through this." He paused, his eyes on the doorway. "Guenivere is here." His hand stopped Branigan from moving towards her. "Wait. She's here to talk to someone. Let her do that first. She knows where you are."

Branigan sighed. "She does. This is hard, you know. Standing back when I want to make it all better for her. But to move in and take over would do her a disservice. She needs to learn to have that hope in God and that trust, doesn't she's?"

"She does. She has more than any of us realized. She called me after she called Will, demanding to know how she was to stay safe if the monster, as she called him, could get into the building and follow her right to her apartment. She's correct in asking that. Security is working on something but if that door had been locked or she had had to key in a passcode, she would not be standing here today."

"That's what frightens me. We seem no further ahead than we were." He looked up as Will spoke his name. "Will, I thought you had left."

"I was in my car when the coroner called. I spoke with Dallas. He'll be out to go over more of the details, but we have a name on the skeleton Guenivere found." He jumped a bit as a sound came from beside him.

Branigan reached for his lady, drawing her close, his eyes back on Will. "Who was it?"

Guenivere spoke. "It was Jason's father, wasn't it?"

Will nodded. "Your guess from the start was correct, Guenivere. We don't know how he died at this point. There was not a lot of evidence that the team could find. When we catch the men after you, I am sure they'll be able to tell us. Stay as safe as you two can. Guenivere, please do not wander around too much on your own. Each one of these men in here have come to myself and Barnabas, offering to escort you where you need to go. That is, if Branigan is not available." He grinned at the look she shot him. "I'm off. Dallas said he'd be out tomorrow."

Branigan began to shake with suppressed laughter at the look of affront on his lady's face, causing her to turn and glare at him in turn before she broke away and walked over to where Brennen was at work, sitting beside him and drawing him out on what he had found.

Breck had watched with amusement, finally grinning openly as he watched the dialogue between the two.

<hr>

"You shouldn't have laughed, you know."

Branigan's grin widened. "I know. I am going to have to apologize for that."

"Nope, not apologize. Grovel would be a good way to go."

"And why would Branigan have to grovel?" Brody spoke from Branigan's other side.

"He laughed at something Will said, tried to hide it and got found out."

Brody grinned. "Then I agree. Grovel it is. Listen, I have found some information on Douglas that I think we need to look further at. It could be a plant, but we need to verify it."

"That bad?" Breck questioned.

"I can't tell for sure. Not until I know for sure it's correct. Listen, I'm off. I have to be on the road by three tomorrow morning. Call me if you need me." He walked away, leaving the two men exchanging glances before Branigan spoke.

"I would hate to think it was Douglas."

"Me, too. He's such a part of their family, but as such would be a good plant. We're looking at all the drivers and the warehouse staff as well."

"I am sure you are. I'm off to draw my lady away and grovel. See you later." He walked towards Guenivere, finding her on her feet, heading his way, taking the hand he had outstretched to her.

Once outside the conference room, they walked slowly to the lobby, finding seats on a couch. Branigan's arm drew her close.

"So, how much grovelling are you planning on doing?" She smirked at him until he laughed.

"Let me guess. Brennen spilled the beans."

"He did. He said the other five men have had to do that, and you thought it was amusing. So it was only fair that you had to." She laughed at the remembrance of the look on Brennen's face before she sobered. "What all did Will have to say?"

"Not much, other than what he said." Branigan grew silent, content to have his lady love in his arms, her hands wrapped around his. The silence grew, both not eager to speak.

"Did you know that Fynn asked Brady to marry her?"

Branigan grinned at the remembrance. "I do. Buckley was there, but kept quiet about it until the two had told us. He doesn't let her forget, you know."

"I can see that. He has quite the sense of humour, needed in his job. He has no one he's dating?"

"None of us did. Not until we met the lady we want to spend the rest of our lives with." His voice died away as he groaned to himself. *Did I really go and say that, Lord? I'm ready for the next step, but I am not sure that Guenivere is.*

Guenivere had been listening closely to his words, her mind stilling as she heard the present tense in his sentence, her heart rising in hope. She finally twisted in his arms so she could look in his face, finding him staring across the room, a contrite expression on his face.

"Did you mean that, Branigan?" Her voice was quiet enough he barely heard her words.

He looked down at her. "I did. I just didn't mean to say them. Not yet."

"But why? Don't you know that gives me hope, hope that I will have someone in my life for the rest of it? Lang took that hope away from me for so long, but you have brought it back. You and God."

Branigan studied her face, drinking in her beauty, seeing her heart once more in her eyes.

"I just thought you needed time. Time to learn to live with the hope I see rising in you."

"But don't you see, you're the one who has helped me do that. You didn't stop asking, looking out for me, taking care of me in a way that no one else ever has."

"I don't want gratitude, Guenivere."

"You will have my gratitude but you're correct when you state that you want to spend the rest of my life with me, is that not true?" At his nod, her hands reached for his. "Don't you see? That's my hope, Branigan. My hope that drives me, keeps me going, helps me to trust God more and more. You have helped me to see it wasn't me, wasn't my fault, that I can and must let go of the past and reach for God and trust Him to lead, no matter what I go through."

Two days later, Branigan stood in the hallway outside of Guenivere's apartment, staring at the open door, the meal he had picked up for them to share dropping to the floor. He reached to touch the door, nodding. He was not seeing anything. The door was open. He walked cautiously in and through the apartment, even checking out the balcony, not finding his love. He spun in a circle, his hand on his head, trying to think of where she would be. She had been adamant that she would be at home. She was working on the contract renewals for some of their clients and was determined to have them done that day.

Blair stopped on his way by, staring down at the bag on the floor before he picked it up, tapping at the door and entering.

"Guenivere? Are you here?" He seemed startled to have Branigan appear at once. "Where's Guenivere?"

"Not here, and she should be. Something is off. She wouldn't have just walked away. Not now."

"No?" Blair's hand drew Branigan from the apartment. "For now, we need to call it in. Come. Sit with me in our apartment. Devaney may know something."

Branigan perked up. "Yes, she might. What are we waiting for?" He headed on a run down the hallway, not waiting for Blair.

Blair dropped his head, shaking it, before he headed for his own home, walking in to find Devaney staring at Branigan, her mouth open.

"No, I haven't seen her today. None of us have. I spoke with her around nine, to see if she wanted to come for lunch, but she said she had contracts that she wanted to get done. Isn't she home?"

"She's not, and the door is wide open. That's not her."

"No, it's not." Devaney spun, reaching for her phone, calling Alice. "Alice? Are you on duty? You are. Good. Listen, Branigan just found Guenivere's door open and no sign of her. He walked through, he said, and then Blair brought him here. No, sorry. Branigan ran for here, Blair following at a slower pace." She made a face at Blair as he shook a finger at her. "Sure. No. We'll be here. Do I need to call it in? Oh, okay, you'll do that? Sure. Come, find us. Branigan?" Her eyes sought the other man, finding him standing, hands on his head, staring at the floor, devastation on his face for a moment. "No, we'll make sure he stays put. Thank you."

Devaney set her phone down, her eyes on Branigan before she glanced at Blair and nodded at the question on his face. She approached Branigan, a hand on his arm bringing him back from wherever it was he had wandered off to.

"Alice is working tonight. She'll come out. She said she'd bring a team with her to search the apartment."

"Thank you." He looked up as Blair handed him a mug of coffee and then with a sigh, shoved him down into a chair. "Where do we search, Blair?"

"For now, we don't. We let Alice and her crew work it through. Then, we spread out." Blair sat, laying his phone on the table. "I sent out a group text. The guys will meet in the conference room. The ladies will meet here. It's our standard plan."

Branigan nodded. "I know. We decided we needed that after you and Devaney. It just doesn't make it any easier, you know."

"No, it doesn't but it helps to have them involved. Buckley responded that he'd make his way here. He was driving back home from that funeral two hours away. He thought he'd be here in about thirty minutes."

"Then, he won't have eaten." Devaney was on her feet, her hand on the fridge door, before her head turned, watching her friend before looking at Blair, who simply shook his head once more.

"Branigan, do you want anything to eat?" Devaney had to ask twice to raise his head up from the folded arms he had laid it on. He *looks tired,* she thought, *tired and worn out. The accident took from his strength. Worrying about Guenivere does not help.*

Branigan took a moment to process what she had asked. "No, I don't think so. Just coffee is fine." He didn't look up, didn't see

———

the sandwich that she set in front of him, reaching automatically for it after Blair had prayed.

Blair and Devaney shook their heads at one another. He's working on autopilot, Blair thought. That is not good. He rose as he heard a quiet tap at the door and stepped outside, not surprised to find both Will and Dallas there.

"Branigan?" Will's voice held concern, concern for Branigan as Guenivere's boyfriend but also concern for a friend.

"He's inside. We managed to get him to eat, but he's not really aware of what he is doing." He looked down the hall past them. "What have you found?"

"They've just gotten started." Dallas turned for a moment. "Do you know who she may have talked to today?"

"Devaney said they spoke around nine. I can't say if she's talked to anyone else. If her phone is there, that should show you."

"It is, but it is password secured." Dallas nodded at the door. "Would Branigan know her password?"

Blair nodded. "Try his first or last name. That might work. Or the town in PEI that he's from."

Dallas thanked him and walked back down the hall. Will stood for a moment, lost in thought. "I need to speak with Branigan, but I have to let him speak to Dallas first. Where can we talk, Blair?"

"Head for the conference room. Most of the guys will be there. The ladies will be heading our way as is Buckley, when he gets in." He watched as Alice approached and quietly asked Will to come with her.

His arm around Lena, Brett began to shake his head as he stared at Will, not believing what he had to say.

"She can't have disappeared. I talked to her about two, going over some details on one of the contracts. She had that one and one other to finish, she said."

"As I said, her door was wide open when Branigan arrived there tonight. We have searched her apartment and are in the process of searching the building and then the surrounding buildings. We'll start a search of the grounds in the morning, bringing in the K-9 units."

"But how, Will? How could she just disappear? She wouldn't have walked out on her own, not knowing that Branigan would be there. She was looking forward to their meal together. They did that every night and then went for walks." Lena's hand covered her mouth for a moment. "I talked to her before work started, and she didn't seem any different than she had."

Will nodded. "Thanks, Brett. Lena. I'm heading back to the Foundation. If you two want to come, Barnabas said he'd make arrangements for you." He paused, a thought crossing his mind. "Where is Douglas?"

"Douglas? Haven't you heard? He was walking across a street down town over the lunch hour and was hit. The car disappeared."

Will paused, a thought crossing his mind. "I'll look into that. I'm on my way back. I just wanted to speak with Douglas, to see if he had thought of anything else that he could remember."

"We talked this morning, Will. He was waiting for me when I got there. He's so distraught. That could be why he didn't see the car. He and his wife, as you know, lost their daughter at age two. Guenivere sort of helped to fill the emptiness for them."

"I remember, and I understand." Will walked away, heading for his vehicle, deep in thought. He slid behind the wheel, but didn't drive off. Something kept his there, his eyes searching through darkness before he was out of his car, running towards the dark form he could see, tackling the younger man and taking him to the ground, before he slapped handcuffs on him. He stood, towering over the man, the man's wallet in his hand, before he reached for his phone and called it in.

Will reached down and yanked the man to his feet, a little rougher than he normally would have.

"Okay, John Jones. Up you go. I have a ride coming for you, and a nice detective to speak with you. I want to know why you were sneaking up on this house. You're not from this neighbourhood, so it really makes me suspicious of your motives."

Dallas sat back, staring at Will. "You found him where?"

"At Brett's. I had stopped by there and something wouldn't let me leave. I found him sneaking up on the house. He had a knapsack with him. I'll leave it for you to talk to him. I'm heading back out."

Dallas stood, following Will down the hallway. "No word?'

Will shook his head. "Not a word. No ransom demand. No note asking for Branigan or Brett to do something." He pulled out his phone, checking the number. "Let me get this and then if we need to talk, come find me. If not, you know where I'll be. I hope we can at least keep the media down to a dull roar."

Dallas gave a slow nod of his head. "It's funny. They would usually be all over this, but Jim, the news editor from the local station, called. They have all agreed to keep it low key and as quiet as they can. The Foundation has done too much good in our community, he said, for them to do them any harm."

"That's a relief. If they keep it low key, then it can be controlled." He walked away, Dallas watching him before he turned, heading for one of the interrogation rooms and John Jones.

Branigan stirred as he felt a hand on his shoulder and looked up from the chair he had slumped down into, not wanting to leave the conference room and the work that was going on there. He started to rise, meeting Brett's eyes and then kept his seat. Brett sat next to him, his face buried in his hands for a moment.

"Brett?" Branigan's voice was quiet, just loud enough that Brett heard him. "Have you heard anything?"

"No." Brett looked up, his chin resting on his hand, the other hand rubbing at the table. "Will stopped by. As he was leaving, he tackled someone sneaking towards our house. I haven't heard yet why or who."

Branigan shook his head. "I wish I knew where to look for Guenivere. I talked to her about three, just to find out what she wanted for her meal. She sounded fine, just like herself."

"And you got here, what about five or so?"

"That's correct." Branigan looked up to find Dallas sliding into a chair at the table, his notepad and pen out. "Dallas?"

Dallas shook his head even as he gave a somber smile. "Just a few questions, Branigan. Brett. I need to clarify something." He turned to Brett. "You said Guenivere was working on contracts?"

Brett nodded. "She was. We have some new clients that we had to have the contracts ready for, and a couple whose contracts were expiring. She always has everything ready well ahead of time, says we can't run a fair or reliable business if we don't." He looked down at his folded hands. "She had emailed me all of them by late this afternoon. I can check the timing of that for you, but when I checked around five, they were waiting for me."

Branigan nodded. "I received a text message around four, just to say she had them done and had some other work waiting." He paused, a thought crossing his mind. "Did she send that text though? How do we know for sure?"

"We don't, not until we find her and can ask her." Dallas looked down at his notes. "I think that's all for now. I will have other questions as we go along." He looked up, assessing the two men he was with. "We'll find her for you. That's a promise."

———

*Chapter 22*

A day passed by without any word, then another and another until two weeks went along and the calendar flipped to a new page. Branigan grew thin and white, the shadows under his eyes creeping darker and darker. He slept little, wandering the fields and forest around the building, searching through their town, moving to other towns and villages in the area. To no avail. He could not find her, no matter how he looked.

Brett and Lena were almost constant companions of the men and ladies of the building, helping to research, trying their best to stay positive but failing. Brett had privately told Barnabas that he had taken Lena to their physician the day before after he came home and found her collapsed on the floor, unconscious. Branigan had spent time with them, and with Douglas. He had searched around the property Brett had his business on to no avail as well. Guenivere had simply disappeared.

His friends were spending every moment they could helping to search, to research, to talk to people. Buckley and Brendon had headed to the streets of the town, talking to everyone and anyone they could. The Foundation board had approached Brett and offered to put up a reward, if it came to that. He had looked at his fellow members and with tears in his eyes and broken words, had thanked them.

Brennen stood for a moment, those two weeks later, his eyes on Branigan as he sat in the lobby, a mug of tea at his side on the table. He had stopped drinking coffee, just why, he couldn't tell them. He approached his friend, dropping into a chair near him, waiting, needing to talk to him, but unsure of how to do just that.

"Brennen? You have news?" Branigan rubbed at his gritty, red eyes.

"I do. I'm just not sure if it's accurate or not. Someone approached me today, one of the down and outers that Buckley

948

ministers to.  He handed me a paper and then took off.  On it was an address.  I looked it up.  It's in Ennis' town."

"We've searched there, haven't we, without finding anything?"

"We have, but somehow, this is different.  I want to go take a look, without alerting anyone.  I think there's a leak somewhere in the investigation, but I can't prove it."

Branigan sat up, an alert look on his face.  "I know.  It's like someone is watching us, knowing what we know, and then staying one or two steps ahead of us."  He looked down.  "I trust Will, Dallas and Alice but someone else is involved."

"I know.  I'm trying to determine who.  Emma's been in touch.  She has some names to run, she said, something she picked up in her investigation.  She'll talk to Barnabas and Will, she said, when she has more information."

"She does?  Good."  Branigan turned his mug around and around on the counter.  "Brennen, are you heading over to Ennis' town?"

"I am.  Listen.  I talked to Fynn's cousin, Eric.  He and his captain are willing to help, on their own time.  I told him to talk to Barnabas, see where they would fit the best."

"That's good."  Branigan gave a huge, down to his toes, sigh as he laid his head back on the couch, slouching down once more.  "I want her home, Brennen."  His phone vibrated against his side and he ignored it, finally pulling it out with a muttered comment when it kept vibrating.  He squinted at it, not recognizing the number, before he answered.

"Hello?  Hello?  Is someone there?"  He waited, hearing soft rustling in the background.  "Who's there?"

"Branigan?"  The voice was ever so faint, but ever so dear to his heart.  "Branigan?  Come get me.  Please?  I need you to come get me."

"Guenivere?  Oh, my love, where are you?"  He was on his feet, heading for the door, Brennen beside him, pointing to his own truck.  "Keep talking to me.  We're coming, but I need to know where you are."

"It's dark, Branigan. It's dark. I can see the sky above me, but I can't climb up. Please, Branigan? Come get me?" Her voice died away, but Branigan could hear the soft whisper of her breathing, and then her soft sobs. It tore at his heart, hearing her but not being able to comfort her.

Brennen's phone was in his hand, his voice quiet as he listened to Branigan, asking to be put through to either Dallas or Will.

"Dallas? Listen. You have Branigan's phone number. Is it possible for you to trace it?" He listened. "I know. It's a long shot, but he's on his phone right now with Guenivere. She can't tell us where she is but it sounds as if she may be underground or down in a hole or well." He listened, his eyes shooting to Branigan. "Over there? Sure. I'll head that way." His phone hit the cup holder in the console, as he drove away rapidly, halting briefly as he met Brady and Bradon coming back in. He could see Bradon's dog, Kade, in the back seat, his chin on Bradon's shoulder.

"Brady. Follow me. Do you have your emergency kit with you?"

"Always." Brady ducked his head to stare through the window at Branigan, watching as his friend spoke quietly on the phone. "What's up?"

"Guenivere. Branigan's on the phone with her. She called, asking him to come find her."

"What?" Bradon leaned over the console to look at Brennen. "How?"

"We are not sure. It is just so bizarre. I asked Dallas to try and trace her call, but he wasn't sure if he could. She seems to be underground or in a hole or something."

"The old mill. There's an abandoned well near there." Bradon shared a look with Brady. "Let's try there. It all seems to come back to that property. Did we ever research that?"

"Burnie muttered something yesterday about it. I think he was." Brennen drove off as quickly as he could, Brady spinning his wheel to turn his truck and follow.

"Where's Doc today?" Bradon's voice broke through the silence in the cab.

―――

"At home. Call him. We may need him."

Bradon was already dialing Doc, speaking rapidly, hearing the sound of surprise in Doc's voice. He pocketed his phone. "He said he'd grab some supplies from the infirmary, including the backboard and collar."

"I don't like the thought of that, but we may well need them."

The trucks parked, the men shot out of them, Kade milling around before he caught a scent and tugged at his leash, pulling Bradon with him.

"Has he picked up something?" Brady shouldered his bag and ran after them, Brennen and Branigan following on his heels.

"He's picked up something. He has that ability to learn the scent of every one of us. Guenivere spent time with us, and Kade had taken to her. I pray that's who he's picking up."

Fifteen minutes later, they slid to a halt, Kade on his belly, head hanging over a hole in the ground, a soft woof echoing back. Bradon reached for the large flashlight he was handed and carefully knelt, aiming the beam downwards. His heart caught for a moment, seeing that the hole was at least fifteen or more feet deep before the light flashed across something. He moved the beam back and a sudden yell from him startled the three men.

"Bradon?" Branigan hardly dared to breathe.

"She's there, Branigan. Kade found her. Now to get down to her." He stood, his hand reaching to grip his friend's shoulder. "I can't see if she's hurt, it's deep enough."

Branigan nodded, reaching for the harness Brady had pulled from his pack. "I'm going down, Brady. I have to."

Brady hesitated, knowing that he should be the one, that if Guenivere was hurt, he had to be the one to bring her up but he didn't have the heart to say no.

"Okay, you go down. Let me know how she is. If I have to, I pull you back up and go down myself."

Branigan stared at him, his hand on the harness that Brady had not released. "That's fine. Just let me go."

Bradon stopped their conversation with a simple statement. "First, we pray. We need to do that, guys."

Branigan hesitated when they were finished, torn between wanting to go down to Guenivere but knowing that he was not the best person. He turned to Brady, finding his friend watching him intently. He stared down at the harness he held in his hand before he thrust it back at Brady.

"You go. You have the training and are used to this. I don't. God help me, I don't want to hurt her, not if I can help it."

Brady's hand was out to grasp the harness, hearing the quiet murmurs of agreement from the other two. "You're sure?"

Branigan gave a quick nod. "I am. Go, before I change my mind."

Brady was into the harness, the rope attached and then tied off on a nearby tree. They had to call Kade back from the edge, Bradon gripping his leash shortly. He was not moving, his whole body seemed to say, not when a friend was down there. He needed to help, his quiet woof said.

Brady dropped to the edge of the hole before his body twisted and he began to feel his way down, hearing bits of dirt and debris falling. The others stayed away from the edge, not wanting to cave it in. Branigan's gloved hands helped to feed the rope, hearing Brady call that he was on the bottom.

Their arrival had disturbed the quietness of the morning, sending the creatures and birds to hiding before they once more came out, their eyes on the men, before they decided that they meant them no harm. The three men had their focus on the rope and Brady, not seeing the man who had approached and then withdrawn to the shadows of the nearby trees, curses coming in from him. He felt for his phone, not finding it. He cursed once more as his eyes sought out Branigan, blaming him for the loss. He had no idea where it was but if they were here, how did they find her? She wasn't to be found. Not yet. Maybe not ever.

Doc approached the three men, Brennen turning as he heard him and walking towards him in a rapid manner.

"Doc?" Brennen reached for the backboard. "We found her. Brady's down in the well with her."

"He is? I thought Branigan would have been."

"He wanted to, but he stopped himself, telling Brady he didn't have the training that Brady had. It was very hard on him to stop himself."

Doc looked behind him. "Barnabas was rounding up the rest of the men, meeting in the conference room. I told him we would call once we knew something." Doc's phone was in his hand. "Barnabas? Good news." A relieved smile broke across Doc's face. "Brennen says they found her. Brady's with her. What's that? No. We don't know much yet. I think Dallas is on the way. Buckley said he would call him, when I saw him just as I was leaving. Good. We'll let you know once we have more information."

His phone pocketed, Doc looked past Brennen. "Branigan?"

"He's relieved, Doc, but there is that uncertainty right now. We don't know if she's hurt or how bad, or even how she got in there."

"No, we don't. Here's Dallas and his team."

Dallas approached cautiously, hope rising but he refused to let it rise all the way until he was sure.

"Brennen? Is she here? I tried to trace her call but couldn't."

"She is, Dallas. I was telling Doc that Brady is down with her."

They turned, walking rapidly back towards the well, seeing Bradon leaning cautiously over, his hand gripped in Branigan's to keep his balance. He looked up and then spoke rapidly to Brady.

"Doc? Brady wants the backboard and collar sent down. He doesn't think she has any injury but he's not wanting to take any chances."

"Send it down. Dallas, are paramedics on the way?"

"They are. I sent in a call once you confirmed she was here. They're ten minutes out."

Bradon looked around, relief on his face to see Doc. Branigan pulled him back from the edge and turned as well, surprise on his face to see Dallas and Doc both.

"Doc? Dallas?"

"We're here, Branigan. How be you move back for now? The paramedics were right behind me and I think they were sending firefighters as well just in case they were needed in the extraction." Dallas' hand on his arm kept Branigan in place before he moved back. "What can you tell me? Brennen said you had a call."

"I did, Dallas. She called me. I wasn't going to answer as I didn't know the number. She asked me to come and find her, that it was dark where she was." Branigan squinted up at the sky, watching as twilight was moving in. "We need to call Brett and Lena."

"Alice is taking care of that. She'll have them taken to the hospital for now." Dallas looked around, watching close before he was off on the run, heading for the trees, the officer approaching them heading his way instead.

The men turned, a frown on each of their faces, before they exchanged glances and then headed for the well.

Brady stood at the bottom, looking up with relief as he heard Doc's voice.

"Doc? You're here. Backboard and collar?"

"On the way down. How is she?"

"She's been talking. She is angry, I can tell you that much. I need help down here but there is not enough room. Let me see what I can do."

They could hear Brady's voice quietly speaking to Guenivere and on occasion, what they hoped was her voice responding. Finally, a tug came on the rope attached to the backboard.

"I'm ready to come up. What I need is to be pulled up at the same time as Guenivere, that way I can help to stabilize her a bit."

"Will do. We're ready." Brennen looked around at the men gathered, his friends, Doc, and the waiting paramedics as well as the crime scene team Dallas had brought with him. We have almost too many volunteers, he thought.

Branigan's breath came out in a rush as Guenivere appeared at the top of the well and hands reached out for the backboard she was strapped to and then for Brady who was on his knees beside her almost before she was on the ground, Doc on the other side, the two paramedics who had been summoned with them. He waited, edging closer, his eyes on his beloved's face.

Doc looked up, and gave a grim smile. "She's alive, Branigan. How serious she is, I can't tell you yet. We need to get her to the hospital. Ready, fellows?"

Willing hands reached to raise her as the men lifted her and then turned to walk away. Guenivere roused, her eyes shooting around in fear, before she spied Branigan, a hand raising for him to grasp. He walked beside her, almost tripping over his own feet, Brennen's hand on his shoulder steadying him.

Doc followed, in quiet conversation with Brady, before he looked up. Surprise overcame him as he saw Dallas and the officer returning with their prisoner. A closer look at the man drew a startled exclamation from Doc.

"Trevor Lang?"

"It is, Doc. He was in the woods waiting. In fact, it was his cell phone that Guenivere used. I did find out that much." Dallas looked with almost anger on the man. "He has a lot to say."

"I want my lawyer." Lang's mouth snapped shut and he refused to say another word, not even when he was shoved forward to walk back towards the road.

Brett and Lena almost ran into the Emergency Department, looking for someone, anyone, who could tell them how Guenivere was. Will had appeared at their doorway, Brett having come home early, just to be with Lena. She was grieving, he knew, certain that they would never see their daughter again. They had looked at Will in shock, Lena's hand going to her mouth, Brett's arms around her before Will hurried them out to and to his car, speeding away with an escort, hoping to arrive at the same time the ambulance did with Guenivere.

Branigan spun as he felt a hand on his back, Lena reaching to hug him, holding on tighter and longer than she normally would, stepping back only when Brett nudged her to, so he could hug Branigan. He knew, not so much from what his daughter had said but what she hadn't said, that Branigan meant the world to her and would be part of their family at some point.

Will directed them to seats out of the way, a wall of men standing in the way to prevent onlookers from gawking at them, and that would happen, he knew. Brett sank into a chair, suddenly weary, before he looked up at Branigan.

"Branigan? What happened? Will said she called you. How? She didn't have her phone."

"She did. I'm not sure how she got ahold of one but she called. I can't tell you how I felt when I realized it was her and she was alive. Brennen spoke with Dallas who mentioned the well near the mill. We tracked her there, thanks to Kade, and the rest, I guess, is really all that matters. Brady went down, brought her up. Doc's with her right now."

Branigan's head drooped, the sudden release of the tension he had been under drawing all his strength at that moment as a huge wave of fatigue washed over him. He heard a faint call before the world darkened. He roused to find a paramedic crouching down in front of him, Brady's partner in fact.

“Branigan?  You okay, man?  You almost face planted on the floor.”

“I guess.  It’s the relief.”

“That would do it.”  Patrick shared a look with Will before he checked Branigan’s vitals.  “You seem alright now.  I would suggest something sweet.”  He held up a hand at the face Branigan pulled.  “You need it.  Your blood pressure likely dropped and I am sure your blood sugar has as well.  You haven’t been eating, now have you?”  As Branigan shook his head, the paramedic reached for the bottle of juice, uncapped it, and shoved it into his hand.  “Drink.  I’ll go see what I can find out for you.  Brady was through but he said he’d stay with your lady as long as they would let him.  Doc as well.”

Branigan nodded, shame filling him for his reaction at that point.  He felt Lena’s arm around him, a mother’s arm that he could not remember having felt in his life, he thought, and appreciated that his lady’s mother was taking him in.  He looked up finally as he heard footsteps and then was on his feet walking towards Brady, an unspoken question on his lips.

Brady pointed to the outside doors, steering Branigan that way.  Patrick had found him, had told him Branigan needed some air, and Doc had shooed him away, stating he would stay with Guenivere until she had been assessed.  They wouldn’t kick him out, he declared, not out of the department he worked in.

Branigan paced away from Brady, who stood, feet planted near the door, watching and assessing his friend.  He turned back, paused, and then approached.

“Brady?”

“She’s dehydrated for one thing, Branigan.  Scrapes.  Bruises.  They’ll do X-rays to look for broken bones.”

“Thank you.”  Branigan’s head dropped back as he stared up at the sky, dark now, the moon and stars hiding intermittently behind the scudding clouds, driven by the wind that was picking up.  “Did she say anything?

Brady groaned to himself, knowing that Branigan just had to ask that, now didn’t he, Lord?  How do I answer when I still have to give my statement?  This is one time, Lord, I would really appreciate You speaking for me.

"Not a whole lot, Branigan.  She didn't seem to understand where she was, being somewhat that disoriented.  She did ask about you."

"I don't care about me.  Is she okay, that's all I want to know."

"She should be.  Brett and Lena will go back but I know you'll be able to.  Doc will make sure of that."

Branigan nodded.  "Did I hear that Dallas had arrested someone?"

"That's what Doc said.  I didn't see him, so I can't say for sure.  He'll be around at some point, likely."  He turned as he heard the door swish open behind him and Brett appeared.

"Brett?"  Branigan's voice held hope?"

"Guenivere is in X-ray right now.  We were able to just have a moment or two with her.  Doc said he'll get you back when she's in a room."  Brett paused, exhaustion draining him.  "She's okay, Branigan.  They don't think any broken bones or a concussion.  Just dehydration."  He looked around before he looked at Branigan.  "I just don't understand the phone."

"Whoever it was likely dropped it.  I'm sure he's missing it by now."  Branigan gave a sudden grin.  "Is this one of those times Buckley would call a God moment?"

The other two men laughed for a moment before a voice spoke beside them.

"That I would, and yes, it was."  Buckley stood there, exhaustion evident in his face.  He had not slept much, spending the time he was unable to in prayer for his friends.  "This is getting old, guys.  I thought we were told no more adventures."

"That we were, but we just don't seem to be able to avoid them."  Branigan paced away, his eyes on a car that was hovering on the street.

The driver saw Branigan coming and sped away, leaving a dark streak of rubber on the pavement.  Branigan stood, his eyes narrowed, unable to get a really good description of the car or driver, and certainly not the license plate number.

*Chapter 25*

A day later, Branigan perched on the arm of the couch in Guenivere's living room, watching as she paced, albeit slowly. She had adamantly refused to go home, not saying why, but he had read the fear she had tried to hide from everyone. She's afraid, isn't she, Lord? Afraid to bring the men to her family. But that's too late. It's already happened. When they told her, that brought it home to the Danbys.

"Sweetheart? Don't you think you should sit?" He rose, stepping into her path and stopping her with his hands on her upper arms before he pulled her into a hug. She stiffened and tried to pull away, before she relaxed against him, her arms coming around to hug him back.

"I'm so afraid, Branigan. So deeply afraid."

"I know you are. We need to talk about what happened and why you're afraid." He turned her to the couch, sitting and drawing her down with him, an arm wrapped around her to hold her tight to him. "What did he threaten you with?"

She shook her head. "It wasn't a him. It was a woman. I know the voice but I can't think of who it was." Her head tilted to look up at him. "I never told you last night what happened. Dallas was there so late to get my statement and then they gave me something to sleep. I hated that."

"I know." His fingers twisted at the ring he had placed on her finger earlier that day, stating simply that he loved her dearly and when she had been gone he didn't want to live. Would she be his? She had simply nodded, exhaustion taking her voice.

"I need to talk. There are some things I couldn't tell Dallas. I have to at some point, but I needed to talk to you first." She stared up at him, distraught, before he leaned over and kissed her.

———

960

"Talk to me, my love. Tell me what happened. I came home that afternoon, with our supper, found your door open and you gone."

Guenivere nodded. "It was. I still don't understand how they got in the building." She frowned for a moment. "They must have come in through the back. That's how they took me out." She looked horrified. "Are the security guys in on it?"

"No. That was Barnabas' first thought but they weren't. Go on."

Guenivere stared ahead at the far wall, gathering her thoughts.

"Okay, so. I was working on those contracts and had just finished them. I think it was just before four. I had walked to the kitchen to make another cup of tea or something like that, I wasn't sure what I actually wanted. I didn't hear the door open. Just felt that I wasn't alone. I didn't get a chance to look around. They slapped a cloth of some kind over my mouth. I struggled to get away, but couldn't escape the hands holding me. I must have passed out at that point, because the next thing I know I'm waking up in a room somewhere. Where I have no idea. It was really rough and damp and cold. I had a blanket to lie on and one to cover me. I was really dizzy when I stood up and reached for a bottle of water. I am not sure now that I should have but I had to have something to drink. My mouth was so dry.

"I was alone I think for about a day, when Trevor Lang appeared. He didn't say anything, just stood and watched me, waiting for something. There was another door in the room, behind me. I heard it open and I know it was a woman's footsteps I heard. He just watched her and then watched me. A paper was dropped on the table near me and then she left. He backed away and locked the door behind him.

"I waited, before I reached for the paper. It had a list of demands, one of which was that I was to provide access to our work computers and to both the office and the warehouse. I can't do that.

"This went on for a couple of weeks. That bottle of water was all I had that first day, a new one given to me each day, with little food provided. The third day or so, he grabbed me by the arm and shoved me out of the room into the sunlight. I couldn't see where I

———

was.  Shoved into a car, he tied my hands and then drove away and around for quite a while.  Finally, he pulled me from the car, pushed me through the field until we came to that abandoned well.  I fought him, trying to get away.  It was no use.  He wrapped a rope around me, tied it and then shoved me over the edge of the well.  I screamed, cried for him not to, but he lowered me to the bottom.  I was spinning at the speed he did that, banging into the wall, trying to fend it away and to protect myself.  I know I was asking God for help, to stop him.  He didn't, Branigan.  He just didn't.

"I don't remember much, other than waking up yesterday I guess it was, and looking up, knowing there was no way I could get out of there on my own.  I finally was able to untie the rope and stand, leaning on the wall.  I saw something on the ground and reached for it, falling back down.  It was a phone, Branigan.  All I could think of was would I be able to open it and would I be able to make a call.  You don't know the relief I felt when I heard your voice."

Guenivere stopped, her emotions and strength draining away, her head slipping down on his shoulder as he tightened his arms around her.  Branigan rested his chin on her head, watching as Brett and Lena had entered and found seats, horrified at what they were hearing.

She slept, Branigan not moving, not willing to wake her.  An hour passed and he took with thanks the plate of food and mug of coffee that Lena set down beside him.  He didn't know if he could eat, but he would try.

Brett had excused himself and walked away, his phone out to talk with Dallas.  His face was grim when he returned, simply shaking his head at Branigan before he glanced at Lena.  They would talk, he seemed to be saying but not right then.

Guenivere had finally awakened, stumbled to her feet and to her bedroom.  Lena had followed, waiting until her daughter had showered, changed into warm pyjamas although the night was warm, and crawled into bed.  She stood, her heart sorrowing for her, raising a prayer for healing.  She could feel anger in her and knew she shouldn't but at the moment she could feel nothing else.  God would understand, she thought, and took her anger to Him.

Brett had walked with Branigan back to the younger man's apartment, few words between them, before he prayed with him, a hand on his shoulder and then watched as Branigan had locked himself away inside.  He paused, not sure where he wanted to be, turning to find Buckley and Brody waiting for him, drawing him down to the chapel in the building, where the other men and the ladies were waiting.  They knew it would only get worse for the couple and they had no choice but to bathe them in prayer.

*Chapter 26*

A few days later, Branigan looked up from his desk in the building before rising and walking towards the door, listening carefully before he opened it to peek out. He frowned. The two men he could see wandering down the hallway did not belong to the building's family and he didn't think they were here for an appointment. That's not how the offices worked. He slipped out of his door, quietly locking it behind him, and walked rapidly to the security desk, finding two of the guards there. A few words and the men were heading for the corridor Branigan had just exited. He heard raised voices before the security officers were back, the two men in handcuffs.

Barnabas stood for a moment, watching with a frown on his face as the men were shoved into the police cruisers and one officer approached him.

"Bob?"

"Branigan found them wandering in the building and your security guys nabbed them. They're known to us. They weren't here for the good of any of you."

"I surmised that. Let me know what transpires with them." Barnabas walked away, finding Branigan waiting for him. "Anything to add?"

Branigan shook his voice. "I just don't get it. How are they getting in? They didn't come in from the front."

"No. They would have been stopped, that's a given." Barnabas walked rapidly towards the back door, pausing at one of the empty suites. He studied the door. "This is how, I have no doubt. This door lock has been tampered with. New locks on it and inside I suspect will be in order. I'll let Dallas know so he can look into it before I make any changes here."

Branigan felt a hand touching his back, and turned. Guenivere stood there, a frown on her face.

———

"Were they here again?" At their nod, she sighed. "Then I guess we need to talk some more. I have had some interesting emails coming to my personal box. I have no idea how they got it."

Branigan stared at her and then at Barnabas, who was already pointing back towards the conference room. "In there. The guys are working, all of them I think."

She nodded and then disappeared down the hall. They heard the door close behind her before Barnabas spoke.

"How did they get that?"

"That's what I don't understand. No one should have it. Unless." Branigan groaned. "The church directory? We have our emails in that. Anyone could pick up an extra from the desk in the foyer."

"That they could. Buckley will see that they are removed right away."

The men who had gathered listened intently as Guenivere explained what she had, handing out copies of the emails. Brennen and Brendon took theirs, putting their heads together for a moment, before looking around and then heading out. Brennen had mentioned quietly that something about the whole thing puzzled him and he needed to do some research in town.

Guenivere finally stood and stretched. She had gotten nowhere, she thought, looking around at the men. She was beginning to get to know them and their personalities as well as some of their likes and dislikes. She named them: Baird, Benen, Blair, Bradon, Brady, Branigan, Brandon, Brendon, Brennen, Brody, Buckley, Burnie, Breck, and of course, Barnabas. Baird's brother-in-law, Darby, was there as was Brady's brother-in-law, Farr, and Farr's cousin, Eric. Dallas had dropped in to get their statements and just stayed. Doc had wandered in and out, ostensibly to see what he could do to help, but she found him watching her and then watching Branigan.

She turned as her phone vibrated, pulling it out, and then frowning at the number. It was not one she knew and let it go to voice mail. Only it never did. That was strange, she thought. It should have gone to voice mail and it didn't. She dropped it on the table and stared at it.

———

Branigan had looked up at that point, and rose to approach her.

"Something wrong with your phone?"

"I think. It should have gone to voice mail, only it hasn't." She looked up, fear on her face. "Did they tamper with it? But this is a new phone. Dallas has my old one."

Branigan reached for it, scrolling through programs before he stopped. "Here. Someone has downloaded something on it. I would hazard a guess it was when it was bought for you. Let Dallas have it and the details where you got it."

Guenivere simply shuddered and walked away, leaving Branigan staring between her and her phone, a puzzled look on his face. He searched through her phone, finding other programs that should never have been on it. He sighed. It was not getting any easier, now was it? Lord, please? We need this to end, but it doesn't seem as if it will any time soon.

Dallas had approached and Branigan handed him the phone, quietly letting him know what he had found. He had changed the password on it as well, letting Dallas have that. Dallas just shook his head.

"What is it with you guys? You just can't find your ladies in the normal way? You have to dash into danger for them?" He was grumbling in a lighthearted way to try and relieve the tension Branigan was under, but he wasn't even sure that it would work.

Branigan had shaken his head and walked away, heading for the outdoors. He needed some air and some alone time. He paced, his head tilted up to the sky, watching the flickering lights from a plane overhead and then just the twinkling of the stars. The night sounds soothed his mind and heart, bringing a peace as he communed with his Lord.

He turned, not seeing the man who had appeared, not until an iron fist connected with his jaw, sending him flying backwards and down to the ground, to lie still, flat on his back, his arms askew above his head. The man looked around and then lifted Branigan up and over his shoulder, disappearing into the darkness with him.

Benen and Blair walked slowly towards the gym building, needing to wear off some energy, they had declared. They had paused at a sound, looked at each other and shrugged, and continued on their way. Neither saw the man or Branigan disappearing.

*Chapter 27*

An hour after Branigan had disappeared from the room, Guenivere looked up, needing to ask him something, frowning as she didn't see him. She rose, heading for the door, to be stopped in her tracks by Buckley, who had just entered.

"Buckley? Was Branigan out there?"

Buckley stopped on his way by, searching her face. "No, I didn't see him. I came in from the back, so if he's out front, I wouldn't have. Why? Lose him?" He grinned as she shook a finger at him.

"No. At least, I don't think so. He was here and now he's not. The last I saw him, he was talking with Dallas about my phone. And by the way, those directories in the church foyer? They need to go. We think someone used them to get my email address. The emails I received were not pretty."

Buckley frowned harder. "That's odd. I removed them a month ago, just because of something like this. So, either it was done before then."

Guenivere paled. "Or it's someone in the church or who has access to someone's."

"That's what I think. Now, let's see if we can find your beau."

"Beau?" She laughed as she headed through the door and to the lobby. "Who talks like that?"

"Your mother and father. That's what they call him."

"They do not!" She spun, laughter on her face, not realizing that was the aim of Buckley's teasing. "They don't!"

"On the contrary, they do. Don't you know that?" Buckley stopped, his head turning as he searched the lobby. "Nope. No Branigan. Where is he hiding? And why would he be hiding? You two have a disagreement?"

Guenivere continued to laugh as she headed for the outside. "No, we did not. He took my phone, talked to Dallas, and then I was involved in what I was looking up. Do you know how many Langs there are in the area?"

"No, but I gather you could tell me." Buckley's hand on her arm stopped her forward motion. "Wait for me. We walk together, Guenivere, please."

She paled at his words. "Of course. I'm sorry. I didn't think."

"And that could spell danger or death for you, just keep that in mind." Buckley peered through the darkness. "His truck is still here. I see lights in the gym. Do you suppose?"

"I guess we could check it out, but I don't see that he would be." Guenivere walked forward, step in step with Buckley, before her eyes dropped to the ground and she froze, not able to move.

Buckley walked forward a few feet, then paused, realizing Guenivere was not with him. He turned, his mouth open to tease when he saw her bend over and pick up something from the ground, giving a low cry as she did so. He was back beside her as quickly as he could move

Guenivere looked up, stalling the question that had risen to his lips. "Branigan's phone. He wouldn't have dropped it and not picked it up." Her face paled. "They've taken him, haven't they?"

Buckley's hand was under her arm as he turned her and rushed her back to the building and into the conference room, the violence of how he shoved the door open stopping all activity and causing some of the men to rise in response.

"Buckley? You flew in here for what reason?" Breck approached.

Buckley held out the phone. "Branigan's. We found it on the ground outside. Only there was no Branigan with it."

Breck paused as he reached for it, his eyes on Guenivere, seeing the terror her own eyes held, even as she tried to control her emotions. "Branigan? He's not out there?"

"No. We were looking for him and couldn't find him in the building. We had headed for the gym when Guenivere found this."

———

"Not another one." Breck spun, his eyes on the men who had stood and were standing behind him. "Fan out, guys. Search the area. See what you can find. Burnie, call it in."

Will stood an hour later, his hand resting on the lobby door, his head bent as he listened to Alice.

"No sign of him?"

"None. We'll need to come back at first light but there doesn't seem to be much disturbance where they found his phone. He's disappeared just like Guenivere did. How do these guys do it?"

"I have no idea. Patrol headed for the mill?"

"They did. They've searched and found nothing. There has to be another building connected to them."

Will held up a finger as his phone chimed and he pulled it out to check a text. "Emma. She's couriering some information on to Dallas. She seems to think she's found something but doesn't want to put it out there on a phone or email."

"It must be big then."

"I would think so. Listen, you're staying here for now. There are two cruisers around as well. I'm heading back into the office. Call if there's any change." He walked away, leaving her staring after him before she turned, a finger tapping at her lips as she thought through what she knew and the buildings in the immediate area. *Where is he, Lord? Can You direct us to him? I don't know that Guenivere can take much more. I look at her tonight and see the hope she had found fading. I don't like that.*

*Chapter 28*

Struggling against the hands that held him flat to the ground, Branigan fought to rise, to escape, his head tossing as he did so. He didn't understand what had happened or where he was. He didn't hear the click of the shackles around his ankles, but felt the cold of the metal against his skin through his socks.

The men holding him finally stood, winded from their fight with him. They had not expected him to awake so soon or to fight them so hard to escape. The older man, heavyset, his face lined with the abuses he had put his body through, the scraggly beard hiding the lower face, shook his head and pointed to the table, his words muttered from a mouth that held broken and stained teeth.

The younger man, on his way to the same state of body, reached for the syringe, their orders specific. First, the shackles, then the sedative. Their employer wanted him docile. Why, they really didn't care. All they cared about was the money they were being paid.

Branigan fought the men again as his arm was held to the ground, the syringe plunging in, a press on the end sending the sedative into his unwilling body. His body twisted as his other hand reached for the syringe to try and grasp it, reached to shove the men away from him, his head raising in his determination to succeed. But his determination and fight were not enough. The sedative began its work, and his body collapsed, his head hitting hard on the concrete floor he was laying on, his eyes rolling back as his consciousness fled. His body relaxed, all fight gone. He could only murmur, God, please help me before he dropped down into a well of darkness.

The men stood, shaking their heads at him. Neither had expected the fight from him, not after the blow he took that rendered him unconscious. They walked away, the door slamming shut behind them. There was no need for a lock. His shackles' chain traced its way across the cold, dirty concrete floor to end in a huge

———

eye hook in the wall.  He would not escape, that they were confident of.

Their employer turned from the window she was staring out of, anger on her face and in her eyes, disdain for the men in front of her hidden.  If she could work in any other way, she would, but she needed them, and she had to acknowledge that they needed her.

"Well?"  Her voice was low and harsh, not fitting the groomed appearance she endeavoured to portray.

"He's out.  He fought us.  He shouldn't have been awake.  The shackles are in place, and the sedative given."  The older man spoke, not looking up as he did so.  He had learned that he didn't look at her.  The blows from her hands and cane had taught him that.

"Good.  Now comes the next part."  She walked towards him, her cane tapping on the floor as it helped her to balance.  "We will need to take pictures of him and send them to that witch."

The younger man shrugged, reaching for the camera, and following as she walked towards where Branigan was held captive. She stood, staring down at him, her cane tapping at his chest, finding he didn't move.

"Good.  Good."  She looked around.  "There.  By that pile of broken blocks.  Lean him against that."

The two men exchanged glances before shrugging once more. The younger man set the camera down and helped to drag Branigan to the pile of debris, positioning as she directed, more than once, until she was satisfied.  His body sagged against the blocks, his head hanging to the side, his hair disheveled, the bruising on his face evident in the bright light the older man had been handed and ordered to shine on him.

The younger man approached, camera in hand, hesitating for the barest second before the camera clicked through a number of shots.  She reached for the camera, almost tearing it away from him in her eagerness to see the pictures, scrolling through them, finding the ones that she wanted, and deleting the others.  Camera in her hand, she turned, walking away, the cane tapping once more on the concrete before the men heard it tapping up the rough stairs to the main floor and then across the floor to the office she had set up.

———

The younger man shook his head.  Somehow, this was not what he had signed on for.  Not at all.  He shot a look at his partner who was standing, staring down at Branigan, before he turned, quietly moving away, finding the door to the outside and once through it, closing it quietly behind him.  He was done, he thought. He would pack up the room he rented and leave this town, this very night.  He would be gone before anyone found out about it.  A new start in a new province.  That was what he had decided to do.

The woman finally turned from her desk, reaching for the photos on the printer, satisfied with the ones she had selected.  She hunted for a large Manila envelope, addressing it to Guenivere in large black block letters, intending to drop it into the mail that night. It would find her.  She would be watching for her reaction, hearing of it from her source.  She cackled with glee.  It was all starting to come together, her plots and plans for revenge.  The Danby's would be destroyed through all this, and that was her end goal.  Take them down.  Wreak havoc on their lives.  Destroy their livelihood.  She had many plots and plans to put in place, but they depended on the reaction she would elicit from these photos.

*Chapter 29*

Two days later, Brett fingered the envelope that had appeared on the reception desk in the office, not sure who or when it had appeared. He didn't remember seeing it the day before, but then, he had not looked at the mail. He sighed, knowing he had to find Guenivere and just not sure where she would be. He detoured by the mechanic shop for a quick word with Douglas and then headed for his car, determined to find his daughter.

Guenivere looked up from the papers she was studying, deep into research on the Langs, as she heard the door to the conference room open. Some of the men were there, each deep into their own research, quiet words and sometimes jokes flying between them. She frowned as her father appeared.

"Dad?" She went to stand but Brett shook his head, taking a seat beside her. "What do you have?"

"I have no idea, Guenivere. I found it on the desk out front this morning. I don't know when it was delivered but it could have been yesterday or even this morning. I was back and forth from the shop and I must admit, I didn't always lock the door, and I should have."

Guenivere shrugged. "They would have just shoved it into the box." She reached reluctant hands for it. "It doesn't look too important. I'll get to it in a bit. I have some information here I'm trying to understand and I think I have found a link of some kind. I want to talk to you about it when I'm done."

Brett studied her for a moment, knowing from experience that she would not open the envelope until she was ready to. He rose, heading for the coffee pot, and then taking a seat near Brody, who was staring at a computer screen.

"It won't bite, Brody."

Brody's head shot around as Brett spoke, finally realizing he wasn't alone, and then grinning at the words. "It won't? Here, along I've been wrong.  I was convinced it would.  What brings you out?"

"I had an envelope to bring to Guenivere."  He leaned back to look over at his daughter.  "She hasn't opened it yet.  She won't until she's ready, and who knows when that will be."

"Was it important?"

Brett shrugged.  "I doubt it.  Probably just some advertising for her.  She gets that all the time and just throws it away.  It has come to the point, she'll look at an envelope and most times won't even touch it."

"That's not good, especially now.  That's how they may communicate with her."

"She knows that, Brody.  Part of it is denial on her side. We've tried to talk to her, Lena and I.  It doesn't make any difference.  Tell me, where are you all in the mystery?  Any word on Branigan?"

"No, there hasn't been.  I don't like that. There should be." Brody was off on a tangent, turning back to his computer, completely forgetting that Brett was waiting for an answer.

Brett pulled out his phone, scrolling through his business emails, and was soon concentrating on them, the noise and conversation in the room fading to the background.  He had looked up on occasion towards Guenivere but found her head bent over the papers in front of her.

A sudden scream split the air in the room about an hour after Brett had entered, the sound of a chair violently shoved across the floor clattering as did the sound of a body hitting the floor as the chair crashed to its side, startling the men, having them on their feet in instant, eyes alert to what had happened.  Brody spun and then was across the room, on his knees beside Guenivere, who lay on her side, reaching to try and raise her to a sitting position.  She lay, curled up, her arms tight around her head, sobs wracking her body.

Brett was there, on his knees on her other side, hands reaching for her as well, drawing back as she flew to her hands and knees and scrambled away from them, to tuck herself into a corner, her knees drawn up, her face buried against them, her arms once more wrapped around her head.

"What happened?" Brett's voice was harsh, as he stared at his daughter, afraid to approach her, afraid not to.

Brady stood by the table, his eyes on the envelope. "Where did this come from?"

Brett rose, fear in his heart for the young couple. "It was at the office. I brought it over to her. Why?"

Brady's pen was out to move the photos of Branigan that had dumped out of the envelope, as Blair and Breck stood behind him, their faces as grim as they could get. "This is why. It's Branigan."

"What?" Brett was at the table, his eyes on the photos, before they slid shut. "I didn't know. I thought it was just advertising, like she's had before." He spun and then was across the room, on his knees beside his daughter, a hand hovering in mid-air as he reached to touch her and then paused.

Brady was beside him, his own hands reaching for Guenivere, moving her arms and then scooping her up into his arms, leaving the room almost on a run, Brett behind him, Braydon running to find Doc and Anna, who were around that day.

Doc stood for a moment in the infirmary doorway, before he approached Guenivere.

"What happened?" When Brett had explained, Doc shook his head. "I see. Let Anna and I have some time with her, Brett, and then I'll have you come back in. You'll need to find Lena."

Brady spoke up. "Blair was on his way to get her."

"Good. Now, clear the room." Doc watched as the door closed behind them before he turned to Anna. "I don't like this, Anna. She's at her limit. This may push her over it."

"I know, Doc. That I do know." Anna's hand stroked down Guenivere's hair. "I've been praying so hard for her. I could see the hope rising in her, hope I haven't seen in her before. Now this. It will set her back."

"I am afraid it will. We need to pray for her and pray hard."

Guenivere roused, her eyes staring around in fright until she focused on Anna. "Anna? Where's Branigan?"

"He's not here, Guenivere. Don't you remember?"

Guenivere's eyes slid shut, as tears flowed. "I do. I am so afraid. I think he was dead in those pictures. Please? Dear Lord, please. Don't let him be dead."

Anna and Doc shared a startled look before Doc was out the door, finding Brett and Breck right outside.

"Those pictures? What was in them?"

Brett shuddered. "Branigan. He was slumped over some broken concrete blocks, I think. He looked dead, but I'm sure that can't be." Brett's face paled even more. "He was shackled, Doc. There was a close up on his ankles. Who does that?" A hand clutched at his chest.

Breck had watched Brett closely, his arms reaching to catch him as he collapsed to the floor, Doc beside him.

"Into the other room, Breck. And then call for the paramedics. I think it's his heart."

Breck lifted Brett and carried him to the other room, then stood, phone in hand as he made the call, watching as Doc worked on their friend. He turned at a tap before the door open, and Brody appeared.

"Breck?"

"We think it's his heart. We have people on the way."

Brock grew stern. "This is not what they need. I'll have Blair change course and head to the hospital with Lena." He stood back as the paramedics entered, watching as they worked on Brett before shifting him to their stretcher and then walking rapidly away, the heart monitor on the stretcher between Brett's feet, the oxygen mask in place. The men and ladies from the building stood, horror and concern on their faces before Breck was away, following the ambulance as siren wailing and emergency lights flashing it sped for the hospital.

Barnabas stood near Doc, his hand on the older man's shoulder, a prayer rising for Brett, Lena and Guenivere.

"Doc?"

"I think it was his heart. They'll assess him. Guenivere? Now, this is not going to help her. She's on the edge, Barnabas. She can't take much more. Those photos almost destroyed her."

"That's what Brady said. He's heading to find Dallas with them. Whoever this is, they're brutal."

Doc hesitated before he spoke. "Somehow, I think you'll find it's a woman. They can have a real cruel streak. This had all the earmarks of that."

Barnabas stared at him before he nodded. "I think you're right, Doc. I really do. And it's someone we know."

"That's what I'm afraid of. I'm going to pull out that church directory. I heard Guenivere's comments and I have a feeling she's right." Doc walked away, his steps as heavy as his heart.

## Chapter 30

Late that same afternoon, Guenivere stood beside her father's hospital bed, her arm around her mother, her eyes studying the monitors connected to him even as the beeps sounded in her ears. They had been lucky, the Emergency Room doctor had declared, even as Lena shook her head and stated emphatically that it was God, not luck. Guenivere had roused in the infirmary in the Foundation building, overhearing Doc's quiet conversation with Anna. She had been on her feet, flying from the room, desperate to find her way to the hospital. Bradon and Brendon were there, rushing her to Bradon's truck, shoving her inside and then speeding as quickly as they could for the hospital.

Guenivere had sat, silent, still, her hands clasped together, even as the men had each taken turns to watch her. She had flown into the Emergency department, finding her mother waiting, Blair hovering near, and was enveloped in her mother's arms. They had finally been taken to Brett's room, the additional comment being that he would be kept in overnight and that he needed to reduce the stress in his life. Guenivere had given a harsh laugh at that, surprising the doctor, and then swallowed hard, suppressing her feelings.

Barnabas watched for a moment from the doorway before he approached, his hand resting lightly on Lena's shoulder.

"Lena?"

"He can go home tomorrow, Barnabas. God was good. It wasn't a heart attack, just stress. The doctor wants to do more testing, but it can be done as an outpatient."

"That's good." He looked past her mother at Guenivere, finding her watching him. "If you like, we can set you up at the building."

Lena shook her head. "No, he'll want to go home. But we can't have Guenivere there. They'll use this to get at her."

"I'm sure they will." Barnabas shook his head in warning as Guenivere opened her mouth, biting back a smile as she snapped it closed, a frown on her face.

"Mom? I can't stay away."

"You must, Guenivere. You must." She looked up at Barnabas. "Barnabas? Please?"

"She's right, Guenivere. They will use this to get to you. This may be all part of the plan, you know."

Guenivere blew out a breath, before she nodded. "I know. I just don't want to be away from Dad." She looked down as she felt a hand cover the one she had resting on the bed beside her father. "Dad? You're awake?"

"I am, Guenivere. I've been laying here, listening and thinking. Barnabas is right. This may be part of their overall plan. If we can keep apart, maybe they will back away. Please stay at the building. You have security there." His finger raised as she went to protest. "I know. Security has been breached. Branigan was taken from there. But it is still likely the safest place for you. Barnabas, the photos?"

"Dallas has them. He's quite disturbed at them, but quite determined to find Branigan. He got word to me that officers are volunteering their off-duty hours to help. Branigan has been there for so many of them over the years with his work as an auxiliary officer.”

“He has been. That’s good. I pray it’s resolved soon.” His eyes closing, Brett drifted off to sleep.

Lena turned to Guenivere. “Go on with Barnabas, dear. I’m not leaving but I would feel better knowing you’re safe.”

Guenivere was torn. She wanted to stay with her parents but she always wanted to be out hunting for Branigan. Neither option seemed available to her, and she felt angry and disgruntled. She hugged her mother, following Barnabas as he led the way out to his car, tucking her inside, before he stood, staring around, not liking that he felt watched. He nodded at the security team that waited in the two vehicles, and pulled away from the hospital, one car in front, the other behind. He was taking no chances, not any more. Whoever it was had proven that they would and could play dirty. Lord, we need to end this. This could have ended today in tragedy. I don’t want that for this family. Please, Lord?

Guenivere glared at the clock in her living room for the umpteenth time. She sighed. It was early morning, and she had not slept, instead spending her time pacing, moving from room to room. She had sought her bed, only to toss and turn, rising to pace, and then to seek her bed once more. This was not working, she thought, slouching down on the couch, her arms crossed over her chest, her chin dropping down with her hair covering her face. She stayed like that as she thought through what she knew, her hands finally coming up to grasp her hair and pull at it.

There has to be an answer somewhere, she thought. Lord, right about now would be a good time to send a hint or two. Her head dropped back and rested on the couch back, and her eyes closed. She envisioned the photos, cringing in fear once more for Branigan, praying that he really was alive and would come back to her. She was losing hope, she knew, and that she didn’t like or even want.

Her mind drifted back to when she was twelve and that incident. She frowned as she tried to remember who had been there. Her brow cleared as she shuddered. She had a good idea now who was behind everything. She just had to prove it, and how to do that, she had no idea.  She needed to talk to someone and was on her feet, almost running for the door, when she slid to a stop.  No, she couldn't awaken anyone in the middle of the night.

She spun, heading for the kitchen, reaching for the carafe to rinse it out and then dumping the water into the coffee pot, knowing she would need it.  She reached for the bread on the counter and then the tomato and lettuce from the fridge, fixing her favourite sandwich. She slapped it down harder than she meant to onto a plate, reaching for a mug, then reaching past that one for the largest one she could find in the cupboard.  Her hand stilled as she caught the verse on it. Psalms, she thought: *I hope in Your word.*  She smiled.  Branigan must have put it there.  I have to ask him that.

Guenivere walked rapidly through to her office, setting down the plate and her mug, pulling up her chair.  She sighed.  The anger, guilt and despair that she felt was weighing her down.  She needed to spend time with God before she did anything else.  Her head went down on her arms as she wept, prayed, and then waited.

Early morning found Guenivere running down the stairs, heading for the conference room, a thought having crossed her mind. She clutched a sheaf of papers in her hand, her other hand sliding lightly down the railing. Breck watched from where he stood near the front doors, dressed for his morning run. He hesitated before shaking his head. He would check in on her when he returned.

Guenivere slipped quietly into the room, her hand reaching to flip on the light switches, hesitating for a moment as the fear from the day before overcame her once more. She shook her head, stiffened her spine, and marched towards the computer she had been using. Booting it up, she hesitated, her hands hovering over the keyboard, her eyes looking up. Lord, I know what I think, who I think it is. I just don't know for sure. I need proof, and it's too well hidden. I need You to step in for me. Please, Lord? I don't know if Branigan is still alive or if he's dead. The pictures tell me that he is dead, my heart says otherwise. Guide our search. We need to find them, whoever it is, and then find him.

Brennen paused as he passed the door a couple of hours later, hearing muttering and then humming coming out through the partially open door. He frowned, and then reached to shove the door open further, looking down at the sneaker holding it open. He grinned, bending to pick up the peach-coloured shoe. Guenivere, he thought. She's in here working, and propped the door open to watch for one of us.

He didn't try to hide his footsteps as he walked across the room, but actually walked a little harder than usual, an amused look crossing his face as Guenivere ignored him. He came to a stop next to her, his mouth open to speak, when her forefinger went up into the air in an abrupt manner, stopping his words, but causing the amusement on his face to deepen. He dropped into a chair beside her, his elbow on the table, head on his hand as he tilted it to watch her face. He frowned at the deep concentration, and then smiled inwardly at the streak of dust on her cheek. What have you been doing, Guenivere, that you found dust? I thought the room was clean.

"Brennen? What is your take on this?" Guenivere suddenly spoke, shoving papers across to him hard enough that he had to slap a hand down on them to stop them from flying from the table.

"What is this?"

"A mess, I think. I need someone to take a look at it, someone who really doesn't know the people involved. That would be one of you." Guenivere turned to face him, devastation showing deep in her eyes. "I know what I think it says, and I know what I don't it to say."

"That doesn't make sense, Guenivere." Brennen frowned at her, his eyes lifting to look past her as he heard a sound at the door, and Brandon, Brendon and Brody appeared, shortly followed by Blair, Bradon and Baird.

"What did you find?"

She shook her head. "Read it, please. Then, talk to me." She dropped her head to her folded arms and the sigh she drew shook her body, causing the men to stare at her before staring at one another.

"Brennen?" Blair finally spoke, even as he slid into a chair, and reached for the keyboard and mouse of the computer he had selected.

"Guenivere has been hard at work, I would say for hours." He gathered up the sheaf of papers and held it up, drawing the men's eyes to first it and then Guenivere. "She's come up with something she needs verified. We can do that, can't we?"

"We can." Baird reached for the papers. "Let me make copies for each of us. Then, each of us can work on it, and pool our thoughts. That's how we do it, Guenivere."

She nodded without raising her head. "I know. It's just I don't like what I found." Her voice was muffled, low enough that they had to strain to catch her words.

The men were soon deep in concentration, amazed at what Guenivere had been able to dig up, but dismay rippling through the room as the people she had named. It would be difficult, Brennen thought, to find the evidence, and he thought he knew Guenivere well enough that she wouldn't say anything without it.

"Guenivere?" When she looked up, Blair smiled. "You've done a lot and just in a short while."

"No, actually. I have been working on it since around two, I think. I did what I could on my own system, but you have programs here that I needed to use." She paled, a thought crossing her mind. "I'm sorry. I shouldn't have used them." She shoved at the table, preparatory to rising and running from the room.

Breck's hand on her back stopped her even though it caused her to jump.

"There is no problem, not that I can see, Guenivere. Those programs are open for any of us to use, us men, the ladies of the family. And believe me, you are one of us, whether you realize it or not. Branigan has staked his claim on you." He paused, as he watched tears pool in her eyes. "Guenivere? What did I say?"

She simply shook her head, overcome by her emotions for a moment, not seeing Cadee until Cadee's arm encircled her shoulders. She looked up, seeing the five younger women had entered as had the rest of the men.

Guenivere sighed to herself. She had to be honest with them, didn't she, Lord? And how did she do just that? Branigan should be the one stating the obvious. They were his friends, those he considered his family.

Looking around at them all, her eyes resting on Barnabas, seeing the knowledge of what she was about to say in his eyes, she sighed once more and then reached for the chain around her neck, pulling it out from under the soft yellow T-shirt she wore.

She didn't look around, afraid of the censure she would see. Cadee reached for the ring on the chain, studying it and then reaching to unclasp the chain, to slide the ruby and gold ring from it. She held it out to her friend.

"Put it on, Guenivere. Put it on where Branigan placed it. He would want to acknowledge that you are his chosen life mate, his helpmeet, his love."

Guenivere had turned to watch her, seeing the acceptance in her friend's face, before she reached to take the ring, her eyes searching each one in the room, finding love and acceptance, not the censure she expected, on each face.

Barnabas nodded as she once more sought him out. "Do what Cadee asked, Guenivere. Branigan would want you to. Don't hide from us. We are, each one of us, trying our best to solve this and bring him home to you. And we will bring him home. That's a guarantee. God has spoken and He is not done with Branigan. Not yet."

*Chapter 32*

A groan pulled deep from within him, Branigan roused in the early morning hours, feeling around for his blankets to pull up over him against the early morning chill.  For some reason, he thought, I can't find them.  That's bizarre.  He roused a bit more and wondered at the lumpy hard mattress he was laying on, that had sharp corners driving into him as he shifted.  He finally pushed himself to a sitting position, leaning back on what he thought was the headboard, but it too felt odd.  It has too hard for the wooden headboard he had, and too cold.  His head spun from his efforts and his eyes slid closed to counter the vertigo assailing him.

Branigan rubbed at his face, feeling the stubble from two days of not shaving.  This can't be right, he thought.  Guenivere and I had dinner out last night, before walking by the river.  His mind drifted back to their dinner.

He had chosen a small family-run British restaurant, a favourite of his, and as it turned out, one of Gueinvere's as well.  They had lingered over their meal, their conversation quiet at times and at times somewhat heated as they got to know one another better.

Branigan had reached for her hand as they left, steering her towards a park near there, mingling with the pedestrians until he found the bench he favoured.  She had nestled down in his arms, content, she said, just to be there and with him.

Talk had been intermittent before he bit at his lip, staring off towards the town.  His gaze dropped to her, her profile to him as she laughed at the antics of some small children and their dog nearby.

"Guenivere?"  His voice was low and hesitant enough that she turned to him, a question on her lips that died away as she searched his face.  "I know we haven't know each other long.  I mean, we've been dating.  We have talked, I think, about so many things.  I love your spirit, your thoughts, your willingness to tell me off, to forgive, your eagerness for life.  I see the change in you.  God is restoring

———

986

your hope." He paused, drawing his upper lip in, before he continued. "I guess what I am trying to say is this. I love you, deeply, and more each day. Will you be mine, to share life with me, to walk beside me, to serve God wherever He would direct us? Will you be my Proverbs 31 lady?" He held up the single ruby ring that had been his mother's, given to him by his father when he was in his teens, to be given, his father said with a sad but loving smile, to the lady who would be his Proverbs 31 lady, just as Branigan's mother had been his.

Guenivere swallowed hard, not believing that he had asked, before she looked away, trying to control her unruly emotions. She felt, rather than saw, the motion of his hand dropping, and could sense the disappointment he felt.

Turning back, she simply nodded, her hand going out to grasp his.

"I will, Branigan. I will. I like what you said. Dad has always described Mom as that."

"He has? That's how Dad looked at my mother. I don't have the memories of her that you do of your mother." He slipped on her ring and then gathered her close.

Branigan had frowned as she slipped it onto a chain, a question on his face.

"It's okay. I will wear it, but we need to talk to Mom and Dad first, unless you have already."

He shook his head at that and then agreed with her, with the stipulation that she would be wearing it on her finger for everyone to see by the next evening.

Branigan's mind drifted back to the present, a groan rising from him again as he tried to raise himself up and stand. He was finally able to draw himself to his feet, a hand planted on the wall, his blurry eyes staring around.

He frowned as he stared down at the pile of broken blocks and wondered just how he had gotten to there. It certainly wasn't his apartment, that much he knew, but where he was? That was the question it seemed he could not answer. God? Are You there? Do You know where I am? Of course, You do. You're God. You would know that.  His thoughts were not the usual organized thoughts he had but scattered and incomplete.

He turned to walk away, surprise on his face that he could not take a normal step.  He frowned at the clank of metal as he once more stepped forward, heading towards the door he could see just a few feet away.

Branigan stared at his face, seeing the bruise on his jaw.  How did I do that, he thought?  I look like I have been in a fight or something.  Running the tap to warm the water, he splashed his face, reaching for a towel to dry it off.

He turned, once more restricted in his steps, the clanging of metal sounding loud in his eyes, echoing through the small room, and intensifying the headache that was pounding in his temples and behind his eyes.

Slumping back to the floor, Branigan stared at his ankles, not quite sure of what he was seeing before he reached to touch and then grasp the shackles binding him.  He shook them and then felt for a way to remove them, finding none.  What did I do, he wondered?  Just where am I?

His head raised as he searched the room, seeing the tray near him with food and a bottle of water.  He reached for the water, twisted off the cap, and drank deeply, before he reached for the sandwich, downing it in a few bites.  He had no idea what day it was, and no way of finding out.  Finished his meal, his hand still holding the partly-full water bottle, his head went back against the wall and he slept, not hearing the door open and the older man enter.

The man stood, his eyes narrowed as he studied first Branigan and then the tray.  He nodded.  Good, he thought.  He did eat and drink.  We need him to do that, to wake up and stay alive.  He reached for the tray to retrieve it and then for the water bottle before shaking his head.  That wouldn't hurt to stay.  He could not defend himself with that.

The door swung shut and the lock snapped into place, Branigan rousing slightly at the noise before he drifted off once more.  His thoughts became muddled dreams where he was being chased or he was chasing an unknown opponent.  He could hear Guenivere's voice calling to him and in his drugged sleep he reached

———

for her, calling her name, before he lurched forward to stand and then fall with a heavy hard thud to the concrete floor, his arms askew over his head.  He lay there, for unknown hours, before the man returned with a new tray, this time near dusk.

His back to the door, Branigan listened to the commands being thrown at him by the older man. He simply shook his head. There was no way, he thought, that he would do anything that would endanger Guenivere, her family, their business or his friends. That was a given.

The man was growing angry. Pressure was being put on him to make Branigan agree. Secretly, he admired the younger man, but he was making it extremely difficult for him to do what he had been charged to do.

"You will make that video. And you will provide the information we need for the security system that you changed. We will have access to their trucks." The man stormed from the room, the door slamming closed behind him.

Branigan drew in a deep breath and let it out slowly. It was what he had thought. They wanted access to Brett's fleet and that would be for likely smuggling or illegal activities of some kind. How did he get away from them and warn Brett?

Lord, I don't know how to do this. Only You can release me and help me to stop this.

He turned to eye the door, knowing he could not reach it, before he began to pace in the little room that he could. He finally slumped back down to the floor, his eyes closing as he slept. He didn't realize that he had been drugged again, part of the way that they were trying to wear him down, to make him pliable in their hands and an accessory to their devious, dirty plans. He didn't know who all they were planning on ensnaring.

The woman stood in the doorway, anger radiating from her. They were on a time crunch, her words lashing at the man standing behind her.

"I don't care how you accomplish it. He will make that video. He will provide the information that we need." She stormed away, her cane tapping in tune with her angry, heavy footsteps, leaving the man staring after her before he moved to the doorway.

"There ain't no way he'll do it." The whine sounded deep in his voice. "There just ain't no way."

Days went by like this, Branigan growing more exhausted and fatigued, the shackles wearing heavy on his ankles, the sore spots appearing where they rubbed. He resolutely refused to do what they asked, simply stating that he couldn't and wouldn't be part of their schemes to destroy a family, a respected business, or his friends. He just turned away from their requests, to stand leaning against the wall, his eyes fastened on the small dirty window that let in what light it could to brighten his day and to make the nights seem shorter.

Finally, the day came. It had been how long, Branigan couldn't tell. He had lost track of time, of days, just knowing that night followed day which followed night. He had paced where he could, tried to free himself from his shackles, had sleep, both a natural sleep and a drugged one. He had been threatened, cajoled, promised freedom if he would only help. Guenivere and her family and then his friends and their ladies had been threatened. He had simply shaken his head and backed away, to stand staring up at the window. Branigan had managed to reach it one day by standing on his toes and using a wet rag had cleaned what he could. It had make his dungeon brighter to a degree. And that was what he was in, a dungeon.

His mind had slipped one day, back to when he was a small boy, and playing cops and robbers with his friends had been their best past-time. His father had smiled at him and then sat him down, explaining what it was like to be one of the good guys and what it was like to be one of the bad guys, as he put it. His explanation had made Branigan determined to be one of the good guys. That was what he had promised his father that day, causing his father to smile and then hug him. Branigan had sat that day, in his prison, his eyes riveted on the door as he thought about that and then remembered how his father had talked about Paul being in a dungeon, that he had still served God there, had praised and prayed, had sent out encouragement to the churches. He had not lost hope. Branigan was determined that he would be the same. He would not lose hope, as difficult as it seemed.

———

Branigan had grown thin, his face covered in a rough beard, his thoughts on his beloved and how she would be coping.  She would have the support of all his friends, he knew, as well as the Foundation board, to say nothing of her parents.

He thought about the board, a frown on his face as he searched his memory, before a groan shook his body and his eyes closed. That was the voice he had kept hearing, in his dreams, outside his dungeon.  It was that board member.  But how did he let them know? How did he reach out to his friends?

Entering the room in the near dusk of that day, the man searched for Branigan, not seeing him at first.  Curses flew from his mouth as he headed back out to find a flashlight, shining it around as he searched.  Branigan was gone, the shackles he had been wearing cut open and laying discarded on the floor.  The man paled, curses flying anew from him, as he searched the room and then backed out, to slam the door and look at the lock.  He couldn't tell if it had been tampered with, he had scratched it so badly with his alcohol-shaky hands.  He turned, heading for the stairs, and then the back door, searching for Branigan, and not finding him.

He stood, as the moonlight became to filter through the trees, his mind blurring, but the cunning he had been known for all his life still active.  He spun to stare at the house, and then spun, running for his truck, the gravel in the driveway spewing from the tires as he gunned the motor and fled.  He had had enough, he decided, and would leave town, just like the younger man had.  He wouldn't even wait to collect what he had in his apartment.  There was nothing there of value and nothing that would identify him.  He had used fake identification to rent it.

Cane tapping on the stairs, the woman approached the door herself.  She had appeared, calling for her henchman and not receiving an answer from him.  Anger had begun to build at him and then at Branigan and then at Brett and his trucking company.  She stood for a moment, shocked to see the door unlocked and open, before she shoved at it with her cane and waited, finally entering, to find it empty, to find the man she had planned to use, destroy and then kill missing.  Rage began to build as she turned for the stairs, her balance unsteady under it.  She tottered on the next to the top step, her balance gone, and she plunged back down the steps, to lie, a crumpled, broken heap that no one would miss or no one might ever find.

Guenivere rose from her seat that day they had discovered her engagement, stretching. She glanced at the clock in shock. She had been settled there for hours, it would appear, and she realized that she was both hungry and thirsty. A hand on her arm turned her towards Ennis, who pulled her with her out of the conference room and to her own apartment. Guenivere stood for a moment, staring at the ladies seated in the living room, her own mother one of them, as well as Anna and her sister, Amy.

"What is going on, Ennis?" She turned to her friend, a puzzled look on her face.

Ennis had just grinned. "We needed to rescue you, that's what. First, you haven't moved from there for hours. I hear you were already working before the guys entered. And that you were up at two working away. You need to eat. Branigan would expect that of you."

Soberly, Guenivere turned to each lady, catching their nods of agreement but something more. She sank down beside her mother, sitting on the floor, her legs folded, as her mother's hand rested on her head.

"Who's with Dad?"

"Doc. He appeared, sent me off with Baird, who told me I was to come here for lunch." She studied her daughter, seeing the strain and stress in her face, but something more. A hope in something or someone, she thought. "He seems to think I needed to talk with you."

Guenivere sighed. "I wanted to tell you the other night when you called, but Branigan and I planned to surprise you with a meal last night. That didn't happen." She held up her hand for her mother to take, hearing the soft intake of her breath. "He calls me his Proverbs 31 lady, just like Dad does with you. He said his father did the same."

Lena reached to hug her daughter, a few tears falling on Guenivere's hair, before she pulled back. "Dad suspected something like this. He said Branigan had approached him one day but wouldn't say why. This must have been it." She looked up at a sound from Fynn.

Guenivere looked around her mother at Fynn. "Fynn? You're up to something. All of you."

The ladies laughed before Berneen spoke. "We are. We know you're missing Branigan and that you're determined to find him. We've been talking. As you know, I married Baird to save his life. Cadee married Benen to escape from a war-torn country. Devaney and Blair were engaged but she walked away to save his life. Ennis and Fynn had a chance to be courted, as they used to say. You're different. You're being courted, but there is also something else going on that we can't understand right now." She paused, biting at her lip, distress on her face. "Maybe this wasn't such a good idea, after all."

Guenivere was puzzled. "What wasn't such a good idea?"

Devaney spoke up. "We just thought, to help you get through this, that we could sort of, you know, help you plan."

"So definite there, Devaney." Cadee grinned at her friend. "What Devaney is stumbling over her words, trying to say, is that we would like to help you put some ideas down for your wedding. I know Branigan and he would say to go for it. He wouldn't care, as long as you were there. In fact, if you showed up in your jeans, a T-shirt and your peach sneakers, he'd still marry you."

The ladies laughed as Guenivere sat back, her eyes wide, her mouth open until she snapped it closed. She felt her mother's arm around her.

"I think it's a wonderful idea, Guenivere. We've talked over the years about what you'd like. I know your heart. You want simple and plain. Let's see what we can come up with. You don't have to do anything we say, but if you would listen and then plan from that, it will help. It will keep your hope up that he's coming back. And he is. I am confident of that."

———

Much laughter filled the room as the most outrageous ideas were thrown at her.  Guenivere suspected they were doing that on purpose, trying to outdo one another.

She finally rose, tucking the notes she had made into the folder handed to her, and walked down the stairs and out to where Benen was waiting for her.  She stood, arms folded around herself, as her mother left, tears near the surface, not seeing both Barnabas and Buckley watching her.

Barnabas approached and with the ease of an old friendship, dropped an arm around her shoulder.  Buckley stood on her other side.

"Well?  We passed by the apartment.  You ladies sounded like you were having fun."  Barnabas grinned down at her.

She shook her head.  "Did you put them up to having me there for lunch and bringing in Mom and Anna and Amy?"

Both men shook their heads.

"No, that was their idea.  Fynn did ask if we thought they should, and we agreed.  You needed a break, Guenivere, and we weren't sure you would take one."  Buckley peered down at the folder in her hand.  "It looks as if it was a productive lunch."

"In some ways, it was.  They are all so sweet.  They wanted to help me come up with ideas for the wedding.  Only, I don't know that there will be one."  She ran from them, unable to stem the flow of tears, the lobby door shutting silently behind her as she ran for her apartment.

Barnabas and Buckley stared after her before they looked at one another.

"It had to happen, Barnabas.  She's been on edge now for days."

Barnabas agree.  "It did.  We've all tried to get her to take a break, to slow down, but she won't.  She wants this over and Branigan home."  He ran his hand through his hair.  "Dad's heading out this way tonight.  We need to talk with him about what we've found.  As the Board chair, he needs to know and help to make plans on where we go with this."

<hr>

"That he does. Let's plan on meeting in your office, spending some time in prayer, and then working through what we have. We don't want to go to the Board yet, not until we have absolute proof."

"No, we can't. Guenivere is right in that respect. No accusations without proof. We'll likely need to call in Will in his official capacity at some point."

"That we will." Buckley opened his mouth to speak again, then shut it, shaking his head before he walked away.

*Chapter 35*

Days passed, and Guenivere grew thin and pale. She slept but she knew her sleep was restless. She would wake early in the morning and just lie in bed, her thoughts on Branigan, her heart in prayer, before she would rise, dress, grab a piece of toast or bagel, and then head for the conference room. Her parents had each taken her aside, and tried to talk to her, but she had just stared past them and continued as she was. Her work for her father was still done, but she didn't have the heart or interest in it any more.

That particular day, she had roused early, glancing at the clock to see that it was only three. She had closed her eyes, seeking her rest again, but unable to find it. Finally rising, she had taken her Bible and a mug of tea this time, and headed for her balcony, to spend the next few hours seeking every verse she could find on hope and praying them through.

Buckley had looked up as she entered the conference room, ready to joke with her as he usually did, but he didn't. There was something different about her that day, he thought. *I wonder what.*

He finally rose and took a seat beside her, his head tilted to study her face. Guenivere knew he was there and looked over at him.

"Buckley?"

"Guenivere. Something has changed."

——

She sighed as she sat back in her chair, a pen tapping on the table. "I don't know, Buckley. I had a horrible feeling about three this morning and just had to get up. I looked up all the verses on hope that I could find." She looked over at him, seeing him nodding. "Does that make any sense at all?"

"It does. Sometimes God will wake us when we need to spend time with Him. I have often woken for days at a certain time, unsure why, but praying through the friends I have, the church family, and just situations that I am aware of. He doesn't expect us to have the answers. He just wants us to search and be willing to listen."

"He does." She looked past him. "I just wish I knew where Branigan was and if he's okay. It's seems so long since he was taken."

"It has been. Not so much in days, but in worry, in stress, in the unknown. In lost hope." He nodded as her gaze came back to him. "That's been a difficulty for you to accept. That you can and have lost hope but God will restore that."

"He has, Barnabas." Guenivere looked past him once more as the door opened and Barnabas appeared with a man she didn't know. "Buckley, who's that?"

He spun on his chair, and then was on his feet, his hand outstretched. "Murphy O'Brien? What brings you here?"

Murphy grinned. He was a friend of Fynn's, a team member for Abe Finlay, who ran a security team. Abe's wife, Emma, had been involved in the search for Branigan, coming aboard to the investigation at Fynn's request.

"To see you all?" He grinned again as Buckley laughed, before he sobered. He walked over to stand in front of Guenivere, who had risen to her feet, her hands clutched in front of her. "This lady brings me here."

"I'm sorry, I don't think I know you."

"You don't. You know my name. What you don't know is that I am employed by a security team. You have heard Fynn speak of Abe and Emma?" At her nod, he continued. "Abe is my employer, or more accurately, I am his partner. He got word yesterday about something and we headed this way today." His hand gently took her arm and seated her, seating himself in the chair Buckley had abandoned. "Abe asked me to come and find you. He wanted one of us to talk to you in person."

Guenivere was staring at him, seeking an answer, seeing something in his eyes and face that gave her hope. "Branigan? Is it Branigan? Do you know where he is? Have you found him? Can you take me to him?"

Murphy gave a quick grin that didn't reach his eyes. "That's why I'm here. I do know where Branigan is. And yes, I can and will take you there." His hand reached out to steady her as she wobbled on her chair. "He's safe, Guenivere. We have him and he's safe."

"Oh, thank You, Lord." Her eyes slid closed as she endeavored to control her emotions before they popped open. "What time?"

"I'm sorry. What do you mean?" Murphy didn't understand how she asked that, instead of how Branigan was.

"What time? What time did you find him and get him out?"

"What time? Somewhere around three this morning." He looked genuinely puzzled as she began to sob, her head down on her folded arms on the table. He looked up at Buckley, who stood, a hand resting on her shoulder. "What did I say?"

"She awoke this morning at that time, and felt compelled to search the scriptures for verses on hope. She somehow knew."

Murphy shook his head. "God does indeed work in mysterious ways. I always say He has a plan and purpose for us we don't know about. Who knows why they had to go through this?'

"He's alive? Please, tell me he's alive." The desperate pleading in her voice broke the men's hearts.

"He is, Guenivere. He roused a bit and tried to fight us, but he didn't stay awake for long." His heart broke for her as she wept, turning as she felt her father beside her, to be hugged to him as she had been when she was a child and hurt.

Brett looked up at Murphy, a silent thank you mouthed to him. When Guenivere could finally control herself, she looked around, taking the handkerchief that Murphy was holding out for her, frowning at it.

"Cloth?  I didn't think anyone used cloth handkerchiefs anymore."

Murphy grinned, glad for a moment to lighten the mood. "You'll find they are still in use.  In fact, all my friends carry them. We did before we married.  A friend, in fact the police chief of our town, told us we had to, that ladies in distress needed the real thing, not paper.  That came from his wife."

"Thank him for me."  She rose, her father's arm still around her. "Can I see him?  Please?  I need to see him."

"That's why I'm here.  That's why your father is here.  We'll take you to him, but we need to take you on your own.  Your father will follow with some of my friends."

She's frowned at him.  "Just how many of there are you?"

"Today?  Let's see.  There's the eight of our team.  Abe's brother-in-law tagged along as did a detective friend of ours and also a paramedic friend.  I can assure you, we were well prepared for what we would find.  And before you ask, we all had what we term now as "adventures"."

She stared at him, not sure he was telling her the truth.  At his nod, she simply shook her head and then walked towards the door, stopping as he laid a hand on her arm.

"Just some rules to follow, Guenivere.  Just for now.  One of us goes through the door first.  That's a given.  No argument, please. If you argue, you don't go anywhere.  I know you trust the men here, but there is someone out there after you.  Your friends are working on that.  Soon, you'll be free to walk around without an escort.  But for now, the word we have received and that Barnabas has received is that you are a target to get to your father.  Think of that."

Guenivere had paled as he talked, knowing he was right.  She nodded, unable to say a word.

Murphy watched the emotions playing across her face. Thanks, Abe, you had to volunteer me, now didn't you?  His hand on her arm led her to the loading dock, where a black SUV waited with the doors open, a second one towards which her father headed. She paused, watching as he was greeted and then tucked inside.

His hand nudging her forward, Murphy tucked her inside the first SUV and then sat beside her, the door closing with an almost silent bang. She frowned at that, leaning around him to gaze at the door.

"Surprised?" Murphy grinned at her nod. "Not what you expected. We made some modifications that we needed to."

"Maybe you could work with Dad on his trucks. Some of those doors really sound loud. But then, the men are always in a hurry." She looked around, taking in the other three men with her, before she turned to the man sitting beside her.

"You're Joseph."

"That would be me. How's your security system?"

"So far, I have no idea. I haven't been working at the office. I'm not allowed." She sat back, sounding disgruntled but a glint of mischief peeked from her eyes. "Who's in front?"

"Ian is our driver. That's Micah in the front passenger seat. Abe, Nathaniel, Luke and Matt are with your Dad. We have Gideon, Frankie and Dave with Branigan."

"I'm still impressed. But where are your ladies? I know you are all married. Didn't you bring them for cover?'

The men shot her a quick glance before breaking out into laughter, which had been her aim.


*Chapter 36*

Waiting almost impatiently in the SUV where Ian had pulled to a stop near the back of the hospital parking lot, Guenivere peered through the darkened windows, her gaze steadfast on the door of the building, knowing Branigan was there, that he was alive, that God had brought him back to her. She knew why she had to wait. She just didn't know because of who. But then, again, maybe she did.

———

She looked around at the men, trying to think of a way to ask what she had to. Ian had been watching her closely and his eyes raised to meet Micah's, who nodded.

"Guenivere?" Ian's voice, though low, caused Guenivere to jump as she looked up at him, her hands twisting against one another. "Who do you suspect? Is it someone close to you?"

She hesitated before she nodded. "I haven't been honest with Barnabas. I've given him some names. One of them is a woman on the board." She frowned. "And there's her brother and his wife. I think they are all involved in crime." She blinked rapidly, taking the handkerchief Joseph handed her with a quiet word of thanks. "I never told Dad about how I was physically assaulted when I was young. I meant to but they weren't home when I got there and when the morning came, I was too scared and too ashamed to. She was there. I had driven that memory too deep to bring up. I wanted to forget." She looked up once more, a woebegone look on her face. "It's my fault, isn't it? My fault that Dad has had to deal with this. That Branigan was kidnapped and then hurt."

"Not at all. You didn't make them do what they did. You did not make them live a life of crime and hide it." Micah's voice was stern. "They made those decisions, not you."

She nodded, not quite convinced that he was correct. She watched as Ian started up the vehicle and pulled closer to the back door, waiting until her father and three of the men with him had entered. Murphy's hand rested on her forearm.

"Just to go back over some things. I know you understand that we are here to protect you. Let us do that. Trust us, please, Guenivere." He watched as she nodded, her eyes fastened on him. "You and I go in through another door from what your father did. Joseph and Micah will follow in a moment. We need to get you in and to the room your police chief has arranged for you. He tells me he was overrun with volunteers to make it safe."

Guenivere nodded, a sober look on her face. "Branigan is an auxiliary officer. They have tried so hard to find him. I just don't understand how you did."

"Abe's wife, Emma, came across an address that seemed to fit but she wasn't sure if it would. Abe talked to your police chief and volunteered us to go in and bring Branigan out if it was true." He watched as her mouth opened and then closed. "It's what we do, Guenivere. It's our livelihood but also our mission."

She nodded once more, a desperate look on her face. "Please? Can I see him?"

"Sure. Just let us do all the looking around. You just stay focused on that door and getting through it." Murphy listened for a moment to Abe's voice through his earpiece before he nodded at the other three. "We're good to go."

Murphy was out of the vehicle, Guenivere's hand in his as he rapidly led her the few feet to the door, opening it quickly and pulling her through. They had researched the hospital with Will's help, trying to judge the best and fastest way to get her in and to the room the hospital had set aside for the family.

A whisper of sound came to Murphy's ear and as he spun towards it, a hard object landing on his head sent him to the ground, Guenivere's scream sounding in his ears before it faded. Guenivere stared down at him and then at the two men in front of her, panic beginning to set in. She backed away, her hand coming up to run along the wall behind her back, trying to reach the door she knew was behind her.

A grubby hand with broken nails grasped her wrist and stopped her in her tracks before she was pulled towards the man, struggling to escape to no avail. She heard the heated words between them, one blaming the other for Murphy being there and then blaming each other because they had to take him out, as they put it.

She pulled with her arm, twisting and turning to break the hard grasp to no avail. She began to flail at her captor, her hand catching at his face, causing him to turn on her in anger, a hand raised that smacked at her face, driving her into the wall and then limply to the floor, the only thing holding her from collapsing totally the hold he had on her.

"Now, what did you do that for?" The second man began to curse in violent terms.

"I had to. You saw her." The first man wiped at his face, his hand finding the blood where Guenivere's nails had caught at the flesh. "She scratched me."

"So. Stop being a baby. We need to get out of here." He turned, ready to pick Guenivere up when he saw the men standing there, grim looks on their faces.

The first man dropped her wrist, starting to back away before he realized his exit was blocked. Their hands raised, the men were herded away by the responding officers and then the door closed behind them.

Micah was on his knees beside Guenivere as Ian dropped beside Murphy.

"Murphy?" He heard a groan from his friend who was sprawled face down. A hand reached for the back of his head.

"Ian? What did I do that I don't remember going and doing?" Murphy slowly raised himself to a sitting position, his hand still cupping the back of his head.

"You got clobbered, is what. But it seems as if Guenivere put up a fight." His head turned towards Micah. "Micah? How is she?"

Micah shook his head, as he stood, then bent to pick her up. "She's out cold, Ian. It looks as if she was slammed into the wall."

Will spoke from behind Ian. "Let's get them to that room. Doc's around. I'll have him come take a look. We have many hands on deck to help."

He stood for a moment, watching as the men walked away, before he turned to Barnabas and Abe.

"I don't like this. They shouldn't have known where they were."

"Those are my thoughts." Abe pondered for a moment. "Guenivere. Her shoes? Purse? Phone? Any jewelry?"

"The only jewelry is the ring Branigan gave her. Her shoes? That's possible. We've been wracking our brains trying to figure out how they knew where she was. She is on, I think, her third or fourth phone in the last few weeks. Branigan has gone over it thoroughly and locked it down as much as he can. He won't even let her have her location app working."

"Good. Now, her purse?"

"She doesn't carry one. She has a folder she sticks what she needs in and that goes into her pocket. Her keys? We've looked them over as well."

"That leaves her shoes, maybe? They may have been watching but someone knew where we were heading and which door we would go in." Abe turned at a sound from Will, whose face was sober.

"I think I know how. The Langs have a young relative, who is close to one of my officers. He was warned not to say anything and to be very careful. It seems that I need to have a chat with him. Care to join me? You can listen in from behind the mirror."

"Gladly, Will. I want whoever it is that did this. Guenivere did not deserve to be hurt again." Barnabas walked away, his anger palpable.

Her head twisting as she roused, Guenivere's hand sought her face, wondering why it felt so cold.  Her hand found her face, or so she thought.  It's cold.  I don't understand why.  She twisted at her hand to free it from the one holding it but couldn't.

Lena stood, her hand on her daughter's, watching as Guenivere turned her head in a restless manner, trying to escape the ice pack the nurse had placed against her face.  The nurse had simply shook her head at Lena and whispered that if she could, would she make sure it stayed in place as much as it could?

Barnabas had been in and out, worried about Guenivere.  He hadn't said much, but Brett had stopped him at one point, a question on his face.

"Barnabas, what news is there?"

The younger man had shrugged, his eyes on his friend's face. Brett had become close to him, becoming almost a mentor to him in some ways.

"I haven't been told much.  Will and Dallas are working on an angle.  Emma is shooting them as much information as they can get. Our guys are working their hardest, taking a leave from their work to do so.  They want this over for Branigan.  It has angered them that he disappeared from his home and it has angered them that Guenivere was tracked down at the hospital and then injured."

Brett ran his hands through his hair before dropping them to his side and clenching them.  "That angers me too.  She's my little girl, Barnabas, always will be.  We couldn't have any more.  She's our life.  I want to see her and Branigan build their own life."  He held up a hand as Barnabas opened his mouth.  "He came to me one day, just asking in general he said.  Would I object if he dated Guenivere?  He was honest.  Told me he had never dated, had had no desire to.  Not until Guenivere."

"We're all like that, Brett. Every single one of the guys at the building. We are waiting on God. I have no idea why the six have gone through what they have, but God does. He has allowed it and it always works out for the couple. Whatever it has been that they have needed to work on, that is how He has dealt with them." He had turned and walked away at that point, leaving Brett to stare after him.

Breck spoke from beside Brett, watching him closely. "He's right, you now. None of us want to put our ladies in danger, but that seems to be the way it is."

Brett turned. "Your ladies? Breck, you're not dating. So why would you say that?"

Breck shrugged, a distant look flickering across his face. "When you're a teenager, you think you know how your life will go, who you'll go out with, who you'll date, who you'll marry. You plan out your life, your work, where you'll live. It doesn't always work out that way." He turned and walked away, a slump to his shoulders that Brett had not seen before.

Lena's arm came around him. "What's with Breck? He looks disheartened."

"He is. I think he had someone in his past and for some reason, they parted ways." He looked down at his wife before dropping a kiss on her forehead. "How's our girl?"

"She's sleeping again, but it's so restless. Doc was by when you were down at the office. He doesn't want to give her too much medication. He says he wants to see how she is. Until she rouses completely, they won't know." She turned him back into the hospital room. "Abe's men are angry."

"Yes, they are. So are the building guys. Buckley said he'd be back around."

Barnabas had found his way down the hall to where Branigan was, hesitating to pray before he entered the room. He searched the hall, a frown on his face, feeling someone watching him. His eye caught the husband of a board member, and he frowned. He should not be here. As far as Barnabas knew, they didn't have any friends or family on this floor.

Instead of pushing the door open, he walked away, his phone out.

"Dallas? Where are you?"

"Barnabas? Just heading for the elevator there. Why?"

"Because Evan Lang is here. He shouldn't be. They don't have anyone on this floor." Barnabas turned to watch, seeing Evan Lang moving towards Branigan's room. "What is he doing? He's heading for Branigan. He shouldn't be. There are no visitors allowed." His phone was in his pocket and he was rapidly striding towards the door, to stop in front of it, a hand held up to stop Lang.

"What is the meaning of this, Carey? I want to see that man. I think he knows something."

"Right at the moment, he is under police guard. No one not on the authorized list gets in there." Barnabas' face was sober, not reflecting the emotions and thoughts flowing through his mind. He caught Dallas moving quickly towards him, a hand on his weapon, a police officer approaching from the other way. "Sorry."

"Step aside, Carey. I will see him."

Barnabas continued to shake his head. "As his next of kin, no, I won't allow it. The physicians have restricted his visitors. Besides, as I said, he is under police guard."

"I don't see any officer." Lang's arrogance was foremost, and Barnabas wondered how they had ever chosen his wife for the Board.

"There's one in the room. Dallas, the detective on the case, is beside you and another officer is to your left."

"Not hardly likely." Lang's hand came up to shove Barnabas to one side, only he never got a chance. His wrist was grasped and quickly twisted behind him, the click of handcuffs sounding loud in the suddenly quiet corridor. "What is the meaning of this? Take this off. I will have your job, you do know that."

Dallas merely shook his head, reading Lang his rights, before he spoke. "Barnabas is correct. You have attempted to breach police protective custody. Besides, we have a laundry list of questions we need to ask you. The first being: Where is your wife?"

"My wife? Either at work or at home. Why?"

"Because we need to speak with her, and no, she is not at home. Nor is she at work. She hasn't been in either place for a day or so, I'm told." Dallas nodded to the officer, who moved off, hand to Lang's arm, who tried to hurry away from them all, knowing the staff and visitors to the floor were watching.

"He'll try to get your badge, you know." Barnabas broke into a grim smile.

"He can try. We have too much on him. Not directly related to you or the Foundation or even to Branigan. I just wish I knew where his wife is."

Barnabas looked behind him, seeing Abe approaching. "Talk to Abe. By the way he coming at us, I would say he has something important." Barnabas disappeared into Branigan's room, leaving Dallas to turn and face Abe.

"Abe, is it?"

Abe grinned. "It is. Listen. This address? That's where we found Branigan. I talked to Will last night and we went in early this morning. You may find your missing piece of the puzzle there."

Dallas stared at him, before he looked down at the piece Abe had thrust at him. "This place? Patrols have been by there, but didn't see anything that alerted them."

"No, there wouldn't have been. The lane is well travelled. Branigan was in a room in the basement." Abe had to stop, to swallow the anger rising in him. "He was shackled, Dallas, shackled to the wall, only able to move a certain number of feet."

"What?" Dallas was shocked. "Well then, I guess I'm on my way out there." He nodded towards the door. "Doc says he's still out, that he's been mistreated. I have an officer inside and more around the floor. I know you and your team were planning on staying for a day or so."

"We were, but we've been asked to go in and retrieve someone else. We have to leave this afternoon. In fact, I have to run." Abe glanced at his watch, and then headed away from Dallas, his long strides covering the hallway rapidly.

<hr>

Dallas stared after him and then down at the paper, sighing as he did so.  How does she do it, he wondered?  How does she find these?

*Chapter 38*

Stirring early the next morning, Guenivere felt at her face. The pain had lessened but she could feel the swelling. A bruise, she thought. Now how did I do that? Memory flooded to her as her eyes crept open and she glanced around, not moving her head. A hospital room. That's right. I was coming to see Branigan, and someone attacked me. I do hope Murphy is okay, she prayed.

She slid from the bed, waiting for the dizziness she expected, and surprised when it didn't hit. She searched for her clothes, finding them and then opening the doors in the room until she found the bathroom. She dressed quickly and looked around for her shoes, not seeing them. Shrugging, she slipped on her socks and then padded for the door.

Guenivere knew Branigan was there, somewhere, and she was determined to find him, if she had to search the entire hospital. She paused outside her door, her eyes narrowed against the light for a moment, before she headed away from her room, spying the officer standing outside one of the room just down from her.

She paused as she neared, finding him watching her, an encouraging smile of his face as he stepped over to push open the door, a hand beckoning her to move forward.

"He's sleeping, Guenivere, but he has been rousing more and more. I sure he'll wake fully when you are there." John, the officer, held the door, watching as she hesitated for a moment before almost running for the bed.

Her eyes on the IV line running down to Branigan's hand, Guenivere stood for a moment, almost afraid to look at him. Her hand reached to cover his, feeling the thinness of it. Branigan stirred for a moment, before his hand moved away and then covered hers, his grasp tight. She raised her eyes to his face, a sob in her throat, as she saw how thin and white it was. Dark shadows lay heavy under his eyes. Her free hand rested against the beard he had grown, feeling the fever that raged in his body.

Branigan's eyes flickered as he sensed someone near him. Not his guard, he thought. Nor Yvette Lang. He glanced around, frowning. He was free? How, he wondered. And a hospital room. Good. God, You were there. You did rescue me. Thank you. But Guenivere. I don't know where she is. I am so afraid for her. He paused in his prayer, feeling lips touching his forehead gently and then his beloved's voice whispering in his ear that she loved him and would he please wake up all the way. She needed that.

Too tired to comply, Branigan's eyes dropped down and he slept, this time a natural healing sleep. Guenivere brushed at the tears of her face, tears of thankfulness, joy, but also worry. He hadn't roused enough, she thought. Fatigue hit her in giant waves, to the point her eyelids felt weighted down. She finally gave in and just crawled up beside him, moving his arm so she could snuggle close. She really didn't care if the staff would complain. Branigan was back to her, and that was all she cared about.

The nurse who entered, paused, and then just shook her head. There is no harm, she thought. I would be doing the same. She moved quietly around the room before the door opened and Doc entered.

Doc stood for a moment, before he looked over at Susan, the nurse, and just smiled.

"How is he?"

"Vitals are getting better. His fever is still there, but it seems to be reducing." She nodded at Guenivere. "I was looking for her and then John at the door told me she was in here."

"And so she is. They've had a rough few weeks, Susan. And until they round up everyone, they are still not safe."

"How close are they?"

Doc shrugged. "I have no idea. Will or Dallas haven't said much to Barnabas or Brett but I'm sure they're working hard to find everyone."

"What was that I heard about Yvette Lang?"

"And that would be?"

"I heard they found her dead, at the bottom of the stairs in her parents' old house."

"That may be. I haven't heard that confirmed."

"If it is true, then I'm glad. She has been nothing but trouble to any of us here or even in town."

Doc frowned at Susan's words. "What do you mean?"

"I mean that she has tried to interfere in anyone's treatment that she has been related to. She has come on the floors and tried to rearrange staffing and how we do things."

"She has? Obviously it didn't work."

"No, it didn't. The hospital director finally had to put her in her place and ban her from here for a while."

Doc nodded, his eyes going to Branigan as he stirred. "Then, if it's true, that is one less thing you will all have to worry about. Now, Branigan is awakening. Let's see how he is. Paul asked me to cover for him for a while. He had a family emergency he had to attend to."

Hearing his name called, thinking the voice sounded familiar, Branigan struggled to open his eyes, finally succeeding, a hand coming up to block the low level of the light in the room. He looked around, finding Doc standing beside him, a hand on his wrist.

"Branigan? You're awake? How are you feeling?"

Branigan swallowed hard, moving his lips, before he could speak, his voice rough and hoarse. "Okay, I think. I'm in a hospital?"

"You are. You're safe." Doc watched the relief that flowed his face. "You're dehydrated, malnourished, and running a fever. You'll be here for a few days."

Branigan nodded, not wanting to ask the obvious, unsure as to why Doc stood there, a grin on his face. He coughed, before he felt a heaviness on his shoulder. "What did I do to the shoulder, Doc?"

"Nothing." Doc continued to grin, not explaining.

Branigan's head twisted, his chin brushing against soft hair, before he stilled, his head raising slightly to stare down at the body he had tight in his arm.

"Guenivere?"

"It is. She was hurt coming in to find you, but now it seems as if her world's all right again. Susan found her here a while ago."

"She just had to do this, didn't she?" Branigan's comment was soft, his face lighting with the love he felt for his lady. "Doc, when can we do a wedding?"

"A wedding, is it?" Doc looked up as he heard a choked sound from Susan, catching the merriment on her face.

"Yes. I had time to think when I was held captive. Too much time. I don't want to wait any longer than I have to. She means too much to me. I want whatever time God has decided we get."

Doc had been watching Guenivere, seeing when her eyes had opened and she had looked up at Branigan, her body staying still.

"I see. I guess you'll be needing then to speak with Brett and Lena and then Buckley."

"We have plans, Branigan, Mom and I. Buckley knows. They all do. He's just waiting for us to give him a date." Guenivere's voice was soft, soft enough that Branigan had trouble following her words.

"We do? You have been busy, my love."

"They know, Branigan. They guessed it the day or so after you were taken. Cadee told me I should be wearing your ring. That you would want me to."

Branigan rested his cheek against her hair, knowing that Doc and Susan had stepped outside, leaving them alone. "I do. We had plans for that night, plans that God saw fit to set aside."

"He did. Now, we need to get you better. Buckley will be around, I have no doubt of that."

He nodded, a frown forming. "It wasn't our guys that came in, was it? We have done things like that before. We went in and found Baird and brought he and Berneen out."

"No. Abe Finlay appeared with his men and three of his friends, I think he said. He talked to Will about an address his wife had found."

"Okay. So it was them. I really didn't know for sure."

She waited for him to continue, but he slept, a deep, dreamless sleep, one that he needed so desperately. Guenivere finally sat up, her eyes on his face before she reached to kiss him and then slipped away from him, heading for the waiting room, knowing she would find friends and likely family there.

Lena stood as her daughter appeared, wrapping her in her arms, tears she could not control on her face. Guenivere leaned back, then hugged her mother tighter.

"I'm okay, Mom. I really am. And so in Branigan. We need to talk about what he went through, but he's been awake." She was aware of movement around her. She looked up, not surprised to see the thirteen friends and the ladies there. "He's going to be okay. Doc said so."

"And if Doc said so, then it must be true." Buckley reached to hug her, a prayer audible in the silence.

"Buckley? Branigan wants to set a day." She laughed, a sudden happy carefree laugh, one they had not heard from her before, and one her mother had not heard in years. "He was awake enough that that was what he asked for."

"That we can do. You just tell me when. We will make it work."

Two weeks later, Branigan dropped down into the chair behind the desk in his office. He was back to work, only part time, but he needed to be, both for his mental health and also for his clients. He flipped through the pile of papers on his desk, and then reached for his office schedule. It was clear for now, but that was usually how it worked. He would take calls, make his appointments, then his assessments, and wait for the client to either accept his recommendations or refuse them.

Deep into his work, multiple phone calls returned, Branigan lifted his head, thinking he had heard the door to the reception area open and close. He shook his head. No, he thought, I locked it. There can't be anyone out there. His concentration went back to his work, before he raised his head again. This time, he knew he had heard a key in the door and the door open. Not many people had keys, Guenivere one of them. He glanced at his watch. That must be her.

"Guenivere? Is that you?" He listened, not hearing anything. He did not like that she didn't respond. Hands on his chair arms, he shoved back, ready to rise, freezing in place as he saw Guenivere appear in his doorway, a hand around her mouth, a gun to her temple. His eyes narrowed in fear as he watched her stop just inside the office. She was angry, he could tell, and he couldn't say that he blamed her, not one bit.

"On your feet, Clery. We're going to go on a little trip."

Branigan stayed where he was, his eyes on Guenivere's, a slight frown marring his forehead. She is up to something, but what? He shook his head.

"Sorry, Langton. Not happening." Branigan rested his arms on the desk top. "We're not going anywhere."

"She dies, if you don't." The gun wavered, Guenivere cringing away from it, not sure if she would survive.

"No, I don't think so." Branigan had heard the door once more, quiet on its opening, and then saw Dallas appear in the background. "Somehow, I don't think so."

Dallas moved forward, his hand on his own weapon, and reached around to grasp the man's wrist, jerking it upright as it fired. Guenivere had dropped to the ground, curling up in a ball, her arms over her head, as far away from the men as they struggled as she could get.

Dallas finally shoved Langton towards the officer. "Take him away. He's one we've been looking for." He turned, ready to help Guenivere, finding Branigan had made it to her first. He had not seen Branigan clear the top of his desk as he raced to his sweetheart.

"Guenivere?" He was on the floor, cradling her to him, his arms tight around her. "Are you okay?"

"I am. Just as mad as a hornet, as my grandmother used to say. How did he get in? The door was locked."

"It was?" Dallas crouched down in front of her. "We'll search him, but he either had a key or picked the lock." He looked up at a sound from Branigan. "Branigan?"

"Look at the newest hire in our security team. He looks like him, but the names are different. I am sure he had a thorough background check, but something is off."

"Something is definitely off. I'll be in touch. Now, can you two please stay out of trouble?" With a wave, he was gone.

Branigan just sat, holding Guenivere, who made no move away from him, content to be held in his arms.

She finally turned, her face close to his. "Branigan, what are we to do? Is he the last?"

"I suspect so. I talked to Dallas earlier. He indicated he had one more person to track down. That would be Langton, I suspect. He'll need some time to wrap it all up, but then he'll tell us all about it." He kissed her, lingering for a moment, before he leaned back. "Now, about that date."

———

"What date?  Are you asking me out on a date?  I accept. High heels. Dress. Makeup. Jewelry. The whole nine yards." She tapped at her chin. "Oh, yes. Tuxedo for you."

Branigan stared at her, open mouthed until her finger tapped under his chin. He swallowed hard. "Yeah, sure. If that's what you want." When she didn't reply, his eyes narrowed. He finally caught the gleam of mischief on her face, earning her another long kiss.

"No, it's okay, Branigan. I know what you're asking." She giggled, suddenly free of the past, of the lost hope, of the lost time she felt she had wasted. "God has restored hope to me, in so many ways. You have been a huge part of how He has worked."

"For both of us, sweetheart. For both of us. Now, about that date?"

Her head on his shoulder, she finally nodded. "I know. We need to set one. Everybody keeps asking." She raised her head to stare at him, wondering at the laughter shaking his body. "What did I say?"

"It's not what you said. It's what happened with Brady and Fynn. Buckley made the mistake of telling Fynn he had a Saturday open, would it do for their wedding. Brady shot his words right back at him, taking him up on his offer."

Guenivere went off in peals of laughter. "That's what he meant, then. He told me he had Saturday free, would it do?"

Branigan shook with deeper laughter. He rose, his hand out to help Guenivere to her feet. "Well, then, we'll track him down and ask if it will do. I don't want to rush you."

"You're not. Mom and I have the plans made. I have my dress, hers actually. You need to arrange for the license or rather we do. You get the flowers. Anna has said the ladies at the church want to do the meal for us, with the ladies here helping." She stopped, her hand over her mouth in shock, causing Branigan to duck his head to stare at her and ask what now. "Who do I choose as my attendant? The five ladies are all so precious to me."

"Then, have them all. They'd be happy to. If it's okay with you, I would like a nice simple ceremony. Not too fancy. You're the main part for me."

———

"Then, I'm glad you said that. That's what Mom and I want. I sure the ladies would have a dress they could wear without any expense."

Branigan paused for a moment. "You do realize that when we marry, you become an employee of the Foundation as well? That you receive a salary from it?"

She nodded. "I do. That's part of my hesitation, I think. Dad has paid me well. I just don't know if I feel comfortable taking one."

That Saturday, Branigan and Guenivere mingled with their friends, glad to be able to do so without any shadow hanging over them. Dallas had been by the day before, having asked to meet with them.

When he left, they had just stared at one another, and then at Brett and Lena, who both sat at their kitchen table, shock on their faces.

"I never knew."  Brett had trouble understanding that his cousin, Donald, had been behind part of what had happened.  That he had made plans to take over Brett's trucking company and use it for smuggling and evil.  Brett had not asked what all the plans were, but from the look on Dallas' face, he decided that he didn't want to know.

"You had no idea, Dad?"  Guenivere turned to her father, her hands rolling her mug.

"None at all, or I would have ended it long before this."  He looked over at Lena.  "You said something years ago but we just let it go."

"I did.  I wondered if he was involved in crime, but he covered it too well for me to be certain."

Branigan had been listened to their conversation, before he spoke.  "Donald?  Is he the one from the central part of the province?  Then, Emma picked up on that.  She couldn't confirm anything, which is unusual for her."

"It is, but he hid it behind companies and people.  There was never a record of him being involved, until the Langs were arrested.  Yvette played us, and we feel the fools for that.  But justice has been served for her.  God looked after that."

"She wasn't well, Dad.  I could see it in her face."  Guenivere paused, not sure how to continue.  "It was hard, what we went through." Her eyes turned to her betrothed and she reached for his hand. "But God was there, every step of the way. He kept us alive. He restored our hope, hope that I never thought would ever return. So, in a way, I am glad."

Lena finally spoke after they had spent time in prayer. "I know, Guenivere, that you have struggled for years. You just wouldn't tell us. But now that the Langs and Langton are charged, we can move on. Your Dad has said he wants to retire. Douglas is willing to buy into the company and run it on a daily basis. He's finding the mechanics work getting to be hard on him. His son wants to take over that. Your Dad would still be involved, but as a silent partner."

"Dad? Really? That's great. Then, you can work in the mission like you wanted to."

"That's exactly it, Guenivere. With what you went through, we realized that God was calling us to move on, to move forward to something new and exciting."

Branigan's attention came back to the present, as Blair and Brady stopped beside him. He could see his other friends mingling with the church family.

"Branigan? You really are okay?" Blair still held concern for his friend.

"I'm getting there. I've been in counselling, not with Buckley, but with a trusted Christian counsellor. That has helped." He nodded towards Guenivere. "Knowing she's safe? That makes a huge difference."

"You two did have an adventure, not as life threatening as Bradon's, but still life changing." Brady hesitated. "The six of us make a team. Barnabas has asked that we meet on a weekly basis for now, to share with one another how we're doing, to pray for one another. Our ladies have already planned on that."

"They have? I can see that. And yes, I think it's a good idea." His arm swept his bride tight to his side. "We'll plan on that. Dallas has asked that he meet with us all in a couple of weeks, just to finalize what he knows. Trevor Lang had a heart attack last night, he tells me. He is not expected to survive."

---

"God's avenging once more."  Guenivere looked at the two other men.  "We can plot our revenge but we have to leave it in God's hands."

*Epilogue*

Two months later, Guenivere turned from her desk, tidying up the paperwork she had been immersed in. Douglas had asked her to stay on in the office and she had agreed to do that part time. His daughter had asked for some training to work the other hours, and Guenivere had agreed happily. She had become involved in the mission with her parents, looking after the little ones for a few hours a week, and enjoying it immensely.

Branigan stood, shoulder propped against the door, his eyes on her, wonder in his heart that she was his. He shoved away and walked over, dropping a kiss on the upturned mouth, before he perched on her desk.

"Done for the day?"

"I am." She sat back, mischief on her face. "And if I hadn't been?"

"Then I would has asked you to play hooky. I had a picnic basket delivered to my office with strict instructions that you and I were to go on a picnic."

"Mom's at it again."

"Actually, no. It wasn't your Mom. It was Barnabas' mother. She arranged for Anna to deliver it. She told me I had to court you, that we had missed out on a couple of weeks, and needed to make up for that."

"She did? She is so sweet." Guenivere stood, to be enveloped in his arms. "We have a picnic waiting, buster." Her comment came when she could breathe again.

He laughed as he stood, his hand reaching for hers. "That we do, my Proverbs 31 bride. That we do."

She laughed at him, knowing he was flirting with her, but enjoying it.

———

"Branigan?  Where can we volunteer together?  You volunteer with the police.  I volunteer with the mission.  But I would really like to see us work together somewhere."

"That we can do.  I heard from a friend today about an animal rescue that is looking for help.  They take in strays that have no homes and train them as service dogs."

"Oh!  Yes!  That sounds like something we could do."

Branigan laughed at her.  "Then, I guess I did okay when I arranged for us to go out there Saturday to look around and see if it's a fit."

Her sudden hug stopped him in his tracks.  He felt blessed, knowing he had the lady God had planned for him, work he enjoyed, and friends he could share his life with.

Dear Readers

Thank you for picking up the story of Branigan and his Proverbs 31 lady, Guenivere.  It was another one of those stories that I was just along for the ride on.  I had no idea where they planned to go.  In fact, Guenivere was to be a Gemma, until I was emphatically told that no, she was not a Gemma.  I was ordered to find another name for her.

Hope. Such a precious thing to have.  When we lose hope in life, in whatever, it destroys part of us.  God does not want that.  He wants us to have the hope of His salvation, and through that, hope in whatever He has for us.  So many times over the years, I have been discouraged, lost hope, but God has always brought me through and restored me to walk correctly in His presence.

Never be afraid to tell Him what and how you are feeling.  It's what He wishes. When we are honest with Him and ask for forgiveness and restoration, He does just that.

My father referred quite often to Proverbs 31 as a picture of a godly woman.  It is so true.  When, as ladies, we walk with God, our lives will reflect the characteristics shown in those verses.  That's what we strive for, isn't it?

Dear Abe and his team just had to show up.  I miss these characters from *His Guardians*.  They seem to like to show up when I least expect them to.  It is never planned.  And in this book, they brought in Gideon from *The Haven* and Frankie from *The Storm*, part of the *Haven of Rest* trilogy and Dave, from *A Touch of His Garment.*  All beloved characters.

God bless each one of you.  May you rest in His love.


Ronna

www.ingramcontent.com/pod-product-compliance
Lightning Source LLC
Chambersburg PA
CBHW070341220726
48294CB00016B/3